Shojo Beat

NANA Vol. 11

Story & Art by Ai Yazawa

Contents

The Story of Nana

Nana "Hachi" Komatsu and Nana Osaki meet by chance on a train headed for Tokyo. Their personalities and the environments they grew up in are very different, but by fate or by chance, they meet again and become roommates...

Nana is bent on driving her band Blast to surpass Trapnest, partly to win back Hachi from Takumi. Blast signed a temporary contract with a major label, but nothing has been happening—until a celebrity gossip TV show suddenly reports that Nana is dating Ren from Trapnest. Because of the major publicity, the label decides to rush Blast's debut release.

Hachi watches the scandal unfold on TV and worries about members of Blast's well-being while Nana drops a personal message to Hachi via a TV interview...

Blast gets sent off to the mountains to record their new album and prepare for their debut. Hachi visits her parents back home while Trapnest hides out in the U.K. And when Takumi returns, it's with lots of souvenirs and an engagement ring...

♥For the complete story, please check out *Nana*, volumes 1 - 10.
Available in bookstores everywhere!!

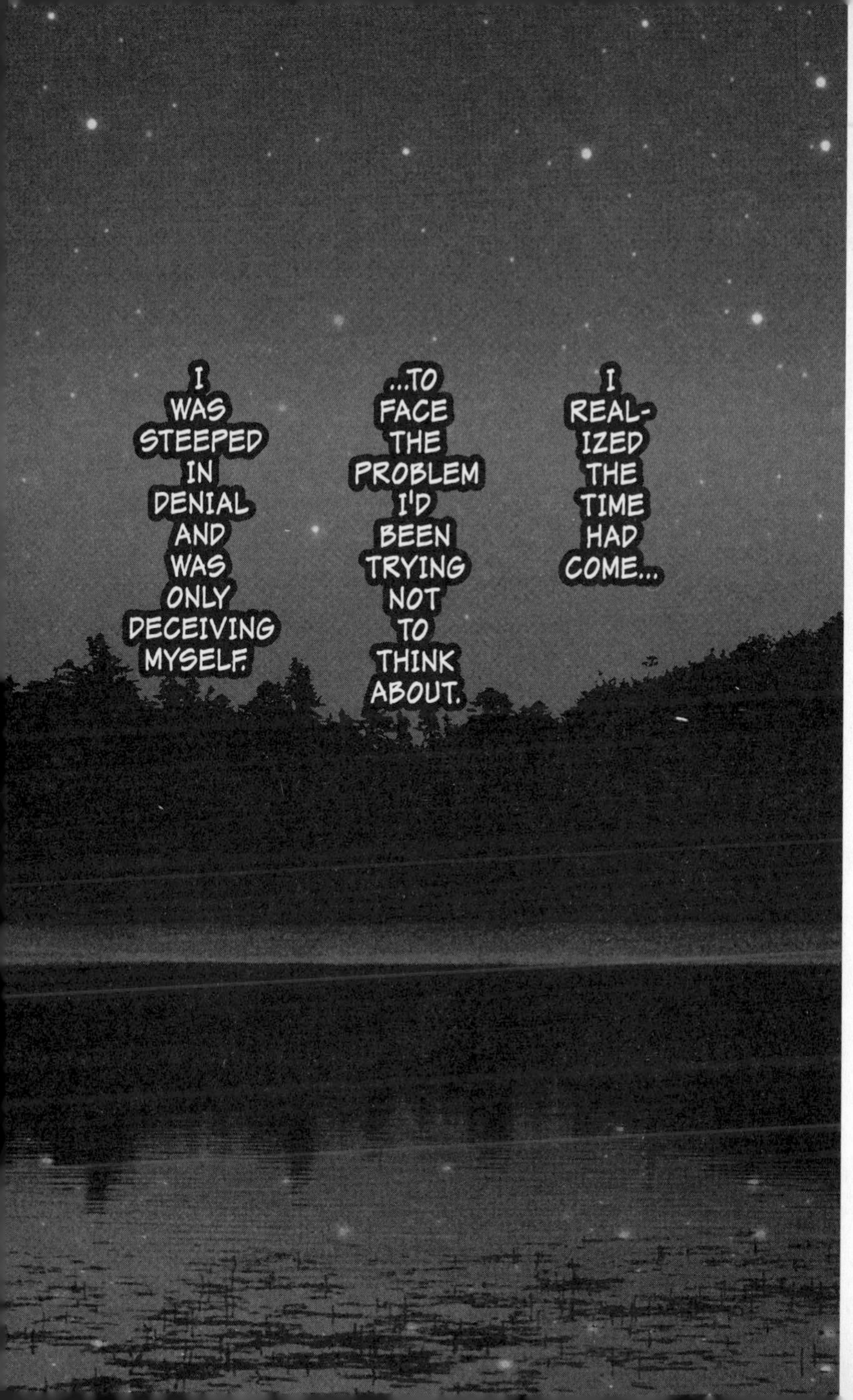
I REALIZED THE TIME HAD COME...
...TO FACE THE PROBLEM I'D BEEN TRYING NOT TO THINK ABOUT.
I WAS STEEPED IN DENIAL AND WAS ONLY DECEIVING MYSELF.

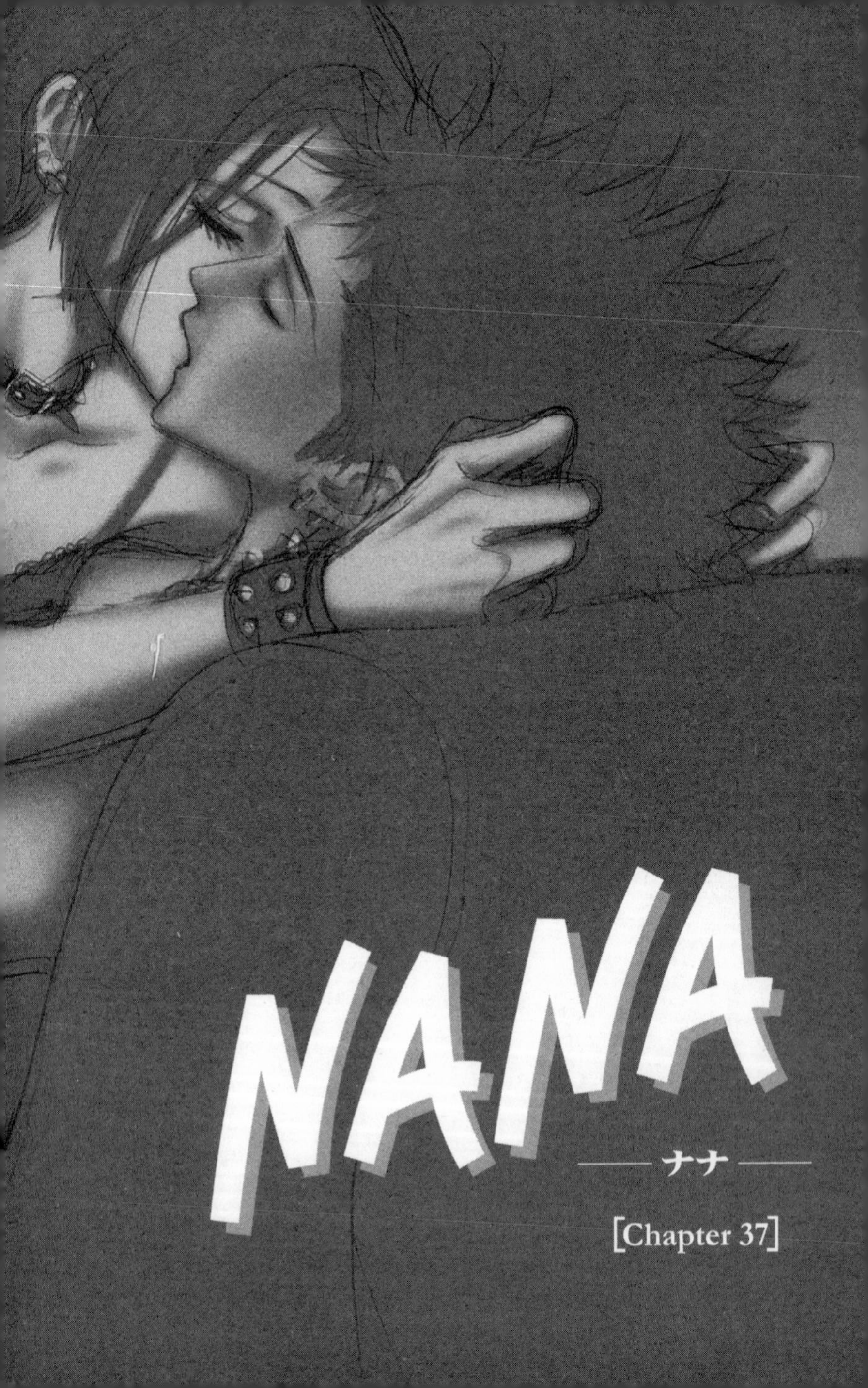
NANA
ナナ
[Chapter 37]

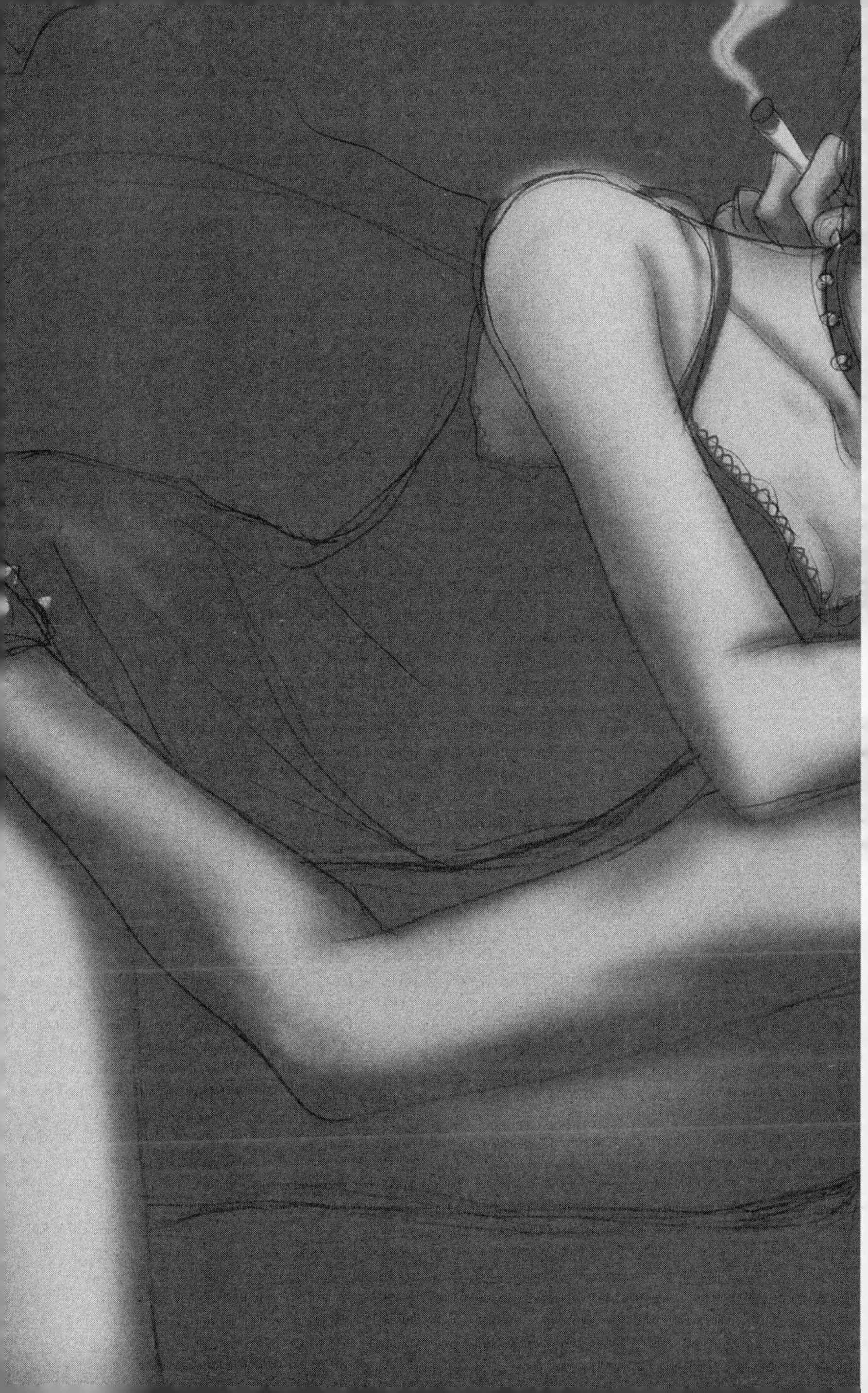

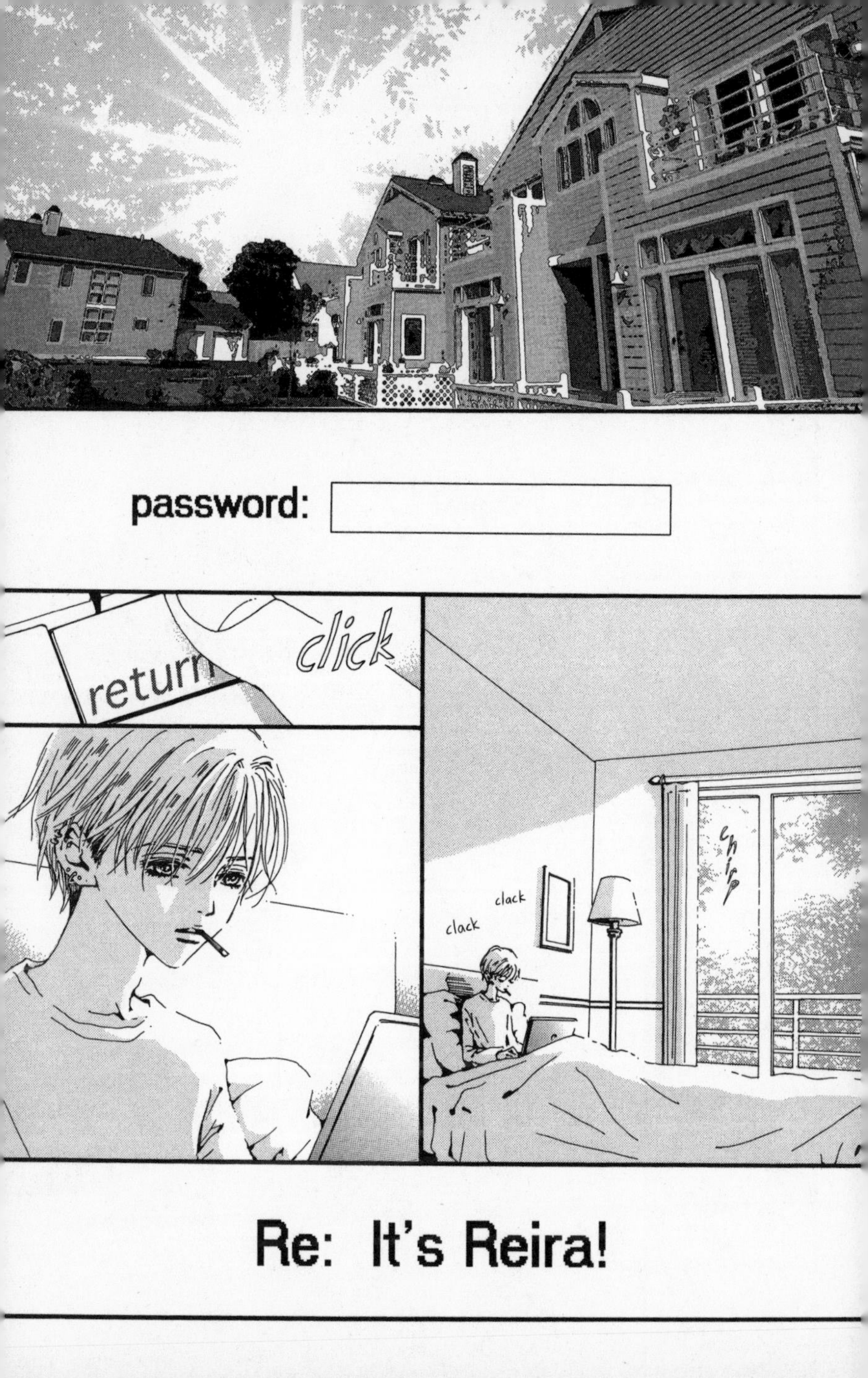
password:
chirp
clack
clack
return
click
Re: It's Reira!

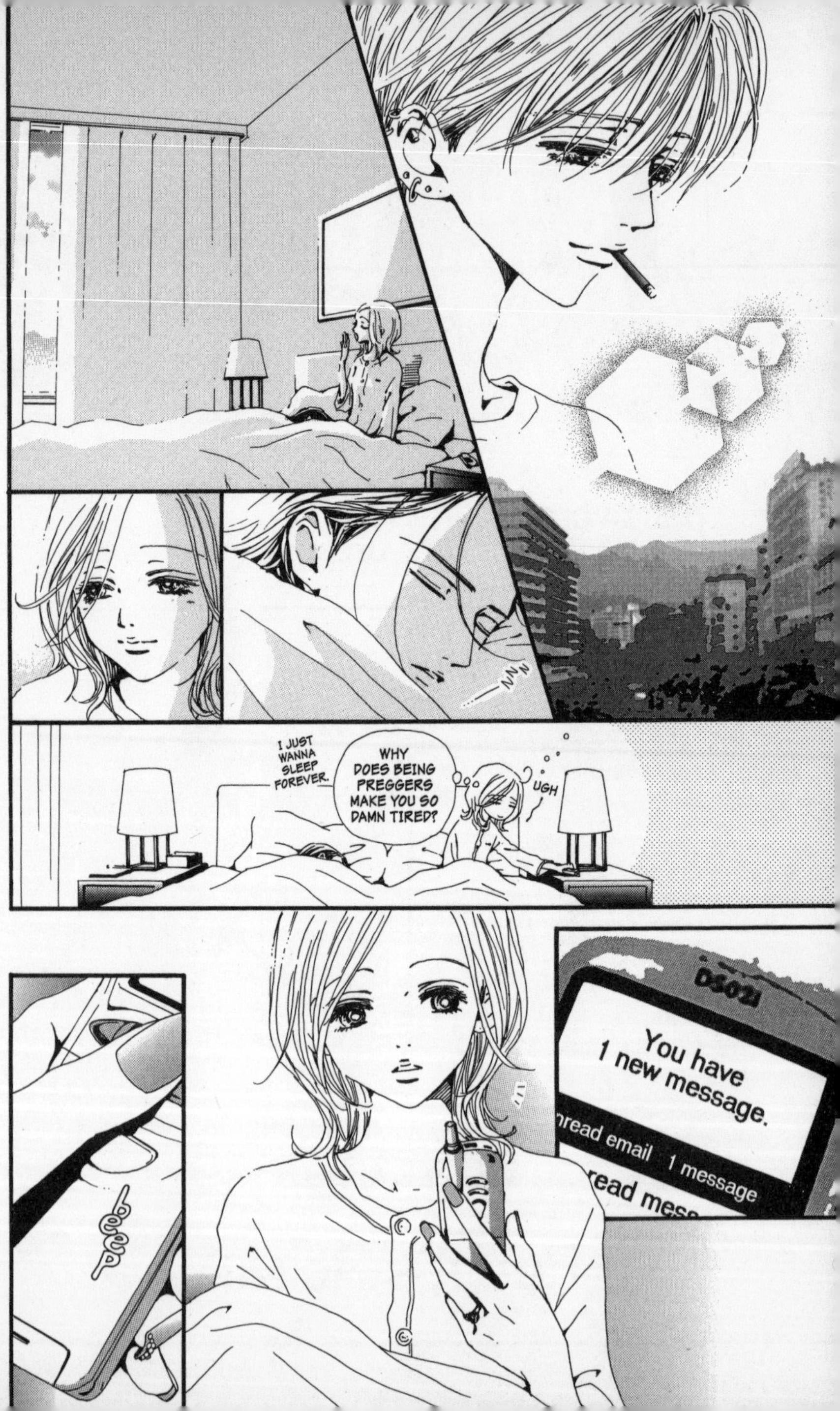
NNN
UGH
WHY DOES BEING PREGGERS MAKE YOU SO DAMN TIRED?
I JUST WANNA SLEEP FOREVER.
DS021
You have 1 new message.
beep

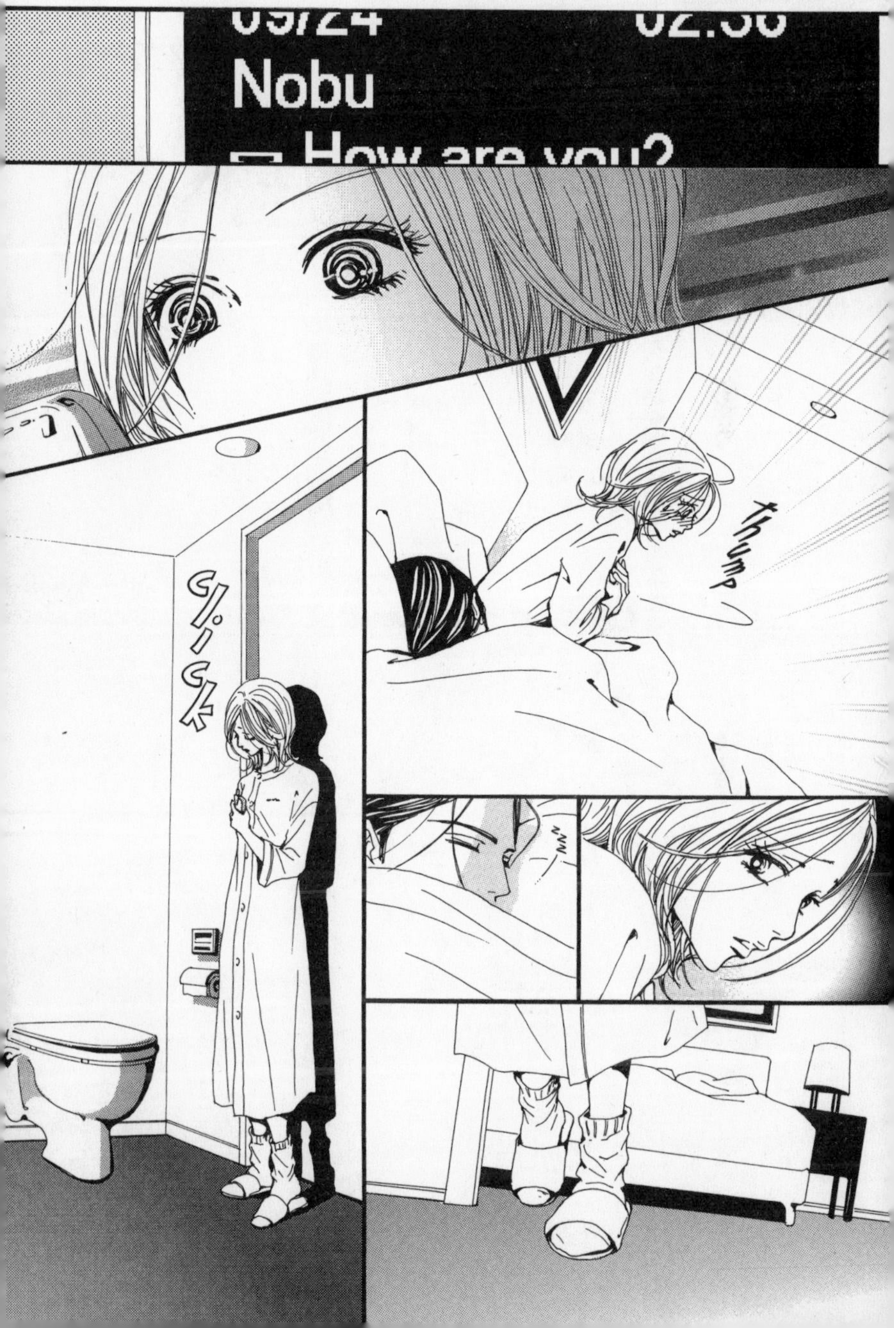
Nobu
thump
click

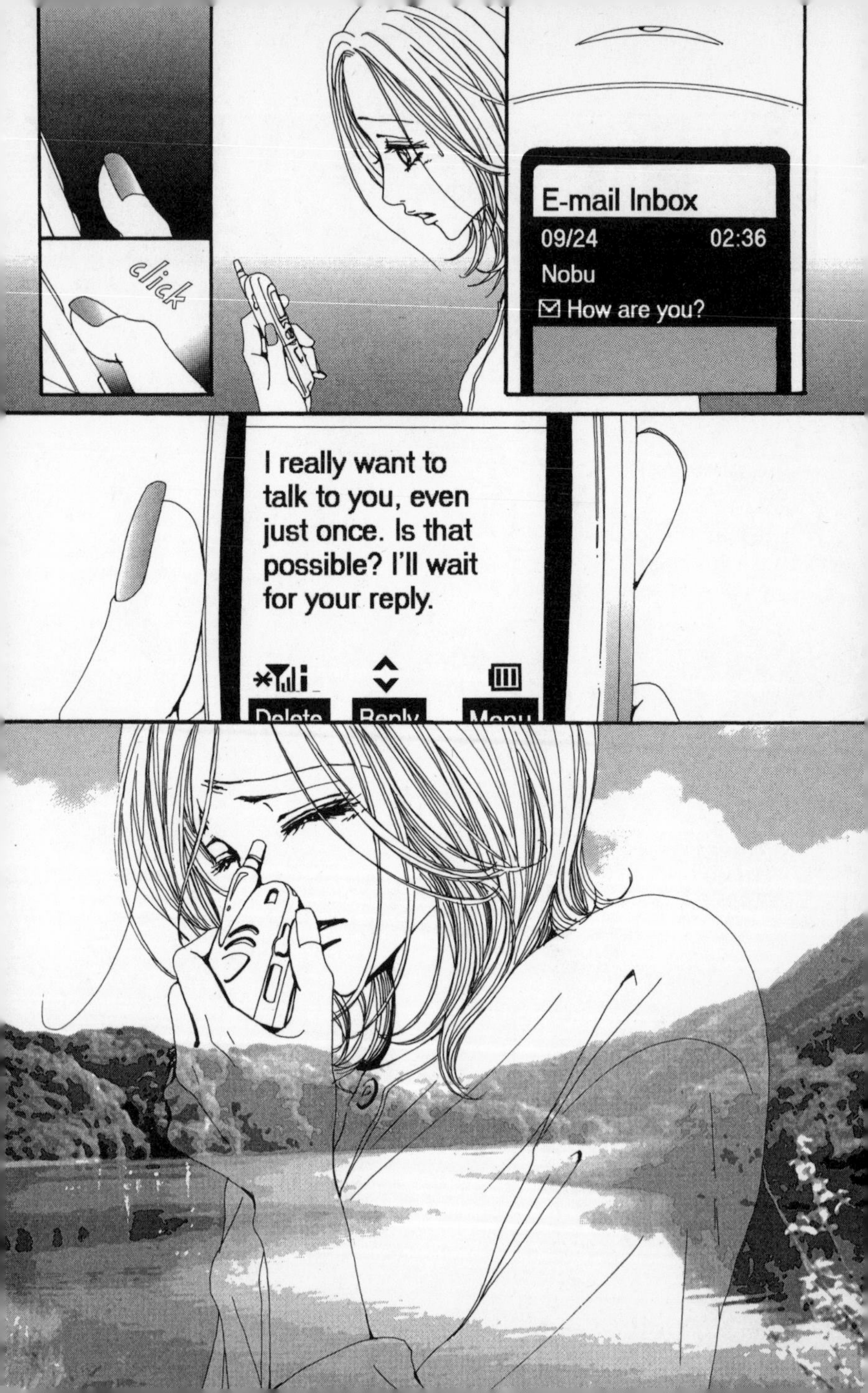
E-mail Inbox
09/24 02:36
Nobu
How are you?
click
I really want to talk to you, even just once. Is that possible? I'll wait for your reply.
Delete
Reply
Menu

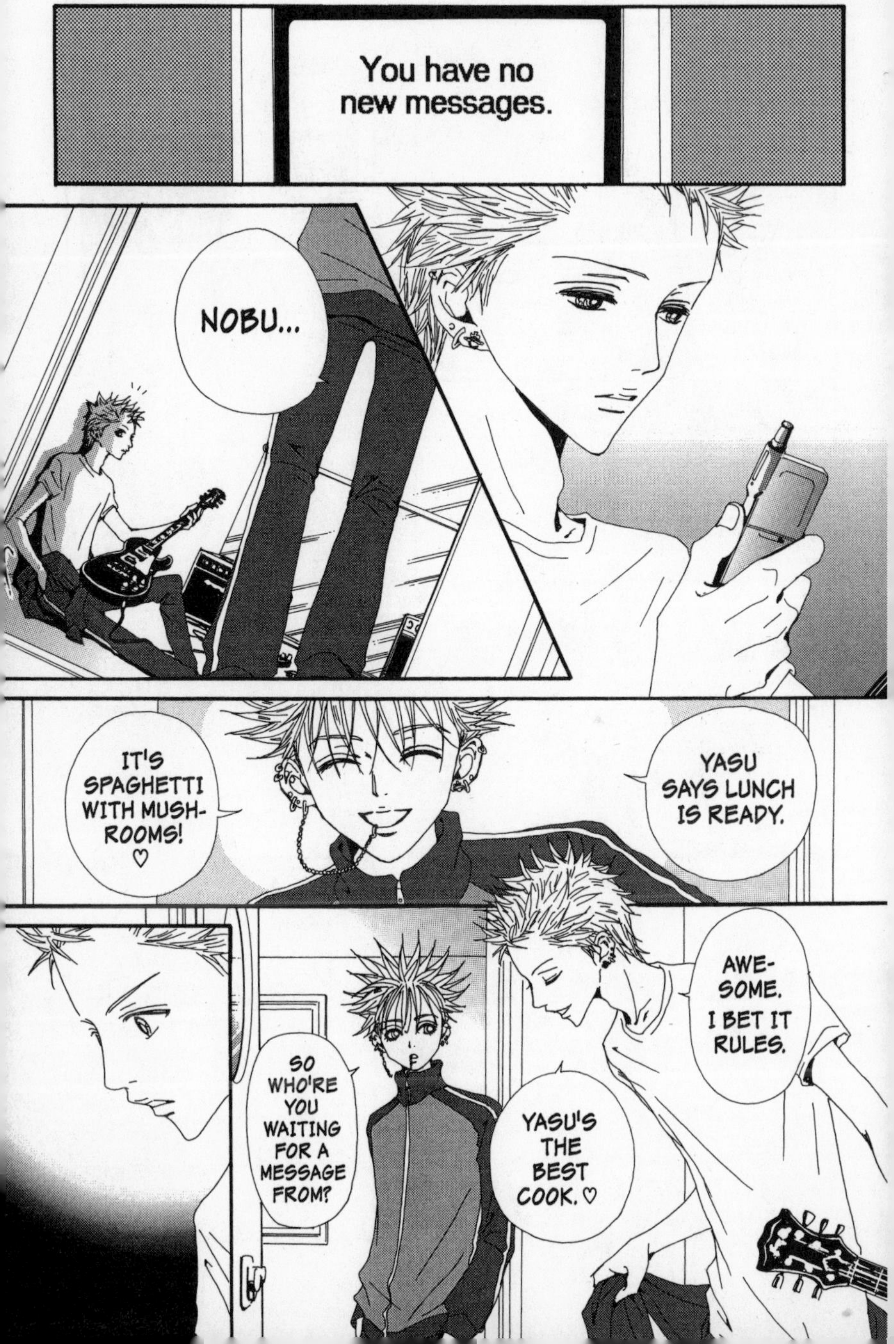
You have no new messages.
NOBU...
YASU SAYS LUNCH IS READY.
IT'S SPAGHETTI WITH MUSHROOMS! ♡
AWESOME. I BET IT RULES.
YASU'S THE BEST COOK. ♡
SO WHO'RE YOU WAITING FOR A MESSAGE FROM?

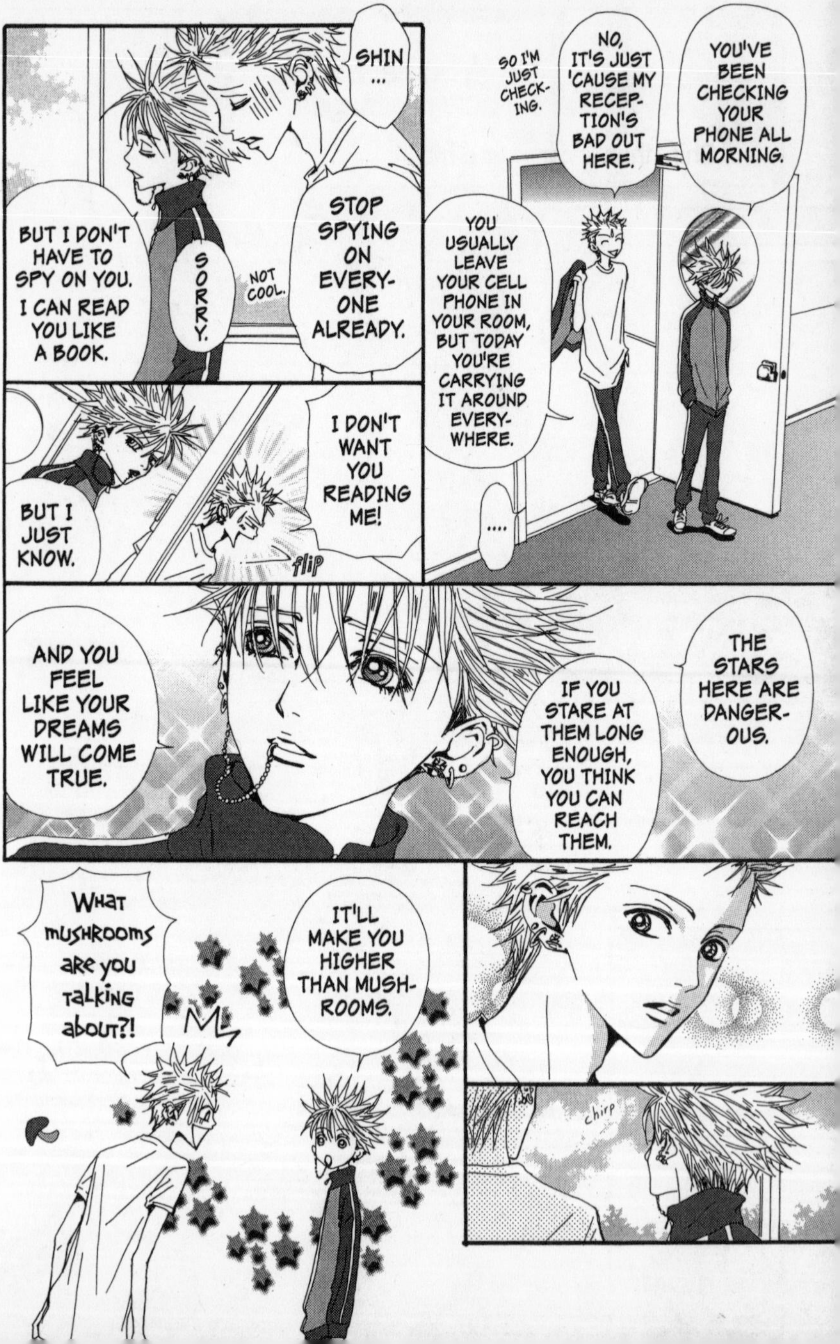
YOU'VE BEEN CHECKING YOUR PHONE ALL MORNING.
NO, IT'S JUST 'CAUSE MY RECEPTION'S BAD OUT HERE.
SO I'M JUST CHECKING.
YOU USUALLY LEAVE YOUR CELL PHONE IN YOUR ROOM, BUT TODAY YOU'RE CARRYING IT AROUND EVERYWHERE.
....
SHIN...
STOP SPYING ON EVERYONE ALREADY.
NOT COOL.
SORRY.
BUT I DON'T HAVE TO SPY ON YOU. I CAN READ YOU LIKE A BOOK.
I DON'T WANT YOU READING ME!
flip
BUT I JUST KNOW.
THE STARS HERE ARE DANGEROUS.
IF YOU STARE AT THEM LONG ENOUGH, YOU THINK YOU CAN REACH THEM.
AND YOU FEEL LIKE YOUR DREAMS WILL COME TRUE.
chirp
IT'LL MAKE YOU HIGHER THAN MUSHROOMS.
What mushrooms are you talking about?!

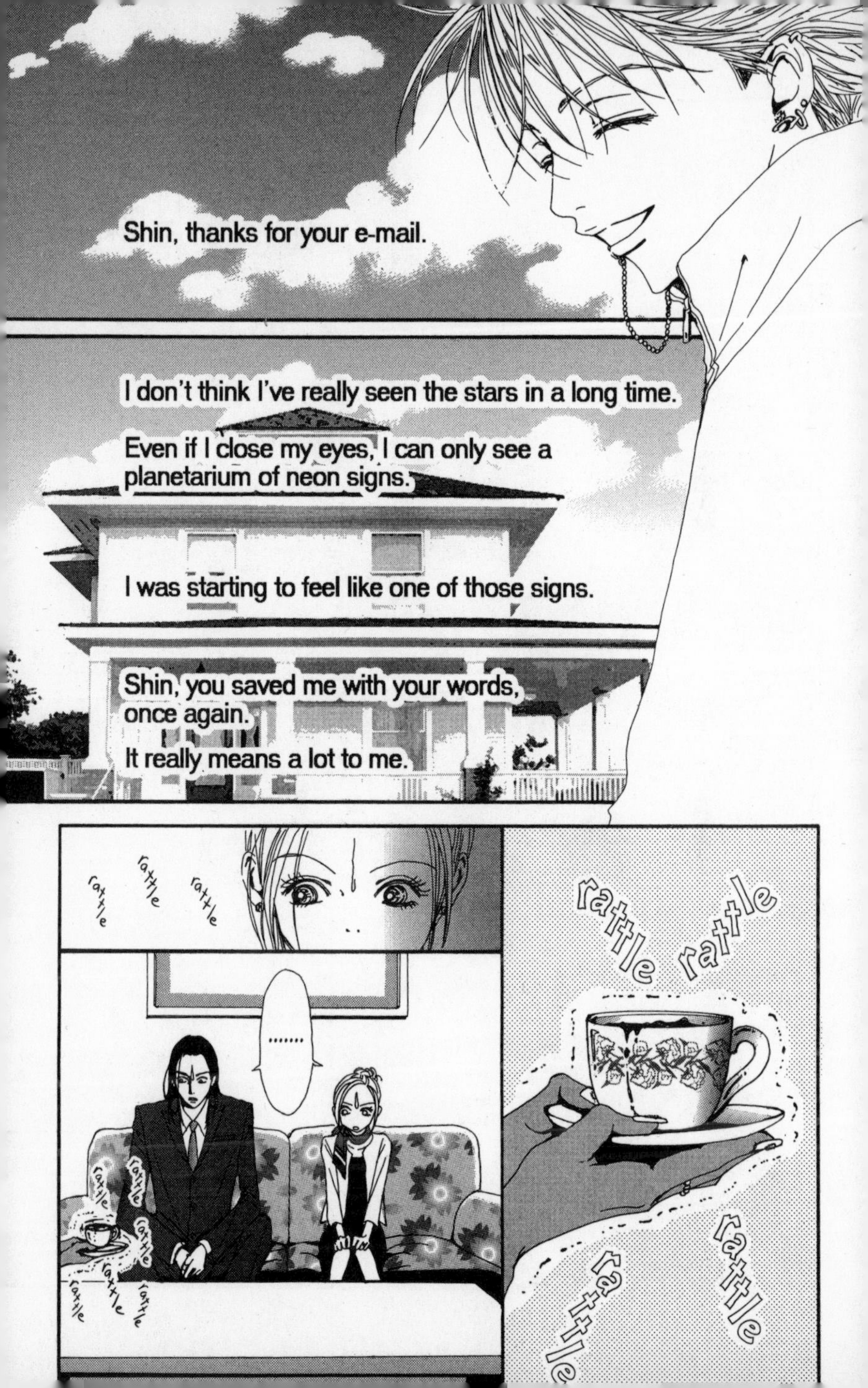
Shin, thanks for your e-mail.
I don't think I've really seen the stars in a long time.
Even if I close my eyes, I can only see a planetarium of neon signs.
I was starting to feel like one of those signs.
Shin, you saved me with your words, once again.
It really means a lot to me.
rattle rattle
rattle rattle
rattle
rattle rattle
rattle
......
rattle
rattle
rattle
rattle
rattle

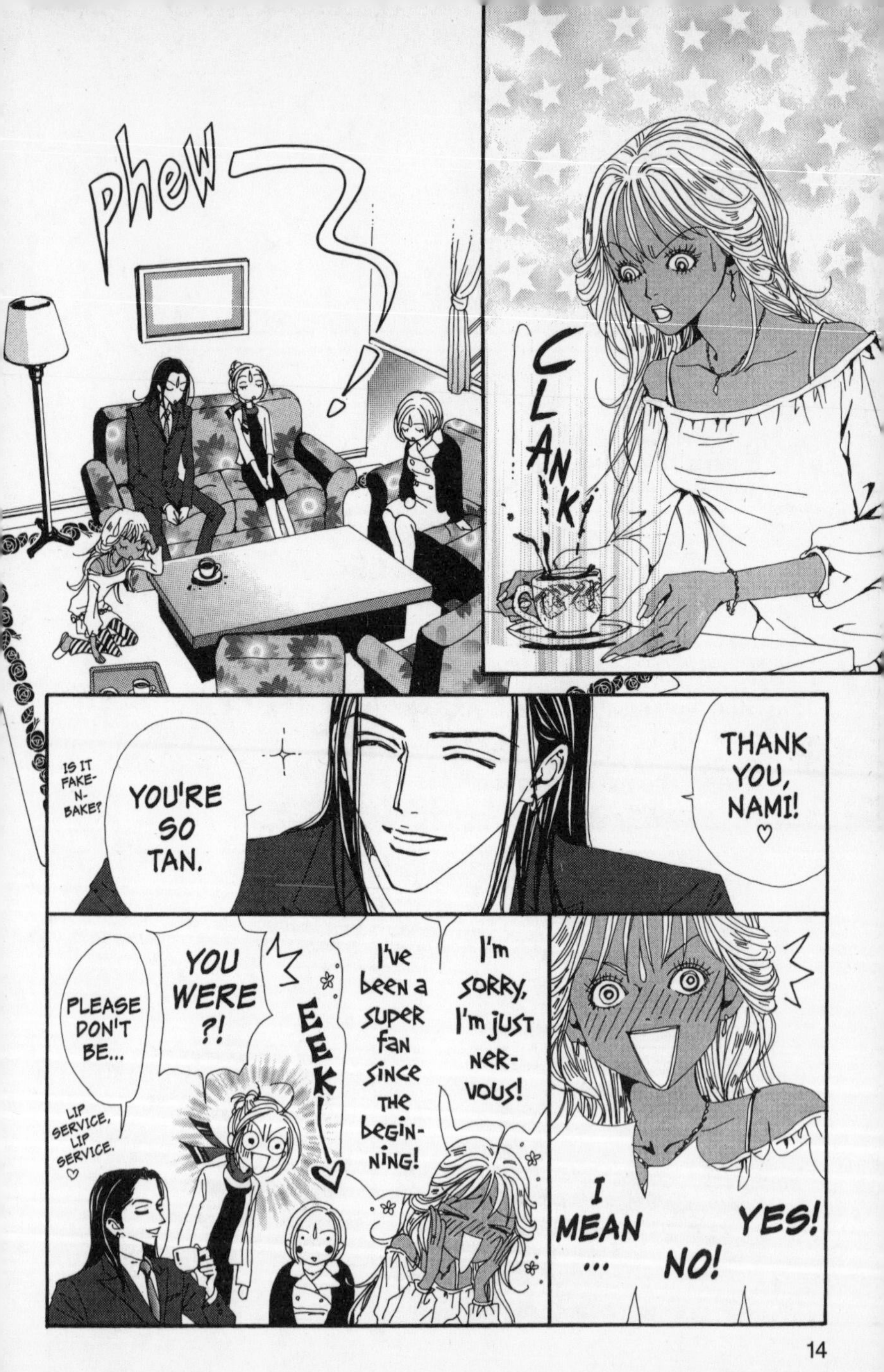
CLANK
phew
THANK YOU, NAMI! ♡
YOU'RE SO TAN.
IS IT FAKE-N-BAKE?
YES!
NO!
I MEAN...
I'm SORRY, I'm JUST NER-VOUS!
I've been a super fan since the begin-ning!
EEK ♡
YOU WERE ?!
PLEASE DON'T BE...
LIP SERVICE, LIP SERVICE. ♡

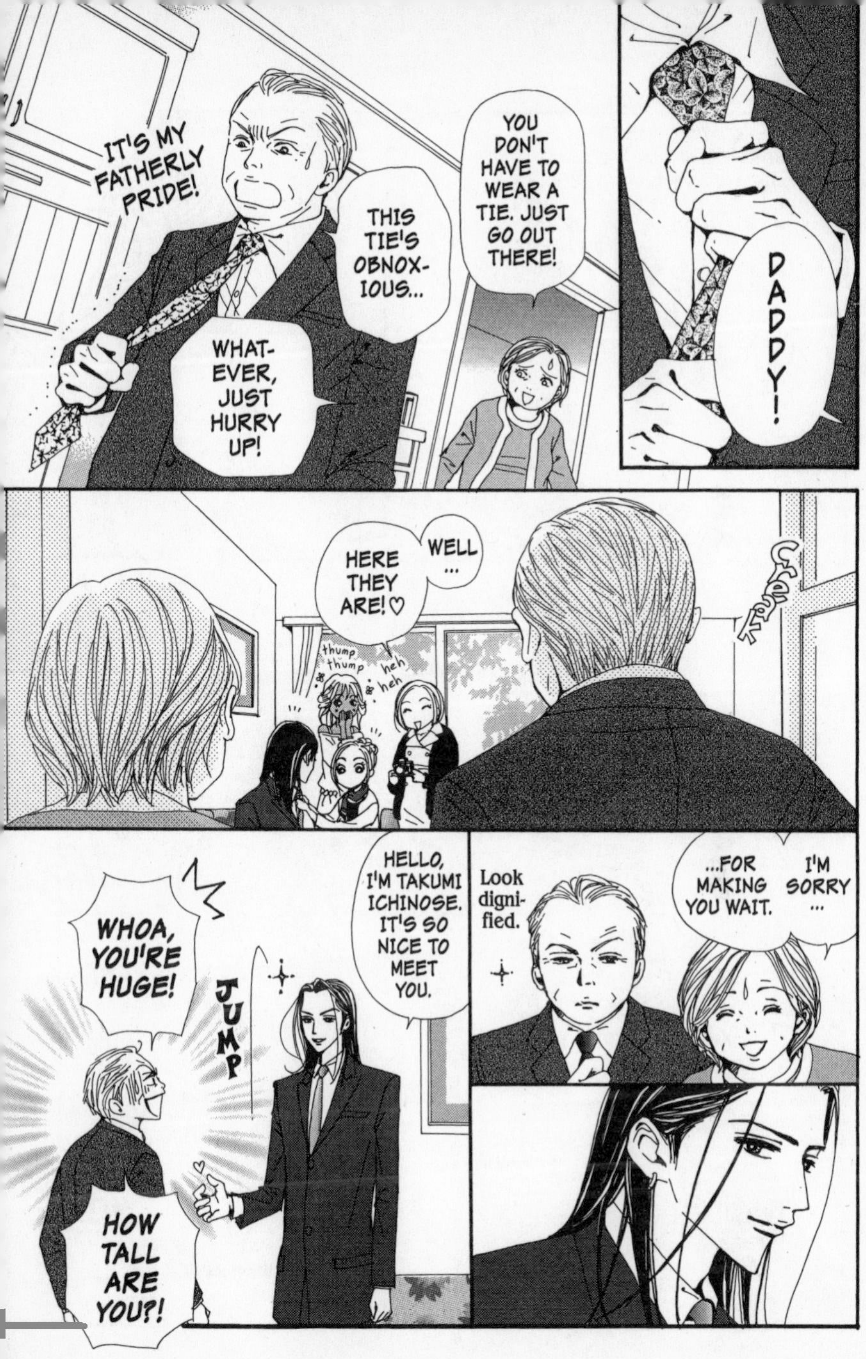
DADDY!
YOU DON'T HAVE TO WEAR A TIE. JUST GO OUT THERE!
THIS TIE'S OBNOX-IOUS...
IT'S MY FATHERLY PRIDE!
WHAT-EVER, JUST HURRY UP!
CREAK
WELL ...
HERE THEY ARE! ♡
thump thump
heh heh
I'M SORRY ...
...FOR MAKING YOU WAIT.
Look digni-fied.
HELLO, I'M TAKUMI ICHINOSE. IT'S SO NICE TO MEET YOU.
JUMP
WHOA, YOU'RE HUGE!
HOW TALL ARE YOU?!

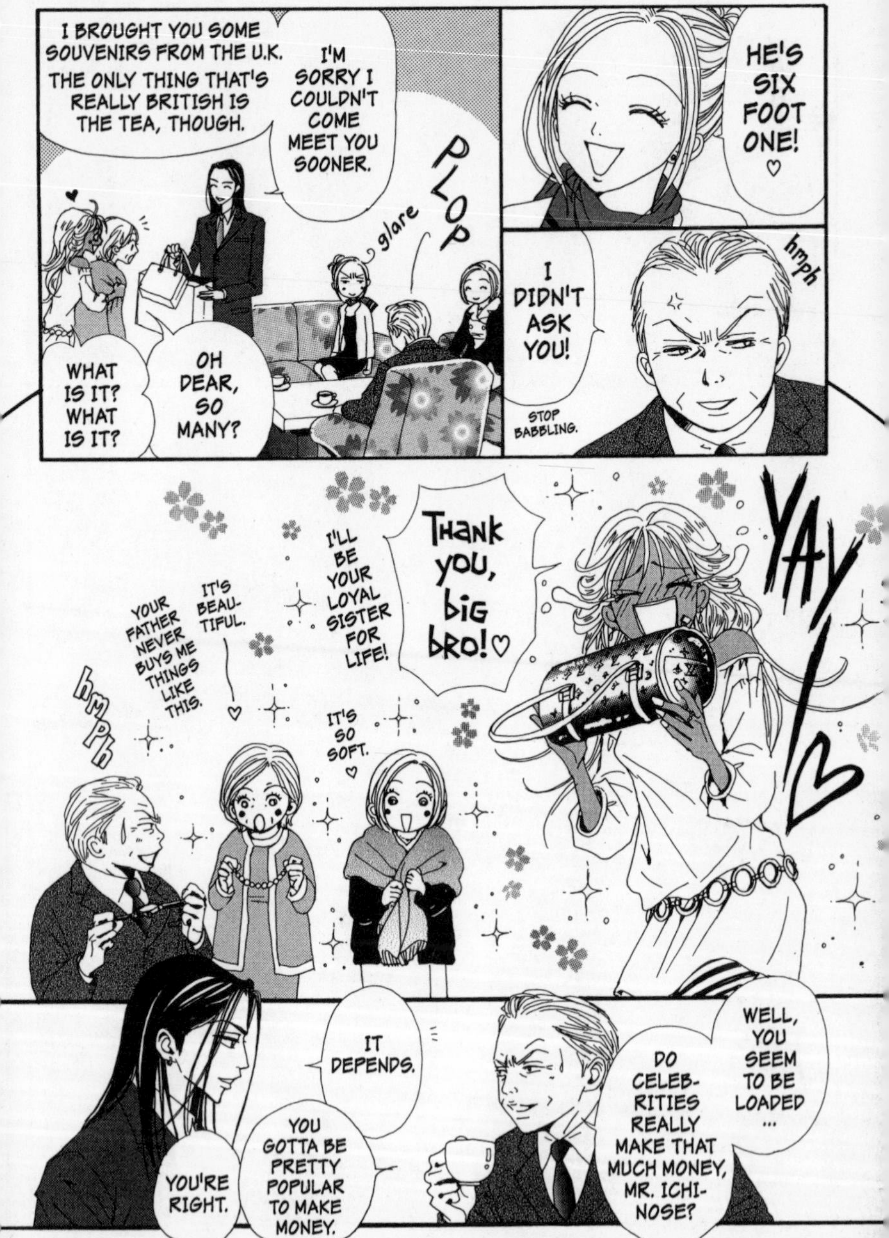
HE'S SIX FOOT ONE! ♡
hmph
I DIDN'T ASK YOU!
STOP BABBLING.
I'M SORRY I COULDN'T COME MEET YOU SOONER.
I BROUGHT YOU SOME SOUVENIRS FROM THE U.K.
THE ONLY THING THAT'S REALLY BRITISH IS THE TEA, THOUGH.
PLOP
glare
OH DEAR, SO MANY?
WHAT IS IT? WHAT IS IT?
YAY ♥
Thank you, big bro! ♡
I'LL BE YOUR LOYAL SISTER FOR LIFE!
IT'S SO SOFT. ♡
IT'S BEAUTIFUL. ♡
YOUR FATHER NEVER BUYS ME THINGS LIKE THIS.
hmph
WELL, YOU SEEM TO BE LOADED...
DO CELEBRITIES REALLY MAKE THAT MUCH MONEY, MR. ICHINOSE?
IT DEPENDS.
YOU GOTTA BE PRETTY POPULAR TO MAKE MONEY.
YOU'RE RIGHT.

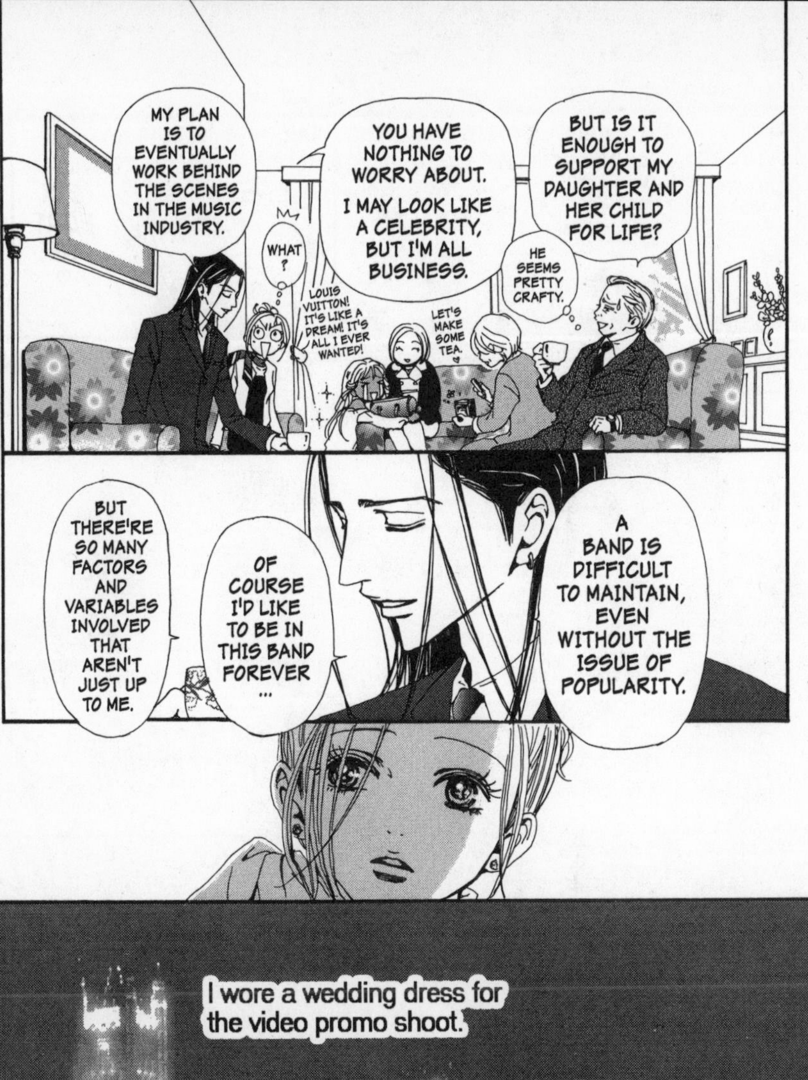
BUT IS IT ENOUGH TO SUPPORT MY DAUGHTER AND HER CHILD FOR LIFE?
HE SEEMS PRETTY CRAFTY.
YOU HAVE NOTHING TO WORRY ABOUT.
I MAY LOOK LIKE A CELEBRITY, BUT I'M ALL BUSINESS.
LET'S MAKE SOME TEA.
WHAT ?
LOUIS VUITTON! IT'S LIKE A DREAM! IT'S ALL I EVER WANTED!
MY PLAN IS TO EVENTUALLY WORK BEHIND THE SCENES IN THE MUSIC INDUSTRY.
A BAND IS DIFFICULT TO MAINTAIN, EVEN WITHOUT THE ISSUE OF POPULARITY.
OF COURSE I'D LIKE TO BE IN THIS BAND FOREVER ...
BUT THERE'RE SO MANY FACTORS AND VARIABLES INVOLVED THAT AREN'T JUST UP TO ME.

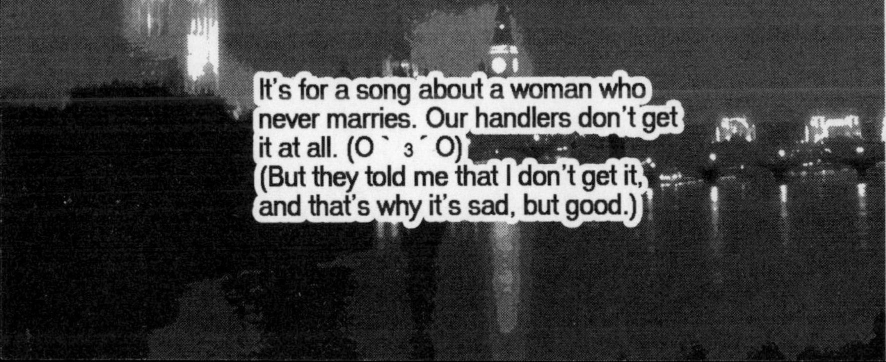
I wore a wedding dress for the video promo shoot.
It's for a song about a woman who never marries. Our handlers don't get it at all. (O ` 3 ´ O)
(But they told me that I don't get it, and that's why it's sad, but good.)

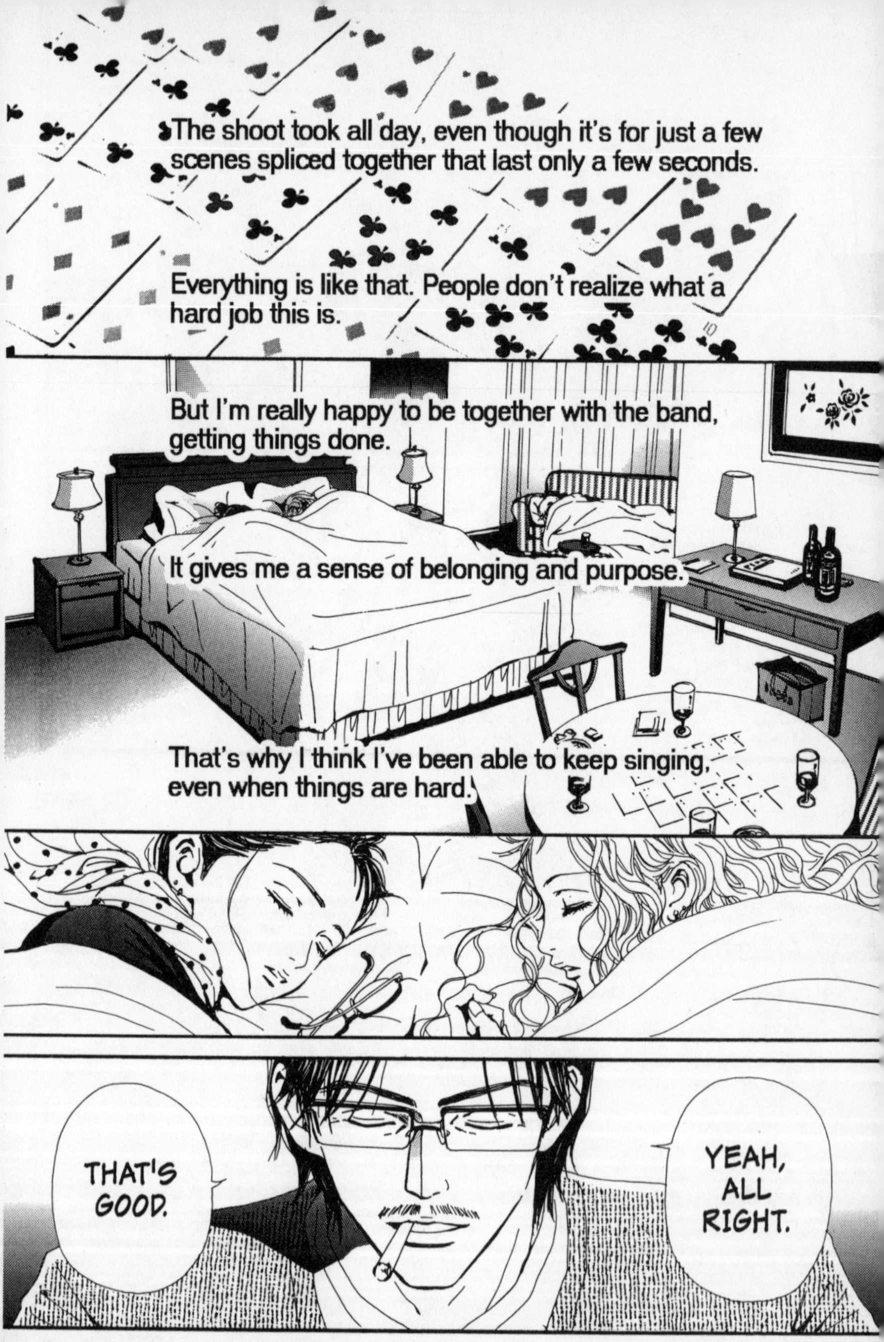
The shoot took all day, even though it's for just a few scenes spliced together that last only a few seconds.
Everything is like that. People don't realize what a hard job this is.
But I'm really happy to be together with the band, getting things done.
It gives me a sense of belonging and purpose.
That's why I think I've been able to keep singing, even when things are hard.
YEAH, ALL RIGHT.
THAT'S GOOD.

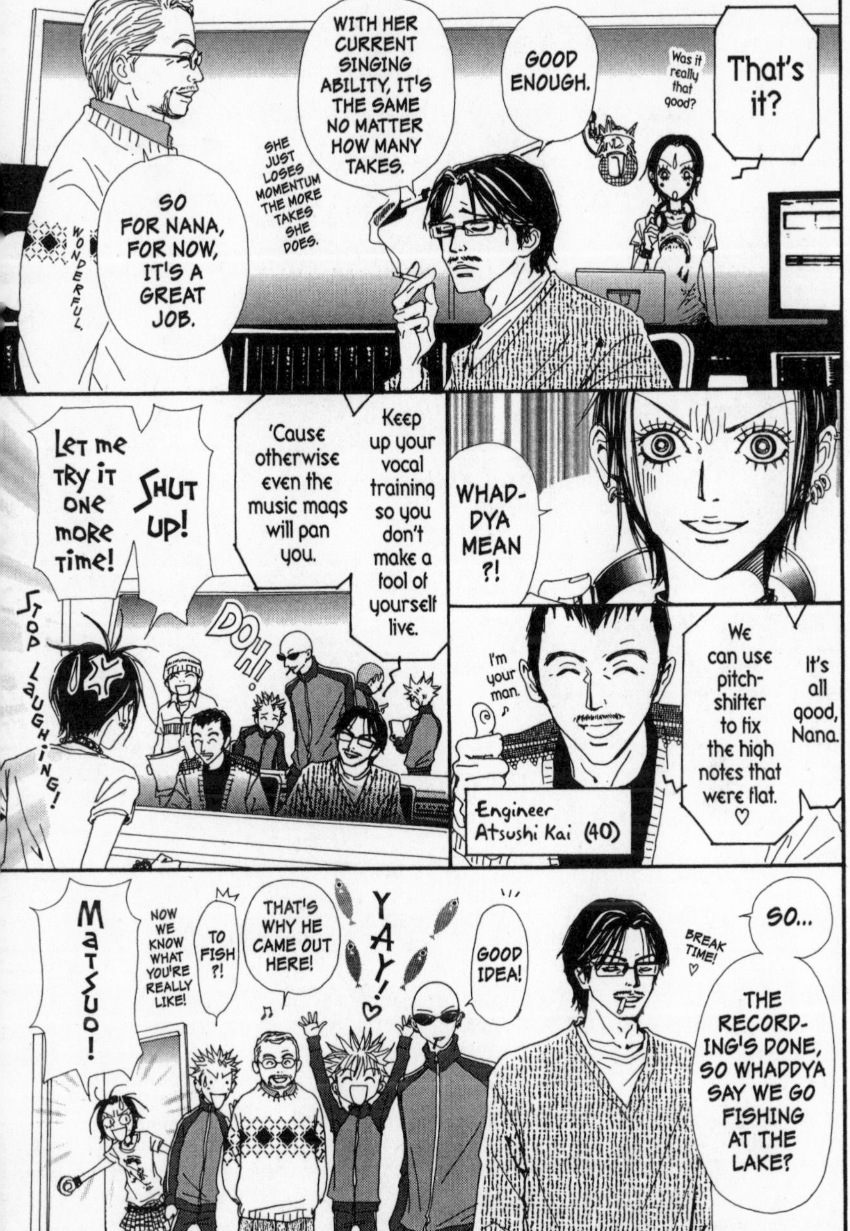

That's it?
Was it really that good?
GOOD ENOUGH.
WITH HER CURRENT SINGING ABILITY, IT'S THE SAME NO MATTER HOW MANY TAKES.
SHE JUST LOSES MOMENTUM THE MORE TAKES SHE DOES.
SO FOR NANA, FOR NOW, IT'S A GREAT JOB.
WONDERFUL.
WHAD-DYA MEAN?!
It's all good, Nana.
We can use pitch-shifter to fix the high notes that were flat. ♡
I'm your man. ♪
Engineer Atsushi Kai (40)
Keep up your vocal training so you don't make a fool of yourself live.
'Cause otherwise even the music mags will pan you.
SHUT UP!
Let me try it one more time!
DOH!
STOP LAUGHING!
SO...
BREAK TIME! ♡
THE RECORD-ING'S DONE, SO WHADDYA SAY WE GO FISHING AT THE LAKE?
GOOD IDEA!
YAY! ♡
THAT'S WHY HE CAME OUT HERE!
TO FISH?!
NOW WE KNOW WHAT YOU'RE REALLY LIKE!
MATSUO!

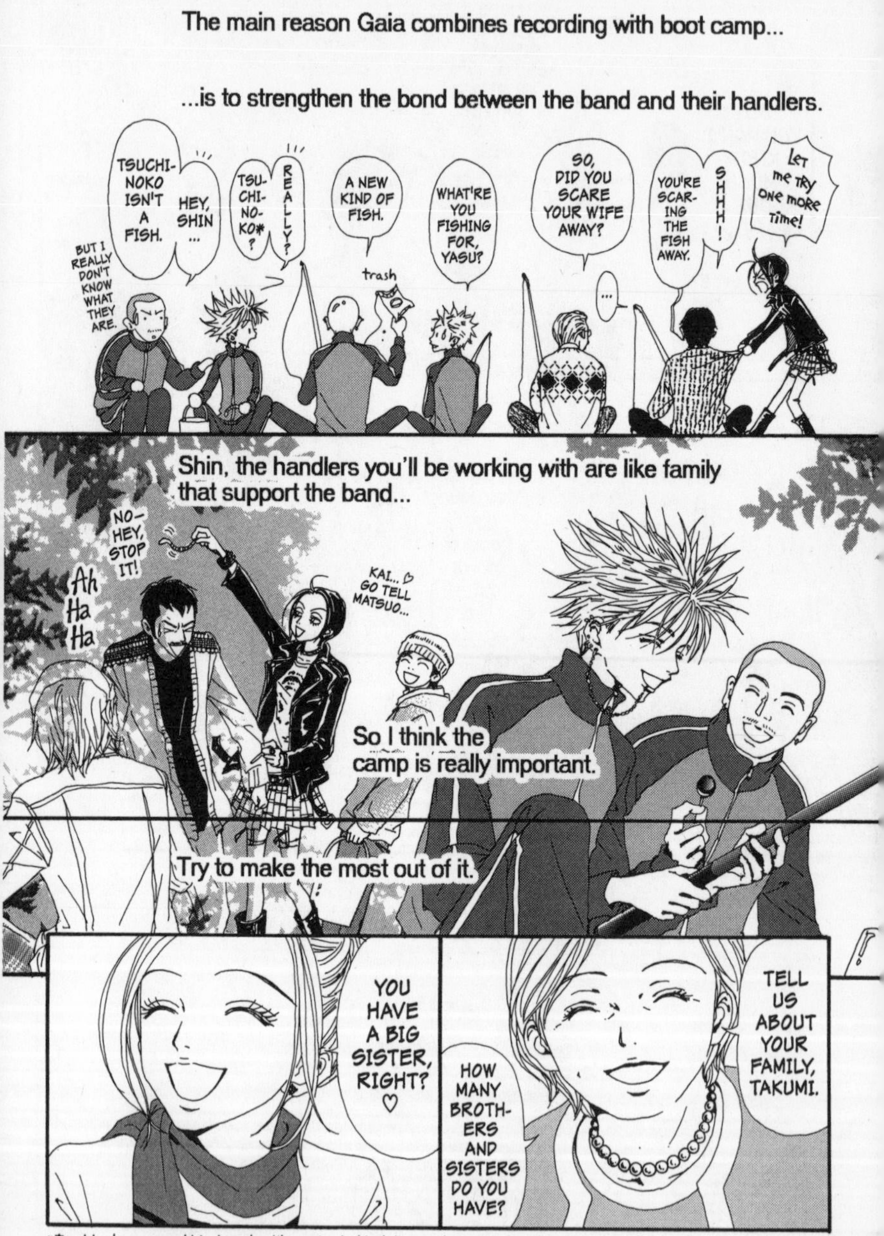
The main reason Gaia combines recording with boot camp...
...is to strengthen the bond between the band and their handlers.
LET me TRY one more Time!
SHHH!
YOU'RE SCARING THE FISH AWAY.
...
SO, DID YOU SCARE YOUR WIFE AWAY?
WHAT'RE YOU FISHING FOR, YASU?
trash
A NEW KIND OF FISH.
REALLY?
TSUCHINOKO*?
HEY, SHIN...
TSUCHINOKO ISN'T A FISH.
BUT I REALLY DON'T KNOW WHAT THEY ARE.
Shin, the handlers you'll be working with are like family that support the band...
KAI... ♡ GO TELL MATSUO...
NO—HEY, STOP IT!
Ah Ha Ha
So I think the camp is really important.
Try to make the most out of it.
TELL US ABOUT YOUR FAMILY, TAKUMI.
HOW MANY BROTHERS AND SISTERS DO YOU HAVE?
YOU HAVE A BIG SISTER, RIGHT? ♡

*Tsuchinoko are mythical snake-like animals that live underground and enjoy alcohol.

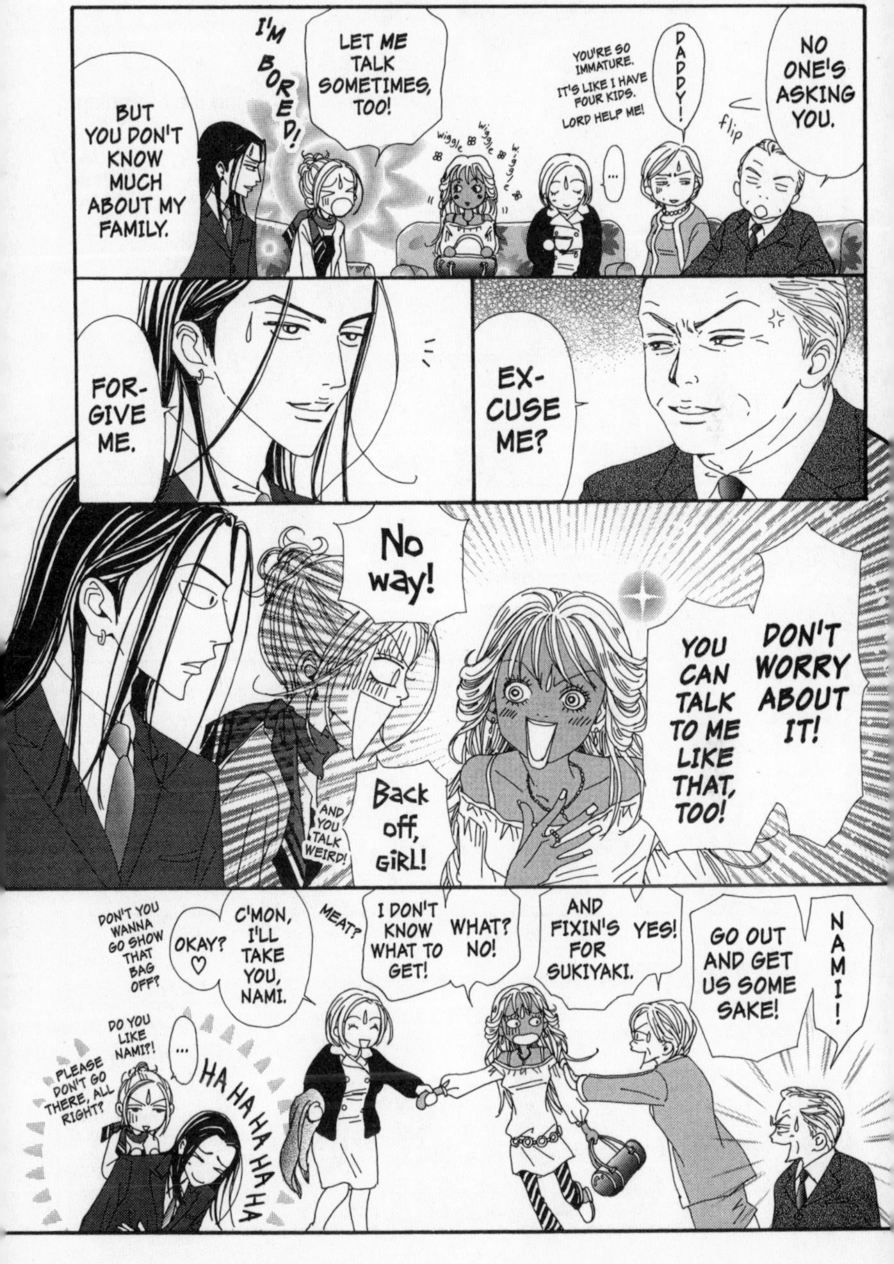
NO ONE'S ASKING YOU.
flip
DADDY!
YOU'RE SO IMMATURE. IT'S LIKE I HAVE FOUR KIDS. LORD HELP ME!
...
wiggle wiggle wiggle
LET ME TALK SOMETIMES, TOO!
I'M BORED!
BUT YOU DON'T KNOW MUCH ABOUT MY FAMILY.
EX-CUSE ME?
FOR-GIVE ME.
DON'T WORRY ABOUT IT!
YOU CAN TALK TO ME LIKE THAT, TOO!
No way!
Back off, GiRL!
AND YOU TALK WEIRD!
NAMI!
GO OUT AND GET US SOME SAKE!
YES!
AND FIXIN'S FOR SUKIYAKI.
WHAT? NO!
I DON'T KNOW WHAT TO GET!
MEAT?
C'MON, I'LL TAKE YOU, NAMI.
OKAY? ♡
DON'T YOU WANNA GO SHOW THAT BAG OFF?
...
DO YOU LIKE NAMI?!
HA HA HA HA HA HA
PLEASE DON'T GO THERE, ALL RIGHT?

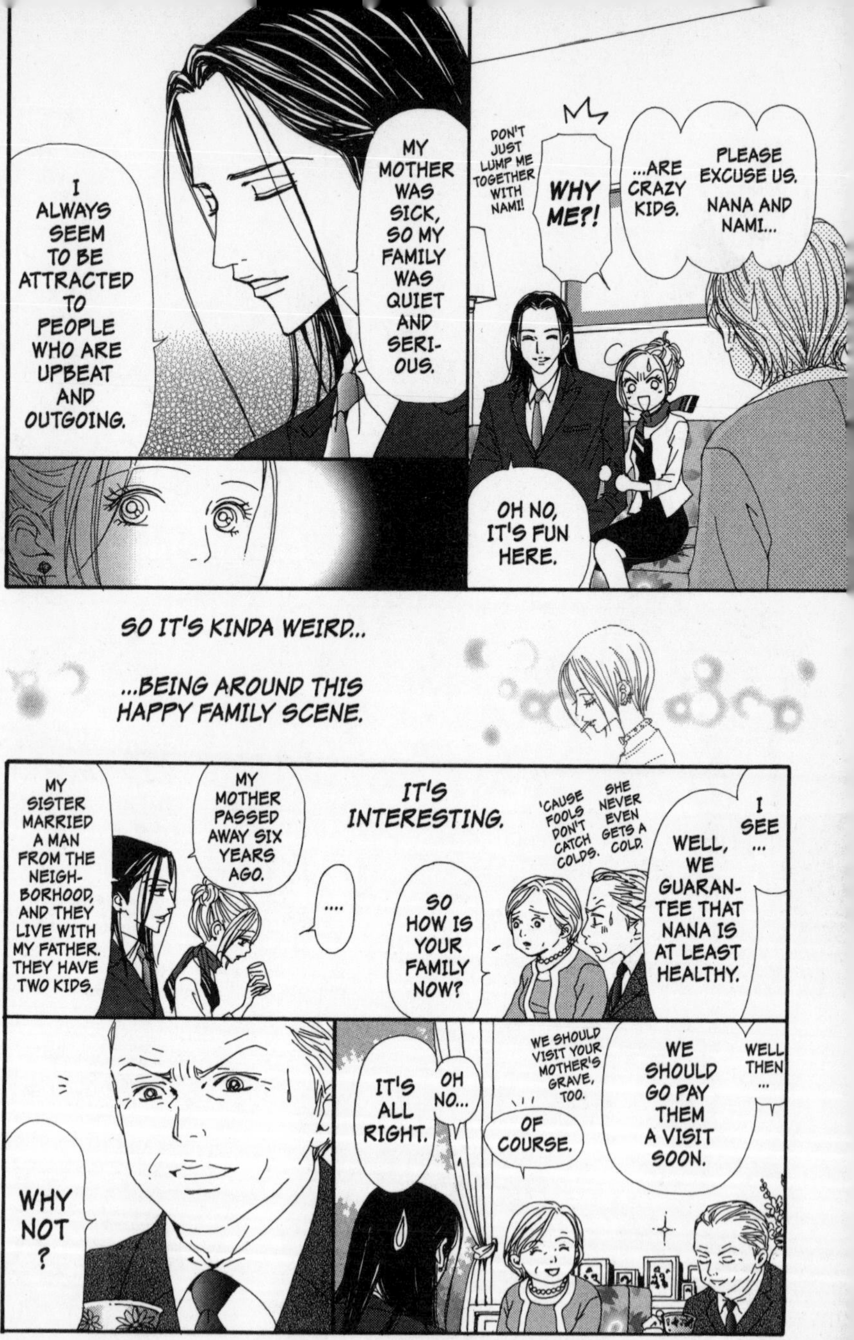
PLEASE EXCUSE US. NANA AND NAMI...
...ARE CRAZY KIDS.
WHY ME?!
DON'T JUST LUMP ME TOGETHER WITH NAMI!
OH NO, IT'S FUN HERE.
MY MOTHER WAS SICK, SO MY FAMILY WAS QUIET AND SERIOUS.
I ALWAYS SEEM TO BE ATTRACTED TO PEOPLE WHO ARE UPBEAT AND OUTGOING.
SO IT'S KINDA WEIRD...
...BEING AROUND THIS HAPPY FAMILY SCENE.
I SEE...
WELL, WE GUARANTEE THAT NANA IS AT LEAST HEALTHY.
SHE NEVER EVEN GETS A COLD.
'CAUSE FOOLS DON'T CATCH COLDS.
IT'S INTERESTING.
SO HOW IS YOUR FAMILY NOW?
....
MY MOTHER PASSED AWAY SIX YEARS AGO.
MY SISTER MARRIED A MAN FROM THE NEIGHBORHOOD, AND THEY LIVE WITH MY FATHER. THEY HAVE TWO KIDS.
WELL THEN...
WE SHOULD GO PAY THEM A VISIT SOON.
WE SHOULD VISIT YOUR MOTHER'S GRAVE, TOO.
OF COURSE.
OH NO...
IT'S ALL RIGHT.
WHY NOT?

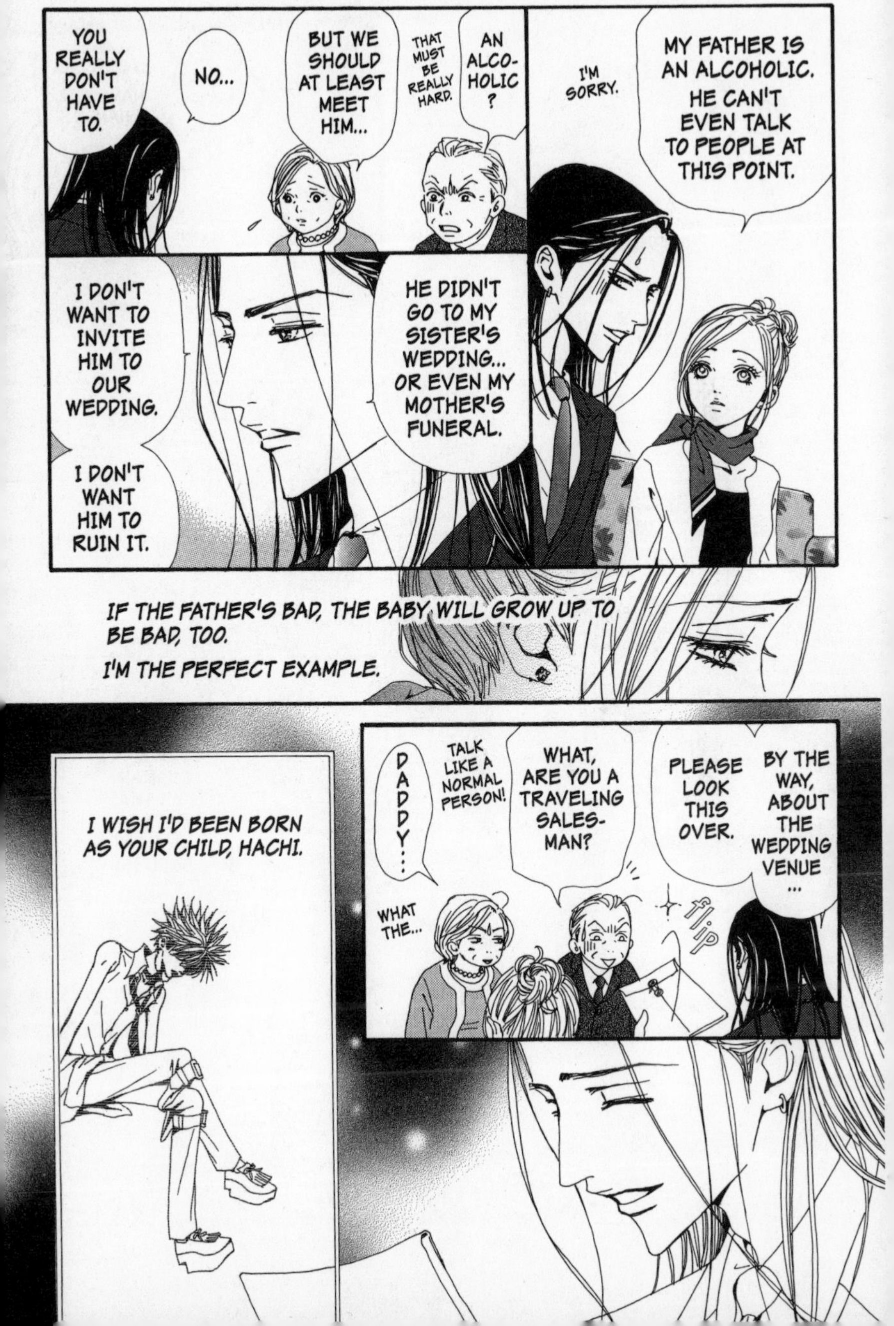
MY FATHER IS AN ALCOHOLIC. HE CAN'T EVEN TALK TO PEOPLE AT THIS POINT.
I'M SORRY.
AN ALCO-HOLIC?
THAT MUST BE REALLY HARD.
BUT WE SHOULD AT LEAST MEET HIM...
NO...
YOU REALLY DON'T HAVE TO.
HE DIDN'T GO TO MY SISTER'S WEDDING... OR EVEN MY MOTHER'S FUNERAL.
I DON'T WANT TO INVITE HIM TO OUR WEDDING.
I DON'T WANT HIM TO RUIN IT.
IF THE FATHER'S BAD, THE BABY WILL GROW UP TO BE BAD, TOO.
I'M THE PERFECT EXAMPLE.
BY THE WAY, ABOUT THE WEDDING VENUE...
PLEASE LOOK THIS OVER.
flip
WHAT, ARE YOU A TRAVELING SALES-MAN?
TALK LIKE A NORMAL PERSON!
DADDY...
WHAT THE...
I WISH I'D BEEN BORN AS YOUR CHILD, HACHI.

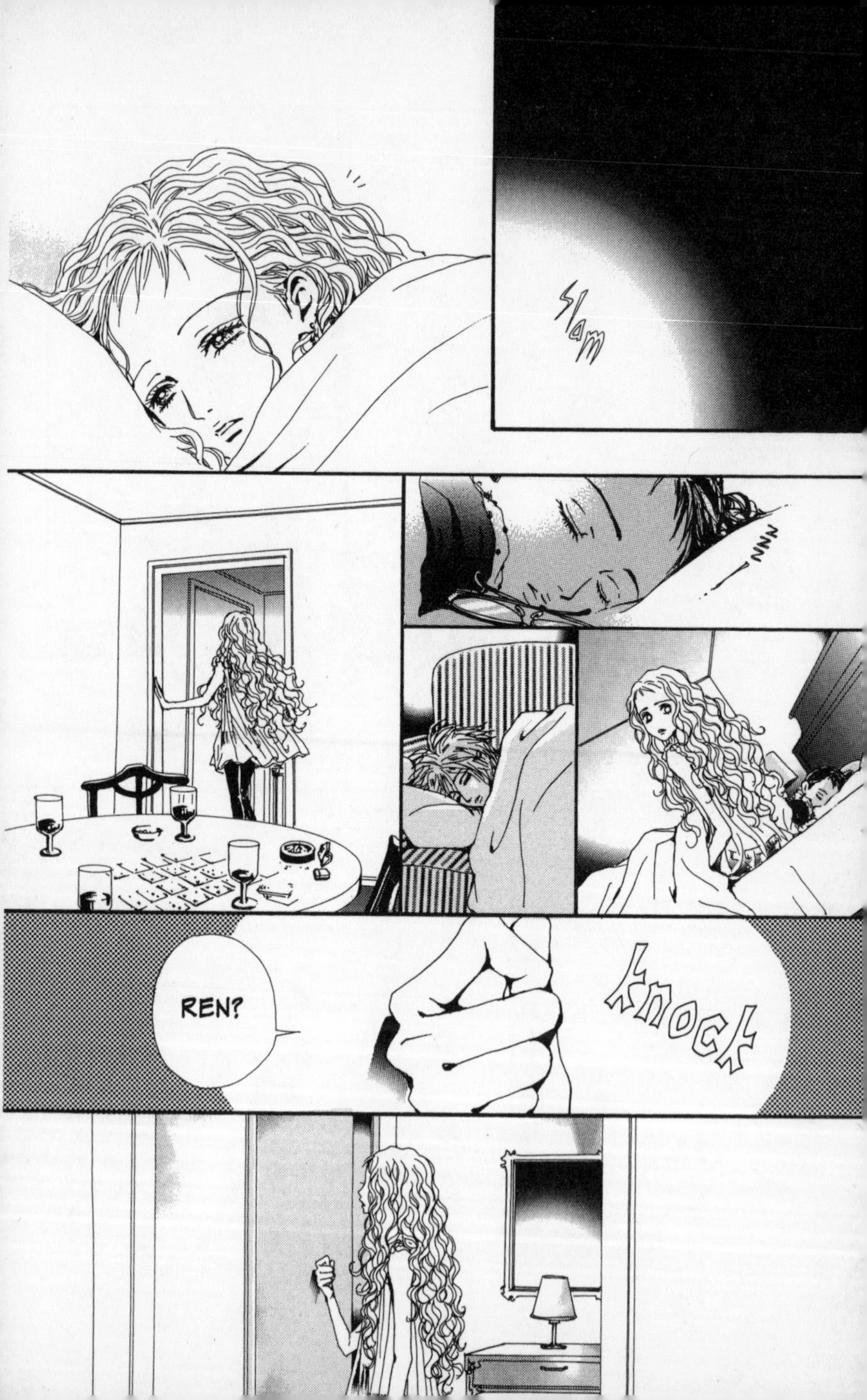
Slam
NNN
knock
REN?

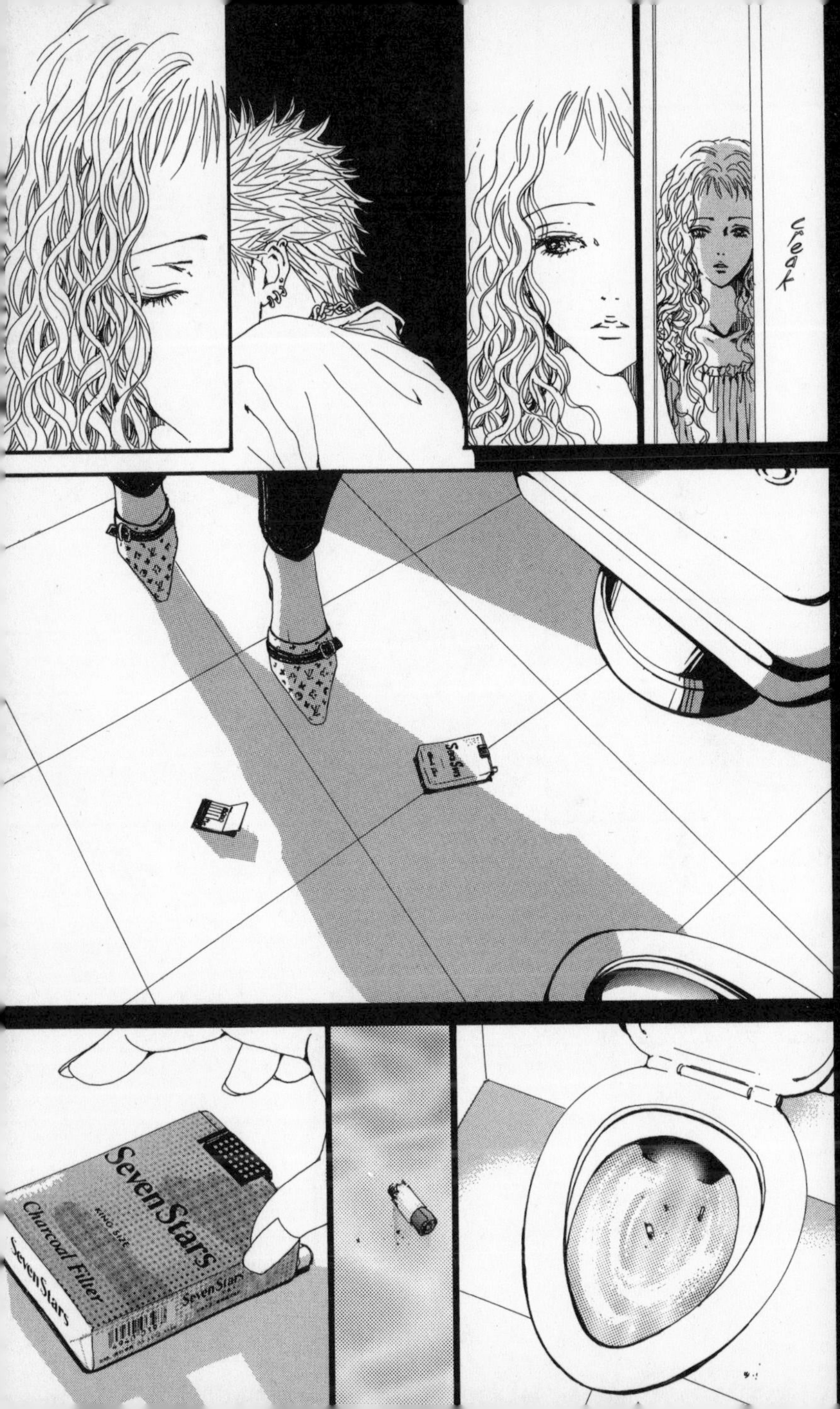
creak
Seven Stars
Charcoal Filter
Seven Stars
Seven Stars

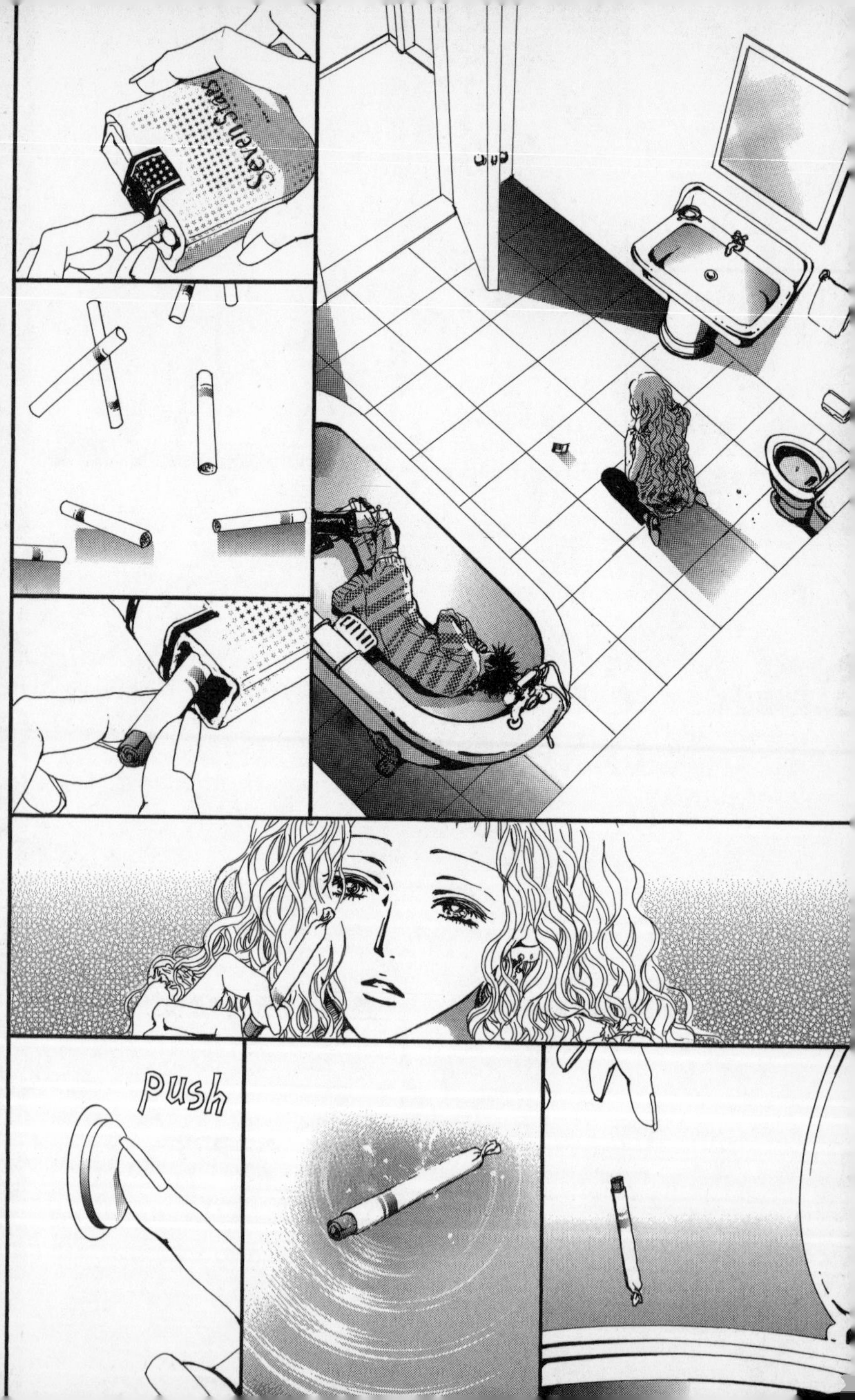
Seven Stars
push

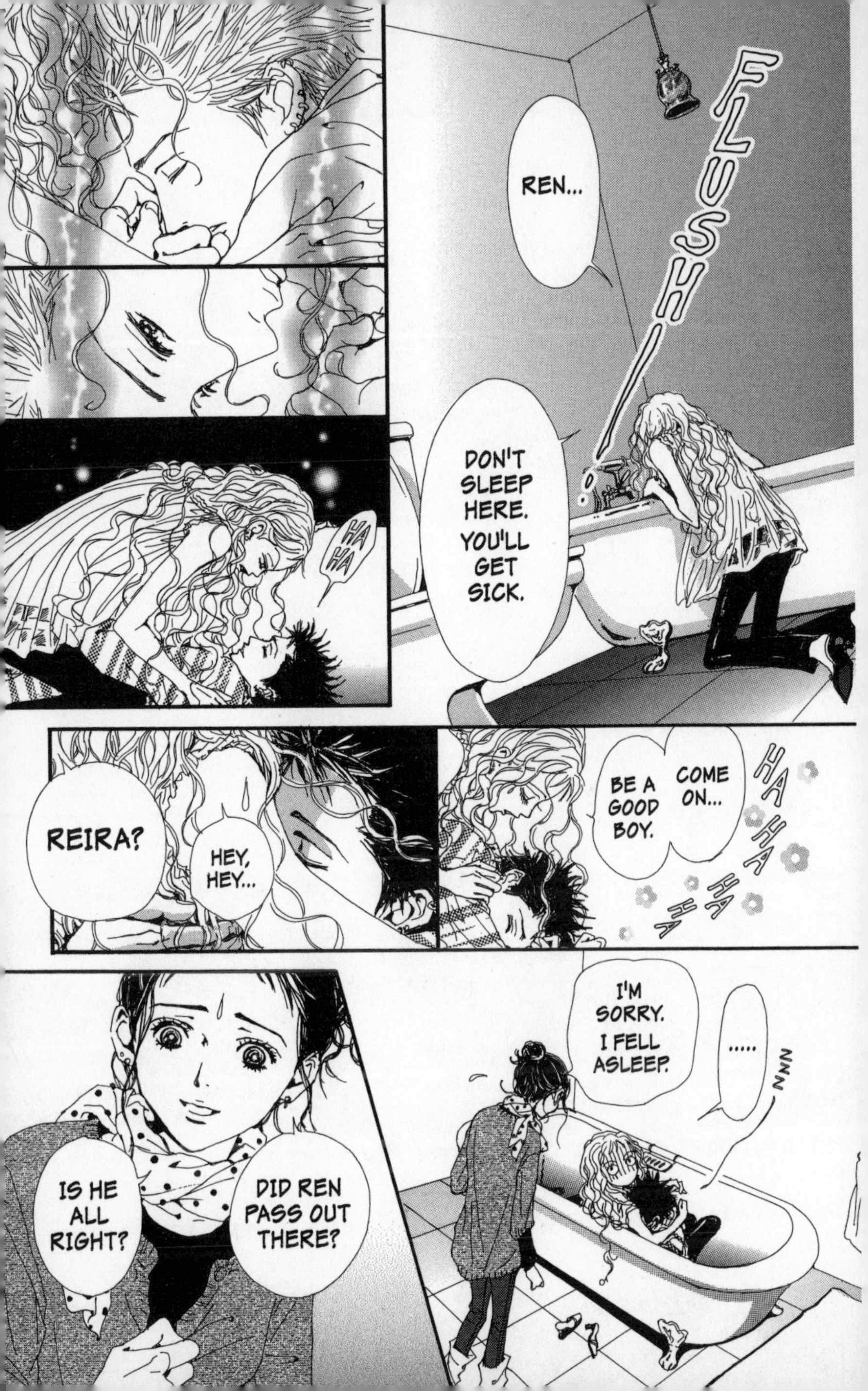
FLUSH
REN...
DON'T SLEEP HERE. YOU'LL GET SICK.
HA HA
HA HA HA HA HA
COME ON...
BE A GOOD BOY.
HEY, HEY...
REIRA?
NNN
.....
I'M SORRY. I FELL ASLEEP.
DID REN PASS OUT THERE?
IS HE ALL RIGHT?

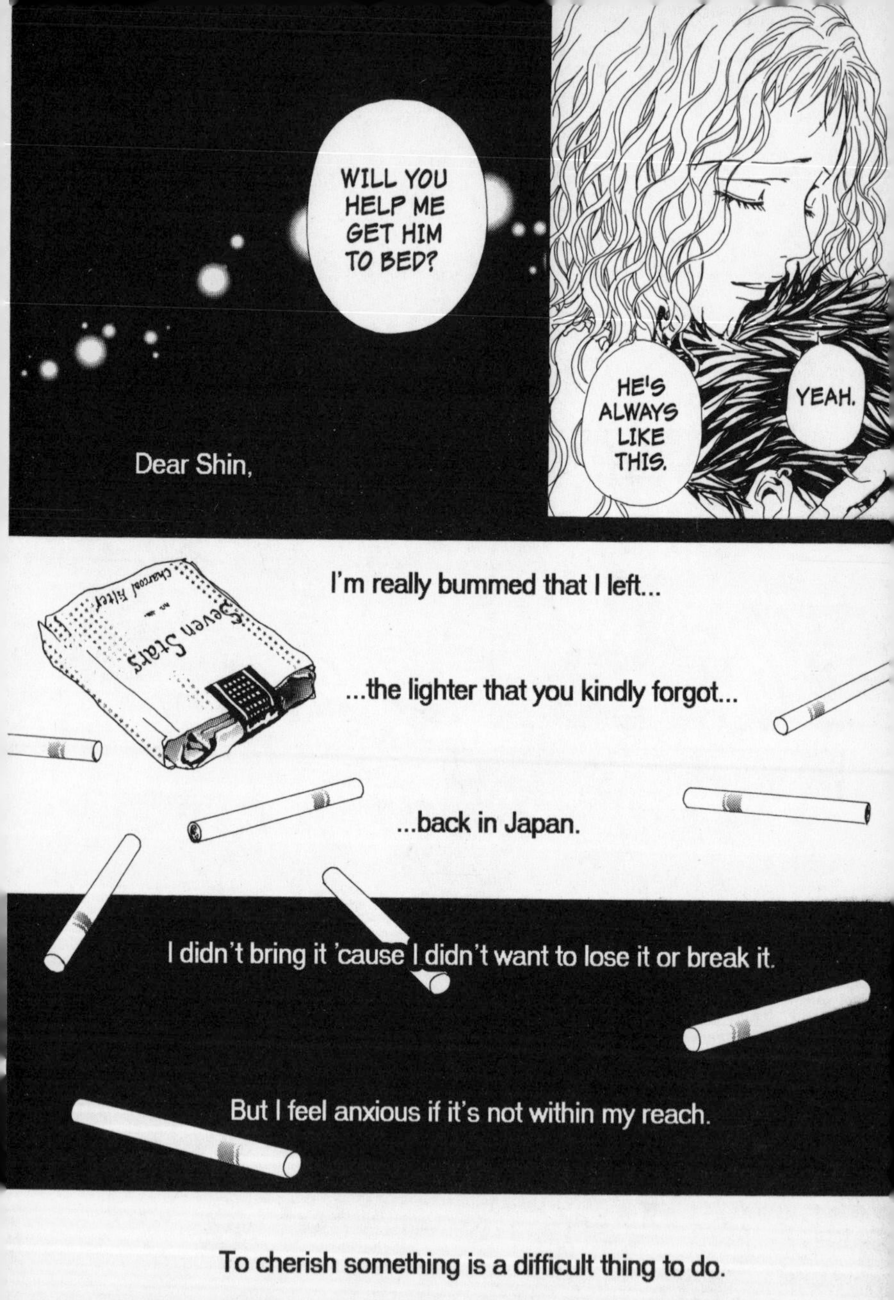
YEAH.
HE'S ALWAYS LIKE THIS.
WILL YOU HELP ME GET HIM TO BED?
Dear Shin,
I'm really bummed that I left...
Seven Stars
Charcoal Filter
...the lighter that you kindly forgot...
...back in Japan.
I didn't bring it 'cause I didn't want to lose it or break it.
But I feel anxious if it's not within my reach.
To cherish something is a difficult thing to do.

I'm flying back to Japan on the 27th.

Will you be back in Tokyo then?

I want to look you in the eye and talk to you.

To look deeply at someone else, with no lies,
is to look at yourself as well.

If you look away, you lose.

I don't want to lose.

Reira Serizawa

F Ren

S A Message for Nana

I got back from the UK today. Please call me.

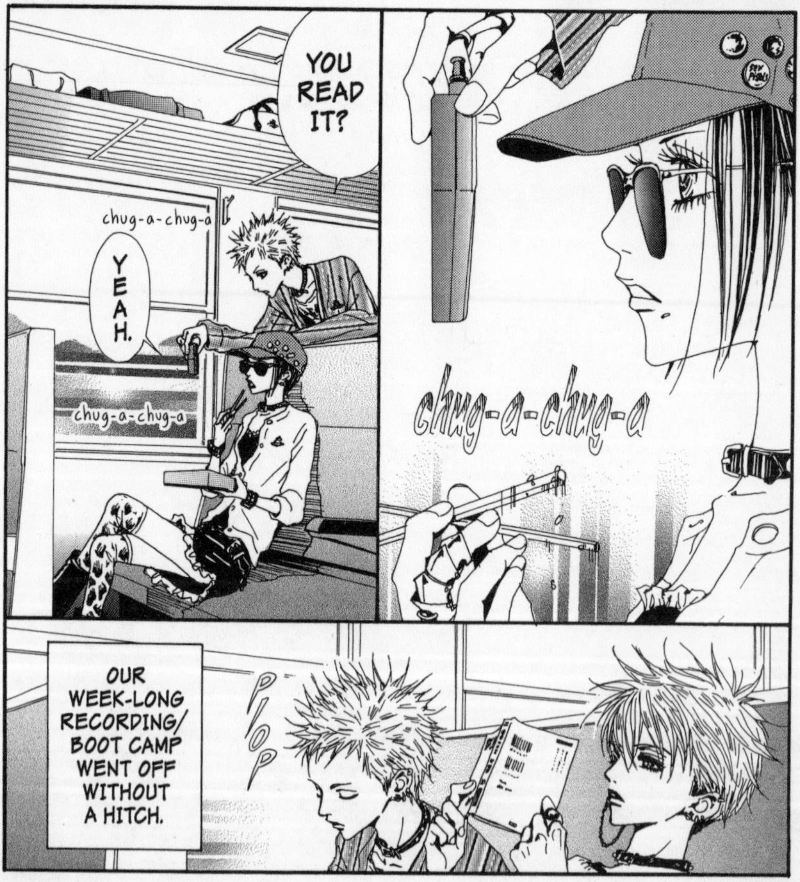
chug-a-chug-a
YOU READ IT?
chug-a-chug-a
YEAH.
chug-a-chug-a
PLOP
OUR WEEK-LONG RECORDING/ BOOT CAMP WENT OFF WITHOUT A HITCH.

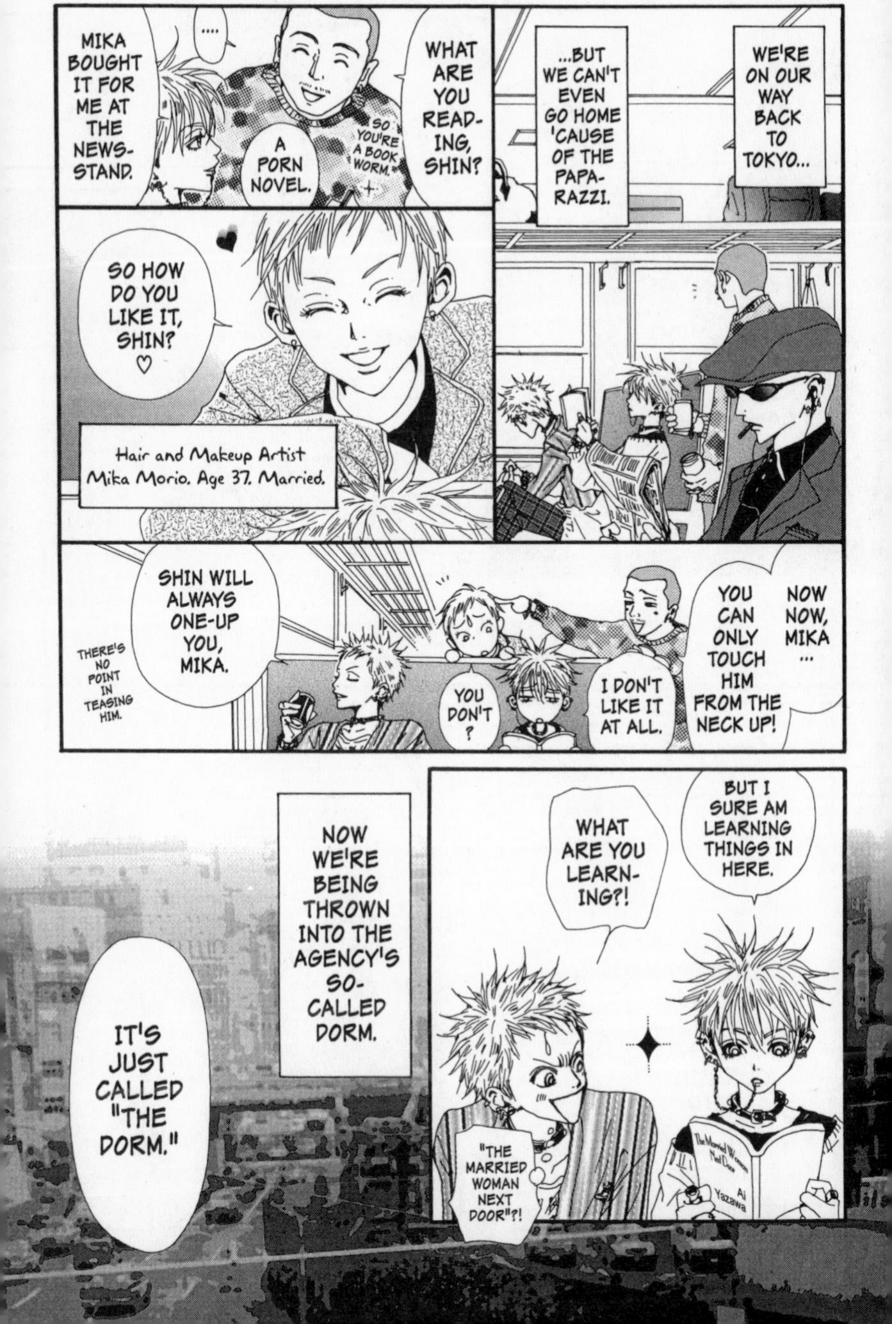
WE'RE ON OUR WAY BACK TO TOKYO...
...BUT WE CAN'T EVEN GO HOME 'CAUSE OF THE PAPARAZZI.
WHAT ARE YOU READING, SHIN?
SO YOU'RE A BOOKWORM.
....
A PORN NOVEL.
MIKA BOUGHT IT FOR ME AT THE NEWSSTAND.
SO HOW DO YOU LIKE IT, SHIN? ♡
Hair and Makeup Artist Mika Morio. Age 37. Married.
NOW NOW, MIKA...
YOU CAN ONLY TOUCH HIM FROM THE NECK UP!
I DON'T LIKE IT AT ALL.
YOU DON'T?
SHIN WILL ALWAYS ONE-UP YOU, MIKA.
THERE'S NO POINT IN TEASING HIM.
BUT I SURE AM LEARNING THINGS IN HERE.
WHAT ARE YOU LEARNING?!
"THE MARRIED WOMAN NEXT DOOR"?!
NOW WE'RE BEING THROWN INTO THE AGENCY'S SO-CALLED DORM.
IT'S JUST CALLED "THE DORM."

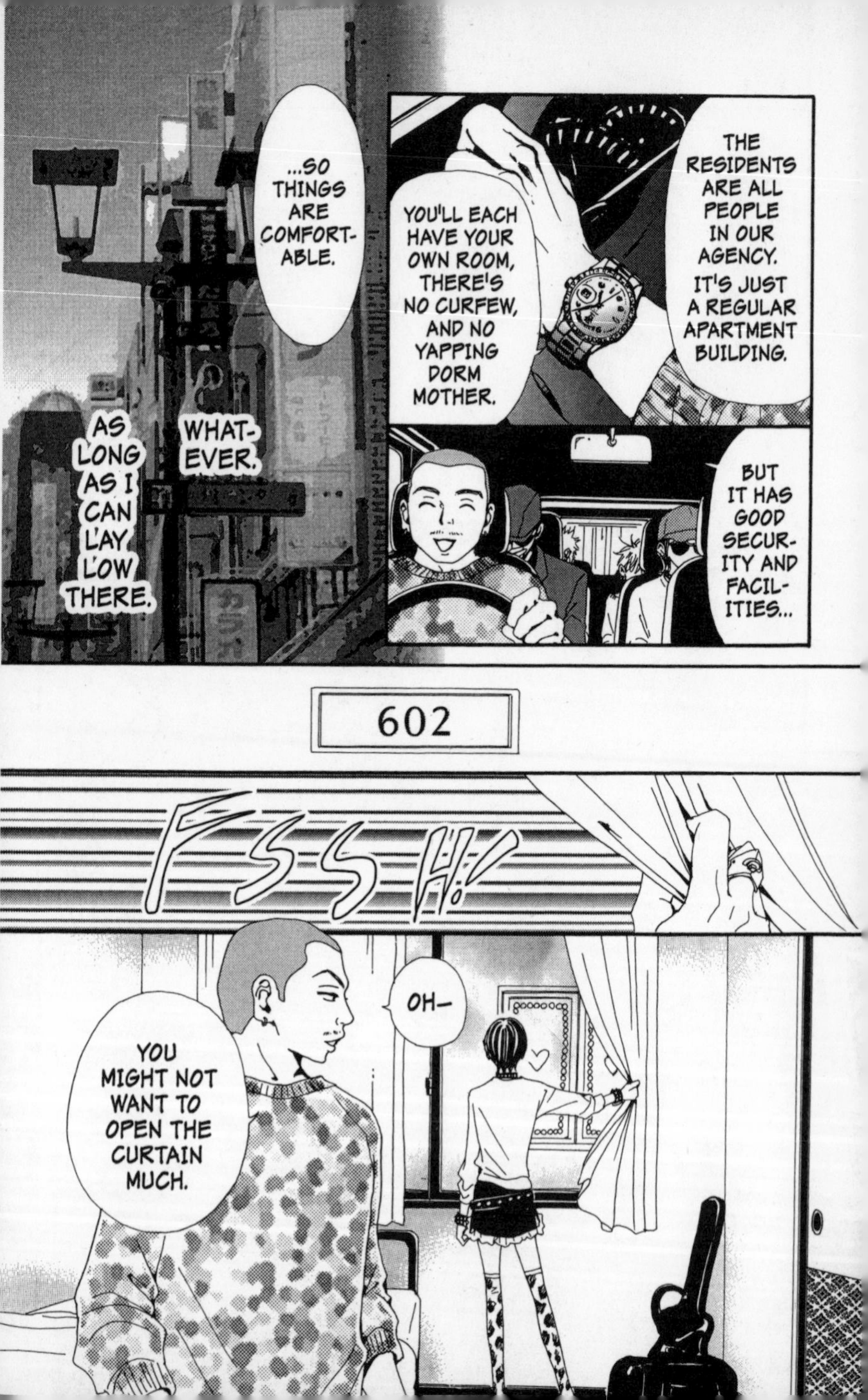
THE RESIDENTS ARE ALL PEOPLE IN OUR AGENCY.
IT'S JUST A REGULAR APARTMENT BUILDING.
YOU'LL EACH HAVE YOUR OWN ROOM, THERE'S NO CURFEW, AND NO YAPPING DORM MOTHER.
BUT IT HAS GOOD SECURITY AND FACILITIES...
...SO THINGS ARE COMFORTABLE.
WHATEVER.
AS LONG AS I CAN LAY LOW THERE.
602
FSSH!
OH—
YOU MIGHT NOT WANT TO OPEN THE CURTAIN MUCH.

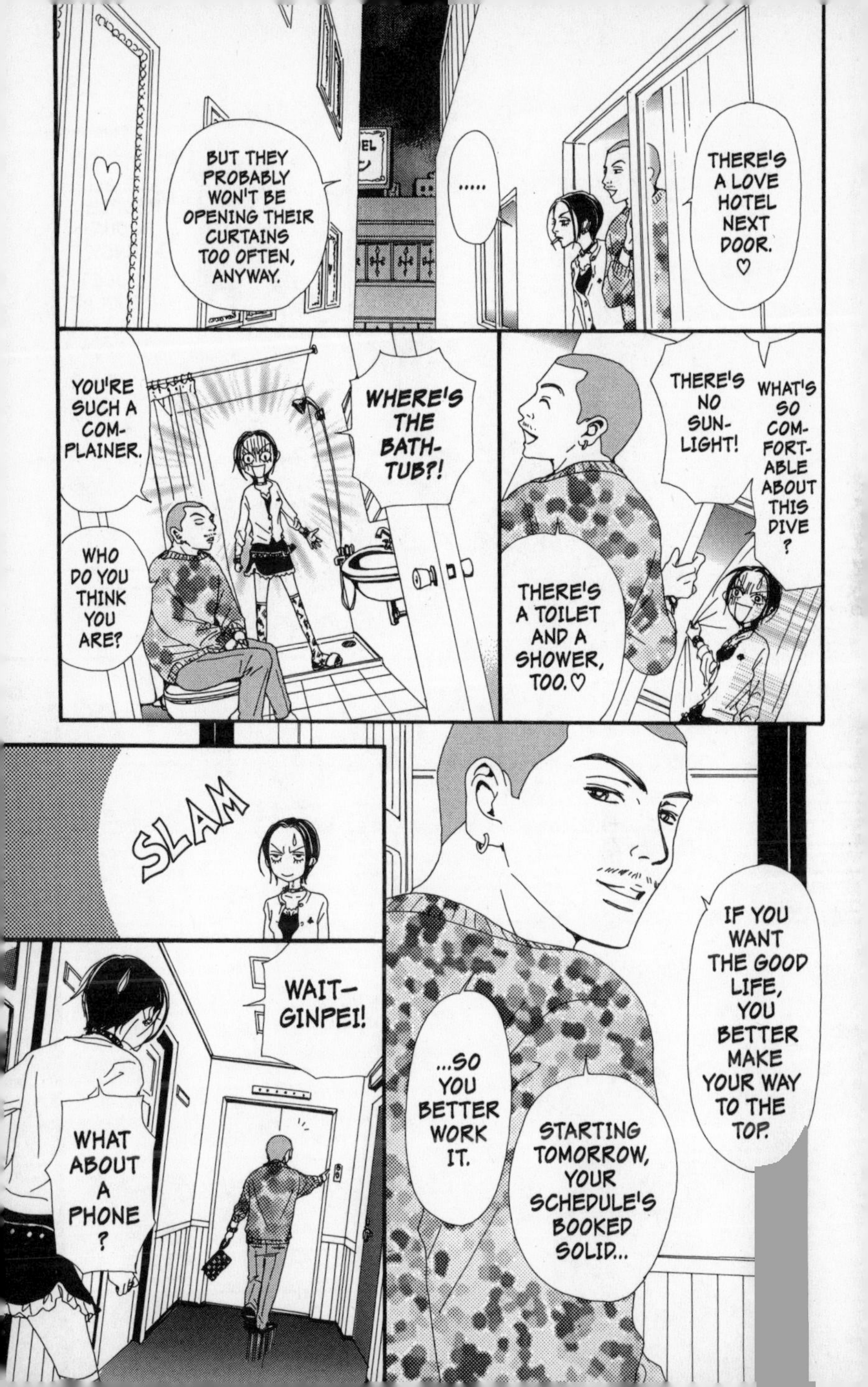
THERE'S A LOVE HOTEL NEXT DOOR. ♡
.....
BUT THEY PROBABLY WON'T BE OPENING THEIR CURTAINS TOO OFTEN, ANYWAY.
WHAT'S SO COMFORTABLE ABOUT THIS DIVE?
THERE'S NO SUNLIGHT!
THERE'S A TOILET AND A SHOWER, TOO. ♡
WHERE'S THE BATHTUB?!
YOU'RE SUCH A COMPLAINER.
WHO DO YOU THINK YOU ARE?
IF YOU WANT THE GOOD LIFE, YOU BETTER MAKE YOUR WAY TO THE TOP.
STARTING TOMORROW, YOUR SCHEDULE'S BOOKED SOLID...
...SO YOU BETTER WORK IT.
SLAM
WAIT-GINPEI!
WHAT ABOUT A PHONE?

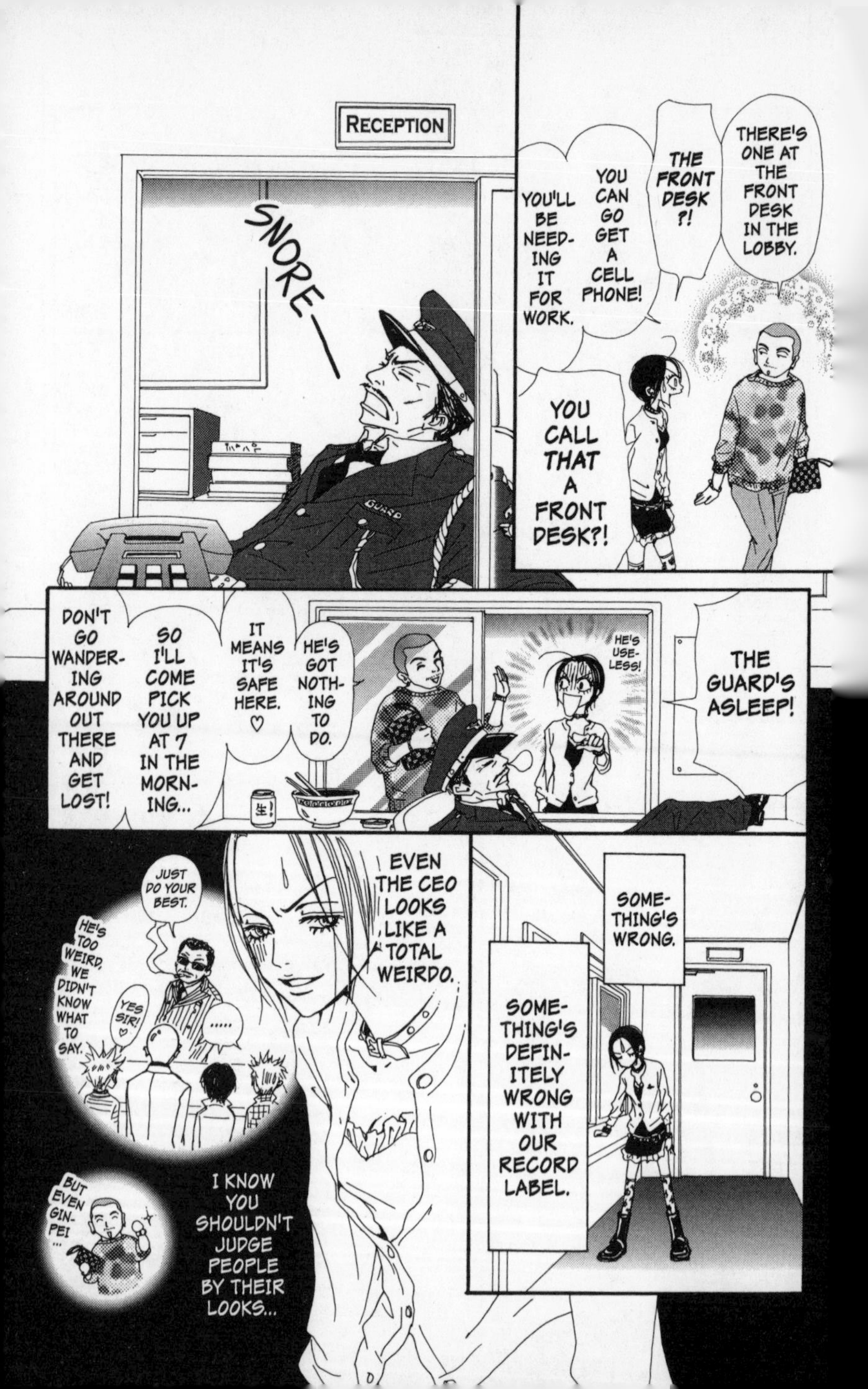
THERE'S ONE AT THE FRONT DESK IN THE LOBBY.
THE FRONT DESK?!
YOU CAN GO GET A CELL PHONE!
YOU'LL BE NEEDING IT FOR WORK.
YOU CALL THAT A FRONT DESK?!
RECEPTION
SNORE—
THE GUARD'S ASLEEP!
HE'S USELESS!
HE'S GOT NOTHING TO DO.
IT MEANS IT'S SAFE HERE. ♡
SO I'LL COME PICK YOU UP AT 7 IN THE MORNING...
DON'T GO WANDERING AROUND OUT THERE AND GET LOST!
SOMETHING'S WRONG.
SOMETHING'S DEFINITELY WRONG WITH OUR RECORD LABEL.
EVEN THE CEO LOOKS LIKE A TOTAL WEIRDO.
JUST DO YOUR BEST.
YES SIR! ♡
......
HE'S TOO WEIRD, WE DIDN'T KNOW WHAT TO SAY.
BUT EVEN GINPEI...
I KNOW YOU SHOULDN'T JUDGE PEOPLE BY THEIR LOOKS...

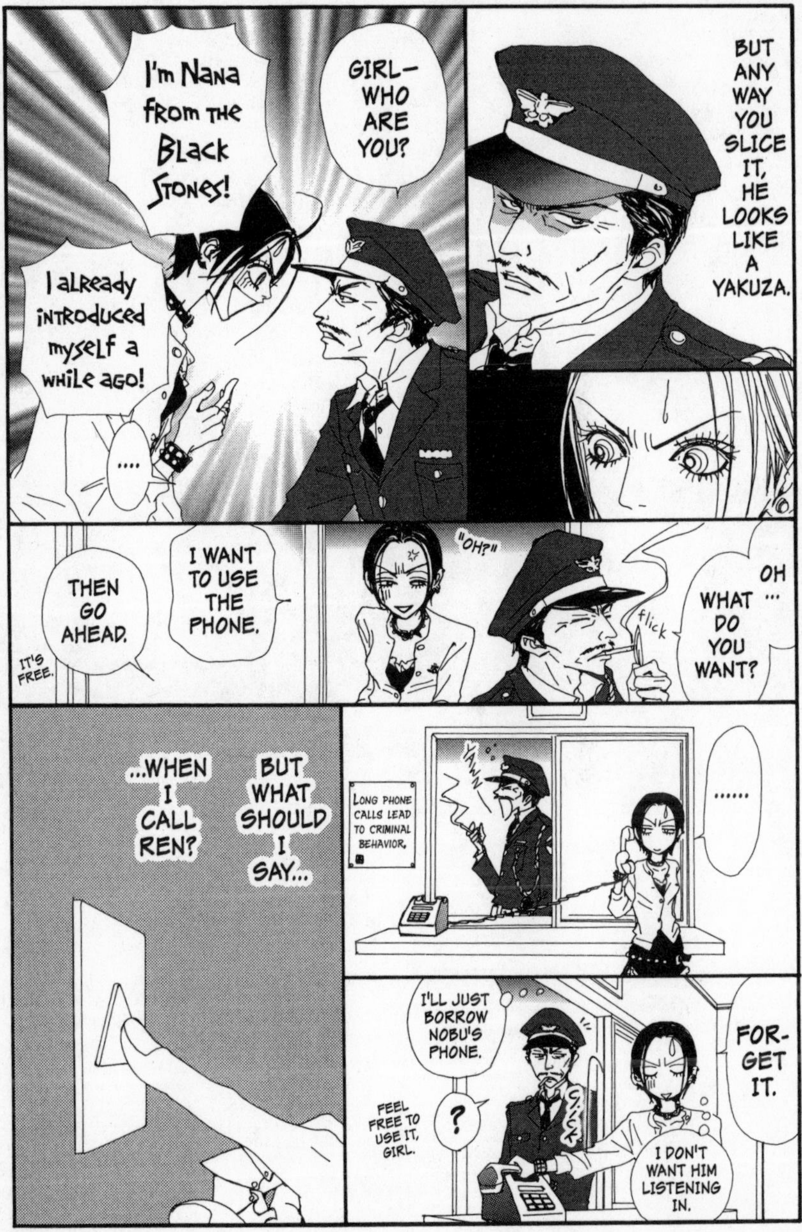
BUT ANY WAY YOU SLICE IT, HE LOOKS LIKE A YAKUZA.
GIRL— WHO ARE YOU?
I'm Nana from the Black Stones!
I already introduced myself a while ago!
....
OH ... WHAT DO YOU WANT?
flick
"OH?"
I WANT TO USE THE PHONE.
THEN GO AHEAD.
IT'S FREE.
......
YAWN
LONG PHONE CALLS LEAD TO CRIMINAL BEHAVIOR.
FOR-GET IT.
I'LL JUST BORROW NOBU'S PHONE.
I DON'T WANT HIM LISTENING IN.
CLICK
?
FEEL FREE TO USE IT, GIRL.
BUT WHAT SHOULD I SAY...
...WHEN I CALL REN?

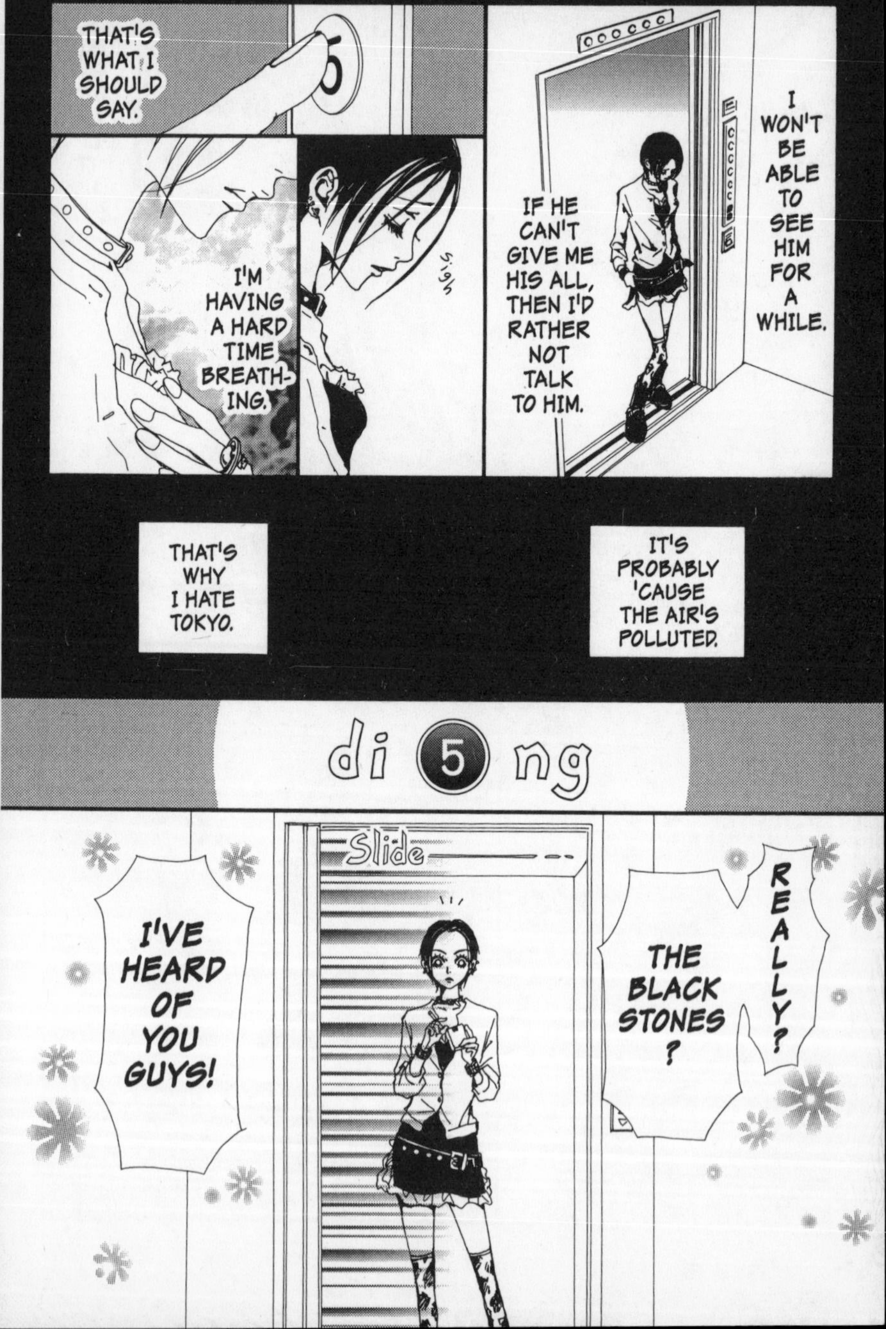
I WON'T BE ABLE TO SEE HIM FOR A WHILE.
IF HE CAN'T GIVE ME HIS ALL, THEN I'D RATHER NOT TALK TO HIM.
THAT'S WHAT I SHOULD SAY.
sigh
I'M HAVING A HARD TIME BREATHING.
IT'S PROBABLY 'CAUSE THE AIR'S POLLUTED.
THAT'S WHY I HATE TOKYO.
di 5 ng
Slide
REALLY?
THE BLACK STONES?
I'VE HEARD OF YOU GUYS!

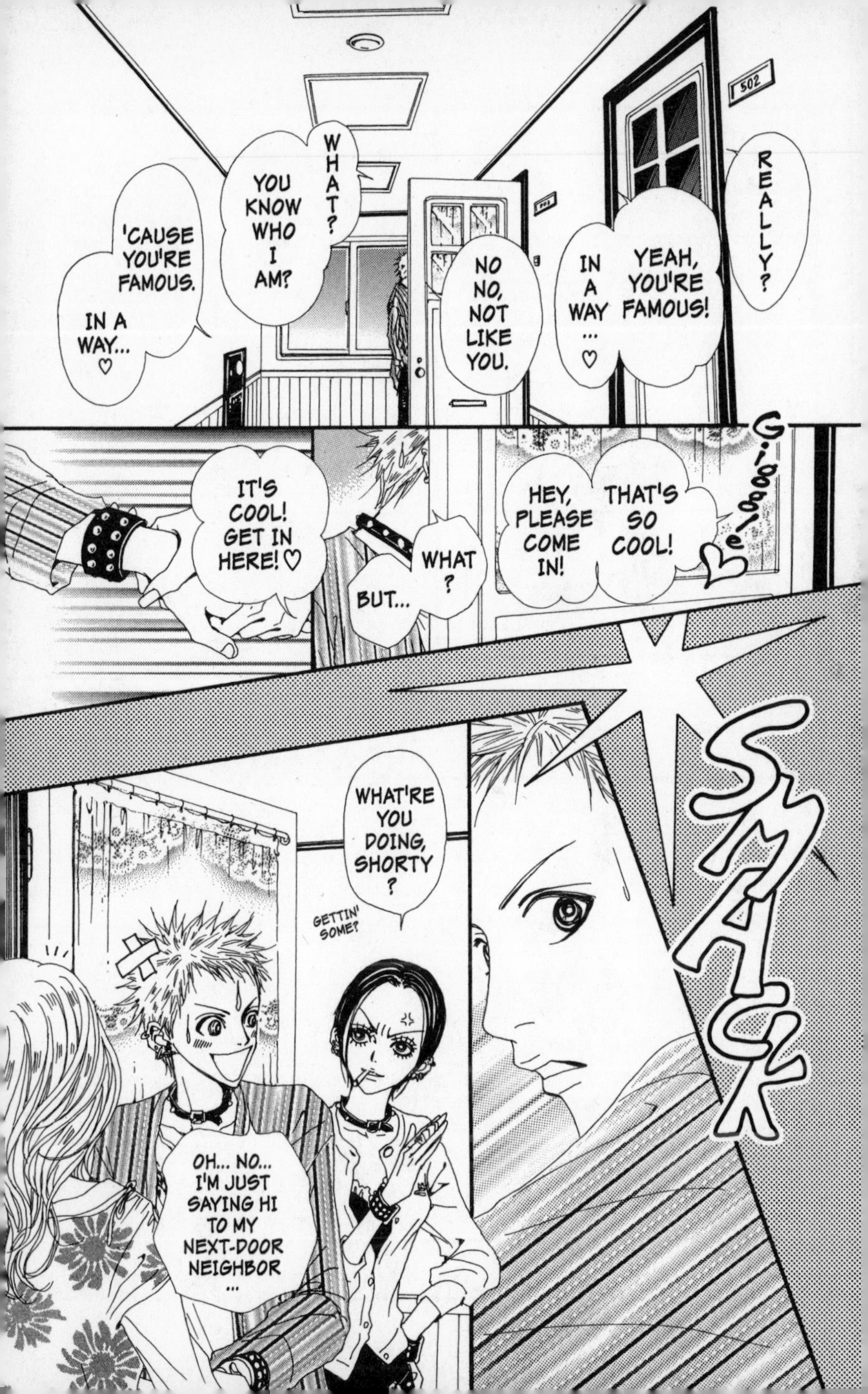
502
REALLY?
YEAH, YOU'RE FAMOUS!
IN A WAY ... ♡
NO NO, NOT LIKE YOU.
WHAT?
YOU KNOW WHO I AM?
'CAUSE YOU'RE FAMOUS.
IN A WAY... ♡
Giggle ♡
THAT'S SO COOL!
HEY, PLEASE COME IN!
WHAT?
BUT...
IT'S COOL! GET IN HERE! ♡
SMACK
WHAT'RE YOU DOING, SHORTY?
GETTIN' SOME?
OH... NO... I'M JUST SAYING HI TO MY NEXT-DOOR NEIGHBOR...

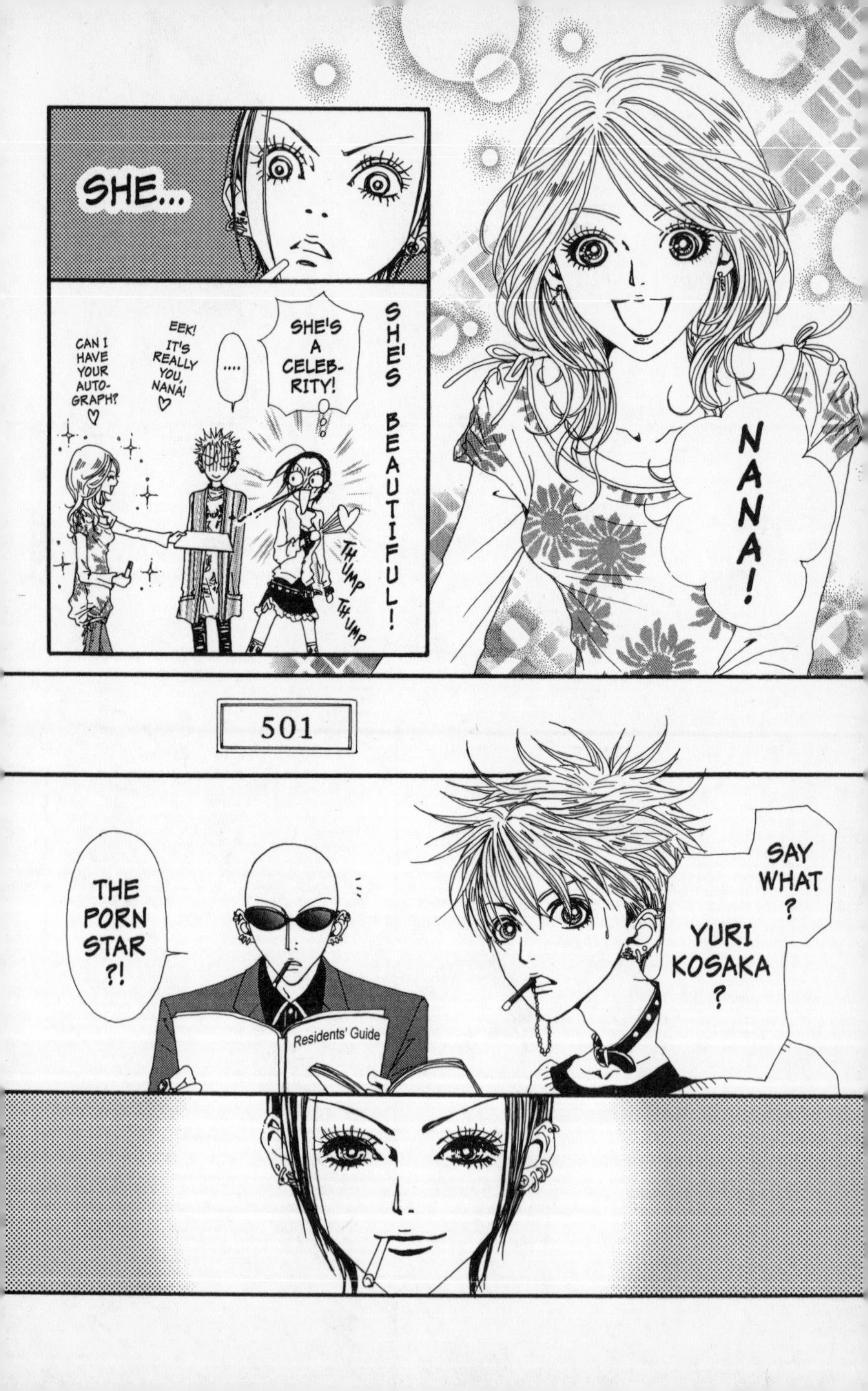
NANA!
SHE...
SHE'S BEAUTIFUL!
SHE'S A CELEBRITY!
....
EEK! IT'S REALLY YOU, NANA! ♡
CAN I HAVE YOUR AUTOGRAPH? ♡
THUMP THUMP
501
SAY WHAT?
YURI KOSAKA?
THE PORN STAR?!
Residents' Guide

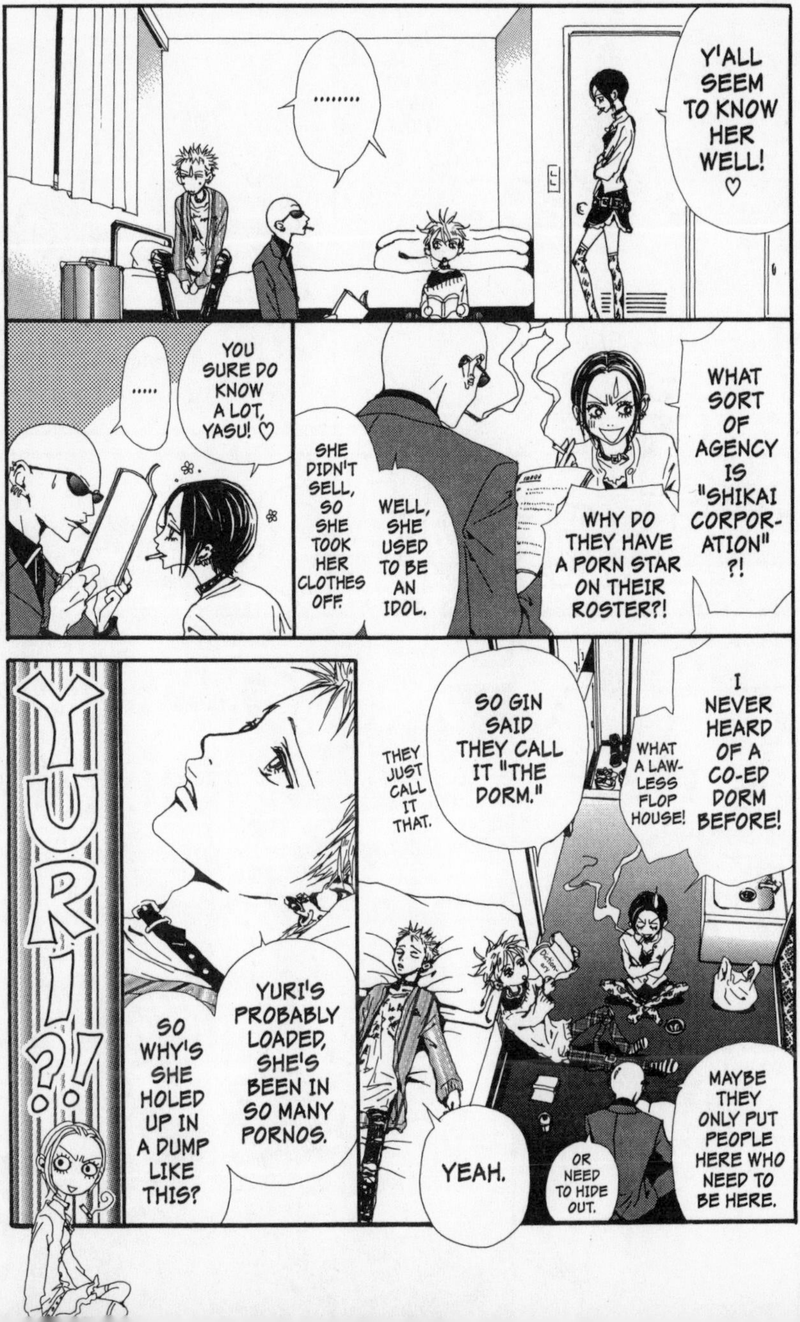
Y'ALL SEEM TO KNOW HER WELL! ♡
....
WHAT SORT OF AGENCY IS "SHIKAI CORPORATION" ?!
WHY DO THEY HAVE A PORN STAR ON THEIR ROSTER?!
WELL, SHE USED TO BE AN IDOL.
SHE DIDN'T SELL, SO SHE TOOK HER CLOTHES OFF.
YOU SURE DO KNOW A LOT, YASU! ♡
.....
I NEVER HEARD OF A CO-ED DORM BEFORE!
WHAT A LAWLESS FLOP HOUSE!
SO GIN SAID THEY CALL IT "THE DORM."
THEY JUST CALL IT THAT.
MAYBE THEY ONLY PUT PEOPLE HERE WHO NEED TO BE HERE.
OR NEED TO HIDE OUT.
YEAH.
YURI'S PROBABLY LOADED, SHE'S BEEN IN SO MANY PORNOS.
SO WHY'S SHE HOLED UP IN A DUMP LIKE THIS?
YURI?!

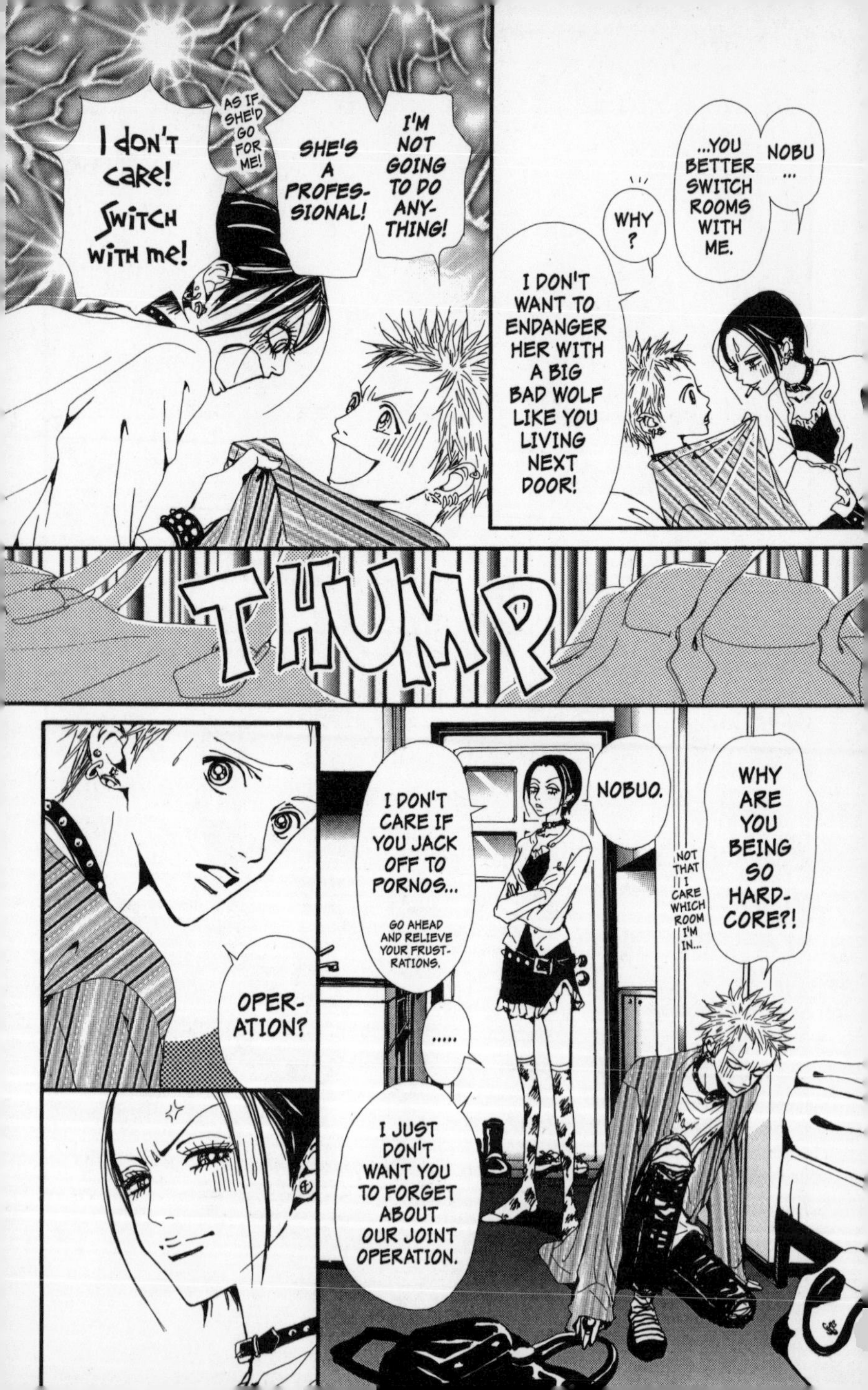
NOBU ...
...YOU BETTER SWITCH ROOMS WITH ME.
WHY ?
I DON'T WANT TO ENDANGER HER WITH A BIG BAD WOLF LIKE YOU LIVING NEXT DOOR!
I'M NOT GOING TO DO ANYTHING!
SHE'S A PROFESSIONAL!
AS IF SHE'D GO FOR ME!
I don't care! Switch with me!
THUMP
WHY ARE YOU BEING SO HARD-CORE?!
NOT THAT I CARE WHICH ROOM I'M IN...
NOBUO.
I DON'T CARE IF YOU JACK OFF TO PORNOS...
GO AHEAD AND RELIEVE YOUR FRUSTRATIONS.
.....
I JUST DON'T WANT YOU TO FORGET ABOUT OUR JOINT OPERATION.
OPERATION?

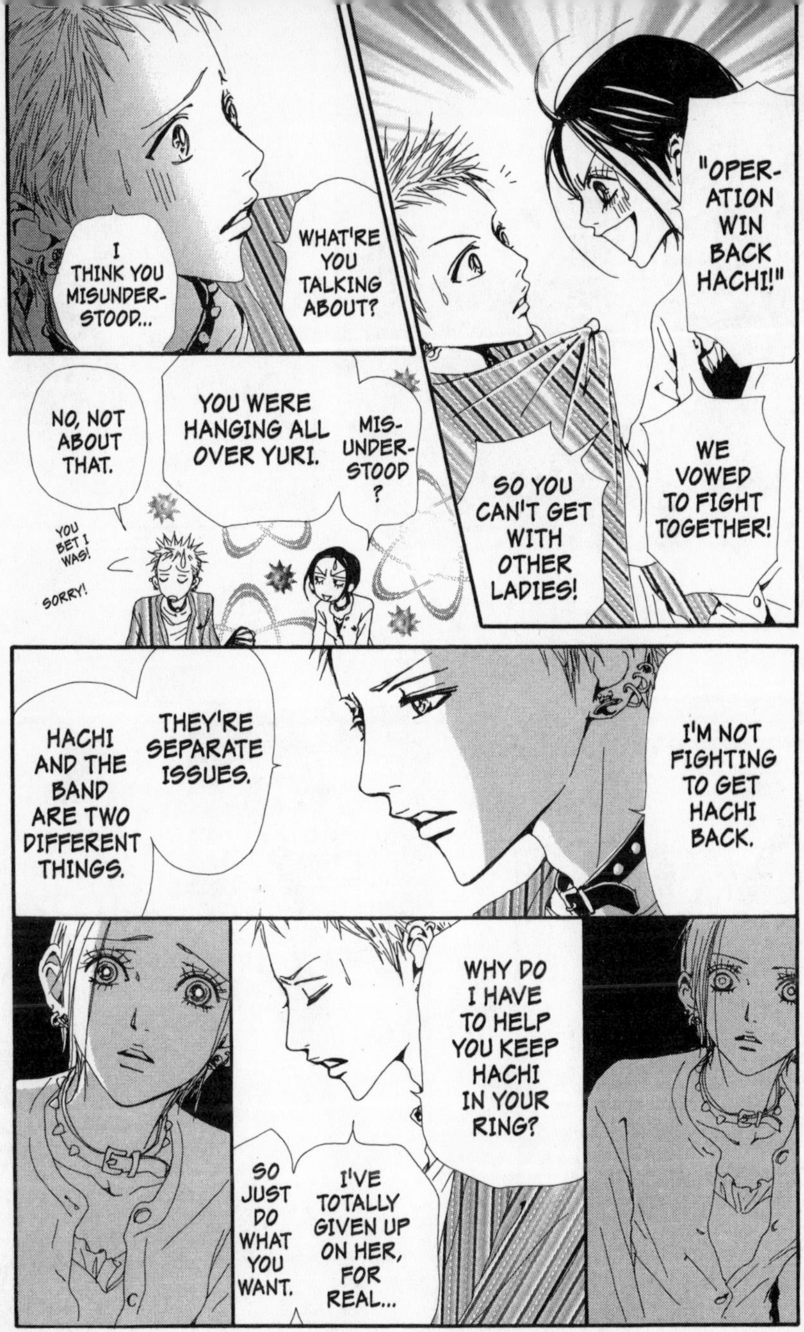
"OPERATION WIN BACK HACHI!!"
WHAT'RE YOU TALKING ABOUT?
I THINK YOU MISUNDERSTOOD...
WE VOWED TO FIGHT TOGETHER!
SO YOU CAN'T GET WITH OTHER LADIES!
MISUNDERSTOOD?
YOU WERE HANGING ALL OVER YURI.
NO, NOT ABOUT THAT.
YOU BET I WAS!
SORRY!
I'M NOT FIGHTING TO GET HACHI BACK.
THEY'RE SEPARATE ISSUES.
HACHI AND THE BAND ARE TWO DIFFERENT THINGS.
WHY DO I HAVE TO HELP YOU KEEP HACHI IN YOUR RING?
I'VE TOTALLY GIVEN UP ON HER, FOR REAL...
SO JUST DO WHAT YOU WANT.

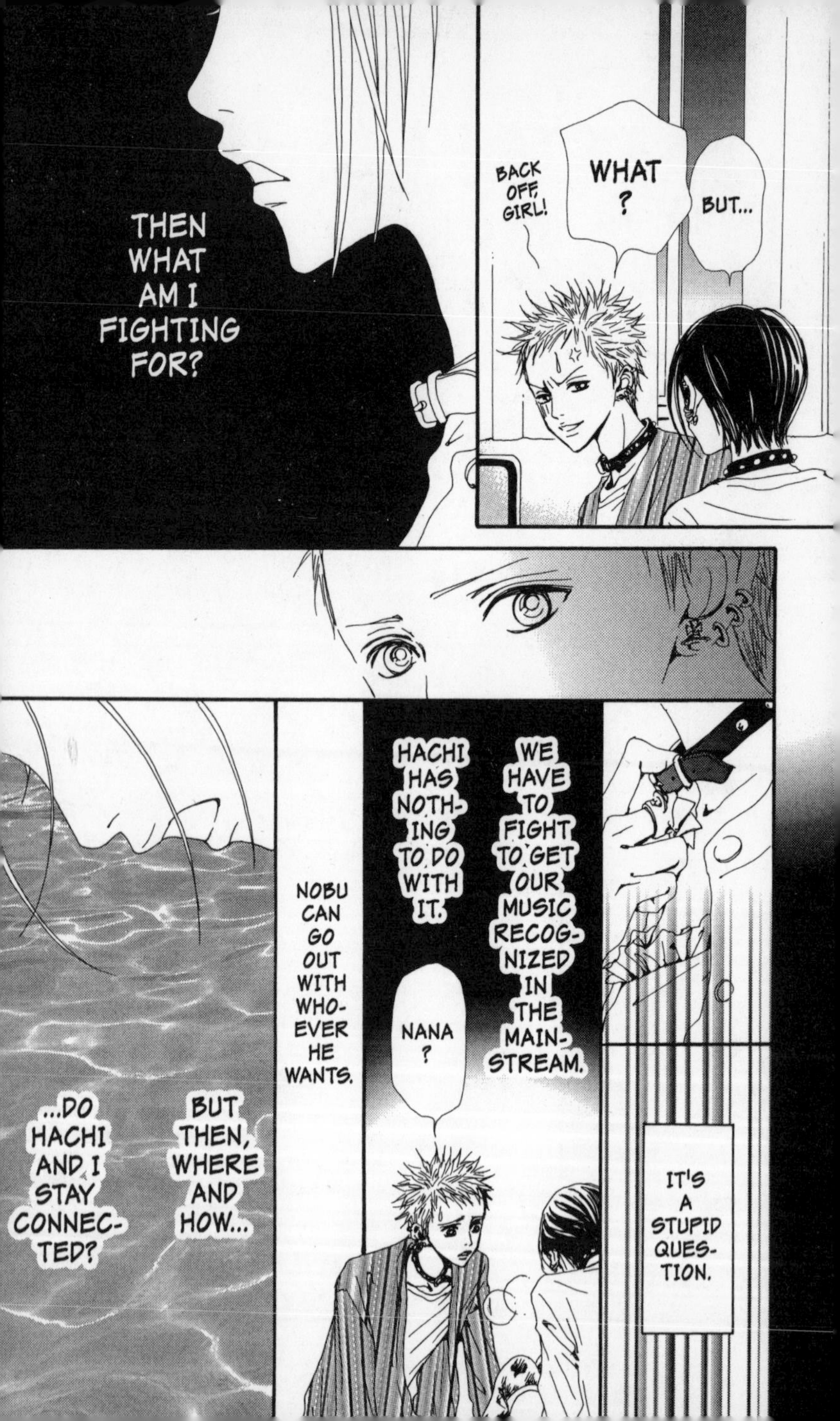
BUT...
WHAT?
BACK OFF, GIRL!
THEN WHAT AM I FIGHTING FOR?
IT'S A STUPID QUESTION.
WE HAVE TO FIGHT TO GET OUR MUSIC RECOGNIZED IN THE MAINSTREAM.
HACHI HAS NOTHING TO DO WITH IT.
NANA?
NOBU CAN GO OUT WITH WHOEVER HE WANTS.
BUT THEN, WHERE AND HOW...
...DO HACHI AND I STAY CONNECTED?

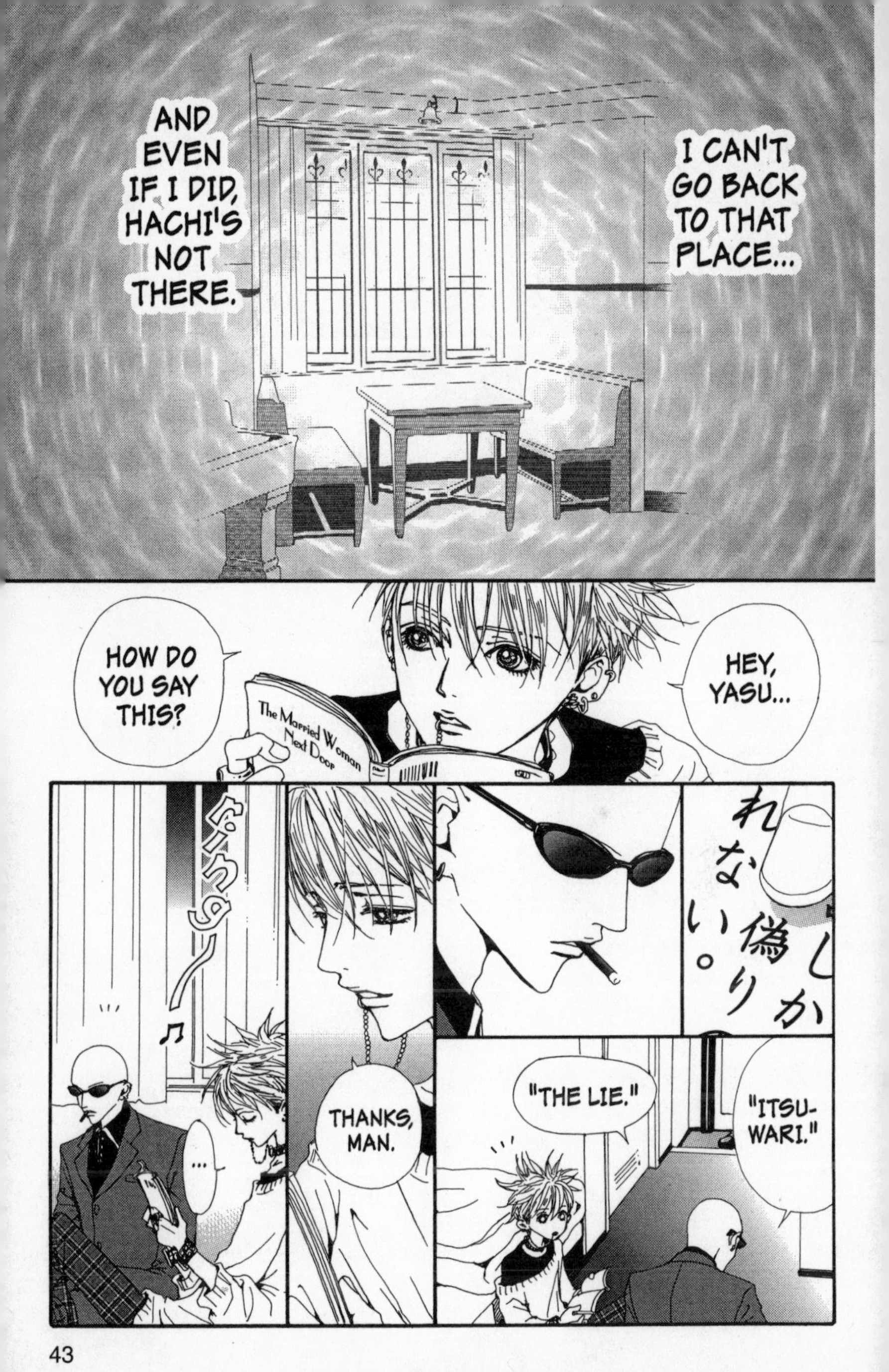
I CAN'T GO BACK TO THAT PLACE...
AND EVEN IF I DID, HACHI'S NOT THERE.
HEY, YASU...
HOW DO YOU SAY THIS?
The Married Woman Next Door
しか偽りれない。
"ITSU-WARI."
"THE LIE."
THANKS, MAN.
ぷうる〜♪
...
...

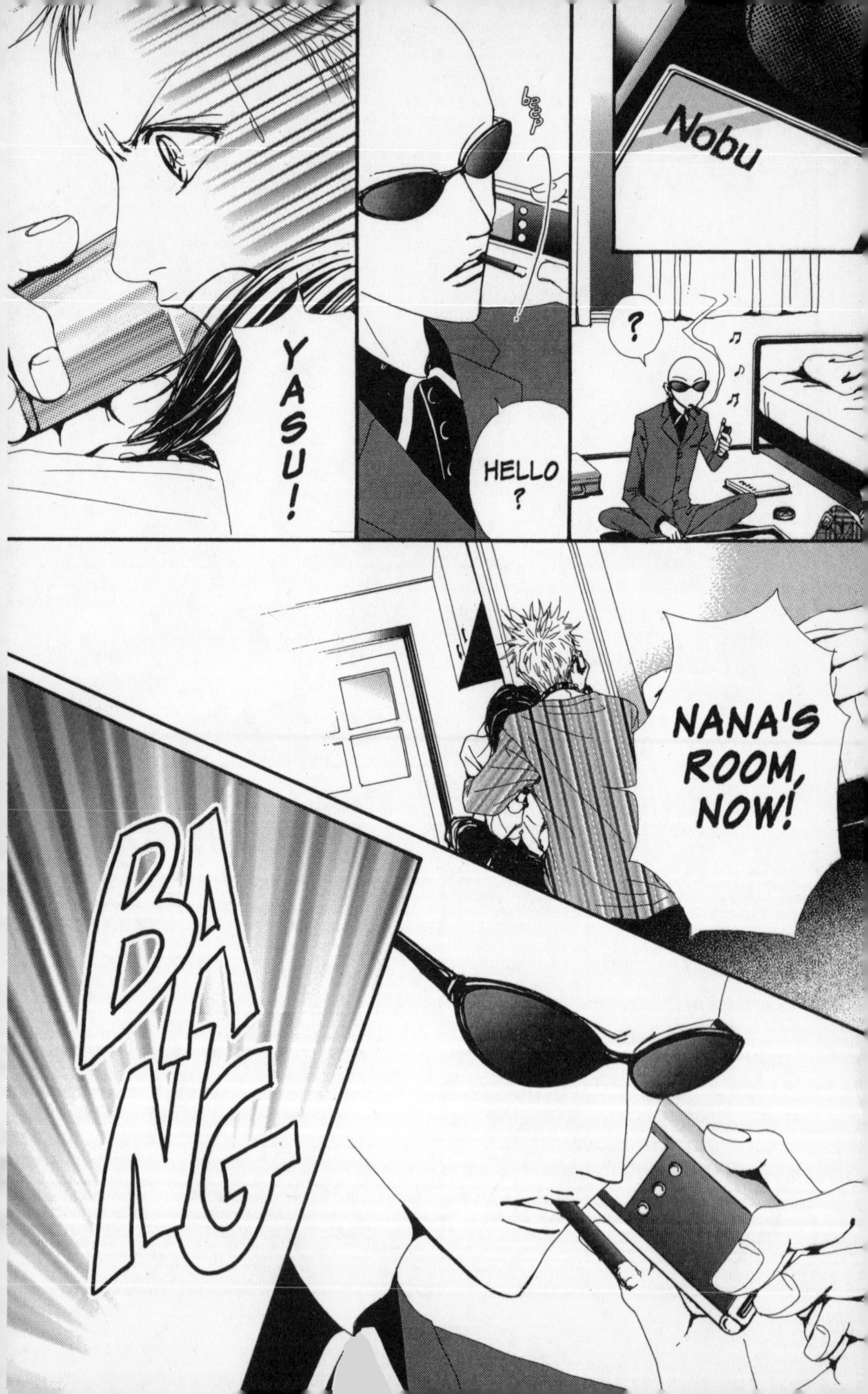
Nobu
?
beep
HELLO ?
YASU!
NANA'S ROOM, NOW!
BANG

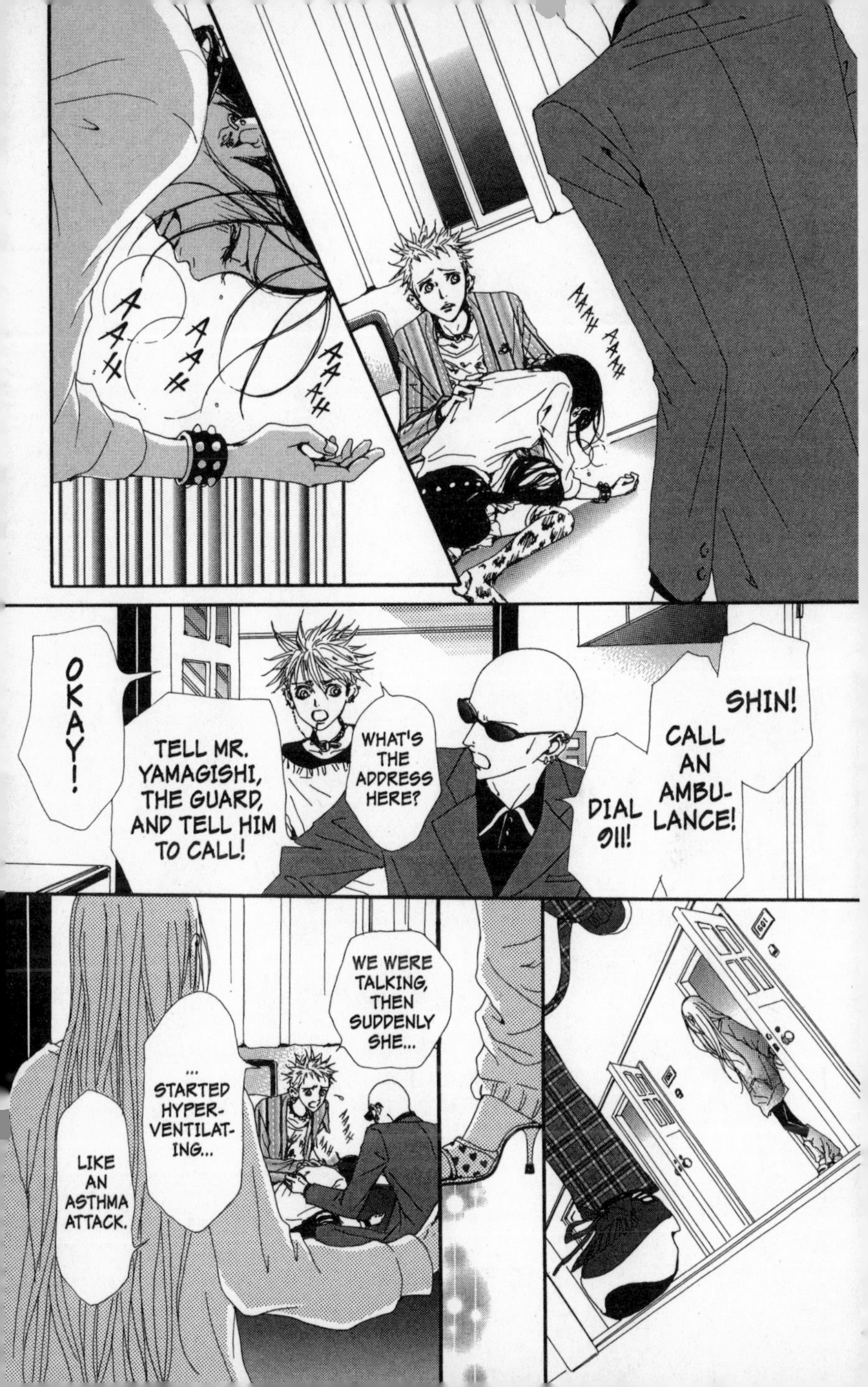
AAAH AAAH
AAAH
AAAH
AAAH
SHIN!
CALL AN AMBULANCE!
DIAL 911!
WHAT'S THE ADDRESS HERE?
TELL MR. YAMAGISHI, THE GUARD, AND TELL HIM TO CALL!
OKAY!
WE WERE TALKING, THEN SUDDENLY SHE...
...STARTED HYPER-VENTILATING...
LIKE AN ASTHMA ATTACK.

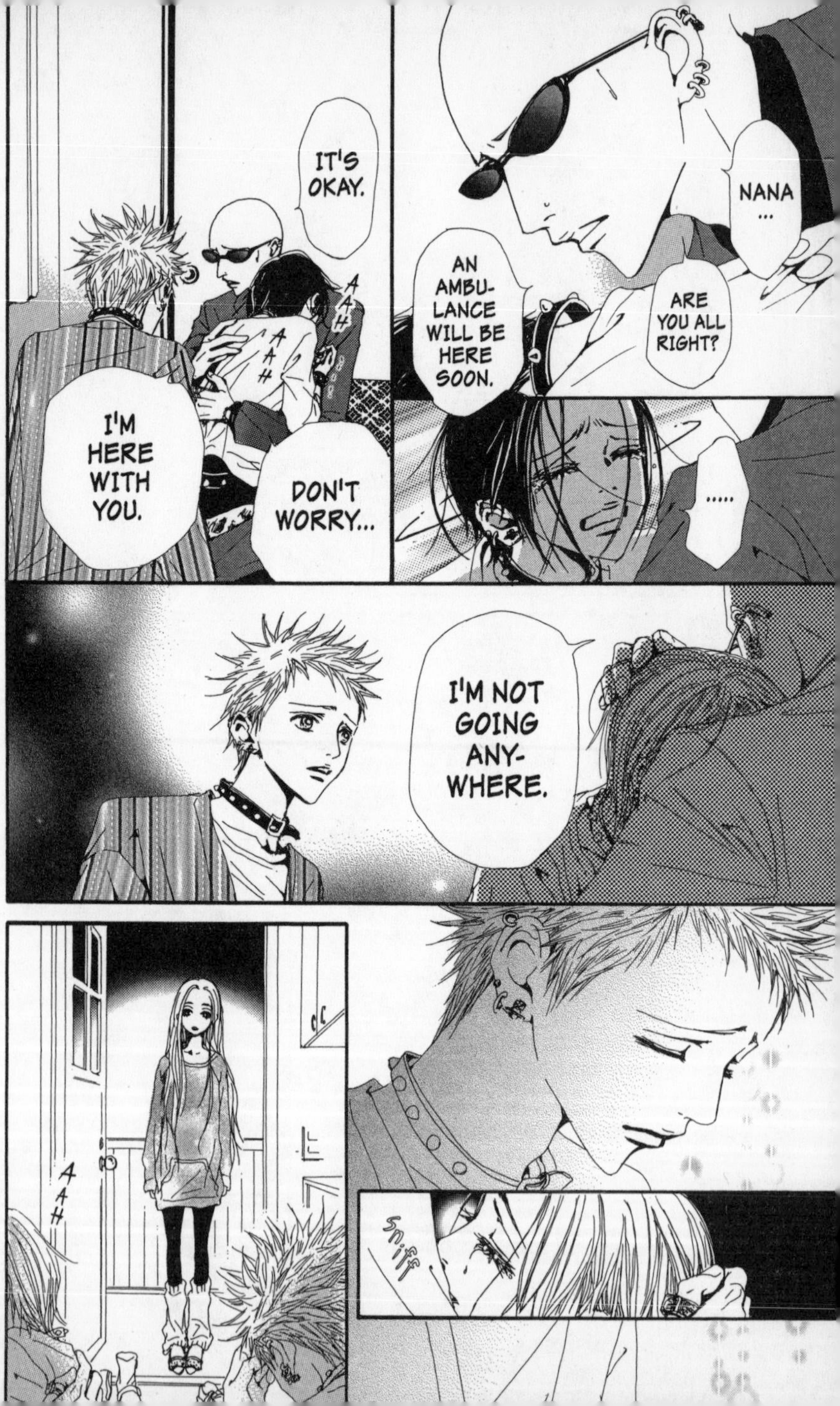

NANA ...
ARE YOU ALL RIGHT?
AN AMBULANCE WILL BE HERE SOON.
.....
IT'S OKAY.
AAH
AAH
I'M HERE WITH YOU.
DON'T WORRY...
I'M NOT GOING ANY-WHERE.
Sniff
AAH

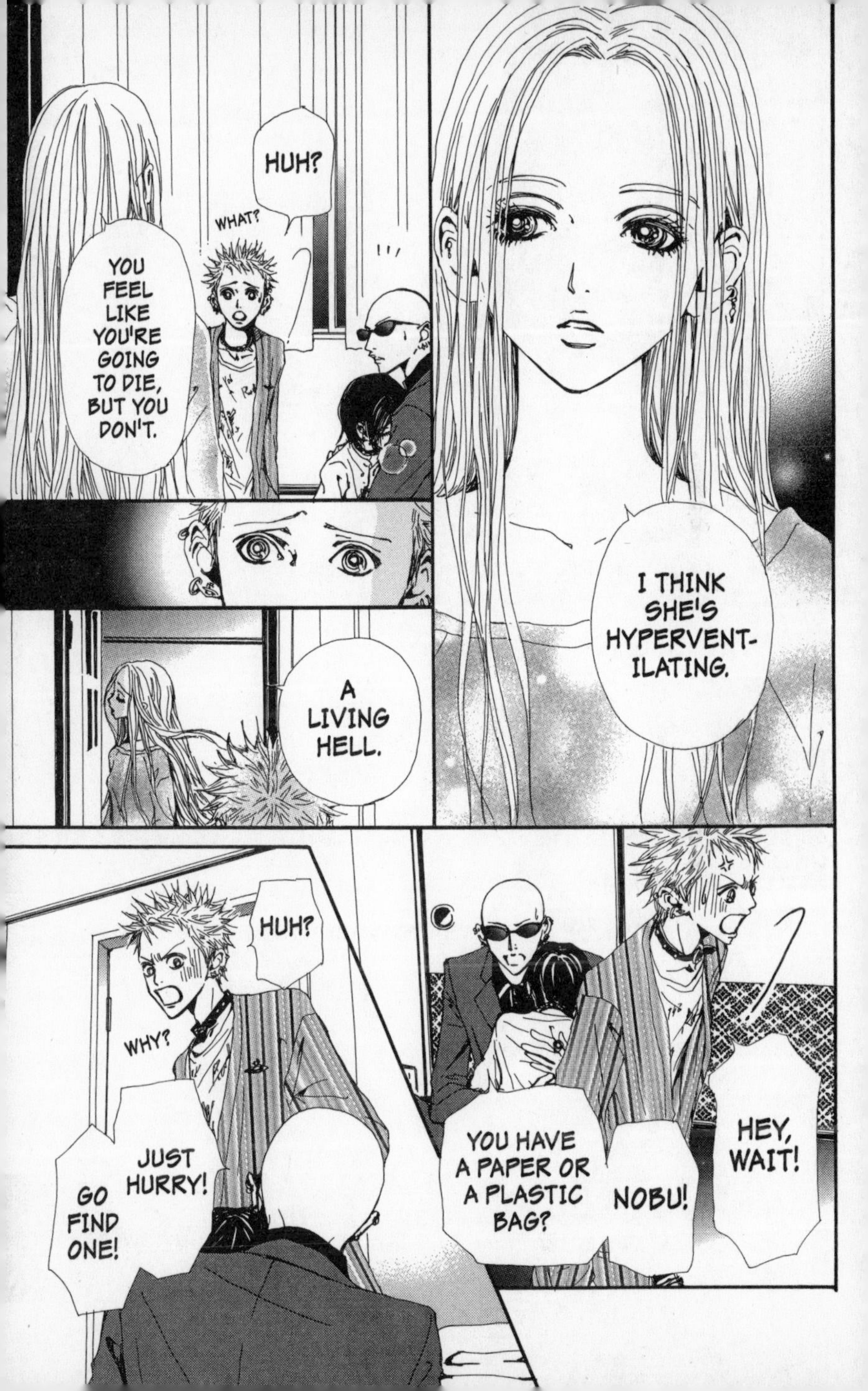
I THINK SHE'S HYPERVENT-ILATING.
HUH?
WHAT?
!!
YOU FEEL LIKE YOU'RE GOING TO DIE, BUT YOU DON'T.
A LIVING HELL.
HEY, WAIT!
NOBU!
YOU HAVE A PAPER OR A PLASTIC BAG?
HUH?
WHY?
JUST HURRY!
GO FIND ONE!

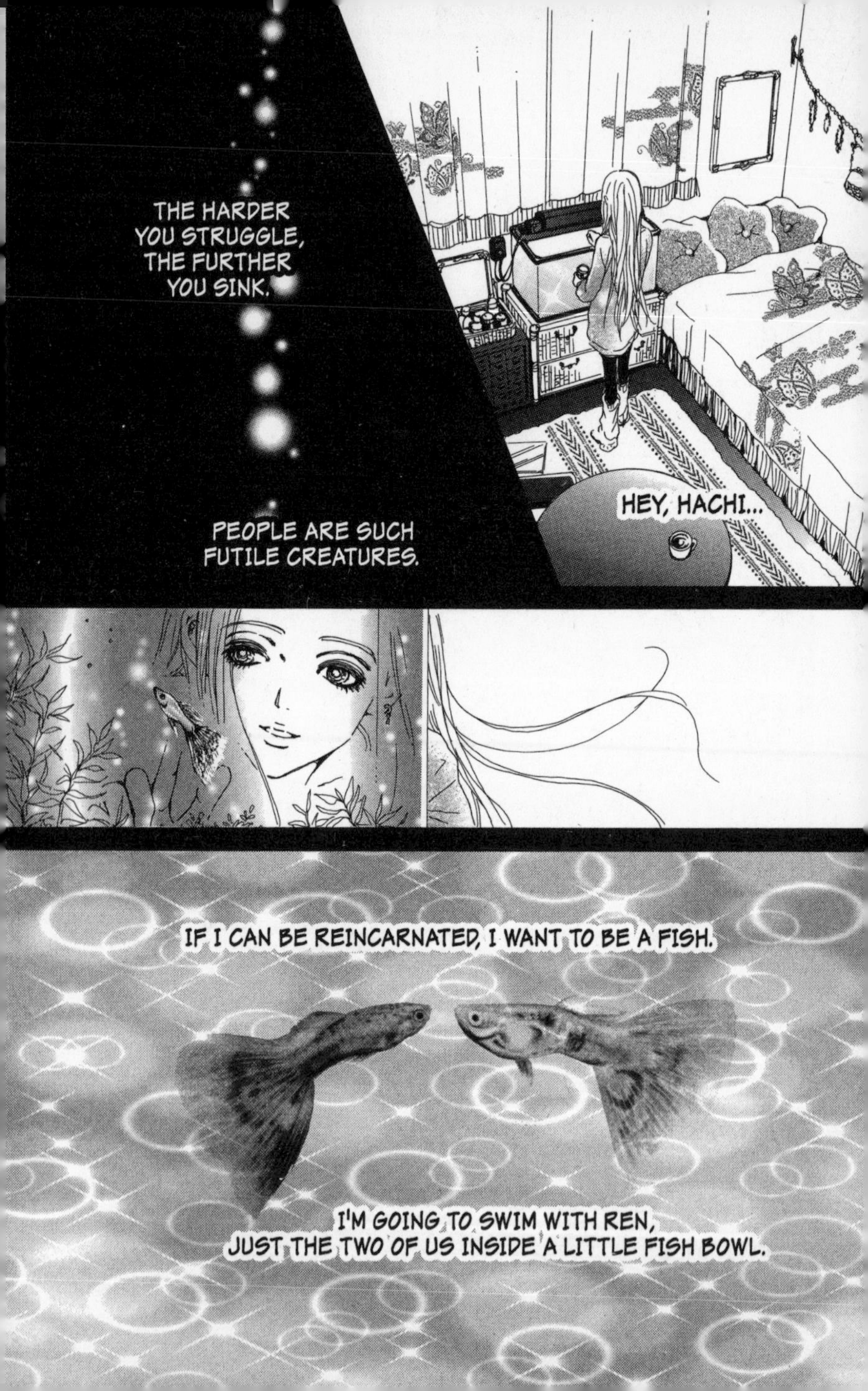
HEY, HACHI...
THE HARDER YOU STRUGGLE, THE FURTHER YOU SINK.
PEOPLE ARE SUCH FUTILE CREATURES.
IF I CAN BE REINCARNATED, I WANT TO BE A FISH.
I'M GOING TO SWIM WITH REN, JUST THE TWO OF US INSIDE A LITTLE FISH BOWL.

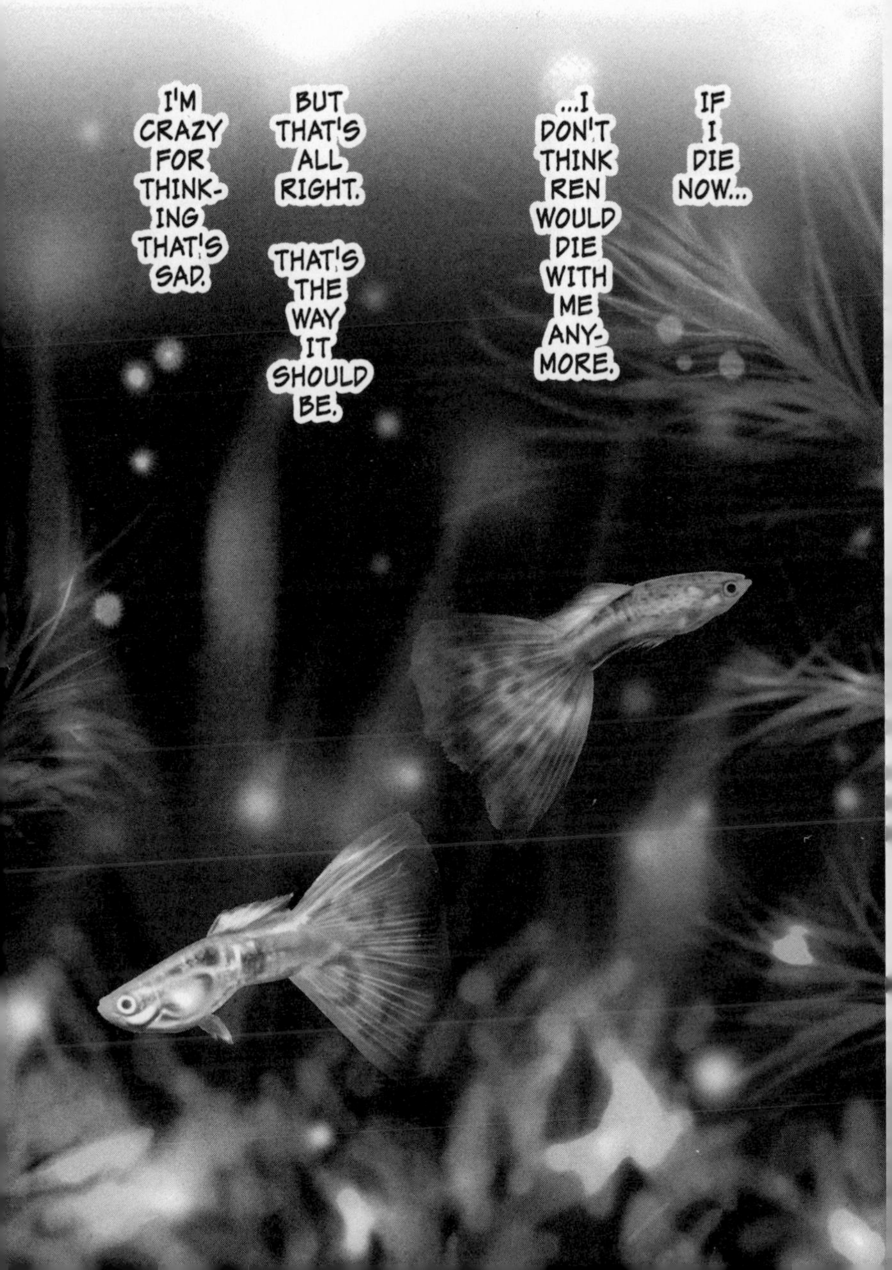
IF I DIE NOW...
...I DON'T THINK REN WOULD DIE WITH ME ANY-MORE.
BUT THAT'S ALL RIGHT.
THAT'S THE WAY IT SHOULD BE.
I'M CRAZY FOR THINK-ING THAT'S SAD.

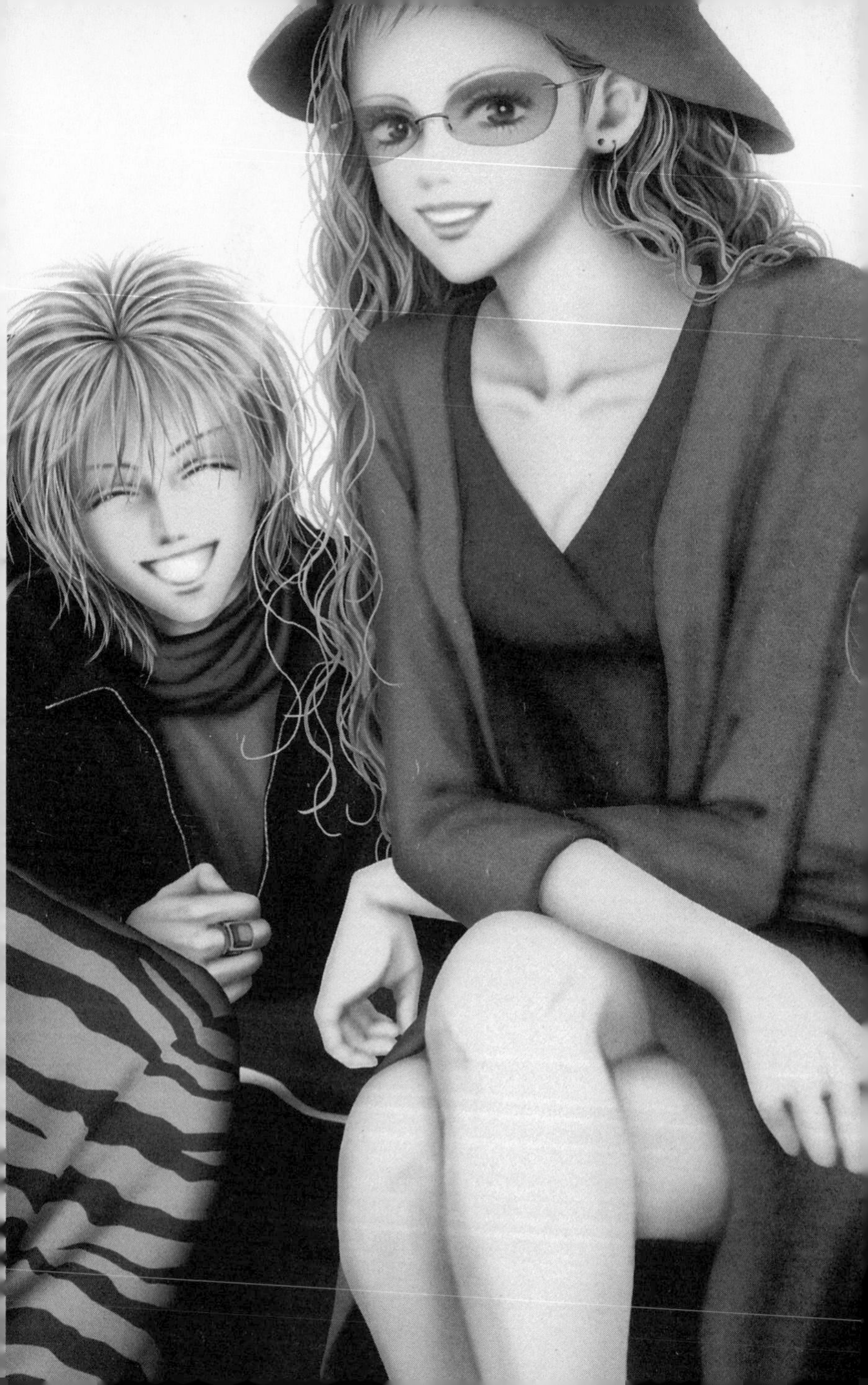

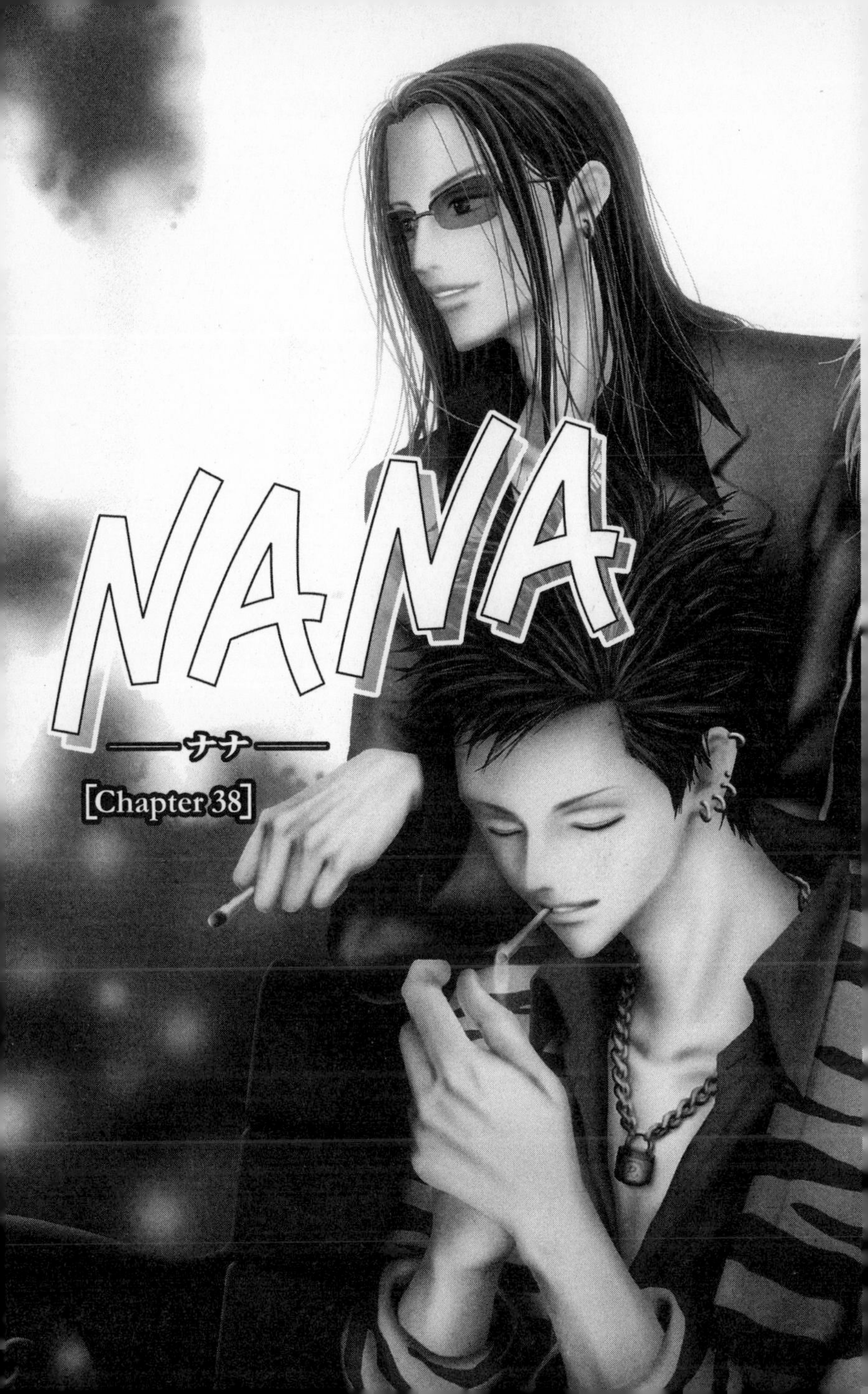
NANA
ナナ
[Chapter 38]

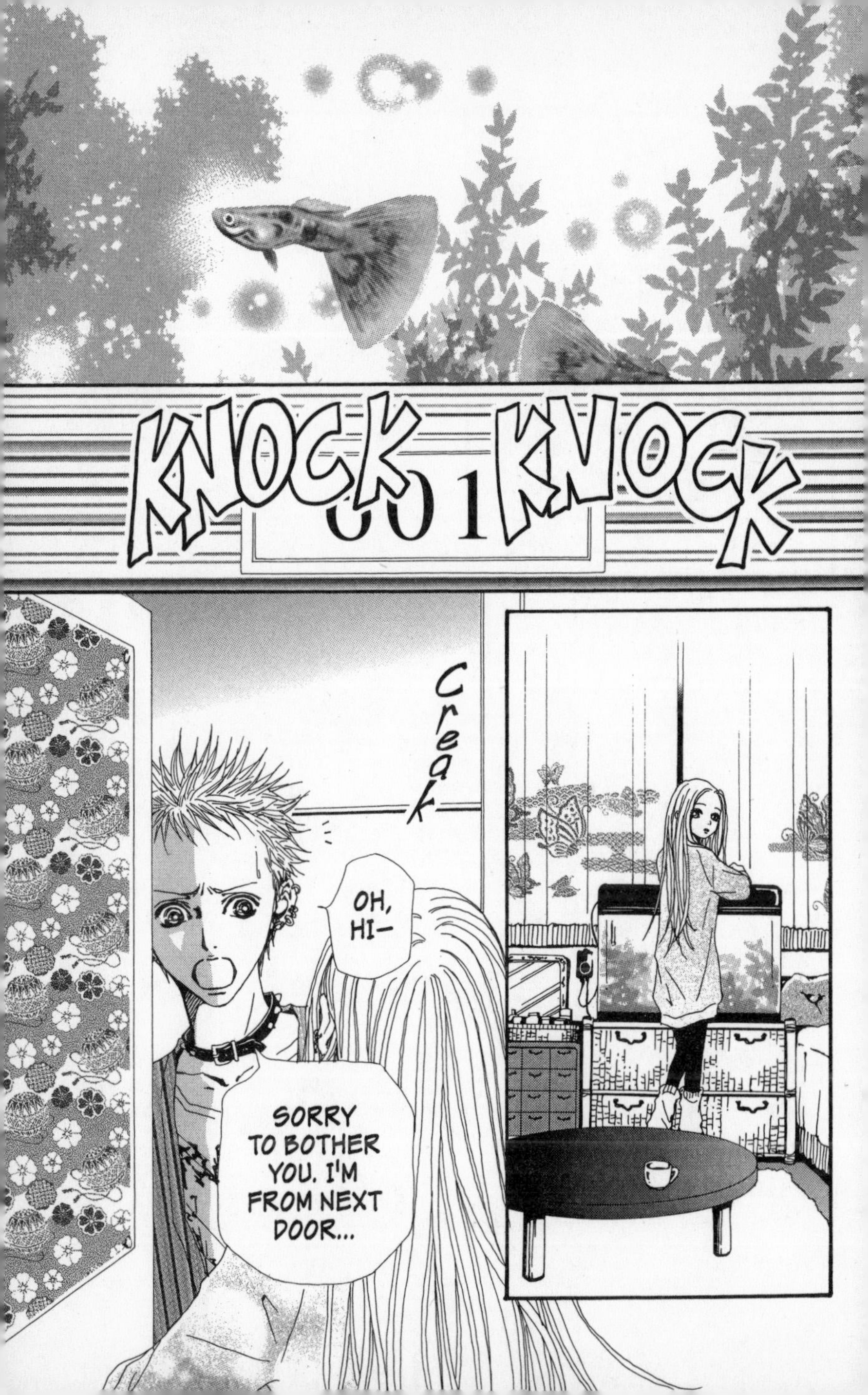
KNOCK KNOCK
001
Creak
OH, HI—
SORRY TO BOTHER YOU. I'M FROM NEXT DOOR...

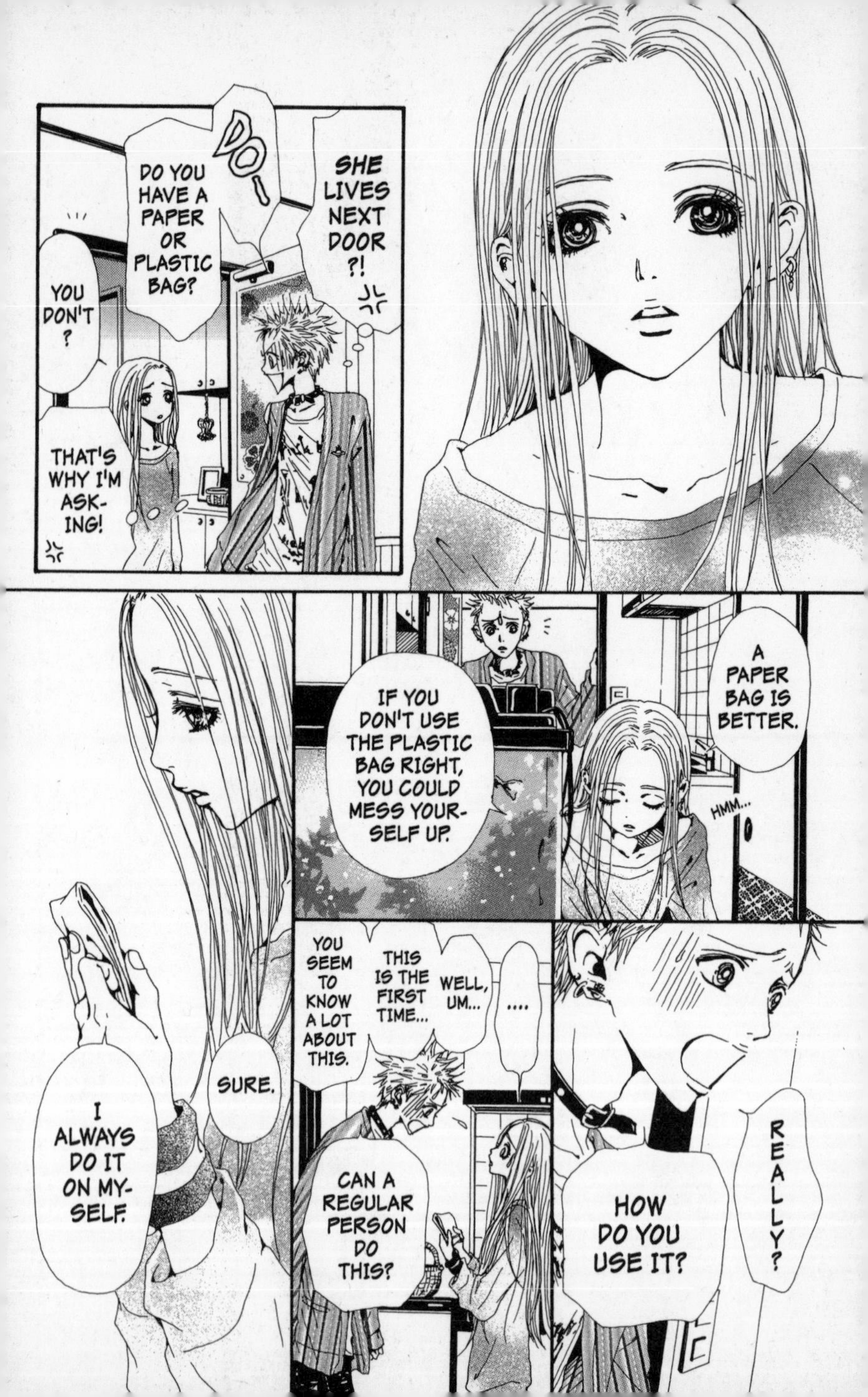
SHE LIVES NEXT DOOR?!
DO-
DO YOU HAVE A PAPER OR PLASTIC BAG?
YOU DON'T?
THAT'S WHY I'M ASK-ING!
A PAPER BAG IS BETTER.
HMM...
IF YOU DON'T USE THE PLASTIC BAG RIGHT, YOU COULD MESS YOUR-SELF UP.
REALLY?
HOW DO YOU USE IT?
....
WELL, UM...
THIS IS THE FIRST TIME...
YOU SEEM TO KNOW A LOT ABOUT THIS.
CAN A REGULAR PERSON DO THIS?
SURE.
I ALWAYS DO IT ON MY-SELF.

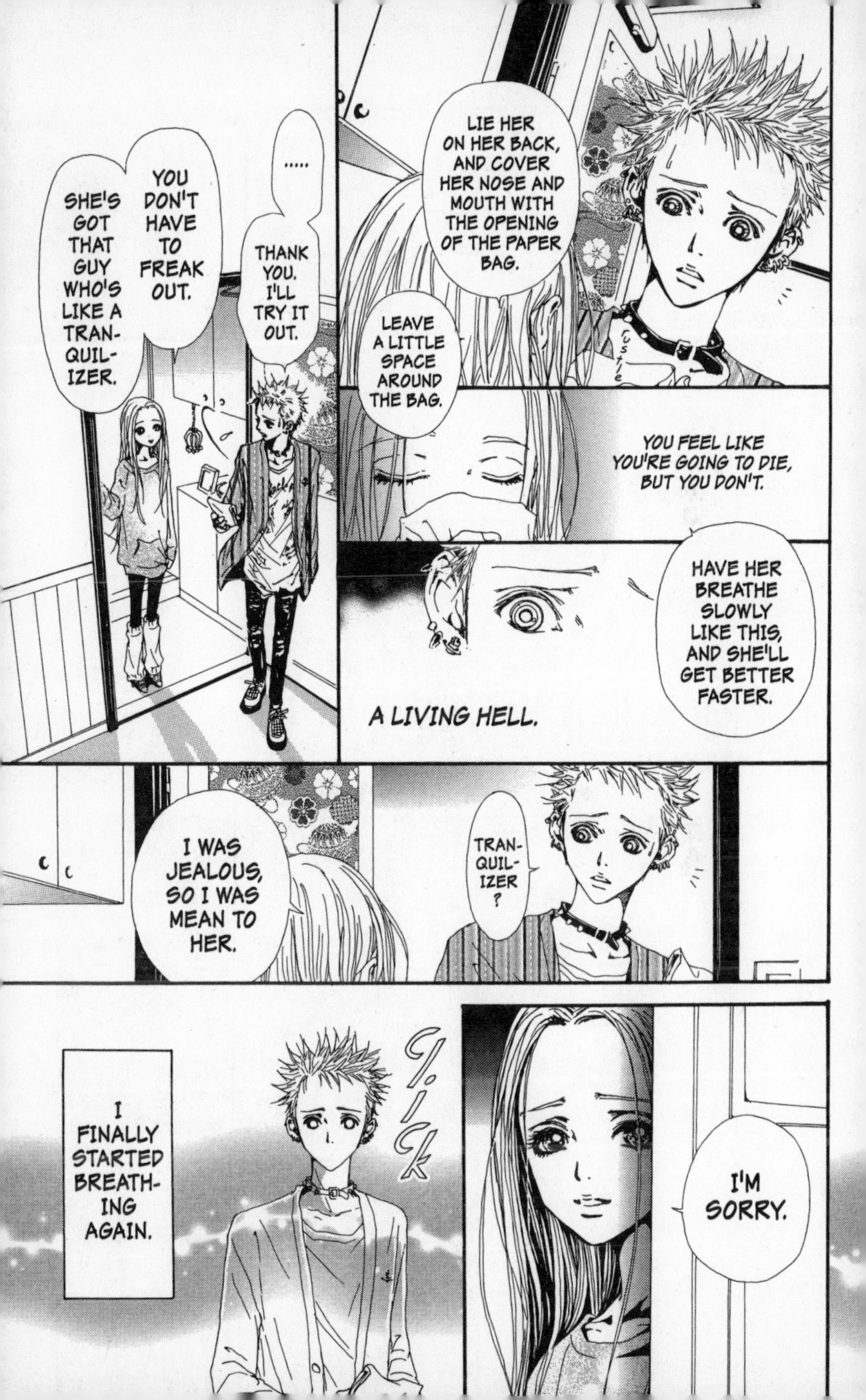
LIE HER ON HER BACK, AND COVER HER NOSE AND MOUTH WITH THE OPENING OF THE PAPER BAG.
LEAVE A LITTLE SPACE AROUND THE BAG.
rustle
YOU FEEL LIKE YOU'RE GOING TO DIE, BUT YOU DON'T.
HAVE HER BREATHE SLOWLY LIKE THIS, AND SHE'LL GET BETTER FASTER.
A LIVING HELL.
.....
THANK YOU. I'LL TRY IT OUT.
YOU DON'T HAVE TO FREAK OUT.
SHE'S GOT THAT GUY WHO'S LIKE A TRANQUILIZER.
TRANQUILIZER?
I WAS JEALOUS, SO I WAS MEAN TO HER.
I'M SORRY.
Click
I FINALLY STARTED BREATHING AGAIN.

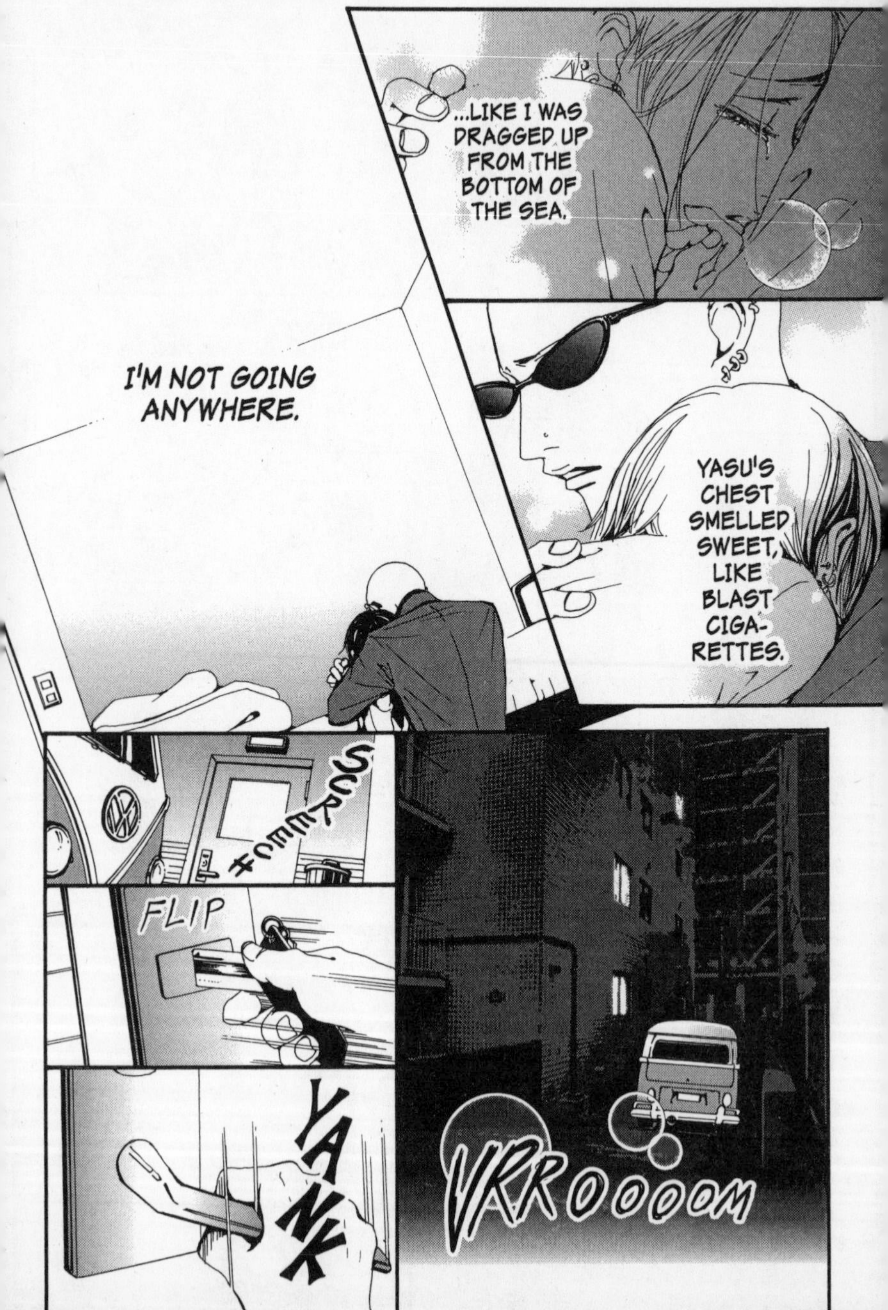
...LIKE I WAS DRAGGED UP FROM THE BOTTOM OF THE SEA.
YASU'S CHEST SMELLED SWEET, LIKE BLAST CIGA-RETTES.
I'M NOT GOING ANYWHERE.
VRROOOOM
SCREECH
FLIP
YANK

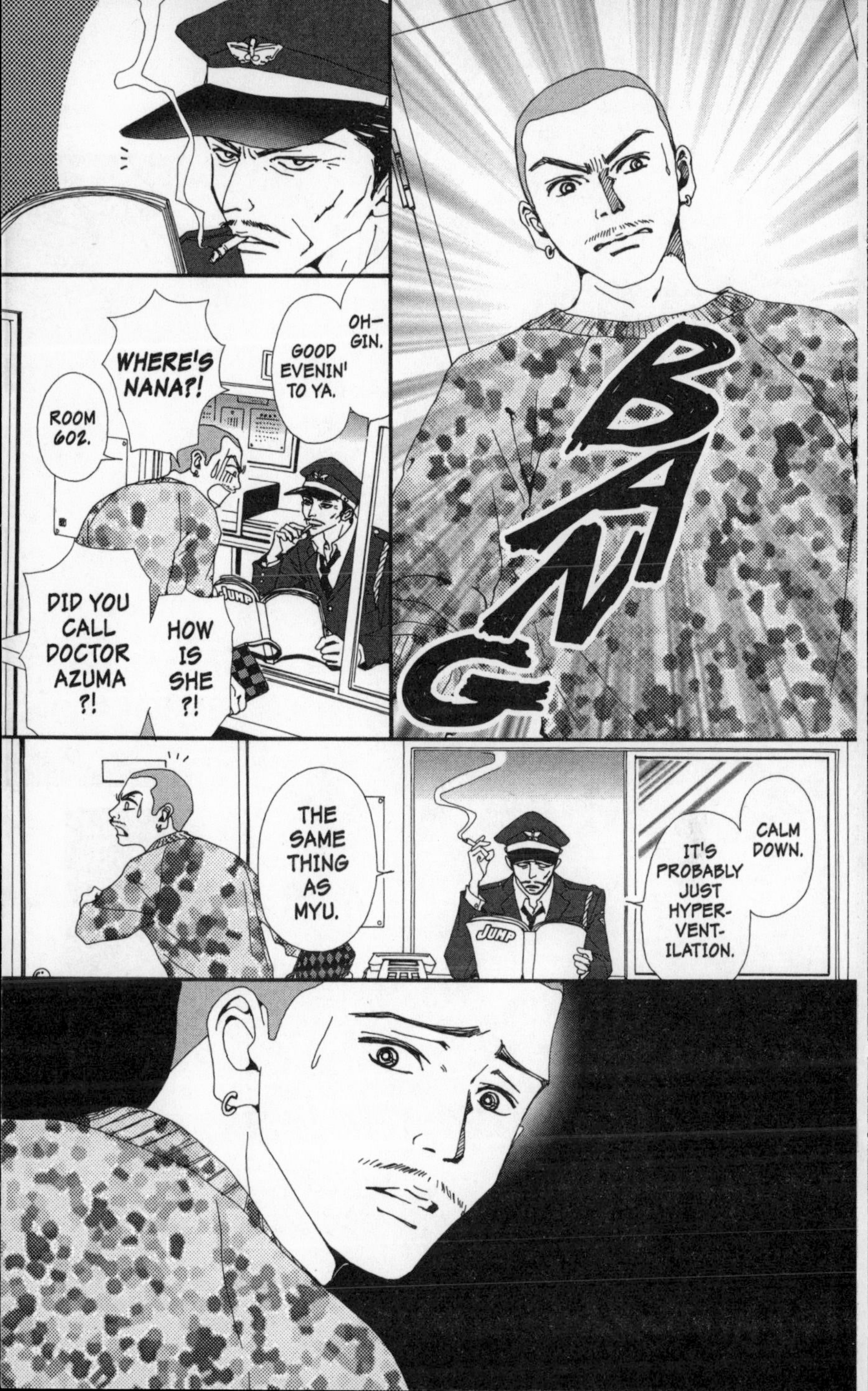
BANG
OH— GIN.
GOOD EVENIN' TO YA.
WHERE'S NANA?!
ROOM 602.
HOW IS SHE ?!
DID YOU CALL DOCTOR AZUMA ?!
CALM DOWN.
IT'S PROBABLY JUST HYPER-VENT-ILATION.
THE SAME THING AS MYU.

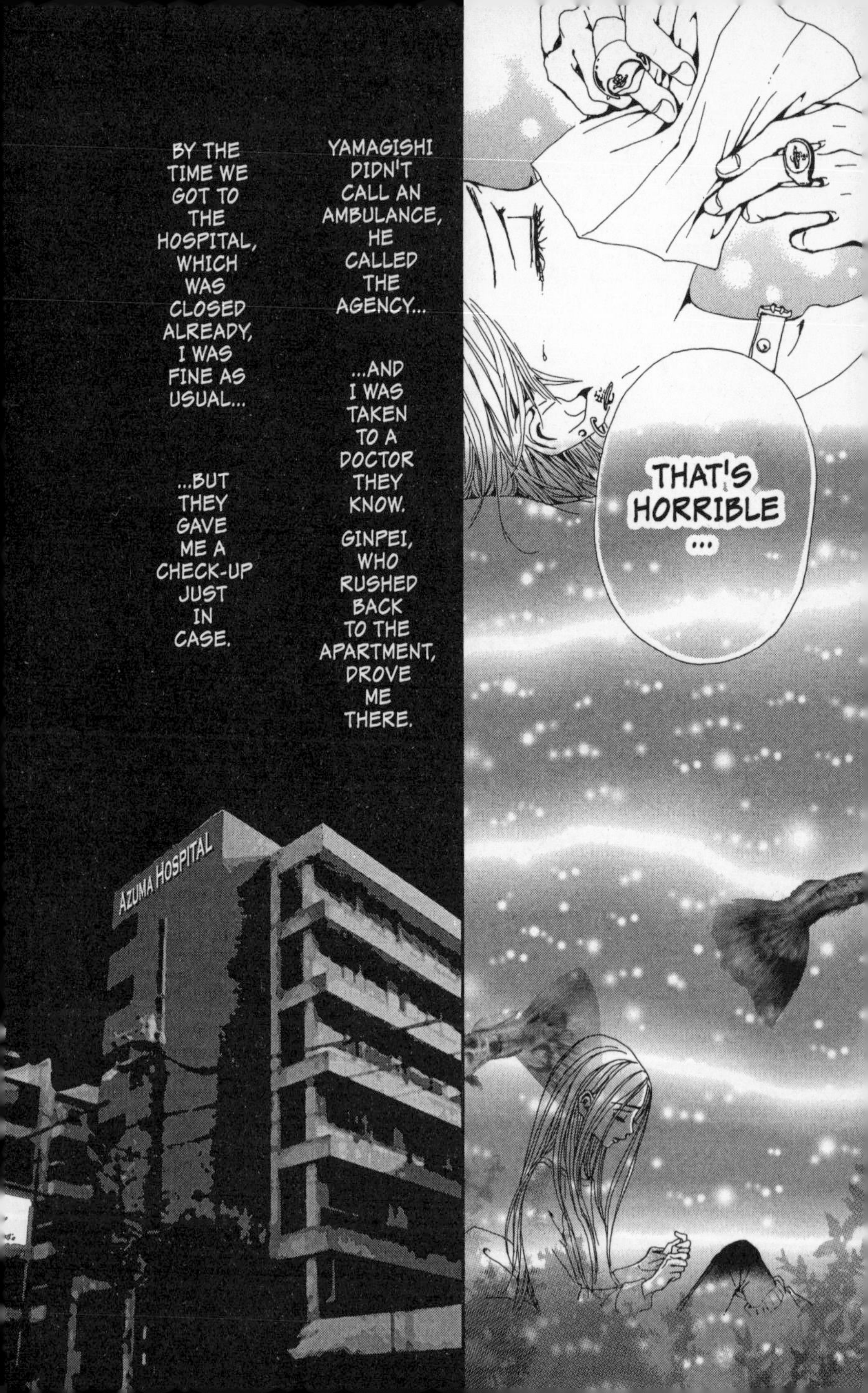
THAT'S HORRIBLE ...
YAMAGISHI DIDN'T CALL AN AMBULANCE, HE CALLED THE AGENCY...
...AND I WAS TAKEN TO A DOCTOR THEY KNOW.
GINPEI, WHO RUSHED BACK TO THE APARTMENT, DROVE ME THERE.
BY THE TIME WE GOT TO THE HOSPITAL, WHICH WAS CLOSED ALREADY, I WAS FINE AS USUAL...
...BUT THEY GAVE ME A CHECK-UP JUST IN CASE.
AZUMA HOSPITAL

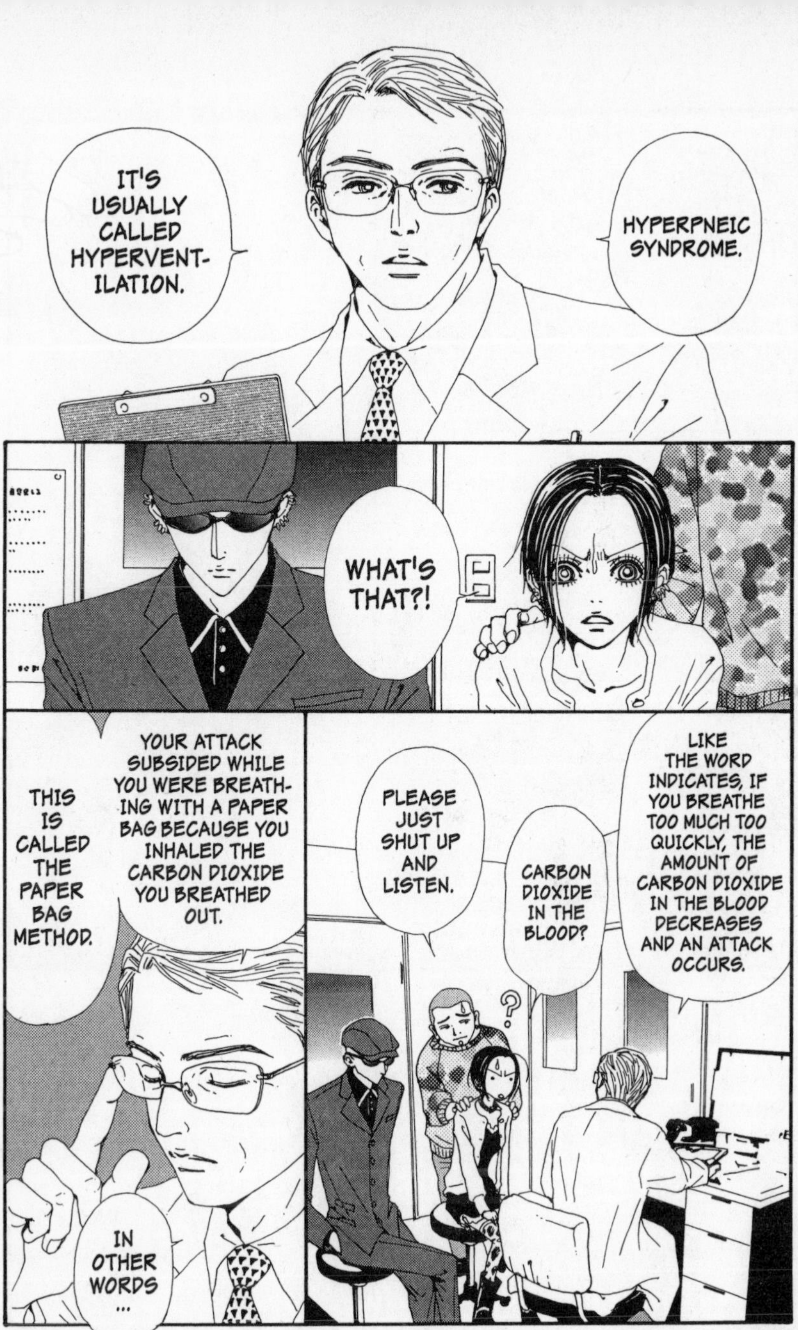
HYPERPNEIC SYNDROME.
IT'S USUALLY CALLED HYPERVENT-ILATION.
WHAT'S THAT?!
LIKE THE WORD INDICATES, IF YOU BREATHE TOO MUCH TOO QUICKLY, THE AMOUNT OF CARBON DIOXIDE IN THE BLOOD DECREASES AND AN ATTACK OCCURS.
CARBON DIOXIDE IN THE BLOOD?
?
PLEASE JUST SHUT UP AND LISTEN.
YOUR ATTACK SUBSIDED WHILE YOU WERE BREATH-ING WITH A PAPER BAG BECAUSE YOU INHALED THE CARBON DIOXIDE YOU BREATHED OUT.
THIS IS CALLED THE PAPER BAG METHOD.
IN OTHER WORDS ...

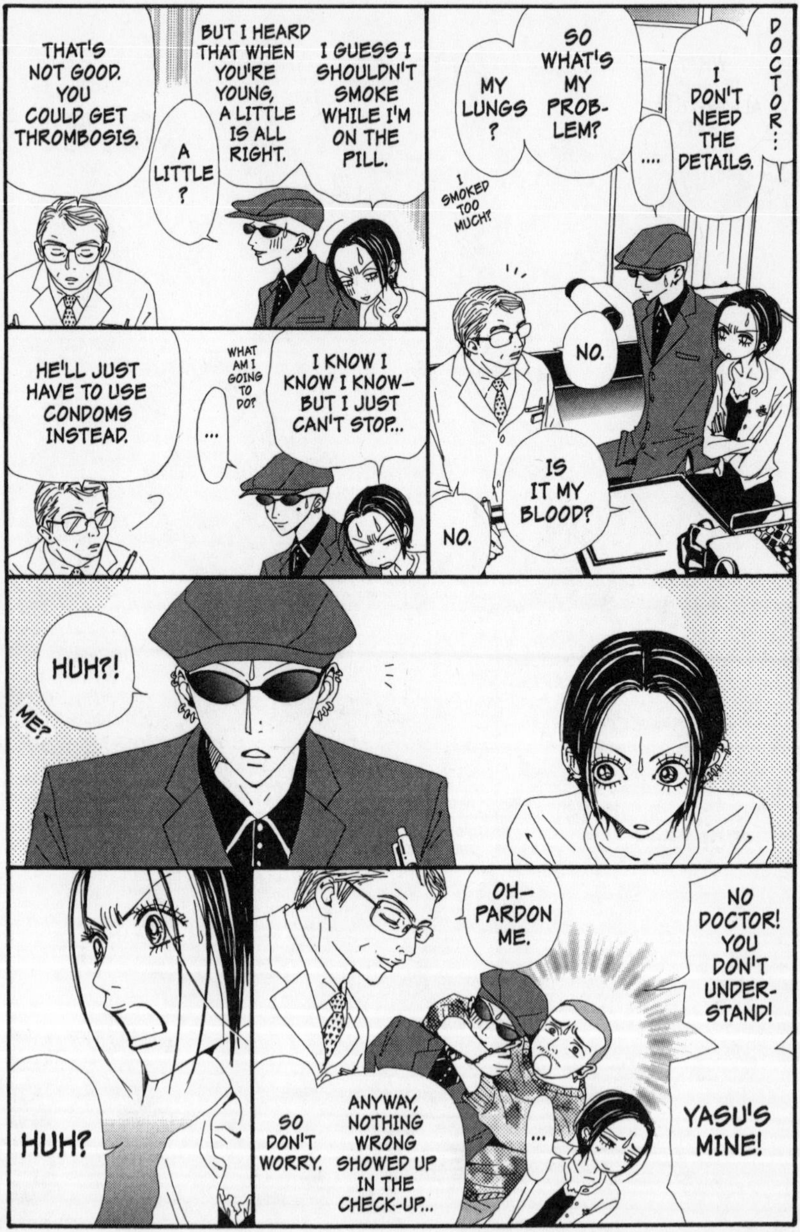
DOCTOR...
I DON'T NEED THE DETAILS.
....
SO WHAT'S MY PROB-LEM?
MY LUNGS?
I SMOKED TOO MUCH?
NO.
IS IT MY BLOOD?
NO.
I GUESS I SHOULDN'T SMOKE WHILE I'M ON THE PILL.
BUT I HEARD THAT WHEN YOU'RE YOUNG, A LITTLE IS ALL RIGHT.
A LITTLE?
THAT'S NOT GOOD. YOU COULD GET THROMBOSIS.
I KNOW I KNOW— BUT I JUST CAN'T STOP...
WHAT AM I GOING TO DO?
...
HE'LL JUST HAVE TO USE CONDOMS INSTEAD.
HUH?!
ME?
NO DOCTOR! YOU DON'T UNDER-STAND!
YASU'S MINE!
OH— PARDON ME.
...
ANYWAY, NOTHING WRONG SHOWED UP IN THE CHECK-UP...
SO DON'T WORRY.
HUH?

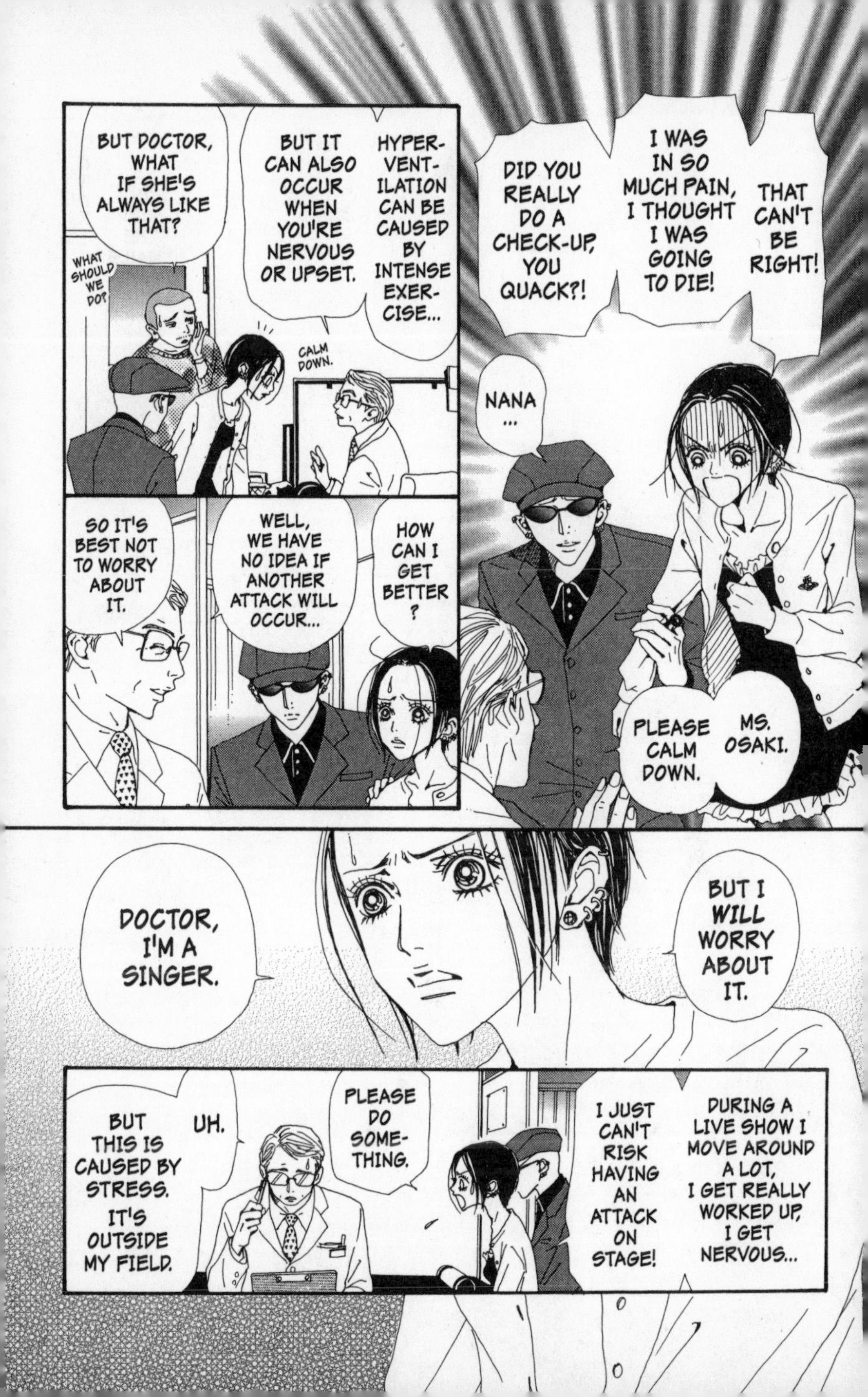
THAT CAN'T BE RIGHT!
I WAS IN SO MUCH PAIN, I THOUGHT I WAS GOING TO DIE!
DID YOU REALLY DO A CHECK-UP, YOU QUACK?!
NANA ...
MS. OSAKI.
PLEASE CALM DOWN.
HYPER-VENT-ILATION CAN BE CAUSED BY INTENSE EXER-CISE...
BUT IT CAN ALSO OCCUR WHEN YOU'RE NERVOUS OR UPSET.
CALM DOWN.
BUT DOCTOR, WHAT IF SHE'S ALWAYS LIKE THAT?
WHAT SHOULD WE DO?
HOW CAN I GET BETTER ?
WELL, WE HAVE NO IDEA IF ANOTHER ATTACK WILL OCCUR...
SO IT'S BEST NOT TO WORRY ABOUT IT.
BUT I WILL WORRY ABOUT IT.
DOCTOR, I'M A SINGER.
DURING A LIVE SHOW I MOVE AROUND A LOT, I GET REALLY WORKED UP, I GET NERVOUS...
I JUST CAN'T RISK HAVING AN ATTACK ON STAGE!
PLEASE DO SOME-THING.
UH.
BUT THIS IS CAUSED BY STRESS. IT'S OUTSIDE MY FIELD.

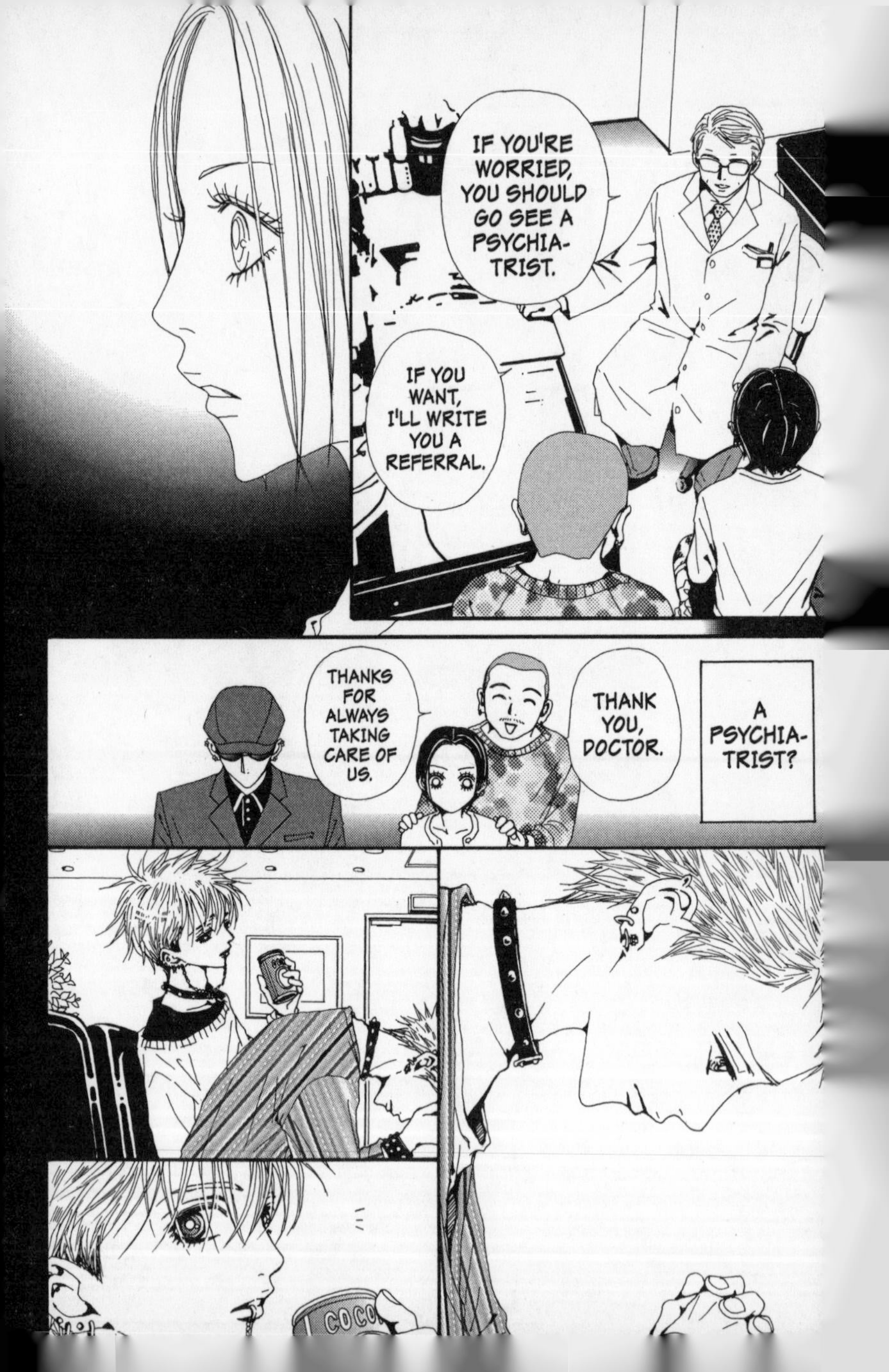
IF YOU'RE WORRIED, YOU SHOULD GO SEE A PSYCHIA-TRIST.
IF YOU WANT, I'LL WRITE YOU A REFERRAL.
A PSYCHIA-TRIST?
THANK YOU, DOCTOR.
THANKS FOR ALWAYS TAKING CARE OF US.
COCO

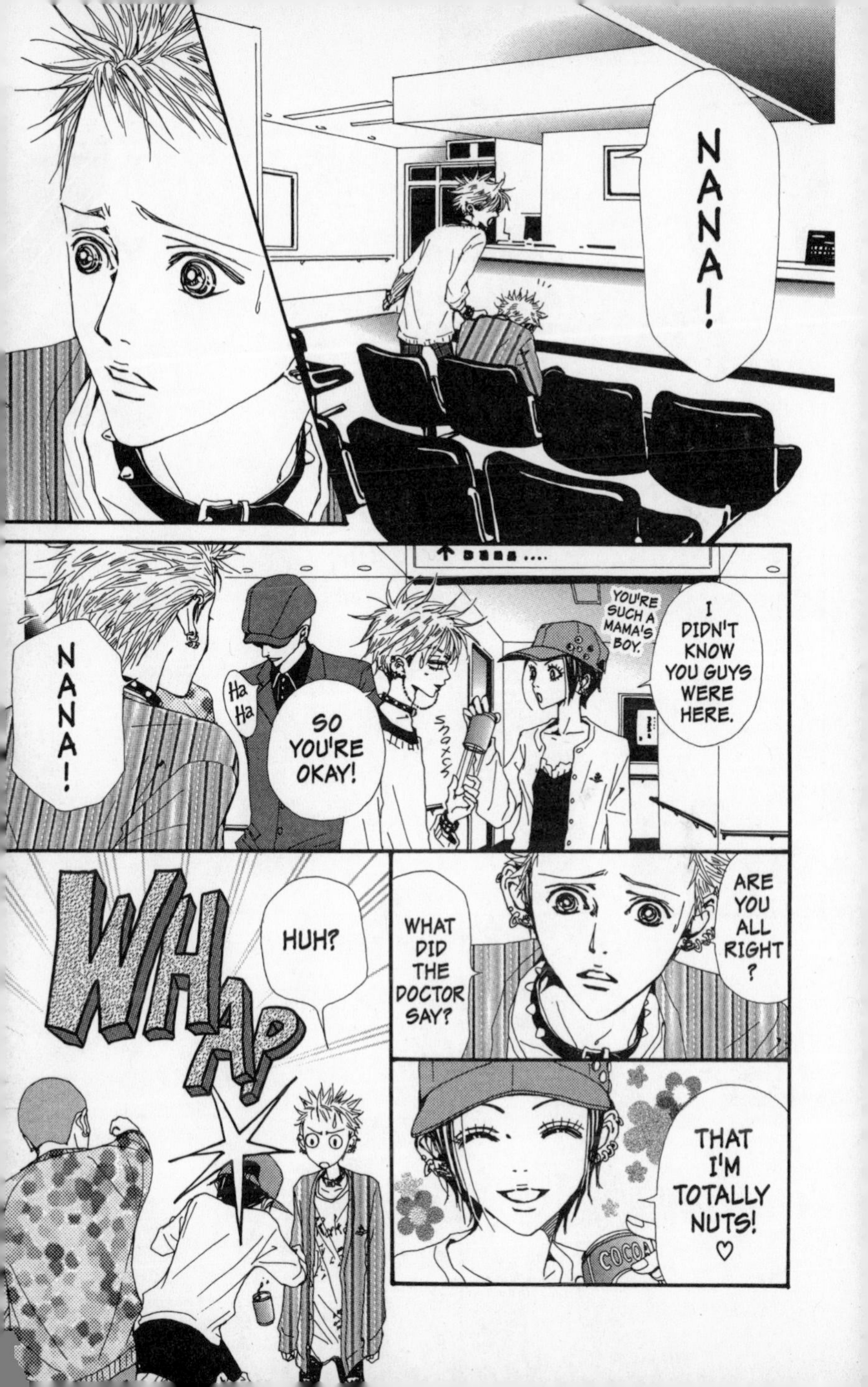

NANA!
I DIDN'T KNOW YOU GUYS WERE HERE.
YOU'RE SUCH A MAMA'S BOY.
SO YOU'RE OKAY!
Ha Ha
NANA!
ARE YOU ALL RIGHT?
WHAT DID THE DOCTOR SAY?
THAT I'M TOTALLY NUTS! ♡
COCOA
HUH?
WHAP

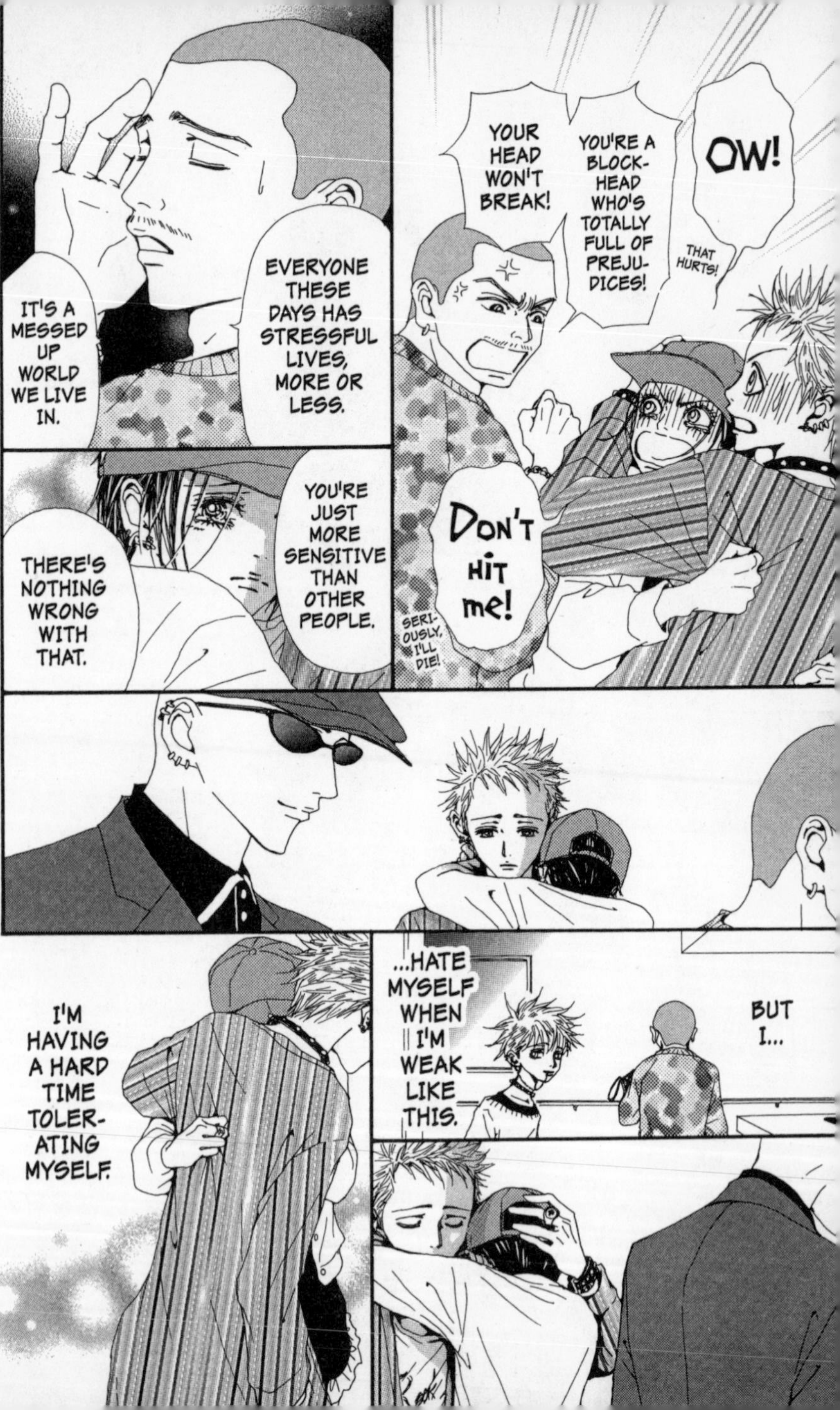
OW!
THAT HURTS!
YOU'RE A BLOCK-HEAD WHO'S TOTALLY FULL OF PREJU-DICES!
YOUR HEAD WON'T BREAK!
Don't hit me!
SERI-OUSLY, I'LL DIE!
EVERYONE THESE DAYS HAS STRESSFUL LIVES, MORE OR LESS.
IT'S A MESSED UP WORLD WE LIVE IN.
YOU'RE JUST MORE SENSITIVE THAN OTHER PEOPLE.
THERE'S NOTHING WRONG WITH THAT.
BUT I...
...HATE MYSELF WHEN I'M WEAK LIKE THIS.
I'M HAVING A HARD TIME TOLER-ATING MYSELF.

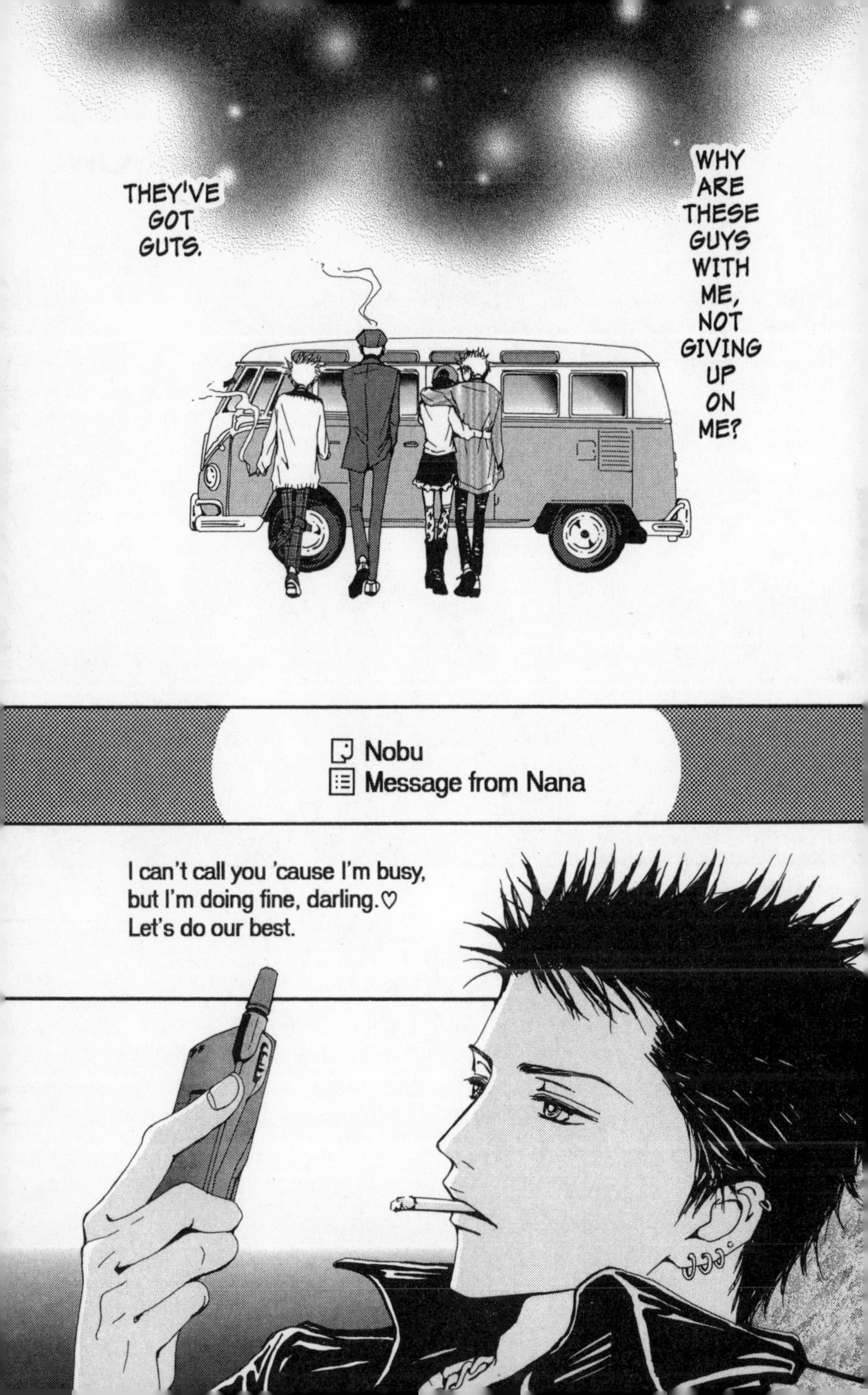
WHY ARE THESE GUYS WITH ME, NOT GIVING UP ON ME?
THEY'VE GOT GUTS.
Nobu
Message from Nana
I can't call you 'cause I'm busy, but I'm doing fine, darling.♡ Let's do our best.

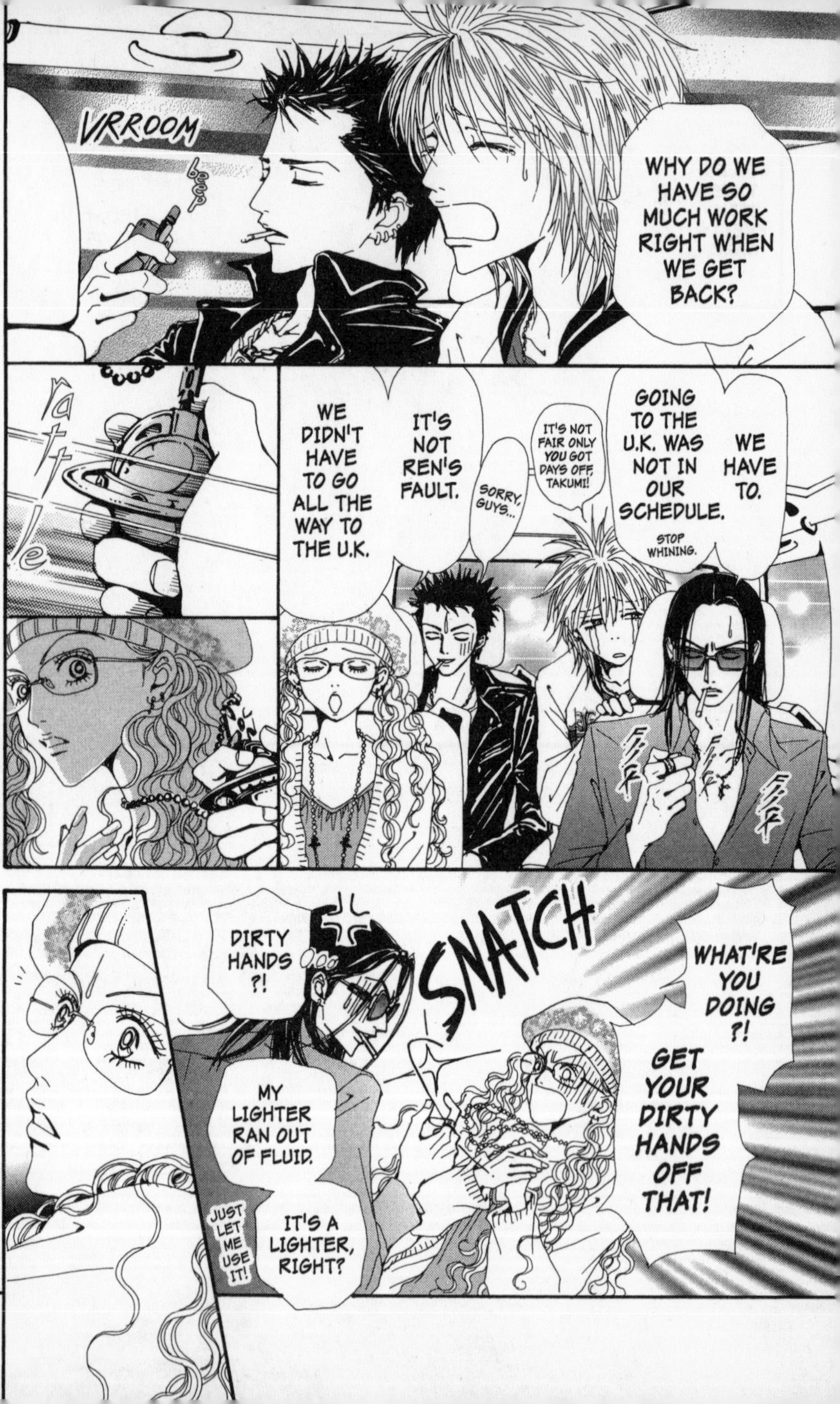
VRROOM
beep
WHY DO WE HAVE SO MUCH WORK RIGHT WHEN WE GET BACK?
WE HAVE TO.
GOING TO THE U.K. WAS NOT IN OUR SCHEDULE.
STOP WHINING.
IT'S NOT FAIR ONLY YOU GOT DAYS OFF, TAKUMI!
SORRY, GUYS...
IT'S NOT REN'S FAULT.
WE DIDN'T HAVE TO GO ALL THE WAY TO THE U.K.
rattle
WHAT'RE YOU DOING ?!
GET YOUR DIRTY HANDS OFF THAT!
SNATCH
DIRTY HANDS ?!
MY LIGHTER RAN OUT OF FLUID.
IT'S A LIGHTER, RIGHT?
JUST LET ME USE IT!

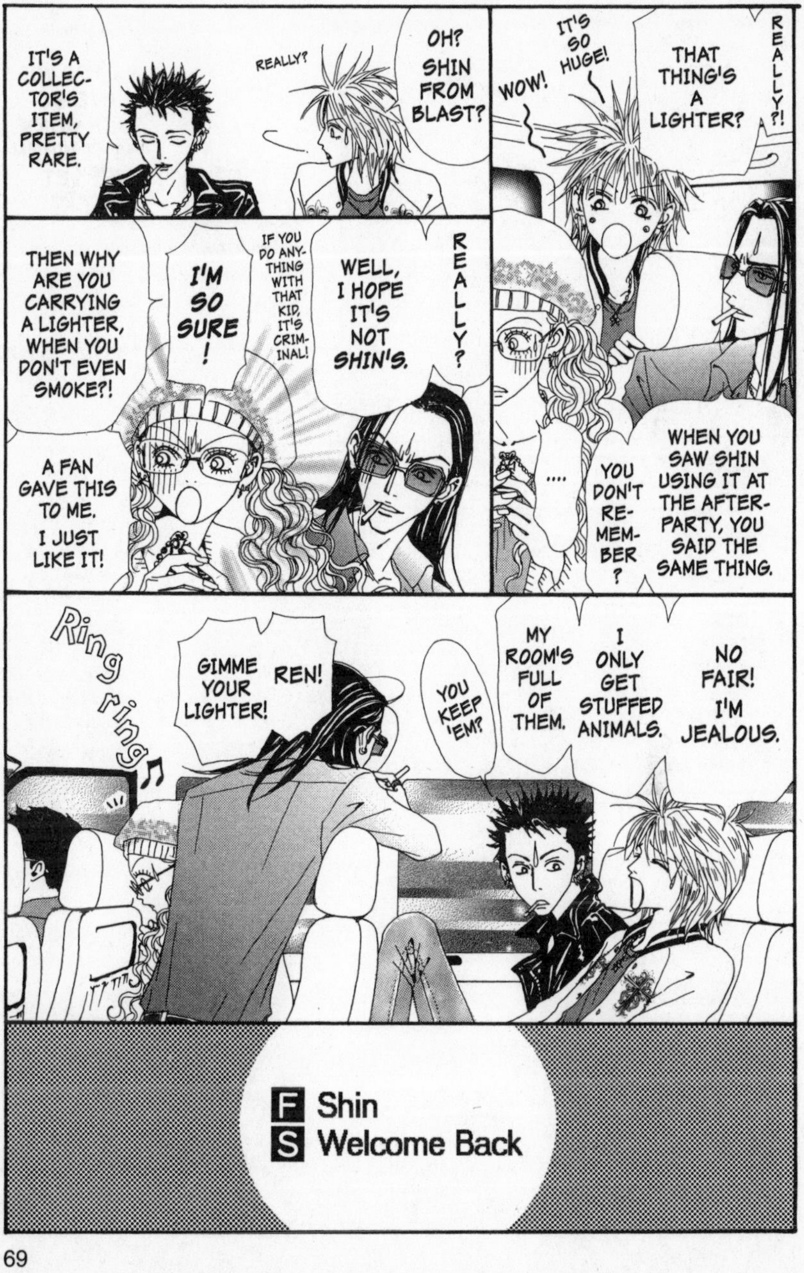
REALLY?!
THAT THING'S A LIGHTER?
IT'S SO HUGE!
WOW!
WHEN YOU SAW SHIN USING IT AT THE AFTER-PARTY, YOU SAID THE SAME THING.
YOU DON'T RE-MEM-BER?
....
OH? SHIN FROM BLAST?
REALLY?
IT'S A COLLECTOR'S ITEM, PRETTY RARE.
REALLY?
WELL, I HOPE IT'S NOT SHIN'S.
IF YOU DO ANY-THING WITH THAT KID, IT'S CRIM-INAL!
I'M SO SURE!
THEN WHY ARE YOU CARRYING A LIGHTER, WHEN YOU DON'T EVEN SMOKE?!
A FAN GAVE THIS TO ME. I JUST LIKE IT!
NO FAIR! I'M JEALOUS.
I ONLY GET STUFFED ANIMALS.
MY ROOM'S FULL OF THEM.
YOU KEEP 'EM?
REN!
GIMME YOUR LIGHTER!
Ring ring
F Shin
S Welcome Back

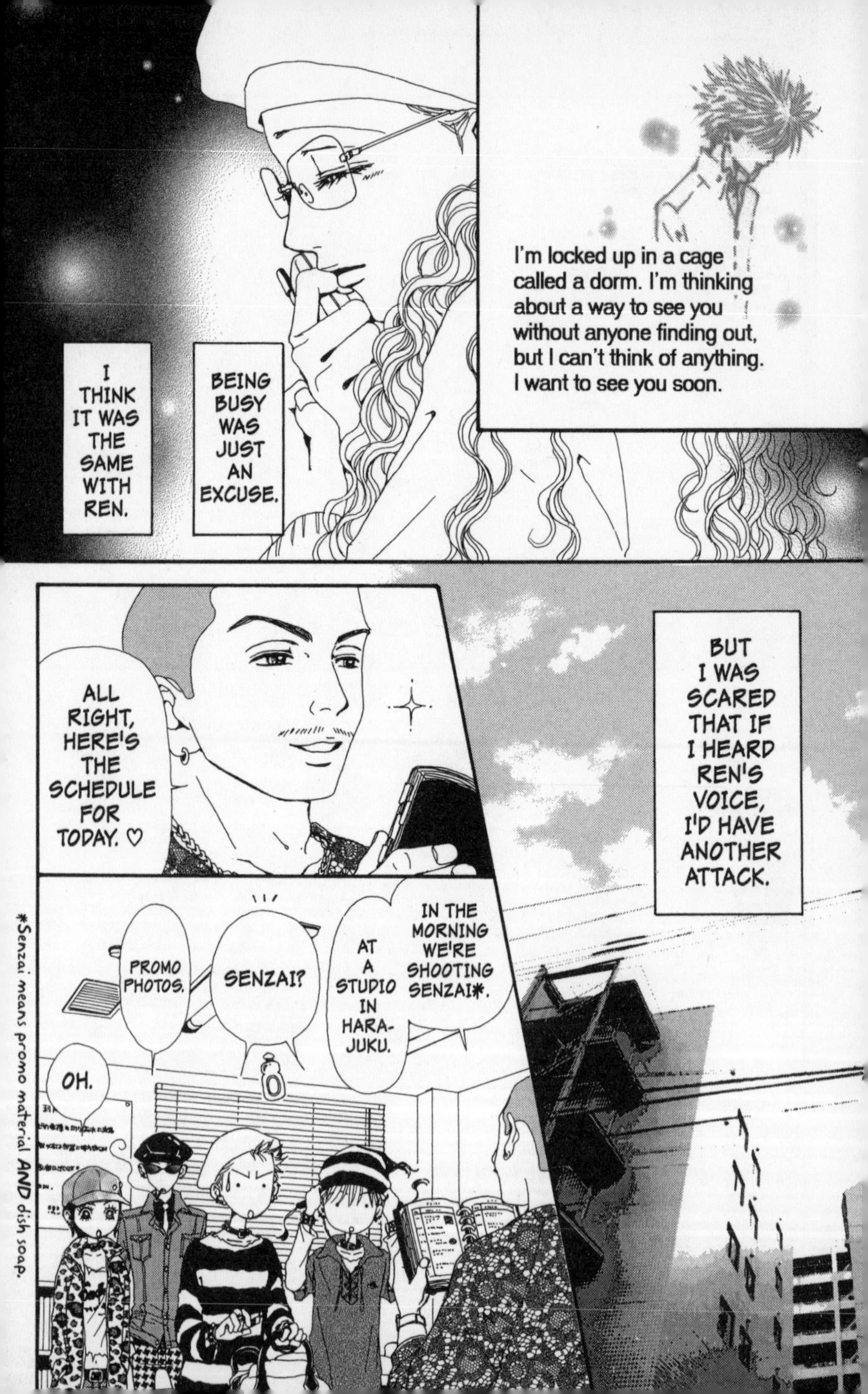
I'm locked up in a cage called a dorm. I'm thinking about a way to see you without anyone finding out, but I can't think of anything. I want to see you soon.
BEING BUSY WAS JUST AN EXCUSE.
I THINK IT WAS THE SAME WITH REN.
BUT I WAS SCARED THAT IF I HEARD REN'S VOICE, I'D HAVE ANOTHER ATTACK.
ALL RIGHT, HERE'S THE SCHEDULE FOR TODAY. ♡
IN THE MORNING WE'RE SHOOTING SENZAI*.
AT A STUDIO IN HARAJUKU.
SENZAI?
PROMO PHOTOS.
OH.

*Senzai means promo material AND dish soap.

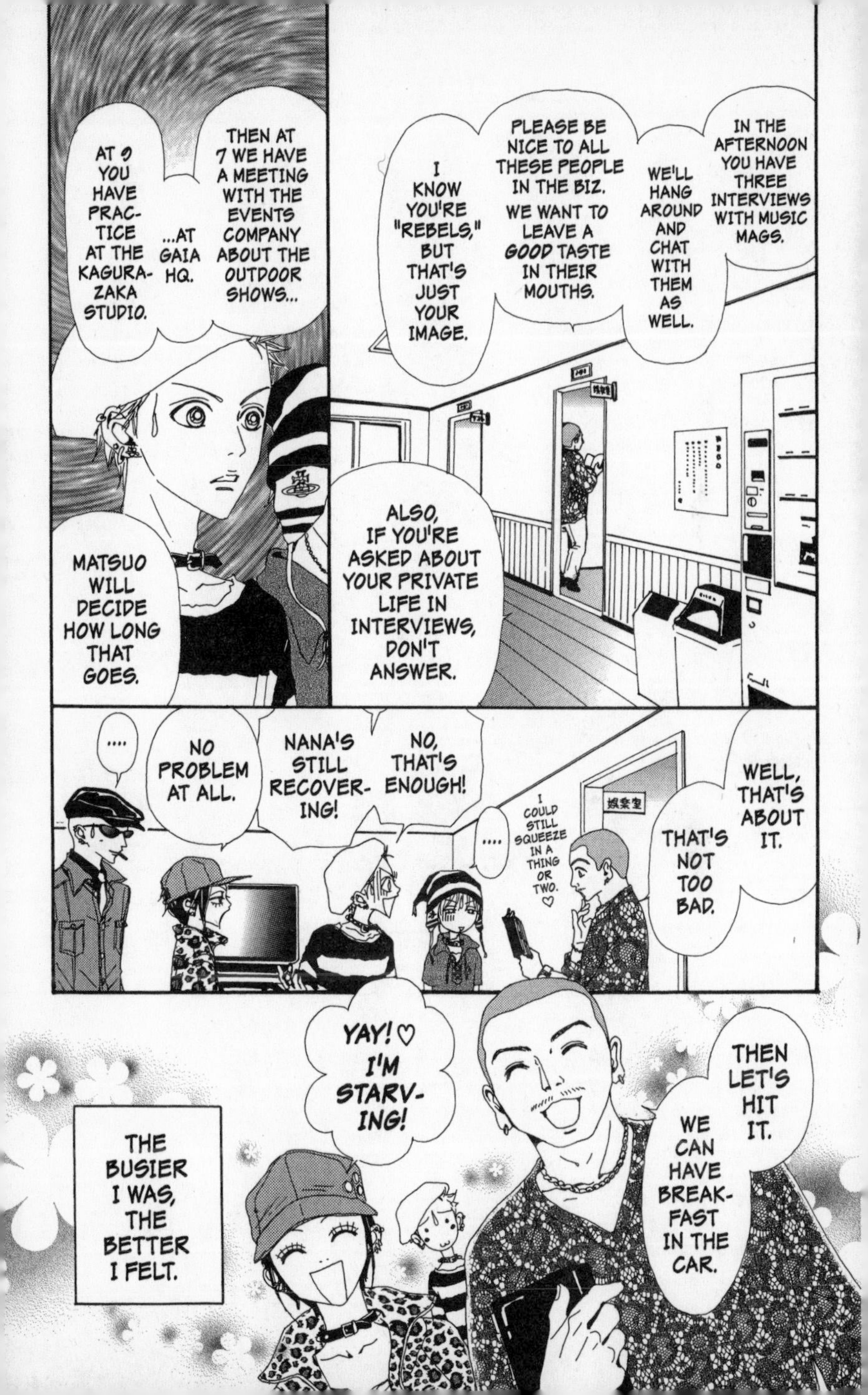
IN THE AFTERNOON YOU HAVE THREE INTERVIEWS WITH MUSIC MAGS.
WE'LL HANG AROUND AND CHAT WITH THEM AS WELL.
PLEASE BE NICE TO ALL THESE PEOPLE IN THE BIZ. WE WANT TO LEAVE A *GOOD* TASTE IN THEIR MOUTHS.
I KNOW YOU'RE "REBELS," BUT THAT'S JUST YOUR IMAGE.
ALSO, IF YOU'RE ASKED ABOUT YOUR PRIVATE LIFE IN INTERVIEWS, DON'T ANSWER.
THEN AT 7 WE HAVE A MEETING WITH THE EVENTS COMPANY ABOUT THE OUTDOOR SHOWS...
...AT GAIA HQ.
AT 9 YOU HAVE PRAC-TICE AT THE KAGURA-ZAKA STUDIO.
MATSUO WILL DECIDE HOW LONG THAT GOES.
WELL, THAT'S ABOUT IT.
THAT'S NOT TOO BAD.
I COULD STILL SQUEEZE IN A THING OR TWO. ♡
....
NO, THAT'S ENOUGH!
NANA'S STILL RECOVER-ING!
NO PROBLEM AT ALL.
....
THEN LET'S HIT IT.
WE CAN HAVE BREAK-FAST IN THE CAR.
YAY! ♡ I'M STARV-ING!
THE BUSIER I WAS, THE BETTER I FELT.

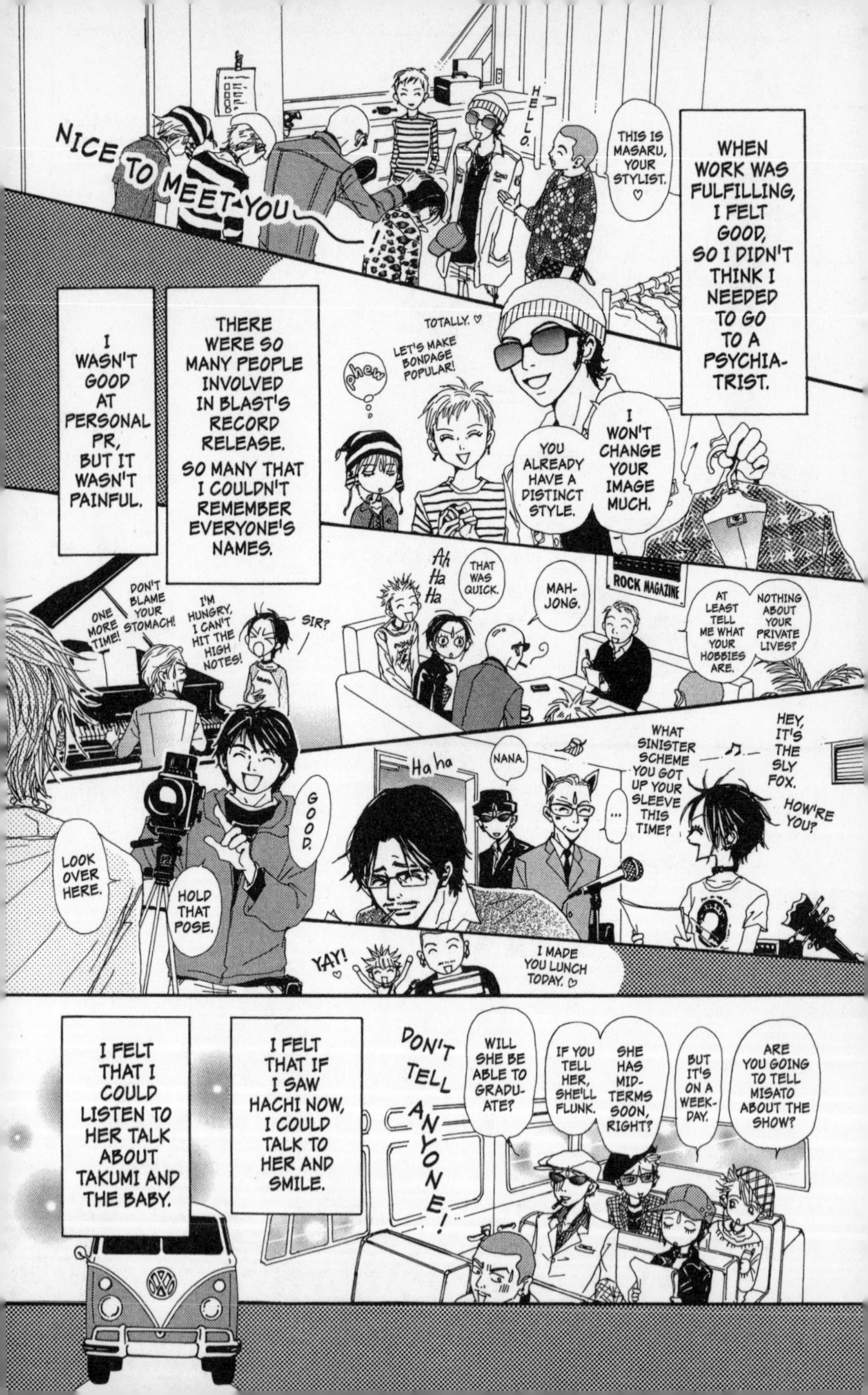
WHEN WORK WAS FULFILLING, I FELT GOOD, SO I DIDN'T THINK I NEEDED TO GO TO A PSYCHIA-TRIST.
THIS IS MASARU, YOUR STYLIST. ♡
HELLO.
NICE TO MEET YOU
I WON'T CHANGE YOUR IMAGE MUCH.
YOU ALREADY HAVE A DISTINCT STYLE.
TOTALLY. ♡
LET'S MAKE BONDAGE POPULAR!
phew
THERE WERE SO MANY PEOPLE INVOLVED IN BLAST'S RECORD RELEASE.
SO MANY THAT I COULDN'T REMEMBER EVERYONE'S NAMES.
I WASN'T GOOD AT PERSONAL PR, BUT IT WASN'T PAINFUL.
NOTHING ABOUT YOUR PRIVATE LIVES?
AT LEAST TELL ME WHAT YOUR HOBBIES ARE.
ROCK MAGAZINE
MAH-JONG.
THAT WAS QUICK.
Ah Ha Ha
SIR?
I'M HUNGRY, I CAN'T HIT THE HIGH NOTES!
DON'T BLAME YOUR STOMACH!
ONE MORE TIME!
HEY, IT'S THE SLY FOX.
HOW'RE YOU?
WHAT SINISTER SCHEME YOU GOT UP YOUR SLEEVE THIS TIME?
...
NANA.
Ha ha
GOOD.
HOLD THAT POSE.
LOOK OVER HERE.
I MADE YOU LUNCH TODAY. ♡
YAY! ♡
ARE YOU GOING TO TELL MISATO ABOUT THE SHOW?
BUT IT'S ON A WEEK-DAY.
SHE HAS MID-TERMS SOON, RIGHT?
IF YOU TELL HER, SHE'LL FLUNK.
WILL SHE BE ABLE TO GRADU-ATE?
DON'T TELL ANYONE!
I FELT THAT IF I SAW HACHI NOW, I COULD TALK TO HER AND SMILE.
I FELT THAT I COULD LISTEN TO HER TALK ABOUT TAKUMI AND THE BABY.

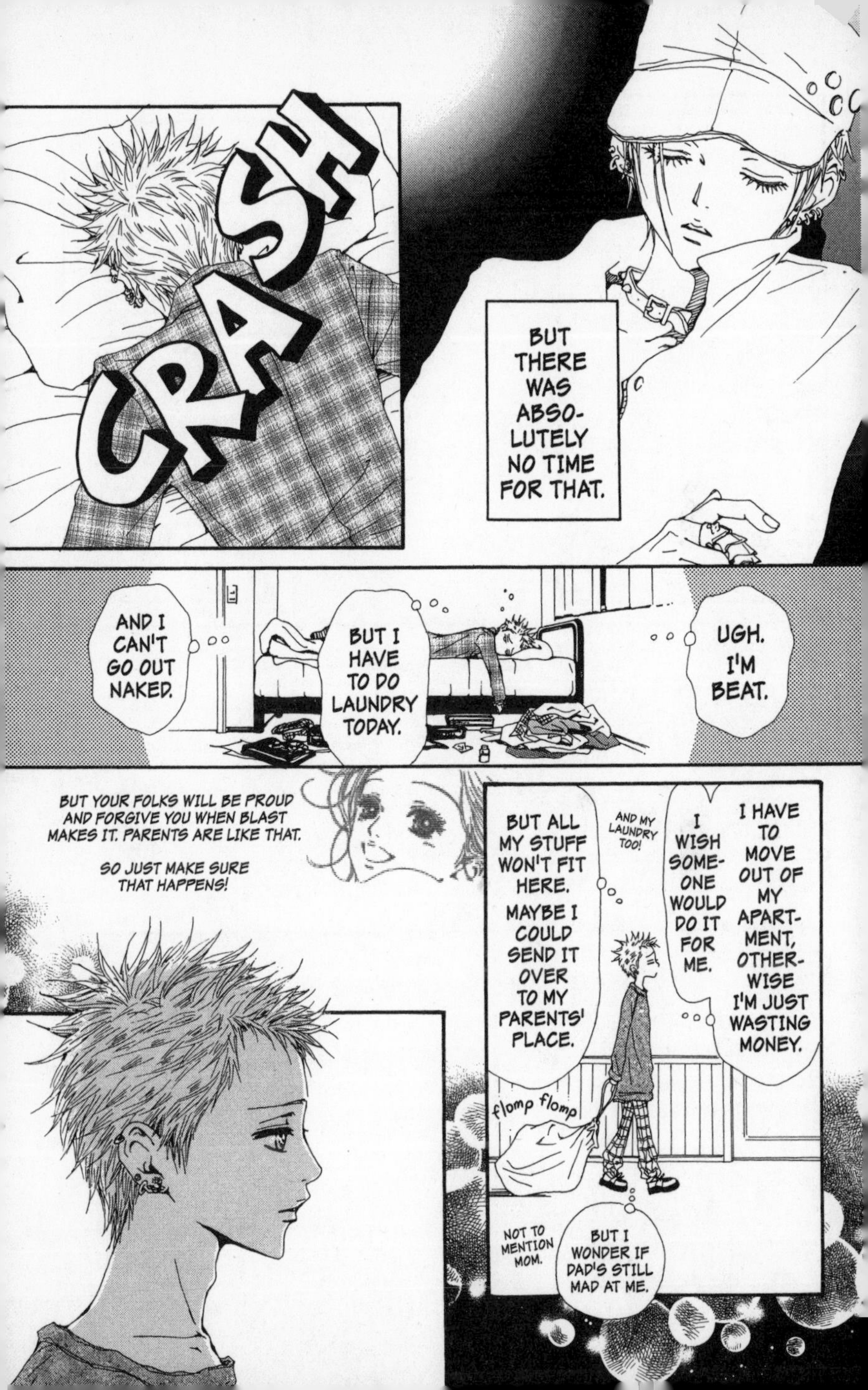
BUT THERE WAS ABSO-LUTELY NO TIME FOR THAT.
CRASH
UGH. I'M BEAT.
BUT I HAVE TO DO LAUNDRY TODAY.
AND I CAN'T GO OUT NAKED.
I HAVE TO MOVE OUT OF MY APART-MENT, OTHER-WISE I'M JUST WASTING MONEY.
I WISH SOME-ONE WOULD DO IT FOR ME.
AND MY LAUNDRY TOO!
BUT ALL MY STUFF WON'T FIT HERE. MAYBE I COULD SEND IT OVER TO MY PARENTS' PLACE.
flomp flomp
BUT I WONDER IF DAD'S STILL MAD AT ME.
NOT TO MENTION MOM.
BUT YOUR FOLKS WILL BE PROUD AND FORGIVE YOU WHEN BLAST MAKES IT. PARENTS ARE LIKE THAT.
SO JUST MAKE SURE THAT HAPPENS!

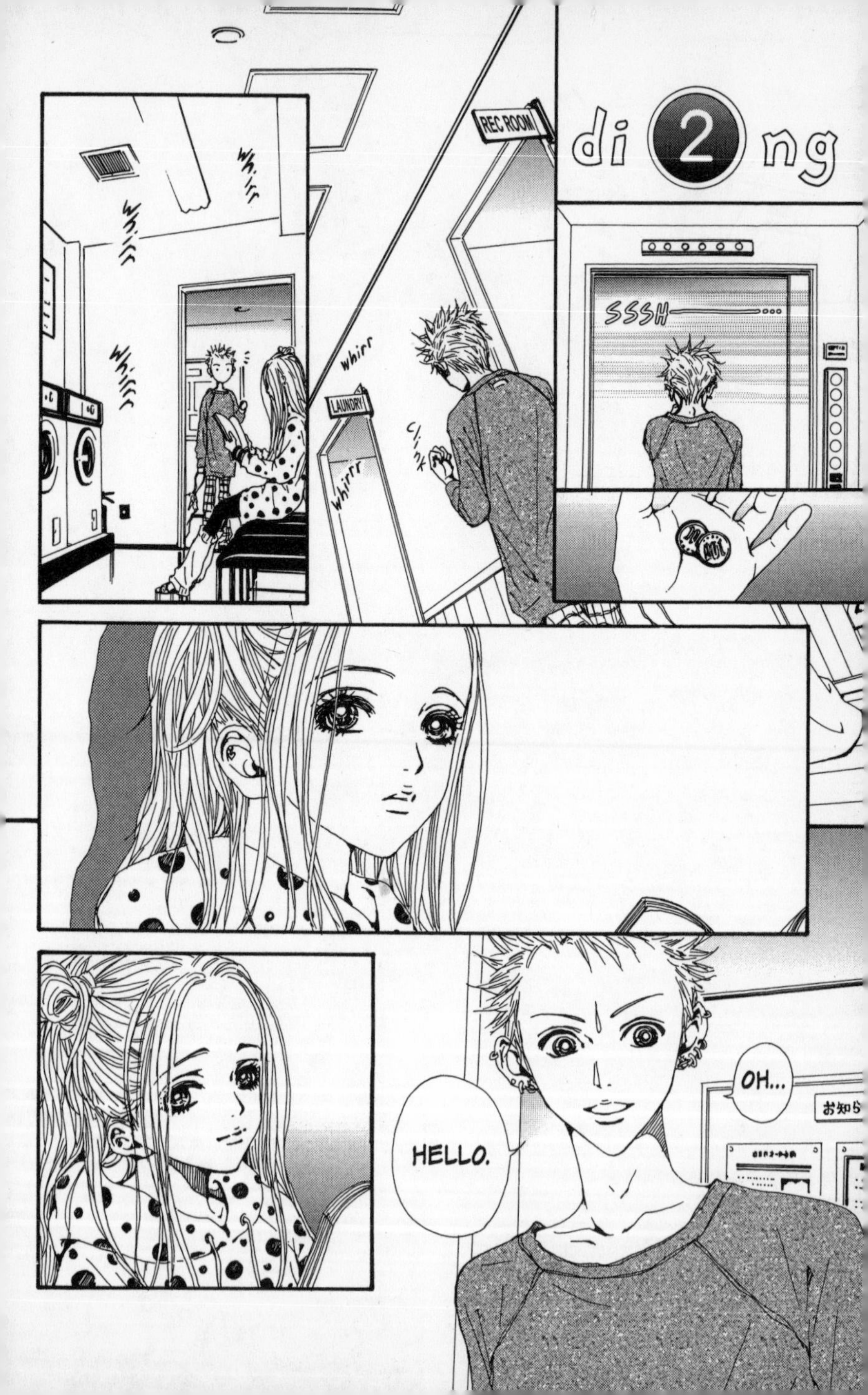

di 2 ng
SSSH———...
REC ROOM
whirr
clink
LAUNDRY
whirrr
OH...
HELLO.

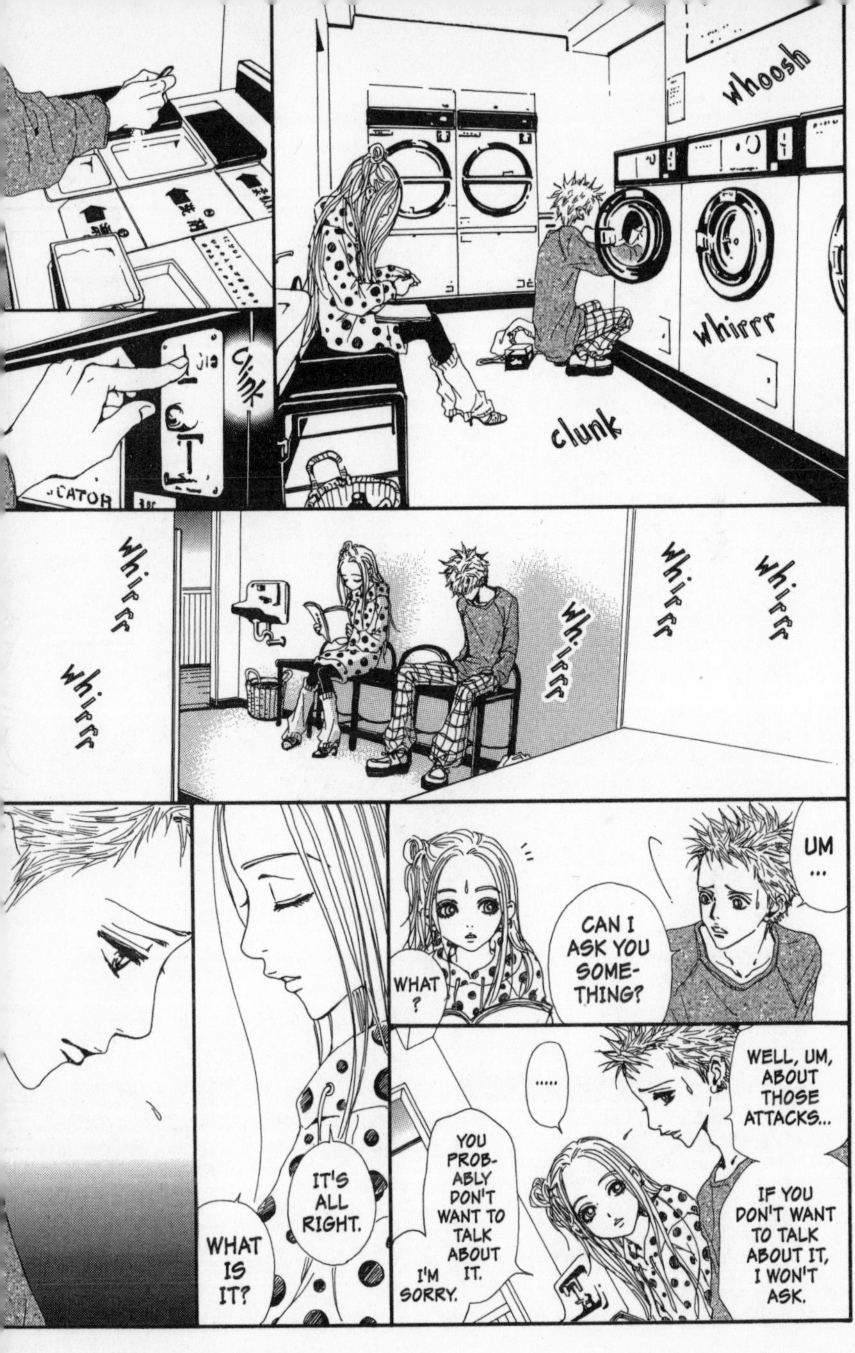
whoosh
whirrr
clunk
clink
whirrr
whirrr
whirrr
whirrr
whirrr
UM...
CAN I ASK YOU SOME-THING?
WHAT?
WELL, UM, ABOUT THOSE ATTACKS...
......
IF YOU DON'T WANT TO TALK ABOUT IT, I WON'T ASK.
YOU PROB-ABLY DON'T WANT TO TALK ABOUT IT.
I'M SORRY.
IT'S ALL RIGHT.
WHAT IS IT?

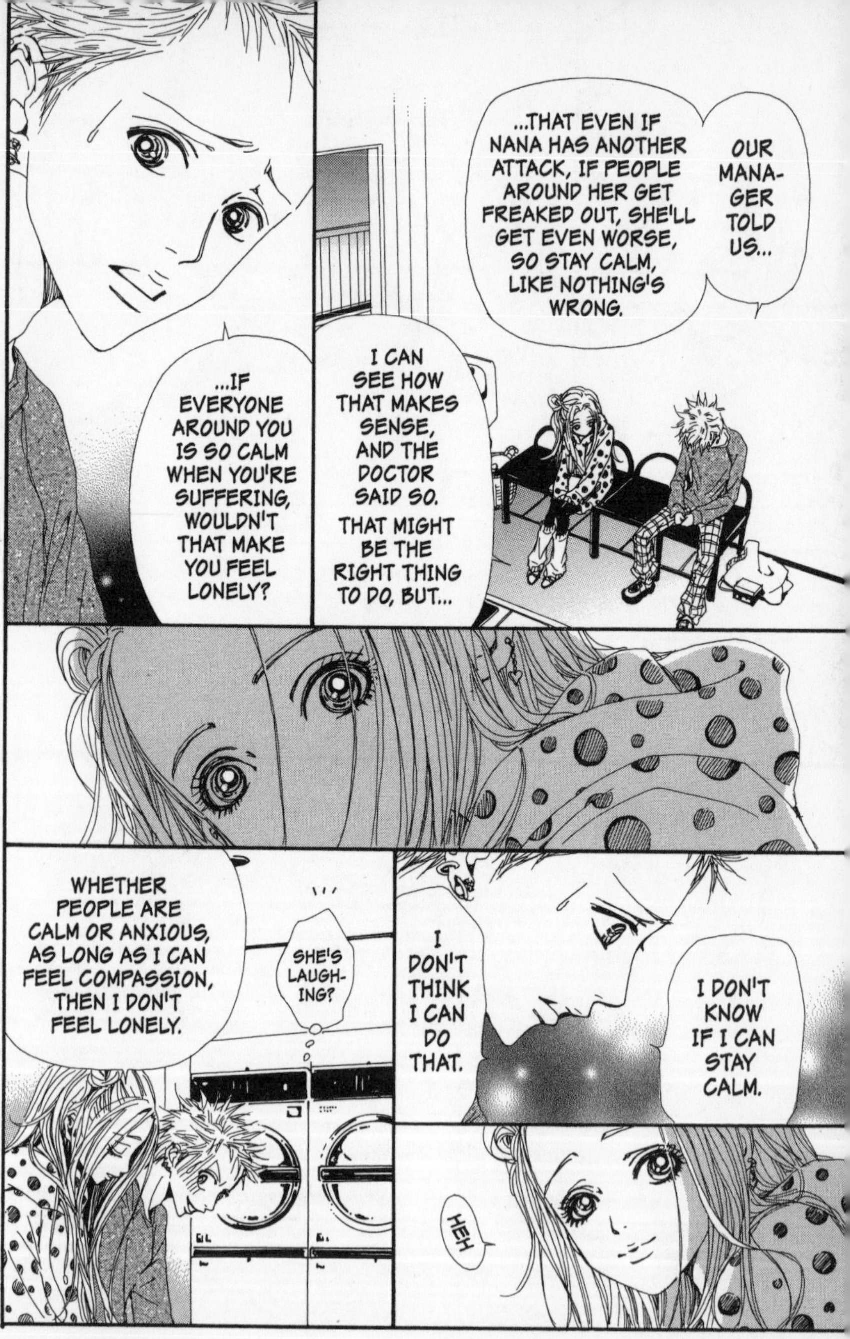

OUR MANAGER TOLD US...
...THAT EVEN IF NANA HAS ANOTHER ATTACK, IF PEOPLE AROUND HER GET FREAKED OUT, SHE'LL GET EVEN WORSE, SO STAY CALM, LIKE NOTHING'S WRONG.
I CAN SEE HOW THAT MAKES SENSE, AND THE DOCTOR SAID SO.
THAT MIGHT BE THE RIGHT THING TO DO, BUT...
...IF EVERYONE AROUND YOU IS SO CALM WHEN YOU'RE SUFFERING, WOULDN'T THAT MAKE YOU FEEL LONELY?
I DON'T KNOW IF I CAN STAY CALM.
I DON'T THINK I CAN DO THAT.
HEH
SHE'S LAUGHING?
WHETHER PEOPLE ARE CALM OR ANXIOUS, AS LONG AS I CAN FEEL COMPASSION, THEN I DON'T FEEL LONELY.

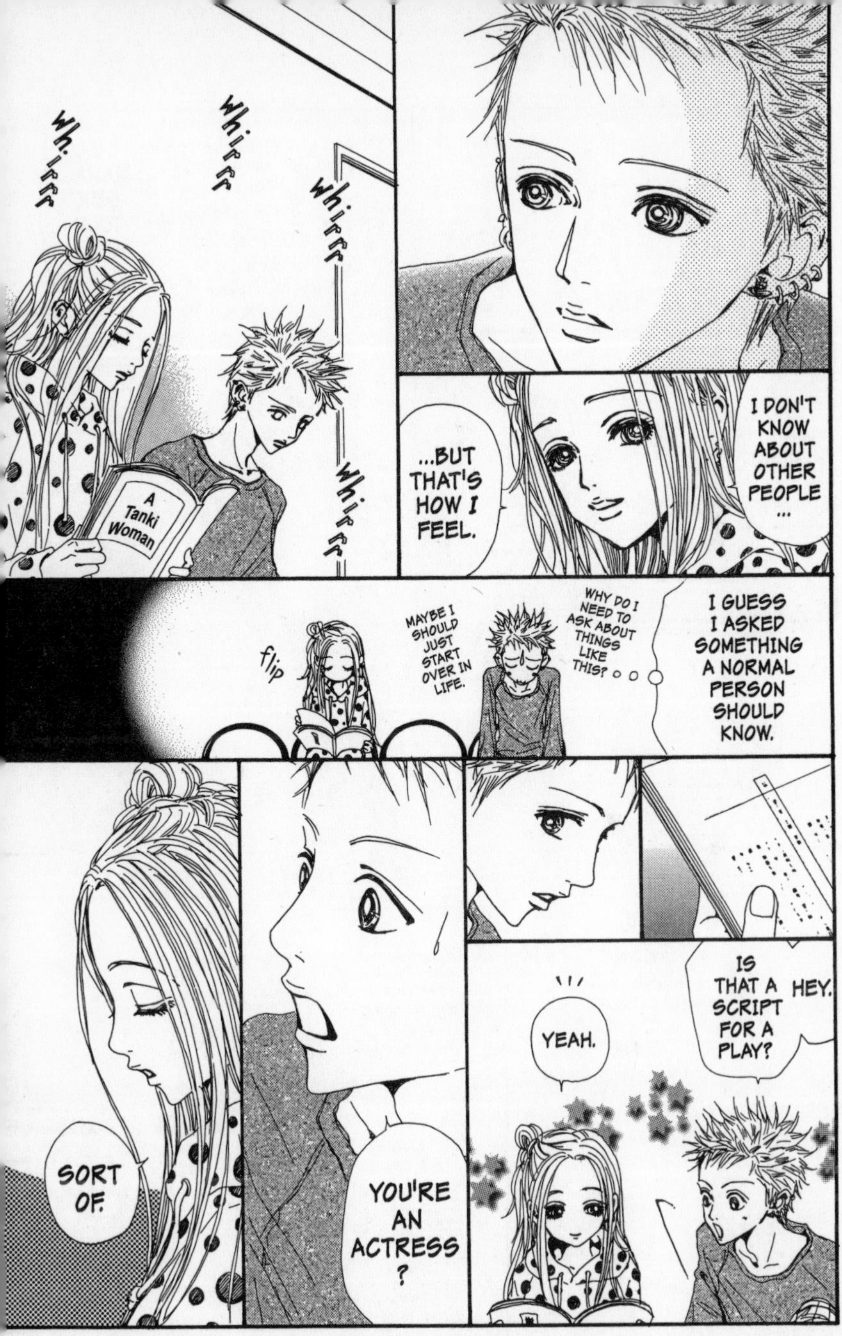
I DON'T KNOW ABOUT OTHER PEOPLE...
...BUT THAT'S HOW I FEEL.
whirrr
whirrr
whirrr
whirrr
A Tanki Woman
I GUESS I ASKED SOMETHING A NORMAL PERSON SHOULD KNOW.
WHY DO I NEED TO ASK ABOUT THINGS LIKE THIS?
MAYBE I SHOULD JUST START OVER IN LIFE.
flip
HEY.
IS THAT A SCRIPT FOR A PLAY?
YEAH.
YOU'RE AN ACTRESS?
SORT OF.

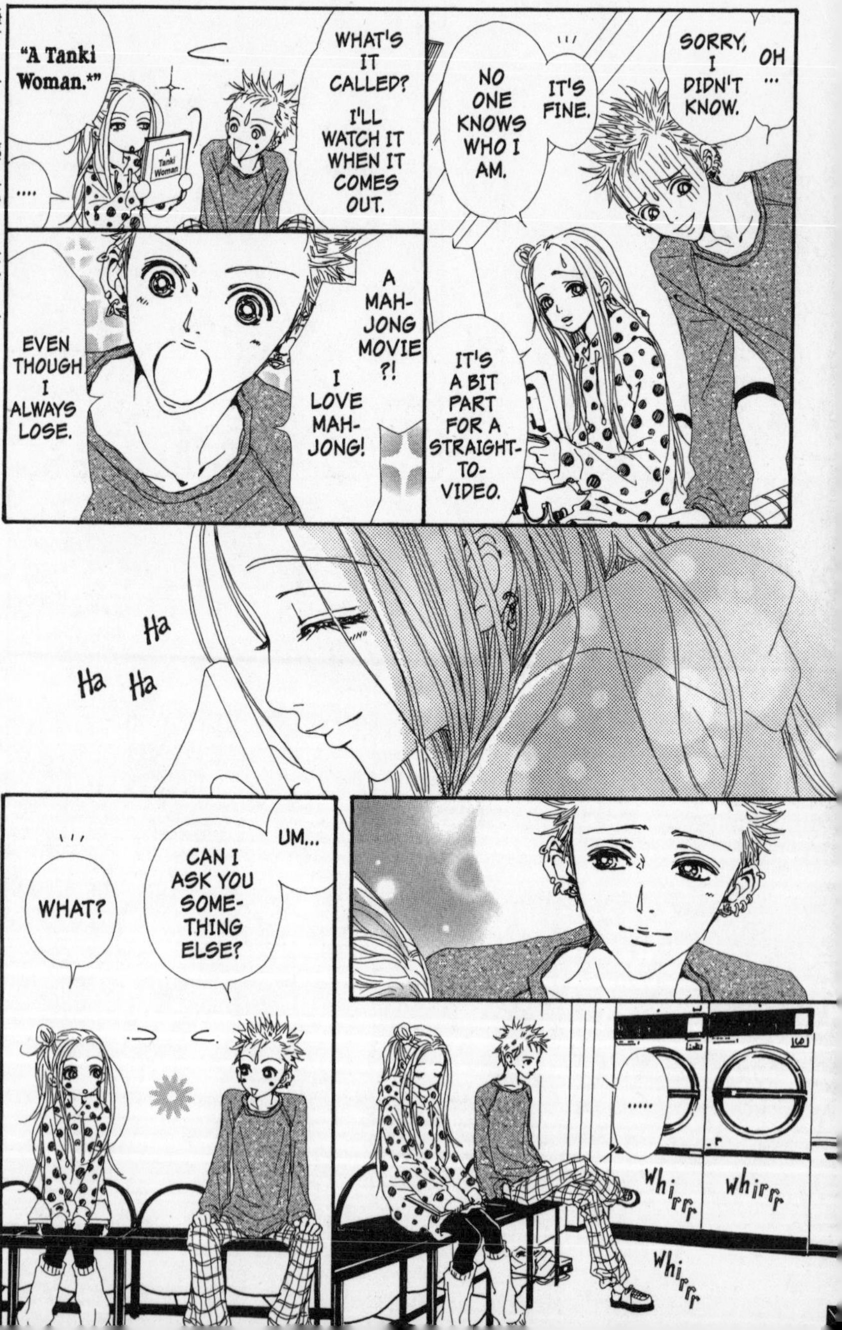
OH ...
SORRY, I DIDN'T KNOW.
IT'S FINE.
NO ONE KNOWS WHO I AM.
IT'S A BIT PART FOR A STRAIGHT-TO-VIDEO.
WHAT'S IT CALLED? I'LL WATCH IT WHEN IT COMES OUT.
"A Tanki Woman.*"
A Tanki Woman
....
A MAH-JONG MOVIE?!
I LOVE MAH-JONG!
EVEN THOUGH I ALWAYS LOSE.
Ha
Ha Ha
UM...
CAN I ASK YOU SOME-THING ELSE?
WHAT?
.....
Whirrr
whirrr
Whirrr

*This can also mean "Short-tempered Woman."

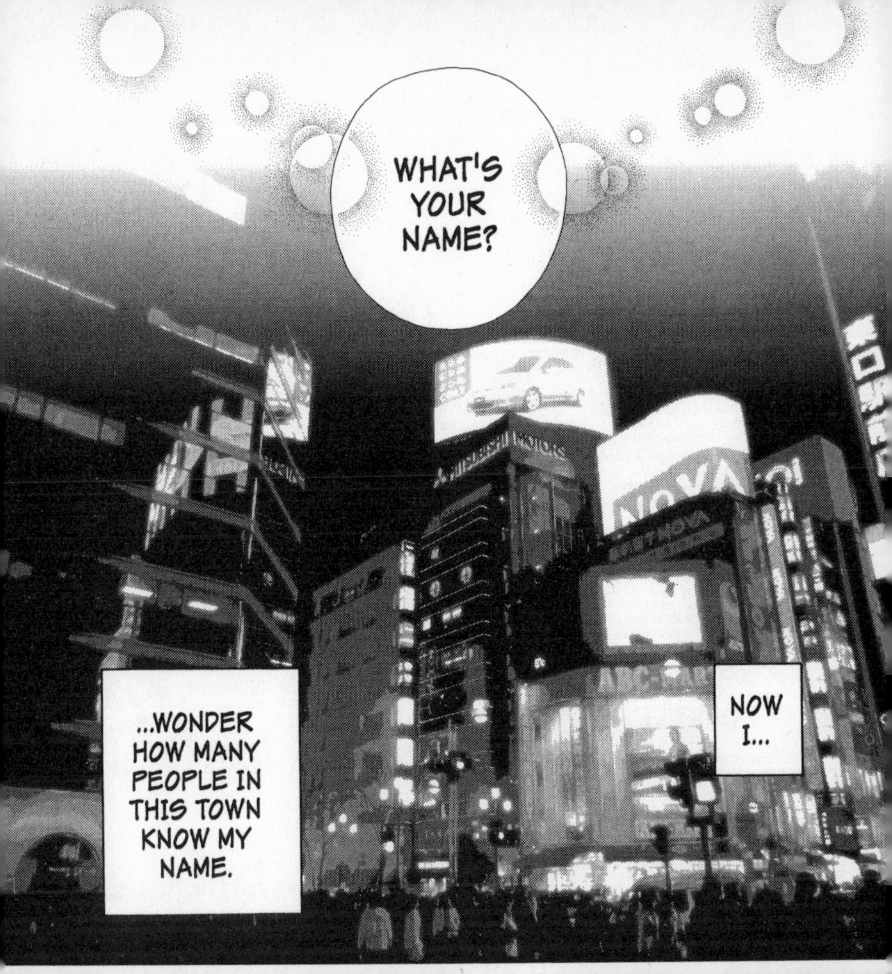
WHAT'S YOUR NAME?
NOVA
NOW I...
...WONDER HOW MANY PEOPLE IN THIS TOWN KNOW MY NAME.

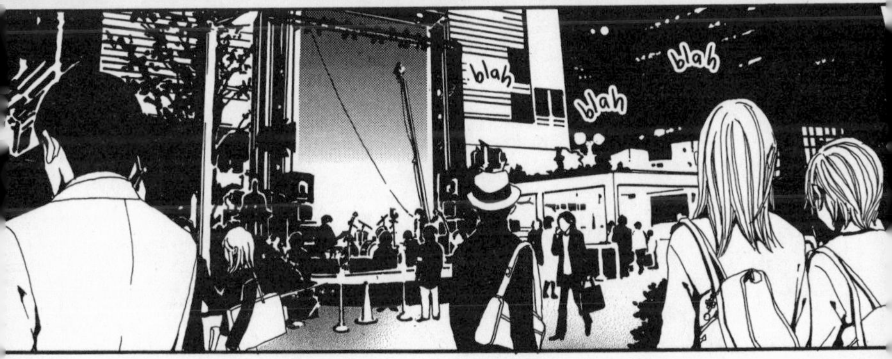
blah
blah
blah

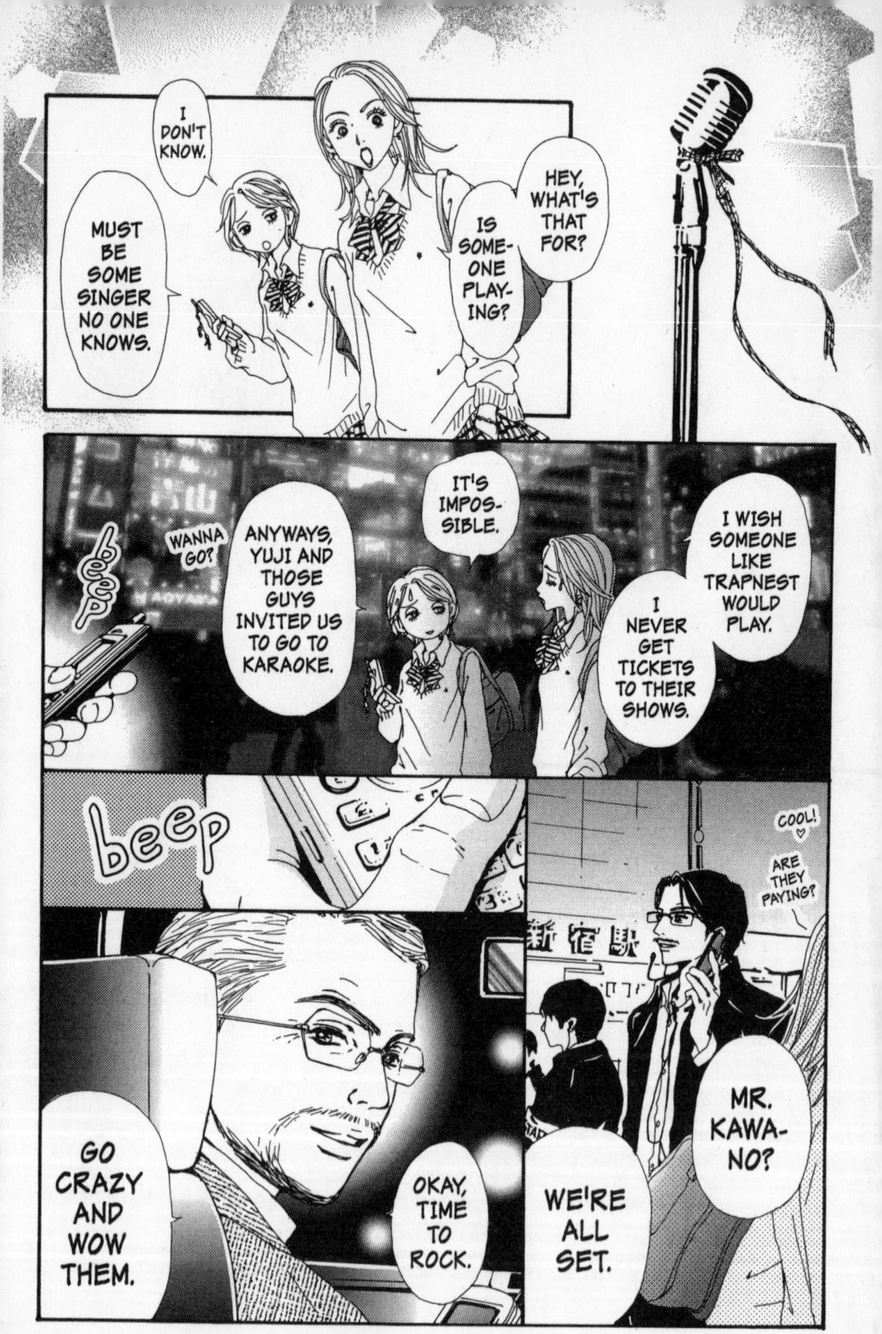
HEY, WHAT'S THAT FOR?
IS SOME-ONE PLAY-ING?
I DON'T KNOW.
MUST BE SOME SINGER NO ONE KNOWS.
I WISH SOMEONE LIKE TRAPNEST WOULD PLAY.
I NEVER GET TICKETS TO THEIR SHOWS.
IT'S IMPOS-SIBLE.
ANYWAYS, YUJI AND THOSE GUYS INVITED US TO GO TO KARAOKE.
WANNA GO?
beep
COOL! ♡
ARE THEY PAYING?
MR. KAWA-NO?
WE'RE ALL SET.
beep
OKAY, TIME TO ROCK.
GO CRAZY AND WOW THEM.

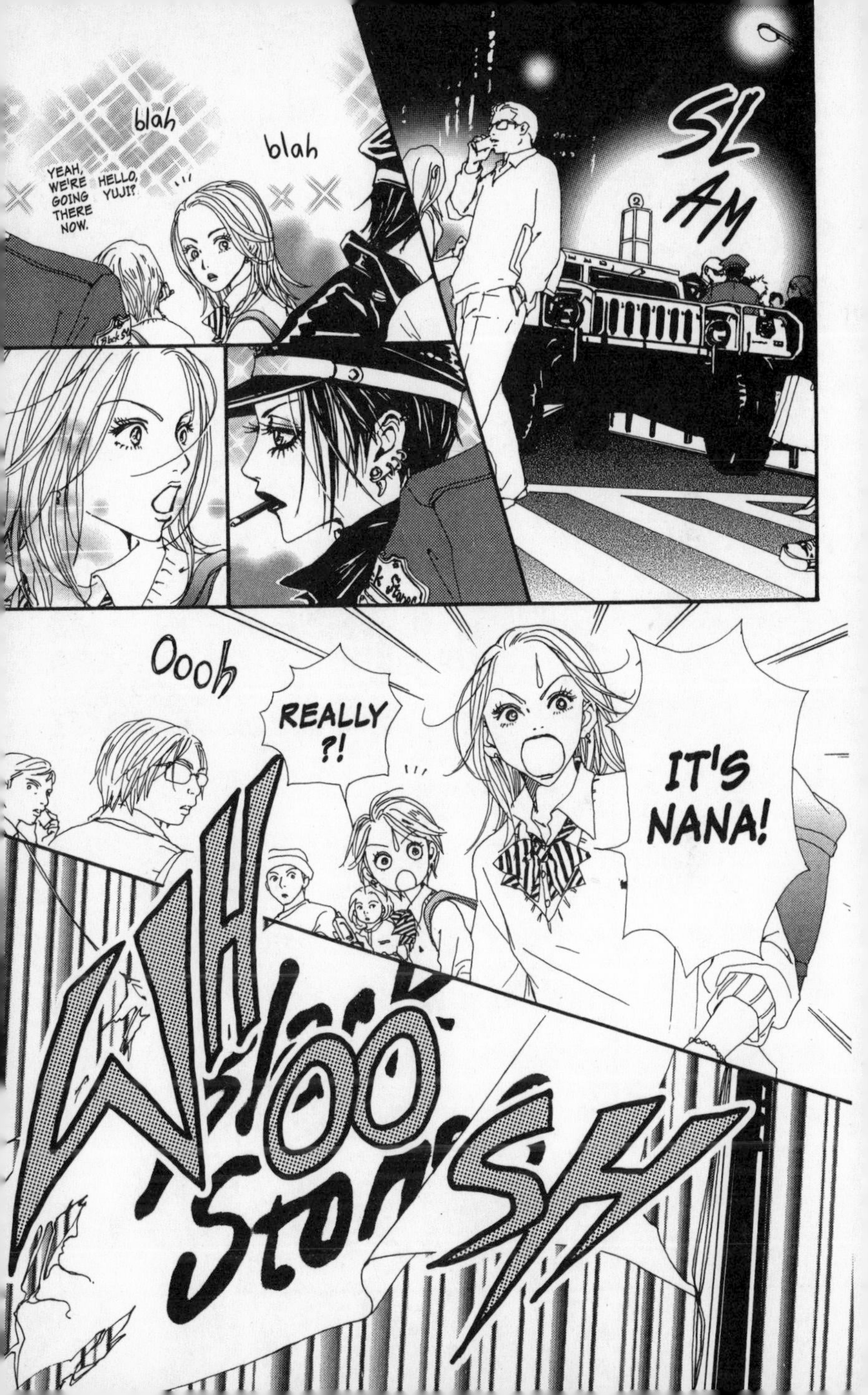
SLAM
blah
blah
HELLO, YUJI?
YEAH, WE'RE GOING THERE NOW.
IT'S NANA!
REALLY ?!
Oooh
WHOOSH

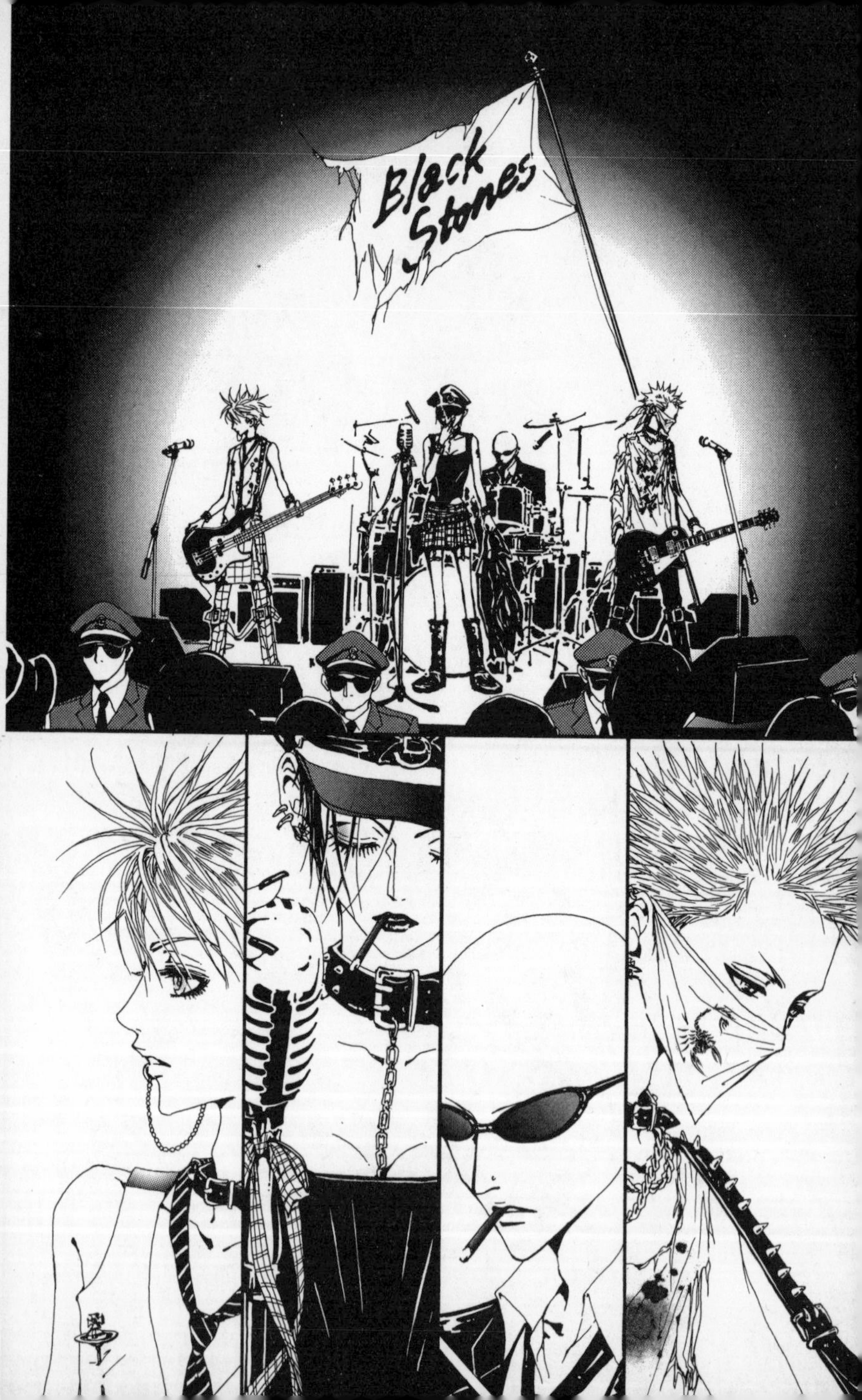
Black Stones

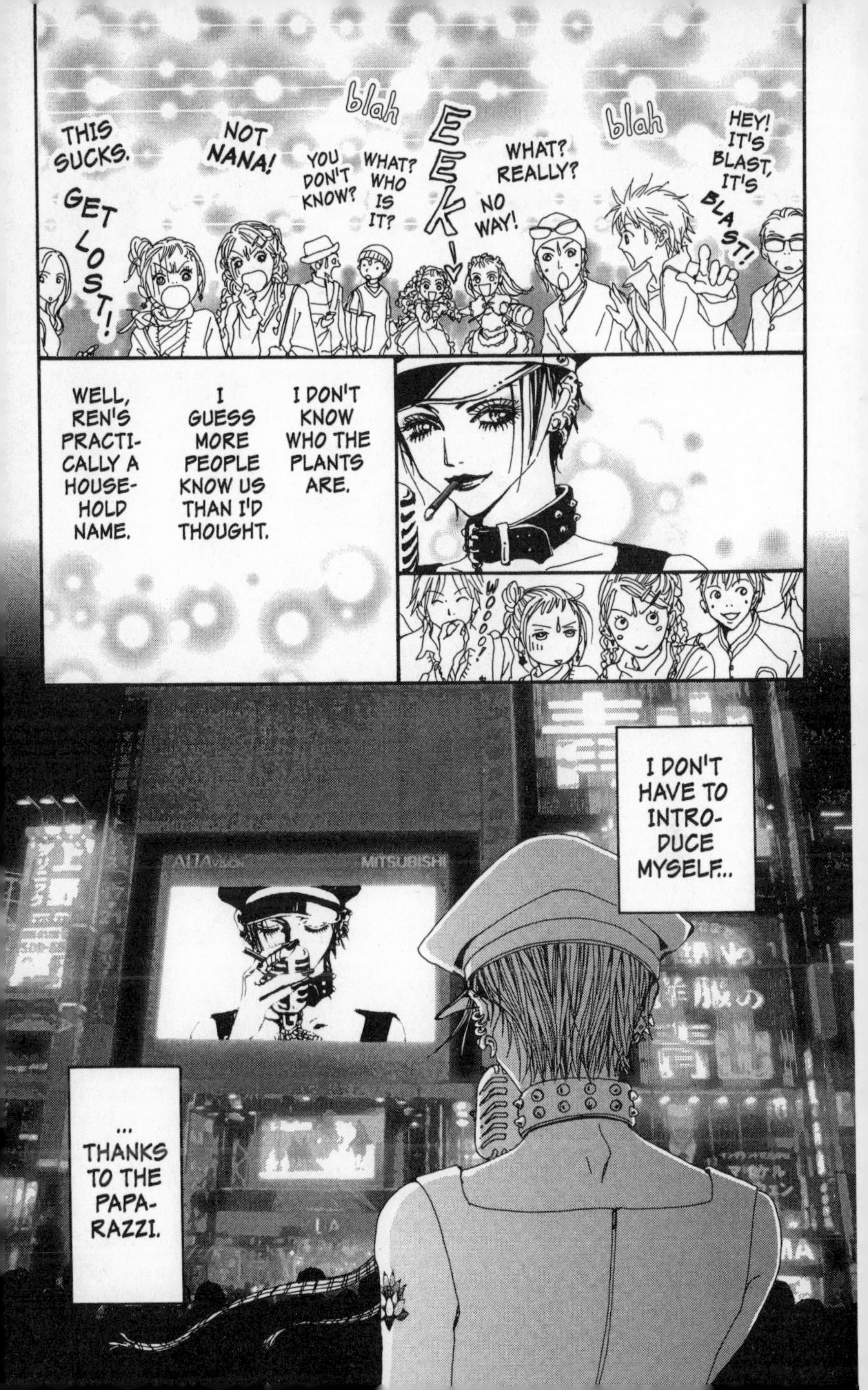
HEY! IT'S BLAST, IT'S BLAST!
blah
WHAT? REALLY?
NO WAY!
EEK!
WHAT? WHO IS IT?
blah
YOU DON'T KNOW?
NOT NANA!
THIS SUCKS.
GET LOST!
WOOOO!
I DON'T KNOW WHO THE PLANTS ARE.
I GUESS MORE PEOPLE KNOW US THAN I'D THOUGHT.
WELL, REN'S PRACTICALLY A HOUSEHOLD NAME.
I DON'T HAVE TO INTRODUCE MYSELF...
MITSUBISHI
... THANKS TO THE PAPARAZZI.

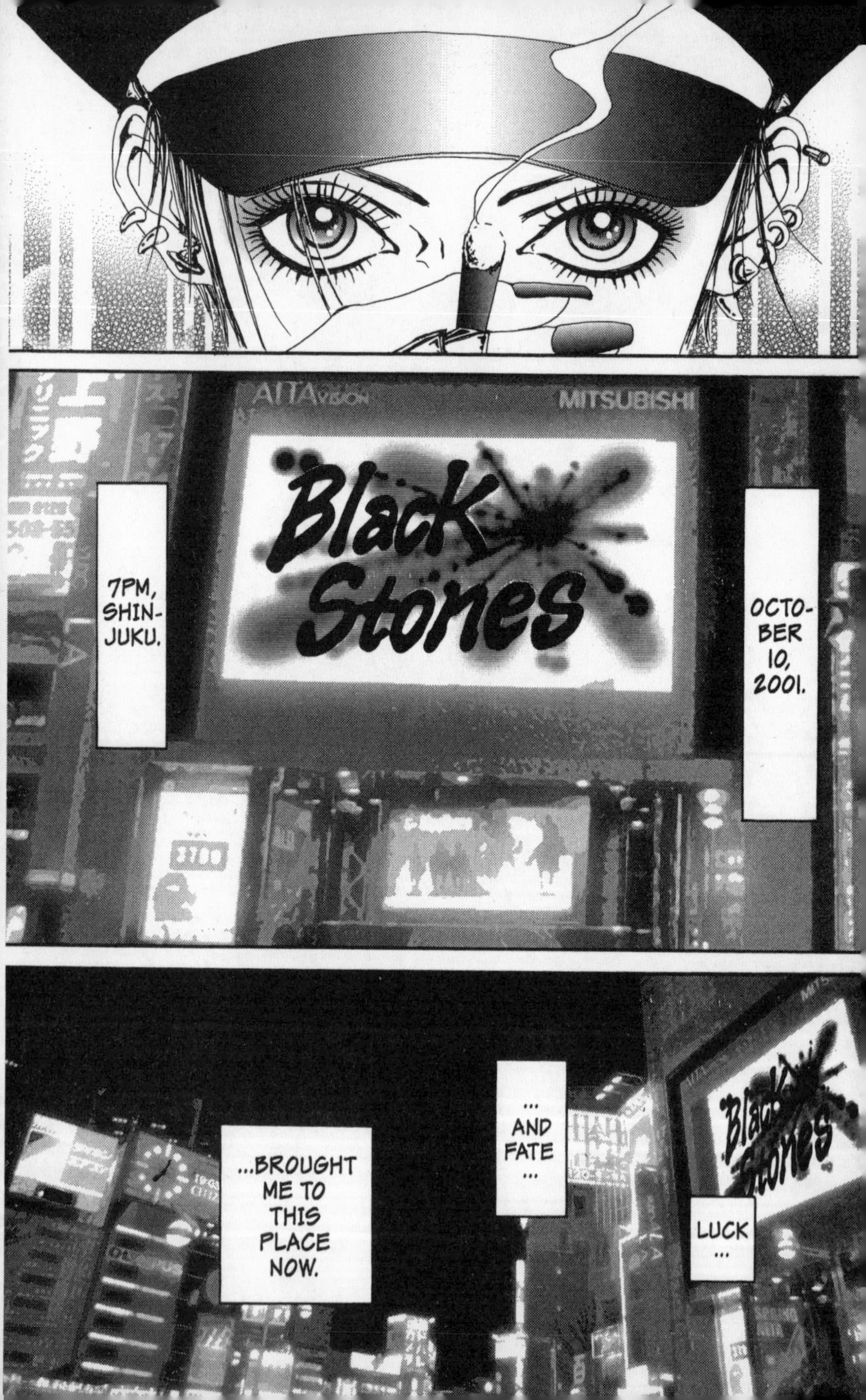
MITSUBISHI
Black Stones
OCTOBER 10, 2001.
7PM, SHINJUKU.
Black Stones
LUCK ...
... AND FATE ...
...BROUGHT ME TO THIS PLACE NOW.

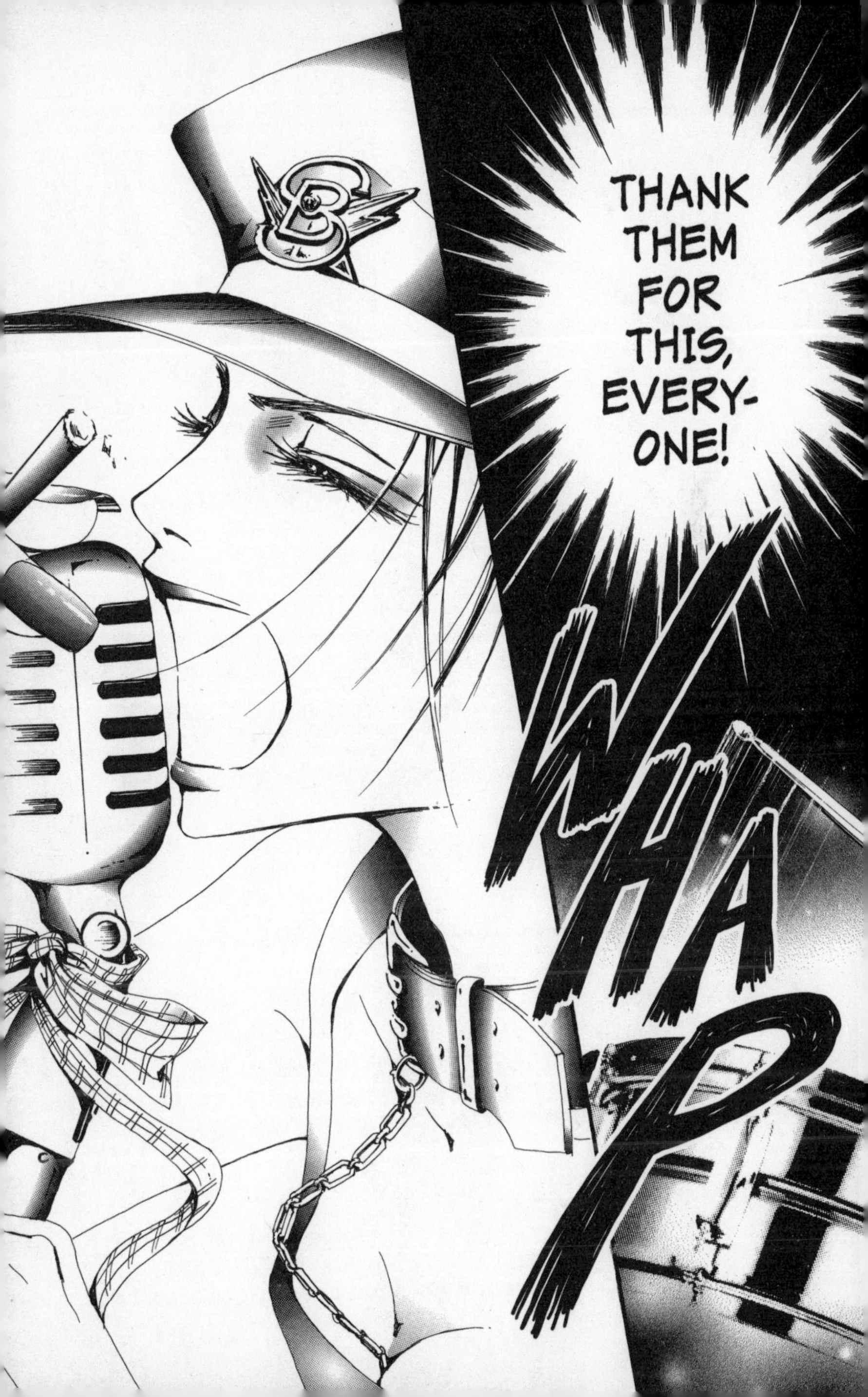
THANK THEM FOR THIS, EVERY-ONE!
WHAP

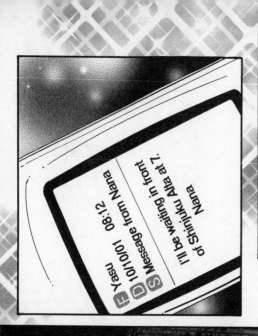

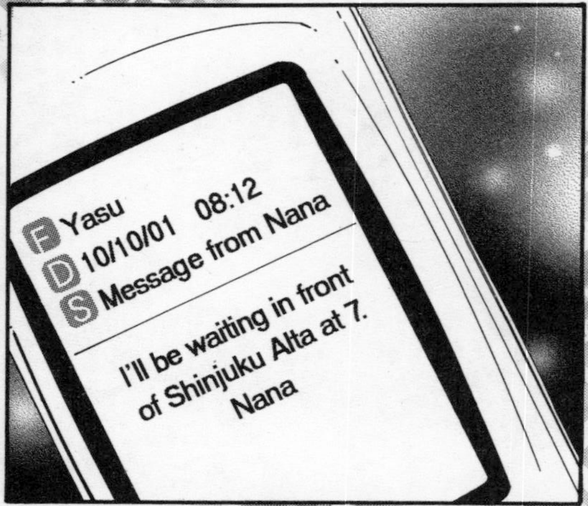
F Yasu
D 10/10/01 08:12
S Message from Nana
I'll be waiting in front of Shinjuku Alta at 7.
Nana
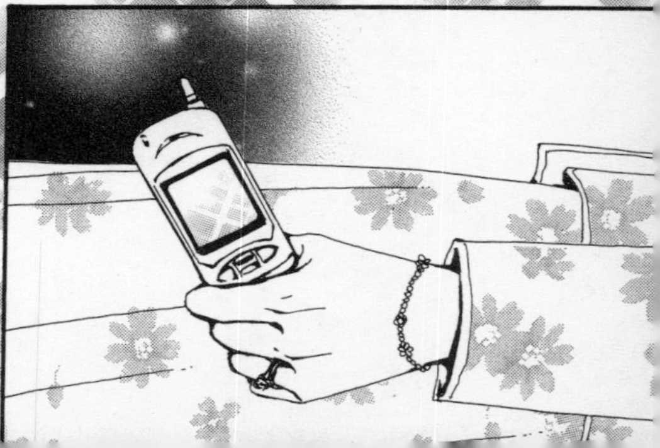
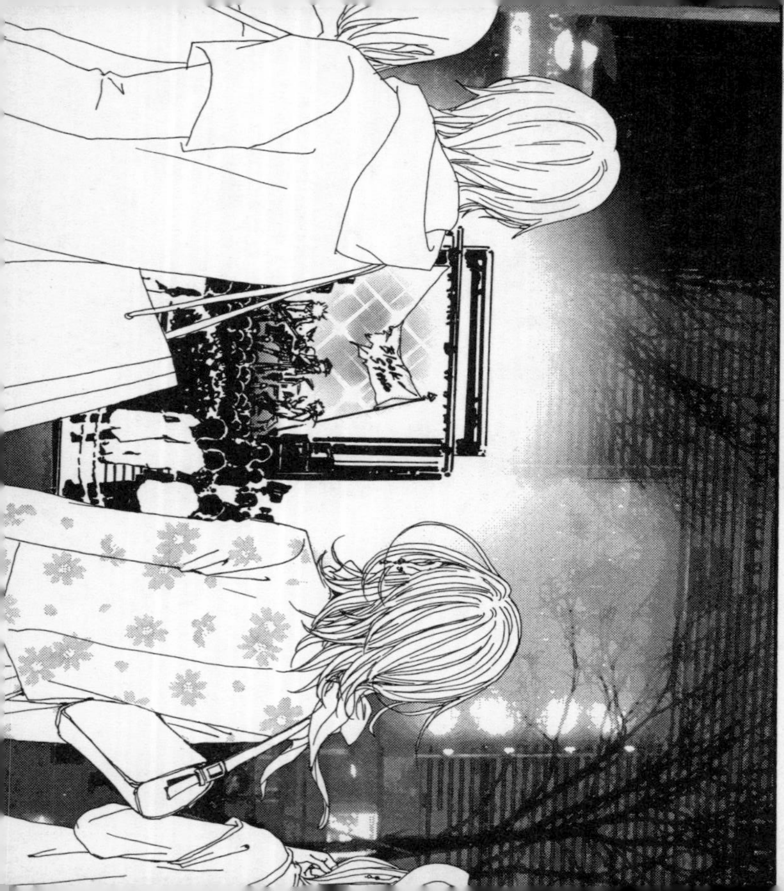

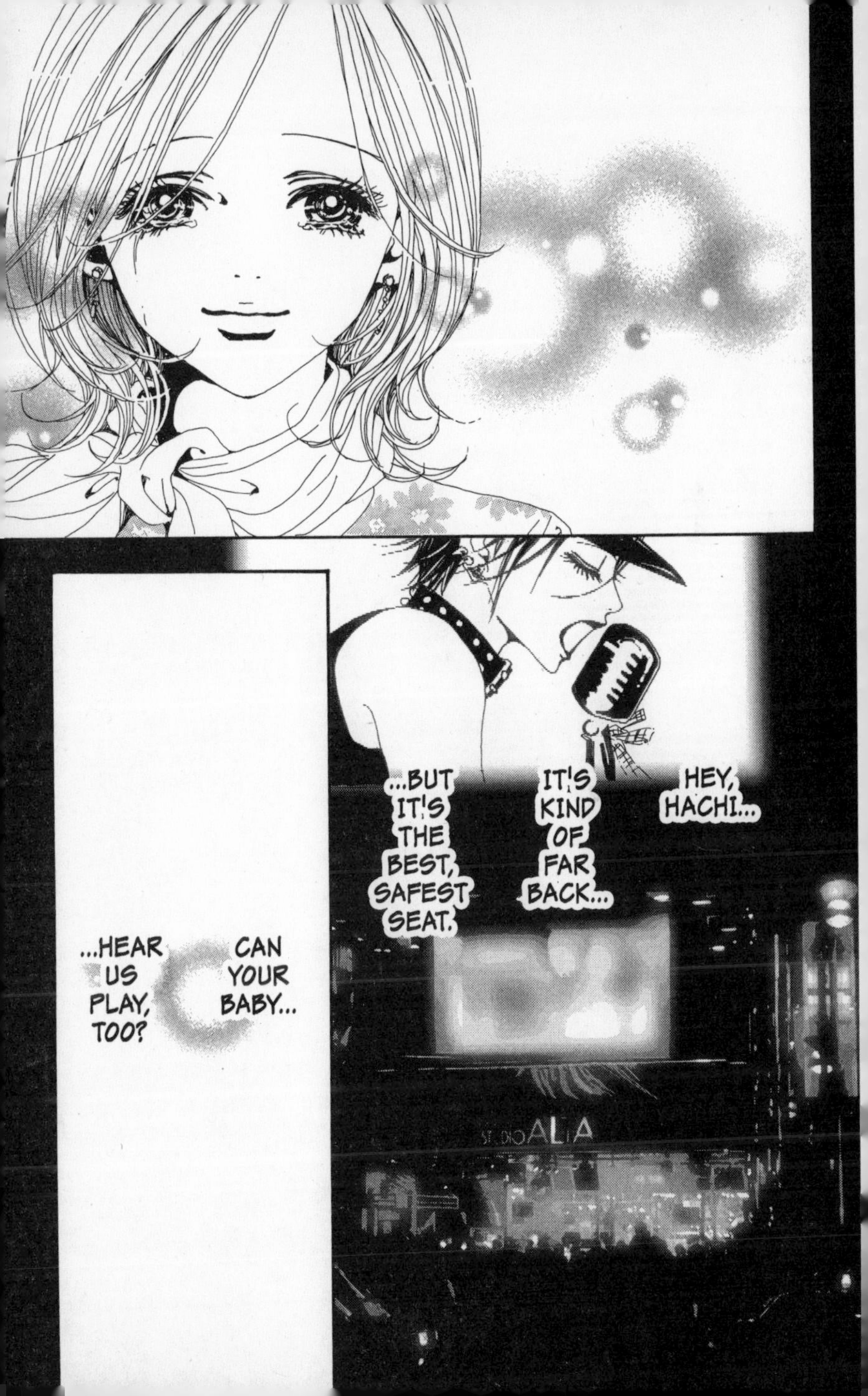
HEY, HACHI...
IT'S KIND OF FAR BACK...
...BUT IT'S THE BEST, SAFEST SEAT.
CAN YOUR BABY...
...HEAR US PLAY, TOO?

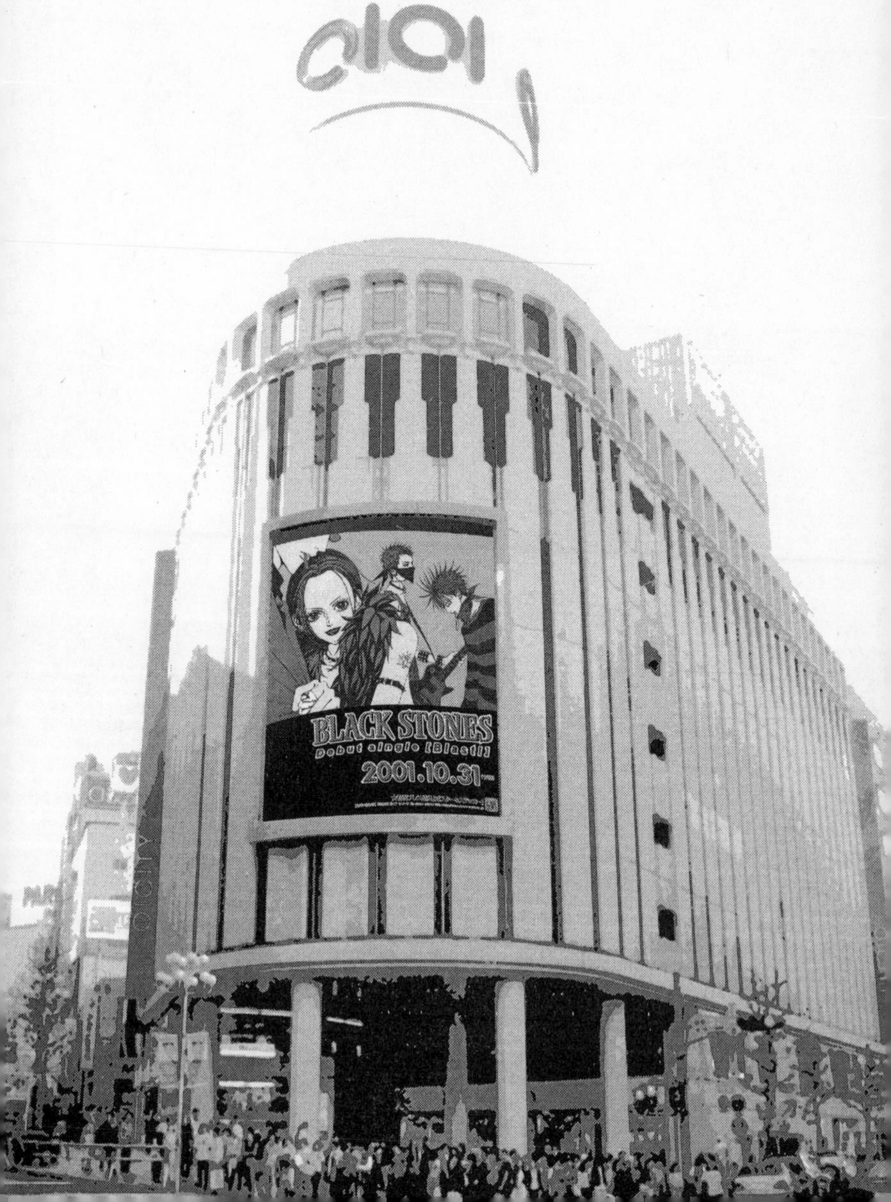
BLACK STONES
Debut single [Blast!]
2001.10.31

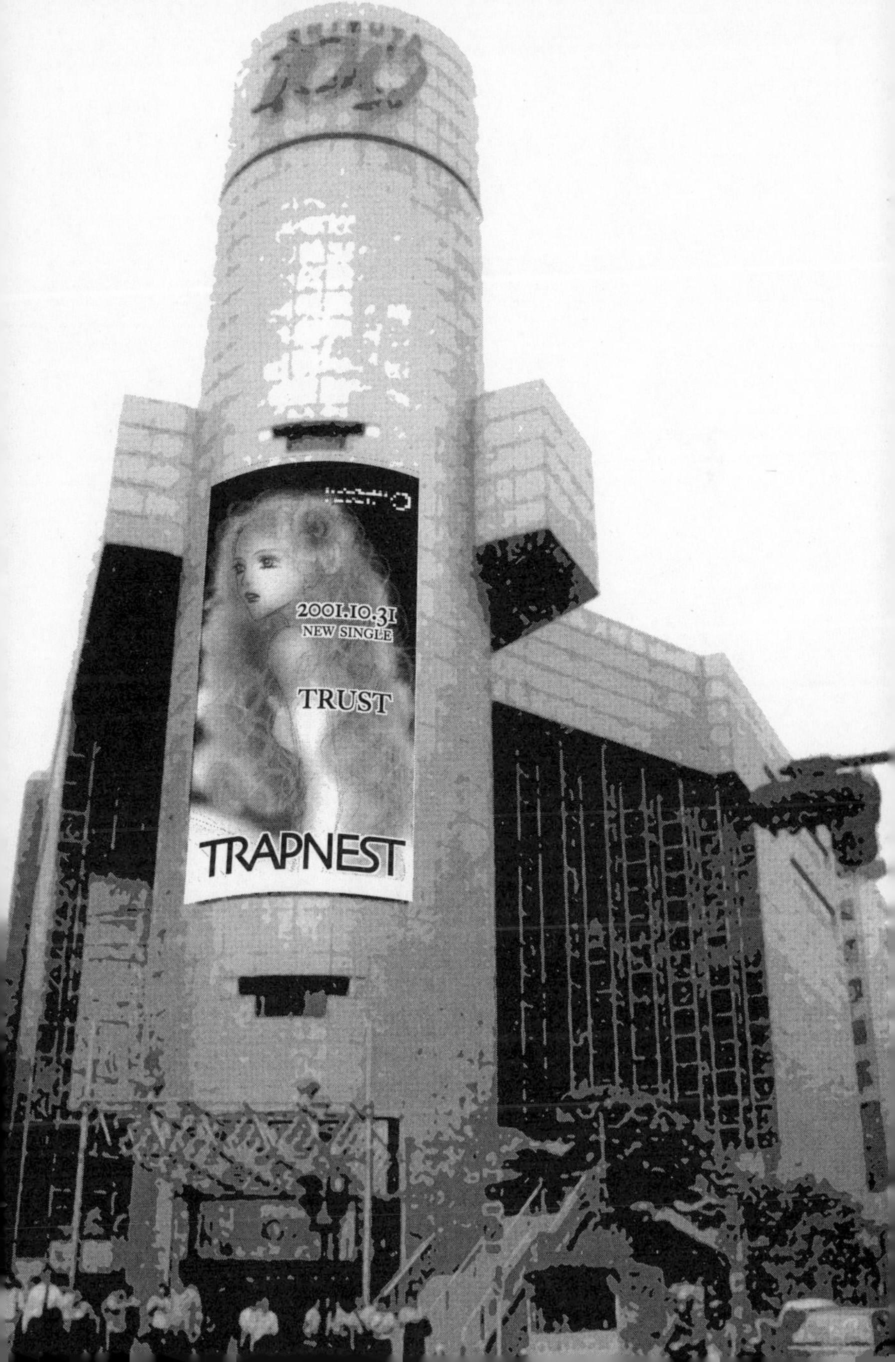
2001.10.31
NEW SINGLE
TRUST
TRAPNEST

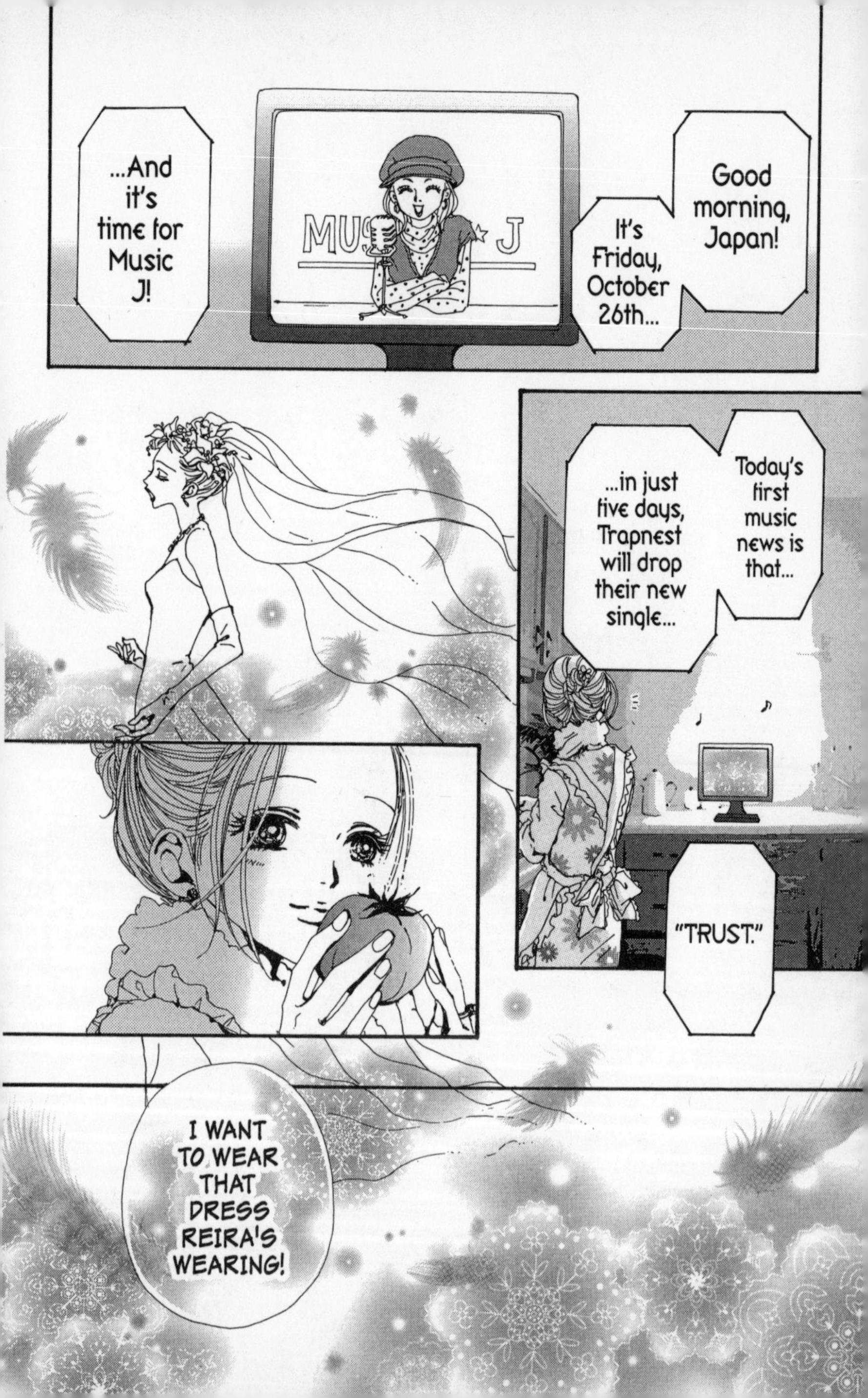
Good morning, Japan!
It's Friday, October 26th...
MUS J
...And it's time for Music J!
Today's first music news is that...
...in just five days, Trapnest will drop their new single...
"TRUST."
I WANT TO WEAR THAT DRESS REIRA'S WEARING!

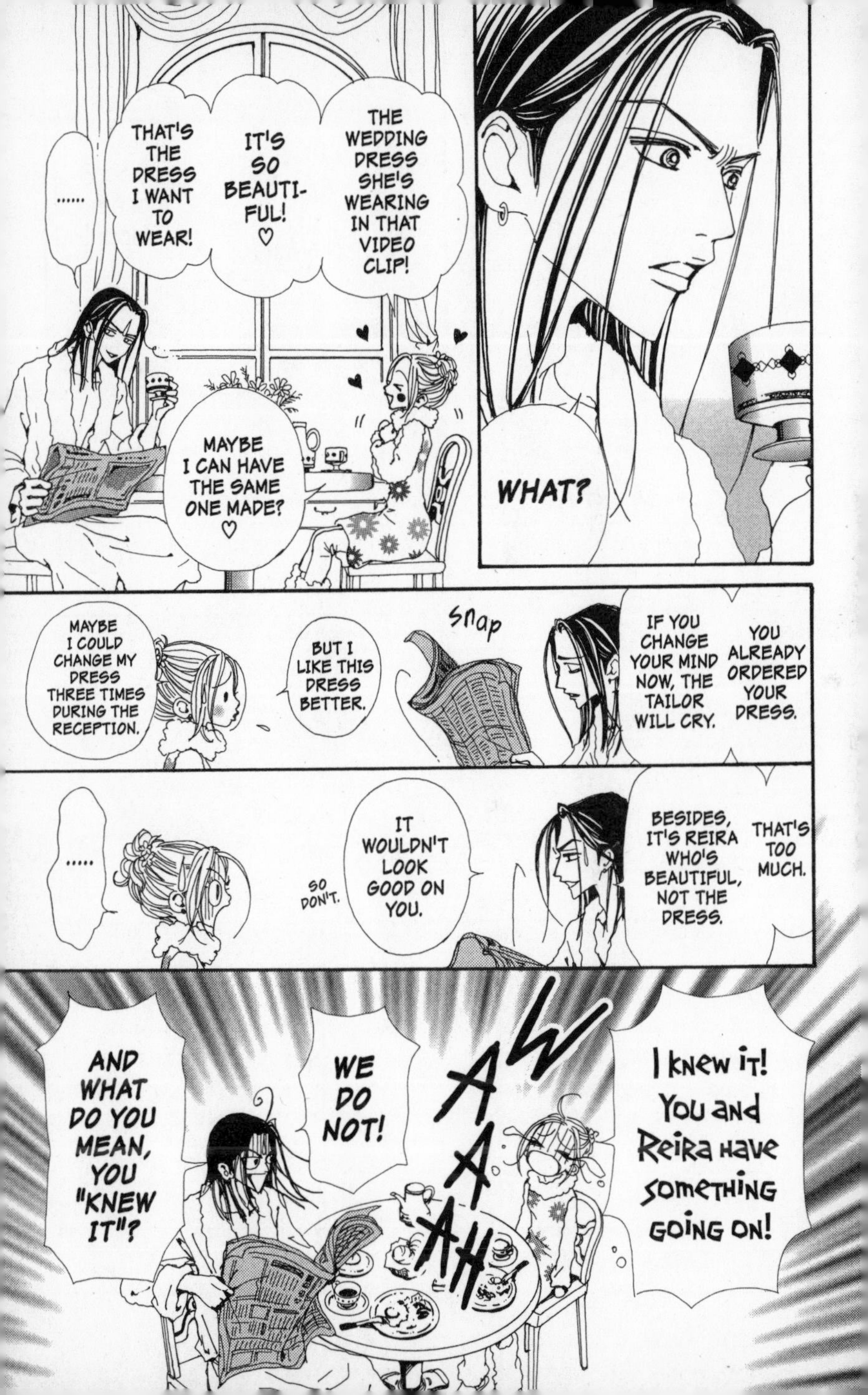
THE WEDDING DRESS SHE'S WEARING IN THAT VIDEO CLIP!
IT'S SO BEAUTIFUL! ♡
THAT'S THE DRESS I WANT TO WEAR!
......
MAYBE I CAN HAVE THE SAME ONE MADE? ♡
WHAT?
YOU ALREADY ORDERED YOUR DRESS.
IF YOU CHANGE YOUR MIND NOW, THE TAILOR WILL CRY.
Snap
BUT I LIKE THIS DRESS BETTER.
MAYBE I COULD CHANGE MY DRESS THREE TIMES DURING THE RECEPTION.
THAT'S TOO MUCH.
BESIDES, IT'S REIRA WHO'S BEAUTIFUL, NOT THE DRESS.
IT WOULDN'T LOOK GOOD ON YOU.
SO DON'T.
......
I knew it! You and Reira have something going on!
AAAAH
AW
WE DO NOT!
AND WHAT DO YOU MEAN, YOU "KNEW IT"?

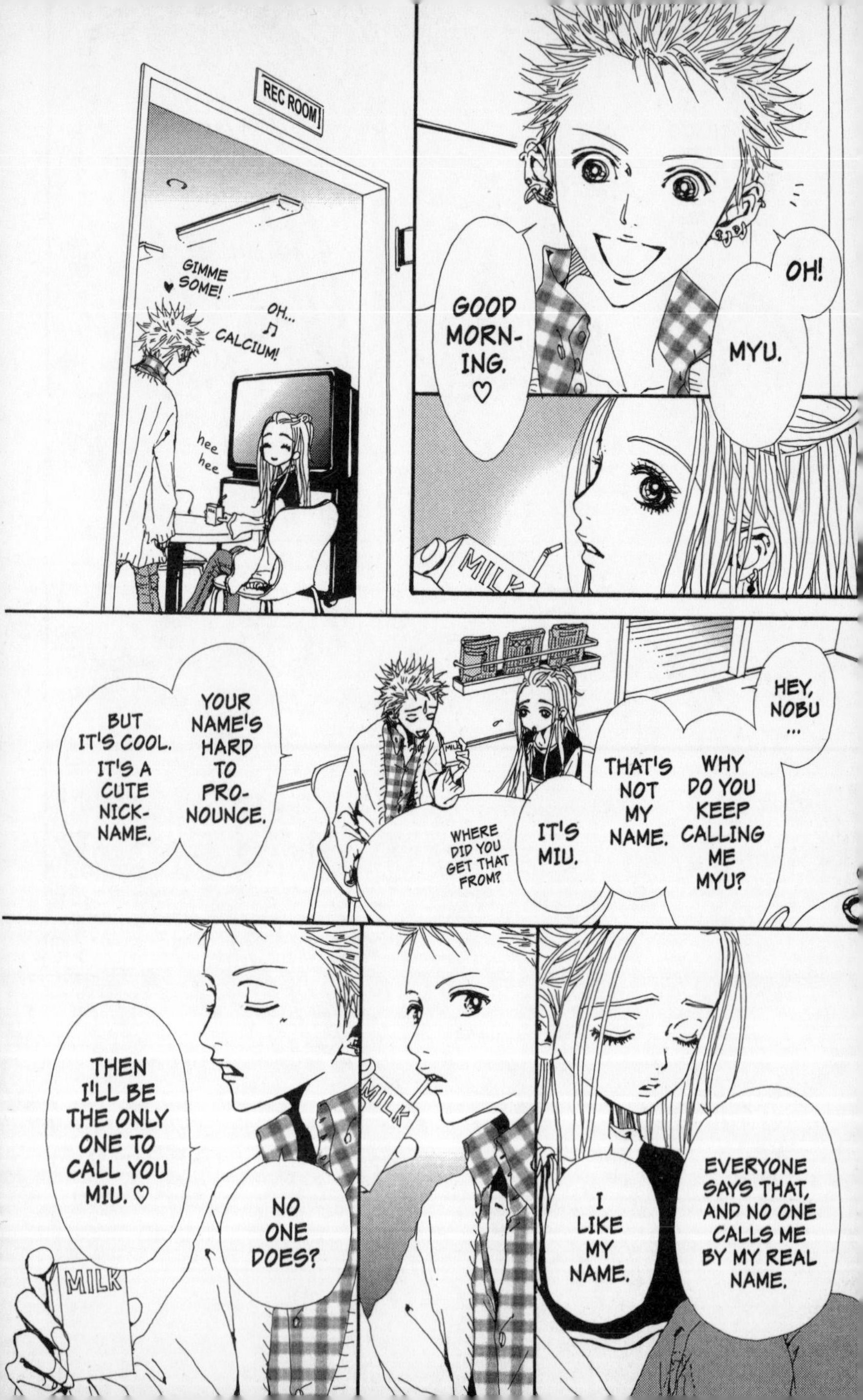
OH!
MYU.
GOOD MORNING. ♡
MILK
REC ROOM
OH... ♫ CALCIUM!
GIMME SOME! ♥
hee hee
HEY, NOBU...
WHY DO YOU KEEP CALLING ME MYU?
THAT'S NOT MY NAME.
IT'S MIU.
WHERE DID YOU GET THAT FROM?
YOUR NAME'S HARD TO PRONOUNCE.
BUT IT'S COOL. IT'S A CUTE NICKNAME.
EVERYONE SAYS THAT, AND NO ONE CALLS ME BY MY REAL NAME.
I LIKE MY NAME.
MILK
NO ONE DOES?
THEN I'LL BE THE ONLY ONE TO CALL YOU MIU. ♡
MILK

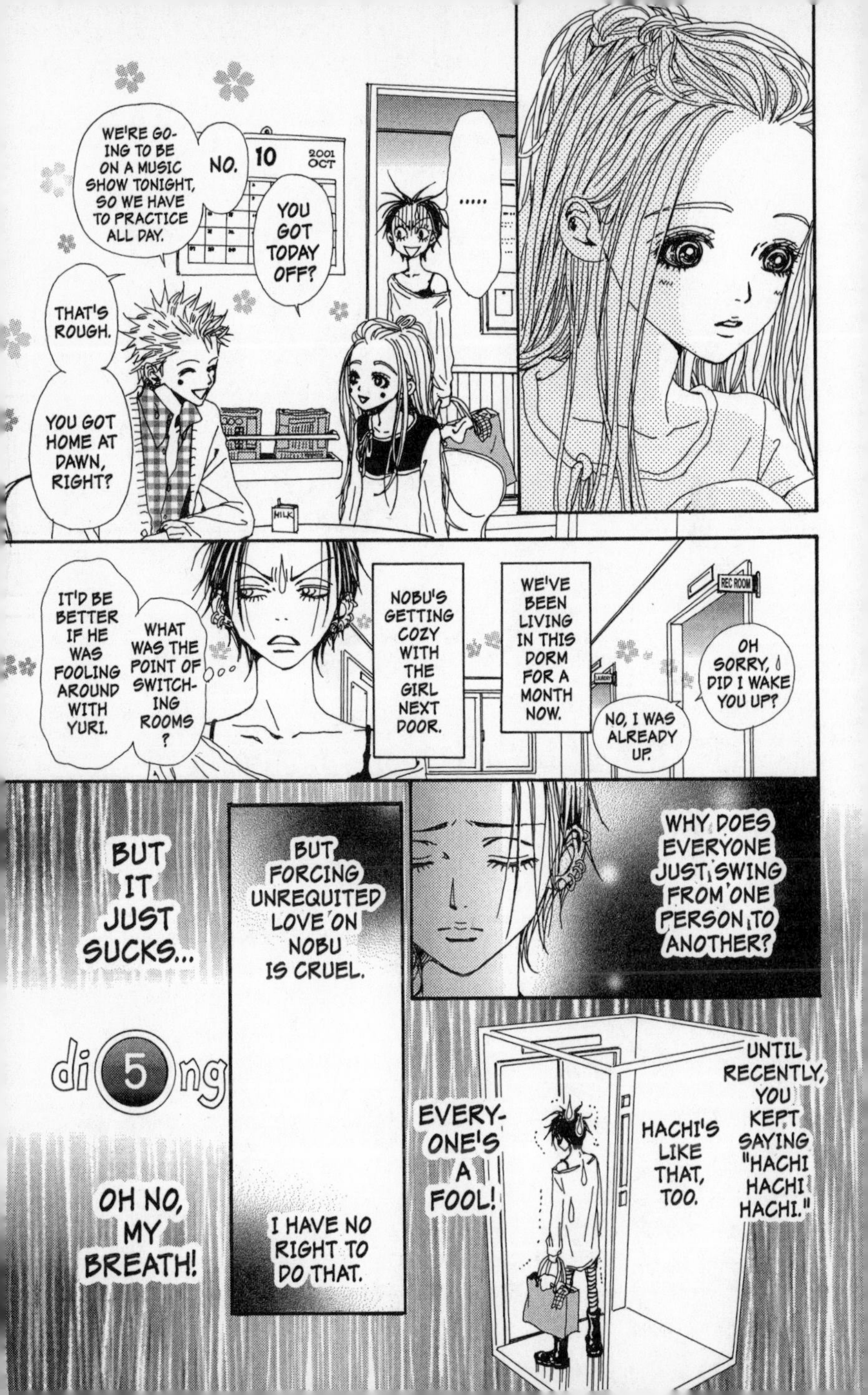
.....
YOU GOT TODAY OFF?
NO.
10
2001 OCT
WE'RE GOING TO BE ON A MUSIC SHOW TONIGHT, SO WE HAVE TO PRACTICE ALL DAY.
THAT'S ROUGH.
YOU GOT HOME AT DAWN, RIGHT?
MILK
REC ROOM
OH SORRY, DID I WAKE YOU UP?
NO, I WAS ALREADY UP.
WE'VE BEEN LIVING IN THIS DORM FOR A MONTH NOW.
NOBU'S GETTING COZY WITH THE GIRL NEXT DOOR.
WHAT WAS THE POINT OF SWITCHING ROOMS?
IT'D BE BETTER IF HE WAS FOOLING AROUND WITH YURI.
WHY DOES EVERYONE JUST SWING FROM ONE PERSON TO ANOTHER?
UNTIL RECENTLY, YOU KEPT SAYING "HACHI HACHI HACHI."
HACHI'S LIKE THAT, TOO.
EVERYONE'S A FOOL!
BUT FORCING UNREQUITED LOVE ON NOBU IS CRUEL.
I HAVE NO RIGHT TO DO THAT.
BUT IT JUST SUCKS...
di5ng
OH NO, MY BREATH!

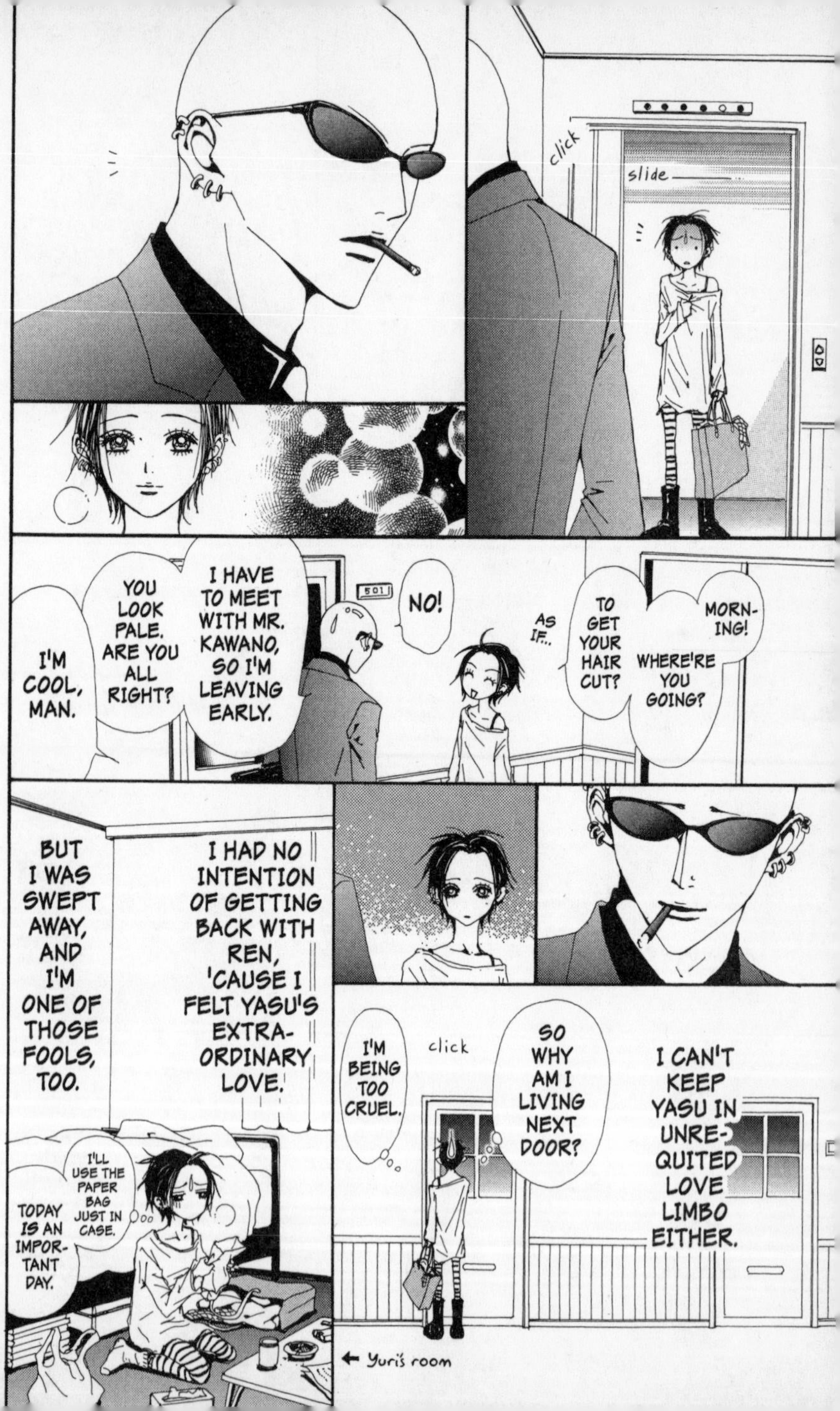
click
slide
501
MORNING! WHERE'RE YOU GOING?
TO GET YOUR HAIR CUT?
AS IF...
NO!
I HAVE TO MEET WITH MR. KAWANO, SO I'M LEAVING EARLY.
YOU LOOK PALE. ARE YOU ALL RIGHT?
I'M COOL, MAN.
I CAN'T KEEP YASU IN UNREQUITED LOVE LIMBO EITHER.
SO WHY AM I LIVING NEXT DOOR?
click
I'M BEING TOO CRUEL.
← Yuri's room
I HAD NO INTENTION OF GETTING BACK WITH REN, 'CAUSE I FELT YASU'S EXTRAORDINARY LOVE.
BUT I WAS SWEPT AWAY, AND I'M ONE OF THOSE FOOLS, TOO.
I'LL USE THE PAPER BAG JUST IN CASE.
TODAY IS AN IMPORTANT DAY.

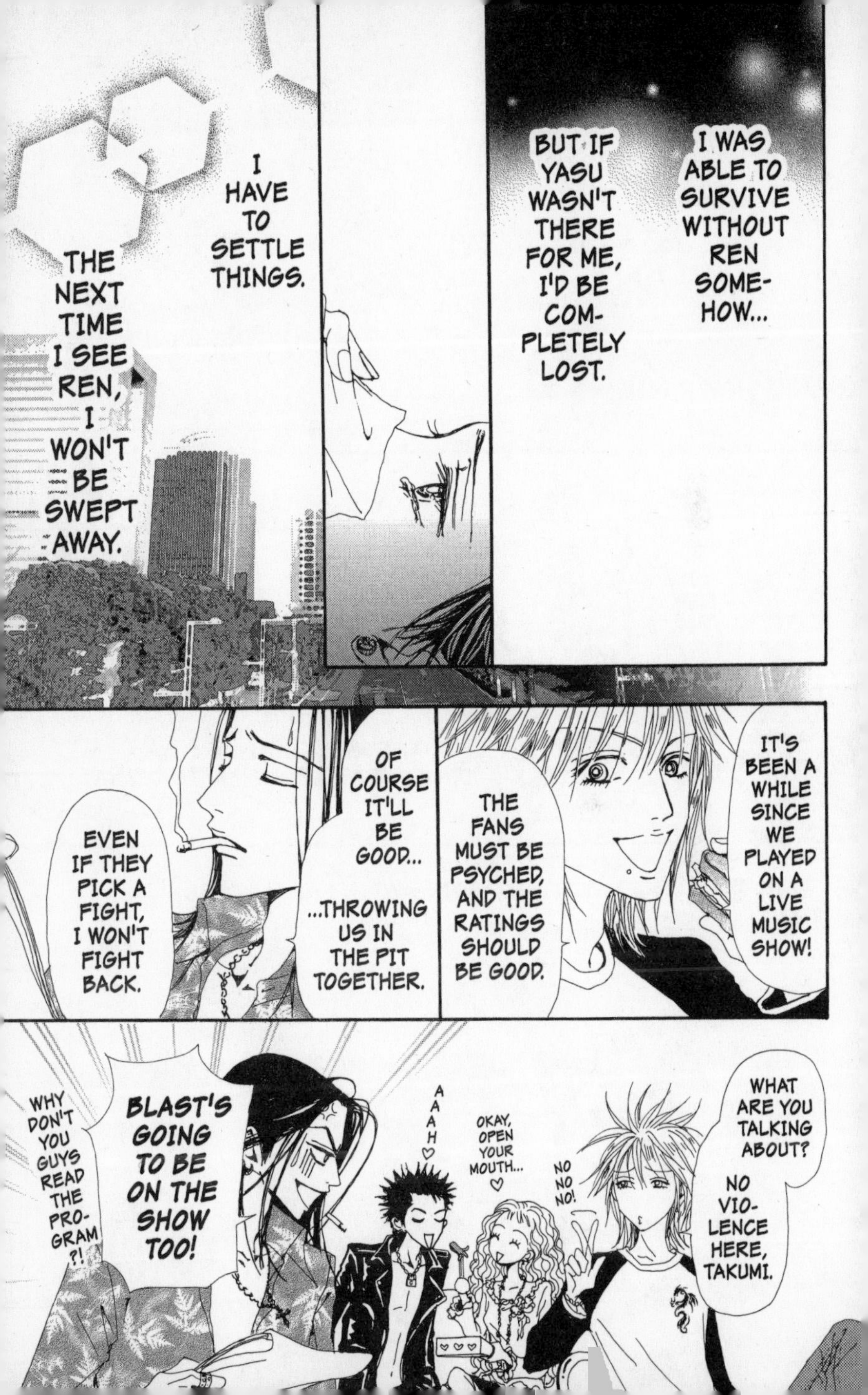
I WAS ABLE TO SURVIVE WITHOUT REN SOMEHOW...
BUT IF YASU WASN'T THERE FOR ME, I'D BE COMPLETELY LOST.
I HAVE TO SETTLE THINGS.
THE NEXT TIME I SEE REN, I WON'T BE SWEPT AWAY.
IT'S BEEN A WHILE SINCE WE PLAYED ON A LIVE MUSIC SHOW!
THE FANS MUST BE PSYCHED, AND THE RATINGS SHOULD BE GOOD.
OF COURSE IT'LL BE GOOD...
...THROWING US IN THE PIT TOGETHER.
EVEN IF THEY PICK A FIGHT, I WON'T FIGHT BACK.
WHAT ARE YOU TALKING ABOUT?
NO VIOLENCE HERE, TAKUMI.
NO NO NO!
OKAY, OPEN YOUR MOUTH... ♡
AAAH ♡
BLAST'S GOING TO BE ON THE SHOW TOO!
WHY DON'T YOU GUYS READ THE PROGRAM?!

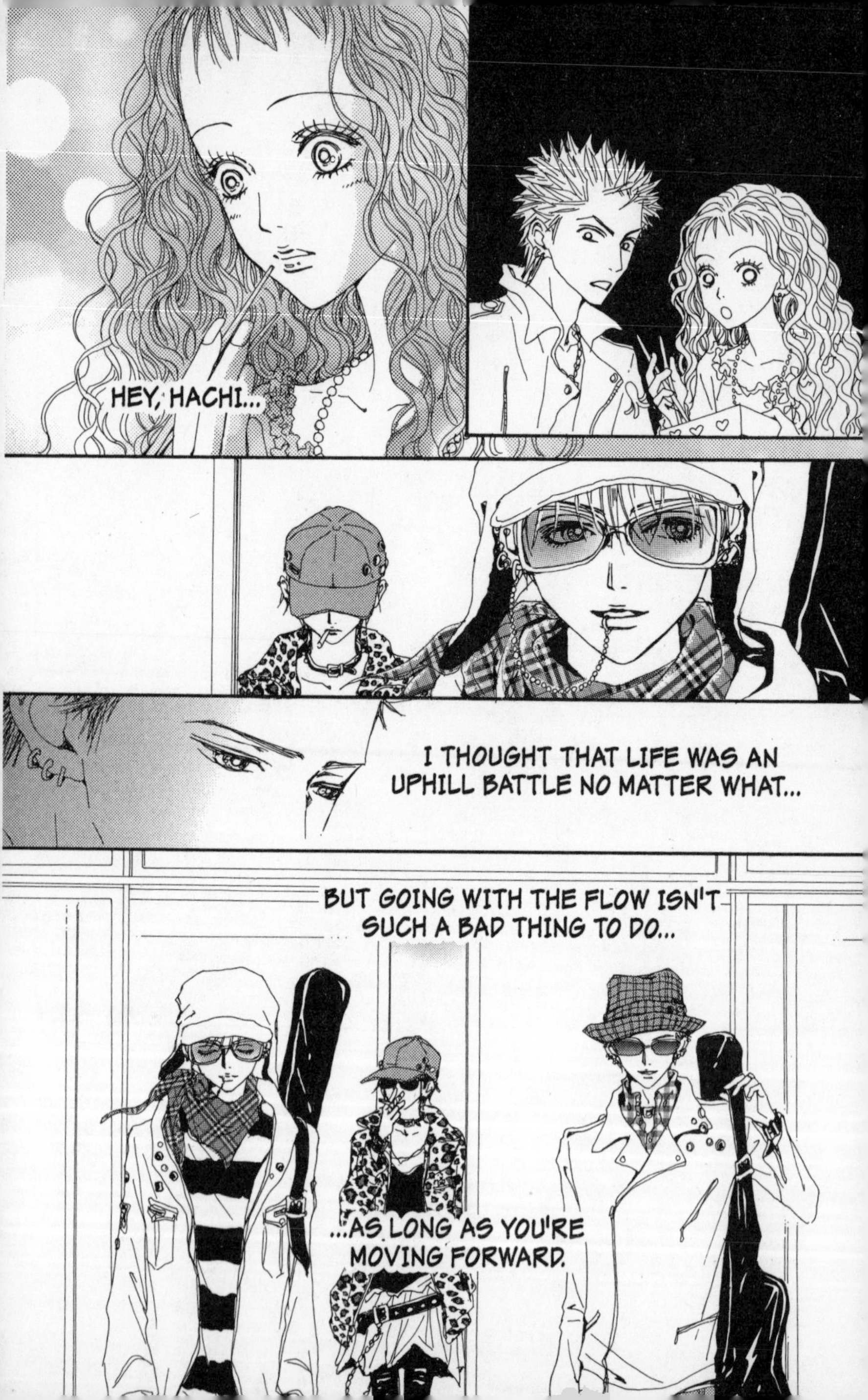
HEY, HACHI...
I THOUGHT THAT LIFE WAS AN UPHILL BATTLE NO MATTER WHAT...
BUT GOING WITH THE FLOW ISN'T SUCH A BAD THING TO DO...
...AS LONG AS YOU'RE MOVING FORWARD.

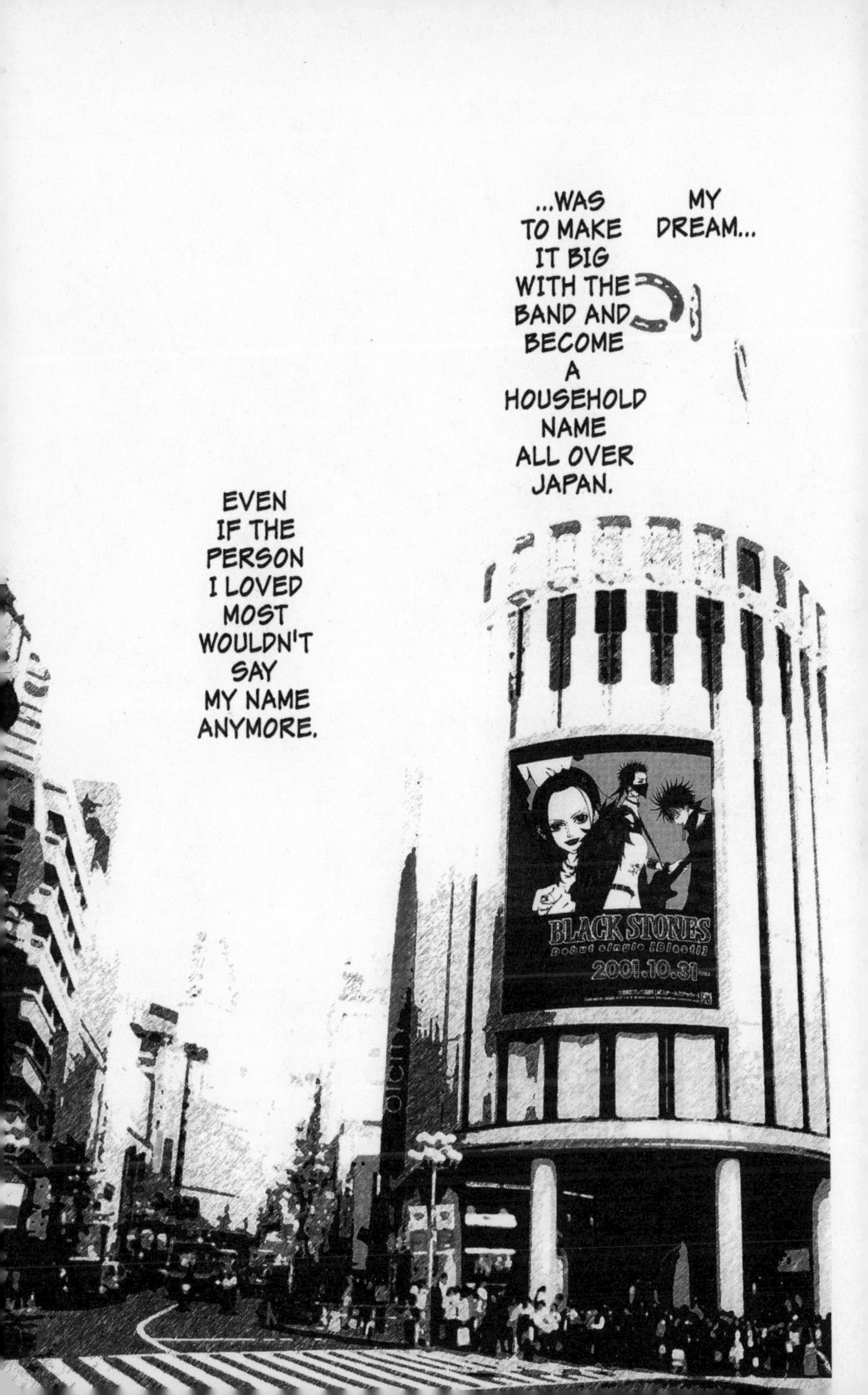
MY DREAM...
...WAS TO MAKE IT BIG WITH THE BAND AND BECOME A HOUSEHOLD NAME ALL OVER JAPAN.
EVEN IF THE PERSON I LOVED MOST WOULDN'T SAY MY NAME ANYMORE.
BLACK STONES
2001.10.31

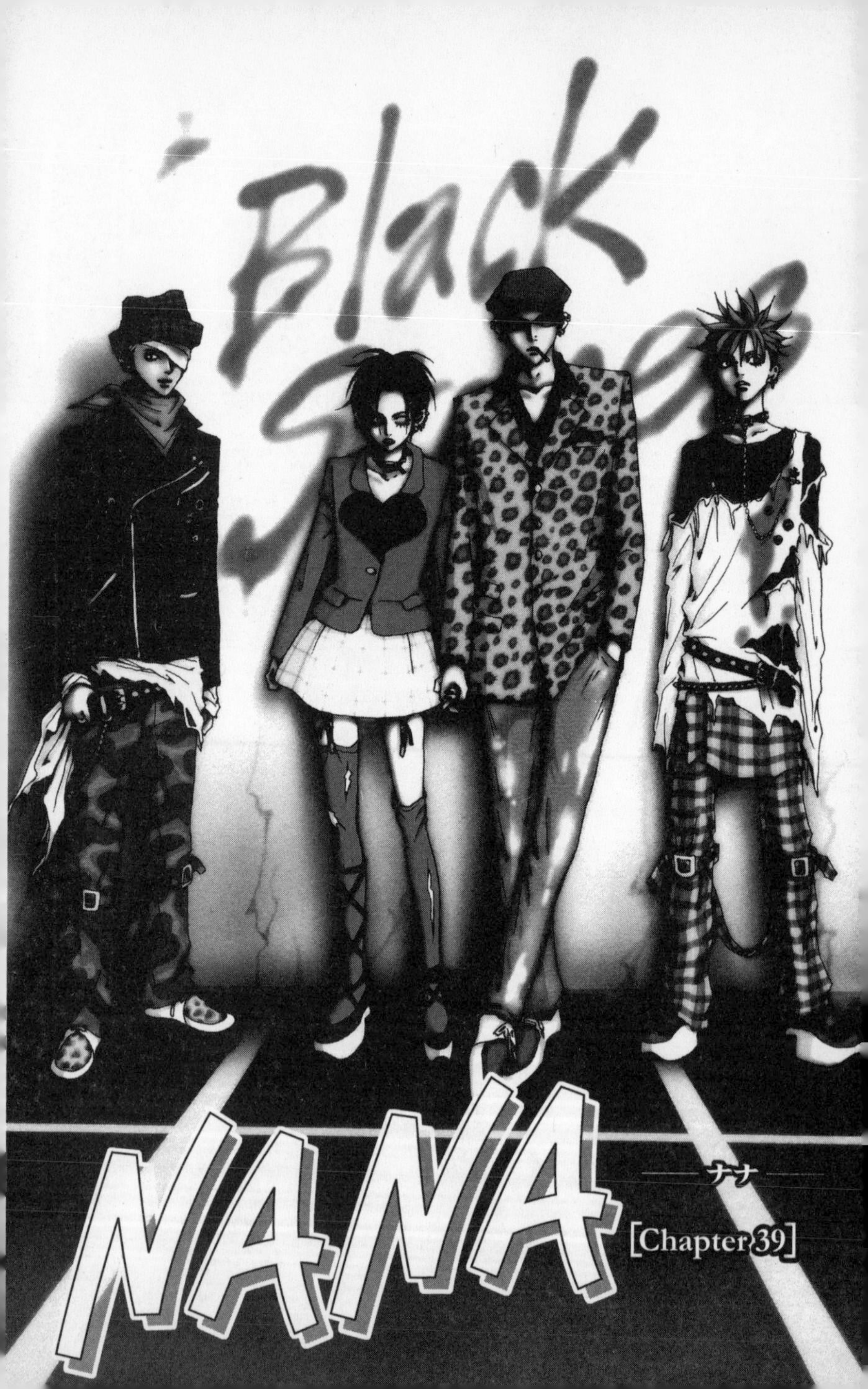
Black
NANA
ナナ
[Chapter 39]

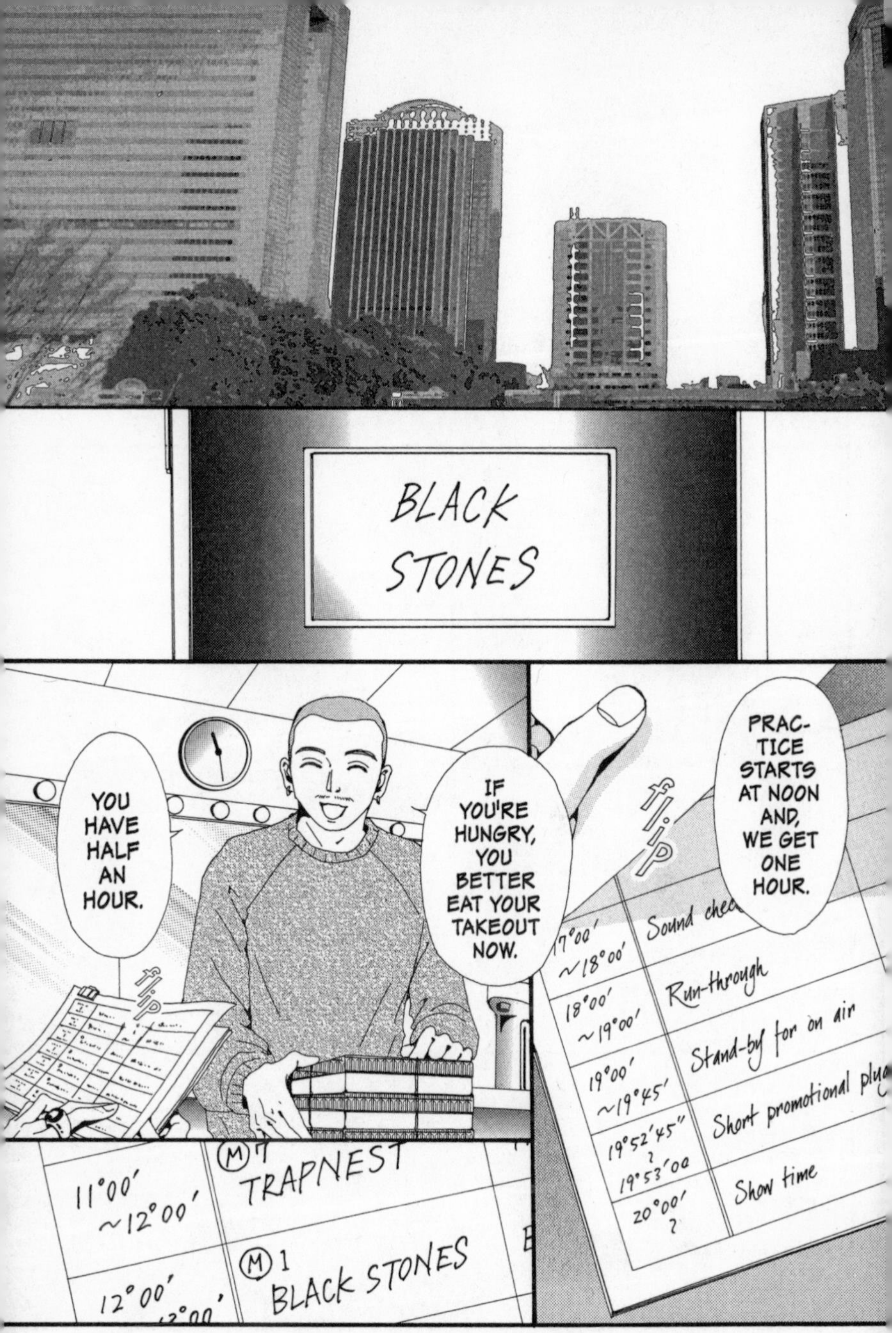
BLACK STONES
flip
PRAC-TICE STARTS AT NOON AND, WE GET ONE HOUR.
17°00' ~18°00' Sound chec
Run-through
18°00' ~19°00' Stand-by for on air
19°00' ~19°45' Short promotional plug
19°52'45" ~ 19°53'00 Show time
20°00' ~
IF YOU'RE HUNGRY, YOU BETTER EAT YOUR TAKEOUT NOW.
YOU HAVE HALF AN HOUR.
flip
11°00' ~12°00' M 7 TRAPNEST
12°00' M 1 BLACK STONES

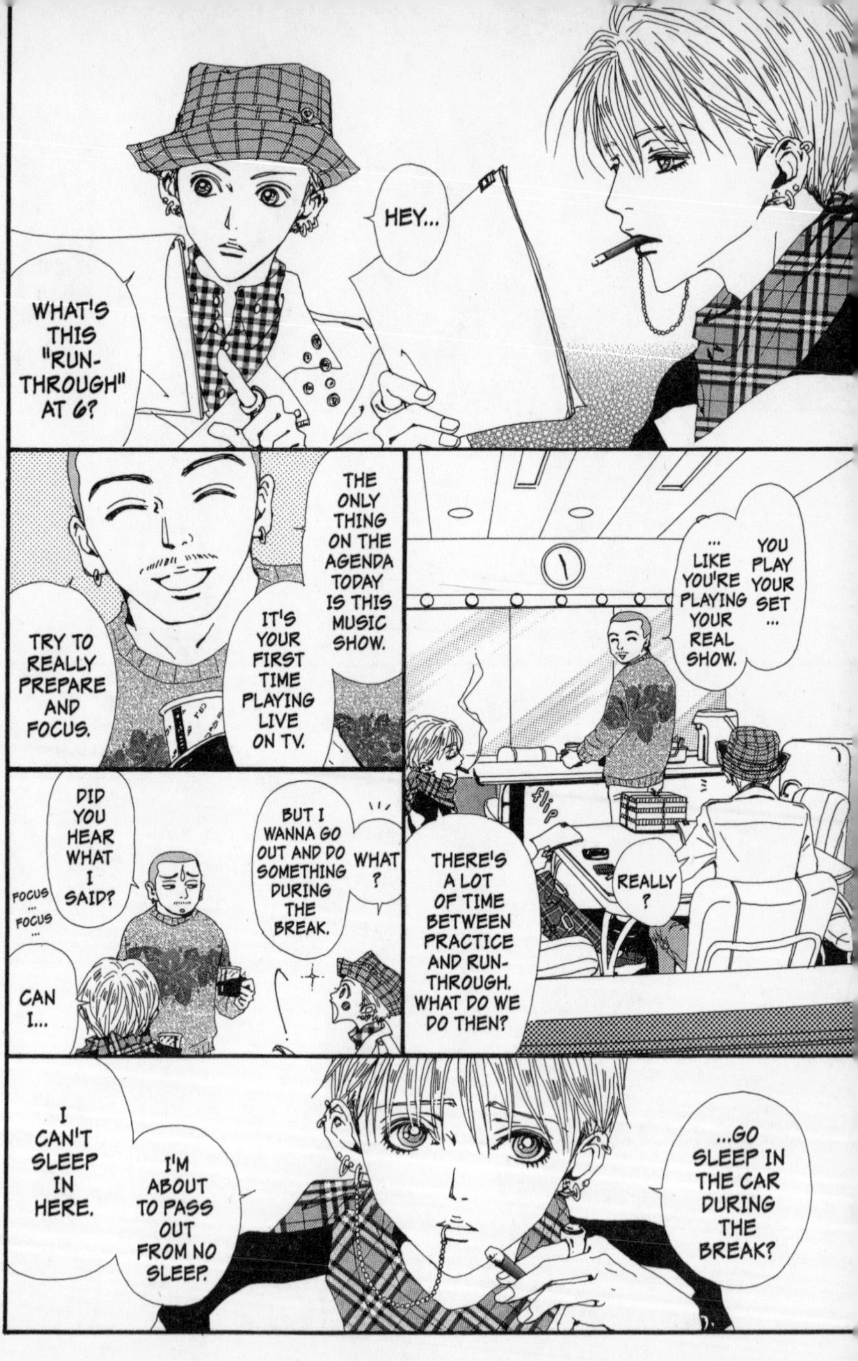
HEY...
WHAT'S THIS "RUN-THROUGH" AT 6?
YOU PLAY YOUR SET ...
... LIKE YOU'RE PLAYING YOUR REAL SHOW.
flip
REALLY?
THERE'S A LOT OF TIME BETWEEN PRACTICE AND RUN-THROUGH. WHAT DO WE DO THEN?
THE ONLY THING ON THE AGENDA TODAY IS THIS MUSIC SHOW.
IT'S YOUR FIRST TIME PLAYING LIVE ON TV.
TRY TO REALLY PREPARE AND FOCUS.
BUT I WANNA GO OUT AND DO SOMETHING DURING THE BREAK.
WHAT?
DID YOU HEAR WHAT I SAID?
FOCUS ... FOCUS ...
CAN I...
...GO SLEEP IN THE CAR DURING THE BREAK?
I'M ABOUT TO PASS OUT FROM NO SLEEP.
I CAN'T SLEEP IN HERE.

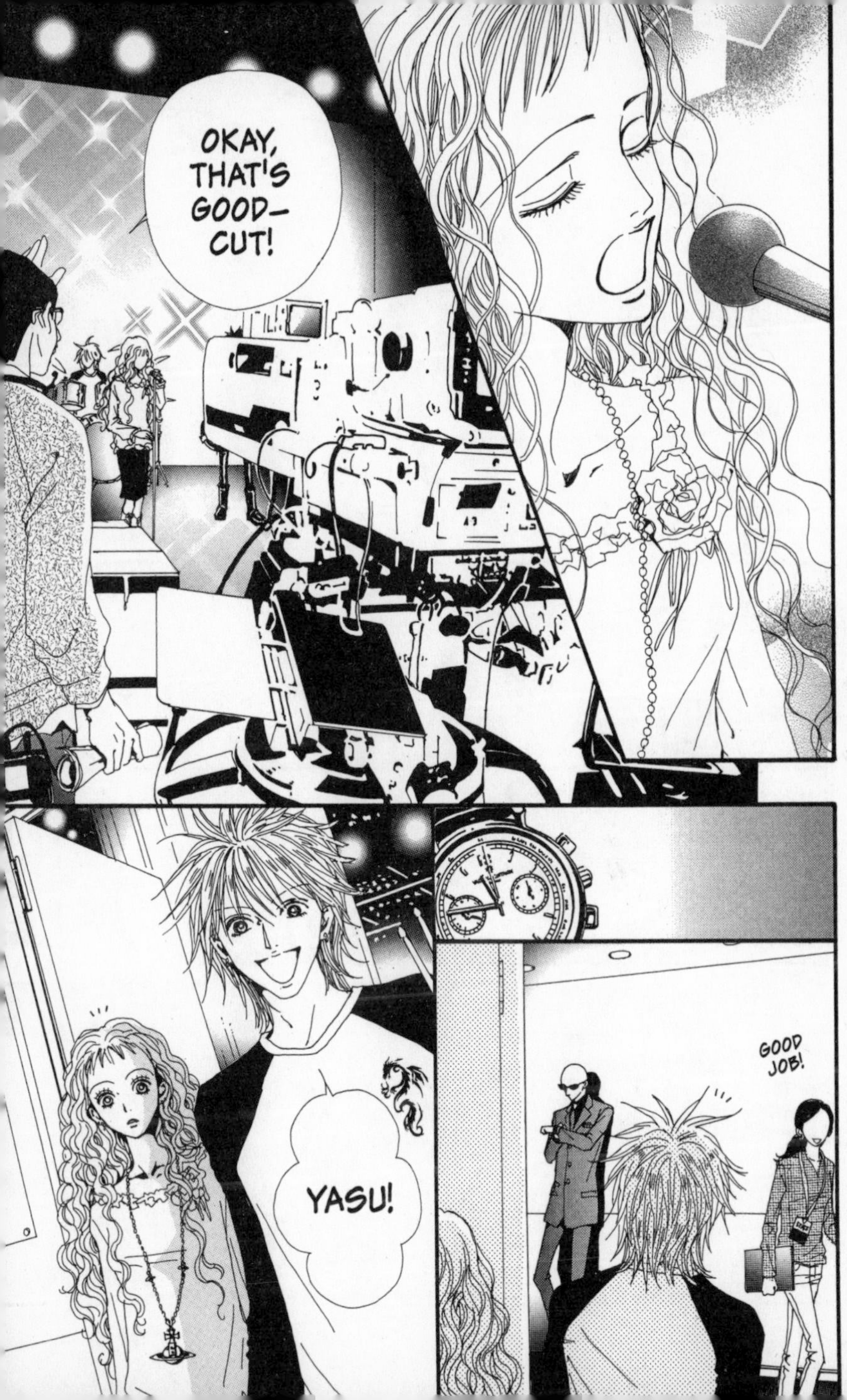
OKAY, THAT'S GOOD—CUT!
GOOD JOB!
YASU!

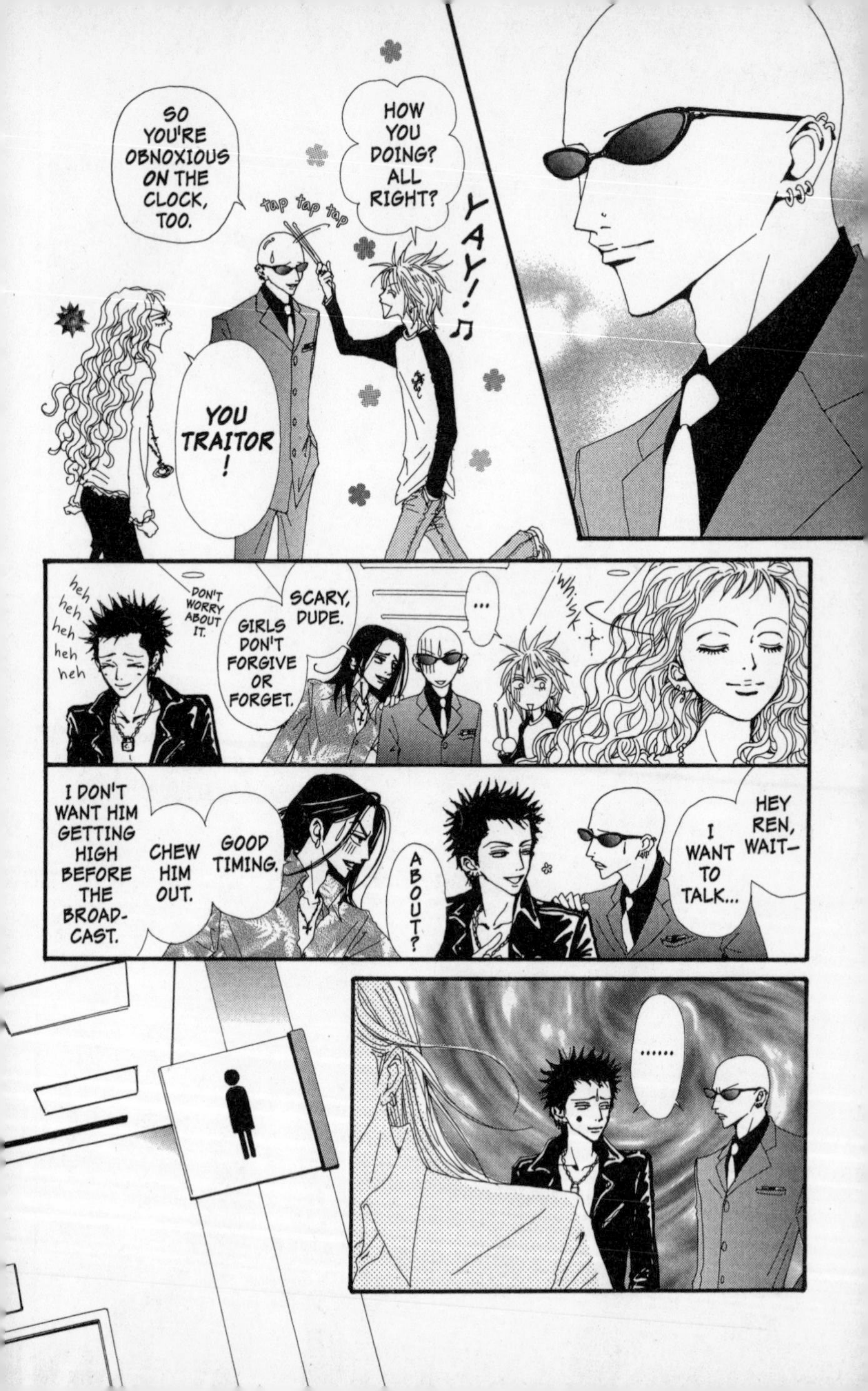
YAY!♪
HOW YOU DOING? ALL RIGHT?
tap tap tap
SO YOU'RE OBNOXIOUS ON THE CLOCK, TOO.
YOU TRAITOR!
whisk
...
SCARY, DUDE.
GIRLS DON'T FORGIVE OR FORGET.
DON'T WORRY ABOUT IT.
heh heh heh heh heh
HEY REN, WAIT—
I WANT TO TALK...
ABOUT?
GOOD TIMING.
CHEW HIM OUT.
I DON'T WANT HIM GETTING HIGH BEFORE THE BROADCAST.
......

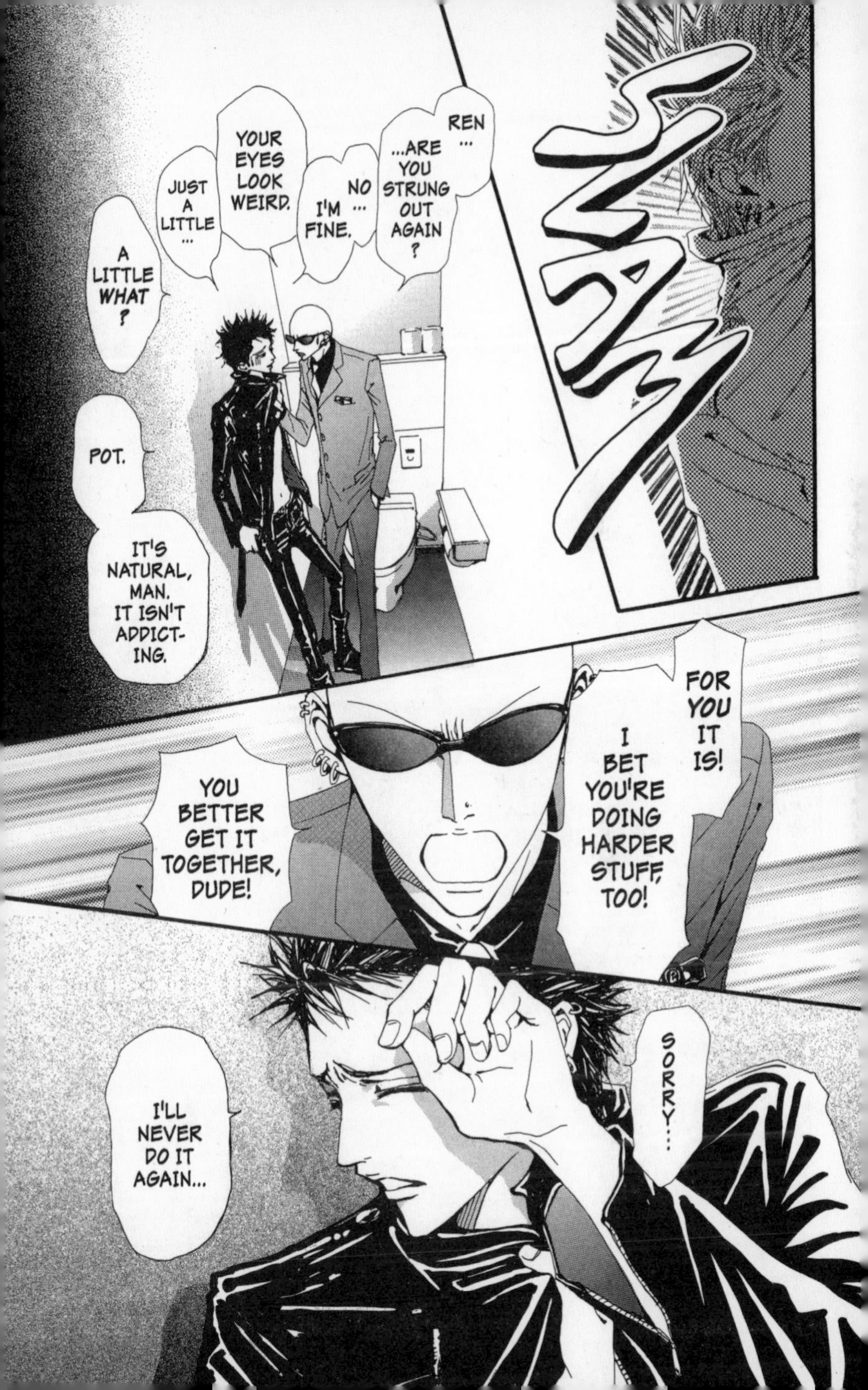
SLAM
REN ... ...ARE YOU STRUNG OUT AGAIN?
NO ... I'M FINE.
YOUR EYES LOOK WEIRD.
JUST A LITTLE ...
A LITTLE WHAT?
POT.
IT'S NATURAL, MAN. IT ISN'T ADDICT-ING.
FOR YOU IT IS!
I BET YOU'RE DOING HARDER STUFF, TOO!
YOU BETTER GET IT TOGETHER, DUDE!
SORRY...
I'LL NEVER DO IT AGAIN...

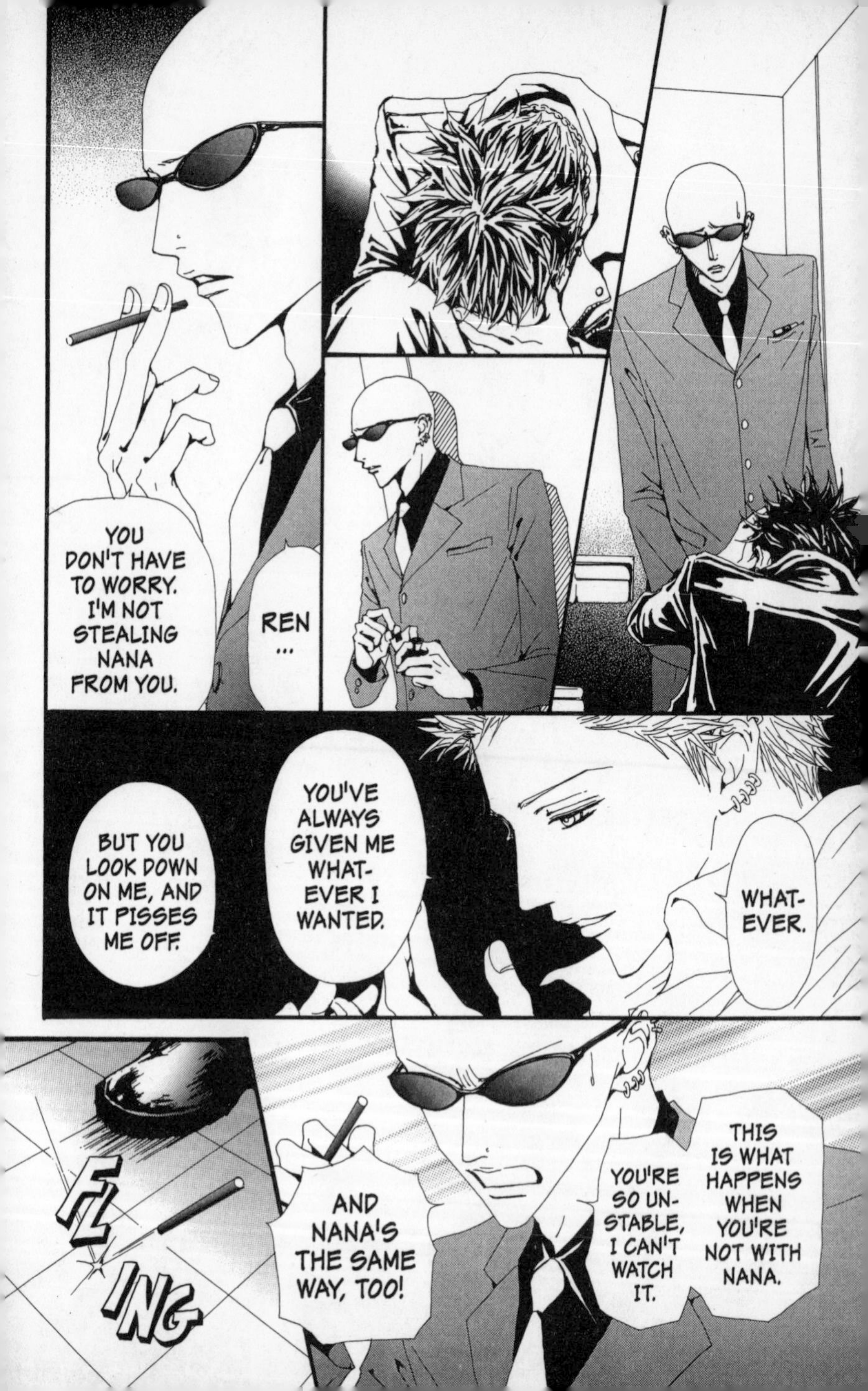
REN ...
YOU DON'T HAVE TO WORRY. I'M NOT STEALING NANA FROM YOU.
WHAT-EVER.
YOU'VE ALWAYS GIVEN ME WHAT-EVER I WANTED.
BUT YOU LOOK DOWN ON ME, AND IT PISSES ME OFF.
THIS IS WHAT HAPPENS WHEN YOU'RE NOT WITH NANA.
YOU'RE SO UN-STABLE, I CAN'T WATCH IT.
AND NANA'S THE SAME WAY, TOO!
FLING

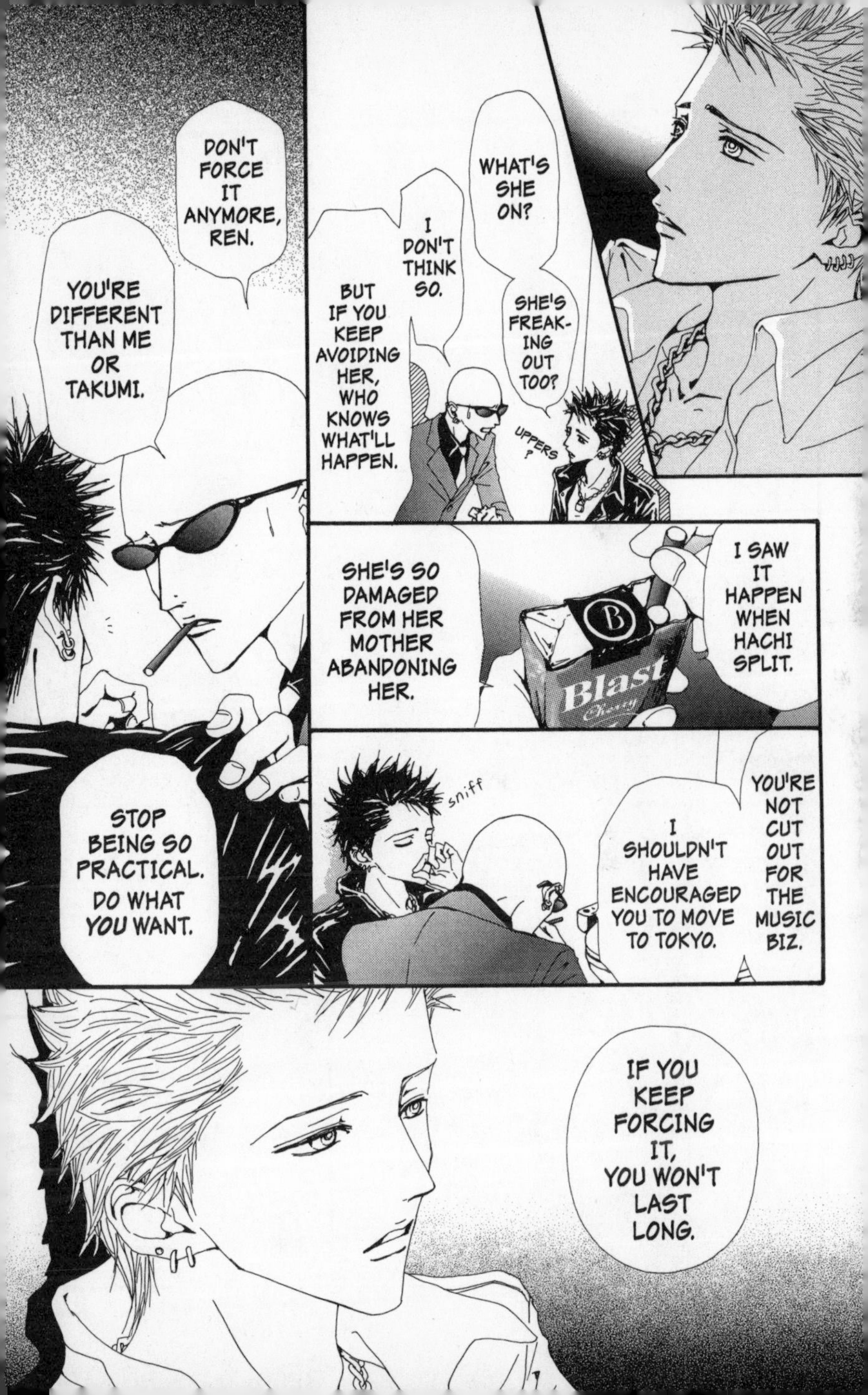
WHAT'S SHE ON?
SHE'S FREAK-ING OUT TOO?
UPPERS?
I DON'T THINK SO.
BUT IF YOU KEEP AVOIDING HER, WHO KNOWS WHAT'LL HAPPEN.
I SAW IT HAPPEN WHEN HACHI SPLIT.
Blast
SHE'S SO DAMAGED FROM HER MOTHER ABANDONING HER.
YOU'RE NOT CUT OUT FOR THE MUSIC BIZ.
I SHOULDN'T HAVE ENCOURAGED YOU TO MOVE TO TOKYO.
sniff
DON'T FORCE IT ANYMORE, REN.
YOU'RE DIFFERENT THAN ME OR TAKUMI.
STOP BEING SO PRACTICAL. DO WHAT *YOU* WANT.
IF YOU KEEP FORCING IT, YOU WON'T LAST LONG.

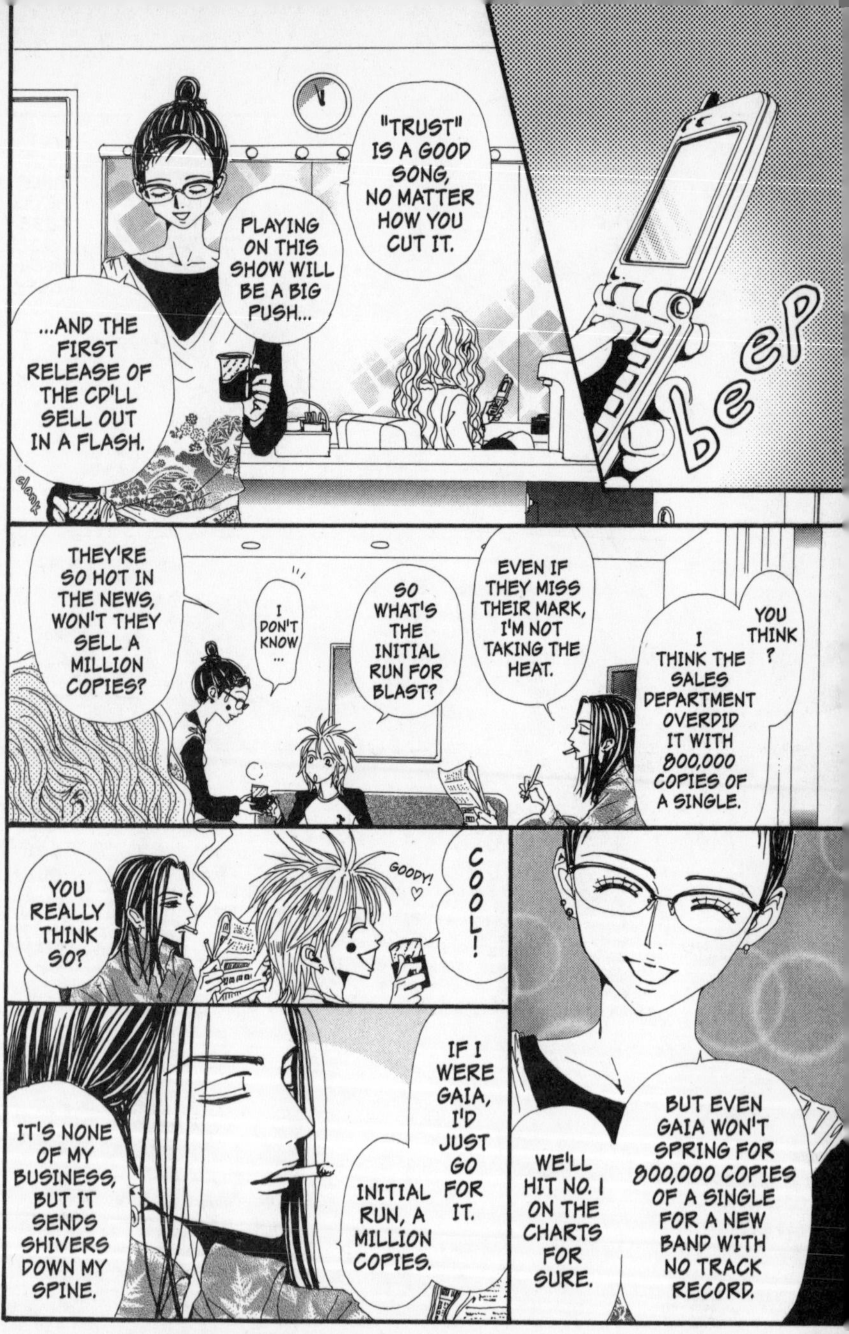
beep
"TRUST" IS A GOOD SONG, NO MATTER HOW YOU CUT IT.
PLAYING ON THIS SHOW WILL BE A BIG PUSH...
...AND THE FIRST RELEASE OF THE CD'LL SELL OUT IN A FLASH.
clank
YOU THINK?
I THINK THE SALES DEPARTMENT OVERDID IT WITH 800,000 COPIES OF A SINGLE.
EVEN IF THEY MISS THEIR MARK, I'M NOT TAKING THE HEAT.
SO WHAT'S THE INITIAL RUN FOR BLAST?
I DON'T KNOW...
THEY'RE SO HOT IN THE NEWS, WON'T THEY SELL A MILLION COPIES?
BUT EVEN GAIA WON'T SPRING FOR 800,000 COPIES OF A SINGLE FOR A NEW BAND WITH NO TRACK RECORD.
WE'LL HIT NO. 1 ON THE CHARTS FOR SURE.
COOL!
GOODY!
YOU REALLY THINK SO?
IF I WERE GAIA, I'D JUST GO FOR IT.
INITIAL RUN, A MILLION COPIES.
IT'S NONE OF MY BUSINESS, BUT IT SENDS SHIVERS DOWN MY SPINE.

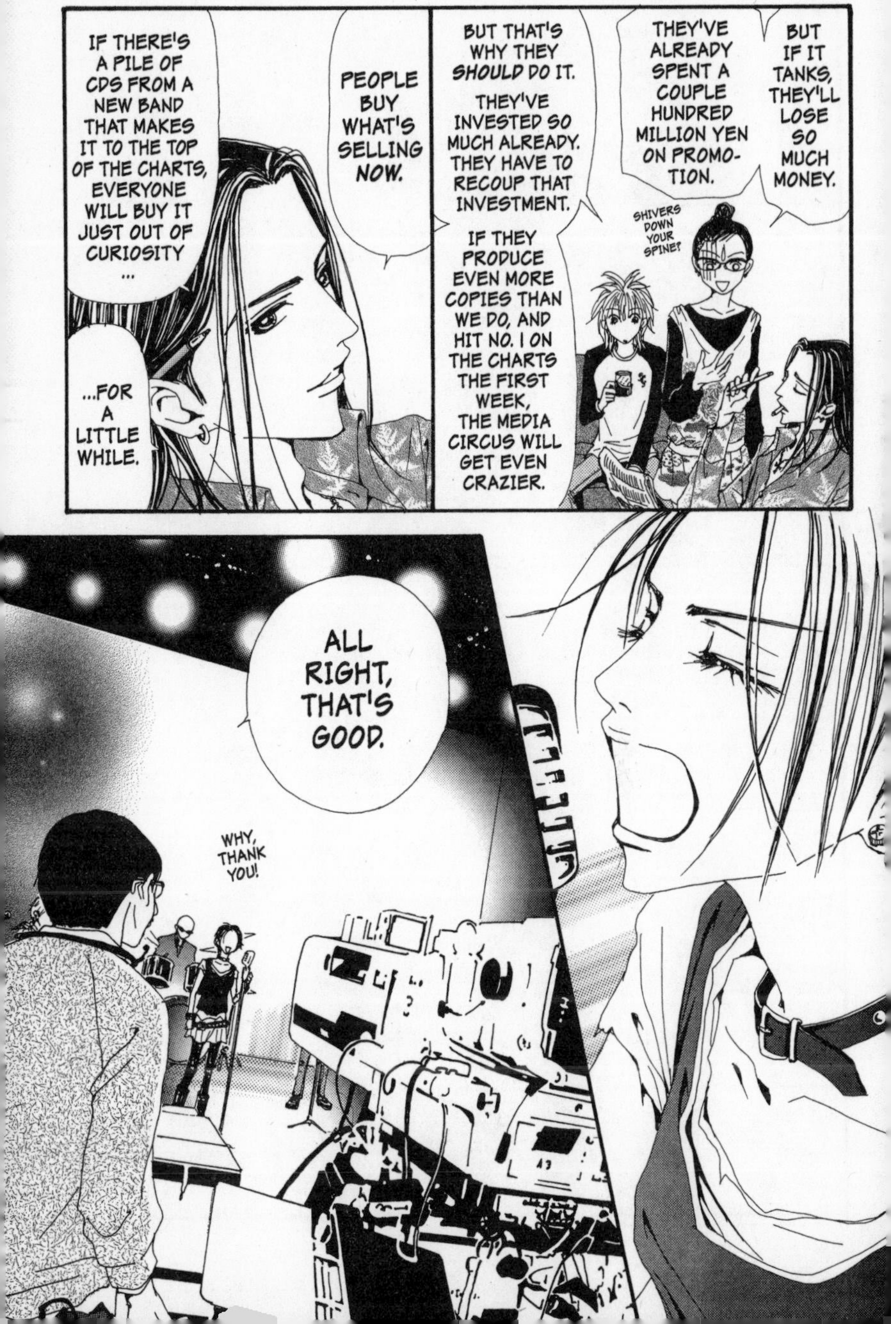
BUT IF IT TANKS, THEY'LL LOSE SO MUCH MONEY.
THEY'VE ALREADY SPENT A COUPLE HUNDRED MILLION YEN ON PROMOTION.
SHIVERS DOWN YOUR SPINE?
BUT THAT'S WHY THEY *SHOULD* DO IT.
THEY'VE INVESTED SO MUCH ALREADY. THEY HAVE TO RECOUP THAT INVESTMENT.
IF THEY PRODUCE EVEN MORE COPIES THAN WE DO, AND HIT NO. 1 ON THE CHARTS THE FIRST WEEK, THE MEDIA CIRCUS WILL GET EVEN CRAZIER.
PEOPLE BUY WHAT'S SELLING *NOW.*
IF THERE'S A PILE OF CDS FROM A NEW BAND THAT MAKES IT TO THE TOP OF THE CHARTS, EVERYONE WILL BUY IT JUST OUT OF CURIOSITY ...
...FOR A LITTLE WHILE.
ALL RIGHT, THAT'S GOOD.
WHY, THANK YOU!

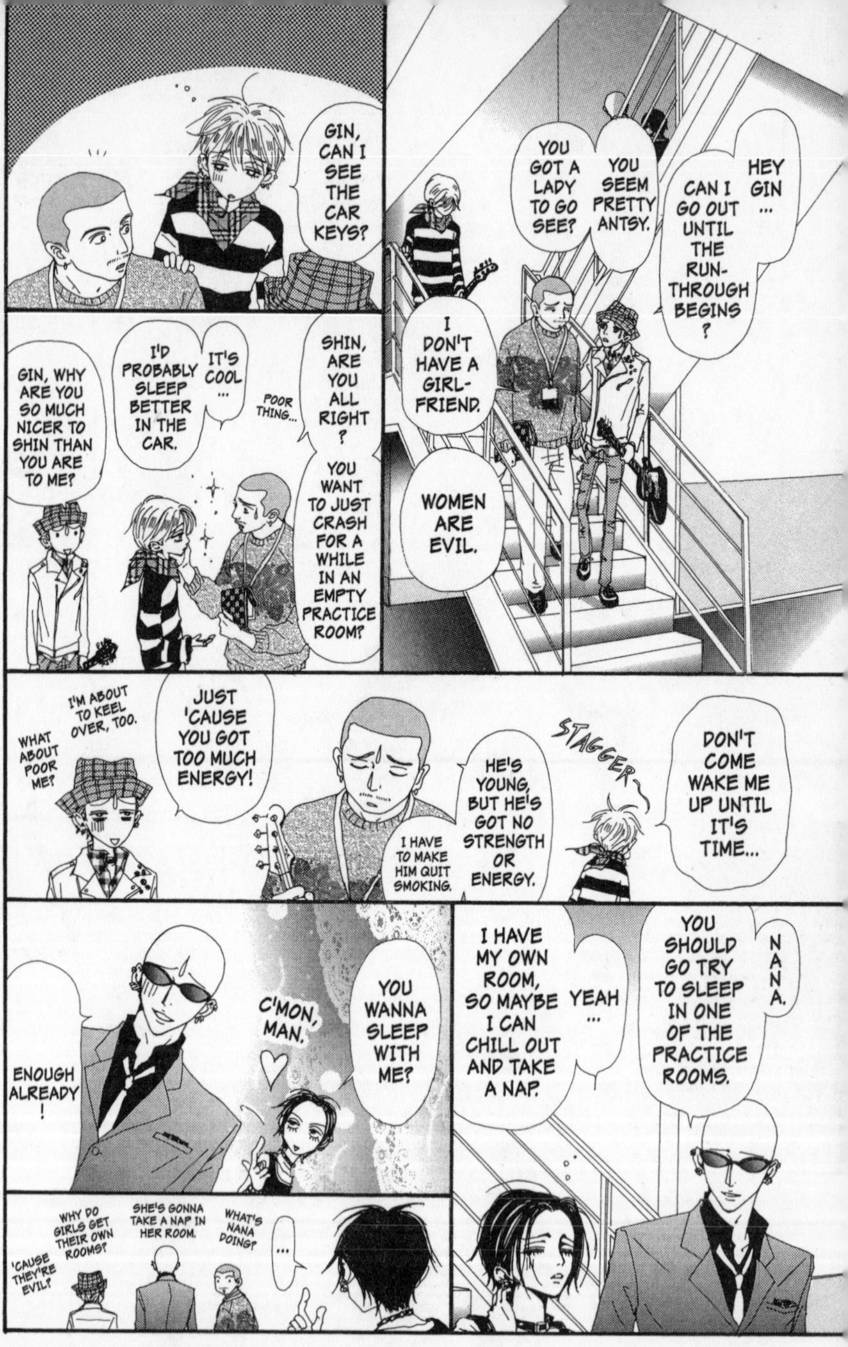
HEY GIN ...
CAN I GO OUT UNTIL THE RUN-THROUGH BEGINS?
YOU SEEM PRETTY ANTSY.
YOU GOT A LADY TO GO SEE?
I DON'T HAVE A GIRLFRIEND.
WOMEN ARE EVIL.
GIN, CAN I SEE THE CAR KEYS?
SHIN, ARE YOU ALL RIGHT?
YOU WANT TO JUST CRASH FOR A WHILE IN AN EMPTY PRACTICE ROOM?
POOR THING...
IT'S COOL ...
I'D PROBABLY SLEEP BETTER IN THE CAR.
GIN, WHY ARE YOU SO MUCH NICER TO SHIN THAN YOU ARE TO ME?
DON'T COME WAKE ME UP UNTIL IT'S TIME...
STAGGER
HE'S YOUNG, BUT HE'S GOT NO STRENGTH OR ENERGY.
I HAVE TO MAKE HIM QUIT SMOKING.
JUST 'CAUSE YOU GOT TOO MUCH ENERGY!
I'M ABOUT TO KEEL OVER, TOO.
WHAT ABOUT POOR ME?
NANA.
YOU SHOULD GO TRY TO SLEEP IN ONE OF THE PRACTICE ROOMS.
YEAH ...
I HAVE MY OWN ROOM, SO MAYBE I CAN CHILL OUT AND TAKE A NAP.
YOU WANNA SLEEP WITH ME?
C'MON, MAN.
ENOUGH ALREADY!
...
WHAT'S NANA DOING?
SHE'S GONNA TAKE A NAP IN HER ROOM.
WHY DO GIRLS GET THEIR OWN ROOMS?
'CAUSE THEY'RE EVIL?

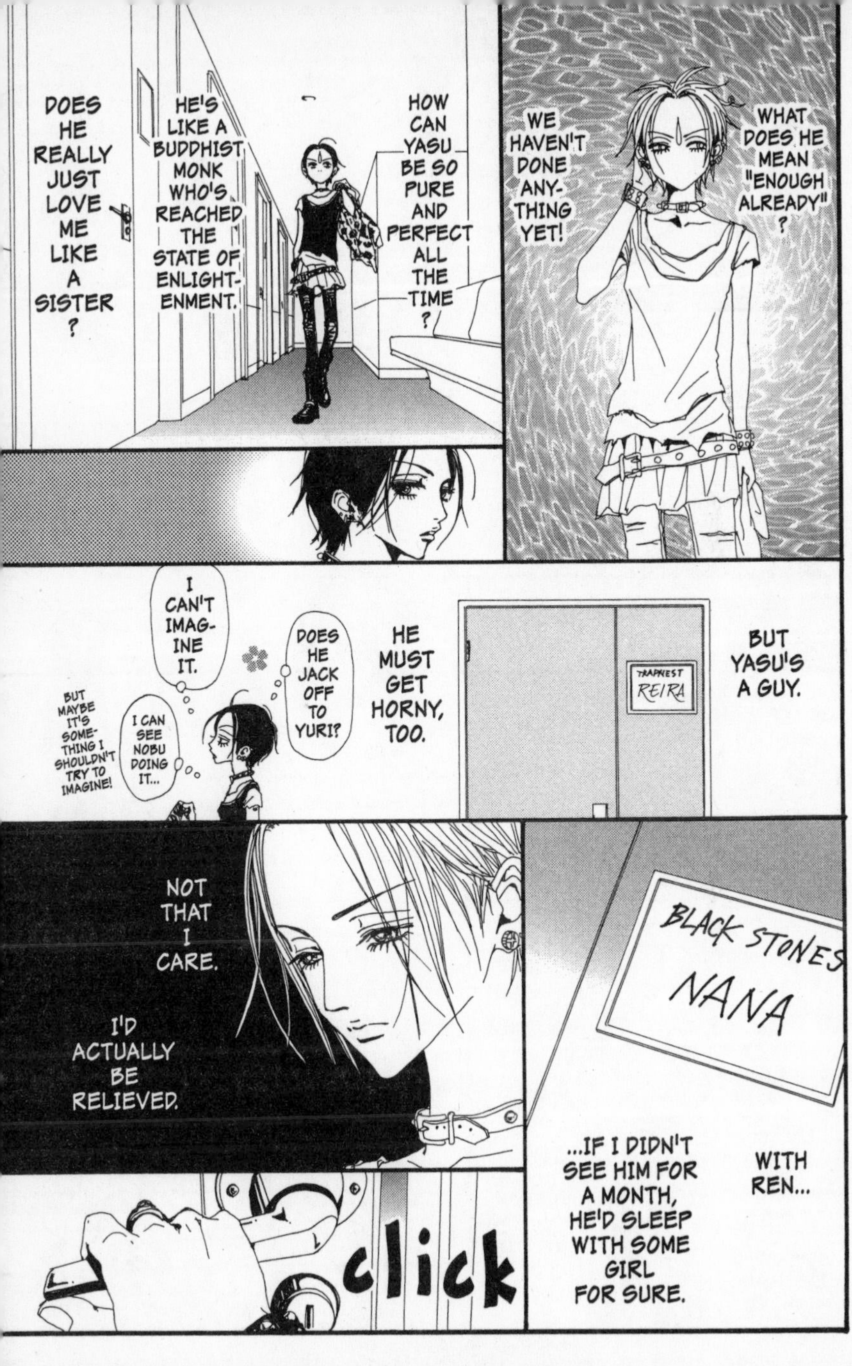
WHAT DOES HE MEAN "ENOUGH ALREADY"?
WE HAVEN'T DONE ANYTHING YET!
HOW CAN YASU BE SO PURE AND PERFECT ALL THE TIME?
HE'S LIKE A BUDDHIST MONK WHO'S REACHED THE STATE OF ENLIGHTENMENT.
DOES HE REALLY JUST LOVE ME LIKE A SISTER?
BUT YASU'S A GUY.
TRAPNEST REIRA
HE MUST GET HORNY, TOO.
DOES HE JACK OFF TO YURI?
I CAN'T IMAGINE IT.
I CAN SEE NOBU DOING IT...
BUT MAYBE IT'S SOMETHING I SHOULDN'T TRY TO IMAGINE!
BLACK STONES NANA
WITH REN...
...IF I DIDN'T SEE HIM FOR A MONTH, HE'D SLEEP WITH SOME GIRL FOR SURE.
NOT THAT I CARE.
I'D ACTUALLY BE RELIEVED.
click

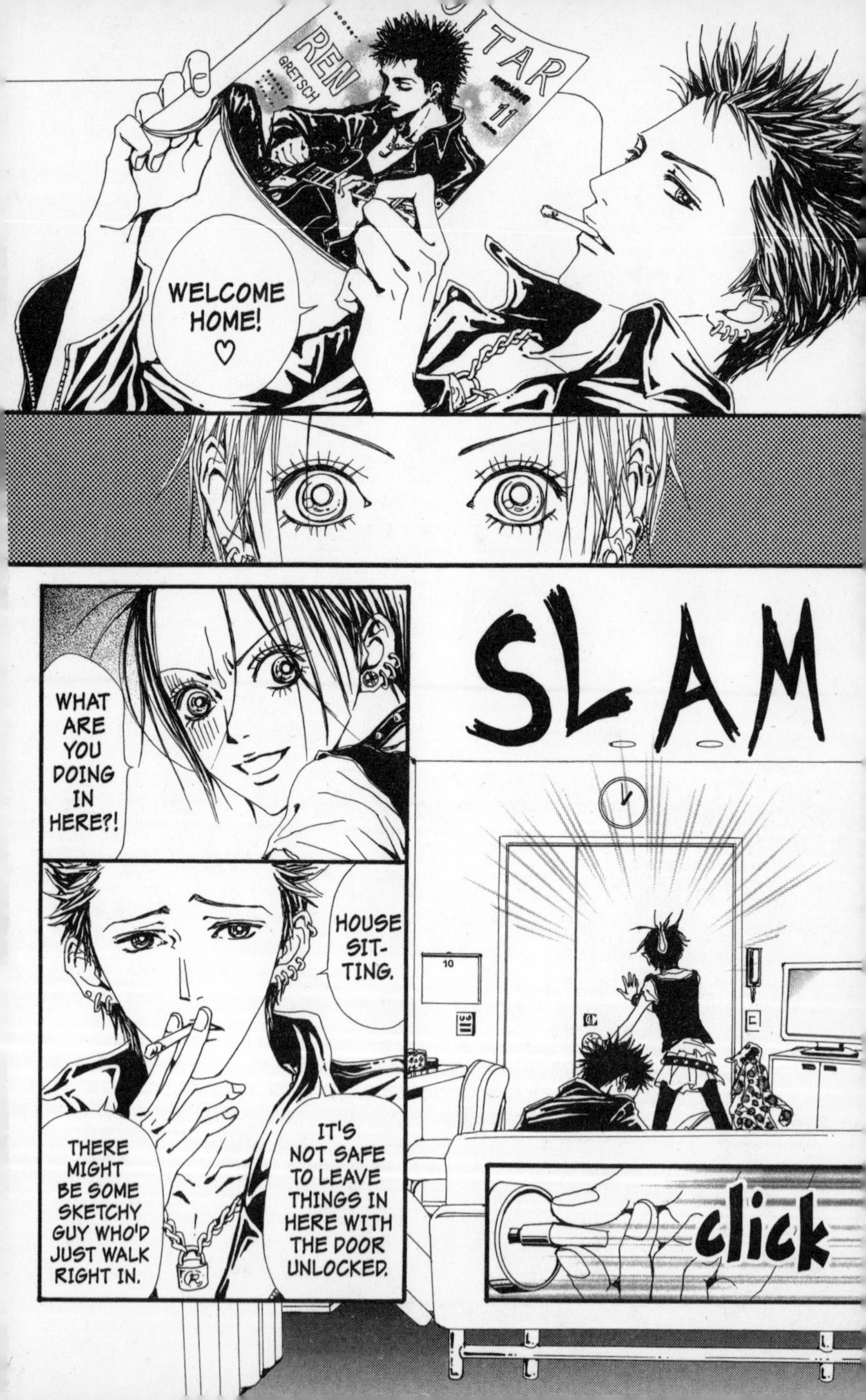
REN
GRETSCH
11
WELCOME HOME! ♡
SLAM
10
click
WHAT ARE YOU DOING IN HERE?!
HOUSE SIT-TING.
IT'S NOT SAFE TO LEAVE THINGS IN HERE WITH THE DOOR UNLOCKED.
THERE MIGHT BE SOME SKETCHY GUY WHO'D JUST WALK RIGHT IN.

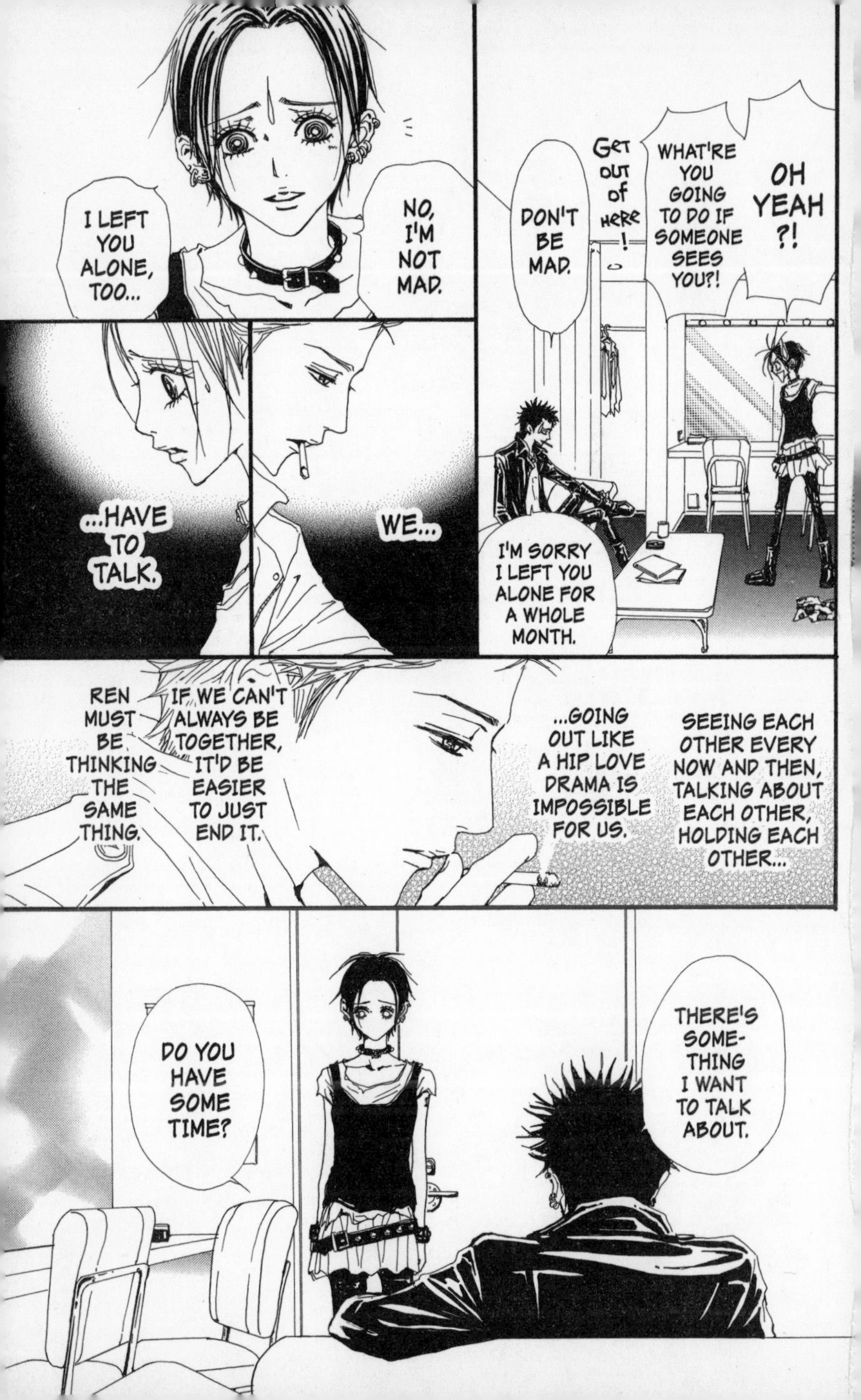
OH YEAH?!
WHAT'RE YOU GOING TO DO IF SOMEONE SEES YOU?!
Get out of here!
DON'T BE MAD.
I'M SORRY I LEFT YOU ALONE FOR A WHOLE MONTH.
NO, I'M NOT MAD.
I LEFT YOU ALONE, TOO...
WE...
...HAVE TO TALK.
SEEING EACH OTHER EVERY NOW AND THEN, TALKING ABOUT EACH OTHER, HOLDING EACH OTHER...
...GOING OUT LIKE A HIP LOVE DRAMA IS IMPOSSIBLE FOR US.
IF WE CAN'T ALWAYS BE TOGETHER, IT'D BE EASIER TO JUST END IT.
REN MUST BE THINKING THE SAME THING.
THERE'S SOME-THING I WANT TO TALK ABOUT.
DO YOU HAVE SOME TIME?

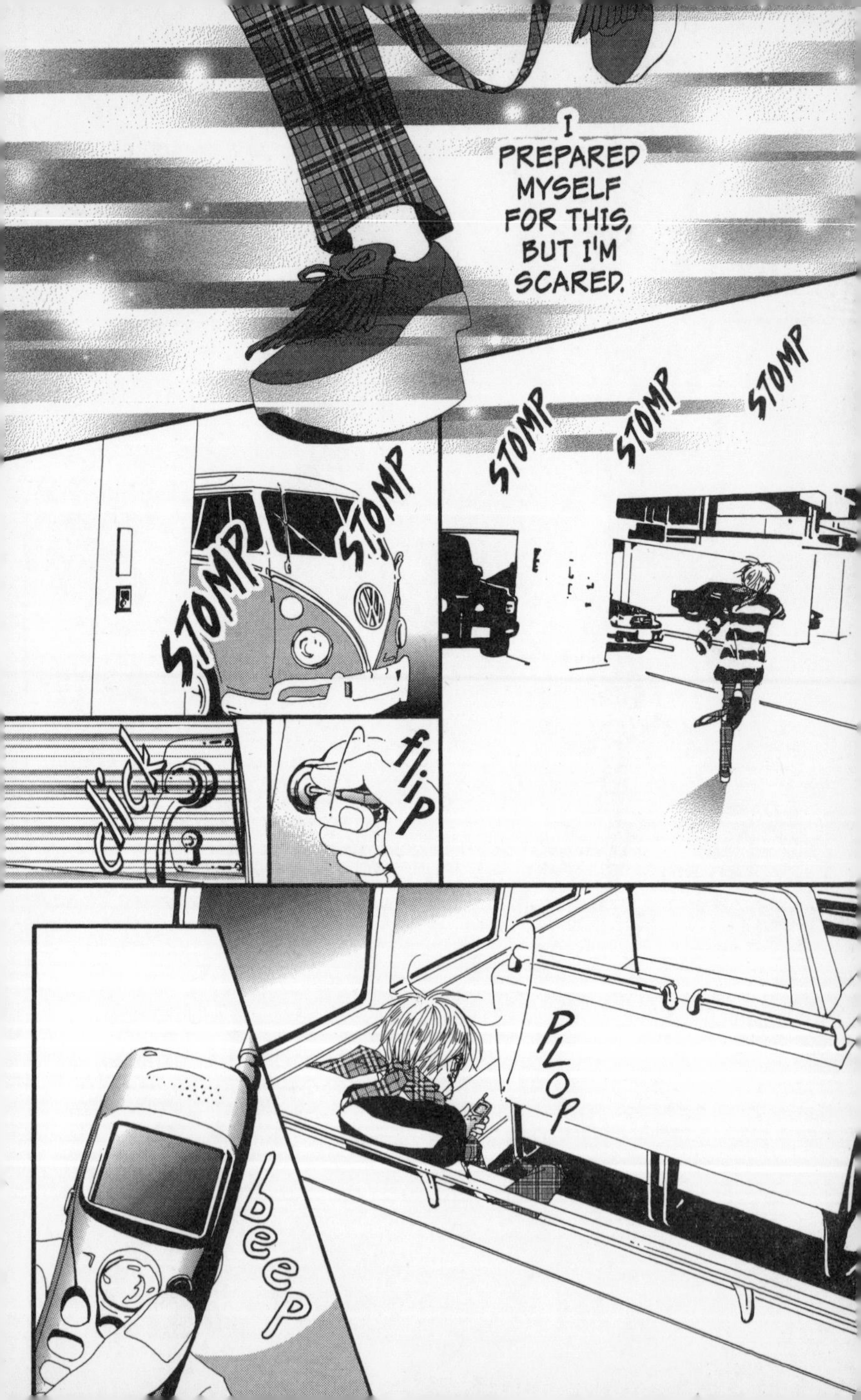
I PREPARED MYSELF FOR THIS, BUT I'M SCARED.
STOMP
STOMP
STOMP
STOMP
STOMP
flip
click
PLOP
beep

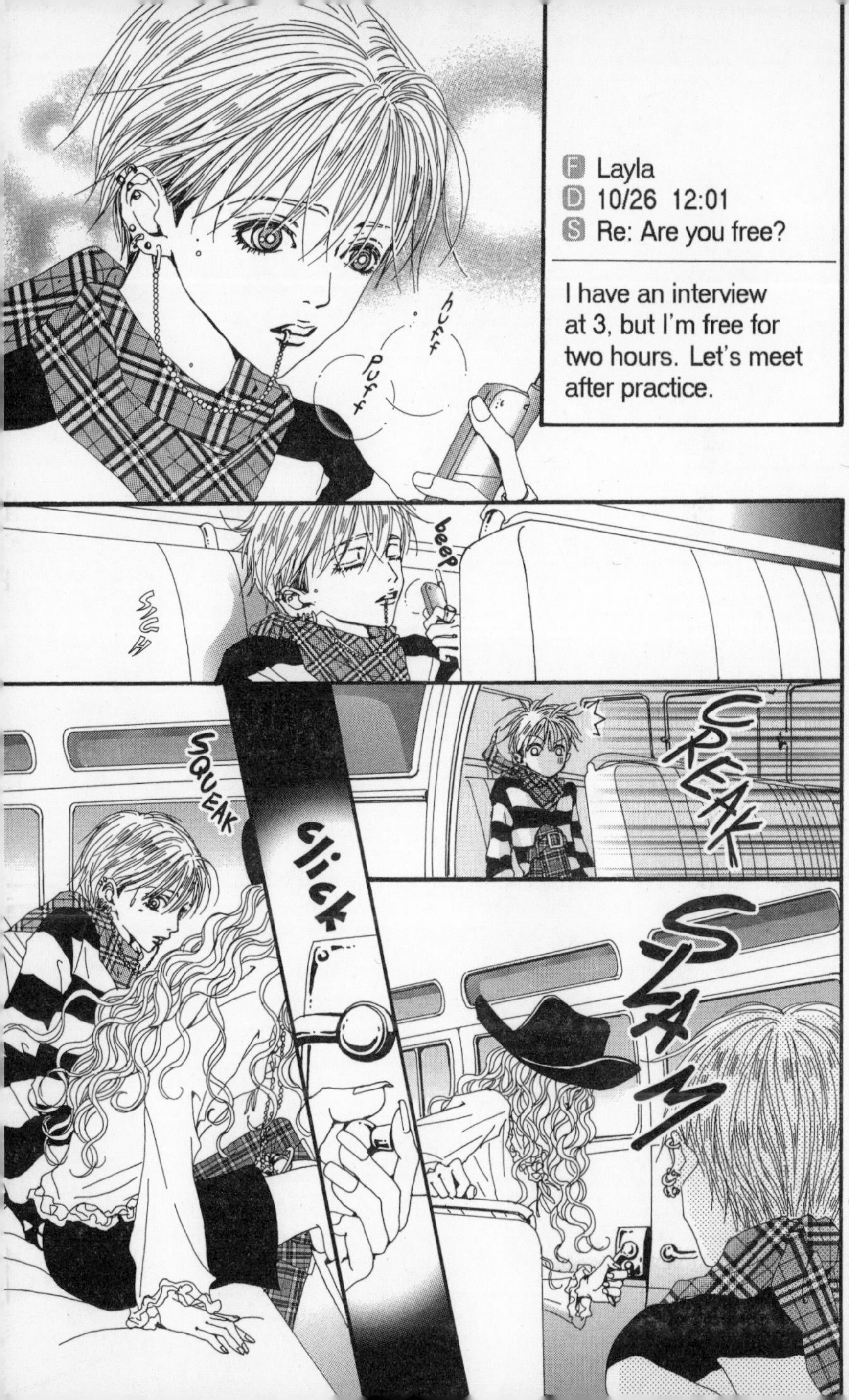
F Layla
D 10/26 12:01
S Re: Are you free?
I have an interview at 3, but I'm free for two hours. Let's meet after practice.
huff
puff
beep
CREAK
SLAM
click
SQUEAK

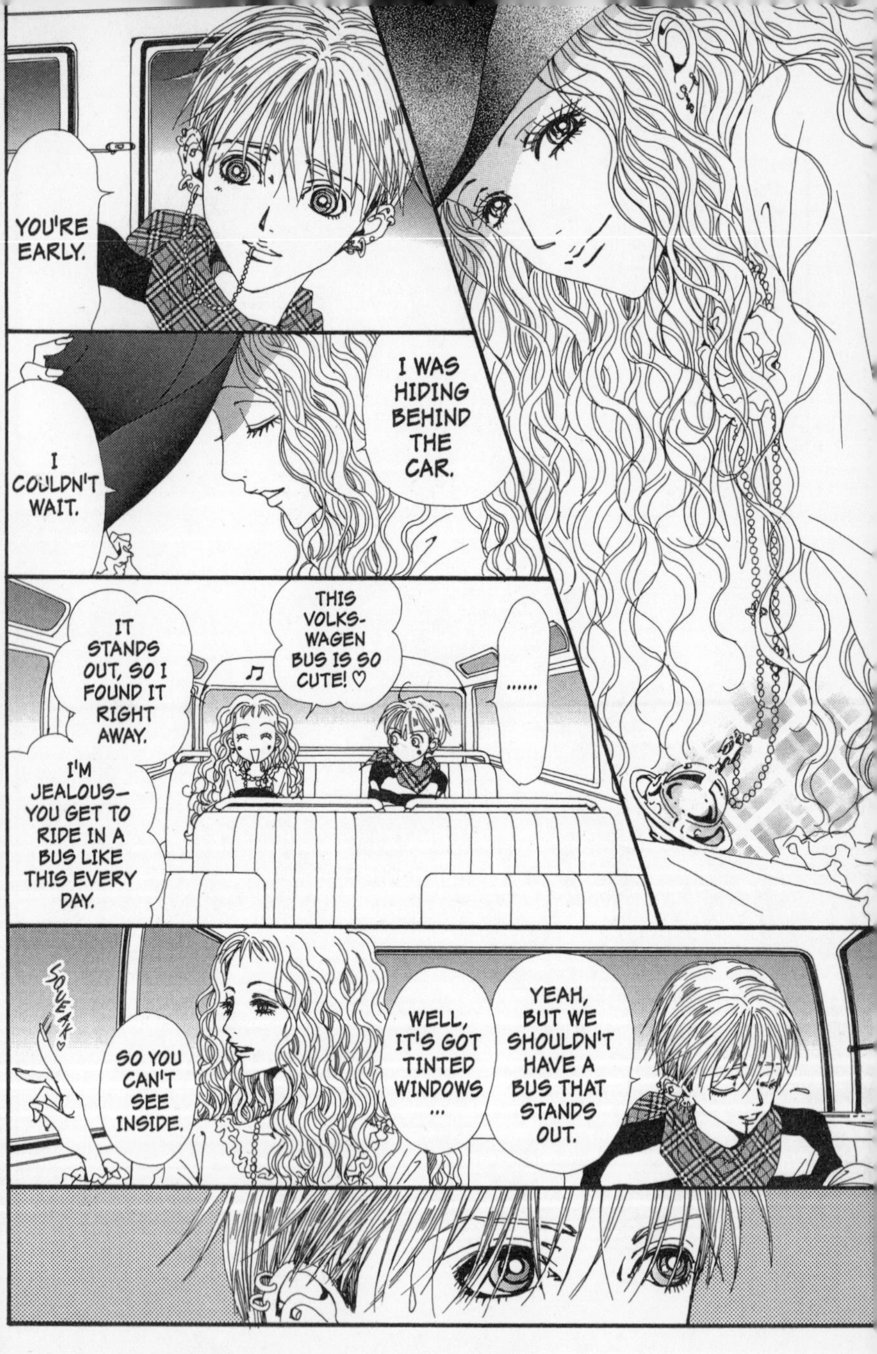
YOU'RE EARLY.
I WAS HIDING BEHIND THE CAR.
I COULDN'T WAIT.
......
THIS VOLKS-WAGEN BUS IS SO CUTE! ♡
♫
IT STANDS OUT, SO I FOUND IT RIGHT AWAY.
I'M JEALOUS—YOU GET TO RIDE IN A BUS LIKE THIS EVERY DAY.
YEAH, BUT WE SHOULDN'T HAVE A BUS THAT STANDS OUT.
WELL, IT'S GOT TINTED WINDOWS ...
SO YOU CAN'T SEE INSIDE.
SQUEAK ♡

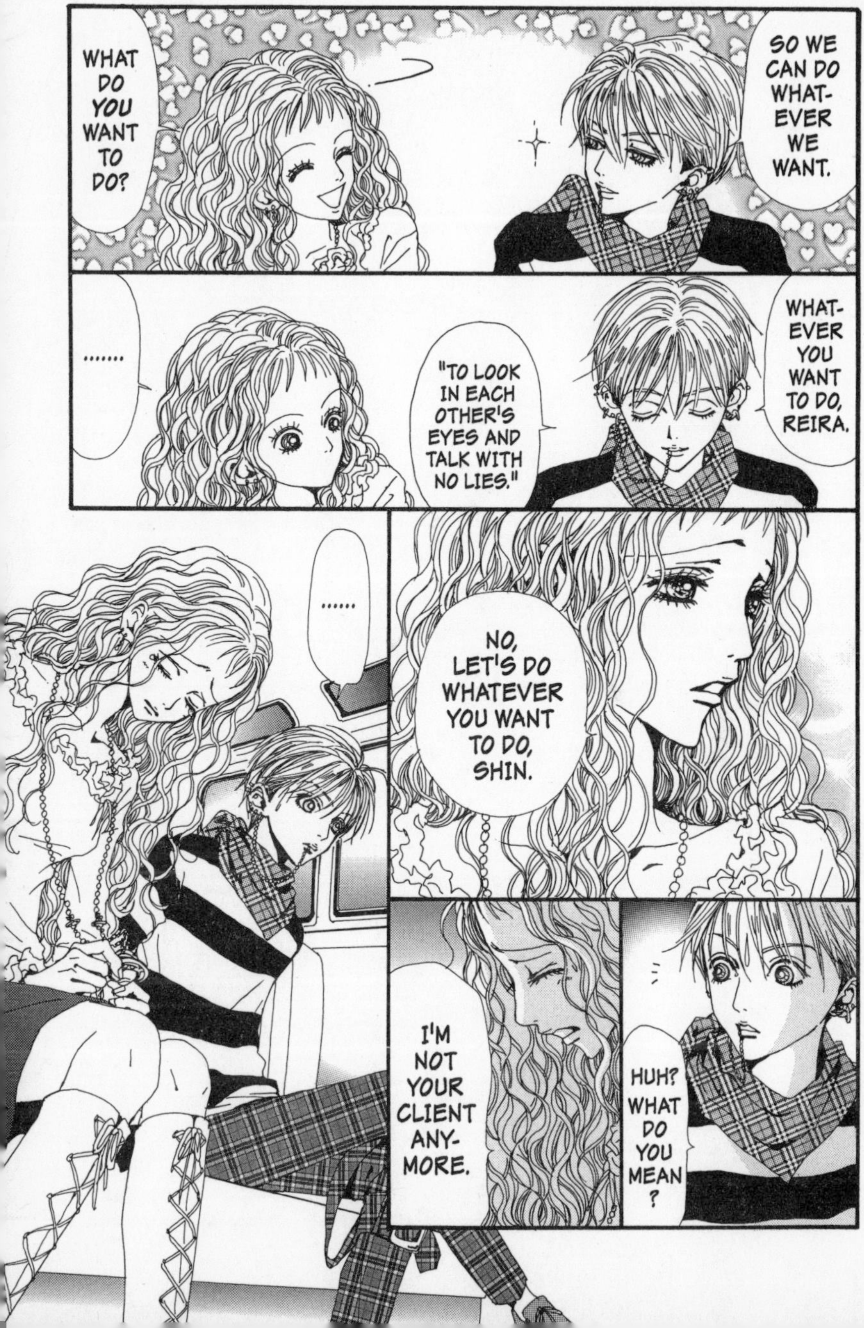
SO WE CAN DO WHATEVER WE WANT.
WHAT DO YOU WANT TO DO?
WHATEVER YOU WANT TO DO, REIRA.
"TO LOOK IN EACH OTHER'S EYES AND TALK WITH NO LIES."
....
NO, LET'S DO WHATEVER YOU WANT TO DO, SHIN.
HUH? WHAT DO YOU MEAN?
I'M NOT YOUR CLIENT ANYMORE.
......

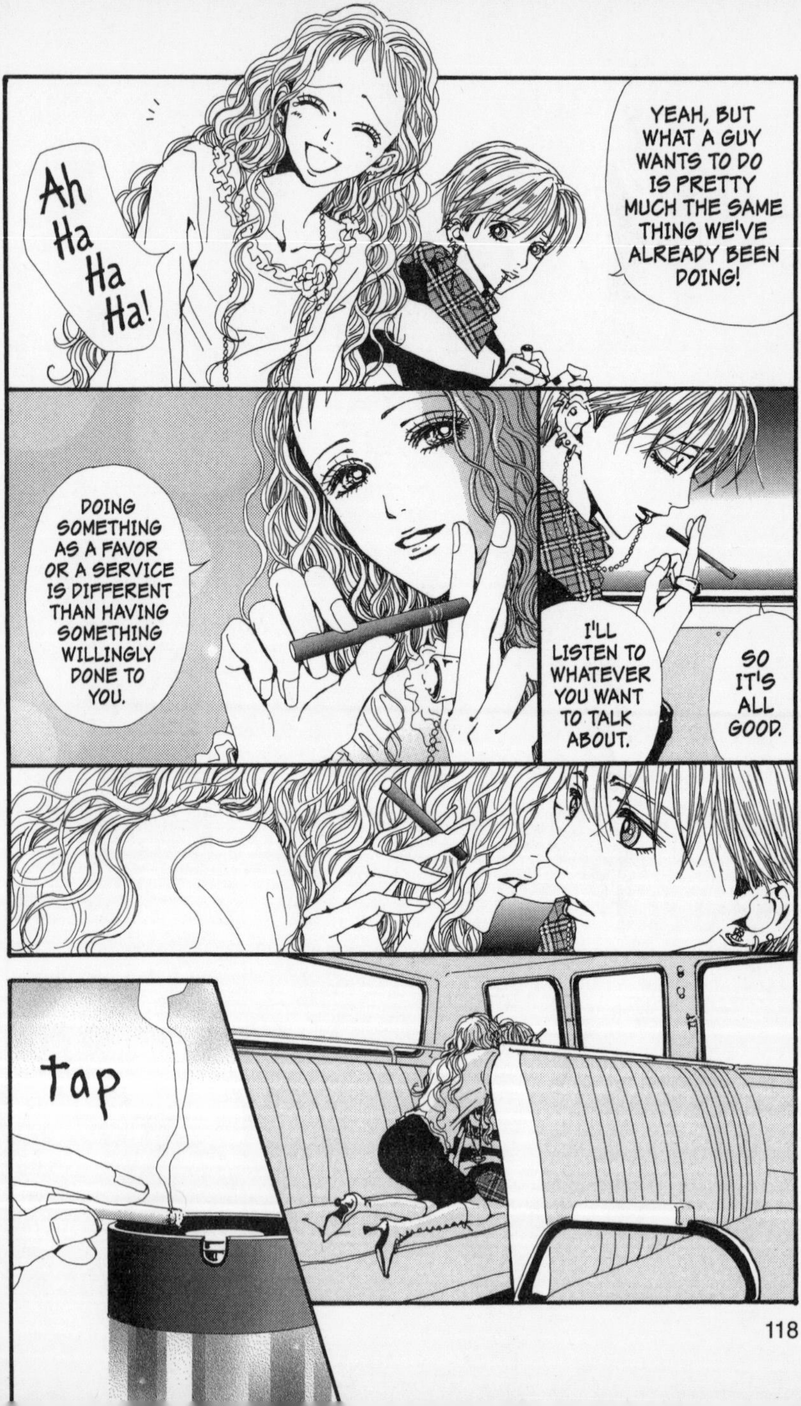
YEAH, BUT WHAT A GUY WANTS TO DO IS PRETTY MUCH THE SAME THING WE'VE ALREADY BEEN DOING!
Ah Ha Ha Ha!
SO IT'S ALL GOOD.
I'LL LISTEN TO WHATEVER YOU WANT TO TALK ABOUT.
DOING SOMETHING AS A FAVOR OR A SERVICE IS DIFFERENT THAN HAVING SOMETHING WILLINGLY DONE TO YOU.
tap

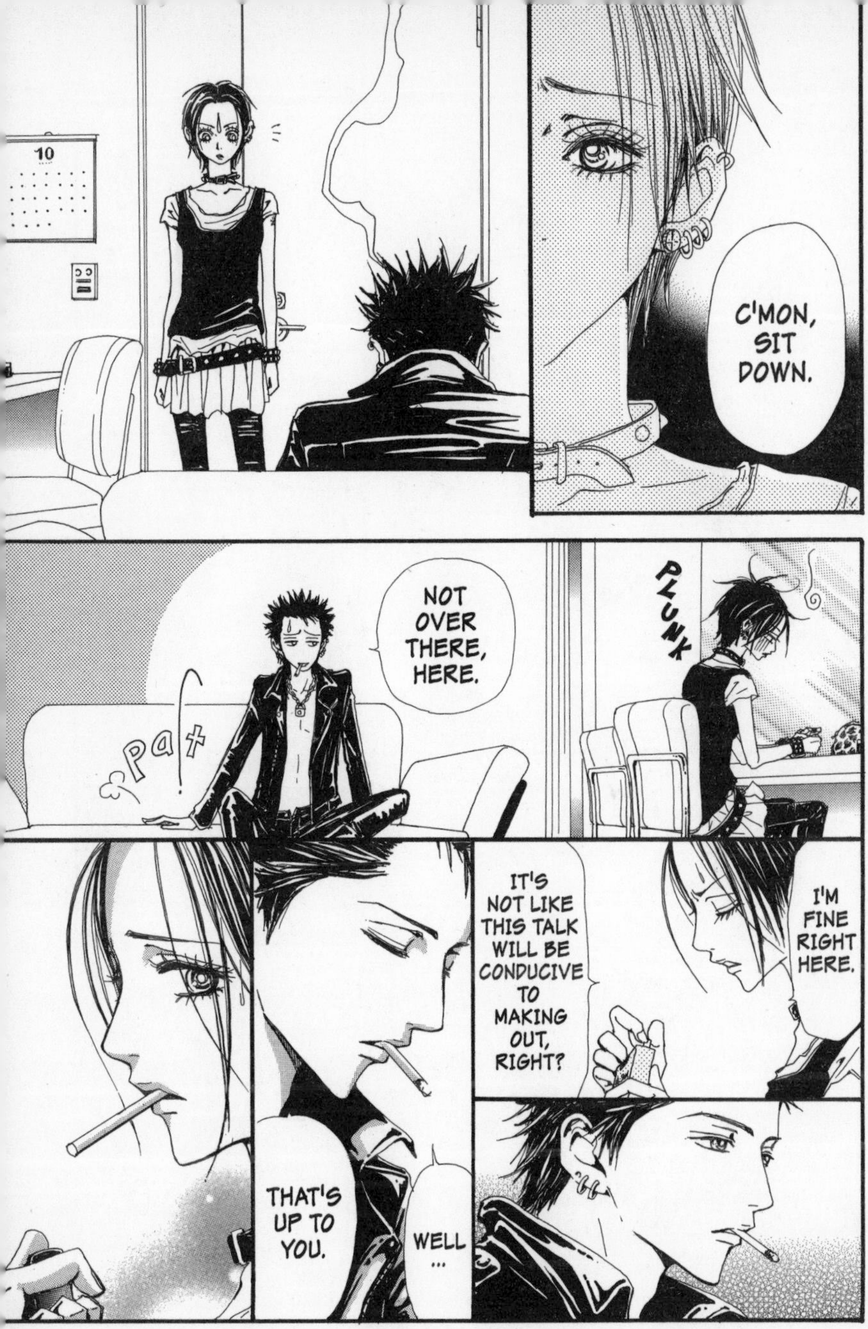
C'MON, SIT DOWN.
10
PLUNK
NOT OVER THERE, HERE.
pat
I'M FINE RIGHT HERE.
IT'S NOT LIKE THIS TALK WILL BE CONDUCIVE TO MAKING OUT, RIGHT?
WELL...
THAT'S UP TO YOU.

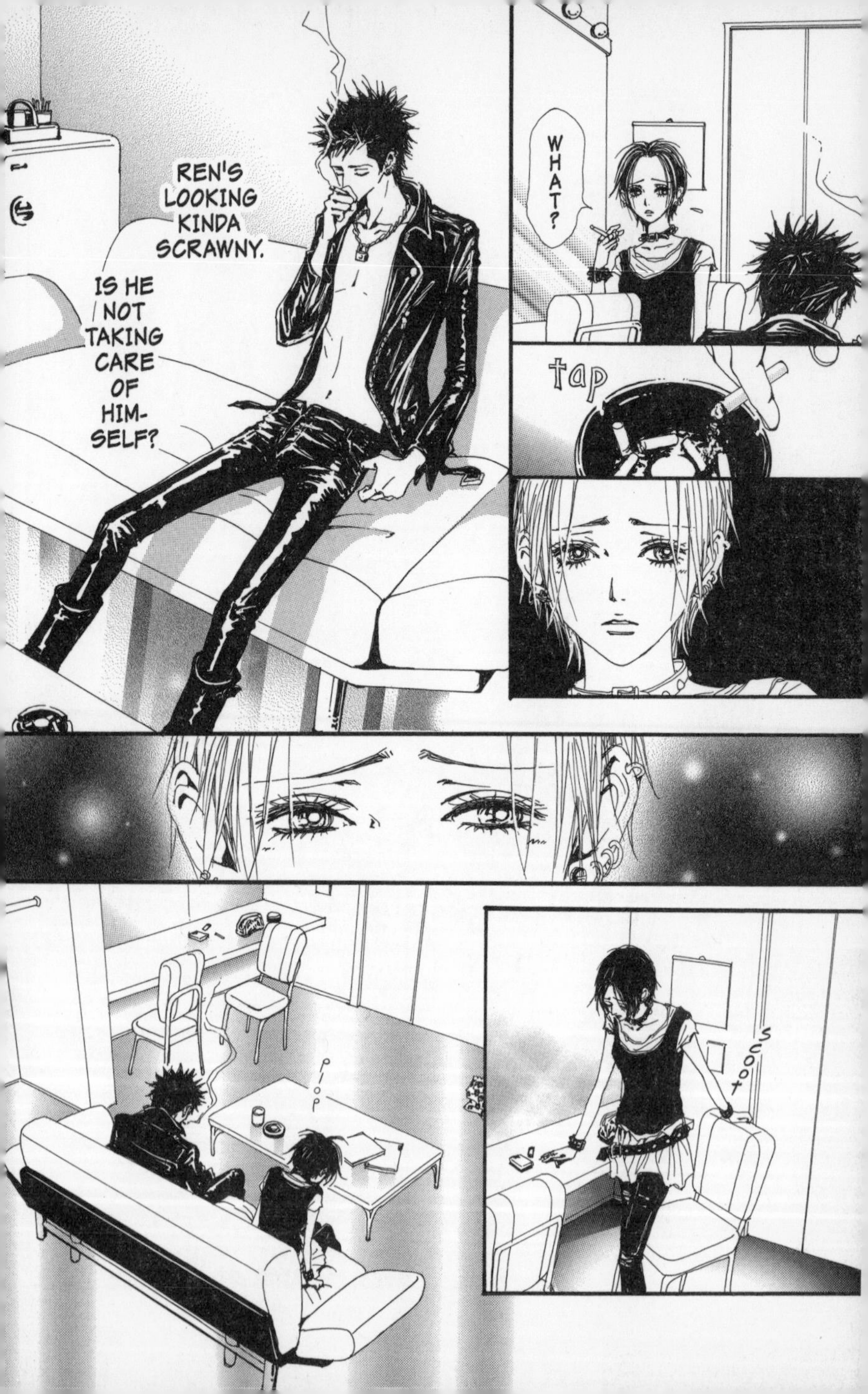
WHAT?
tap
REN'S LOOKING KINDA SCRAWNY.
IS HE NOT TAKING CARE OF HIM-SELF?
scoot
plop

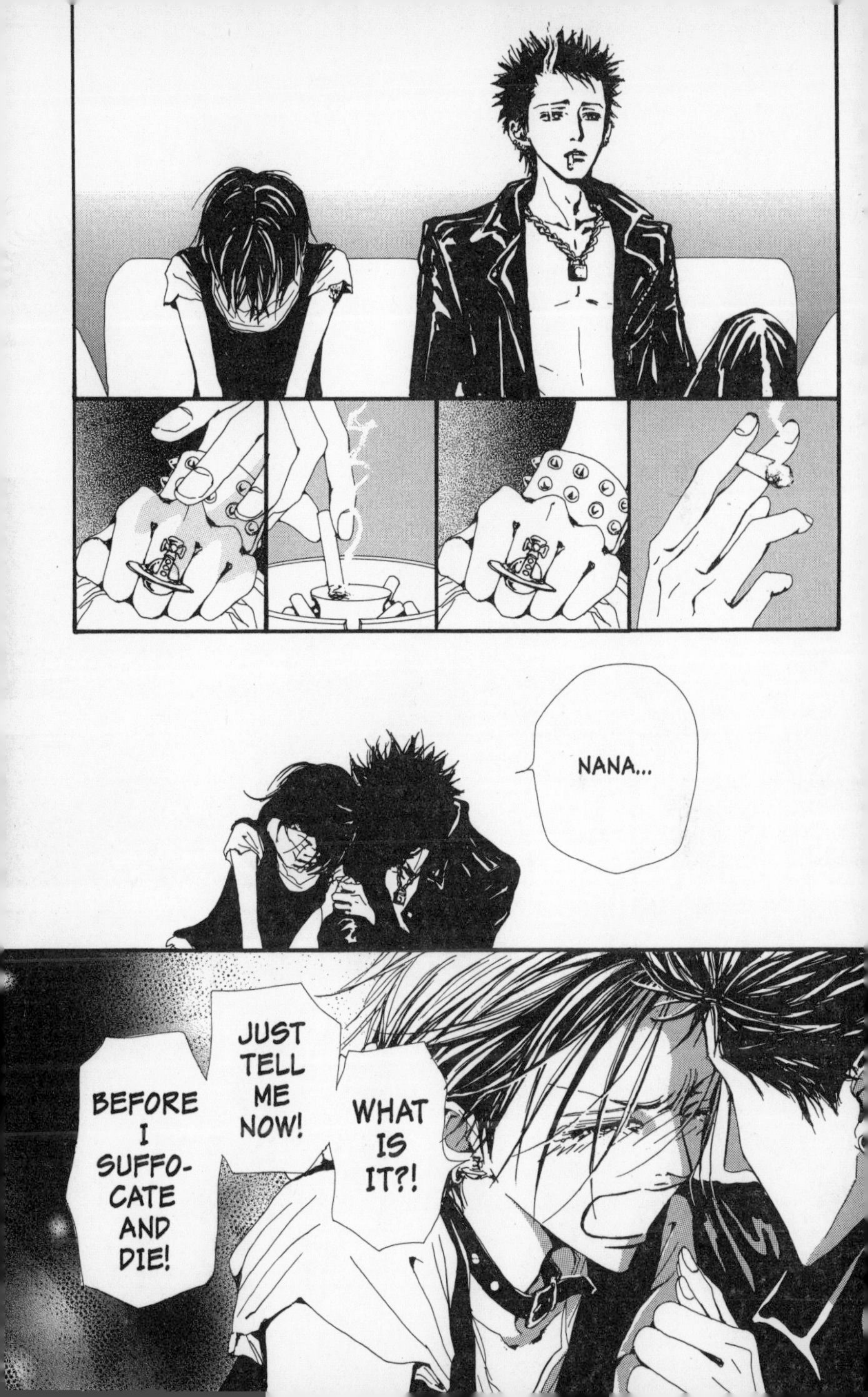
NANA...
WHAT IS IT?!
JUST TELL ME NOW!
BEFORE I SUFFOCATE AND DIE!

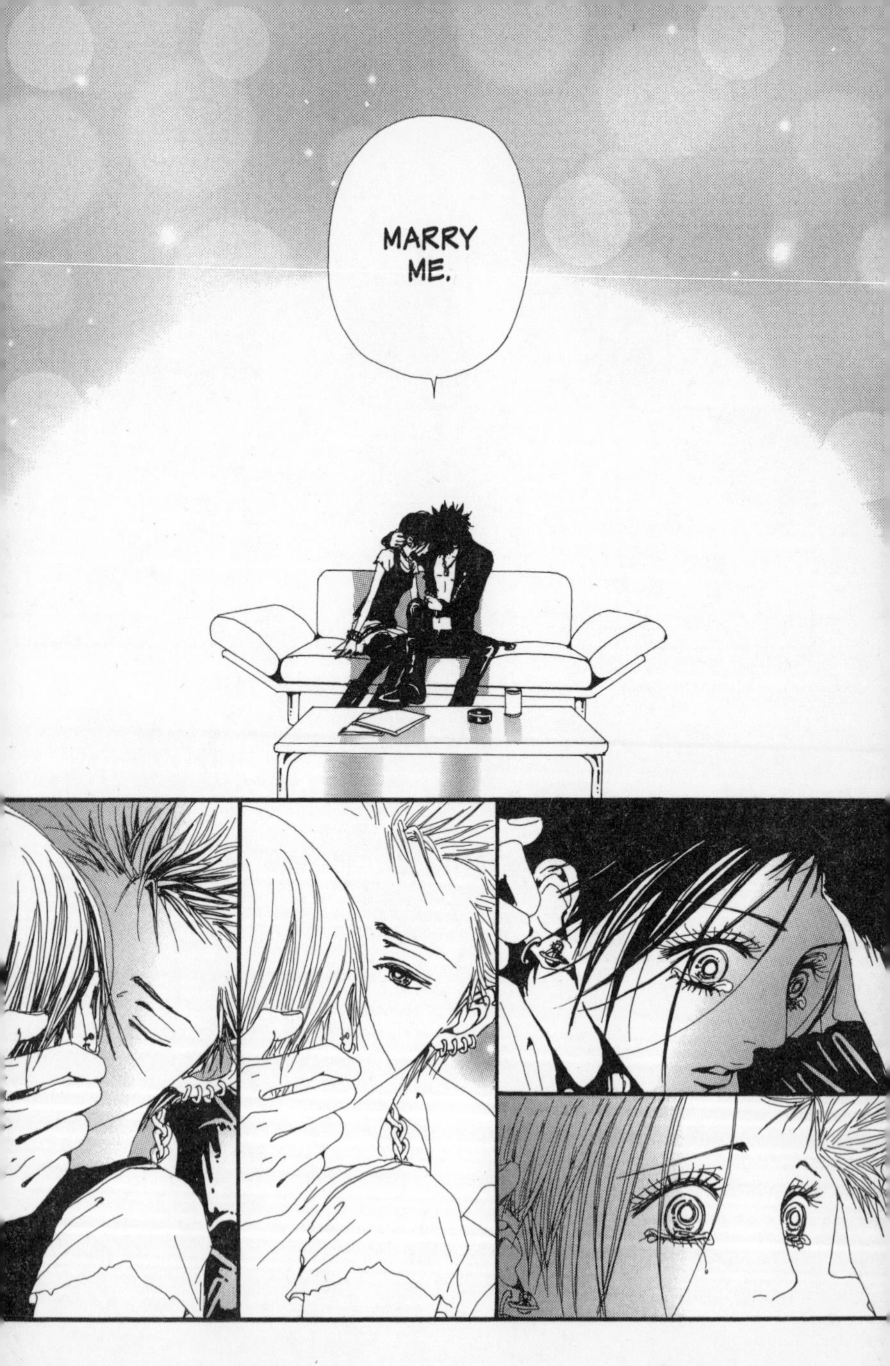
MARRY ME.

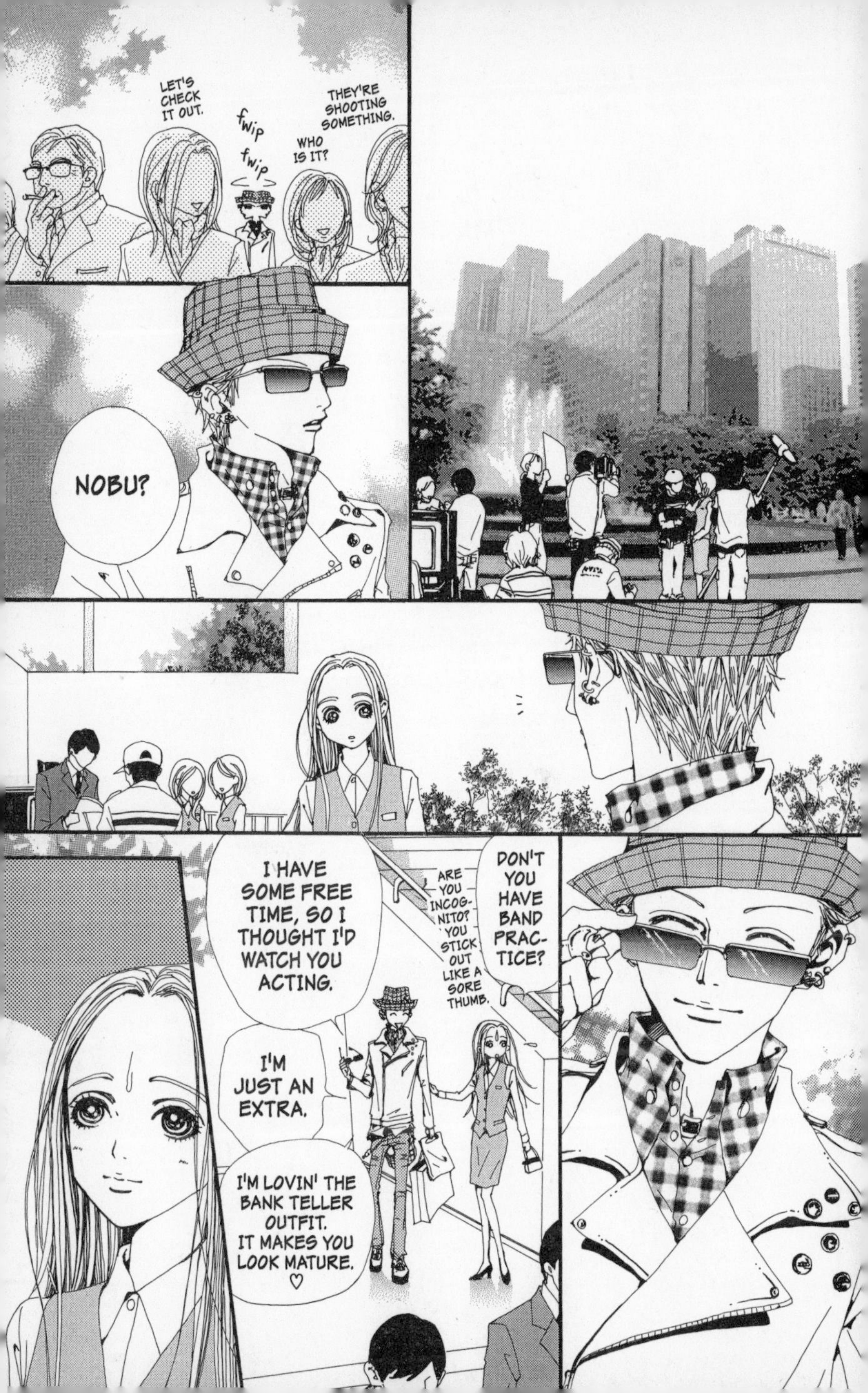

THEY'RE SHOOTING SOMETHING.
WHO IS IT?
fwip fwip
LET'S CHECK IT OUT.
NOBU?
DON'T YOU HAVE BAND PRAC-TICE?
ARE YOU INCOG-NITO? YOU STICK OUT LIKE A SORE THUMB.
I HAVE SOME FREE TIME, SO I THOUGHT I'D WATCH YOU ACTING.
I'M JUST AN EXTRA.
I'M LOVIN' THE BANK TELLER OUTFIT. IT MAKES YOU LOOK MATURE. ♡

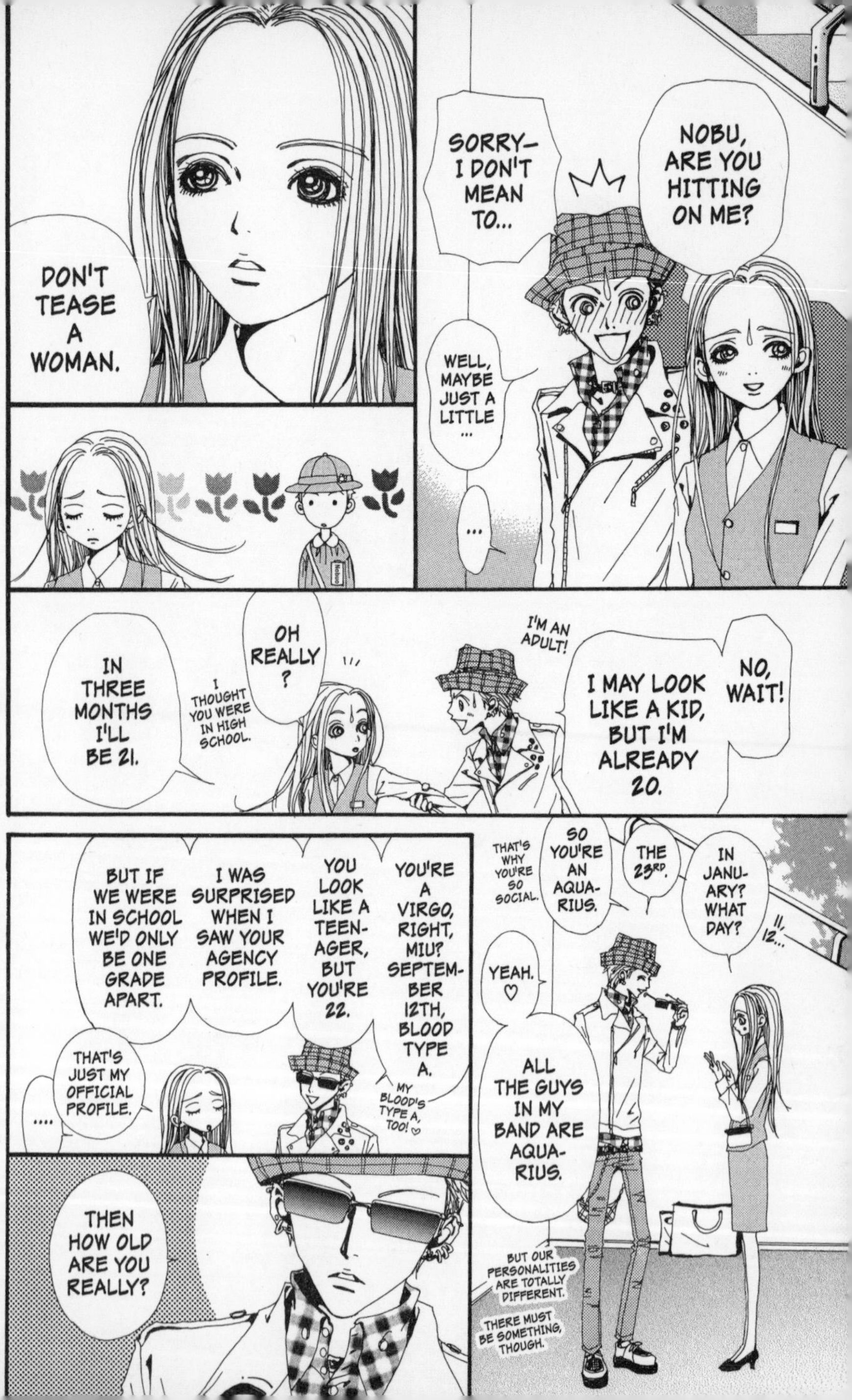
NOBU, ARE YOU HITTING ON ME?
SORRY— I DON'T MEAN TO...
WELL, MAYBE JUST A LITTLE ...
...
DON'T TEASE A WOMAN.
NO, WAIT!
I MAY LOOK LIKE A KID, BUT I'M ALREADY 20.
I'M AN ADULT!
OH REALLY ?
I THOUGHT YOU WERE IN HIGH SCHOOL.
IN THREE MONTHS I'LL BE 21.
IN JANUARY? WHAT DAY?
12...
THE 23RD.
SO YOU'RE AN AQUARIUS.
THAT'S WHY YOU'RE SO SOCIAL.
YEAH. ♡
ALL THE GUYS IN MY BAND ARE AQUARIUS.
BUT OUR PERSONALITIES ARE TOTALLY DIFFERENT.
THERE MUST BE SOMETHING, THOUGH.
YOU'RE A VIRGO, RIGHT, MIU? SEPTEMBER 12TH, BLOOD TYPE A.
MY BLOOD'S TYPE A, TOO! ♡
YOU LOOK LIKE A TEENAGER, BUT YOU'RE 22.
I WAS SURPRISED WHEN I SAW YOUR AGENCY PROFILE.
BUT IF WE WERE IN SCHOOL WE'D ONLY BE ONE GRADE APART.
THAT'S JUST MY OFFICIAL PROFILE.
....
THEN HOW OLD ARE YOU REALLY?

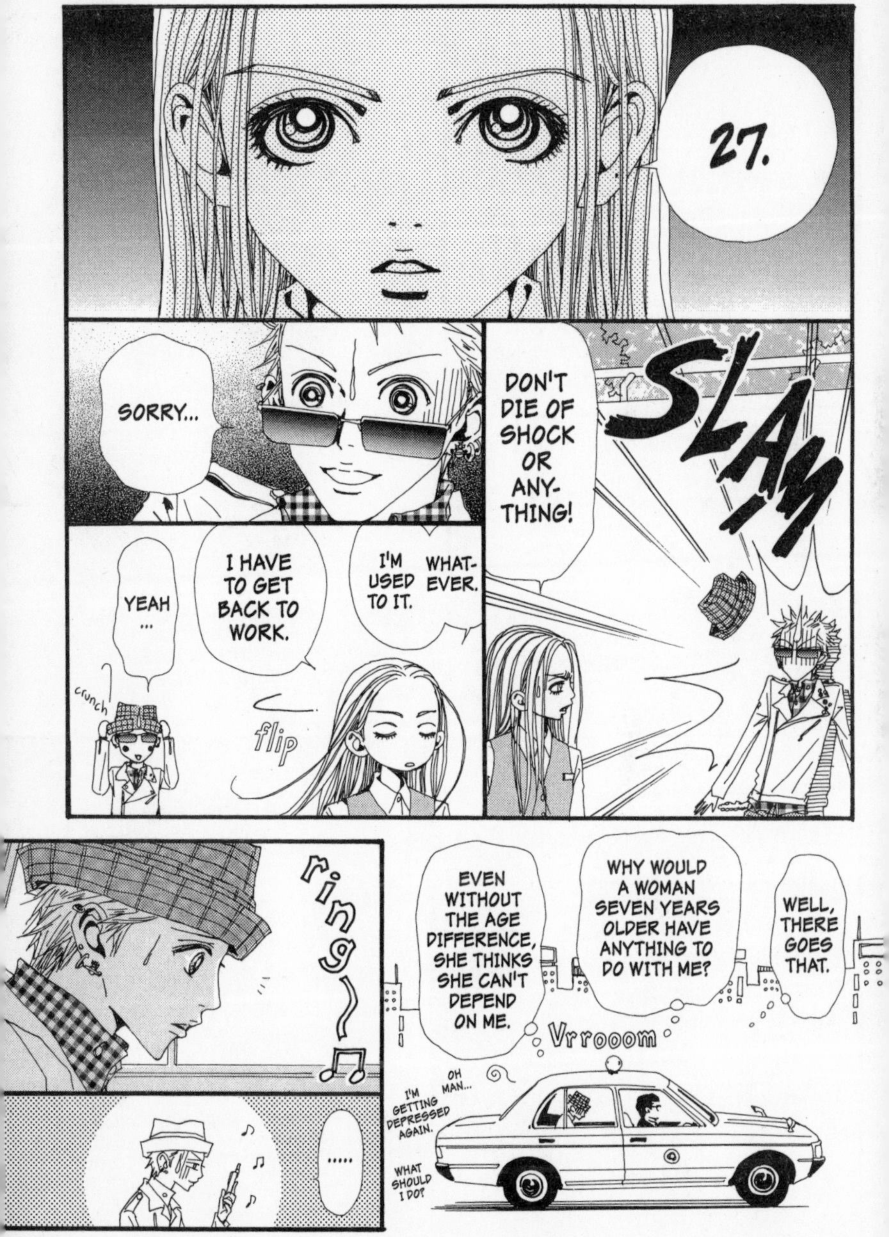
27.
DON'T DIE OF SHOCK OR ANYTHING!
SLAM
SORRY...
WHATEVER.
I'M USED TO IT.
I HAVE TO GET BACK TO WORK.
flip
YEAH...
crunch
WELL, THERE GOES THAT.
WHY WOULD A WOMAN SEVEN YEARS OLDER HAVE ANYTHING TO DO WITH ME?
EVEN WITHOUT THE AGE DIFFERENCE, SHE THINKS SHE CAN'T DEPEND ON ME.
Vrrooom
OH MAN...
I'M GETTING DEPRESSED AGAIN.
WHAT SHOULD I DO?
ring~♫
......

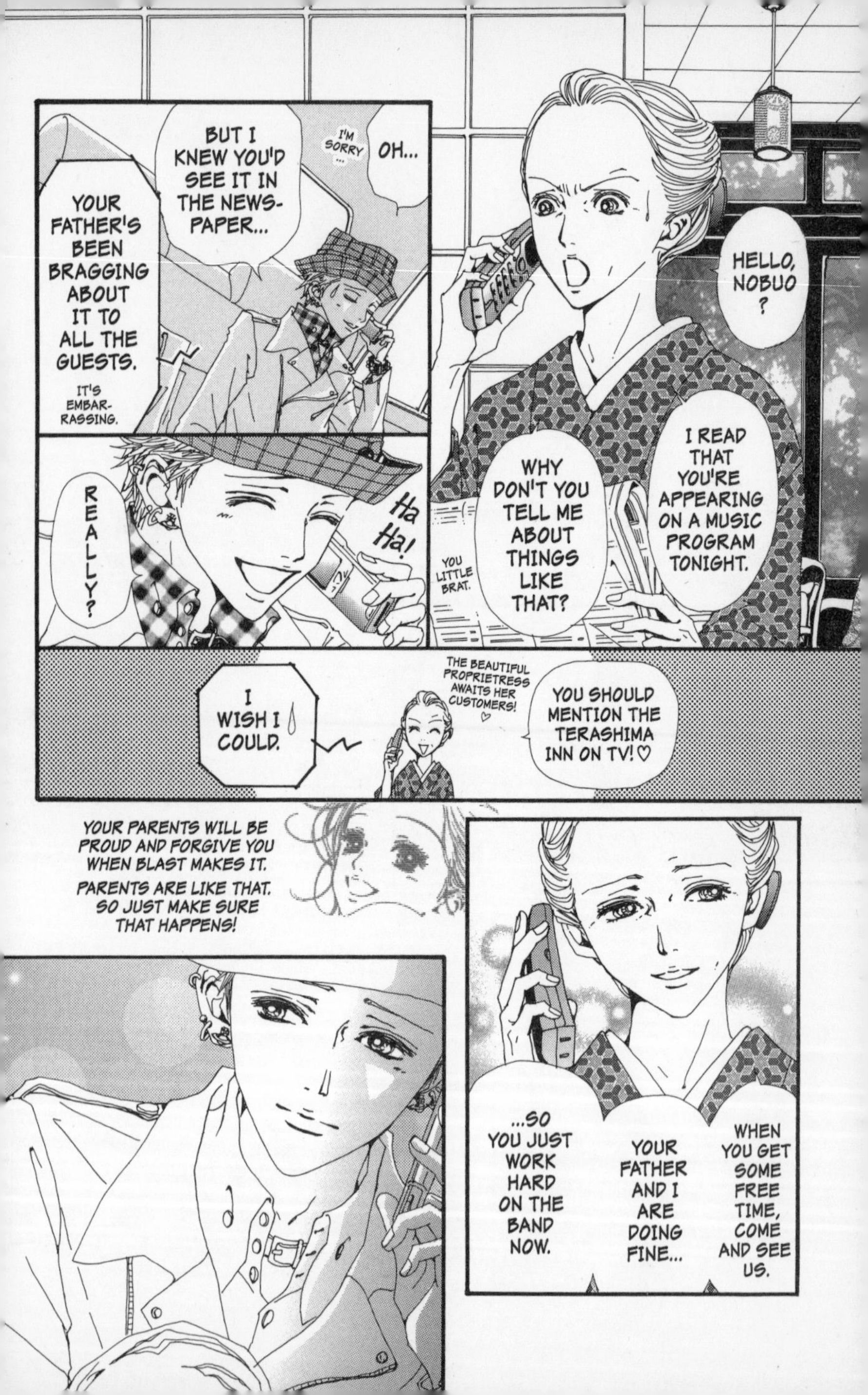
HELLO, NOBUO?
I READ THAT YOU'RE APPEARING ON A MUSIC PROGRAM TONIGHT.
WHY DON'T YOU TELL ME ABOUT THINGS LIKE THAT?
YOU LITTLE BRAT.
OH...
I'M SORRY ...
BUT I KNEW YOU'D SEE IT IN THE NEWS-PAPER...
YOUR FATHER'S BEEN BRAGGING ABOUT IT TO ALL THE GUESTS.
IT'S EMBAR-RASSING.
Ha Ha!
REALLY?
YOU SHOULD MENTION THE TERASHIMA INN ON TV! ♡
THE BEAUTIFUL PROPRIETRESS AWAITS HER CUSTOMERS! ♡
I WISH I COULD.
WHEN YOU GET SOME FREE TIME, COME AND SEE US.
YOUR FATHER AND I ARE DOING FINE...
...SO YOU JUST WORK HARD ON THE BAND NOW.
YOUR PARENTS WILL BE PROUD AND FORGIVE YOU WHEN BLAST MAKES IT.
PARENTS ARE LIKE THAT.
SO JUST MAKE SURE THAT HAPPENS!

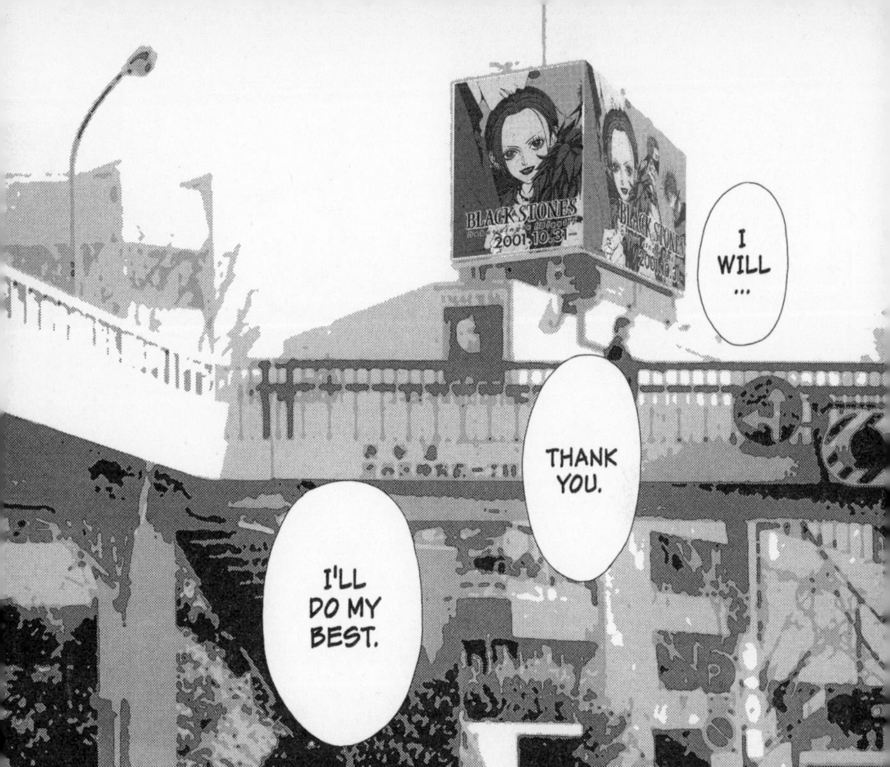
BLACK STONES
2001.10.31-
I WILL ...
THANK YOU.
I'LL DO MY BEST.

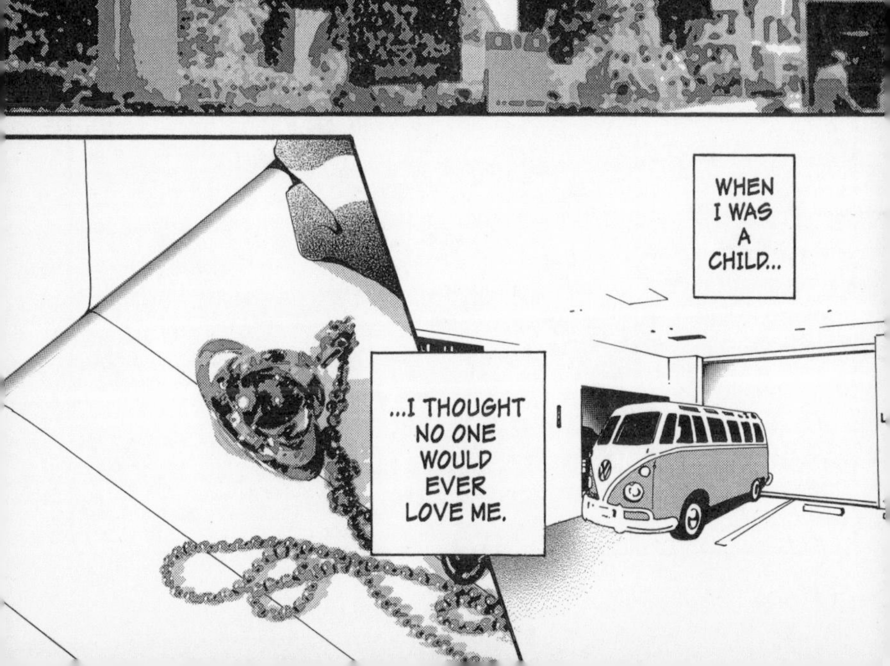
WHEN I WAS A CHILD...
...I THOUGHT NO ONE WOULD EVER LOVE ME.

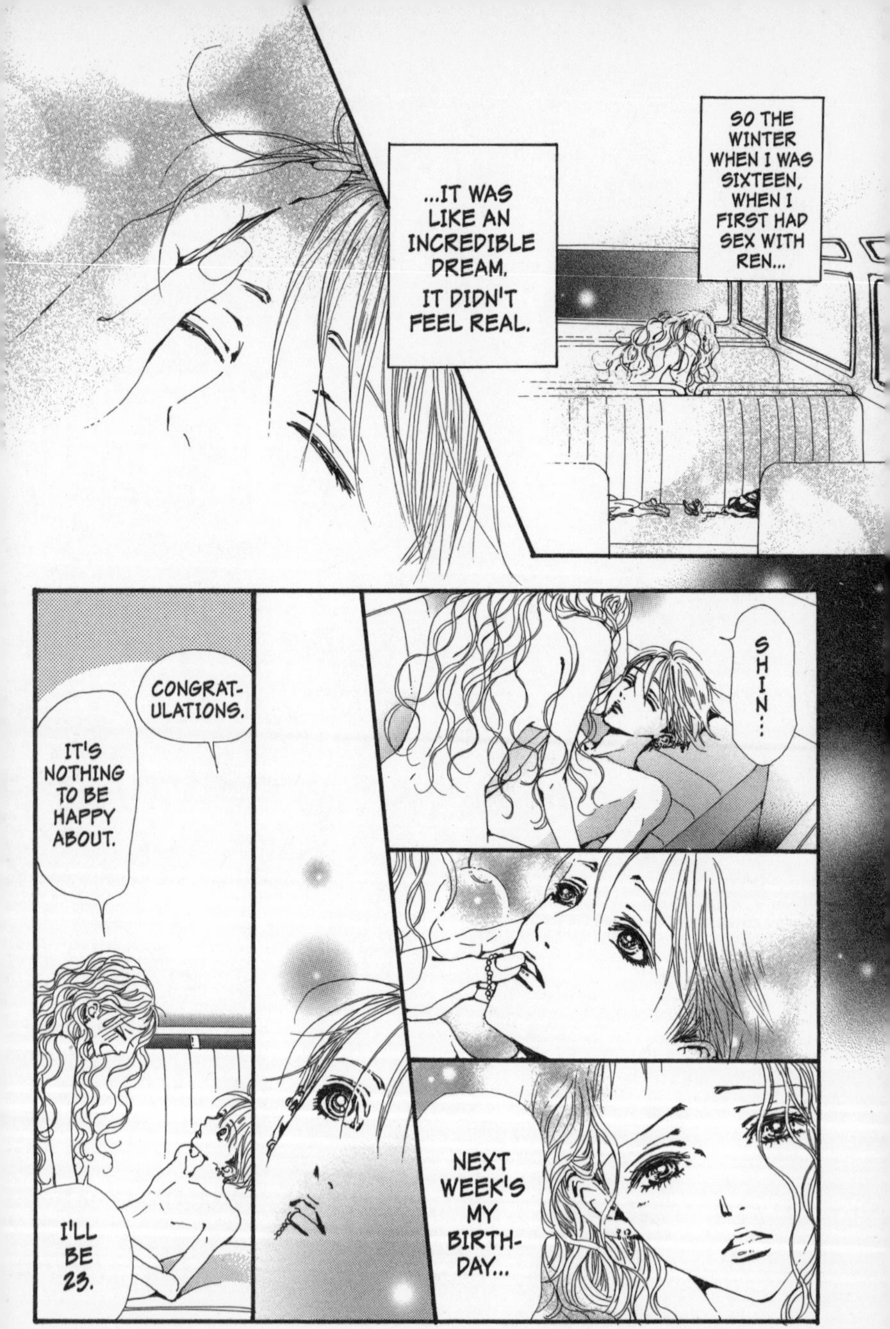
SO THE WINTER WHEN I WAS SIXTEEN, WHEN I FIRST HAD SEX WITH REN...
...IT WAS LIKE AN INCREDIBLE DREAM.
IT DIDN'T FEEL REAL.
SHIN...
NEXT WEEK'S MY BIRTHDAY...
I'LL BE 23.
CONGRATULATIONS.
IT'S NOTHING TO BE HAPPY ABOUT.

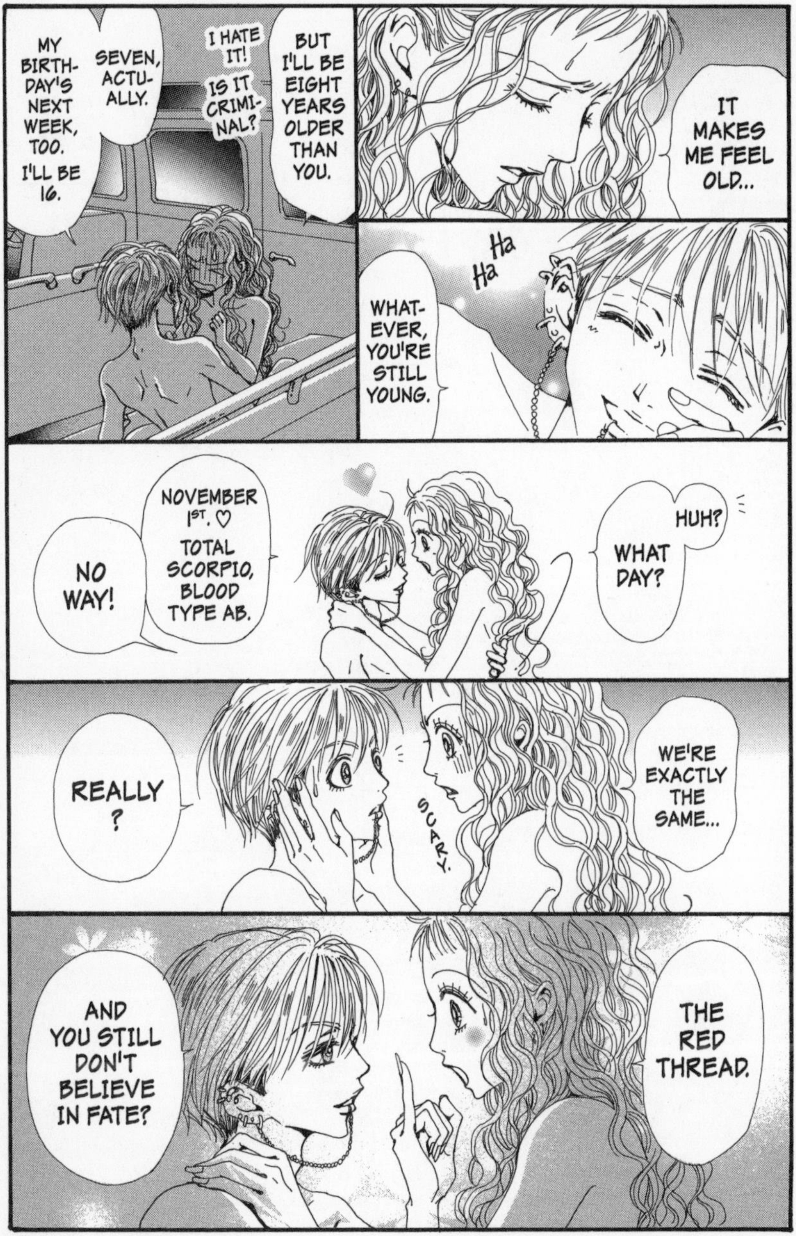
IT MAKES ME FEEL OLD...
Ha Ha
WHATEVER, YOU'RE STILL YOUNG.
BUT I'LL BE EIGHT YEARS OLDER THAN YOU.
I HATE IT! IS IT CRIMINAL?
SEVEN, ACTUALLY.
MY BIRTHDAY'S NEXT WEEK, TOO. I'LL BE 16.
HUH? WHAT DAY?
NOVEMBER 1ST. ♡ TOTAL SCORPIO, BLOOD TYPE AB.
NO WAY!
WE'RE EXACTLY THE SAME...
SCARY.
REALLY?
THE RED THREAD.
AND YOU STILL DON'T BELIEVE IN FATE?

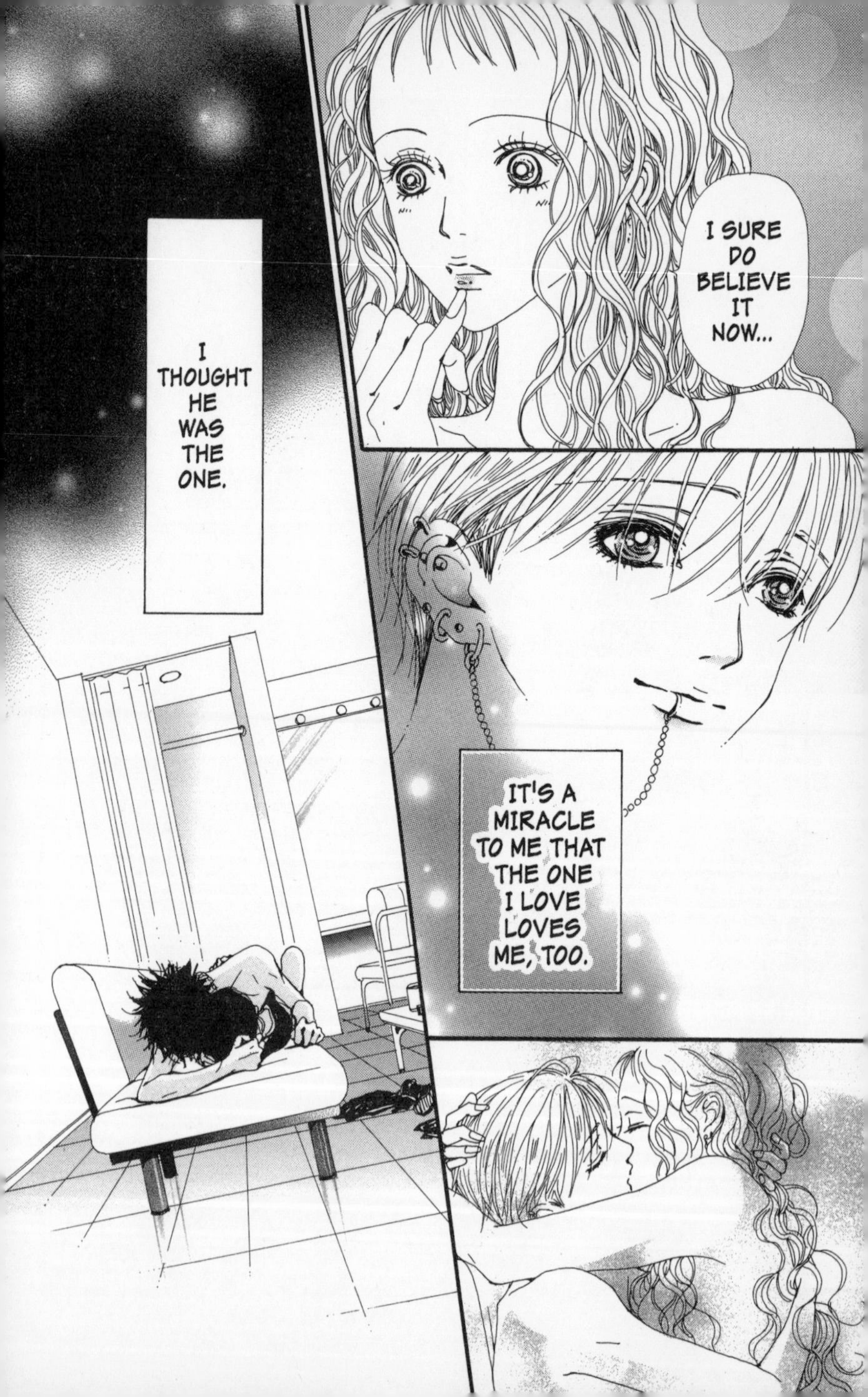
I SURE DO BELIEVE IT NOW...
IT'S A MIRACLE TO ME THAT THE ONE I LOVE LOVES ME, TOO.
I THOUGHT HE WAS THE ONE.

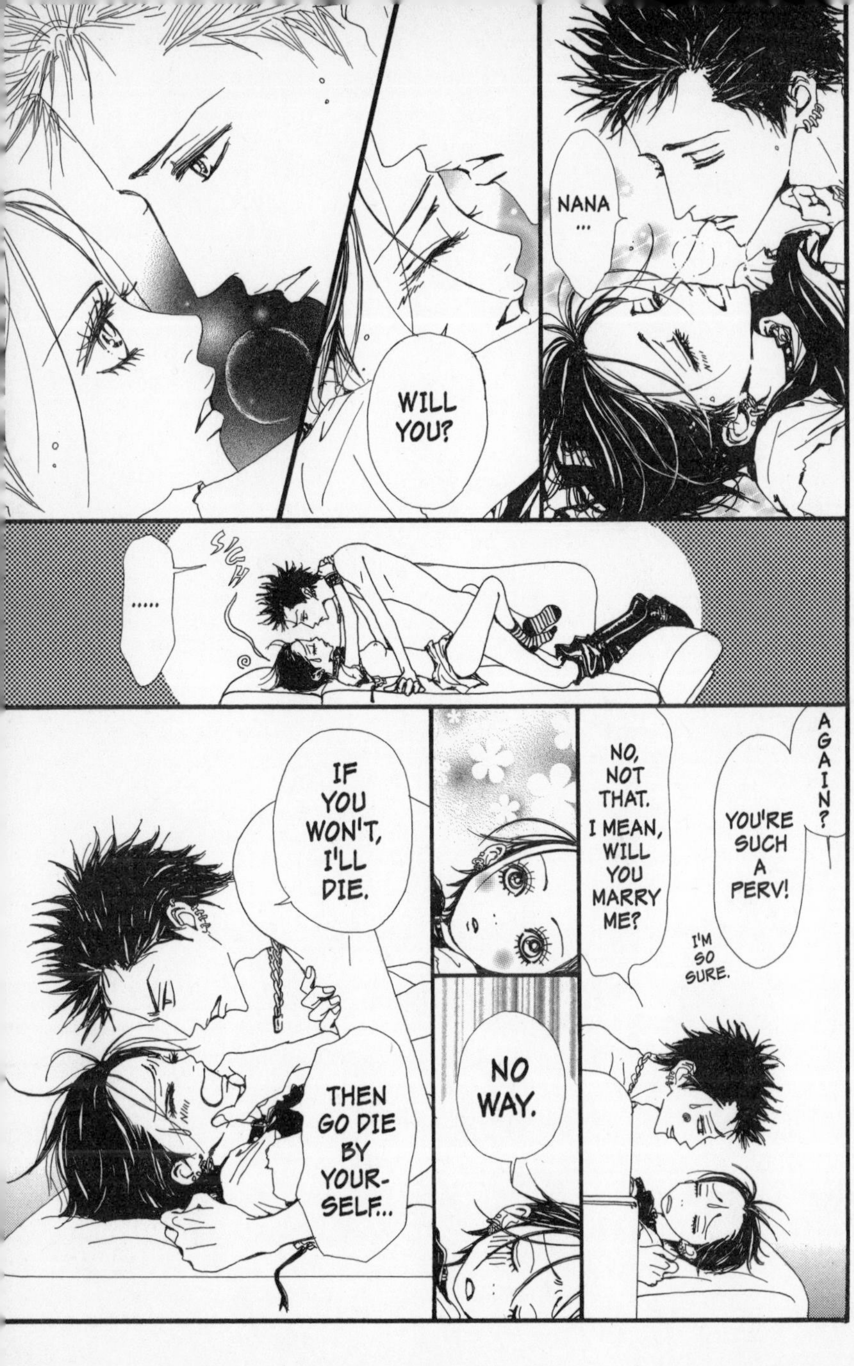

NANA ...
WILL YOU?
SIGH
.....
AGAIN?
YOU'RE SUCH A PERV!
NO, NOT THAT. I MEAN, WILL YOU MARRY ME?
I'M SO SURE.
NO WAY.
IF YOU WON'T, I'LL DIE.
THEN GO DIE BY YOURSELF...

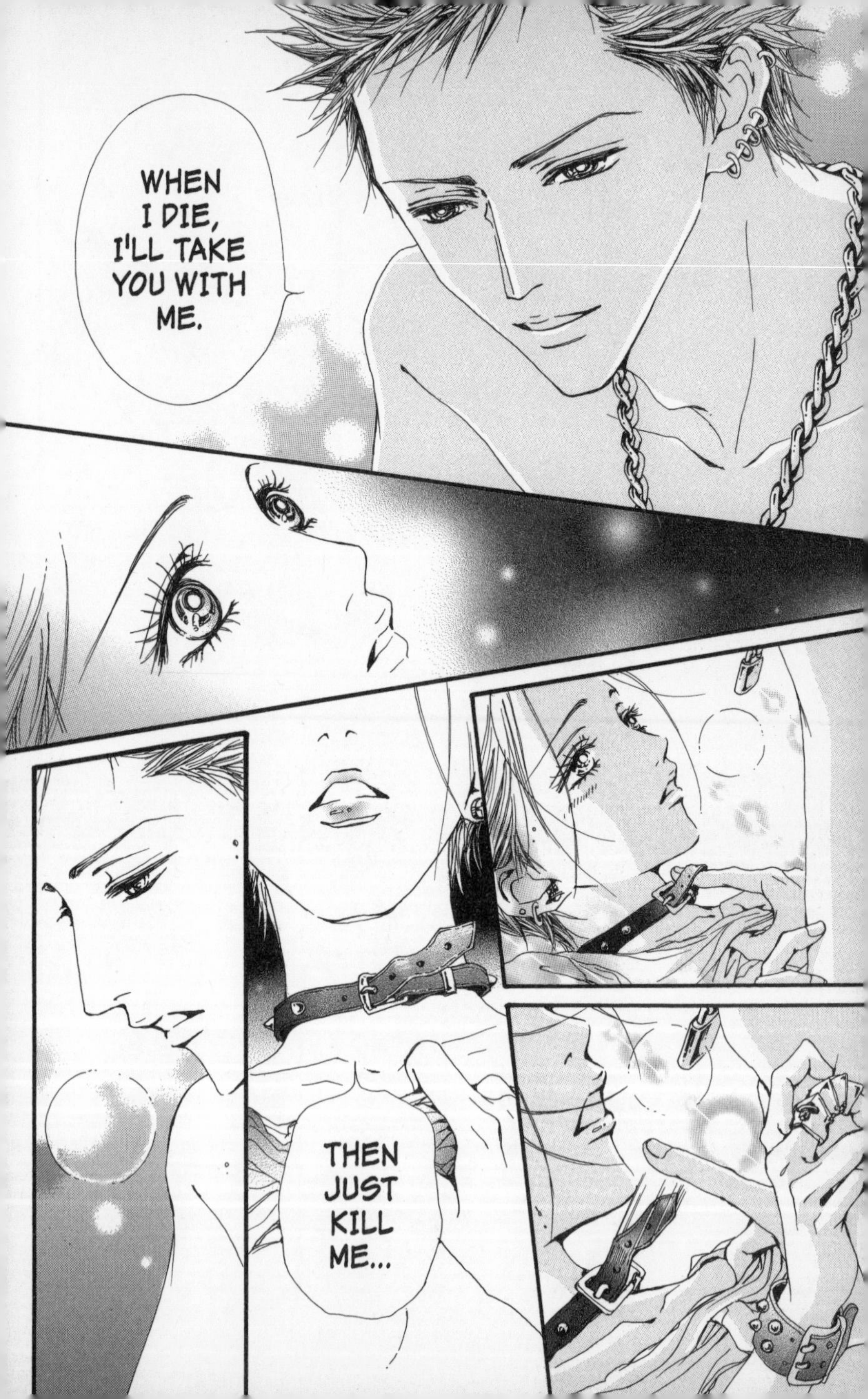
WHEN I DIE, I'LL TAKE YOU WITH ME.
THEN JUST KILL ME...

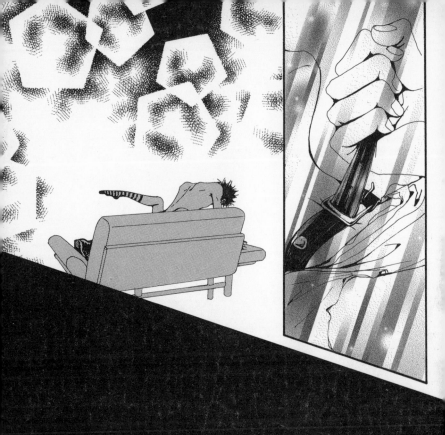

HE HALF-KILLED ME, AND I WENT TO HEAVEN WITH HIM.

I'M A PERVERT, TOO.

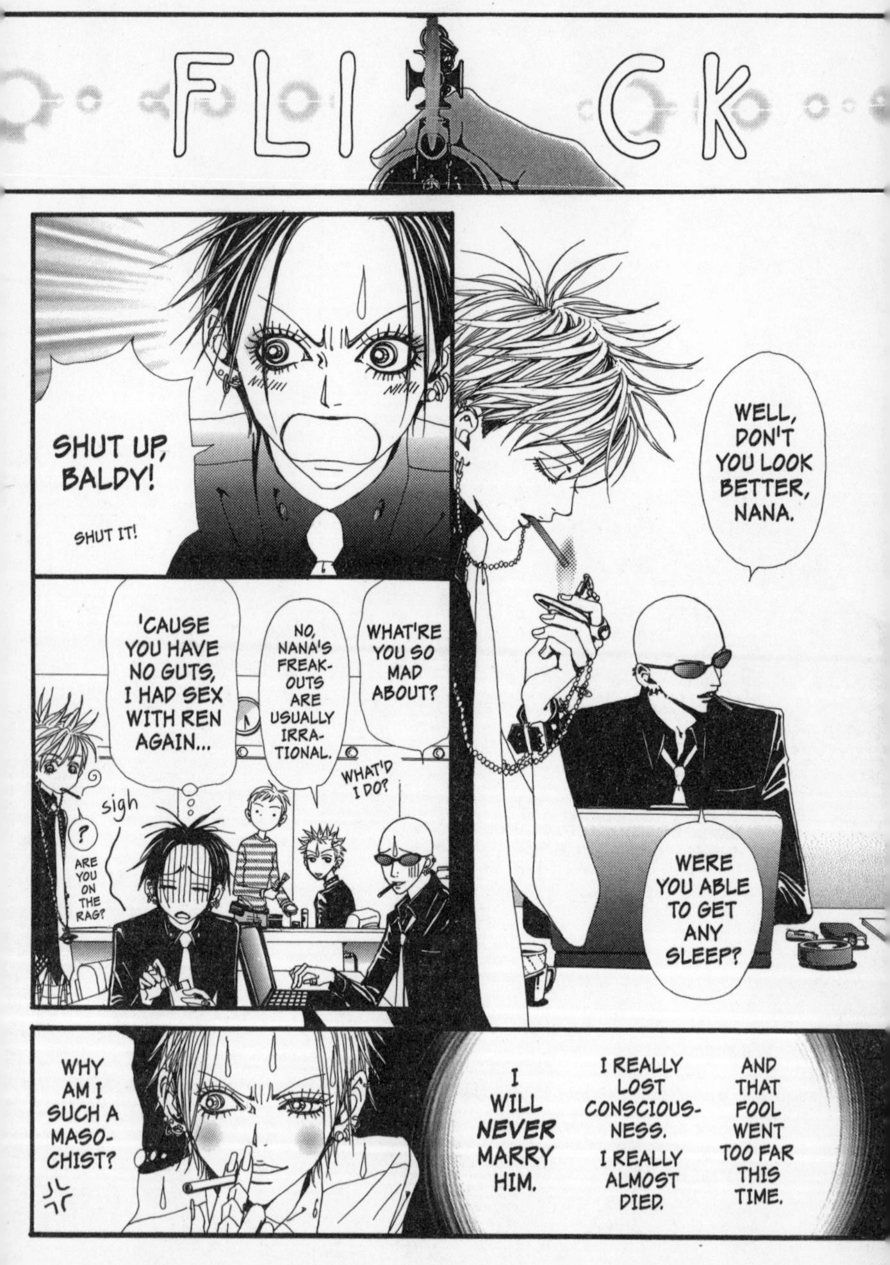
FLICK
WELL, DON'T YOU LOOK BETTER, NANA.
WERE YOU ABLE TO GET ANY SLEEP?
SHUT UP, BALDY!
SHUT IT!
WHAT'RE YOU SO MAD ABOUT?
NO, NANA'S FREAK-OUTS ARE USUALLY IRRATIONAL.
WHAT'D I DO?
'CAUSE YOU HAVE NO GUTS, I HAD SEX WITH REN AGAIN...
sigh
?
ARE YOU ON THE RAG?
AND THAT FOOL WENT TOO FAR THIS TIME.
I REALLY LOST CONSCIOUSNESS.
I REALLY ALMOST DIED.
I WILL NEVER MARRY HIM.
WHY AM I SUCH A MASOCHIST?

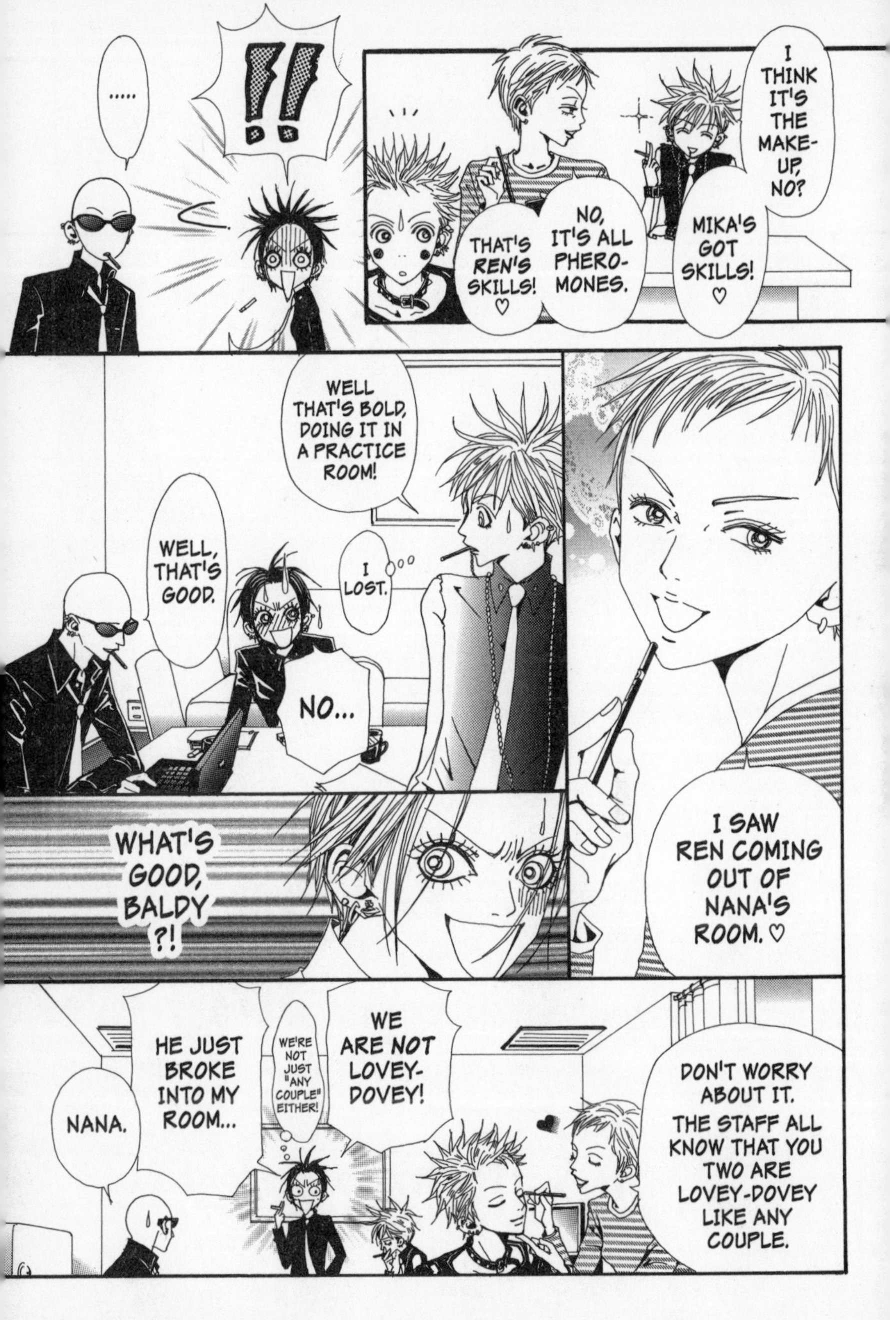
I THINK IT'S THE MAKE-UP, NO?
MIKA'S GOT SKILLS! ♡
NO, IT'S ALL PHERO-MONES.
THAT'S REN'S SKILLS! ♡
!!
......
I SAW REN COMING OUT OF NANA'S ROOM. ♡
WELL THAT'S BOLD, DOING IT IN A PRACTICE ROOM!
I LOST.
WELL, THAT'S GOOD.
NO...
WHAT'S GOOD, BALDY ?!
DON'T WORRY ABOUT IT. THE STAFF ALL KNOW THAT YOU TWO ARE LOVEY-DOVEY LIKE ANY COUPLE.
WE ARE NOT LOVEY-DOVEY!
WE'RE NOT JUST "ANY COUPLE" EITHER!
HE JUST BROKE INTO MY ROOM...
NANA.

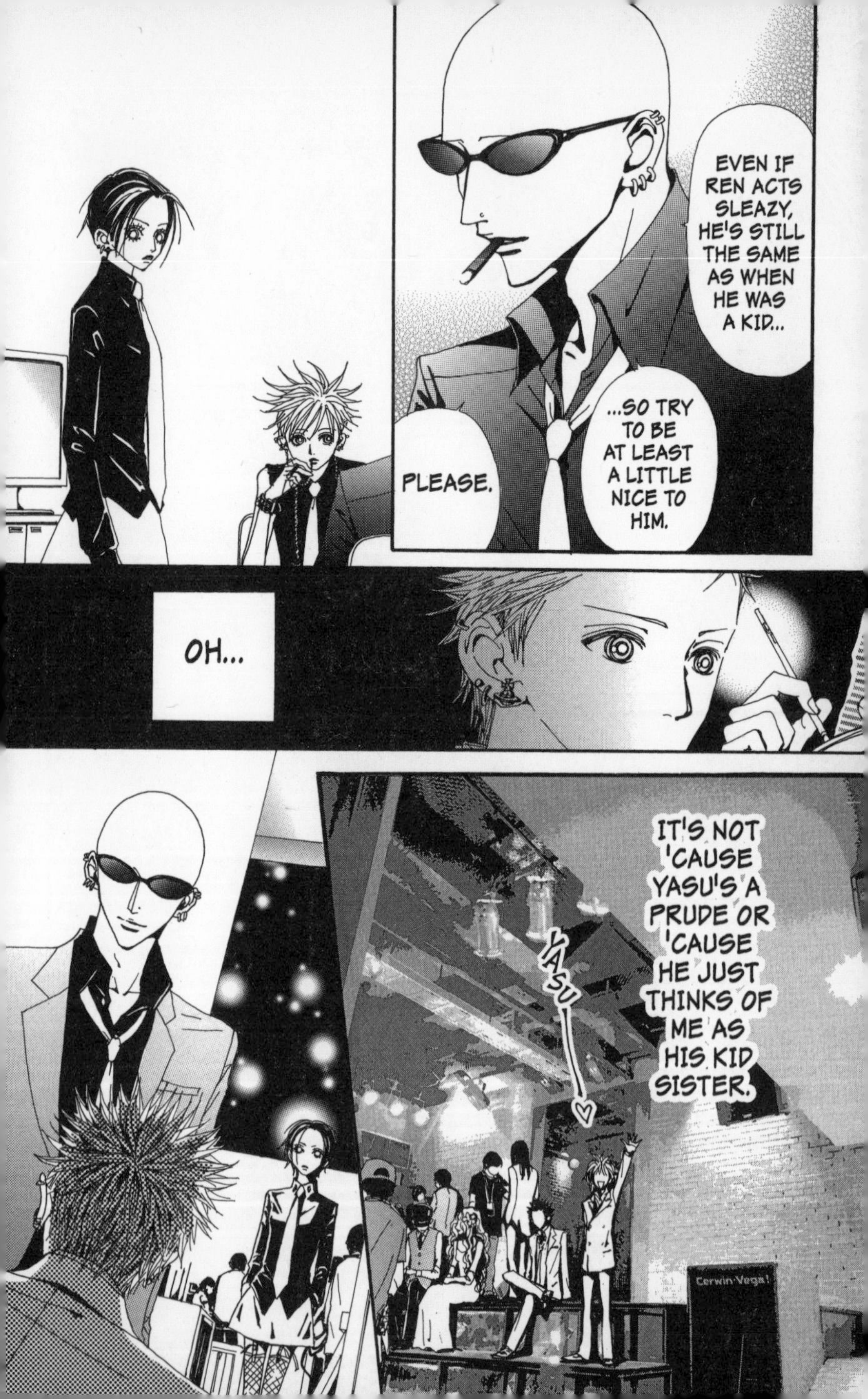
EVEN IF REN ACTS SLEAZY, HE'S STILL THE SAME AS WHEN HE WAS A KID...
...SO TRY TO BE AT LEAST A LITTLE NICE TO HIM.
PLEASE.
OH...
IT'S NOT 'CAUSE YASU'S A PRUDE OR 'CAUSE HE JUST THINKS OF ME AS HIS KID SISTER.
YASU ♥
Cerwin-Vega!

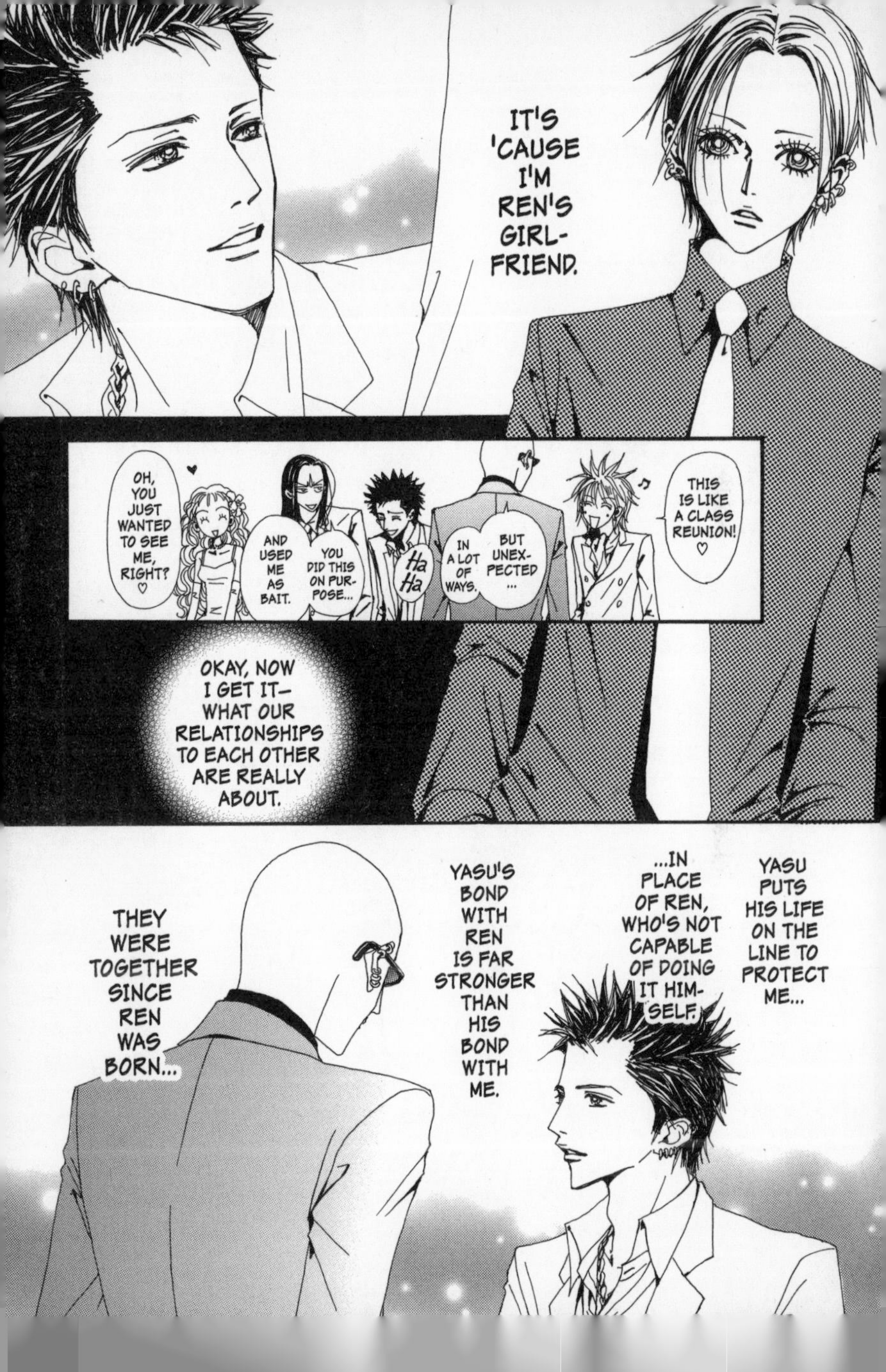
IT'S 'CAUSE I'M REN'S GIRL-FRIEND.
THIS IS LIKE A CLASS REUNION! ♡
BUT UNEX-PECTED ...
IN A LOT OF WAYS.
Ha Ha
YOU DID THIS ON PUR-POSE...
AND USED ME AS BAIT.
OH, YOU JUST WANTED TO SEE ME, RIGHT? ♡
OKAY, NOW I GET IT— WHAT OUR RELATIONSHIPS TO EACH OTHER ARE REALLY ABOUT.
YASU PUTS HIS LIFE ON THE LINE TO PROTECT ME...
...IN PLACE OF REN, WHO'S NOT CAPABLE OF DOING IT HIM-SELF.
YASU'S BOND WITH REN IS FAR STRONGER THAN HIS BOND WITH ME.
THEY WERE TOGETHER SINCE REN WAS BORN...

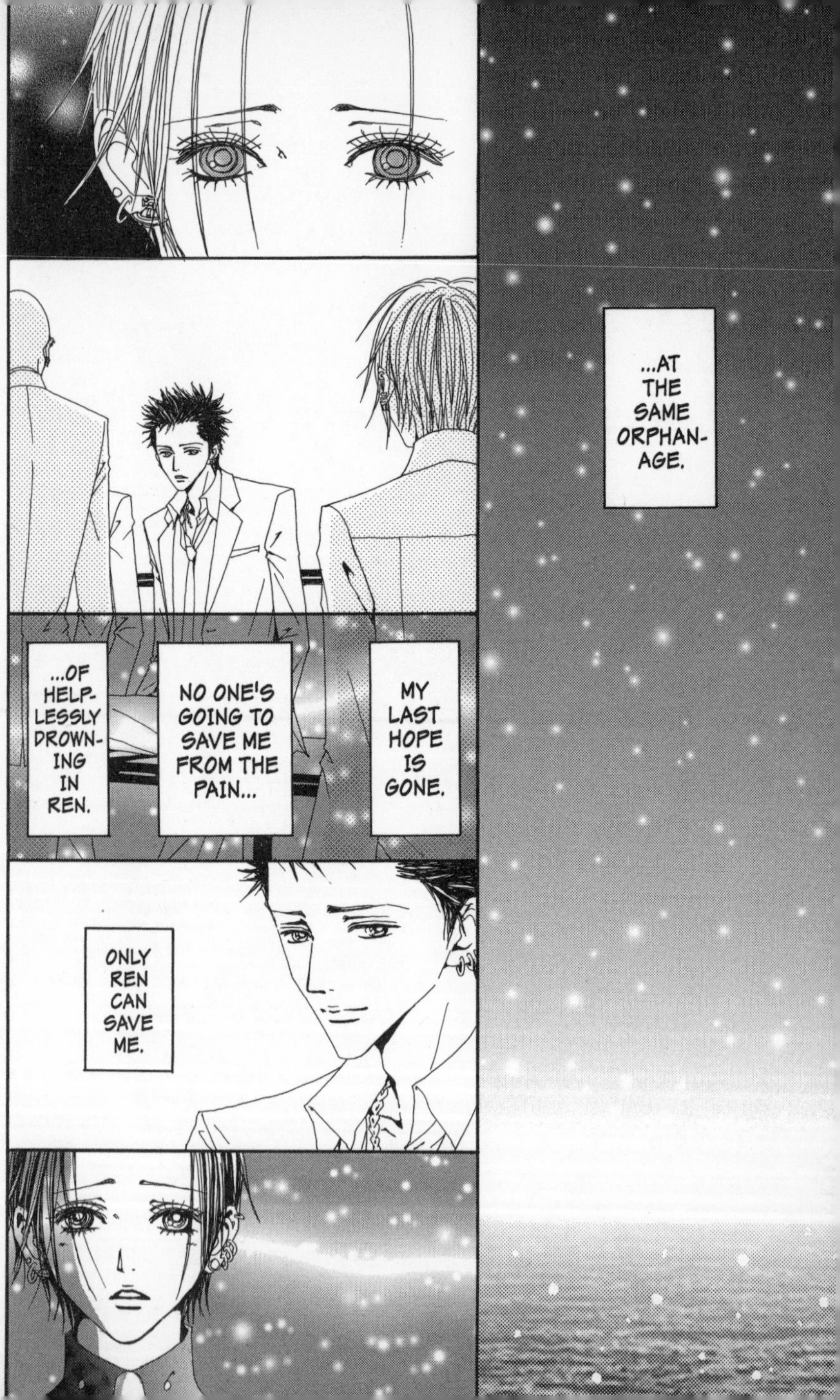
...AT THE SAME ORPHAN-AGE.
MY LAST HOPE IS GONE.
NO ONE'S GOING TO SAVE ME FROM THE PAIN...
...OF HELP-LESSLY DROWN-ING IN REN.
ONLY REN CAN SAVE ME.

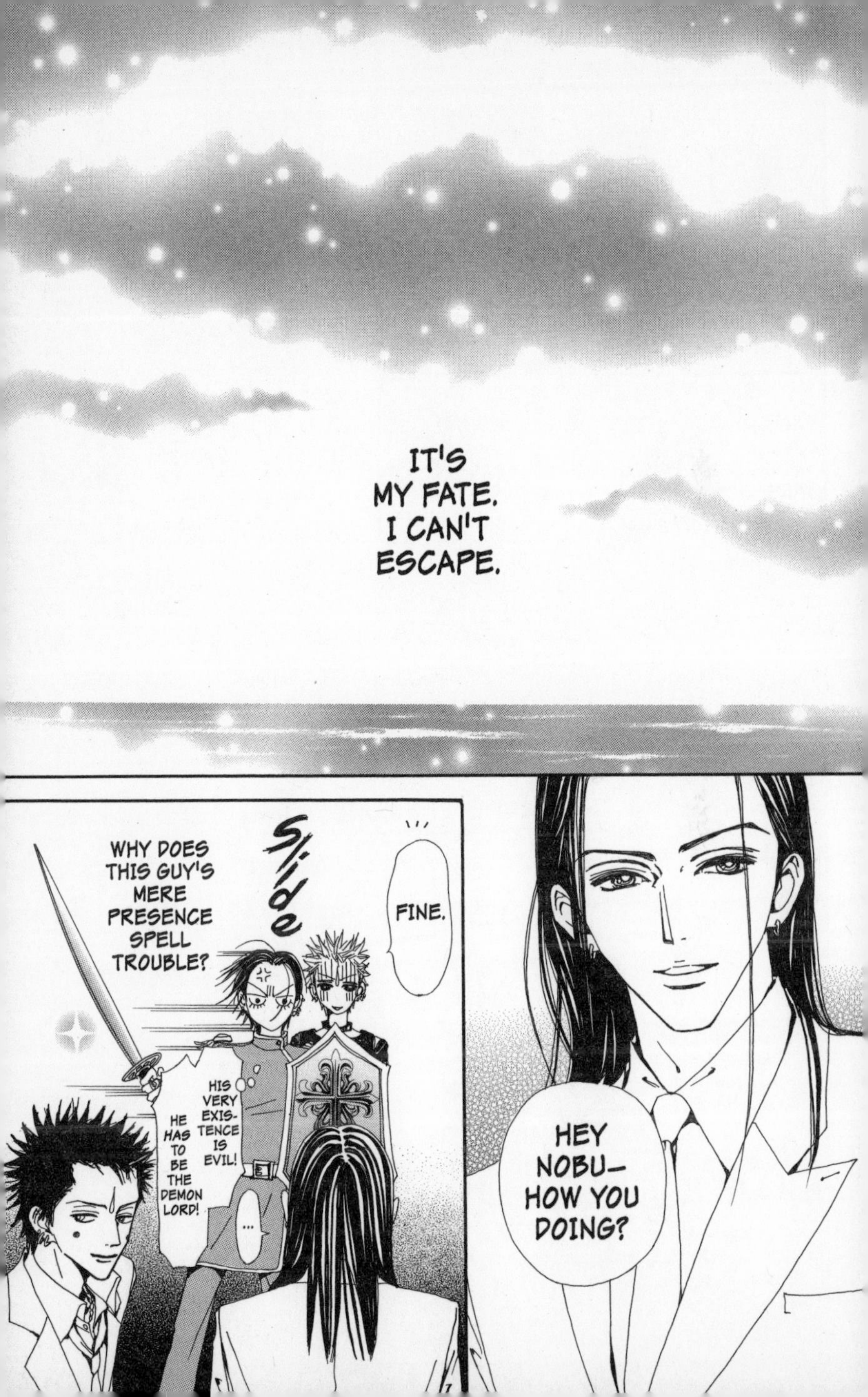
IT'S MY FATE. I CAN'T ESCAPE.
HEY NOBU— HOW YOU DOING?
FINE.
Slide
WHY DOES THIS GUY'S MERE PRESENCE SPELL TROUBLE?
HIS VERY EXISTENCE IS EVIL!
HE HAS TO BE THE DEMON LORD!
...

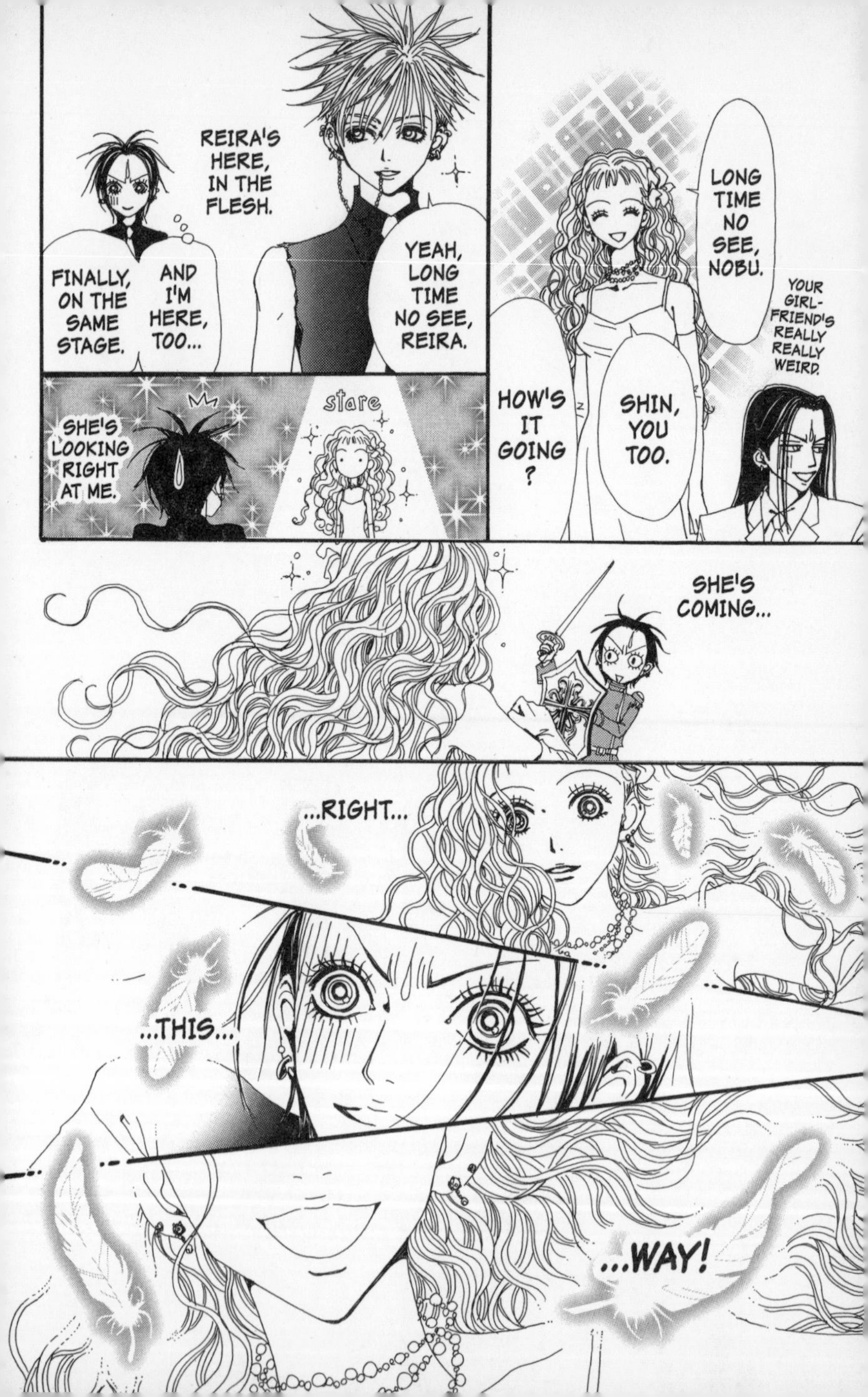

LONG TIME NO SEE, NOBU.
YOUR GIRL-FRIEND'S REALLY REALLY WEIRD.
SHIN, YOU TOO.
HOW'S IT GOING?
REIRA'S HERE, IN THE FLESH.
YEAH, LONG TIME NO SEE, REIRA.
AND I'M HERE, TOO...
FINALLY, ON THE SAME STAGE.
stare
SHE'S LOOKING RIGHT AT ME.
SHE'S COMING...
...RIGHT...
...THIS...
...WAY!

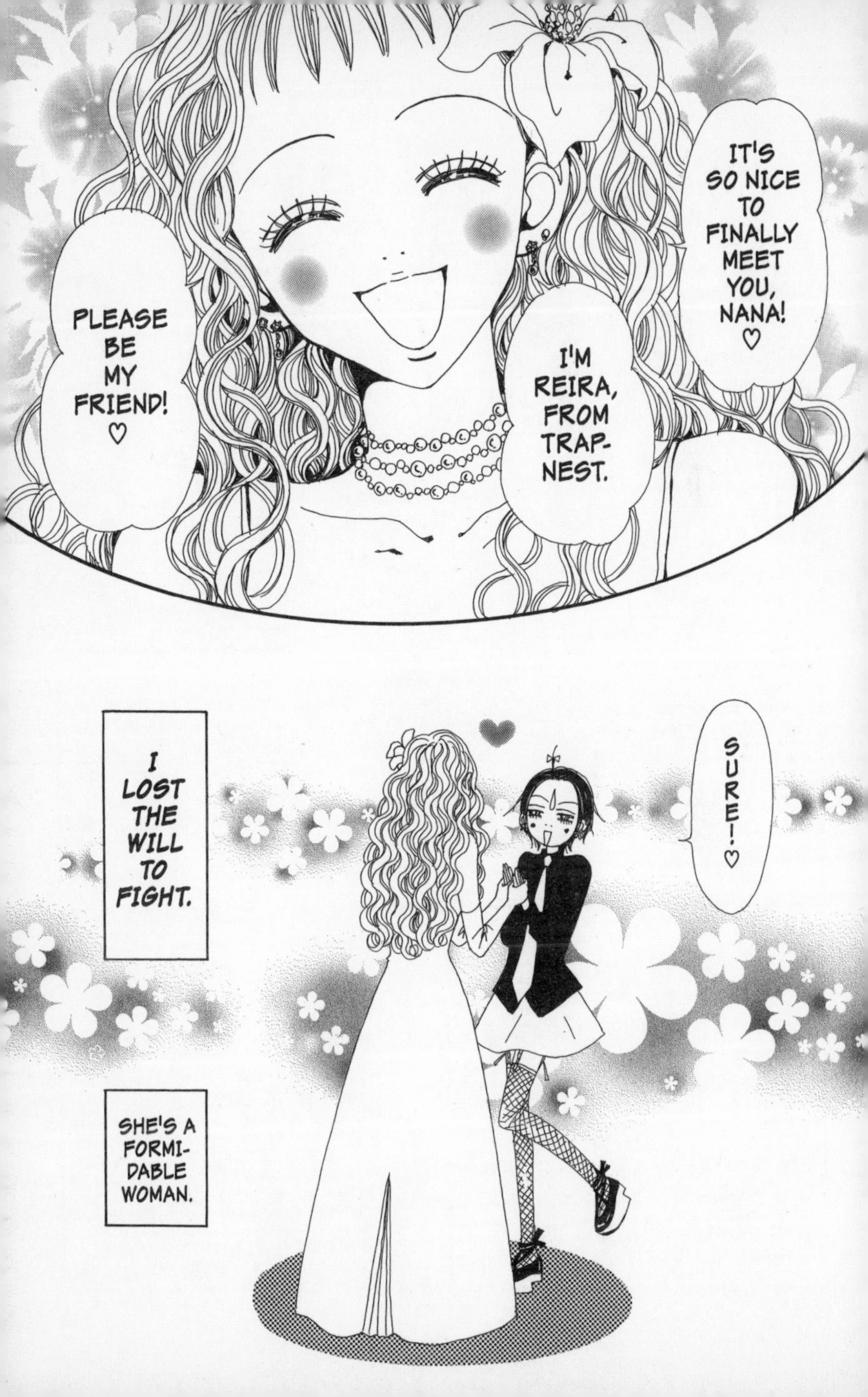
IT'S SO NICE TO FINALLY MEET YOU, NANA! ♡
I'M REIRA, FROM TRAP-NEST.
PLEASE BE MY FRIEND! ♡
SURE! ♡
I LOST THE WILL TO FIGHT.
SHE'S A FORMI-DABLE WOMAN.

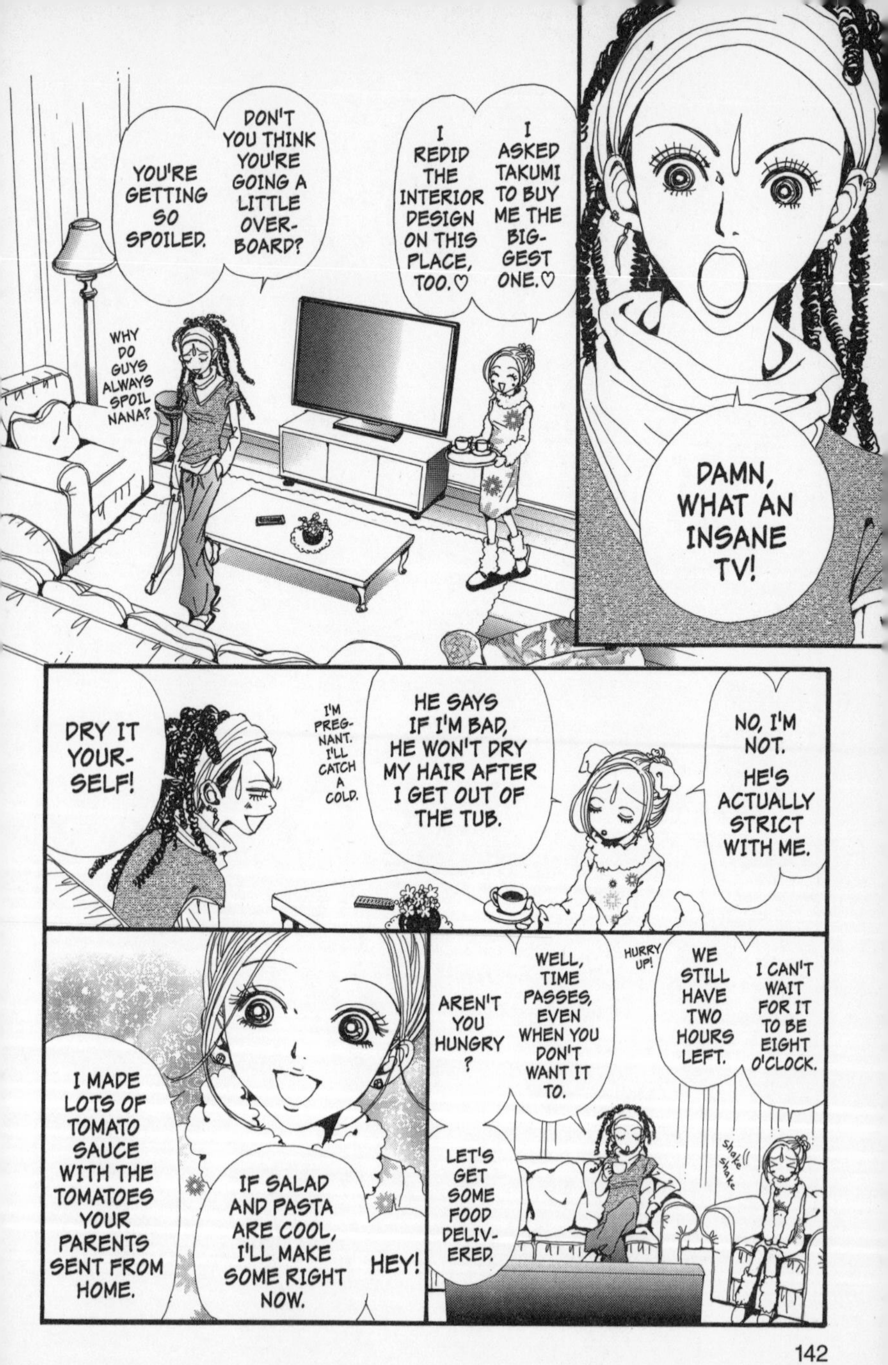
DAMN, WHAT AN INSANE TV!
I ASKED TAKUMI TO BUY ME THE BIGGEST ONE.♡
I REDID THE INTERIOR DESIGN ON THIS PLACE, TOO.♡
DON'T YOU THINK YOU'RE GOING A LITTLE OVERBOARD?
YOU'RE GETTING SO SPOILED.
WHY DO GUYS ALWAYS SPOIL NANA?
NO, I'M NOT.
HE'S ACTUALLY STRICT WITH ME.
HE SAYS IF I'M BAD, HE WON'T DRY MY HAIR AFTER I GET OUT OF THE TUB.
I'M PREGNANT. I'LL CATCH A COLD.
DRY IT YOURSELF!
I CAN'T WAIT FOR IT TO BE EIGHT O'CLOCK.
WE STILL HAVE TWO HOURS LEFT.
HURRY UP!
WELL, TIME PASSES, EVEN WHEN YOU DON'T WANT IT TO.
AREN'T YOU HUNGRY?
LET'S GET SOME FOOD DELIVERED.
shake shake
HEY!
IF SALAD AND PASTA ARE COOL, I'LL MAKE SOME RIGHT NOW.
I MADE LOTS OF TOMATO SAUCE WITH THE TOMATOES YOUR PARENTS SENT FROM HOME.

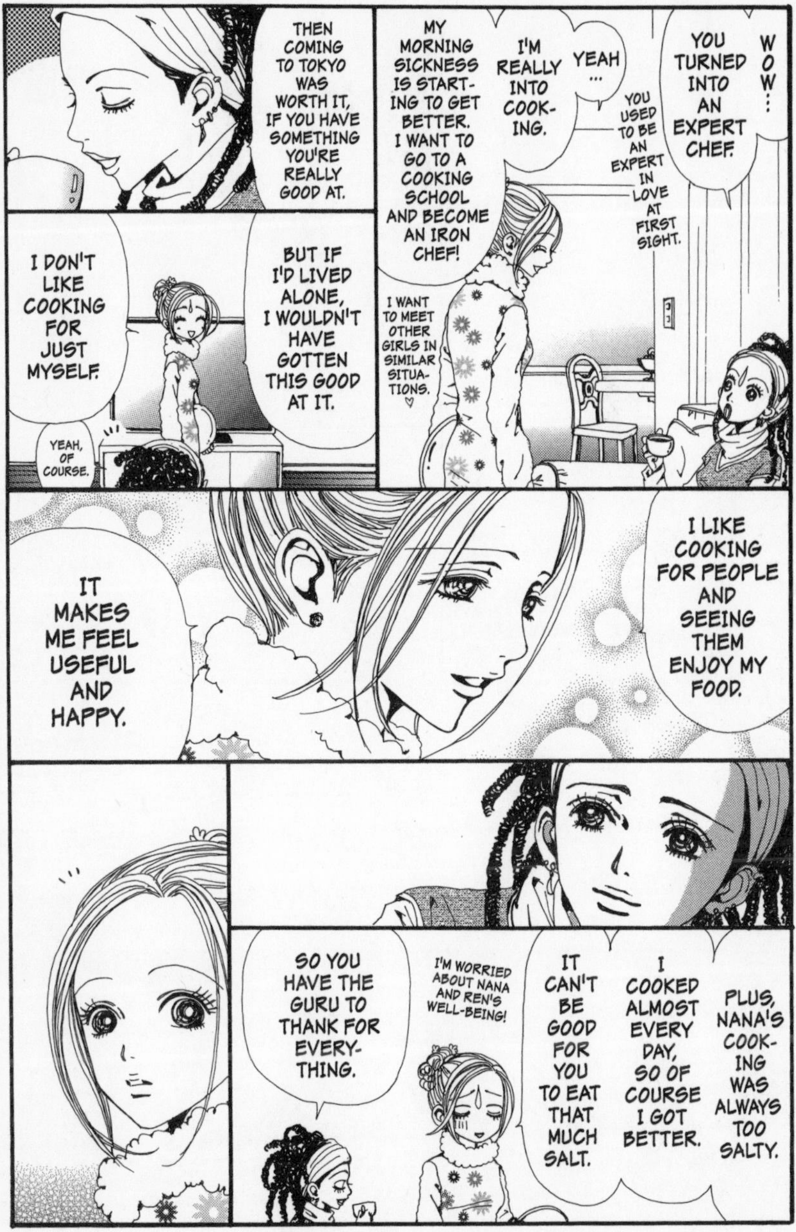
WOW...
YOU TURNED INTO AN EXPERT CHEF.
YOU USED TO BE AN EXPERT IN LOVE AT FIRST SIGHT.
YEAH...
I'M REALLY INTO COOKING.
MY MORNING SICKNESS IS STARTING TO GET BETTER. I WANT TO GO TO A COOKING SCHOOL AND BECOME AN IRON CHEF!
I WANT TO MEET OTHER GIRLS IN SIMILAR SITUATIONS. ♡
THEN COMING TO TOKYO WAS WORTH IT, IF YOU HAVE SOMETHING YOU'RE REALLY GOOD AT.
BUT IF I'D LIVED ALONE, I WOULDN'T HAVE GOTTEN THIS GOOD AT IT.
I DON'T LIKE COOKING FOR JUST MYSELF.
YEAH, OF COURSE.
I LIKE COOKING FOR PEOPLE AND SEEING THEM ENJOY MY FOOD.
IT MAKES ME FEEL USEFUL AND HAPPY.
PLUS, NANA'S COOKING WAS ALWAYS TOO SALTY.
I COOKED ALMOST EVERY DAY, SO OF COURSE I GOT BETTER.
IT CAN'T BE GOOD FOR YOU TO EAT THAT MUCH SALT.
I'M WORRIED ABOUT NANA AND REN'S WELL-BEING!
SO YOU HAVE THE GURU TO THANK FOR EVERYTHING.

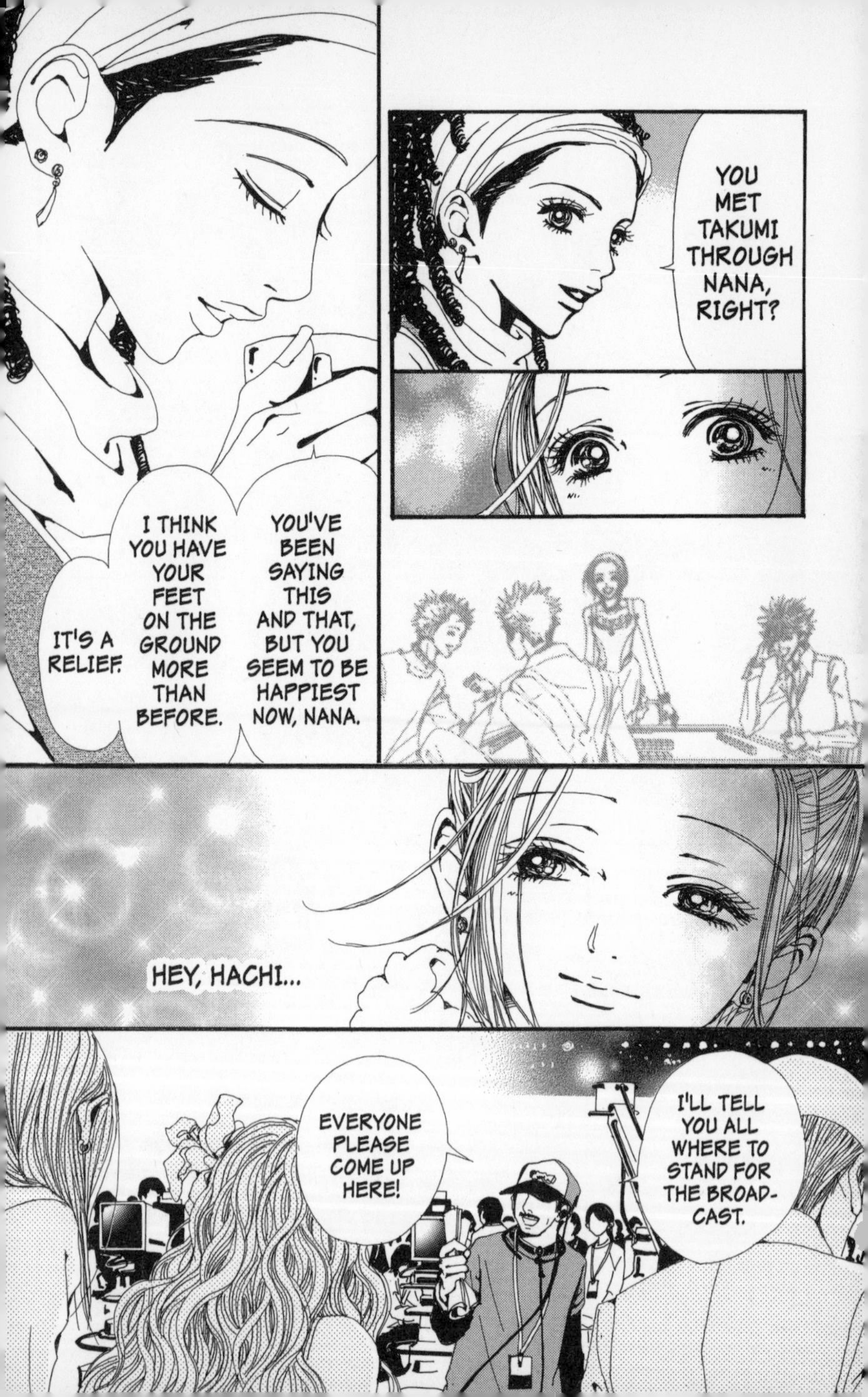
YOU MET TAKUMI THROUGH NANA, RIGHT?
YOU'VE BEEN SAYING THIS AND THAT, BUT YOU SEEM TO BE HAPPIEST NOW, NANA.
I THINK YOU HAVE YOUR FEET ON THE GROUND MORE THAN BEFORE.
IT'S A RELIEF.
HEY, HACHI...
I'LL TELL YOU ALL WHERE TO STAND FOR THE BROAD-CAST.
EVERYONE PLEASE COME UP HERE!

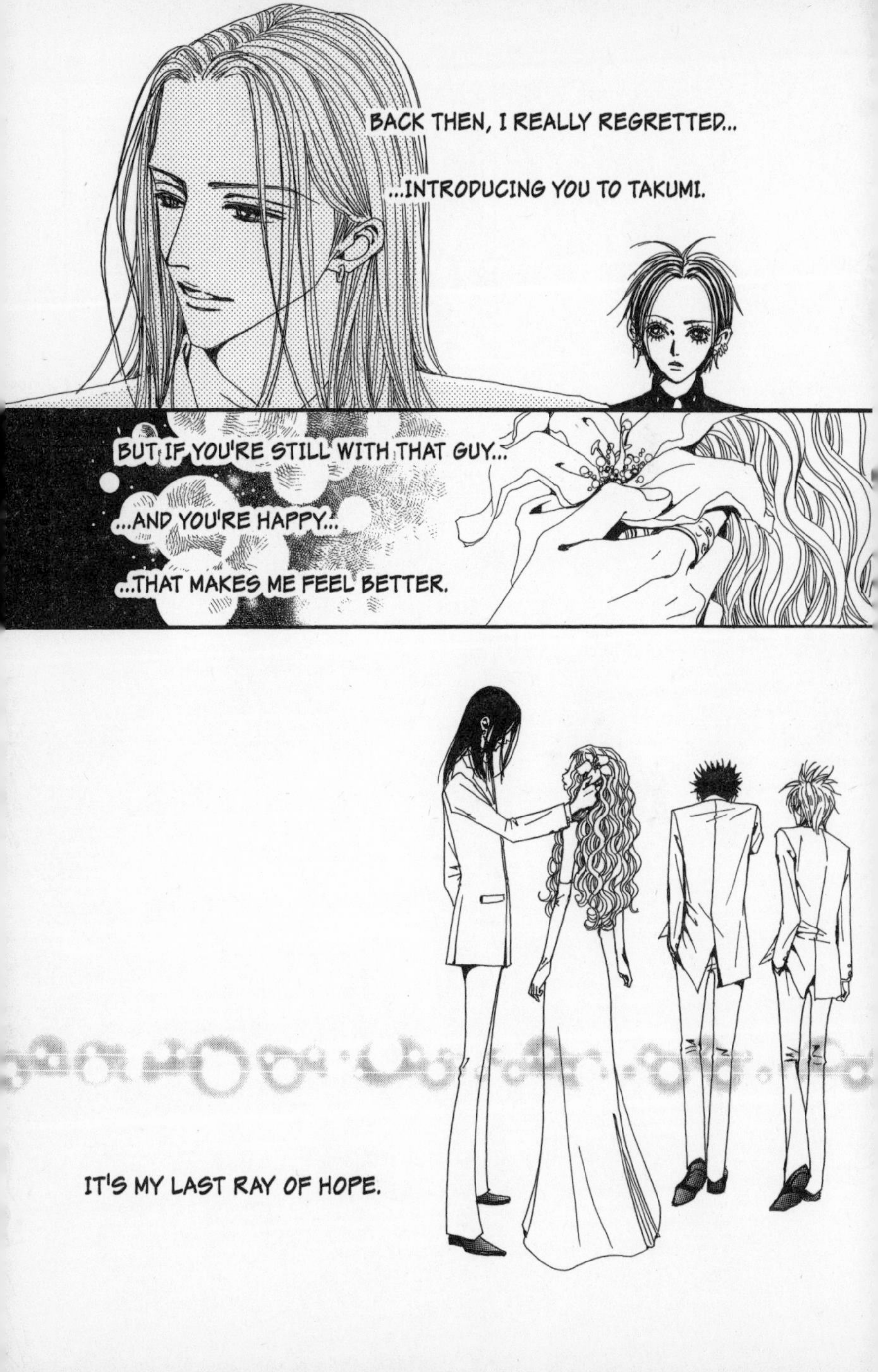
BACK THEN, I REALLY REGRETTED...
...INTRODUCING YOU TO TAKUMI.
BUT IF YOU'RE STILL WITH THAT GUY...
...AND YOU'RE HAPPY...
...THAT MAKES ME FEEL BETTER.
IT'S MY LAST RAY OF HOPE.

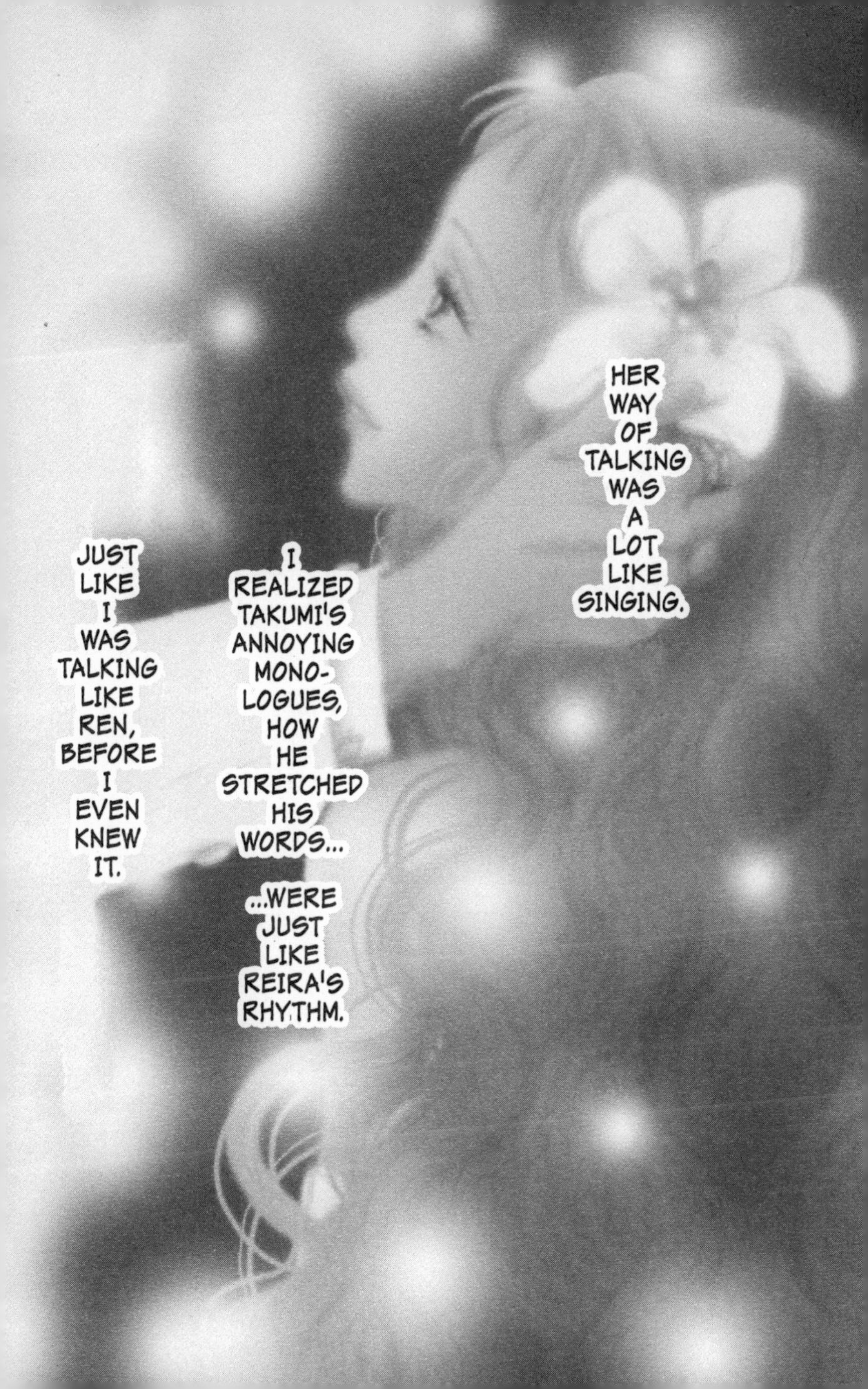
HER WAY OF TALKING WAS A LOT LIKE SINGING.
I REALIZED TAKUMI'S ANNOYING MONOLOGUES, HOW HE STRETCHED HIS WORDS...
...WERE JUST LIKE REIRA'S RHYTHM.
JUST LIKE I WAS TALKING LIKE REN, BEFORE I EVEN KNEW IT.

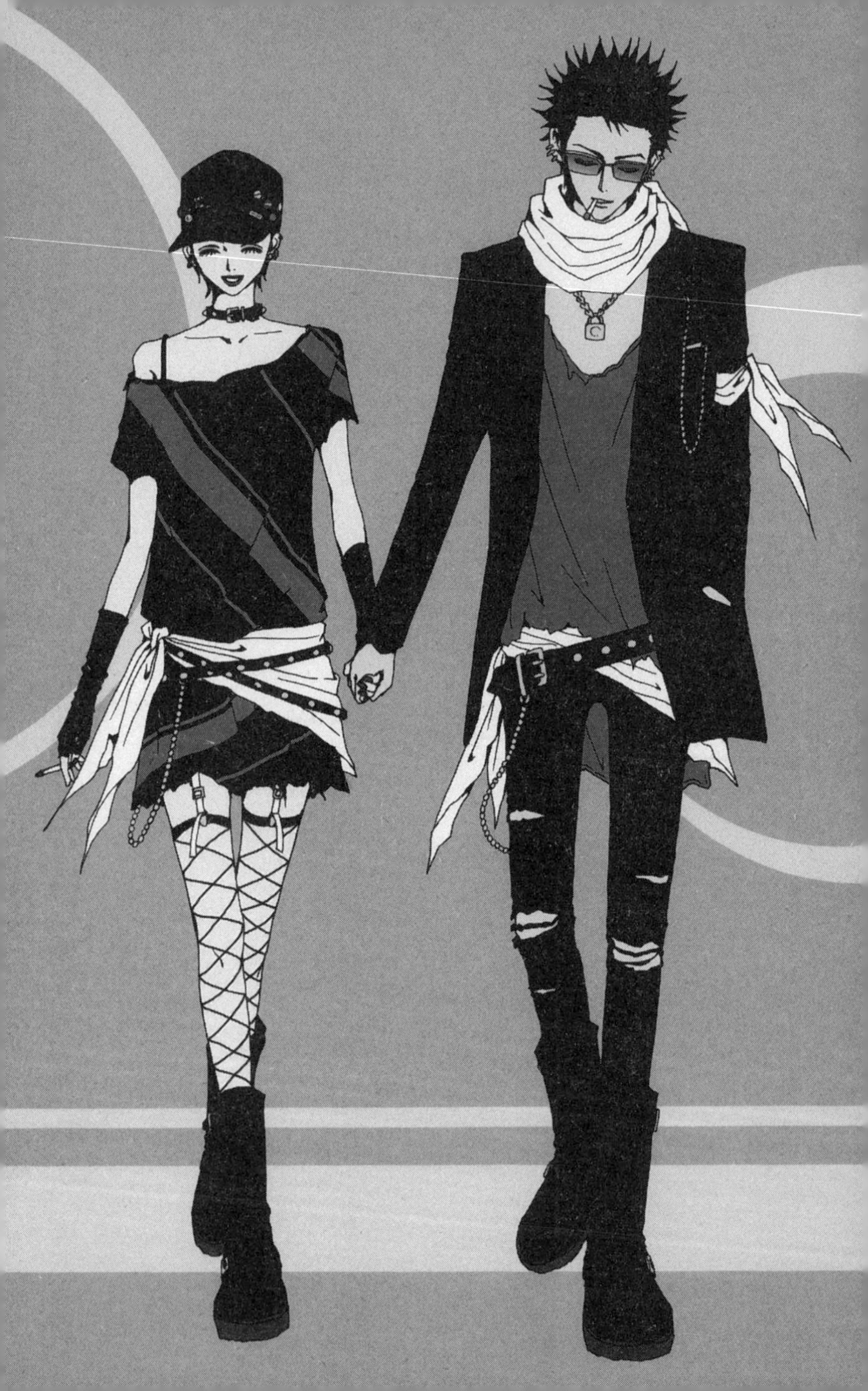

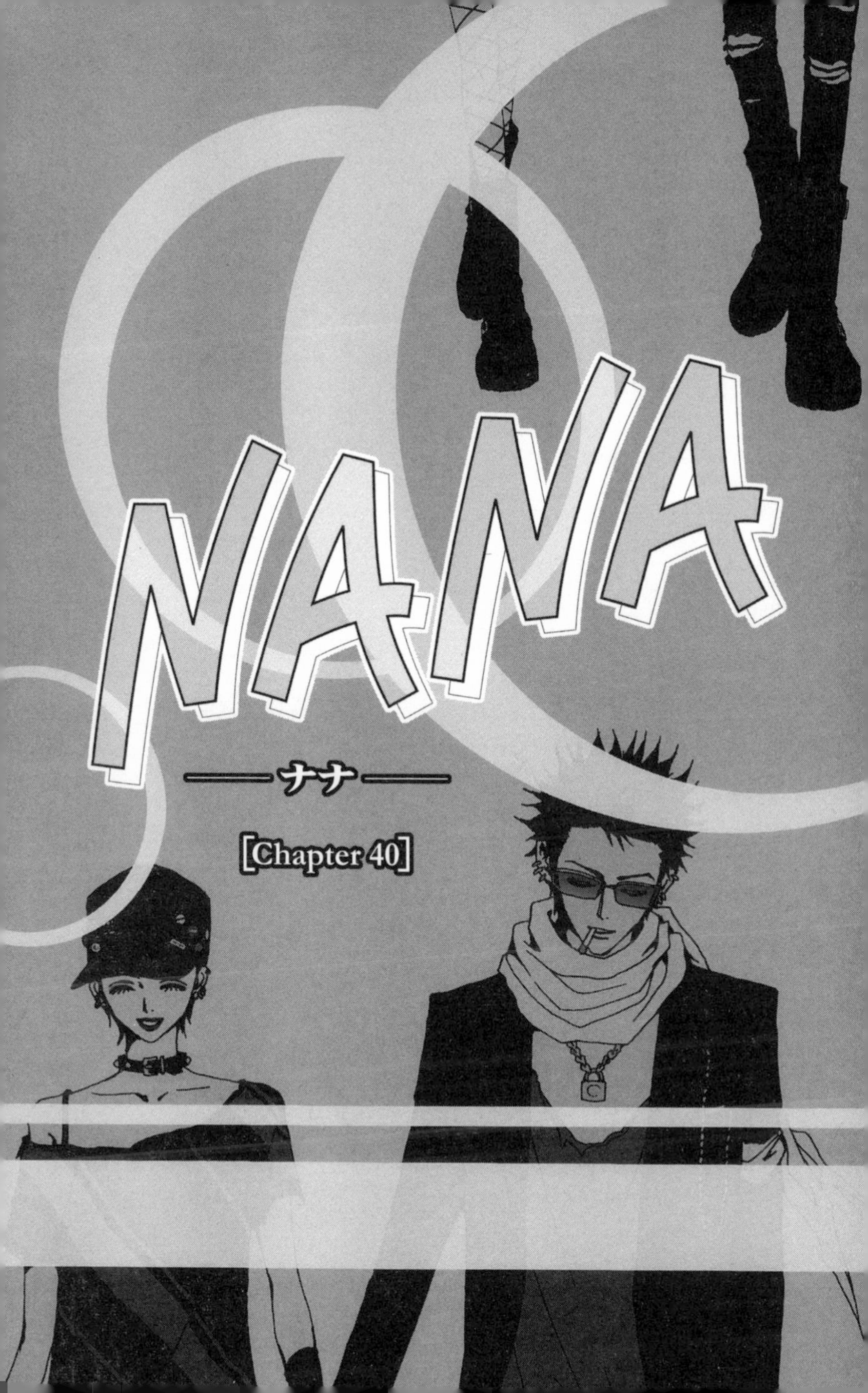
NANA
ナナ
[Chapter 40]

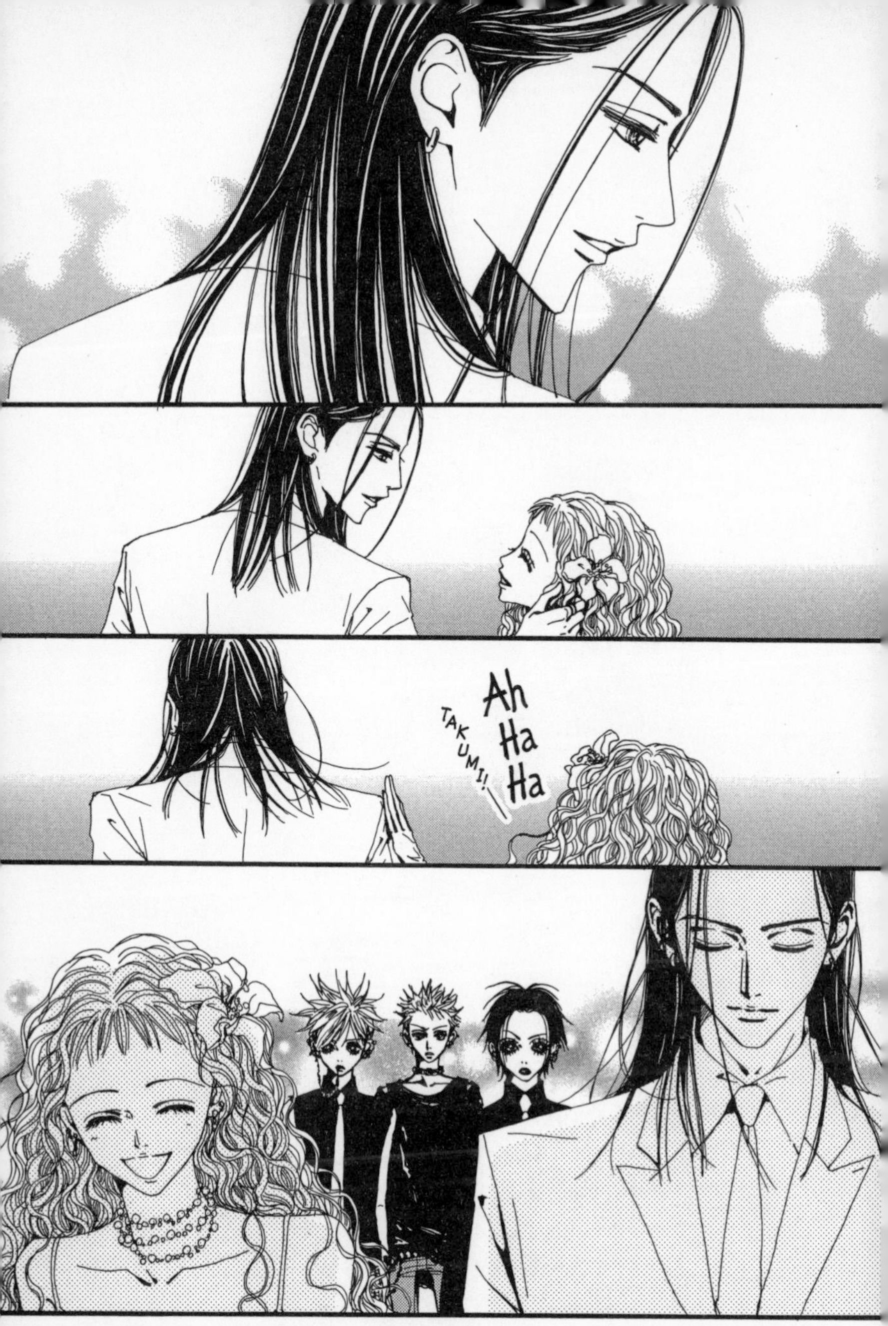

Ah Ha Ha
TAKUMI!

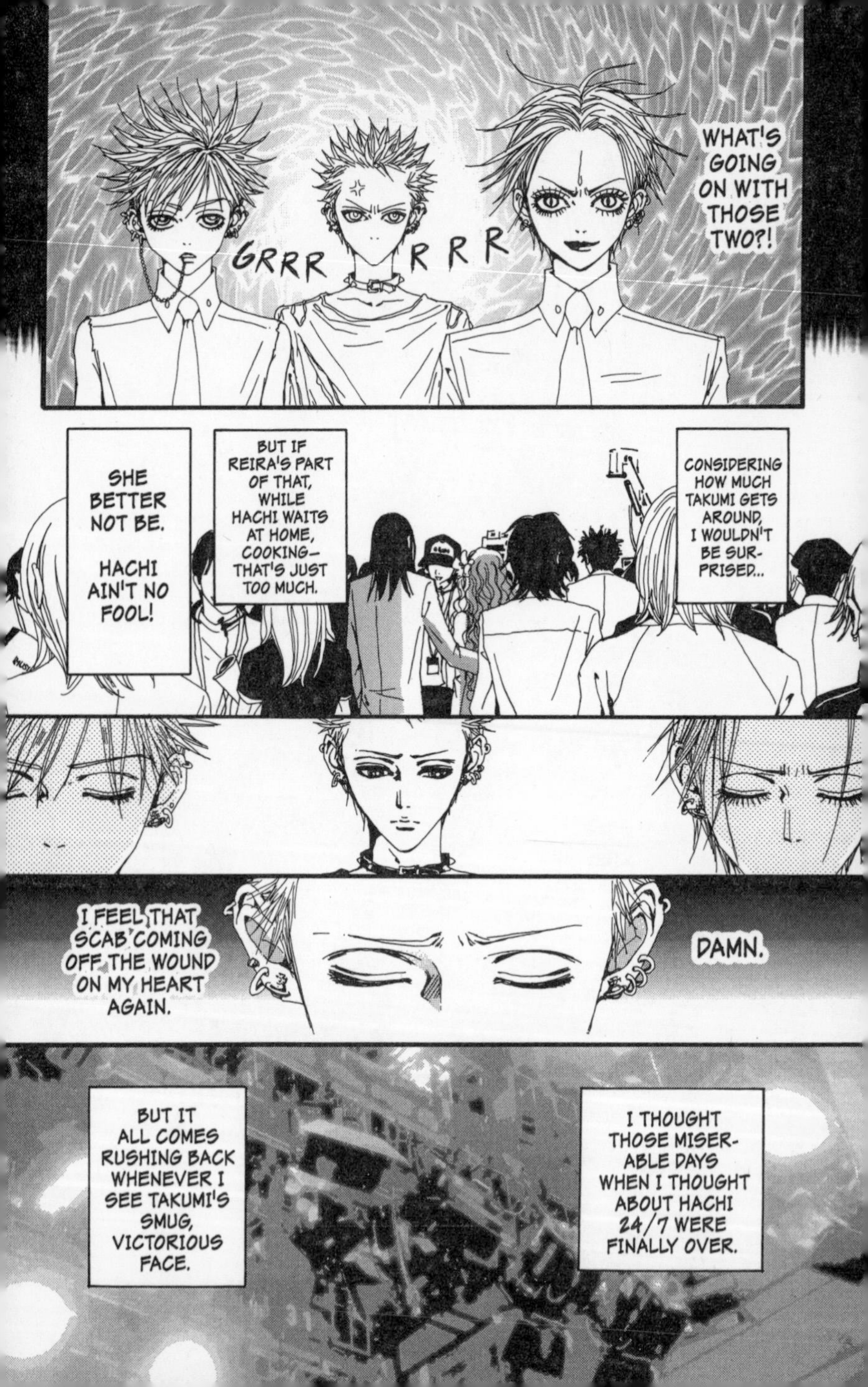
WHAT'S GOING ON WITH THOSE TWO?!
GRRR RRR
CONSIDERING HOW MUCH TAKUMI GETS AROUND, I WOULDN'T BE SURPRISED...
BUT IF REIRA'S PART OF THAT, WHILE HACHI WAITS AT HOME, COOKING—THAT'S JUST TOO MUCH.
SHE BETTER NOT BE.
HACHI AIN'T NO FOOL!
DAMN.
I FEEL THAT SCAB COMING OFF THE WOUND ON MY HEART AGAIN.
I THOUGHT THOSE MISERABLE DAYS WHEN I THOUGHT ABOUT HACHI 24/7 WERE FINALLY OVER.
BUT IT ALL COMES RUSHING BACK WHENEVER I SEE TAKUMI'S SMUG, VICTORIOUS FACE.

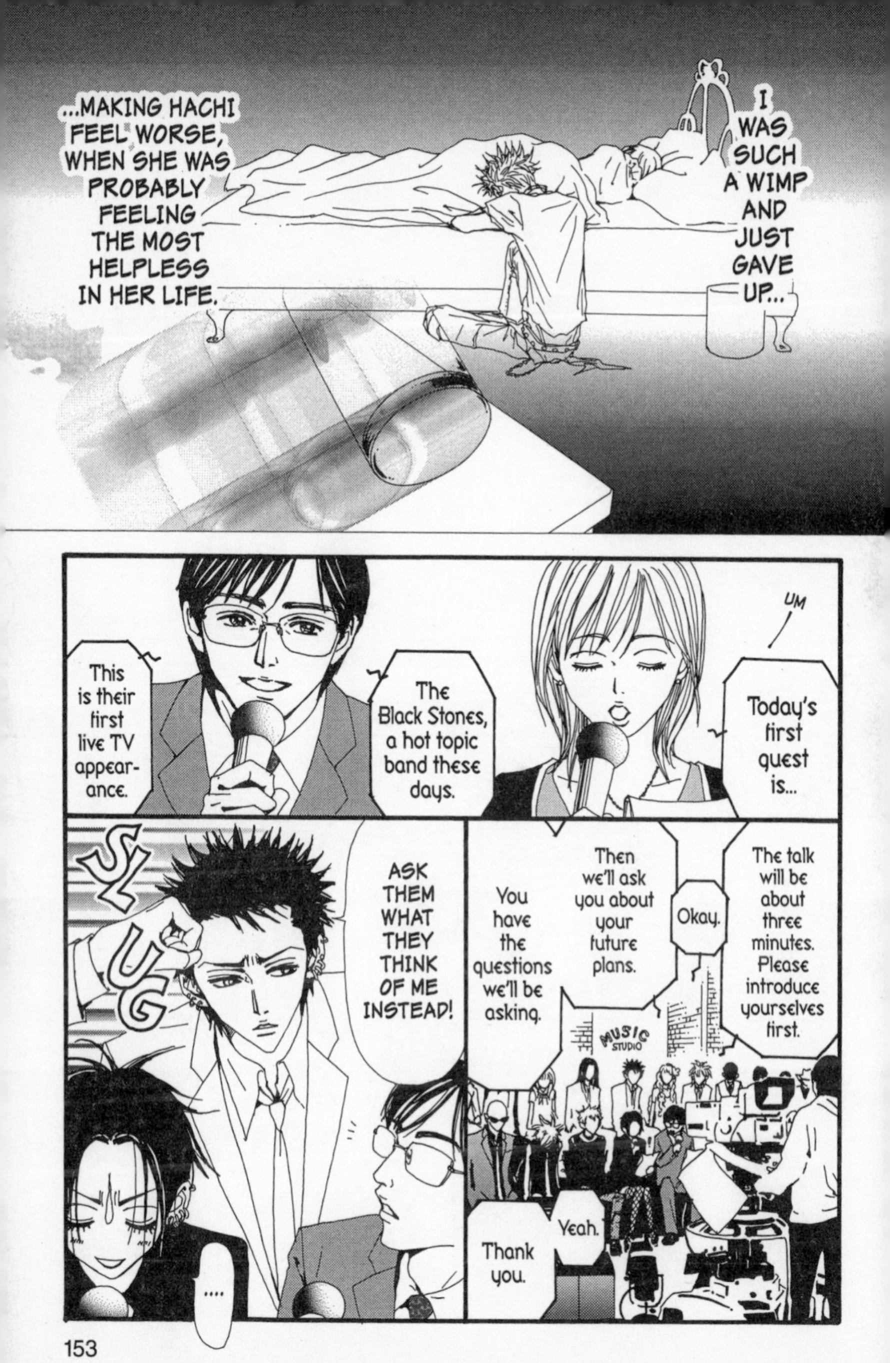
I WAS SUCH A WIMP AND JUST GAVE UP...
...MAKING HACHI FEEL WORSE, WHEN SHE WAS PROBABLY FEELING THE MOST HELPLESS IN HER LIFE.
UM
Today's first guest is...
The Black Stones, a hot topic band these days.
This is their first live TV appearance.
The talk will be about three minutes. Please introduce yourselves first.
Okay.
Then we'll ask you about your future plans.
You have the questions we'll be asking.
MUSIC STUDIO
Yeah.
Thank you.
ASK THEM WHAT THEY THINK OF ME INSTEAD!
SLUG
....

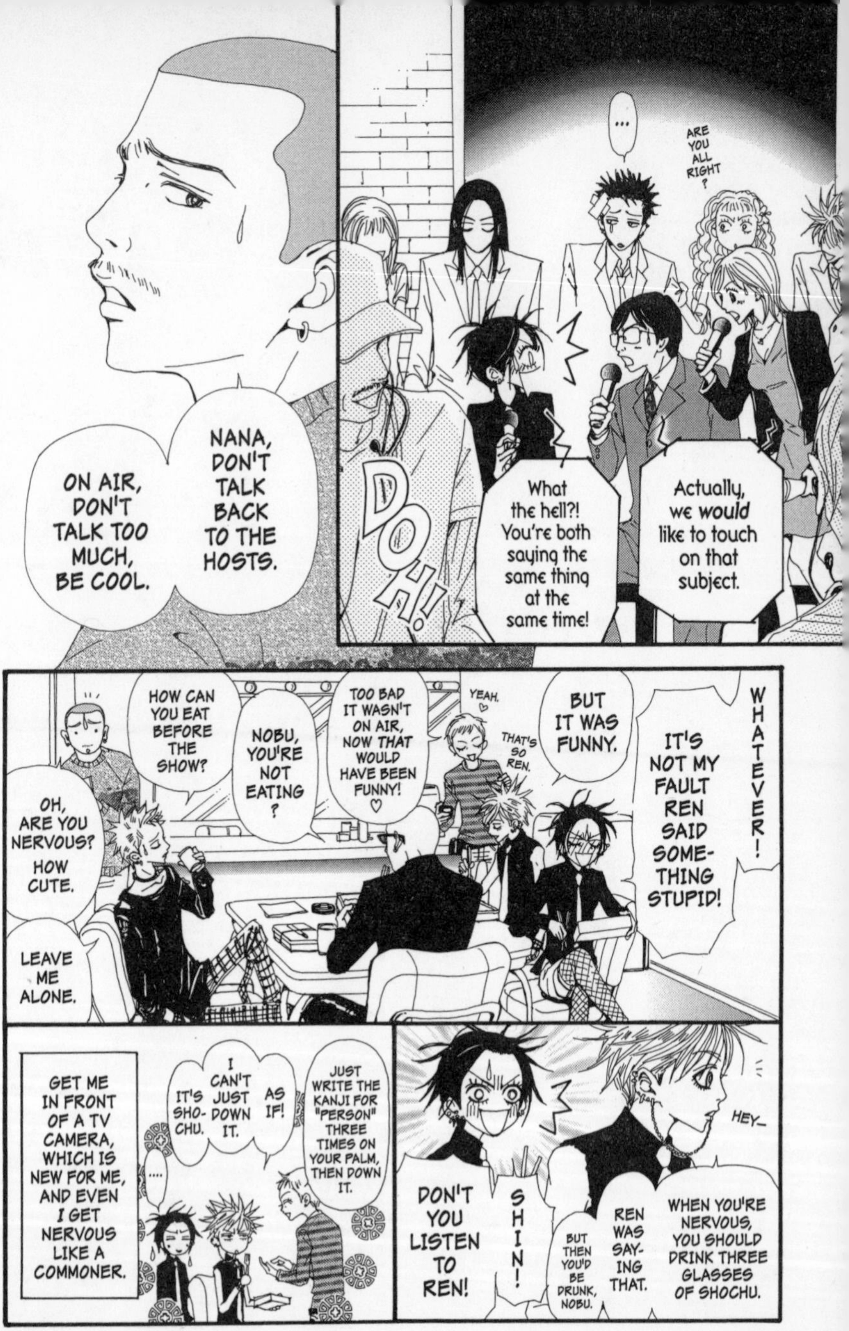
...
ARE YOU ALL RIGHT?
Actually, we would like to touch on that subject.
What the hell?! You're both saying the same thing at the same time!
DOH!
NANA, DON'T TALK BACK TO THE HOSTS.
ON AIR, DON'T TALK TOO MUCH, BE COOL.
WHATEVER!
IT'S NOT MY FAULT REN SAID SOME-THING STUPID!
BUT IT WAS FUNNY.
YEAH. ♡
THAT'S SO REN.
TOO BAD IT WASN'T ON AIR, NOW THAT WOULD HAVE BEEN FUNNY! ♡
NOBU, YOU'RE NOT EATING?
HOW CAN YOU EAT BEFORE THE SHOW?
OH, ARE YOU NERVOUS? HOW CUTE.
LEAVE ME ALONE.
HEY_
WHEN YOU'RE NERVOUS, YOU SHOULD DRINK THREE GLASSES OF SHOCHU.
REN WAS SAY-ING THAT.
BUT THEN YOU'D BE DRUNK, NOBU.
SHIN!
DON'T YOU LISTEN TO REN!
JUST WRITE THE KANJI FOR "PERSON" THREE TIMES ON YOUR PALM, THEN DOWN IT.
AS IF!
I CAN'T JUST DOWN IT.
IT'S SHO-CHU.
....
GET ME IN FRONT OF A TV CAMERA, WHICH IS NEW FOR ME, AND EVEN I GET NERVOUS LIKE A COMMONER.

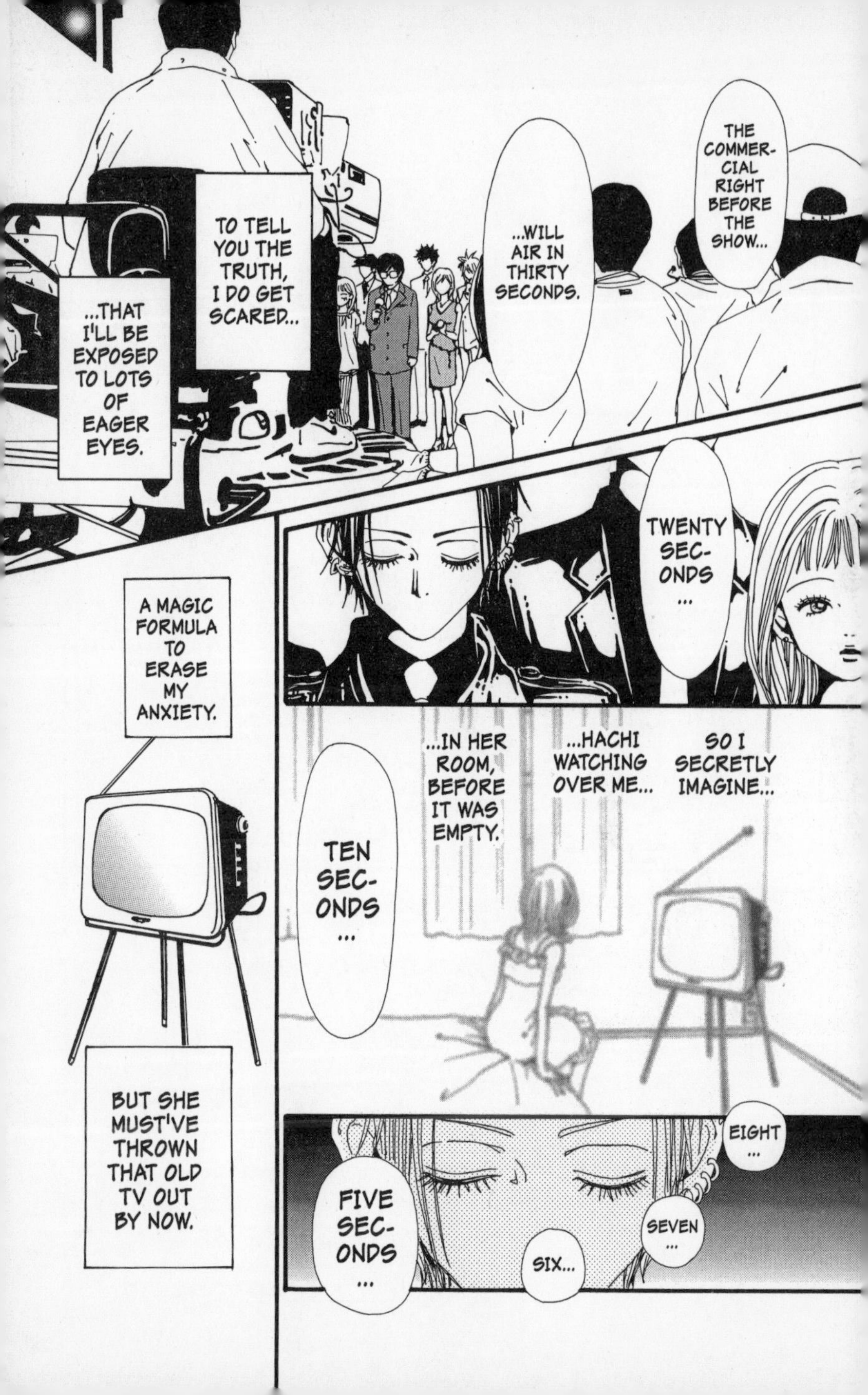
THE COMMERCIAL RIGHT BEFORE THE SHOW...
...WILL AIR IN THIRTY SECONDS.
TO TELL YOU THE TRUTH, I DO GET SCARED...
...THAT I'LL BE EXPOSED TO LOTS OF EAGER EYES.
TWENTY SECONDS...
SO I SECRETLY IMAGINE...
...HACHI WATCHING OVER ME...
...IN HER ROOM, BEFORE IT WAS EMPTY.
TEN SECONDS...
EIGHT...
SEVEN...
SIX...
FIVE SECONDS...
A MAGIC FORMULA TO ERASE MY ANXIETY.
BUT SHE MUST'VE THROWN THAT OLD TV OUT BY NOW.

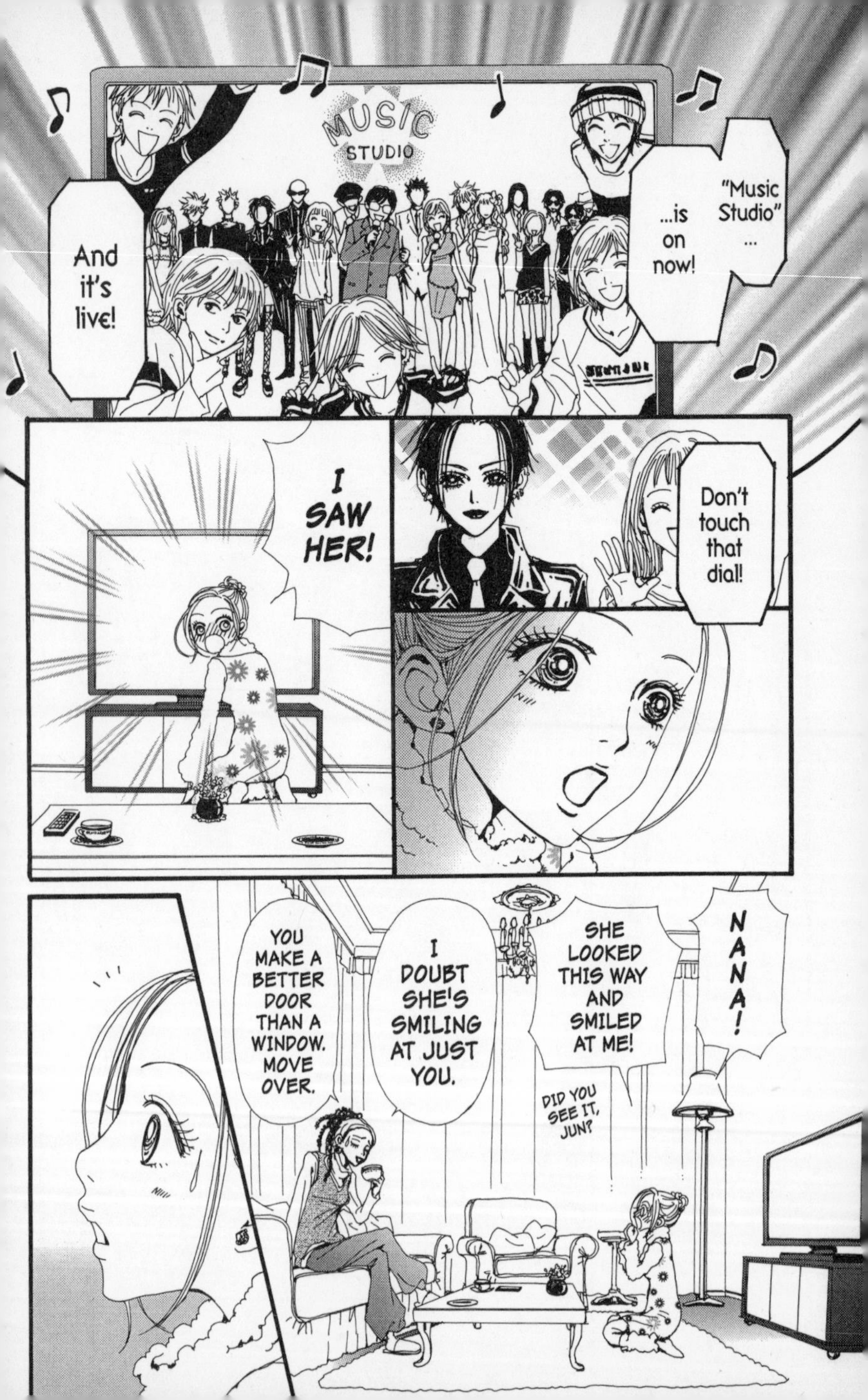
"Music Studio"...
...is on now!
MUSIC STUDIO
And it's live!
Don't touch that dial!
I SAW HER!
NANA!
SHE LOOKED THIS WAY AND SMILED AT ME!
DID YOU SEE IT, JUN?
I DOUBT SHE'S SMILING AT JUST YOU.
YOU MAKE A BETTER DOOR THAN A WINDOW. MOVE OVER.

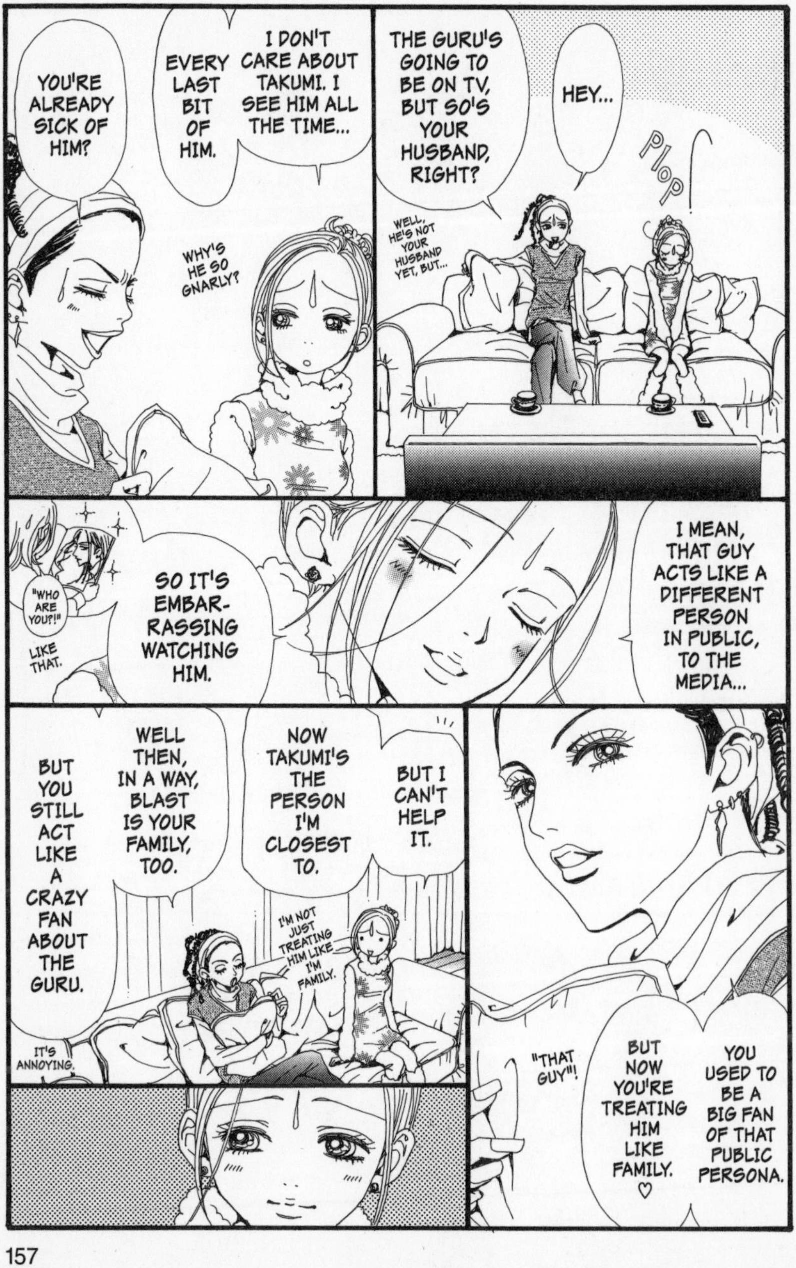
HEY...
PLOP
THE GURU'S GOING TO BE ON TV, BUT SO'S YOUR HUSBAND, RIGHT?
WELL, HE'S NOT YOUR HUSBAND YET, BUT...
I DON'T CARE ABOUT TAKUMI. I SEE HIM ALL THE TIME...
EVERY LAST BIT OF HIM.
YOU'RE ALREADY SICK OF HIM?
WHY'S HE SO GNARLY?
I MEAN, THAT GUY ACTS LIKE A DIFFERENT PERSON IN PUBLIC, TO THE MEDIA...
SO IT'S EMBAR-RASSING WATCHING HIM.
"WHO ARE YOU?!"
LIKE THAT.
YOU USED TO BE A BIG FAN OF THAT PUBLIC PERSONA.
BUT NOW YOU'RE TREATING HIM LIKE FAMILY. ♡
"THAT GUY"!
BUT I CAN'T HELP IT.
NOW TAKUMI'S THE PERSON I'M CLOSEST TO.
WELL THEN, IN A WAY, BLAST IS YOUR FAMILY, TOO.
BUT YOU STILL ACT LIKE A CRAZY FAN ABOUT THE GURU.
I'M NOT JUST TREATING HIM LIKE I'M FAMILY.
IT'S ANNOYING.

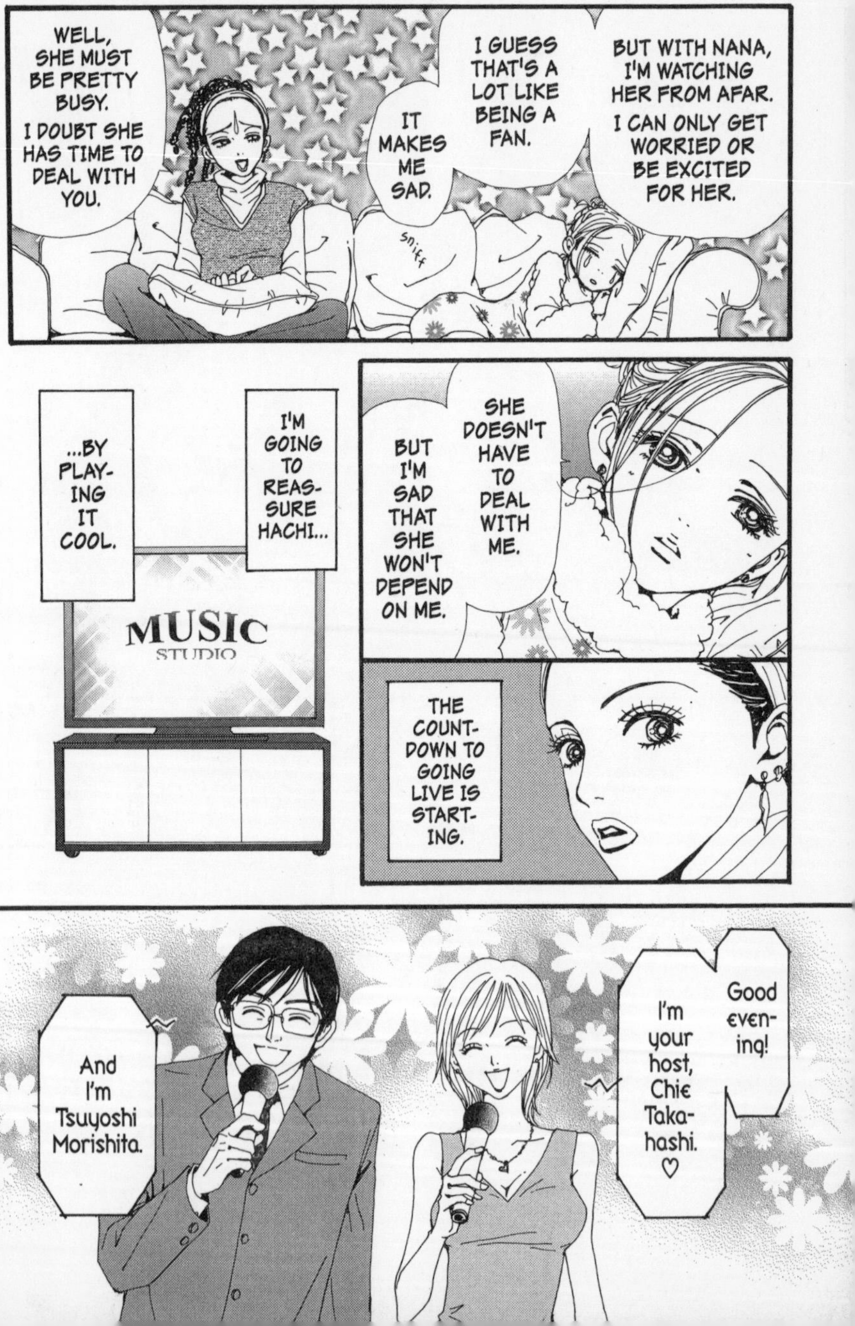
BUT WITH NANA, I'M WATCHING HER FROM AFAR. I CAN ONLY GET WORRIED OR BE EXCITED FOR HER.
I GUESS THAT'S A LOT LIKE BEING A FAN.
IT MAKES ME SAD.
sniff
WELL, SHE MUST BE PRETTY BUSY. I DOUBT SHE HAS TIME TO DEAL WITH YOU.
SHE DOESN'T HAVE TO DEAL WITH ME.
BUT I'M SAD THAT SHE WON'T DEPEND ON ME.
THE COUNTDOWN TO GOING LIVE IS STARTING.
I'M GOING TO REASSURE HACHI...
...BY PLAYING IT COOL.
MUSIC
STUDIO
Good evening!
I'm your host, Chie Takahashi. ♡
And I'm Tsuyoshi Morishita.

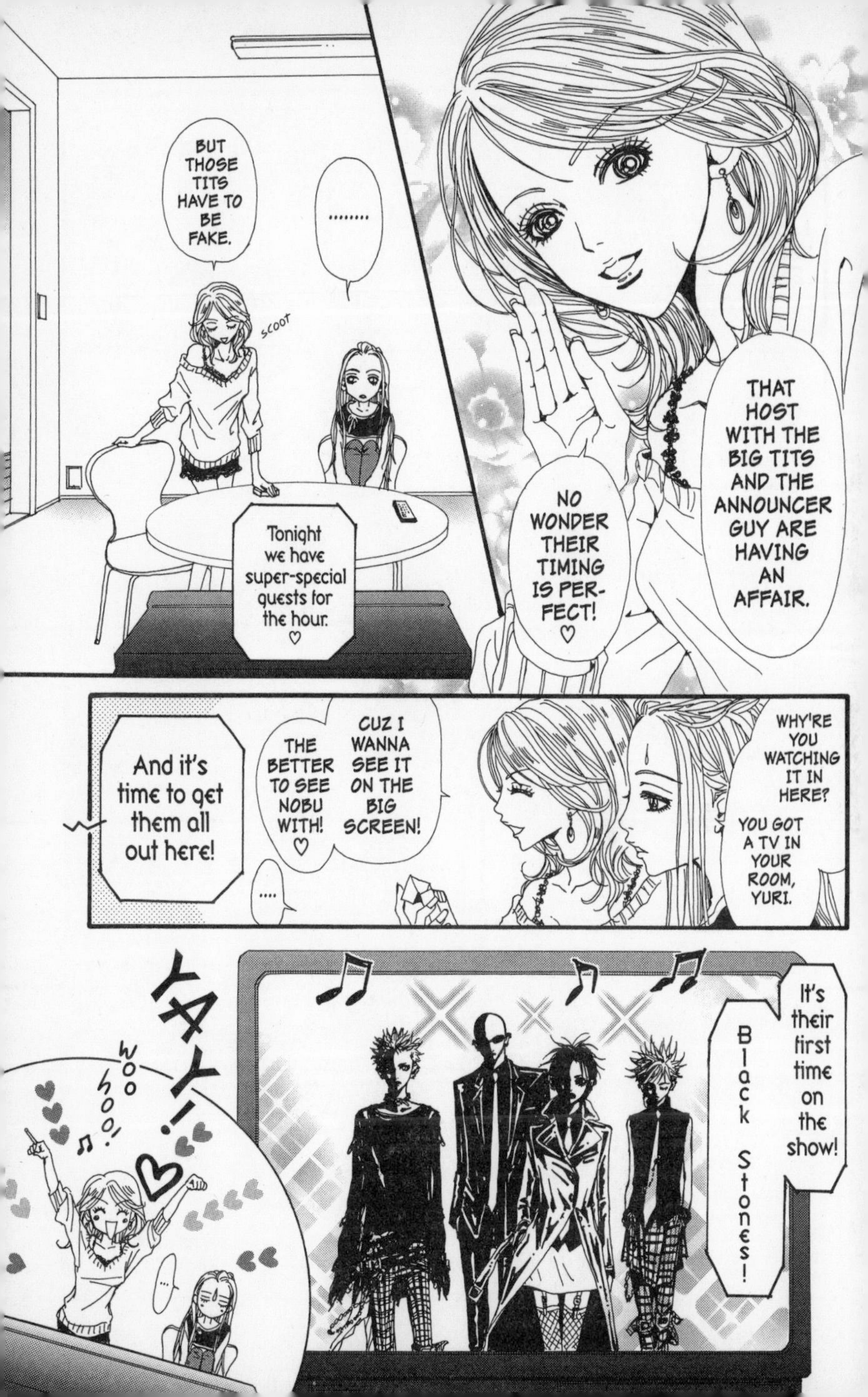
THAT HOST WITH THE BIG TITS AND THE ANNOUNCER GUY ARE HAVING AN AFFAIR.
NO WONDER THEIR TIMING IS PER-FECT! ♡
BUT THOSE TITS HAVE TO BE FAKE.
....
SCOOT
Tonight we have super-special guests for the hour. ♡
WHY'RE YOU WATCHING IT IN HERE?
YOU GOT A TV IN YOUR ROOM, YURI.
CUZ I WANNA SEE IT ON THE BIG SCREEN!
THE BETTER TO SEE NOBU WITH! ♡
....
And it's time to get them all out here!
It's their first time on the show!
Black Stones!
YAY!
WOO HOO!
....

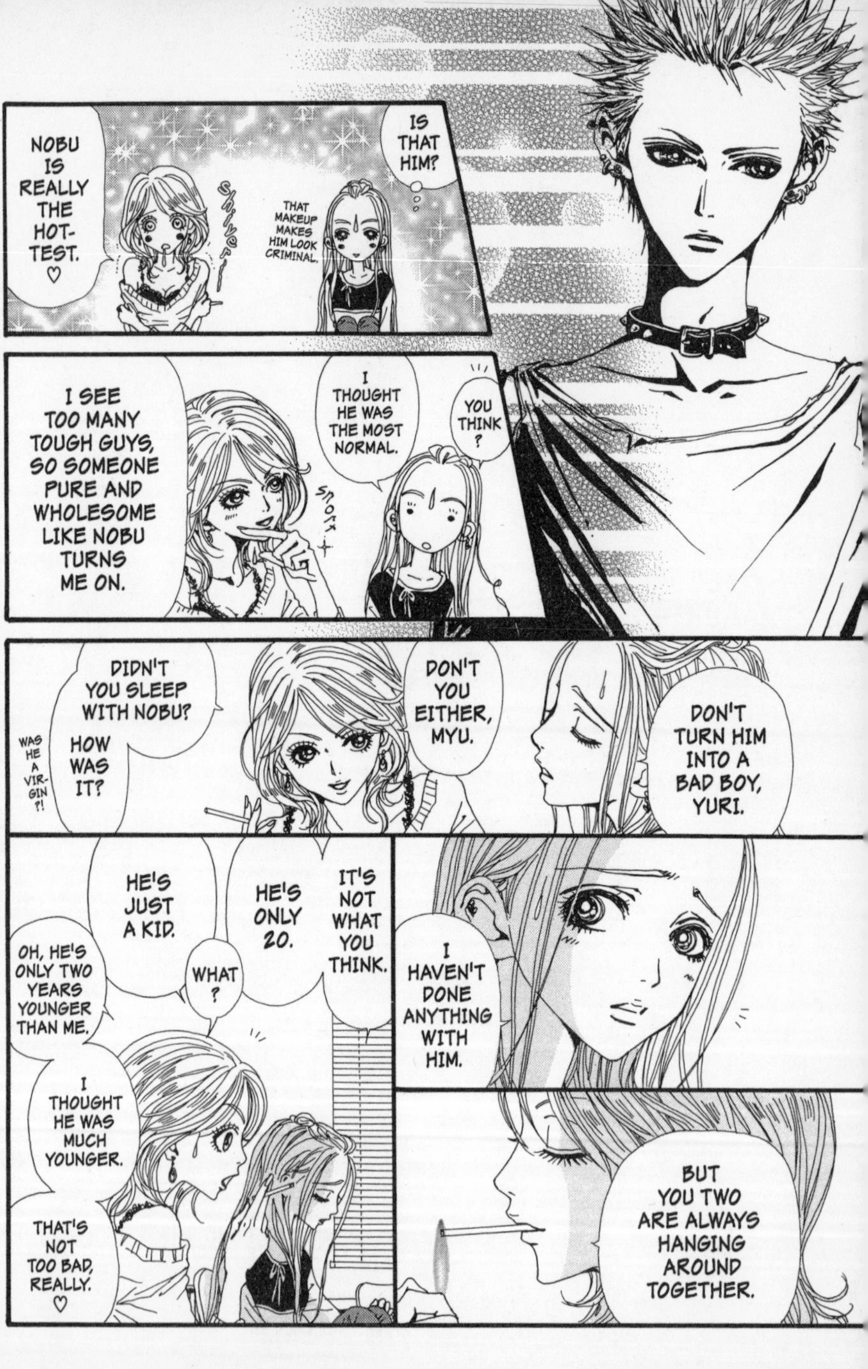
IS THAT HIM?
THAT MAKEUP MAKES HIM LOOK CRIMINAL.
shiver
NOBU IS REALLY THE HOT-TEST. ♡
YOU THINK?
I THOUGHT HE WAS THE MOST NORMAL.
snort
I SEE TOO MANY TOUGH GUYS, SO SOMEONE PURE AND WHOLESOME LIKE NOBU TURNS ME ON.
DON'T TURN HIM INTO A BAD BOY, YURI.
DON'T YOU EITHER, MYU.
DIDN'T YOU SLEEP WITH NOBU?
HOW WAS IT?
WAS HE A VIR-GIN?!
I HAVEN'T DONE ANYTHING WITH HIM.
BUT YOU TWO ARE ALWAYS HANGING AROUND TOGETHER.
IT'S NOT WHAT YOU THINK.
HE'S ONLY 20.
HE'S JUST A KID.
WHAT?
OH, HE'S ONLY TWO YEARS YOUNGER THAN ME.
I THOUGHT HE WAS MUCH YOUNGER.
THAT'S NOT TOO BAD, REALLY. ♡

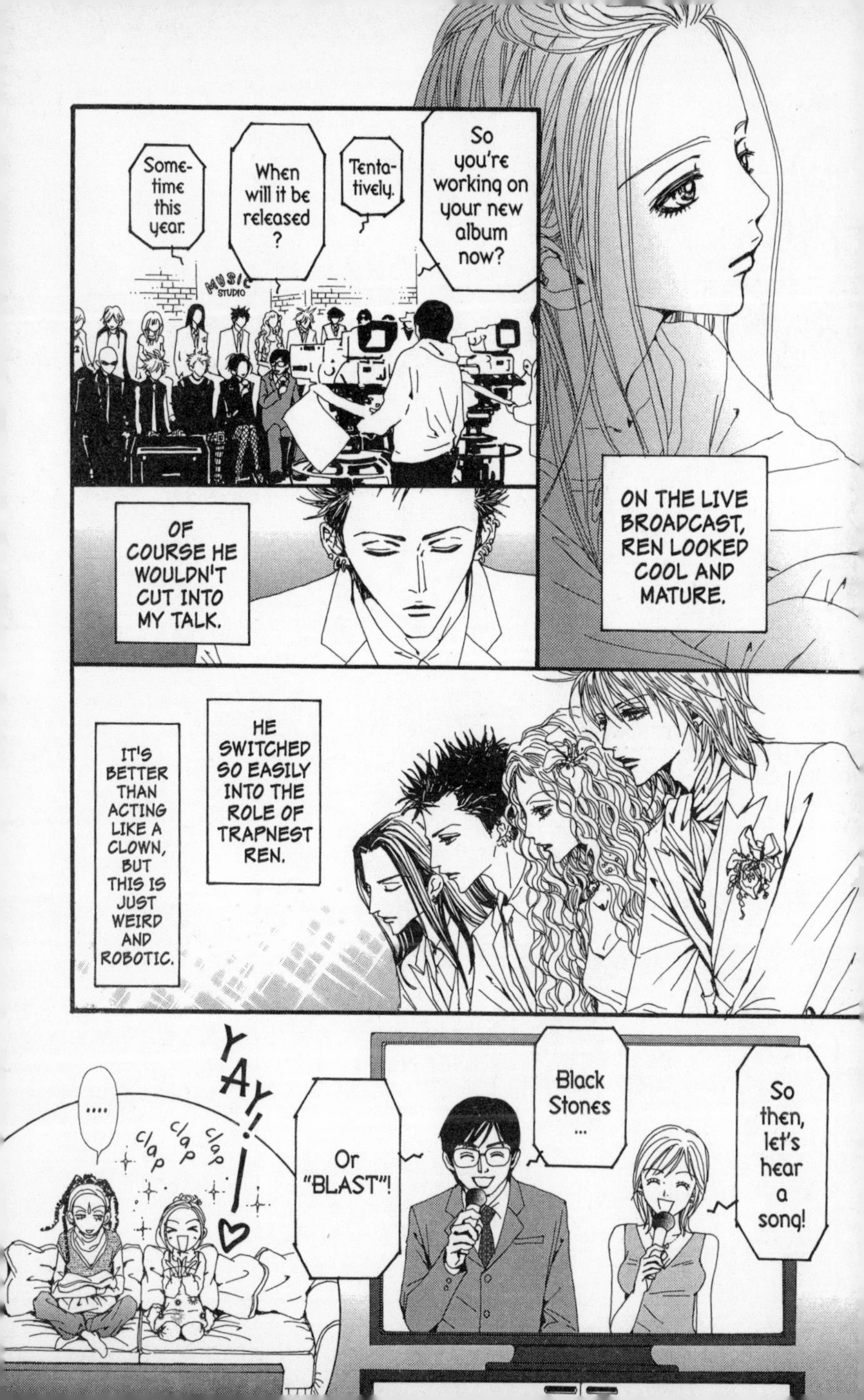
ON THE LIVE BROADCAST, REN LOOKED COOL AND MATURE.
So you're working on your new album now?
Tentatively.
When will it be released?
Sometime this year.
MUSIC STUDIO
OF COURSE HE WOULDN'T CUT INTO MY TALK.
HE SWITCHED SO EASILY INTO THE ROLE OF TRAPNEST REN.
IT'S BETTER THAN ACTING LIKE A CLOWN, BUT THIS IS JUST WEIRD AND ROBOTIC.
So then, let's hear a song!
Black Stones ...
Or "BLAST"!
YAY!
clap clap clap
....

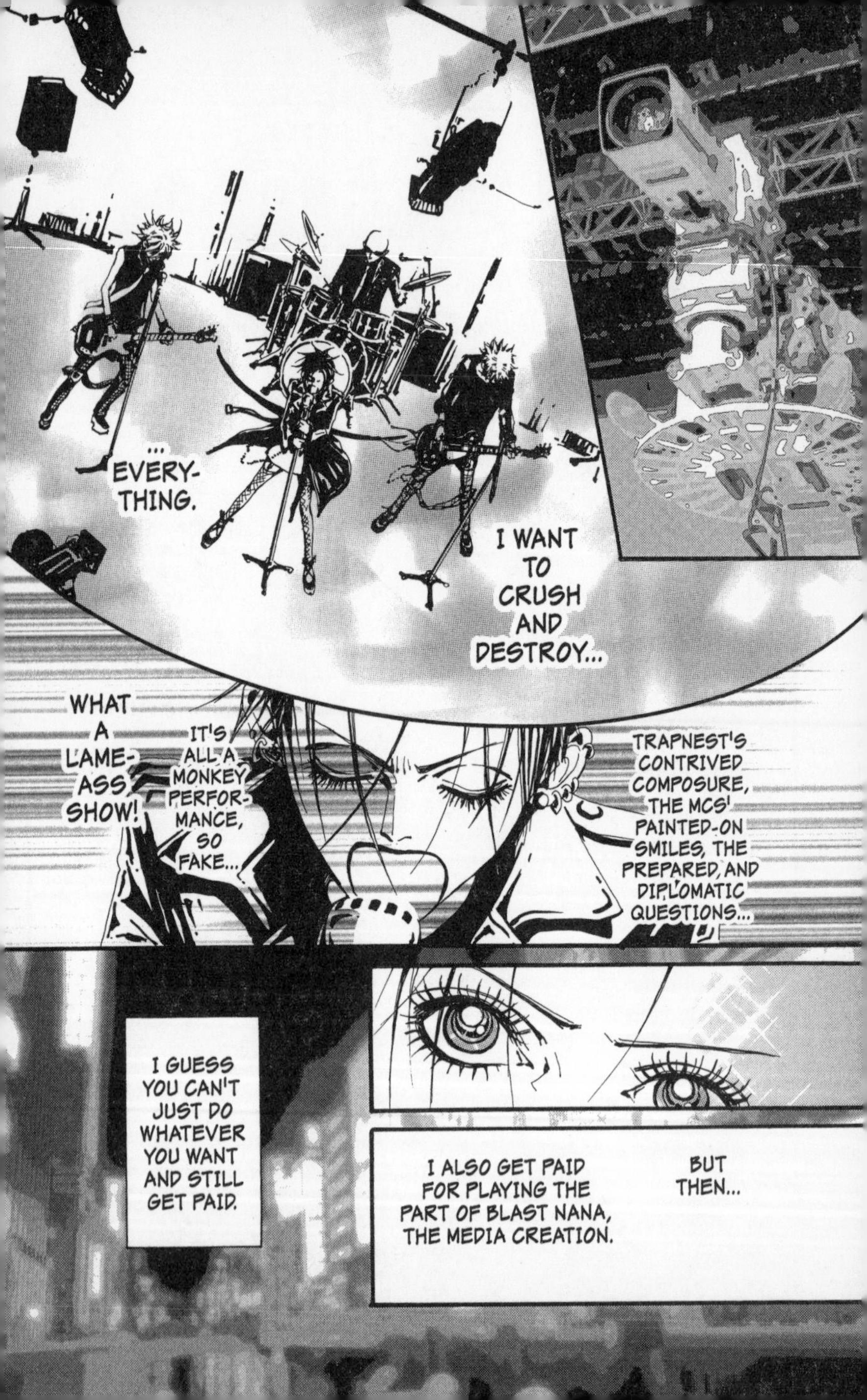
I WANT TO CRUSH AND DESTROY...
... EVERYTHING.
TRAPNEST'S CONTRIVED COMPOSURE, THE MCS' PAINTED-ON SMILES, THE PREPARED, AND DIPLOMATIC QUESTIONS...
IT'S ALL A MONKEY PERFORMANCE, SO FAKE...
WHAT A LAME-ASS SHOW!
I GUESS YOU CAN'T JUST DO WHATEVER YOU WANT AND STILL GET PAID.
BUT THEN...
I ALSO GET PAID FOR PLAYING THE PART OF BLAST NANA, THE MEDIA CREATION.

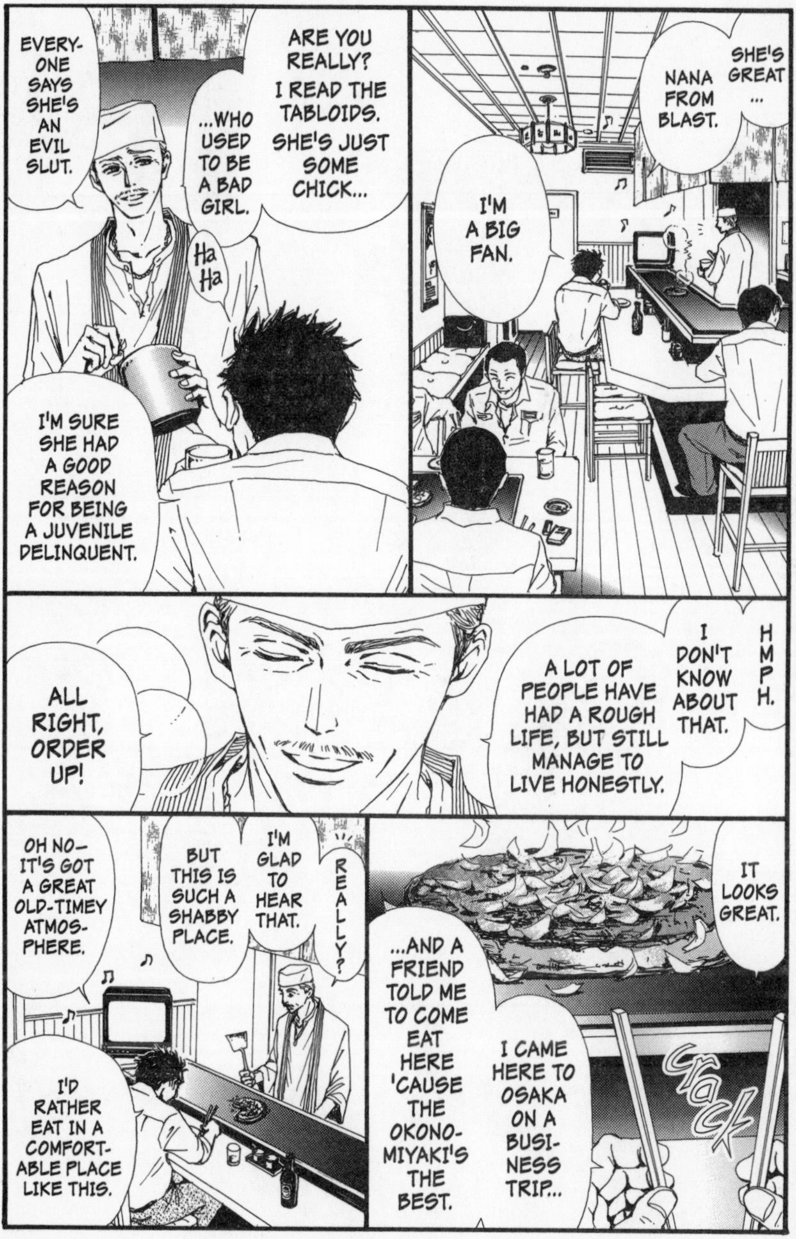
SHE'S GREAT...
NANA FROM BLAST.
I'M A BIG FAN.
ARE YOU REALLY? I READ THE TABLOIDS. SHE'S JUST SOME CHICK...
...WHO USED TO BE A BAD GIRL.
EVERYONE SAYS SHE'S AN EVIL SLUT.
Ha Ha
I'M SURE SHE HAD A GOOD REASON FOR BEING A JUVENILE DELINQUENT.
HMPH.
I DON'T KNOW ABOUT THAT.
A LOT OF PEOPLE HAVE HAD A ROUGH LIFE, BUT STILL MANAGE TO LIVE HONESTLY.
ALL RIGHT, ORDER UP!
IT LOOKS GREAT.
I CAME HERE TO OSAKA ON A BUSINESS TRIP...
...AND A FRIEND TOLD ME TO COME EAT HERE 'CAUSE THE OKONOMIYAKI'S THE BEST.
Crack
REALLY?
I'M GLAD TO HEAR THAT.
BUT THIS IS SUCH A SHABBY PLACE.
OH NO—IT'S GOT A GREAT OLD-TIMEY ATMOSPHERE.
I'D RATHER EAT IN A COMFORTABLE PLACE LIKE THIS.

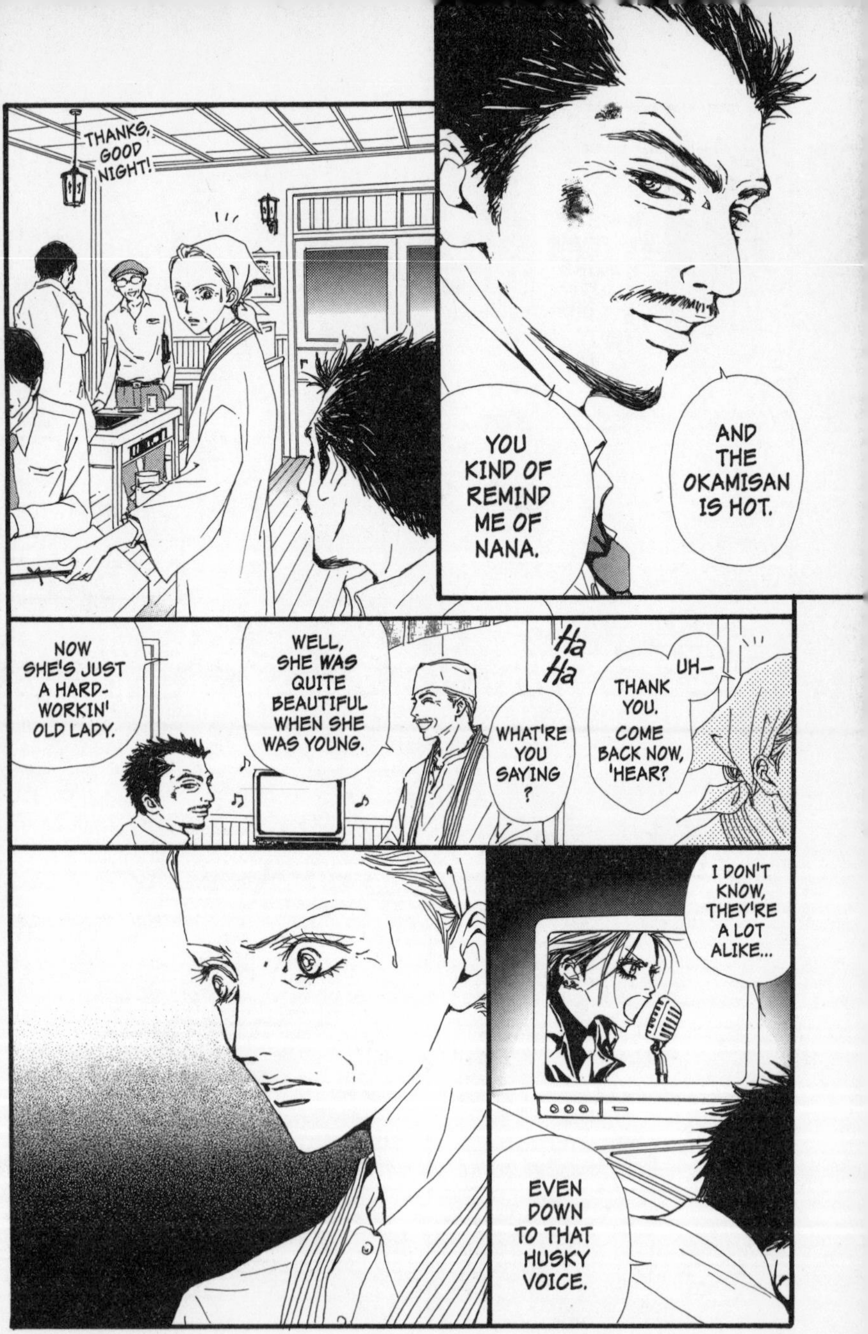
AND THE OKAMISAN IS HOT.
YOU KIND OF REMIND ME OF NANA.
THANKS, GOOD NIGHT!
UH—
THANK YOU. COME BACK NOW, 'HEAR?
WHAT'RE YOU SAYING?
Ha Ha
WELL, SHE WAS QUITE BEAUTIFUL WHEN SHE WAS YOUNG.
NOW SHE'S JUST A HARD-WORKIN' OLD LADY.
I DON'T KNOW, THEY'RE A LOT ALIKE...
EVEN DOWN TO THAT HUSKY VOICE.

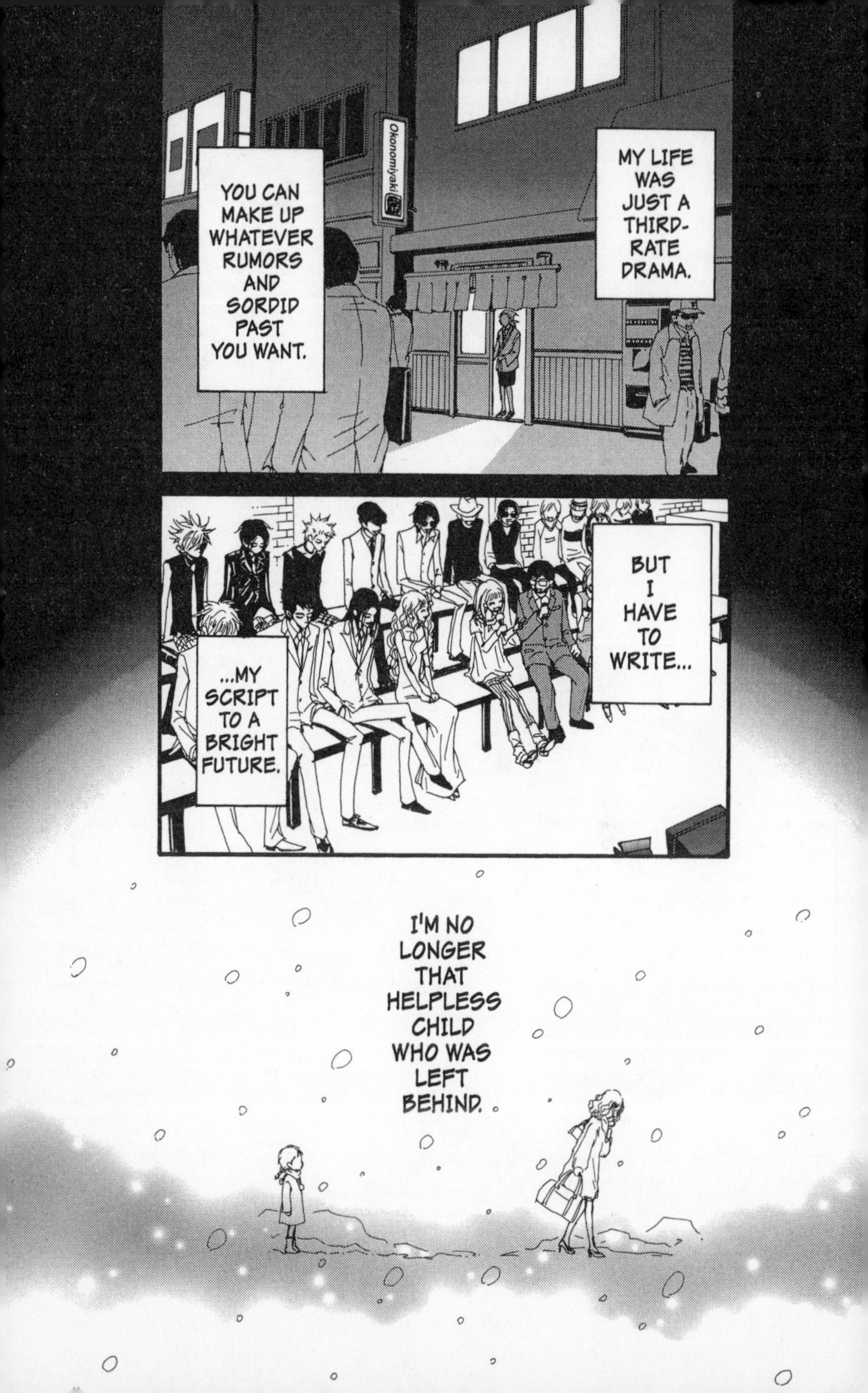
MY LIFE WAS JUST A THIRD-RATE DRAMA.
Okonomiyaki
YOU CAN MAKE UP WHATEVER RUMORS AND SORDID PAST YOU WANT.
BUT I HAVE TO WRITE...
...MY SCRIPT TO A BRIGHT FUTURE.
I'M NO LONGER THAT HELPLESS CHILD WHO WAS LEFT BEHIND.

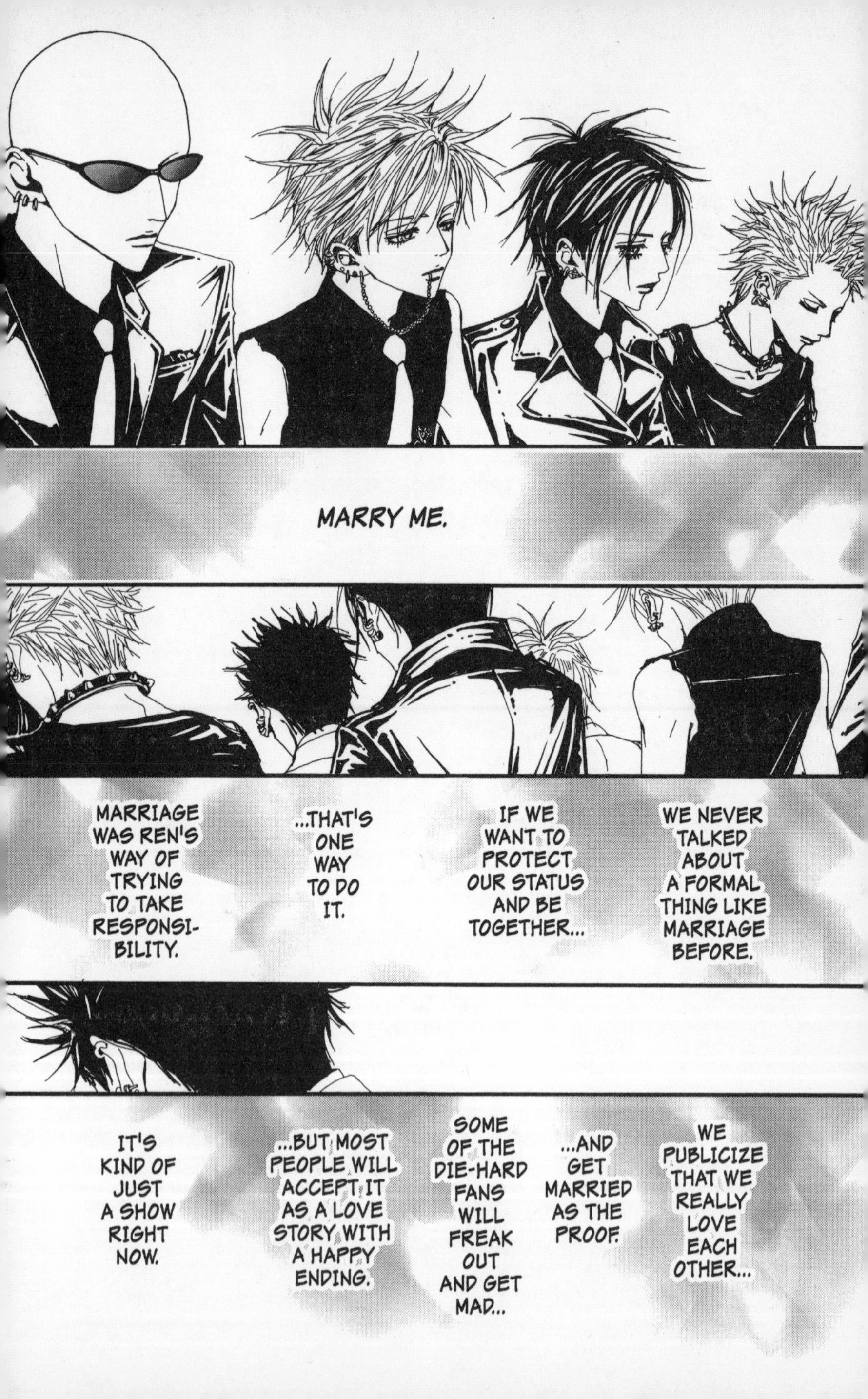
MARRY ME.
WE NEVER TALKED ABOUT A FORMAL THING LIKE MARRIAGE BEFORE.
IF WE WANT TO PROTECT OUR STATUS AND BE TOGETHER...
...THAT'S ONE WAY TO DO IT.
MARRIAGE WAS REN'S WAY OF TRYING TO TAKE RESPONSI-BILITY.
WE PUBLICIZE THAT WE REALLY LOVE EACH OTHER...
...AND GET MARRIED AS THE PROOF.
SOME OF THE DIE-HARD FANS WILL FREAK OUT AND GET MAD...
...BUT MOST PEOPLE WILL ACCEPT IT AS A LOVE STORY WITH A HAPPY ENDING.
IT'S KIND OF JUST A SHOW RIGHT NOW.

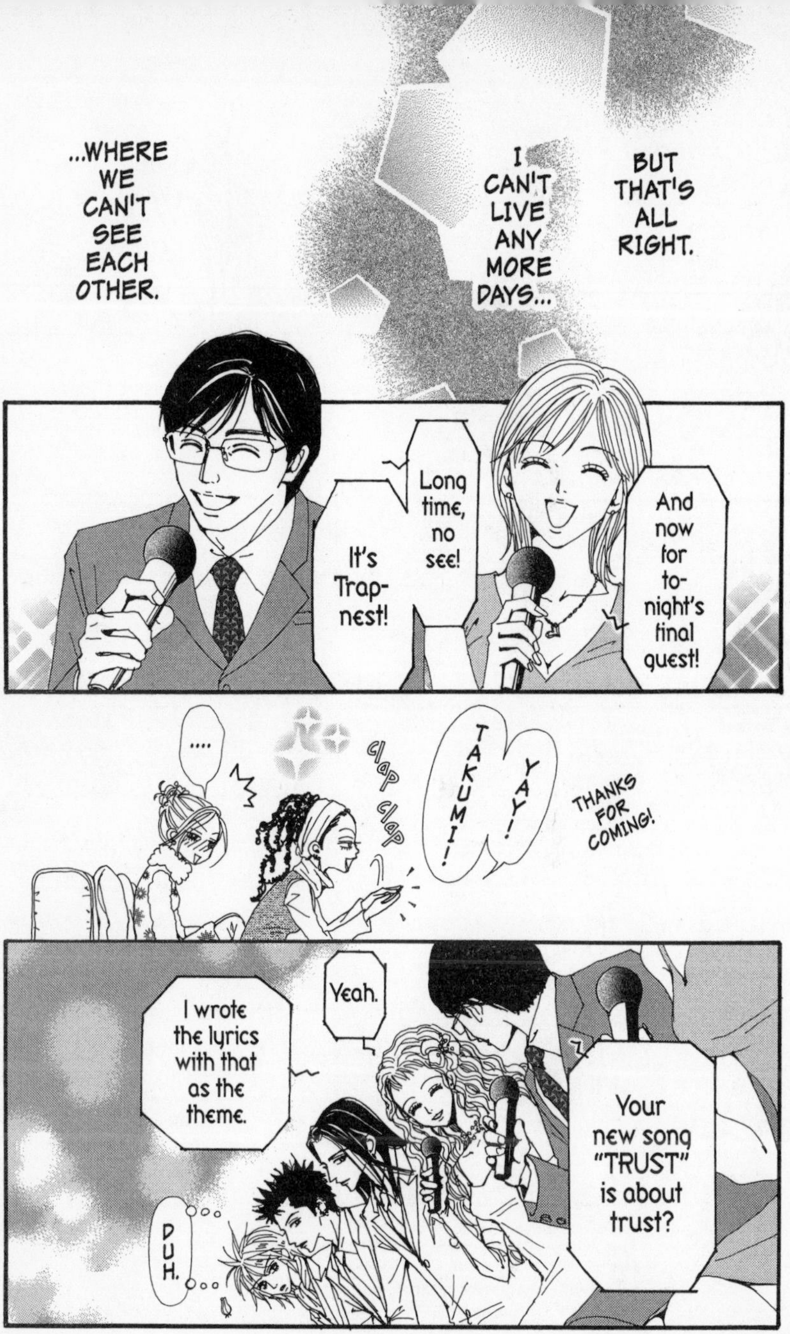
BUT THAT'S ALL RIGHT.
I CAN'T LIVE ANY MORE DAYS...
...WHERE WE CAN'T SEE EACH OTHER.
And now for to-night's final guest!
Long time, no see!
It's Trap-nest!
THANKS FOR COMING!
YAY!
TAKUMI!
clap clap
....
Your new song "TRUST" is about trust?
Yeah.
I wrote the lyrics with that as the theme.
DUH.

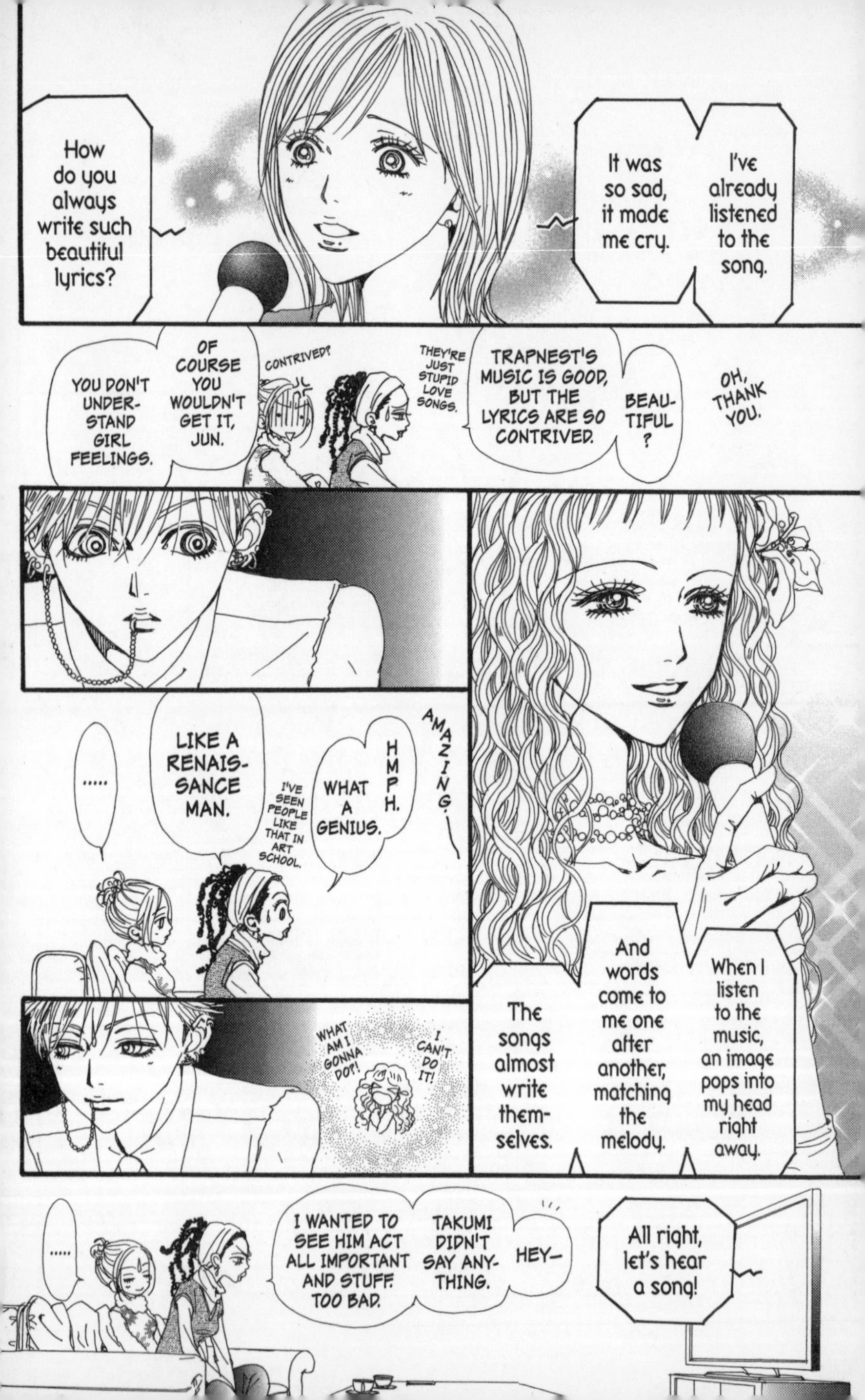
I've already listened to the song.
It was so sad, it made me cry.
How do you always write such beautiful lyrics?
OH, THANK YOU.
BEAUTIFUL?
TRAPNEST'S MUSIC IS GOOD, BUT THE LYRICS ARE SO CONTRIVED.
THEY'RE JUST STUPID LOVE SONGS.
CONTRIVED?
OF COURSE YOU WOULDN'T GET IT, JUN.
YOU DON'T UNDERSTAND GIRL FEELINGS.
When I listen to the music, an image pops into my head right away.
And words come to me one after another, matching the melody.
The songs almost write themselves.
AMAZING.
HMPH.
WHAT A GENIUS.
I'VE SEEN PEOPLE LIKE THAT IN ART SCHOOL.
LIKE A RENAISSANCE MAN.
......
I CAN'T DO IT!
WHAT AM I GONNA DO?!
All right, let's hear a song!
HEY—
TAKUMI DIDN'T SAY ANYTHING.
I WANTED TO SEE HIM ACT ALL IMPORTANT AND STUFF. TOO BAD.
......

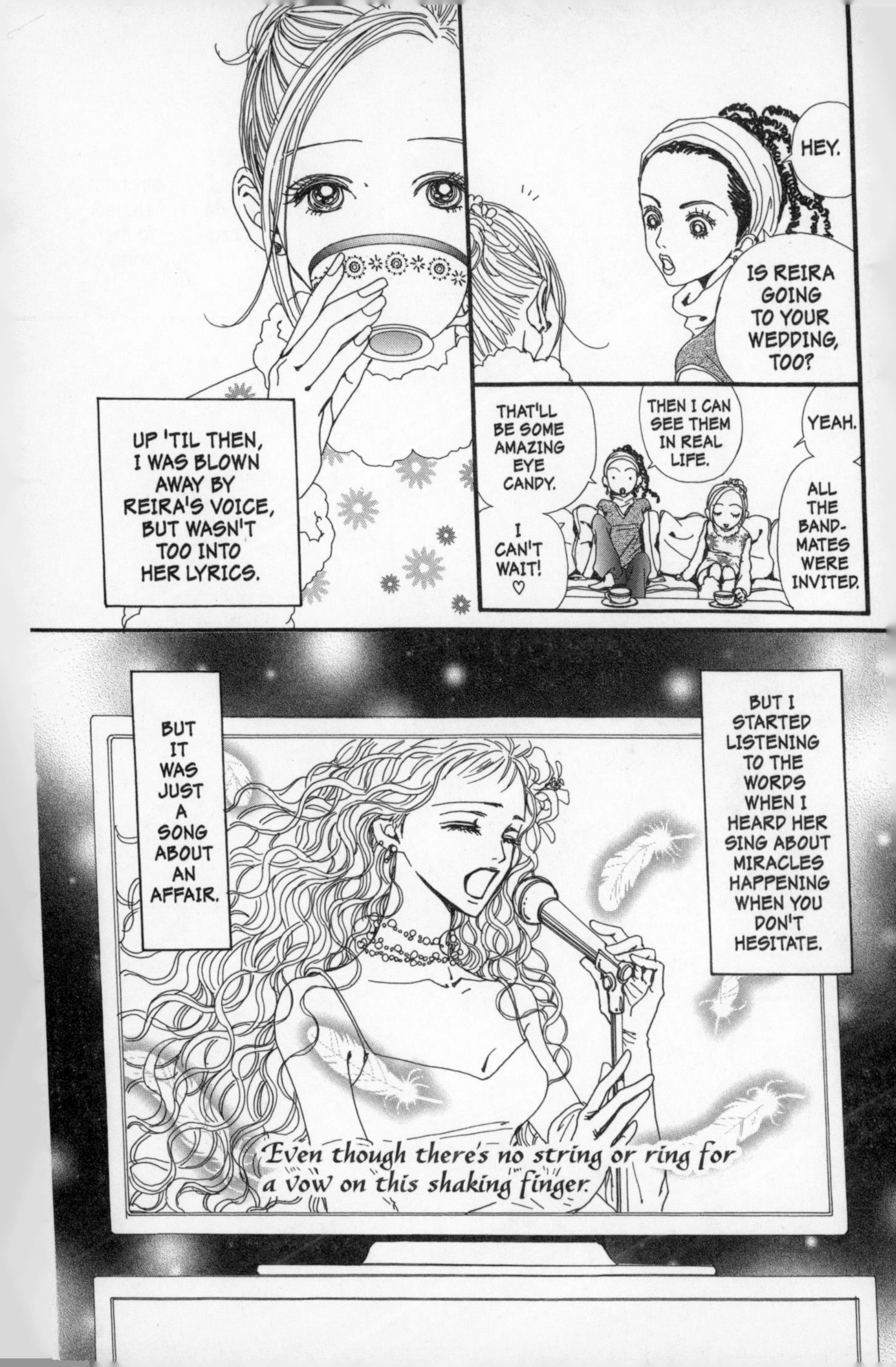
HEY.
IS REIRA GOING TO YOUR WEDDING, TOO?
YEAH.
ALL THE BANDMATES WERE INVITED.
THEN I CAN SEE THEM IN REAL LIFE.
THAT'LL BE SOME AMAZING EYE CANDY.
I CAN'T WAIT! ♡
UP 'TIL THEN, I WAS BLOWN AWAY BY REIRA'S VOICE, BUT WASN'T TOO INTO HER LYRICS.
BUT I STARTED LISTENING TO THE WORDS WHEN I HEARD HER SING ABOUT MIRACLES HAPPENING WHEN YOU DON'T HESITATE.
BUT IT WAS JUST A SONG ABOUT AN AFFAIR.
Even though there's no string or ring for a vow on this shaking finger.

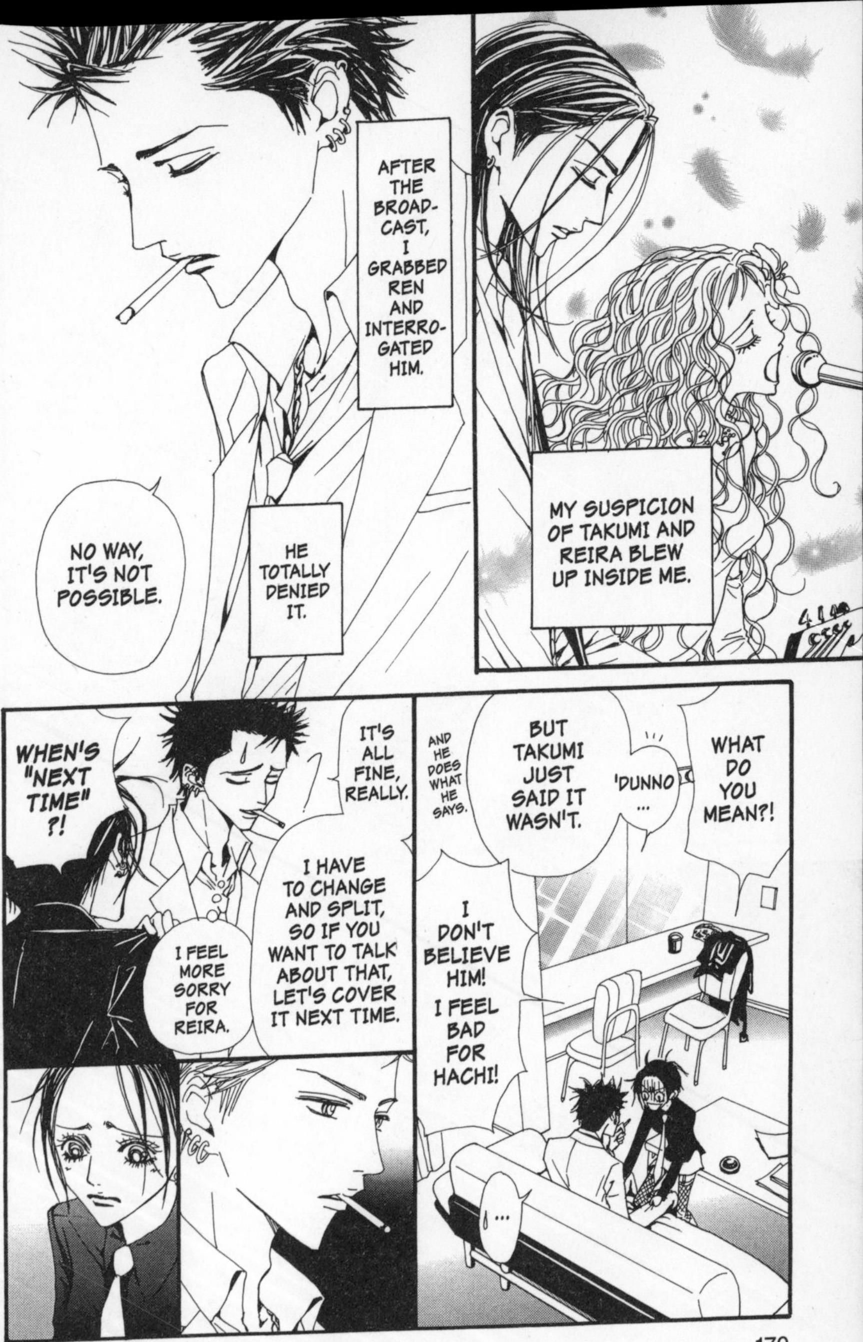
MY SUSPICION OF TAKUMI AND REIRA BLEW UP INSIDE ME.
AFTER THE BROAD-CAST, I GRABBED REN AND INTERRO-GATED HIM.
HE TOTALLY DENIED IT.
NO WAY, IT'S NOT POSSIBLE.
WHAT DO YOU MEAN?!
'DUNNO ...
BUT TAKUMI JUST SAID IT WASN'T.
AND HE DOES WHAT HE SAYS.
I DON'T BELIEVE HIM! I FEEL BAD FOR HACHI!
! ...
IT'S ALL FINE, REALLY.
WHEN'S "NEXT TIME"?!
I HAVE TO CHANGE AND SPLIT, SO IF YOU WANT TO TALK ABOUT THAT, LET'S COVER IT NEXT TIME.
I FEEL MORE SORRY FOR REIRA.

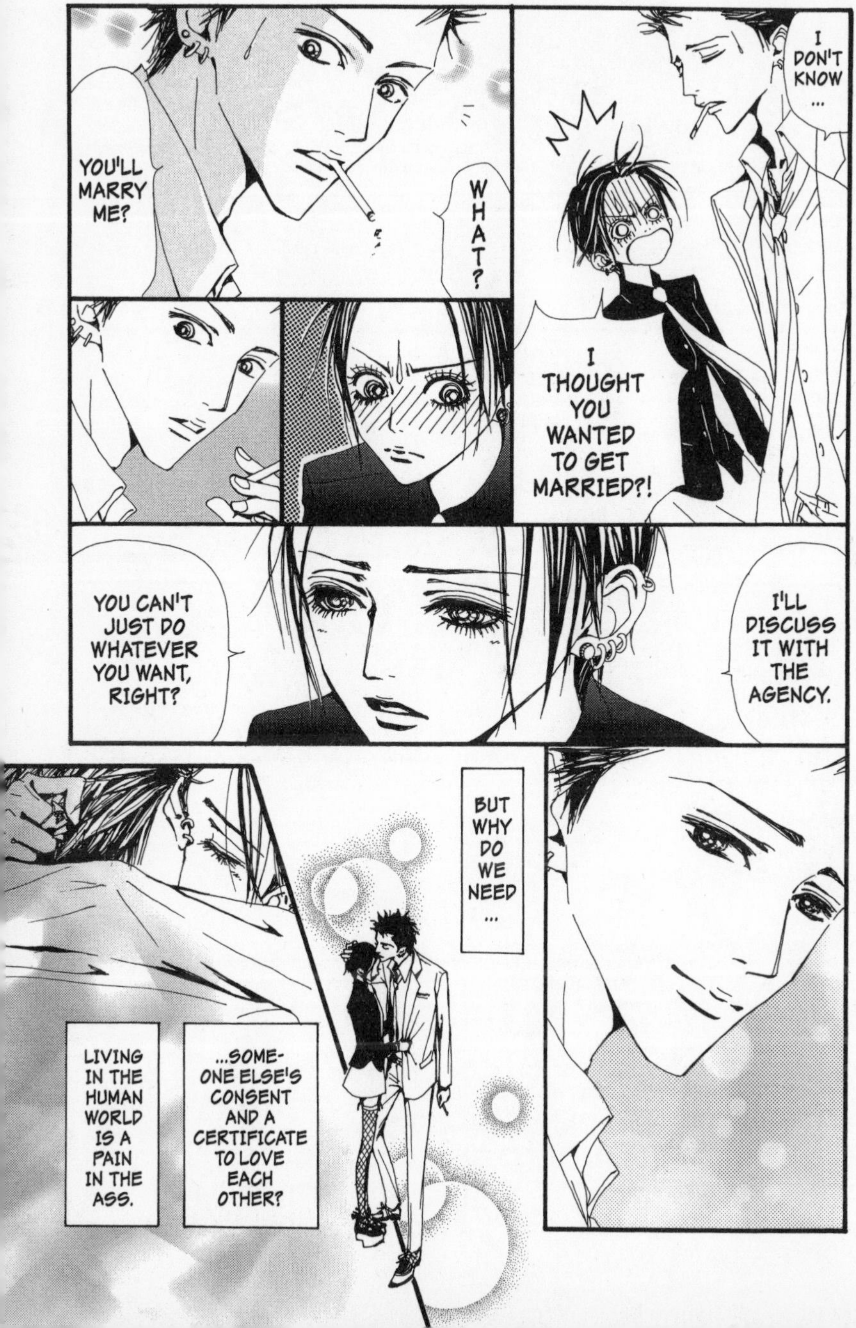
I DON'T KNOW ...
I THOUGHT YOU WANTED TO GET MARRIED?!
YOU'LL MARRY ME?
WHAT?
I'LL DISCUSS IT WITH THE AGENCY.
YOU CAN'T JUST DO WHATEVER YOU WANT, RIGHT?
BUT WHY DO WE NEED ...
...SOME-ONE ELSE'S CONSENT AND A CERTIFICATE TO LOVE EACH OTHER?
LIVING IN THE HUMAN WORLD IS A PAIN IN THE ASS.

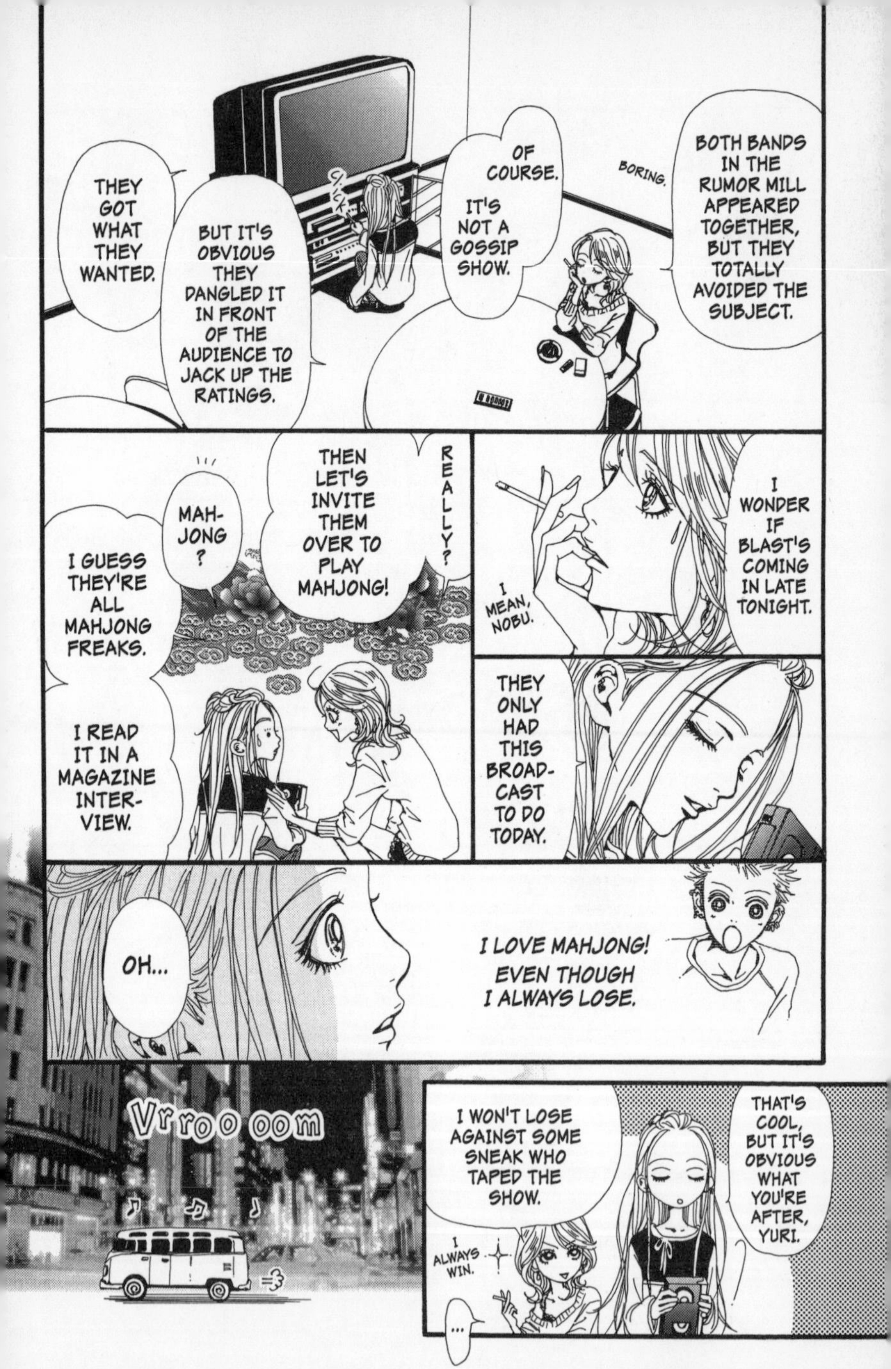
BOTH BANDS IN THE RUMOR MILL APPEARED TOGETHER, BUT THEY TOTALLY AVOIDED THE SUBJECT.
BORING.
OF COURSE.
IT'S NOT A GOSSIP SHOW.
BUT IT'S OBVIOUS THEY DANGLED IT IN FRONT OF THE AUDIENCE TO JACK UP THE RATINGS.
THEY GOT WHAT THEY WANTED.
I WONDER IF BLAST'S COMING IN LATE TONIGHT.
I MEAN, NOBU.
THEY ONLY HAD THIS BROADCAST TO DO TODAY.
REALLY?
THEN LET'S INVITE THEM OVER TO PLAY MAHJONG!
MAH-JONG?
I GUESS THEY'RE ALL MAHJONG FREAKS.
I READ IT IN A MAGAZINE INTER-VIEW.
I LOVE MAHJONG! EVEN THOUGH I ALWAYS LOSE.
OH...
THAT'S COOL, BUT IT'S OBVIOUS WHAT YOU'RE AFTER, YURI.
I WON'T LOSE AGAINST SOME SNEAK WHO TAPED THE SHOW.
I ALWAYS WIN.
...
Vrroo oom

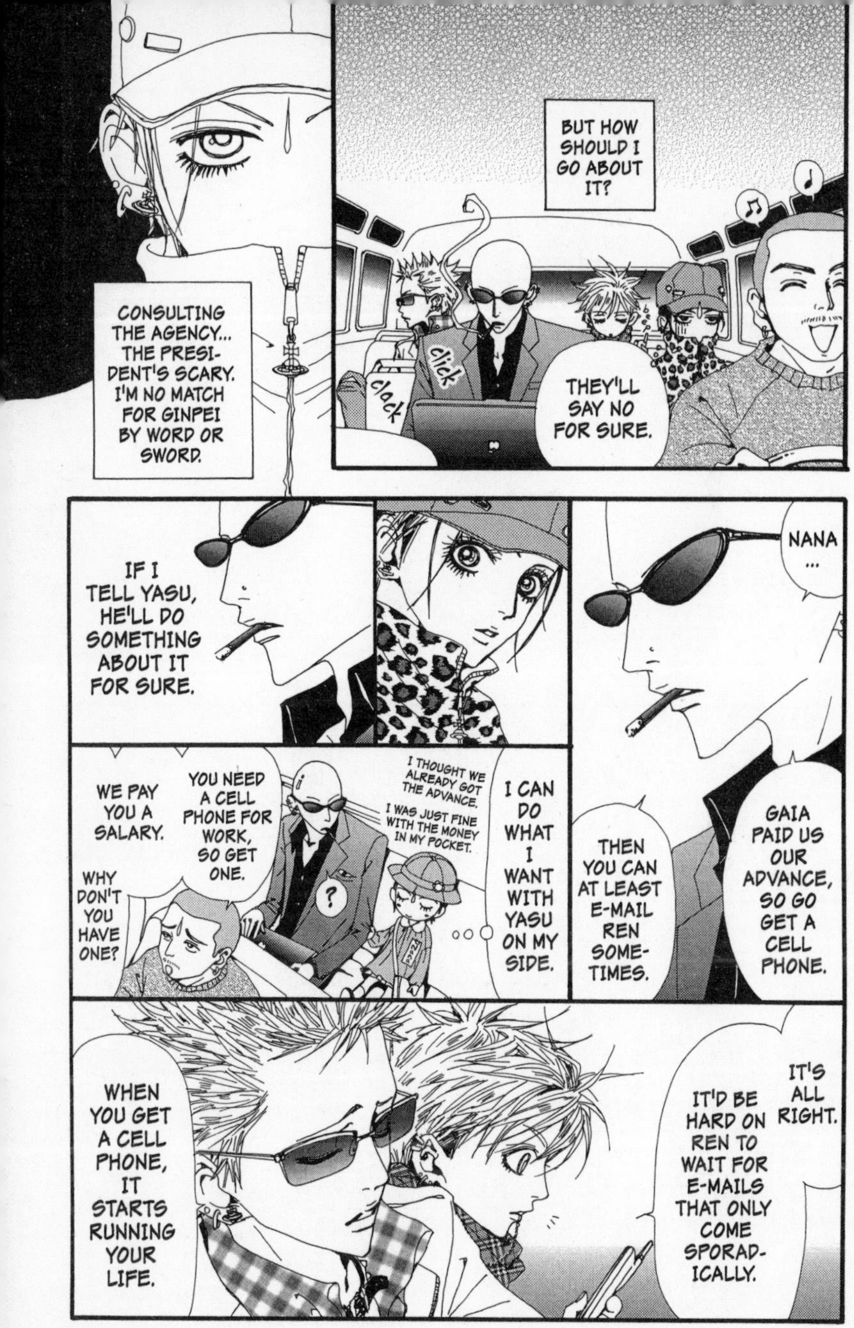
BUT HOW SHOULD I GO ABOUT IT?
click
clack
THEY'LL SAY NO FOR SURE.
CONSULTING THE AGENCY... THE PRESIDENT'S SCARY. I'M NO MATCH FOR GINPEI BY WORD OR SWORD.
NANA ...
GAIA PAID US OUR ADVANCE, SO GO GET A CELL PHONE.
THEN YOU CAN AT LEAST E-MAIL REN SOMETIMES.
IF I TELL YASU, HE'LL DO SOMETHING ABOUT IT FOR SURE.
I CAN DO WHAT I WANT WITH YASU ON MY SIDE.
I THOUGHT WE ALREADY GOT THE ADVANCE.
I WAS JUST FINE WITH THE MONEY IN MY POCKET.
?
YOU NEED A CELL PHONE FOR WORK, SO GET ONE.
WE PAY YOU A SALARY.
WHY DON'T YOU HAVE ONE?
IT'S ALL RIGHT.
IT'D BE HARD ON REN TO WAIT FOR E-MAILS THAT ONLY COME SPORADICALLY.
WHEN YOU GET A CELL PHONE, IT STARTS RUNNING YOUR LIFE.

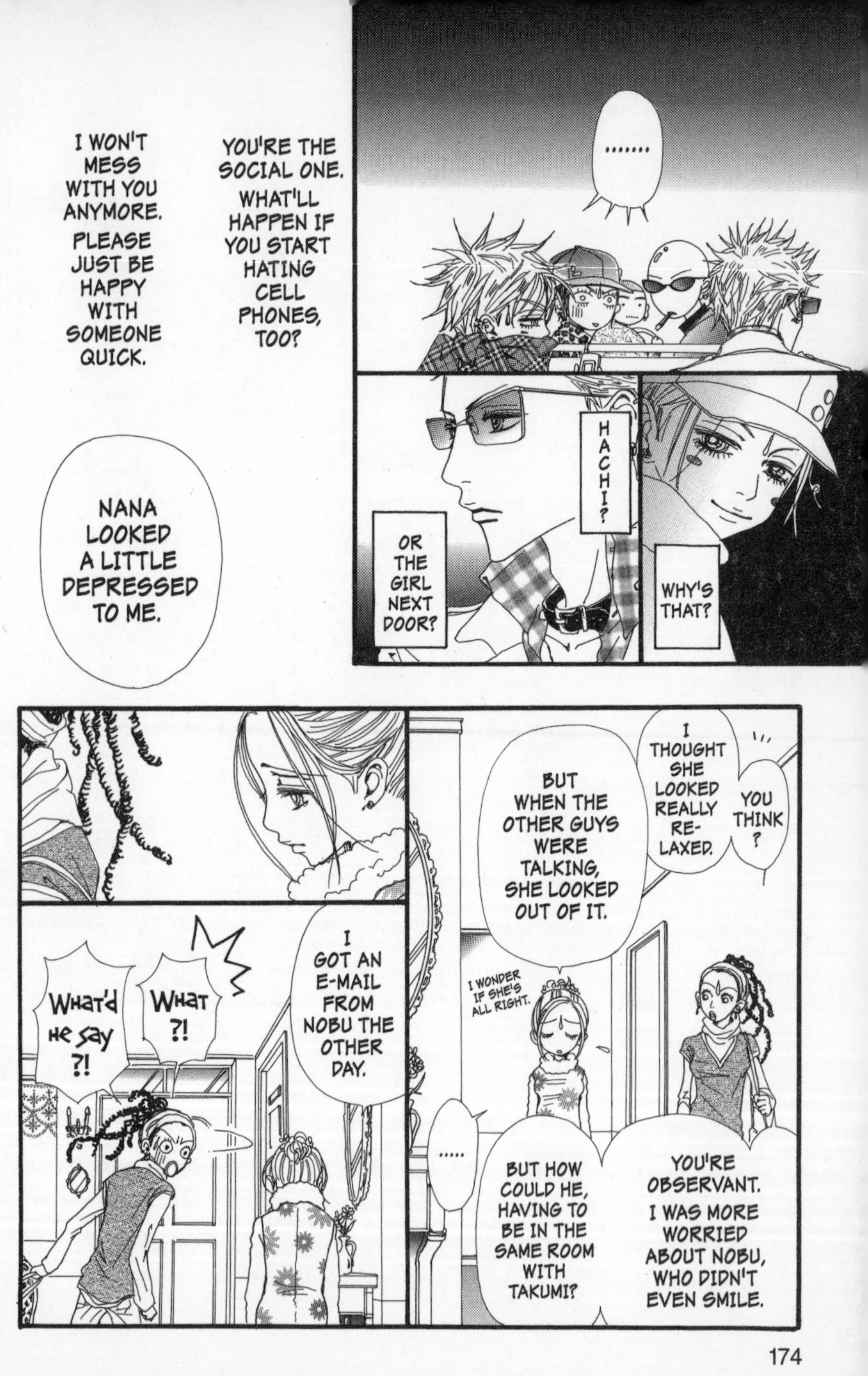

....
YOU'RE THE SOCIAL ONE. WHAT'LL HAPPEN IF YOU START HATING CELL PHONES, TOO?
I WON'T MESS WITH YOU ANYMORE. PLEASE JUST BE HAPPY WITH SOMEONE QUICK.
WHY'S THAT?
HACHI?
OR THE GIRL NEXT DOOR?
NANA LOOKED A LITTLE DEPRESSED TO ME.
YOU THINK?
I THOUGHT SHE LOOKED REALLY RE-LAXED.
BUT WHEN THE OTHER GUYS WERE TALKING, SHE LOOKED OUT OF IT.
I WONDER IF SHE'S ALL RIGHT.
YOU'RE OBSERVANT. I WAS MORE WORRIED ABOUT NOBU, WHO DIDN'T EVEN SMILE.
BUT HOW COULD HE, HAVING TO BE IN THE SAME ROOM WITH TAKUMI?
.....
I GOT AN E-MAIL FROM NOBU THE OTHER DAY.
WHAT?!
WHAT'D HE SAY?!

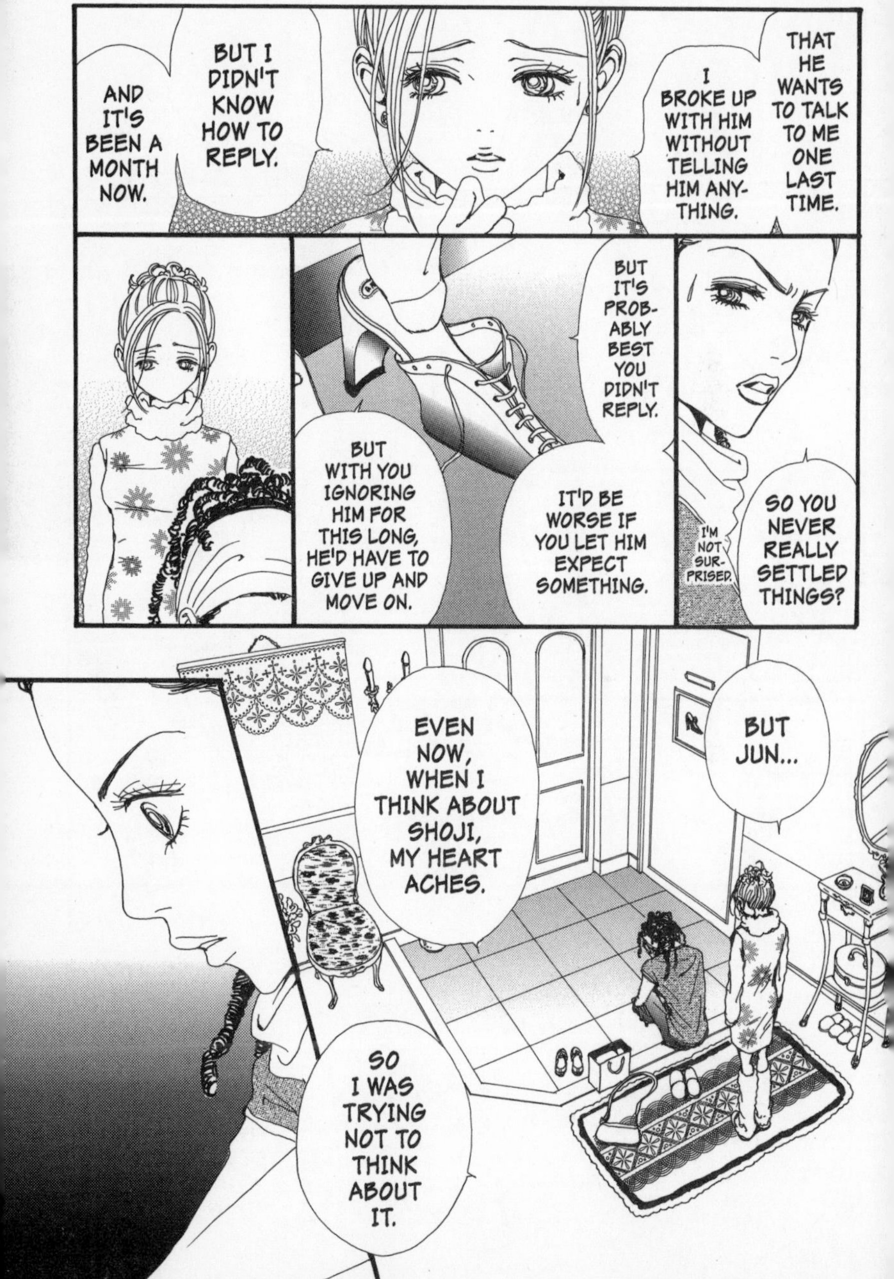
THAT HE WANTS TO TALK TO ME ONE LAST TIME.
I BROKE UP WITH HIM WITHOUT TELLING HIM ANY-THING.
BUT I DIDN'T KNOW HOW TO REPLY.
AND IT'S BEEN A MONTH NOW.
SO YOU NEVER REALLY SETTLED THINGS?
I'M NOT SUR-PRISED.
BUT IT'S PROB-ABLY BEST YOU DIDN'T REPLY.
IT'D BE WORSE IF YOU LET HIM EXPECT SOMETHING.
BUT WITH YOU IGNORING HIM FOR THIS LONG, HE'D HAVE TO GIVE UP AND MOVE ON.
BUT JUN...
EVEN NOW, WHEN I THINK ABOUT SHOJI, MY HEART ACHES.
SO I WAS TRYING NOT TO THINK ABOUT IT.

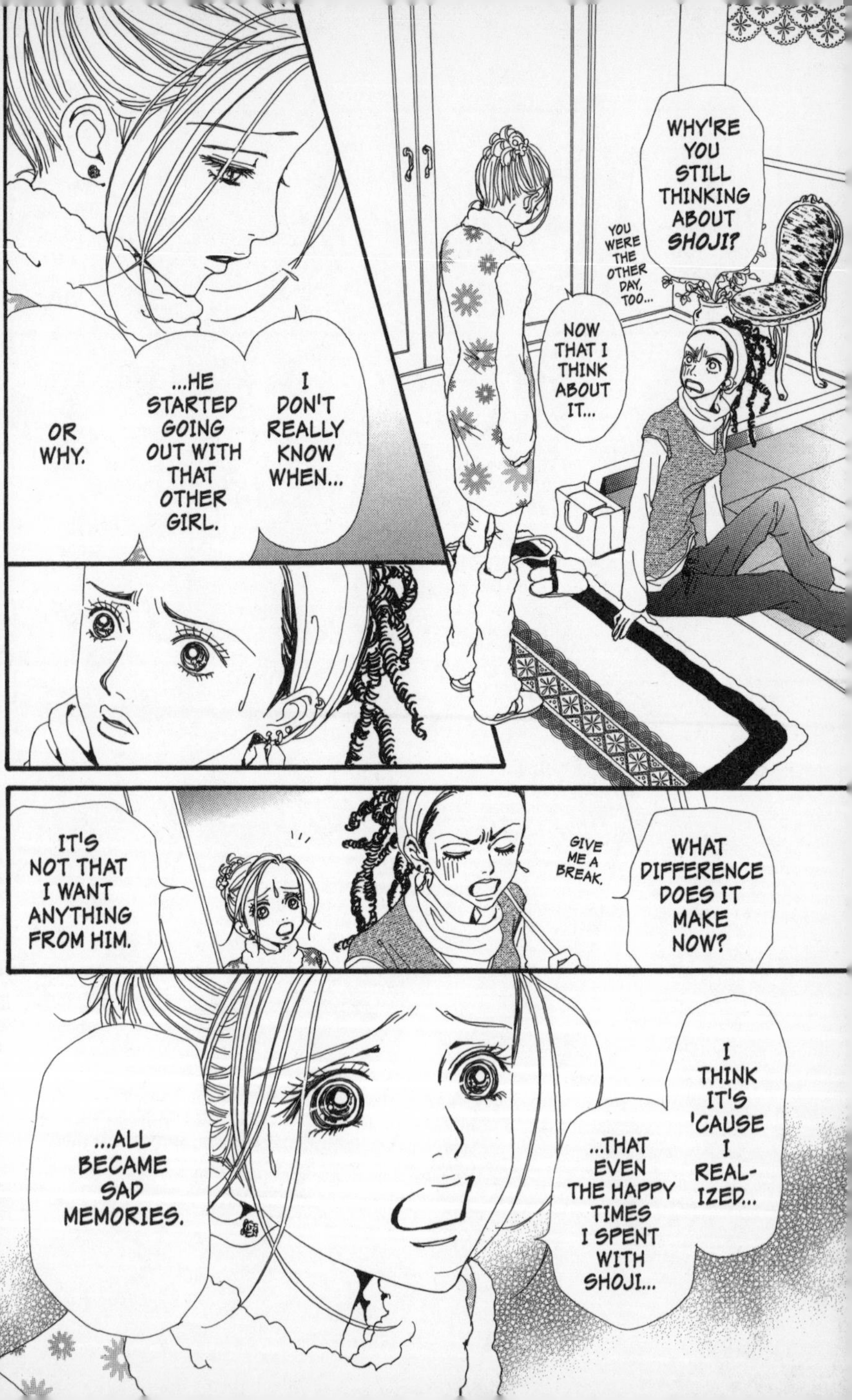
WHY'RE YOU STILL THINKING ABOUT SHOJI?
YOU WERE THE OTHER DAY, TOO...
NOW THAT I THINK ABOUT IT...
I DON'T REALLY KNOW WHEN...
...HE STARTED GOING OUT WITH THAT OTHER GIRL.
OR WHY.
WHAT DIFFERENCE DOES IT MAKE NOW?
GIVE ME A BREAK.
IT'S NOT THAT I WANT ANYTHING FROM HIM.
I THINK IT'S 'CAUSE I REALIZED...
...THAT EVEN THE HAPPY TIMES I SPENT WITH SHOJI...
...ALL BECAME SAD MEMORIES.

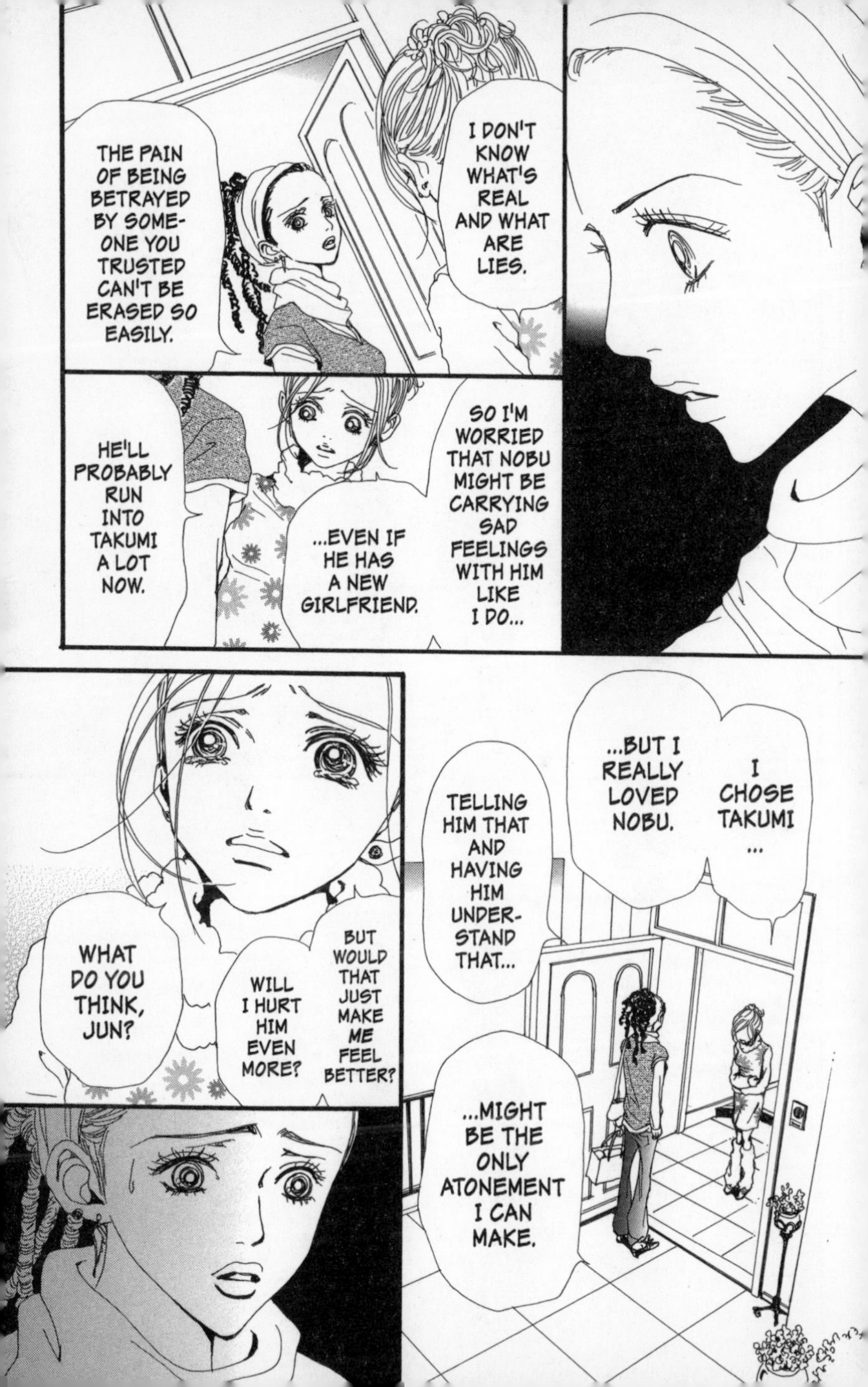
I DON'T KNOW WHAT'S REAL AND WHAT ARE LIES.
THE PAIN OF BEING BETRAYED BY SOME-ONE YOU TRUSTED CAN'T BE ERASED SO EASILY.
SO I'M WORRIED THAT NOBU MIGHT BE CARRYING SAD FEELINGS WITH HIM LIKE I DO...
...EVEN IF HE HAS A NEW GIRLFRIEND.
HE'LL PROBABLY RUN INTO TAKUMI A LOT NOW.
I CHOSE TAKUMI...
...BUT I REALLY LOVED NOBU.
TELLING HIM THAT AND HAVING HIM UNDER-STAND THAT...
...MIGHT BE THE ONLY ATONEMENT I CAN MAKE.
BUT WOULD THAT JUST MAKE ME FEEL BETTER?
WILL I HURT HIM EVEN MORE?
WHAT DO YOU THINK, JUN?

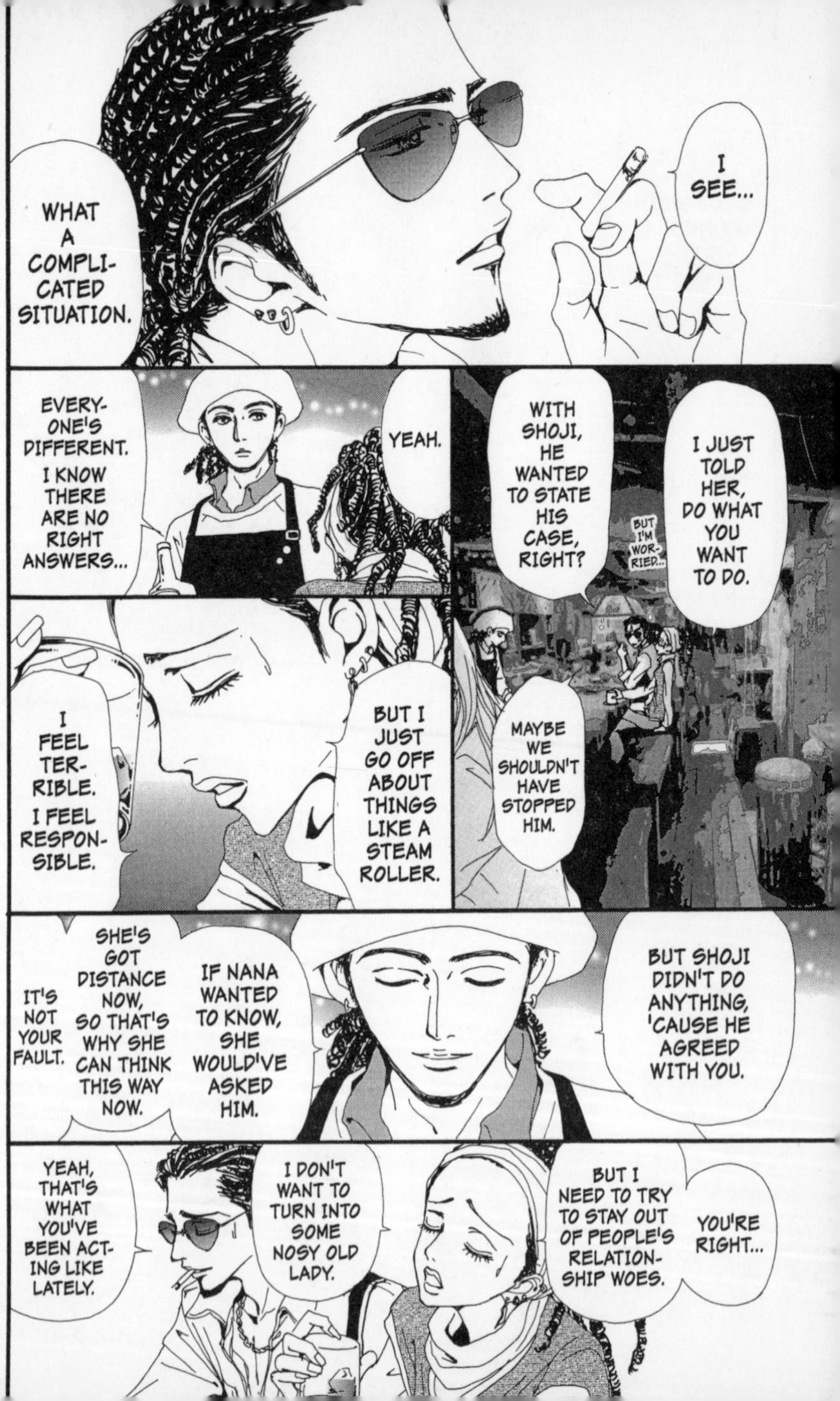
I SEE...
WHAT A COMPLICATED SITUATION.
I JUST TOLD HER, DO WHAT YOU WANT TO DO.
BUT I'M WORRIED...
WITH SHOJI, HE WANTED TO STATE HIS CASE, RIGHT?
MAYBE WE SHOULDN'T HAVE STOPPED HIM.
YEAH.
EVERYONE'S DIFFERENT. I KNOW THERE ARE NO RIGHT ANSWERS...
BUT I JUST GO OFF ABOUT THINGS LIKE A STEAM ROLLER.
I FEEL TERRIBLE. I FEEL RESPONSIBLE.
BUT SHOJI DIDN'T DO ANYTHING, 'CAUSE HE AGREED WITH YOU.
IF NANA WANTED TO KNOW, SHE WOULD'VE ASKED HIM.
SHE'S GOT DISTANCE NOW, SO THAT'S WHY SHE CAN THINK THIS WAY NOW.
IT'S NOT YOUR FAULT.
YOU'RE RIGHT...
BUT I NEED TO TRY TO STAY OUT OF PEOPLE'S RELATIONSHIP WOES.
I DON'T WANT TO TURN INTO SOME NOSY OLD LADY.
YEAH, THAT'S WHAT YOU'VE BEEN ACTING LIKE LATELY.

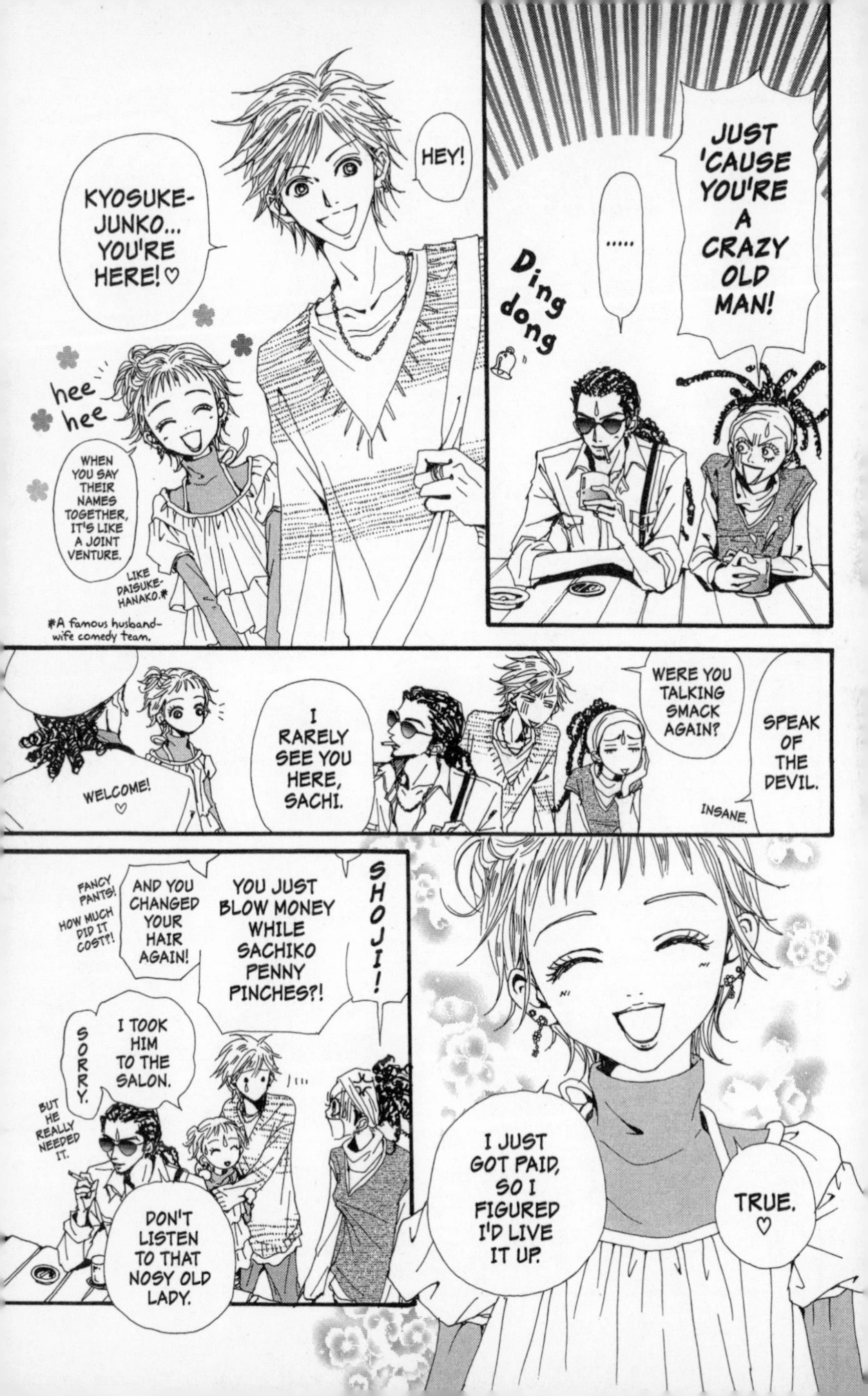
JUST 'CAUSE YOU'RE A CRAZY OLD MAN!
.....
Ding dong
HEY!
KYOSUKE-JUNKO... YOU'RE HERE! ♡
hee hee
WHEN YOU SAY THEIR NAMES TOGETHER, IT'S LIKE A JOINT VENTURE.
LIKE DAISUKE-HANAKO.*
*A famous husband-wife comedy team.
SPEAK OF THE DEVIL.
WERE YOU TALKING SMACK AGAIN?
INSANE.
I RARELY SEE YOU HERE, SACHI.
WELCOME! ♡
TRUE. ♡
I JUST GOT PAID, SO I FIGURED I'D LIVE IT UP.
SHOJI!
YOU JUST BLOW MONEY WHILE SACHIKO PENNY PINCHES?!
AND YOU CHANGED YOUR HAIR AGAIN!
FANCY PANTS! HOW MUCH DID IT COST?!
SORRY.
I TOOK HIM TO THE SALON.
BUT HE REALLY NEEDED IT.
DON'T LISTEN TO THAT NOSY OLD LADY.

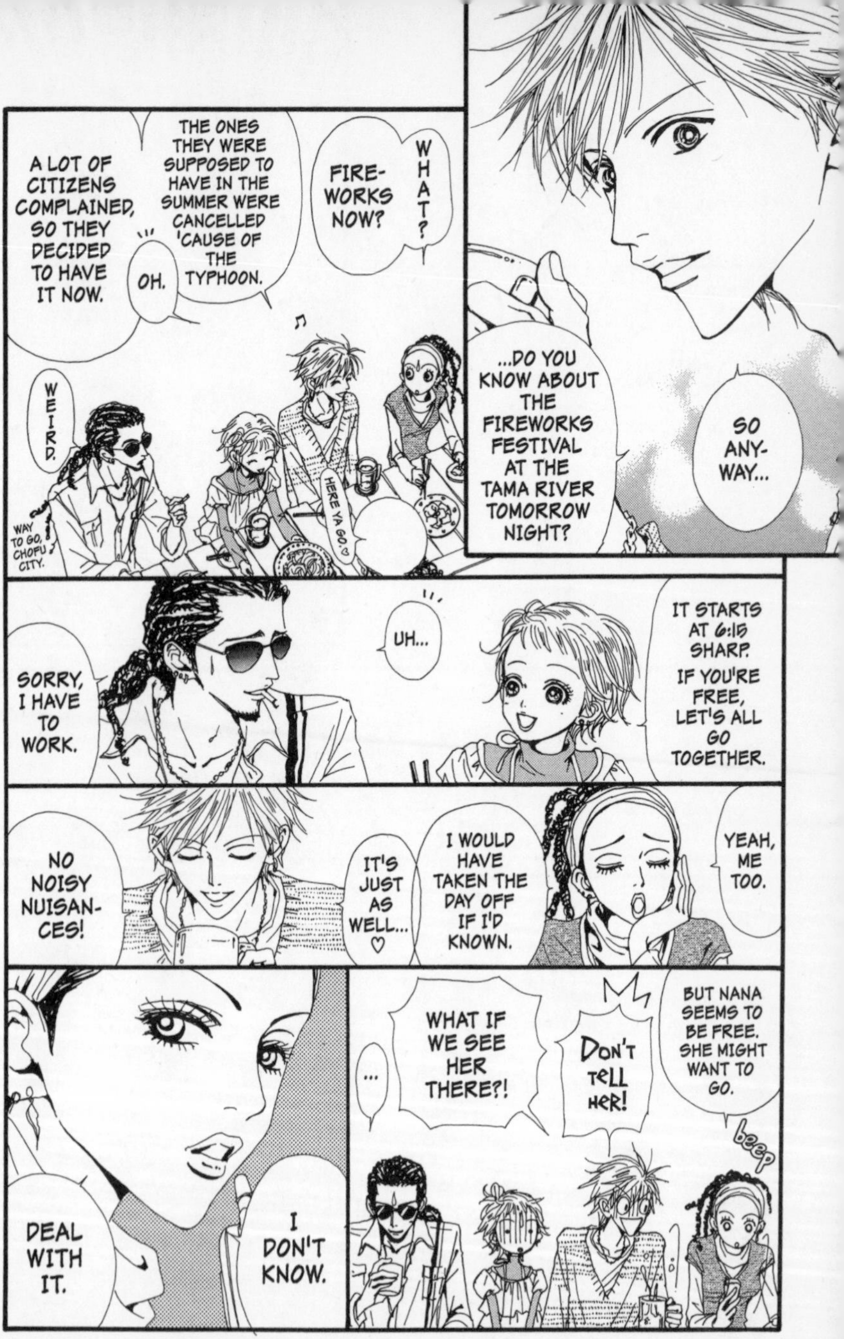
SO ANYWAY...
...DO YOU KNOW ABOUT THE FIREWORKS FESTIVAL AT THE TAMA RIVER TOMORROW NIGHT?
WHAT?
FIREWORKS NOW?
THE ONES THEY WERE SUPPOSED TO HAVE IN THE SUMMER WERE CANCELLED 'CAUSE OF THE TYPHOON.
OH.
A LOT OF CITIZENS COMPLAINED, SO THEY DECIDED TO HAVE IT NOW.
HERE YA GO.♡
WEIRD.
WAY TO GO, CHOFU CITY.
IT STARTS AT 6:15 SHARP. IF YOU'RE FREE, LET'S ALL GO TOGETHER.
UH...
SORRY, I HAVE TO WORK.
YEAH, ME TOO.
I WOULD HAVE TAKEN THE DAY OFF IF I'D KNOWN.
IT'S JUST AS WELL...♡
NO NOISY NUISANCES!
BUT NANA SEEMS TO BE FREE. SHE MIGHT WANT TO GO.
beep
DON'T TELL HER!
WHAT IF WE SEE HER THERE?!
...
I DON'T KNOW.
DEAL WITH IT.

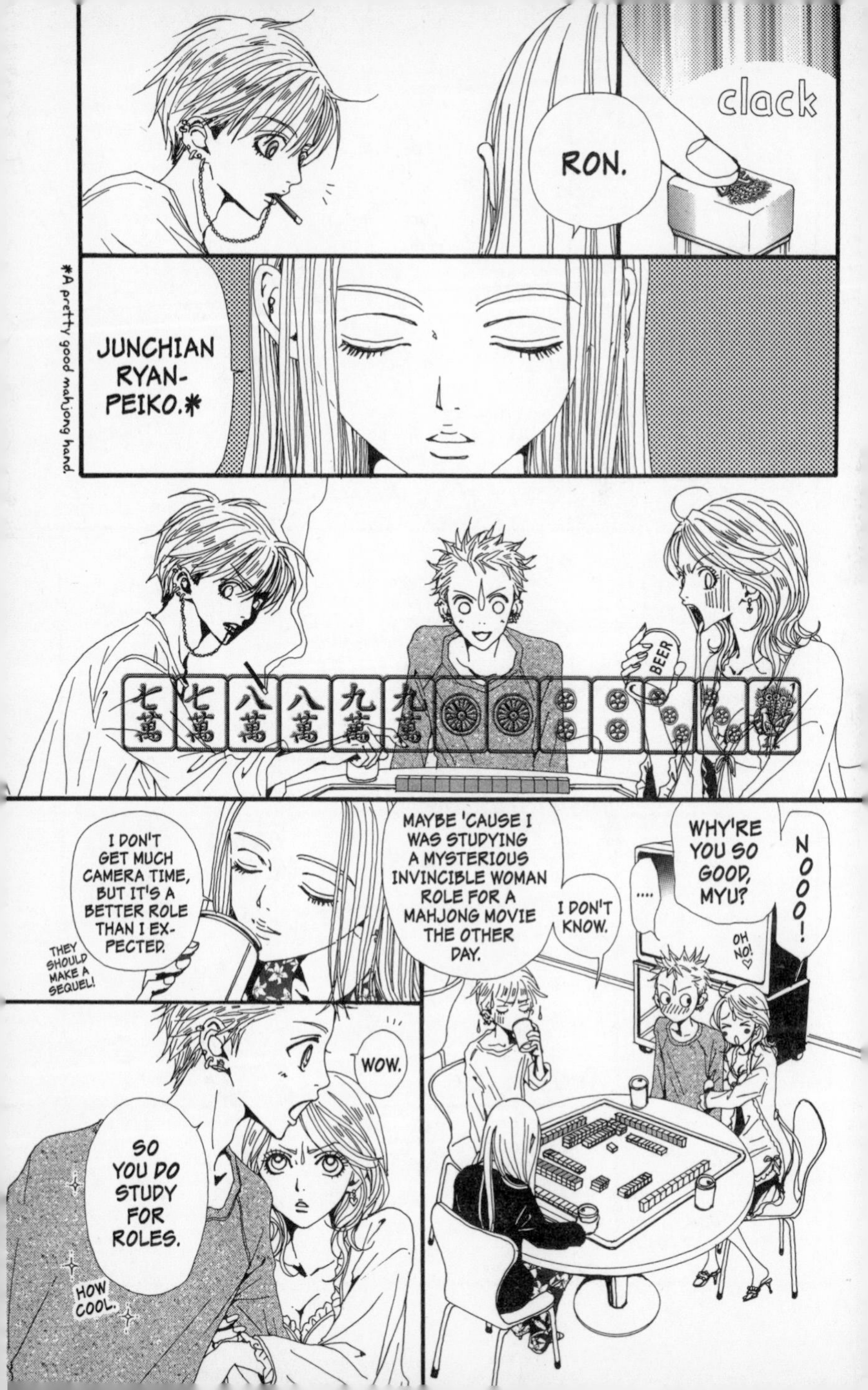
clack
RON.
JUNCHIAN RYAN-PEIKO.*
BEER
NOOOO!
WHY'RE YOU SO GOOD, MYU?
....
OH NO! ♡
I DON'T KNOW.
MAYBE 'CAUSE I WAS STUDYING A MYSTERIOUS INVINCIBLE WOMAN ROLE FOR A MAHJONG MOVIE THE OTHER DAY.
I DON'T GET MUCH CAMERA TIME, BUT IT'S A BETTER ROLE THAN I EXPECTED.
THEY SHOULD MAKE A SEQUEL!
WOW.
SO YOU DO STUDY FOR ROLES.
HOW COOL.

*A pretty good mahjong hand.

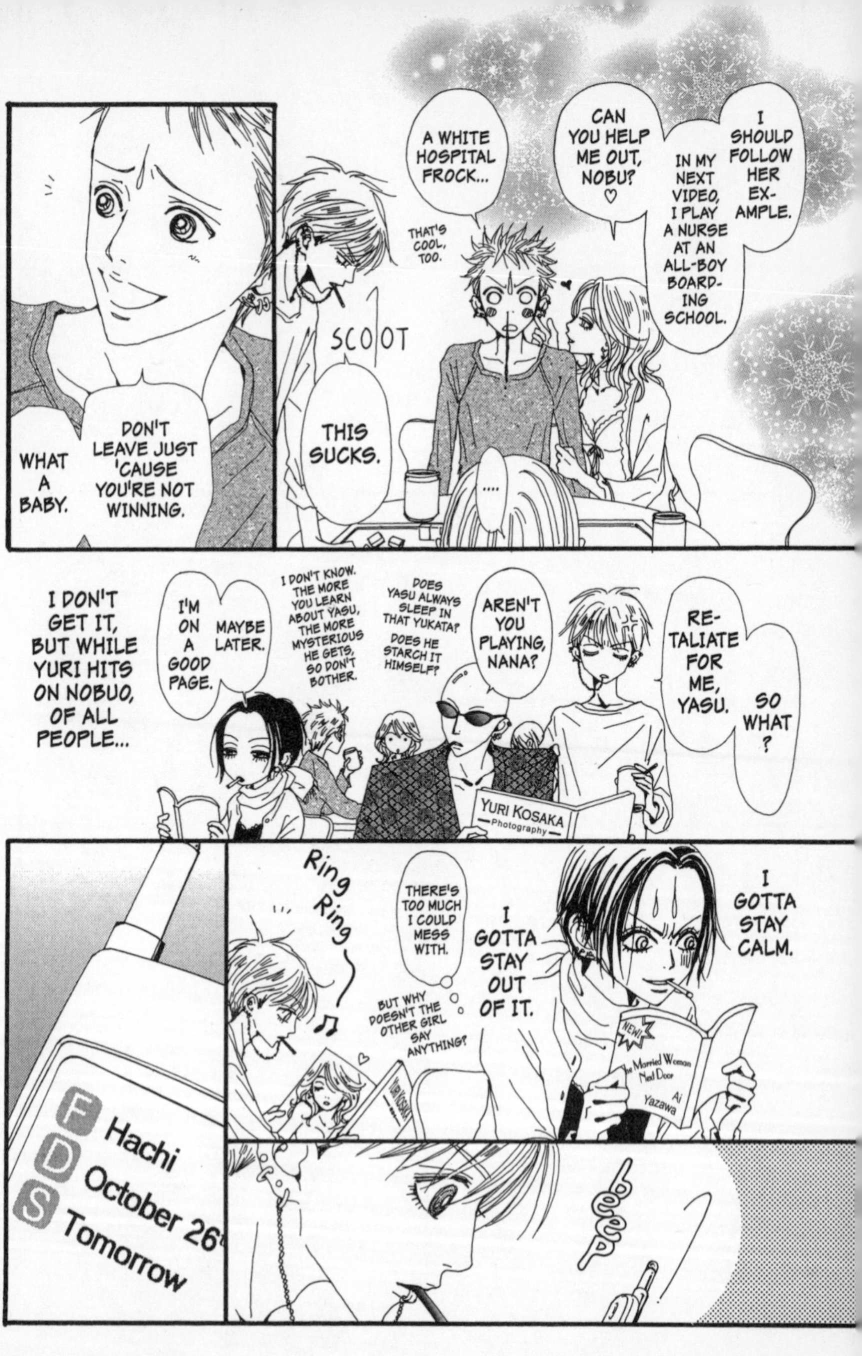
I SHOULD FOLLOW HER EX-AMPLE.
IN MY NEXT VIDEO, I PLAY A NURSE AT AN ALL-BOY BOARD-ING SCHOOL.
CAN YOU HELP ME OUT, NOBU? ♡
A WHITE HOSPITAL FROCK...
THAT'S COOL, TOO.
SCOOT
THIS SUCKS.
....
DON'T LEAVE JUST 'CAUSE YOU'RE NOT WINNING.
WHAT A BABY.
SO WHAT?
RE-TALIATE FOR ME, YASU.
AREN'T YOU PLAYING, NANA?
DOES YASU ALWAYS SLEEP IN THAT YUKATA? DOES HE STARCH IT HIMSELF?
I DON'T KNOW. THE MORE YOU LEARN ABOUT YASU, THE MORE MYSTERIOUS HE GETS, SO DON'T BOTHER.
YURI KOSAKA Photography
MAYBE LATER.
I'M ON A GOOD PAGE.
I DON'T GET IT, BUT WHILE YURI HITS ON NOBUO, OF ALL PEOPLE...
I GOTTA STAY CALM.
NEW! The Married Woman Next Door Ai Yazawa
I GOTTA STAY OUT OF IT.
THERE'S TOO MUCH I COULD MESS WITH.
BUT WHY DOESN'T THE OTHER GIRL SAY ANYTHING?
Ring Ring
beep
F Hachi
D October 26th
S Tomorrow

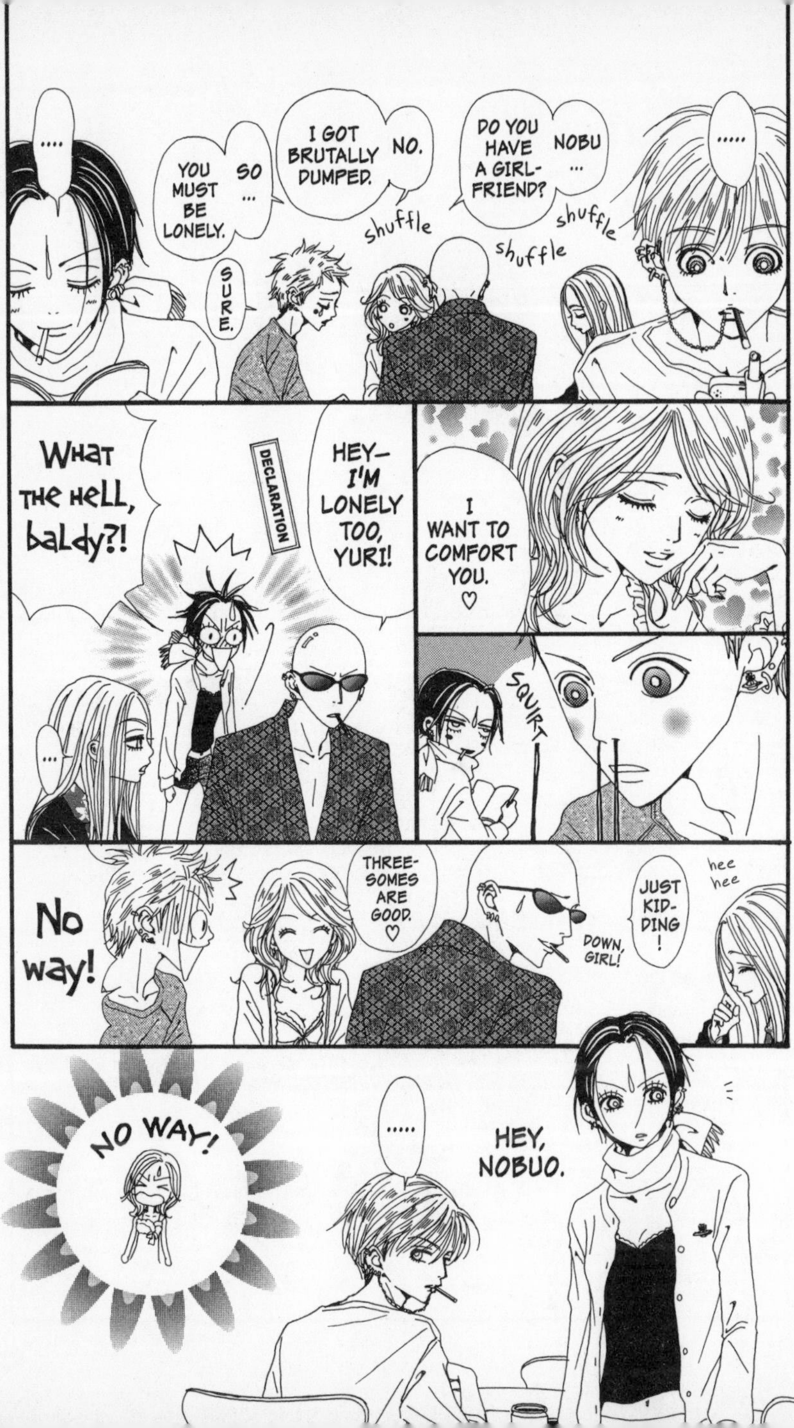
.....
NOBU ...
DO YOU HAVE A GIRL-FRIEND?
shuffle
shuffle
shuffle
NO.
I GOT BRUTALLY DUMPED.
SO ...
YOU MUST BE LONELY.
SURE.
.....
I WANT TO COMFORT YOU. ♡
SQUIRT
HEY— I'M LONELY TOO, YURI!
DECLARATION
WHAT THE HELL, baldy?!
...
hee hee
JUST KIDDING!
DOWN, GIRL!
THREESOMES ARE GOOD. ♡
No way!
HEY, NOBUO.
.....
NO WAY!

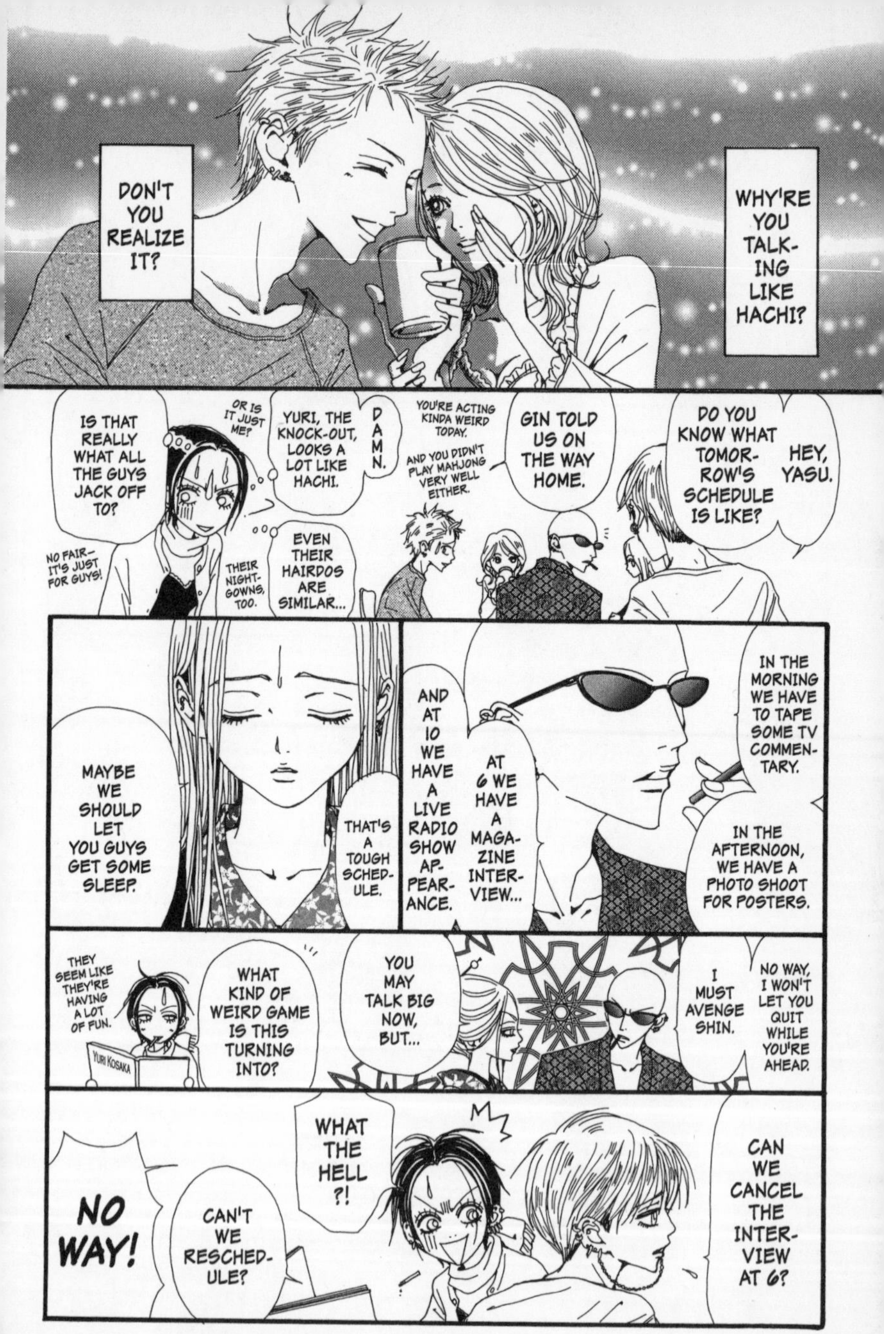
WHY'RE YOU TALKING LIKE HACHI?
DON'T YOU REALIZE IT?
HEY, YASU.
DO YOU KNOW WHAT TOMORROW'S SCHEDULE IS LIKE?
GIN TOLD US ON THE WAY HOME.
YOU'RE ACTING KINDA WEIRD TODAY.
AND YOU DIDN'T PLAY MAHJONG VERY WELL EITHER.
DAMN.
YURI, THE KNOCK-OUT, LOOKS A LOT LIKE HACHI.
OR IS IT JUST ME?
EVEN THEIR HAIRDOS ARE SIMILAR...
THEIR NIGHTGOWNS, TOO.
IS THAT REALLY WHAT ALL THE GUYS JACK OFF TO?
NO FAIR--IT'S JUST FOR GUYS!
IN THE MORNING WE HAVE TO TAPE SOME TV COMMENTARY.
IN THE AFTERNOON, WE HAVE A PHOTO SHOOT FOR POSTERS.
AT 6 WE HAVE A MAGAZINE INTERVIEW...
AND AT 10 WE HAVE A LIVE RADIO SHOW APPEARANCE.
THAT'S A TOUGH SCHEDULE.
MAYBE WE SHOULD LET YOU GUYS GET SOME SLEEP.
NO WAY, I WON'T LET YOU QUIT WHILE YOU'RE AHEAD.
I MUST AVENGE SHIN.
YOU MAY TALK BIG NOW, BUT...
WHAT KIND OF WEIRD GAME IS THIS TURNING INTO?
THEY SEEM LIKE THEY'RE HAVING A LOT OF FUN.
YURI KOSAKA
CAN WE CANCEL THE INTERVIEW AT 6?
WHAT THE HELL?!
CAN'T WE RESCHEDULE?
NO WAY!

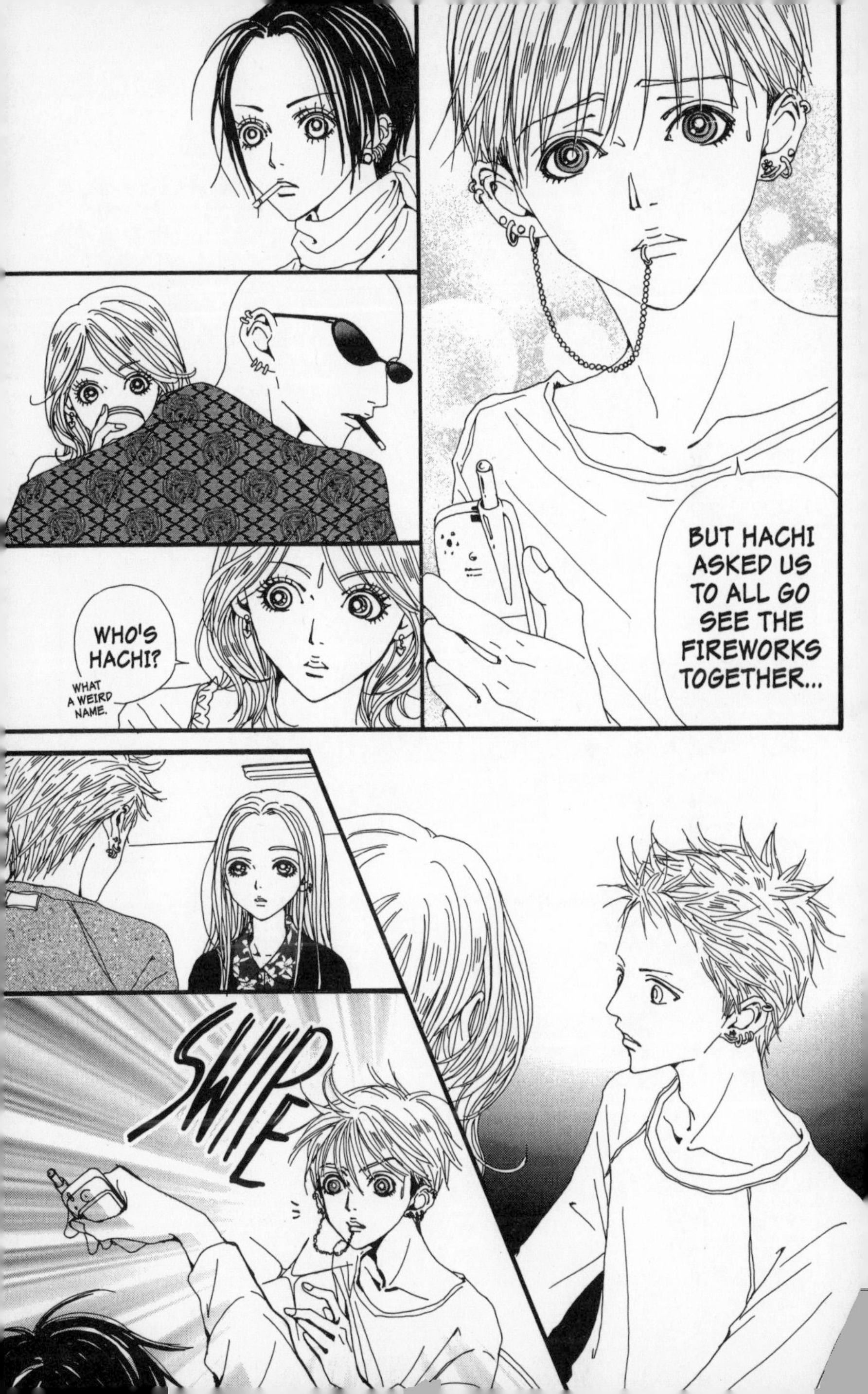
BUT HACHI ASKED US TO ALL GO SEE THE FIREWORKS TOGETHER...
WHO'S HACHI?
WHAT A WEIRD NAME.
SWIPE

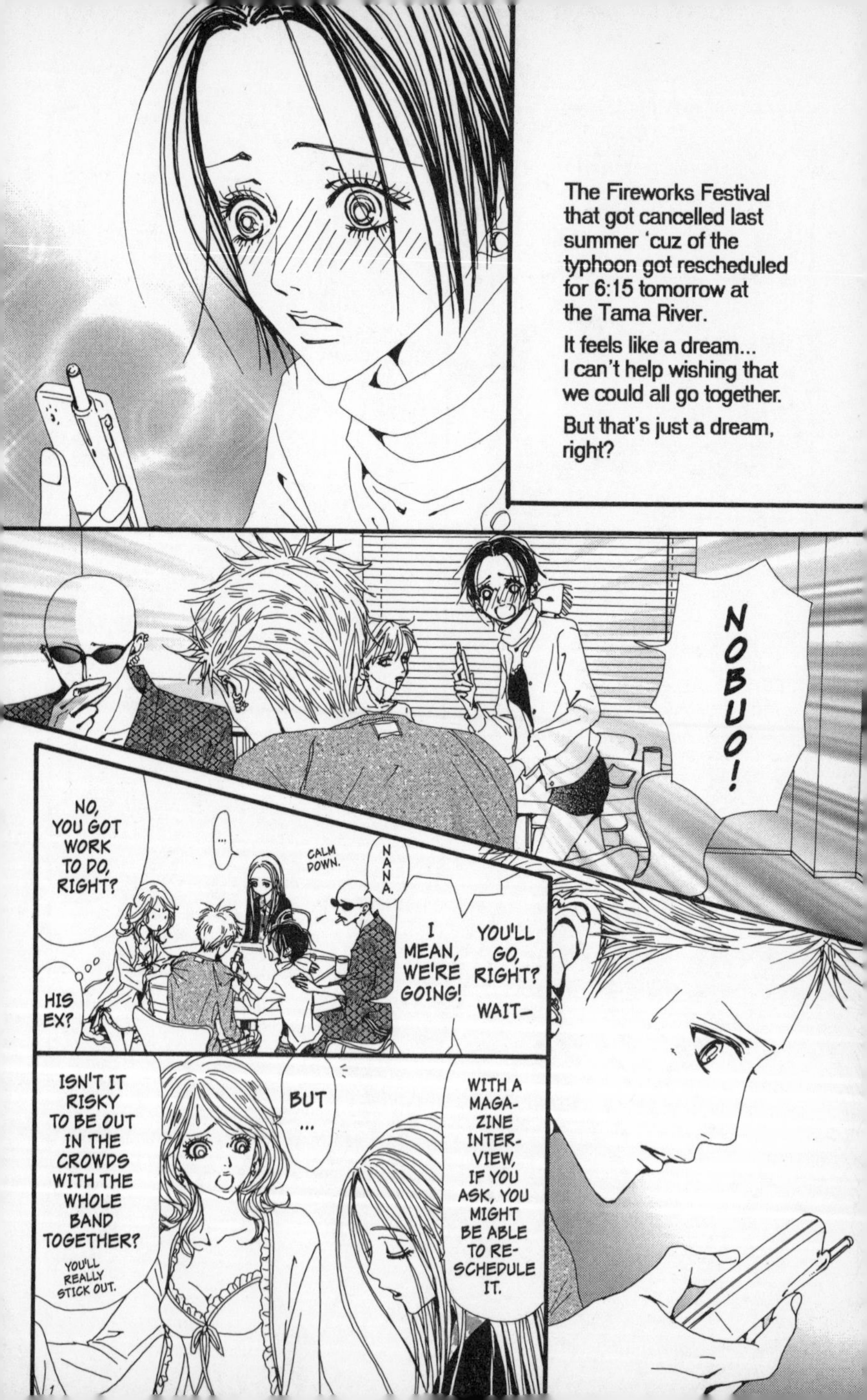
The Fireworks Festival that got cancelled last summer 'cuz of the typhoon got rescheduled for 6:15 tomorrow at the Tama River.
It feels like a dream... I can't help wishing that we could all go together.
But that's just a dream, right?
NOBUO!
NANA.
CALM DOWN.
YOU'LL GO, RIGHT?
WAIT—
I MEAN, WE'RE GOING!
...
NO, YOU GOT WORK TO DO, RIGHT?
HIS EX?
WITH A MAGAZINE INTERVIEW, IF YOU ASK, YOU MIGHT BE ABLE TO RESCHEDULE IT.
BUT...
ISN'T IT RISKY TO BE OUT IN THE CROWDS WITH THE WHOLE BAND TOGETHER?
YOU'LL REALLY STICK OUT.

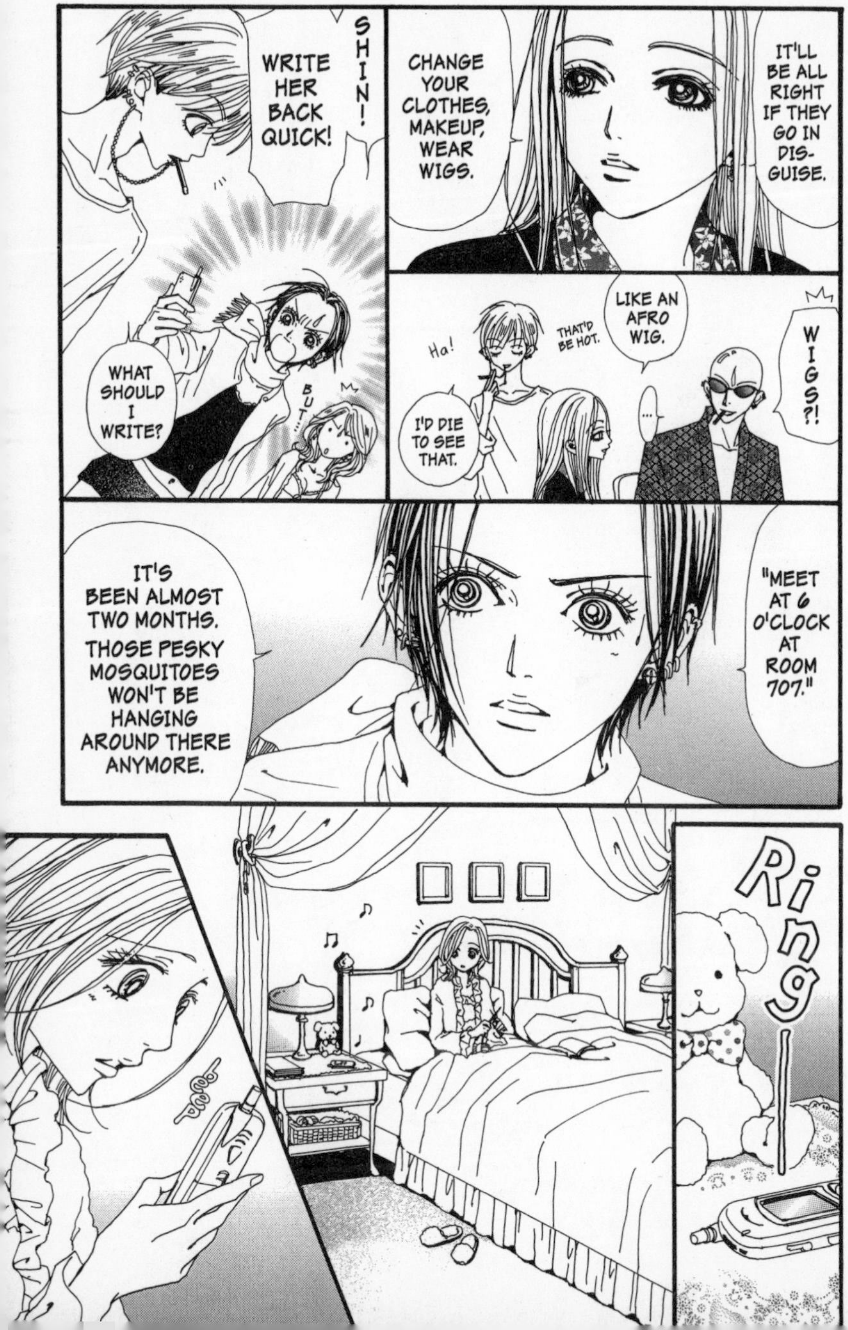
IT'LL BE ALL RIGHT IF THEY GO IN DIS-GUISE.
CHANGE YOUR CLOTHES, MAKEUP, WEAR WIGS.
WIGS?!
...
LIKE AN AFRO WIG.
THAT'D BE HOT.
Ha!
I'D DIE TO SEE THAT.
SHIN!
WRITE HER BACK QUICK!
BUT...
WHAT SHOULD I WRITE?
"MEET AT 6 O'CLOCK AT ROOM 707."
IT'S BEEN ALMOST TWO MONTHS. THOSE PESKY MOSQUITOES WON'T BE HANGING AROUND THERE ANYMORE.
Ring!

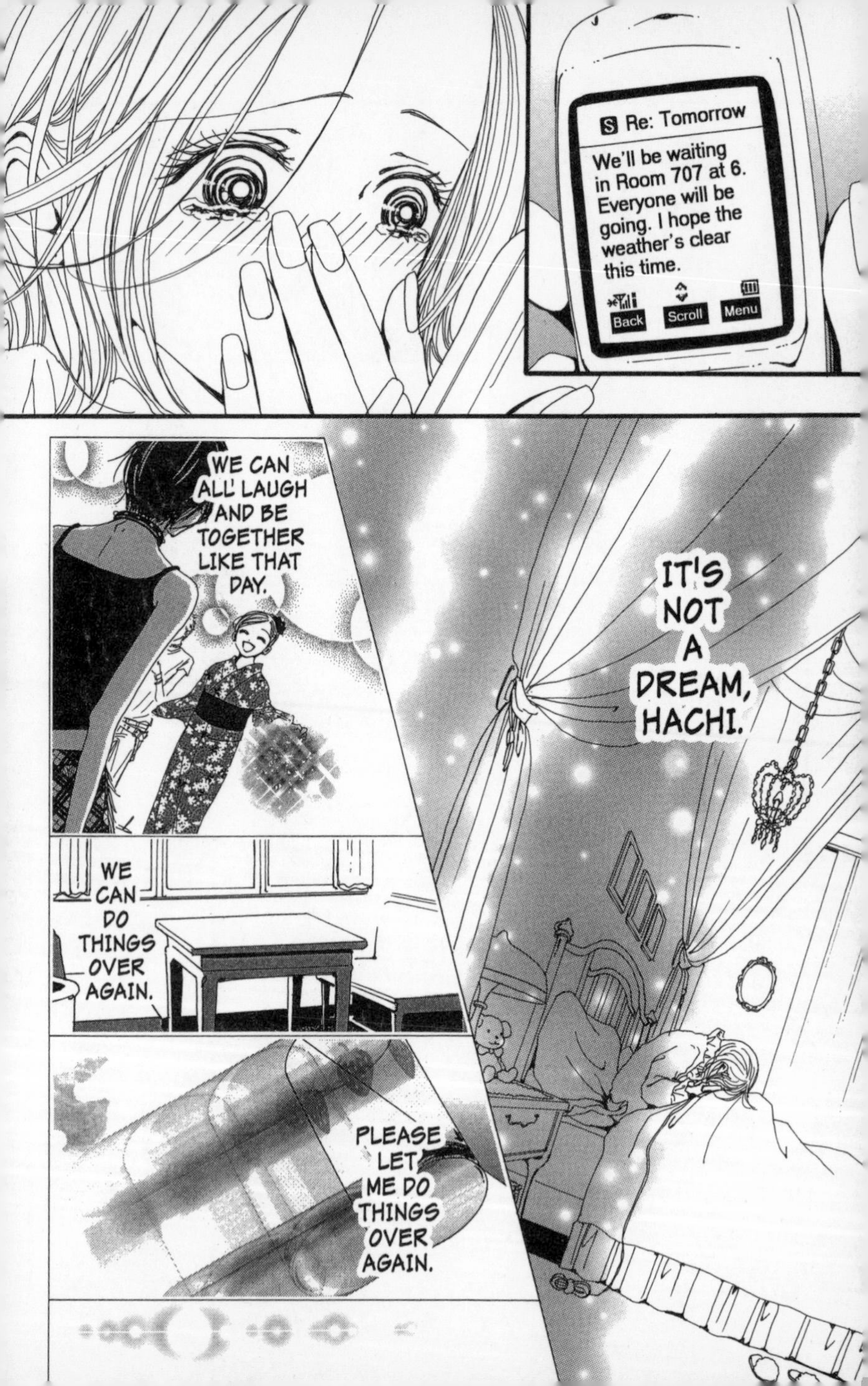
Re: Tomorrow
We'll be waiting in Room 707 at 6. Everyone will be going. I hope the weather's clear this time.
Back
Scroll
Menu
IT'S NOT A DREAM, HACHI.
WE CAN ALL LAUGH AND BE TOGETHER LIKE THAT DAY.
WE CAN DO THINGS OVER AGAIN.
PLEASE LET ME DO THINGS OVER AGAIN.

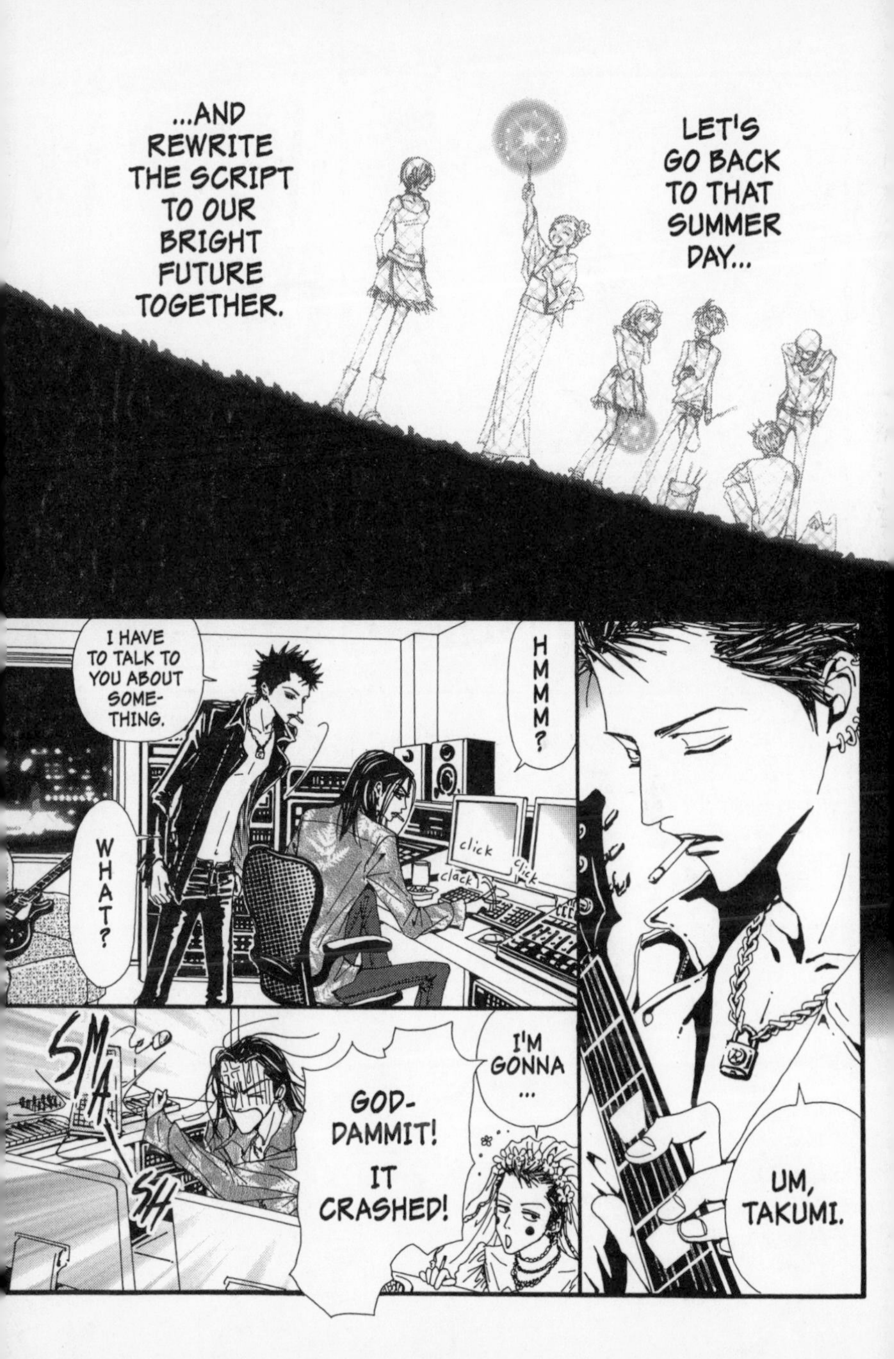
LET'S GO BACK TO THAT SUMMER DAY...
...AND REWRITE THE SCRIPT TO OUR BRIGHT FUTURE TOGETHER.
UM, TAKUMI.
HMMM?
I HAVE TO TALK TO YOU ABOUT SOME-THING.
WHAT?
click
click
clack
I'M GONNA ...
GOD-DAMMIT! IT CRASHED!
SMASH

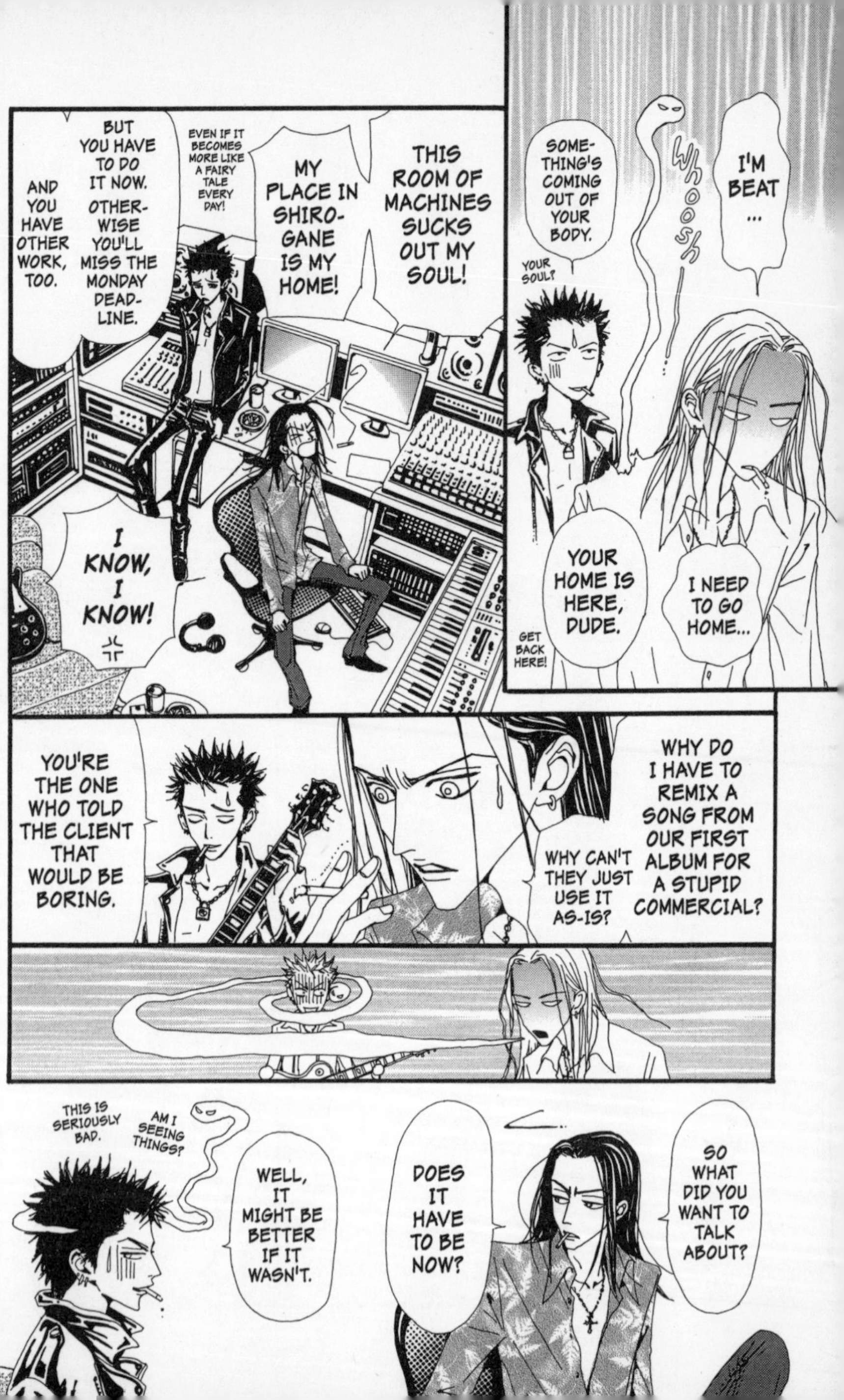
I'M BEAT...
Whoosh
SOMETHING'S COMING OUT OF YOUR BODY.
YOUR SOUL?
I NEED TO GO HOME...
YOUR HOME IS HERE, DUDE.
GET BACK HERE!
THIS ROOM OF MACHINES SUCKS OUT MY SOUL!
MY PLACE IN SHIROGANE IS MY HOME!
EVEN IF IT BECOMES MORE LIKE A FAIRY TALE EVERY DAY!
BUT YOU HAVE TO DO IT NOW. OTHERWISE YOU'LL MISS THE MONDAY DEADLINE.
AND YOU HAVE OTHER WORK, TOO.
I KNOW, I KNOW!
WHY DO I HAVE TO REMIX A SONG FROM OUR FIRST ALBUM FOR A STUPID COMMERCIAL?
WHY CAN'T THEY JUST USE IT AS-IS?
YOU'RE THE ONE WHO TOLD THE CLIENT THAT WOULD BE BORING.
SO WHAT DID YOU WANT TO TALK ABOUT?
DOES IT HAVE TO BE NOW?
WELL, IT MIGHT BE BETTER IF IT WASN'T.
AM I SEEING THINGS?
THIS IS SERIOUSLY BAD.

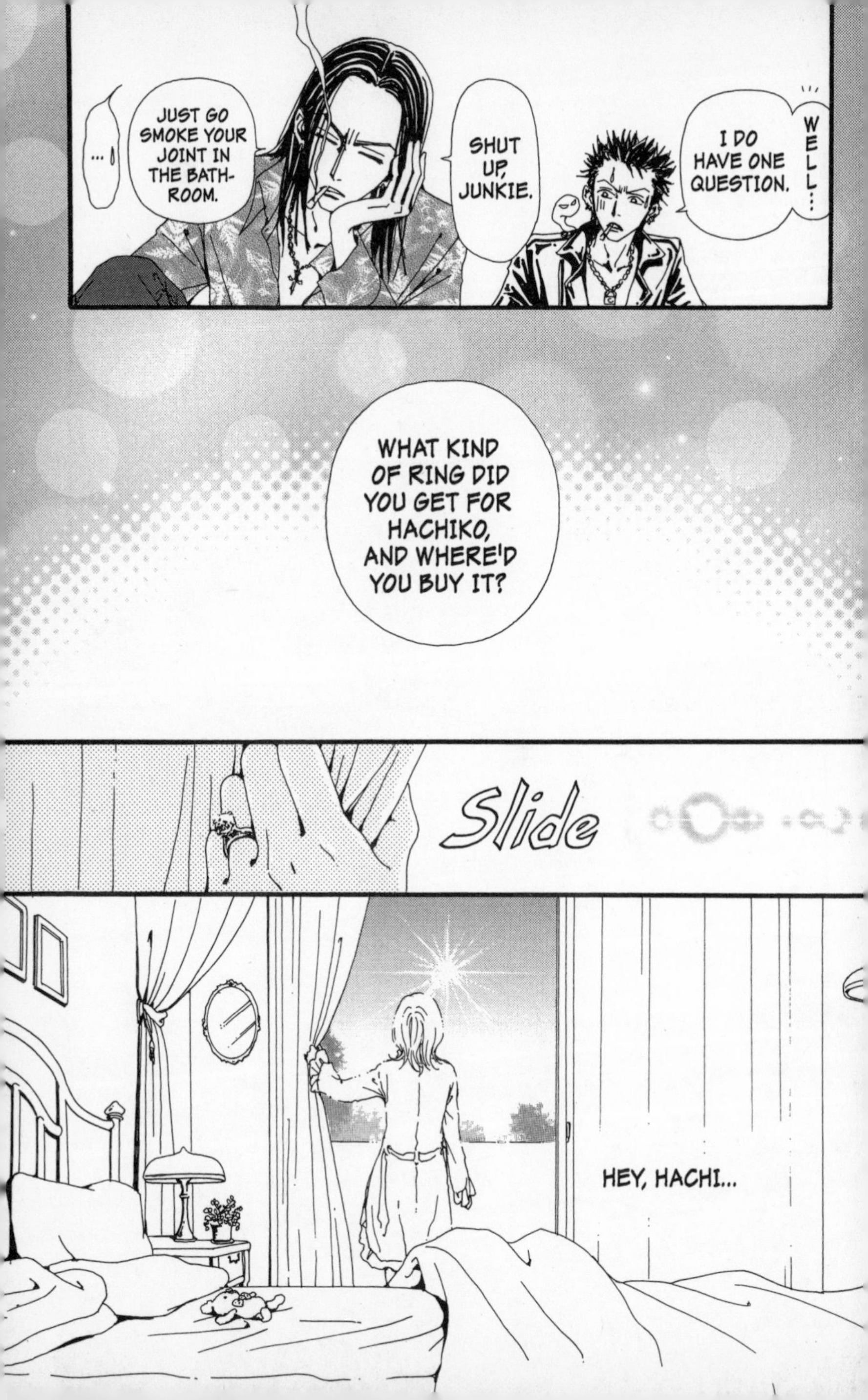
WELL...
I DO HAVE ONE QUESTION.
SHUT UP, JUNKIE.
JUST GO SMOKE YOUR JOINT IN THE BATH-ROOM.
...
WHAT KIND OF RING DID YOU GET FOR HACHIKO, AND WHERE'D YOU BUY IT?
Slide
HEY, HACHI...

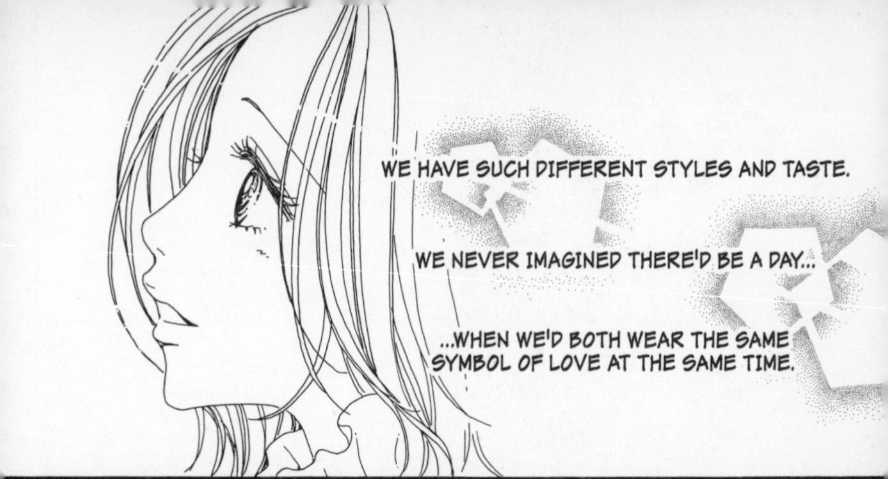
WE HAVE SUCH DIFFERENT STYLES AND TASTE.
WE NEVER IMAGINED THERE'D BE A DAY...
...WHEN WE'D BOTH WEAR THE SAME SYMBOL OF LOVE AT THE SAME TIME.
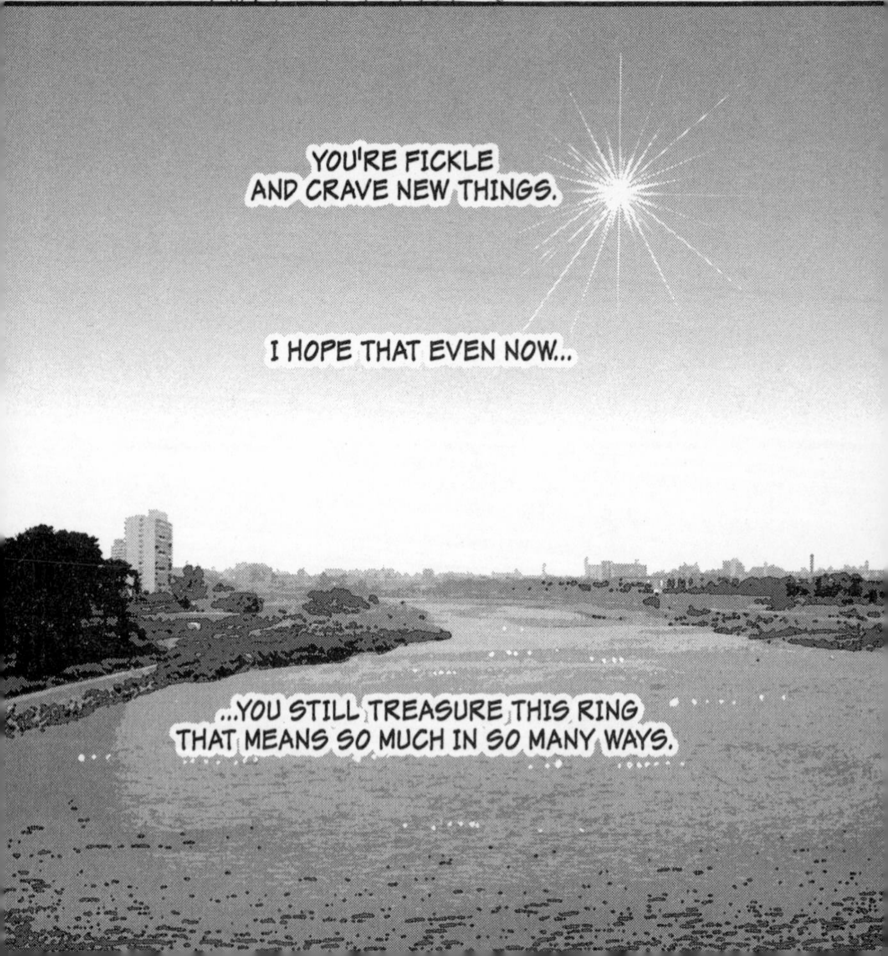
YOU'RE FICKLE AND CRAVE NEW THINGS.
I HOPE THAT EVEN NOW...
...YOU STILL TREASURE THIS RING THAT MEANS SO MUCH IN SO MANY WAYS.

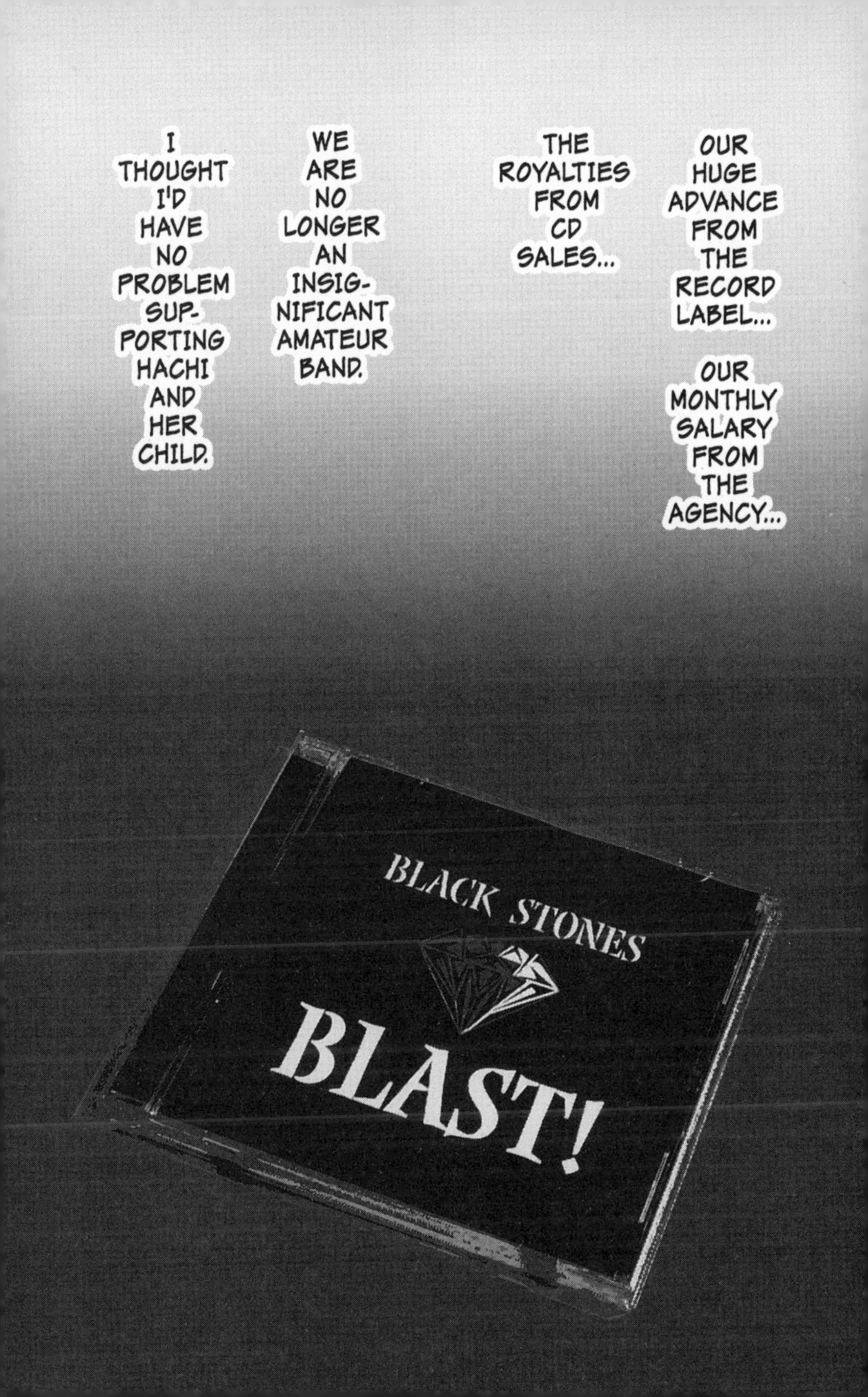
OUR HUGE ADVANCE FROM THE RECORD LABEL...
OUR MONTHLY SALARY FROM THE AGENCY...
THE ROYALTIES FROM CD SALES...
WE ARE NO LONGER AN INSIG-NIFICANT AMATEUR BAND.
I THOUGHT I'D HAVE NO PROBLEM SUP-PORTING HACHI AND HER CHILD.
BLACK STONES
BLAST!

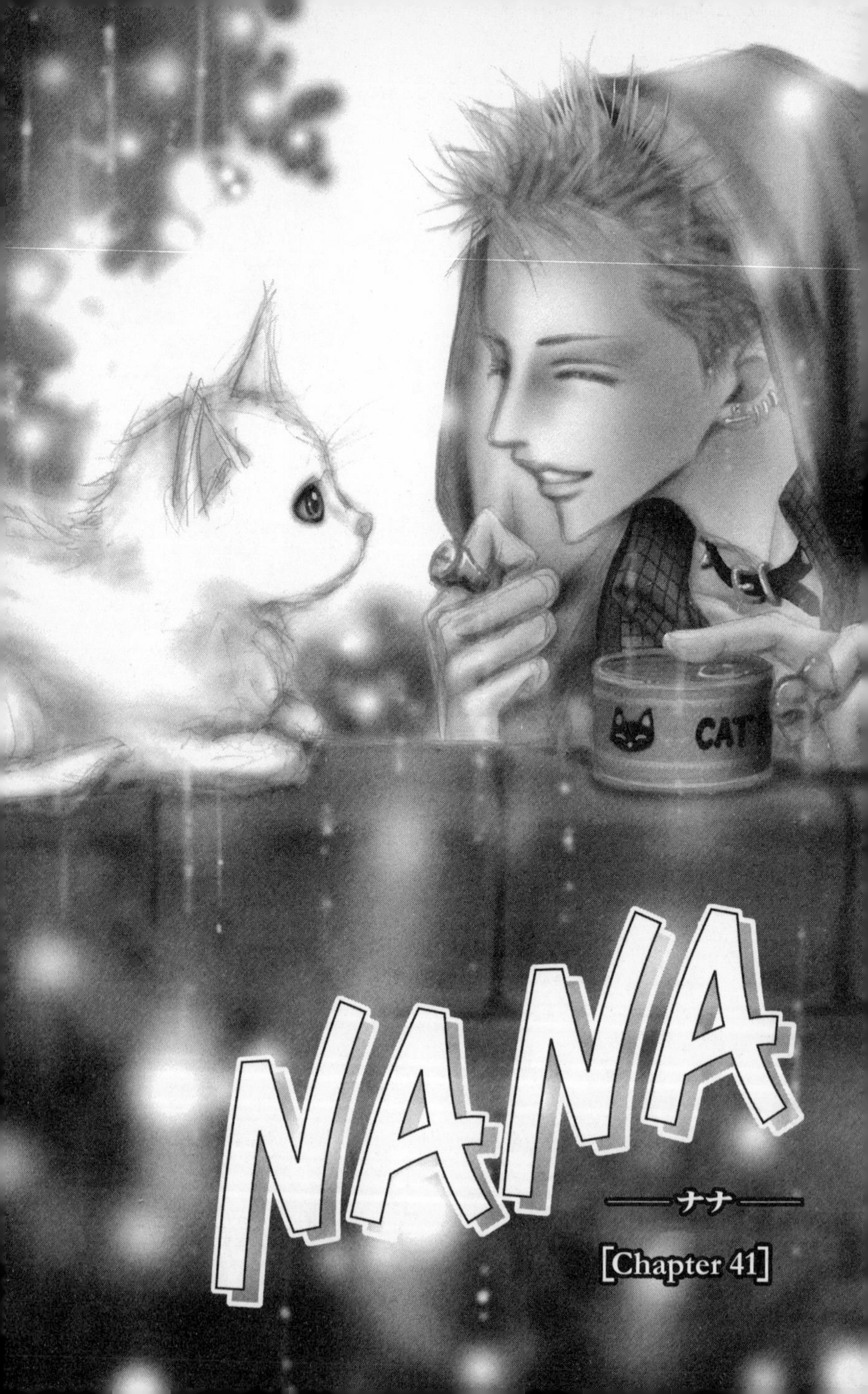
CAT
NANA
ナナ
[Chapter 41]

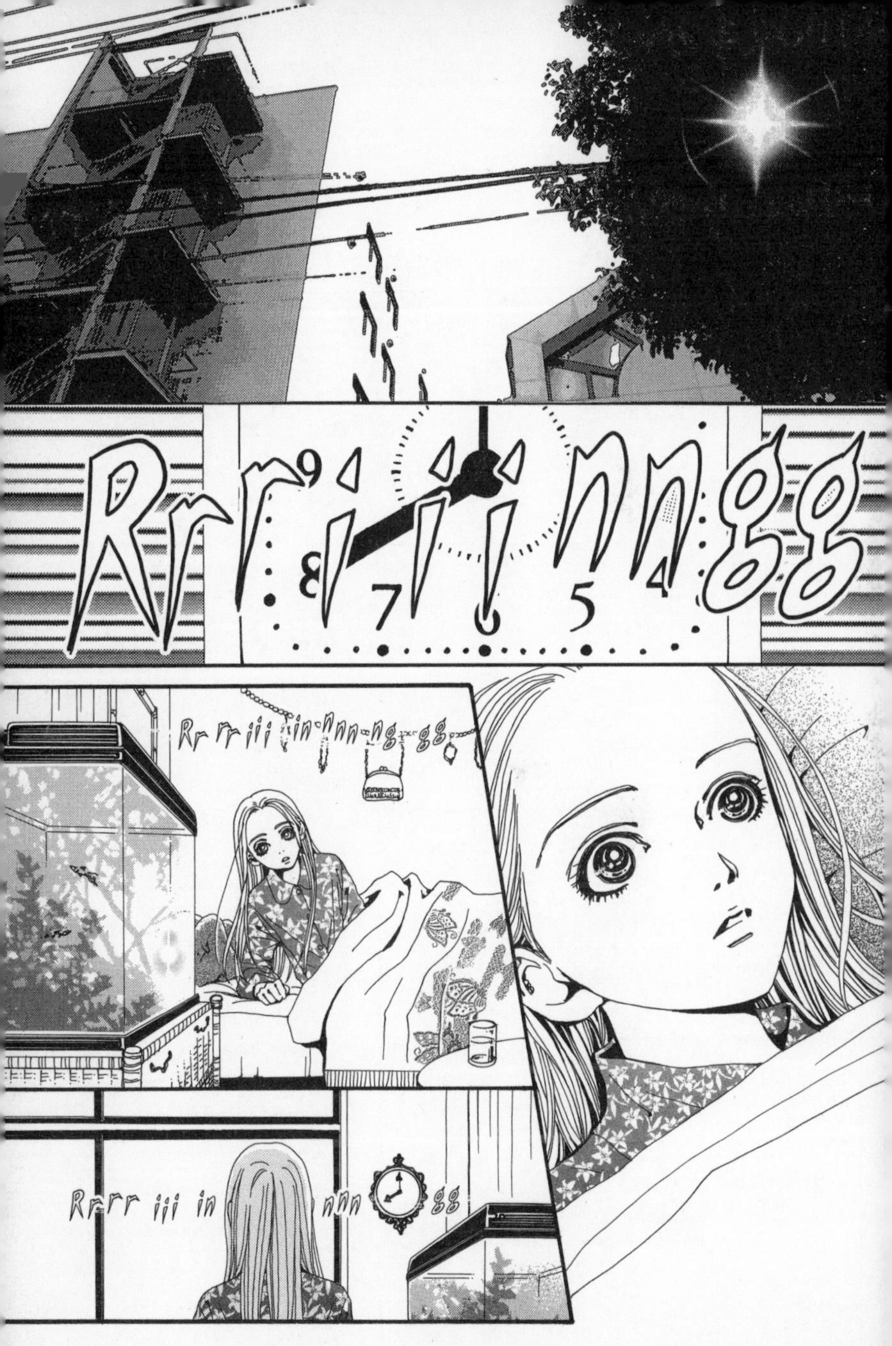
Rrriiinngg
Rr rr iii iin nnn ng gg
Rrrr iii in nnn gg

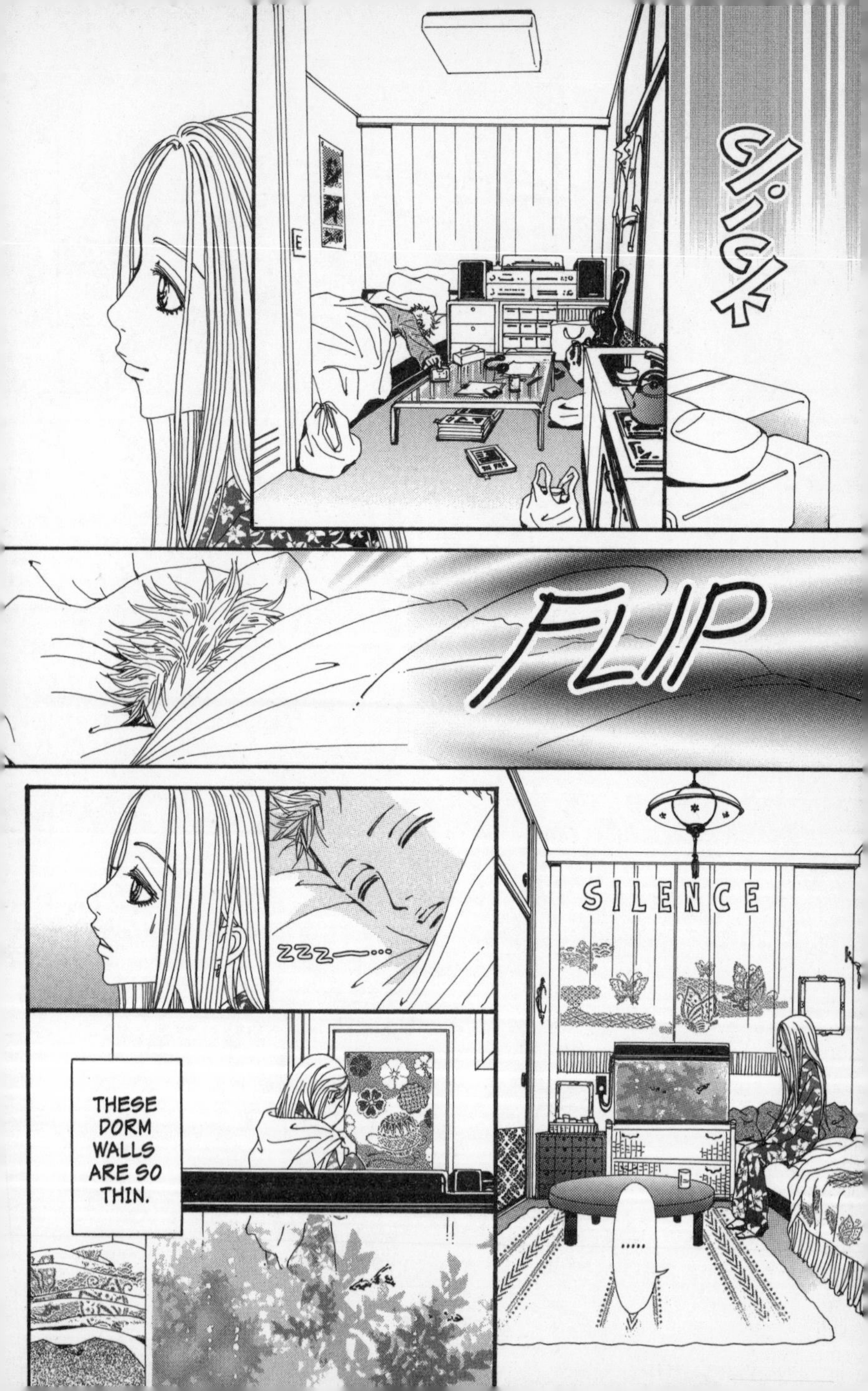
click
FLIP
SILENCE
......
zzz—...
THESE DORM WALLS ARE SO THIN.
!!

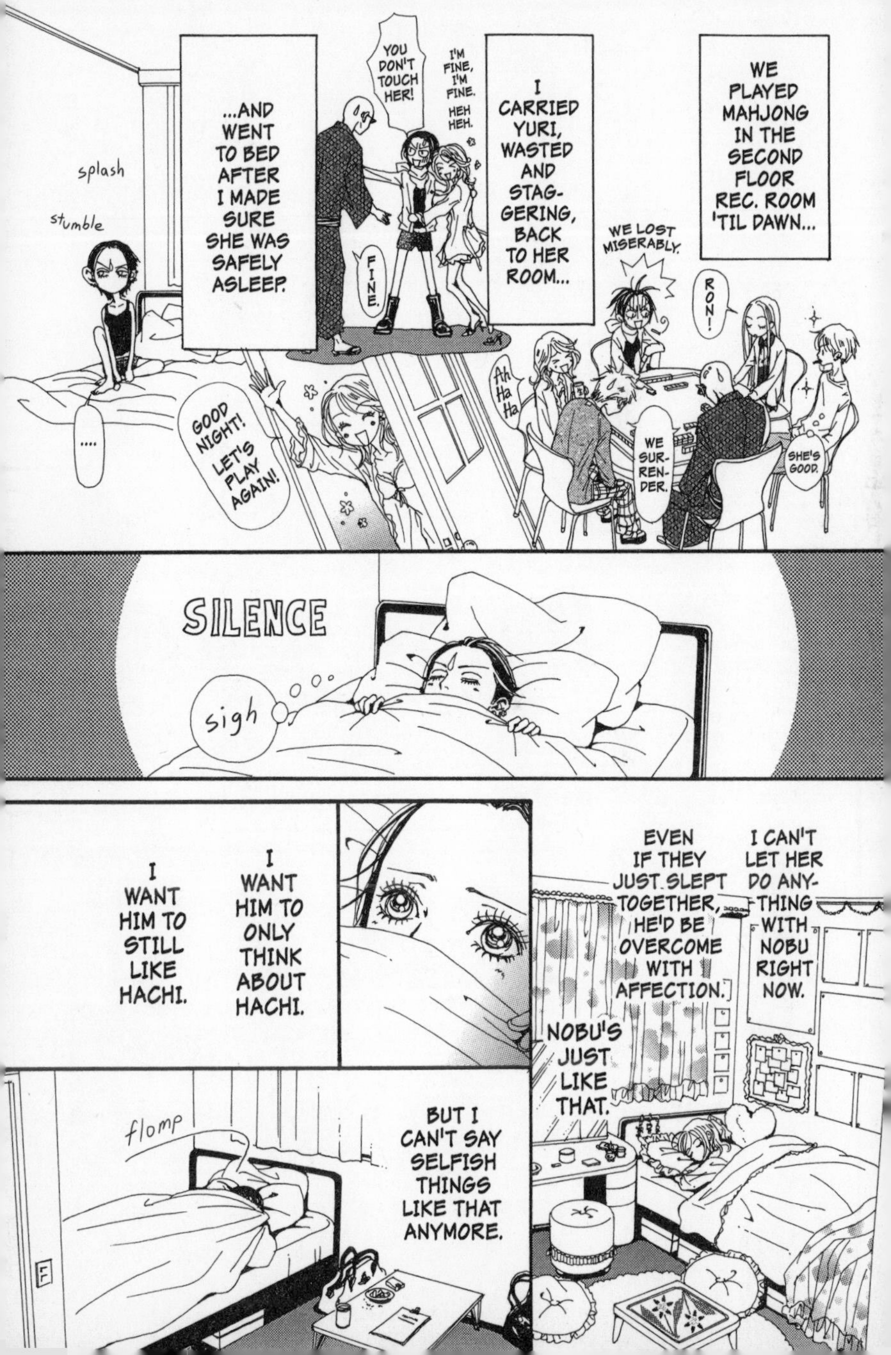
WE PLAYED MAHJONG IN THE SECOND FLOOR REC. ROOM 'TIL DAWN...
RON!
SHE'S GOOD.
WE LOST MISERABLY.
WE SURRENDER.
Ah Ha Ha
I CARRIED YURI, WASTED AND STAGGERING, BACK TO HER ROOM...
I'M FINE, I'M FINE. HEH HEH.
YOU DON'T TOUCH HER!
FINE.
GOOD NIGHT! LET'S PLAY AGAIN!
...AND WENT TO BED AFTER I MADE SURE SHE WAS SAFELY ASLEEP.
splash
stumble
....
SILENCE
sigh
I CAN'T LET HER DO ANYTHING WITH NOBU RIGHT NOW.
EVEN IF THEY JUST SLEPT TOGETHER, HE'D BE OVERCOME WITH AFFECTION.
NOBU'S JUST LIKE THAT.
I WANT HIM TO ONLY THINK ABOUT HACHI.
I WANT HIM TO STILL LIKE HACHI.
flomp
BUT I CAN'T SAY SELFISH THINGS LIKE THAT ANYMORE.

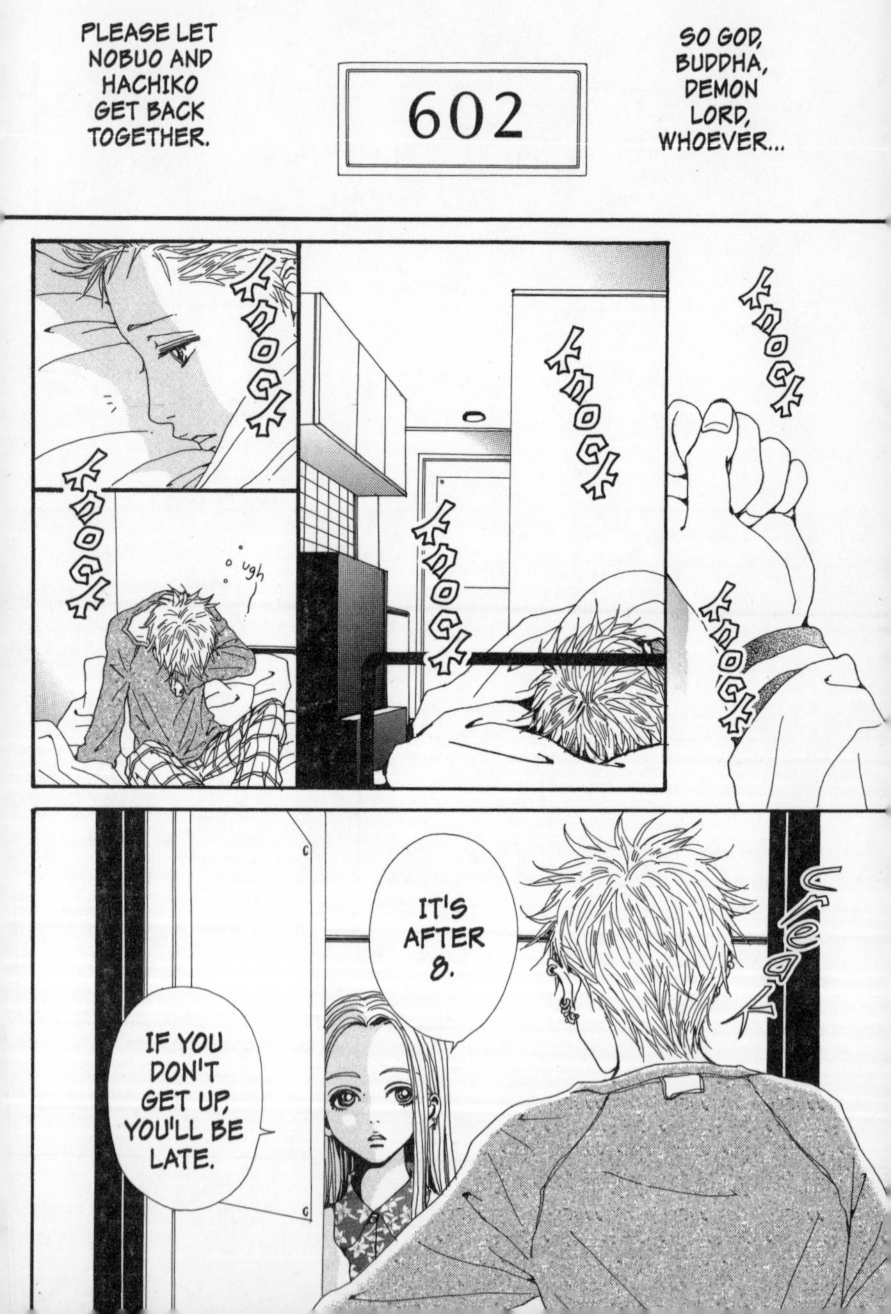
SO GOD, BUDDHA, DEMON LORD, WHOEVER...
602
PLEASE LET NOBUO AND HACHIKO GET BACK TOGETHER.
KNOCK
KNOCK
KNOCK
KNOCK
KNOCK
KNOCK
ugh
CREAK
IT'S AFTER 8.
IF YOU DON'T GET UP, YOU'LL BE LATE.

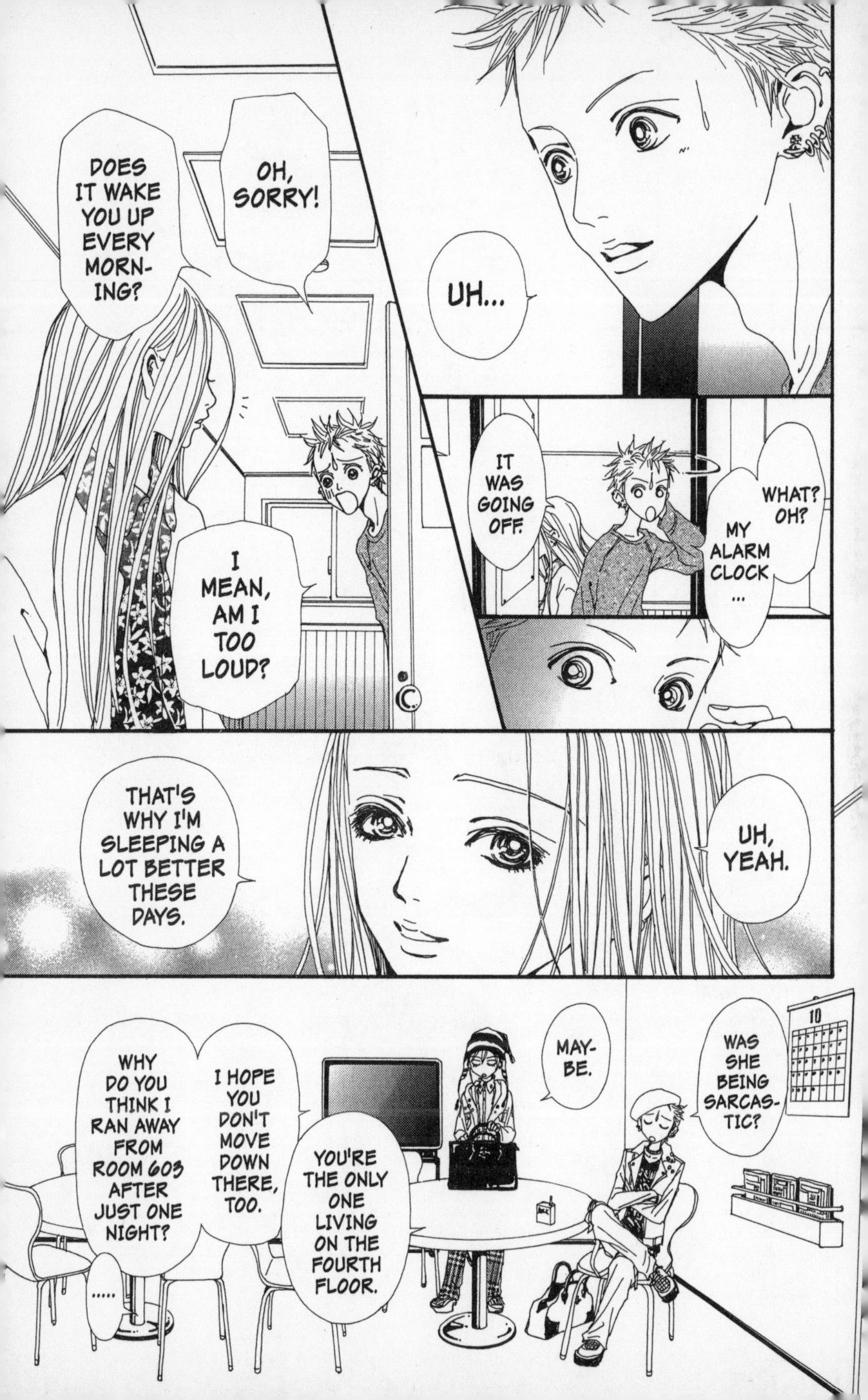
UH...
WHAT? OH?
MY ALARM CLOCK ...
IT WAS GOING OFF.
OH, SORRY!
DOES IT WAKE YOU UP EVERY MORNING?
I MEAN, AM I TOO LOUD?
UH, YEAH.
THAT'S WHY I'M SLEEPING A LOT BETTER THESE DAYS.
WAS SHE BEING SARCASTIC?
MAY-BE.
YOU'RE THE ONLY ONE LIVING ON THE FOURTH FLOOR.
I HOPE YOU DON'T MOVE DOWN THERE, TOO.
WHY DO YOU THINK I RAN AWAY FROM ROOM 603 AFTER JUST ONE NIGHT?
.....

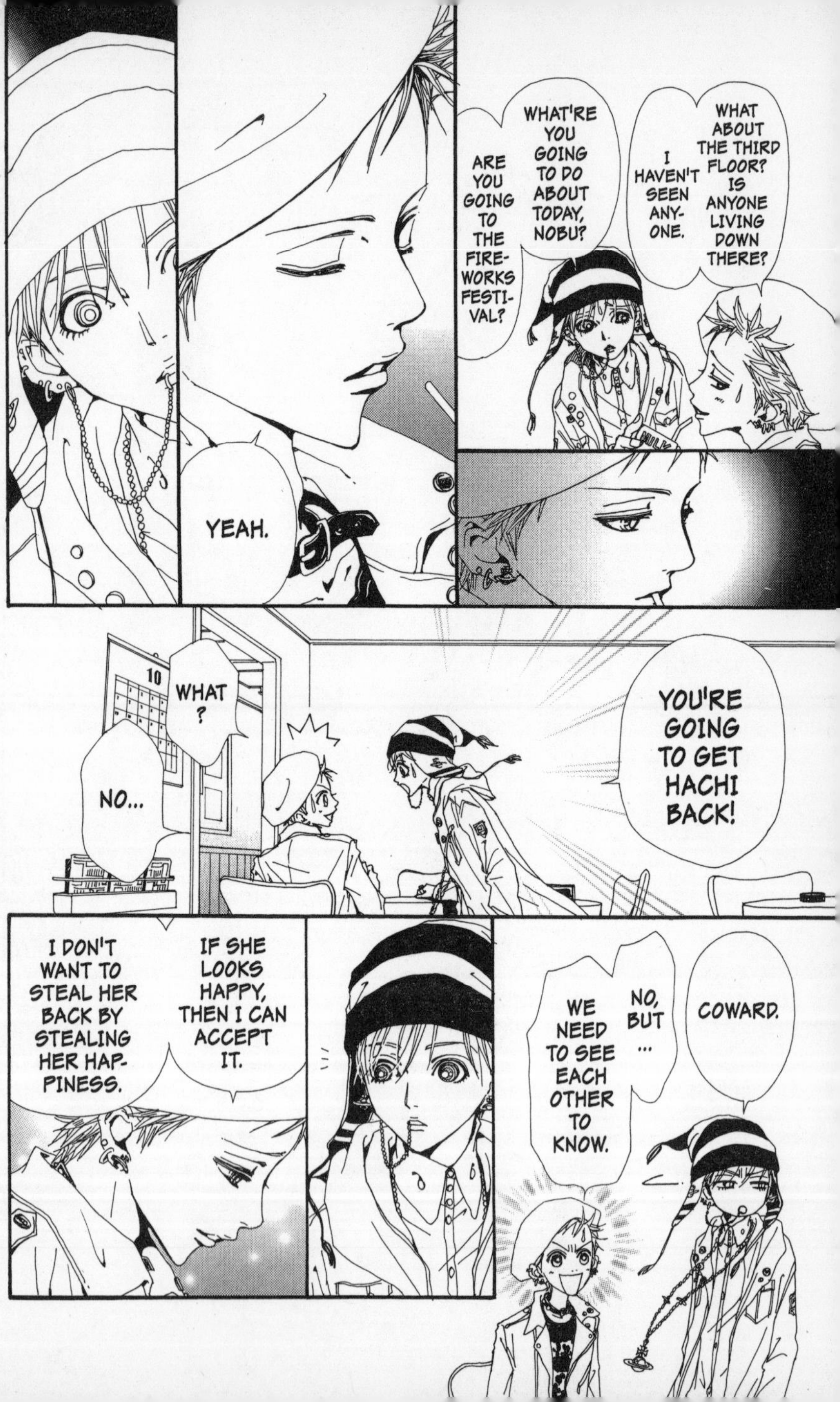
WHAT ABOUT THE THIRD FLOOR? IS ANYONE LIVING DOWN THERE?
I HAVEN'T SEEN ANYONE.
WHAT'RE YOU GOING TO DO ABOUT TODAY, NOBU?
ARE YOU GOING TO THE FIREWORKS FESTIVAL?
YEAH.
YOU'RE GOING TO GET HACHI BACK!
WHAT?
NO...
COWARD.
NO, BUT ...
WE NEED TO SEE EACH OTHER TO KNOW.
IF SHE LOOKS HAPPY, THEN I CAN ACCEPT IT.
I DON'T WANT TO STEAL HER BACK BY STEALING HER HAPPINESS.

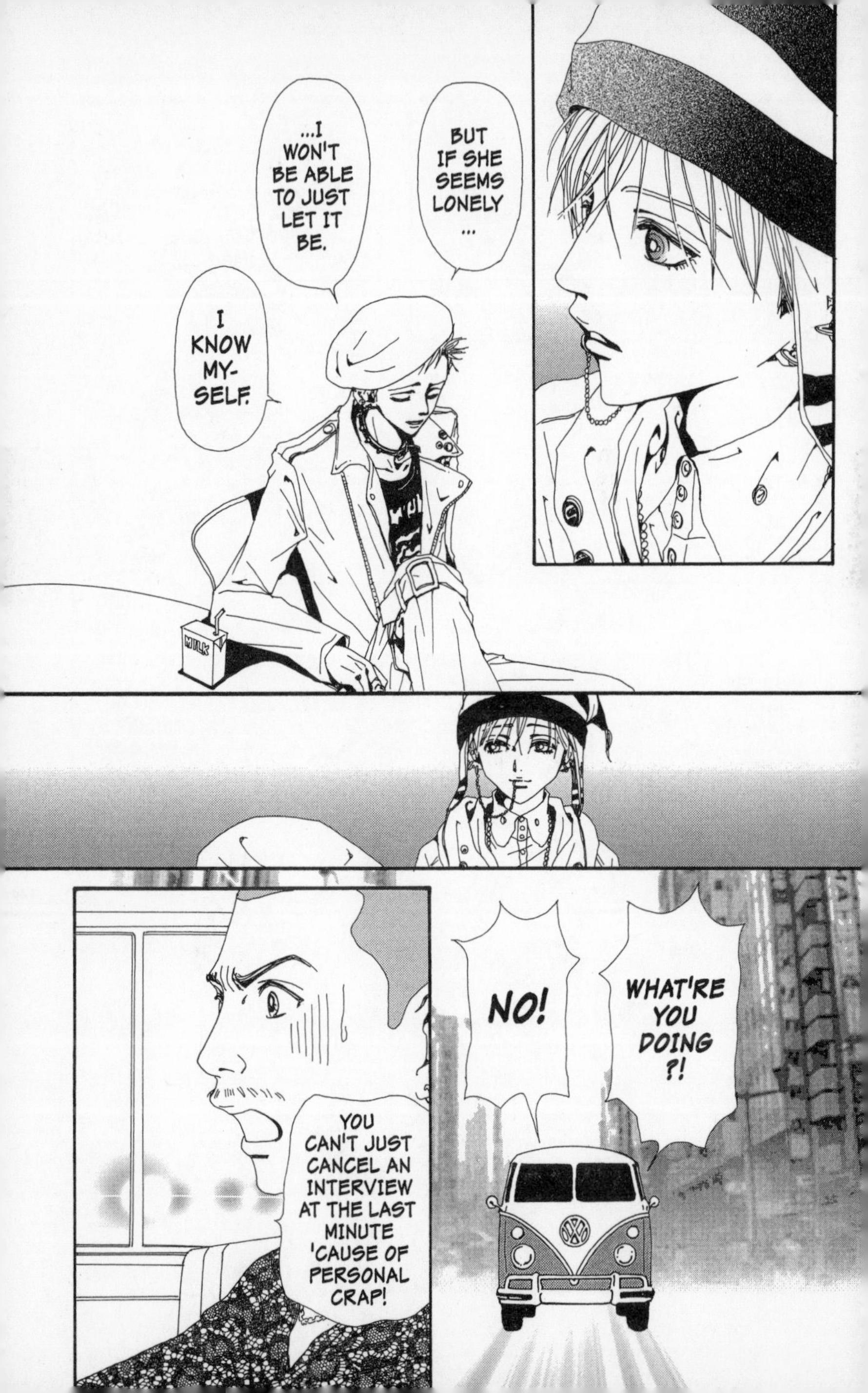
BUT IF SHE SEEMS LONELY ...
...I WON'T BE ABLE TO JUST LET IT BE.
I KNOW MY-SELF.
MILK
WHAT'RE YOU DOING ?!
NO!
YOU CAN'T JUST CANCEL AN INTERVIEW AT THE LAST MINUTE 'CAUSE OF PERSONAL CRAP!

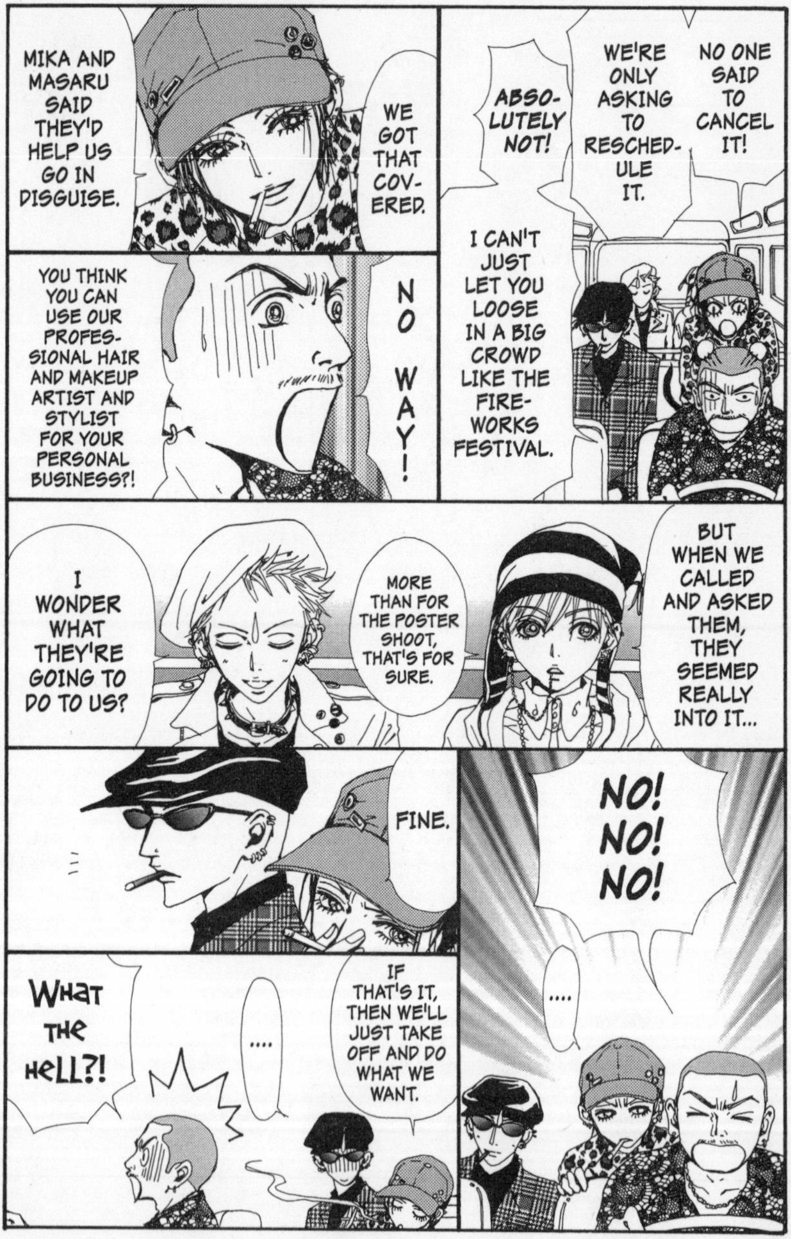
NO ONE SAID TO CANCEL IT!
WE'RE ONLY ASKING TO RESCHEDULE IT.
ABSOLUTELY NOT!
I CAN'T JUST LET YOU LOOSE IN A BIG CROWD LIKE THE FIREWORKS FESTIVAL.
WE GOT THAT COVERED.
MIKA AND MASARU SAID THEY'D HELP US GO IN DISGUISE.
NO WAY!
YOU THINK YOU CAN USE OUR PROFESSIONAL HAIR AND MAKEUP ARTIST AND STYLIST FOR YOUR PERSONAL BUSINESS?!
BUT WHEN WE CALLED AND ASKED THEM, THEY SEEMED REALLY INTO IT...
MORE THAN FOR THE POSTER SHOOT, THAT'S FOR SURE.
I WONDER WHAT THEY'RE GOING TO DO TO US?
NO! NO! NO!
....
FINE.
IF THAT'S IT, THEN WE'LL JUST TAKE OFF AND DO WHAT WE WANT.
....
WHAT THE HELL?!

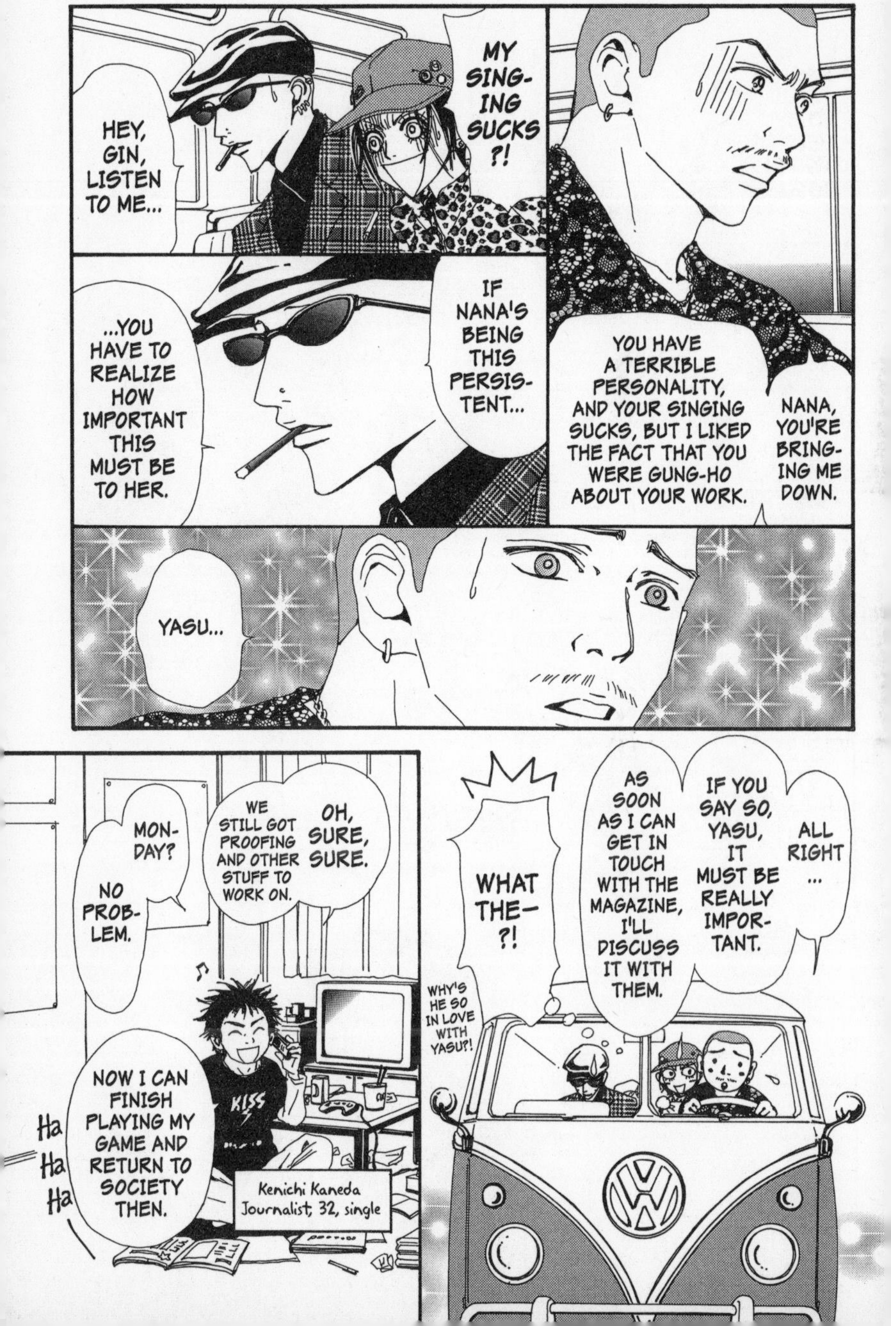
NANA, YOU'RE BRINGING ME DOWN.
YOU HAVE A TERRIBLE PERSONALITY, AND YOUR SINGING SUCKS, BUT I LIKED THE FACT THAT YOU WERE GUNG-HO ABOUT YOUR WORK.
MY SINGING SUCKS?!
HEY, GIN, LISTEN TO ME...
IF NANA'S BEING THIS PERSISTENT...
...YOU HAVE TO REALIZE HOW IMPORTANT THIS MUST BE TO HER.
YASU...
ALL RIGHT ...
IF YOU SAY SO, YASU, IT MUST BE REALLY IMPORTANT.
AS SOON AS I CAN GET IN TOUCH WITH THE MAGAZINE, I'LL DISCUSS IT WITH THEM.
WHAT THE—?!
WHY'S HE SO IN LOVE WITH YASU?!
OH, SURE, SURE.
WE STILL GOT PROOFING AND OTHER STUFF TO WORK ON.
MONDAY?
NO PROBLEM.
NOW I CAN FINISH PLAYING MY GAME AND RETURN TO SOCIETY THEN.
Ha Ha Ha
Kenichi Kaneda
Journalist, 32, single

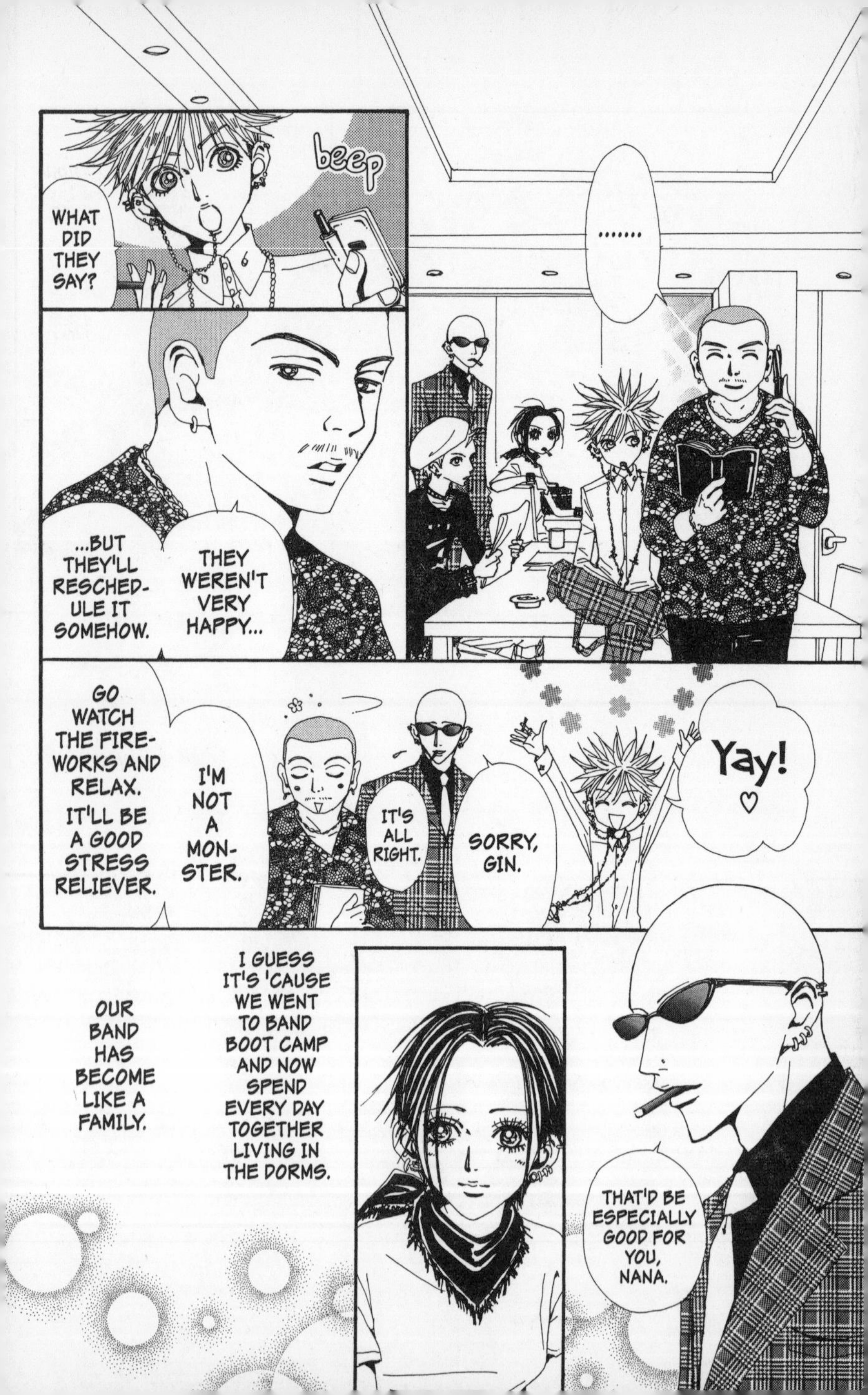

......
beep
WHAT DID THEY SAY?
THEY WEREN'T VERY HAPPY...
...BUT THEY'LL RESCHEDULE IT SOMEHOW.
Yay! ♡
SORRY, GIN.
IT'S ALL RIGHT.
I'M NOT A MONSTER.
GO WATCH THE FIREWORKS AND RELAX. IT'LL BE A GOOD STRESS RELIEVER.
THAT'D BE ESPECIALLY GOOD FOR YOU, NANA.
I GUESS IT'S 'CAUSE WE WENT TO BAND BOOT CAMP AND NOW SPEND EVERY DAY TOGETHER LIVING IN THE DORMS.
OUR BAND HAS BECOME LIKE A FAMILY.

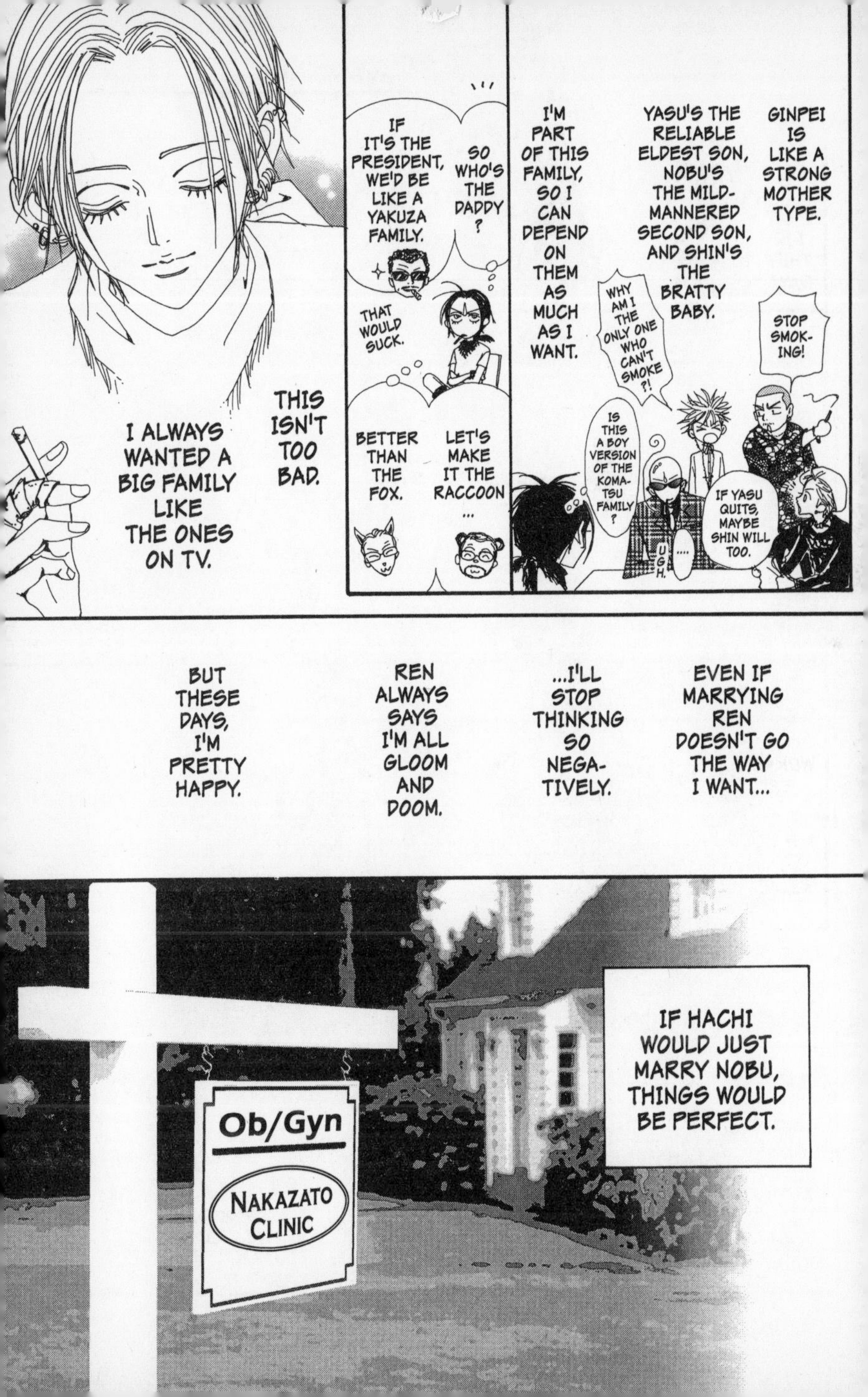
GINPEI IS LIKE A STRONG MOTHER TYPE.
YASU'S THE RELIABLE ELDEST SON, NOBU'S THE MILD-MANNERED SECOND SON, AND SHIN'S THE BRATTY BABY.
I'M PART OF THIS FAMILY, SO I CAN DEPEND ON THEM AS MUCH AS I WANT.
STOP SMOKING!
WHY AM I THE ONLY ONE WHO CAN'T SMOKE?!
IS THIS A BOY VERSION OF THE KOMATSU FAMILY?
IF YASU QUITS, MAYBE SHIN WILL TOO.
....
UGH.
SO WHO'S THE DADDY?
IF IT'S THE PRESIDENT, WE'D BE LIKE A YAKUZA FAMILY.
THAT WOULD SUCK.
LET'S MAKE IT THE RACCOON...
BETTER THAN THE FOX.
THIS ISN'T TOO BAD.
I ALWAYS WANTED A BIG FAMILY LIKE THE ONES ON TV.
EVEN IF MARRYING REN DOESN'T GO THE WAY I WANT...
...I'LL STOP THINKING SO NEGATIVELY.
REN ALWAYS SAYS I'M ALL GLOOM AND DOOM.
BUT THESE DAYS, I'M PRETTY HAPPY.
IF HACHI WOULD JUST MARRY NOBU, THINGS WOULD BE PERFECT.
Ob/Gyn
NAKAZATO CLINIC

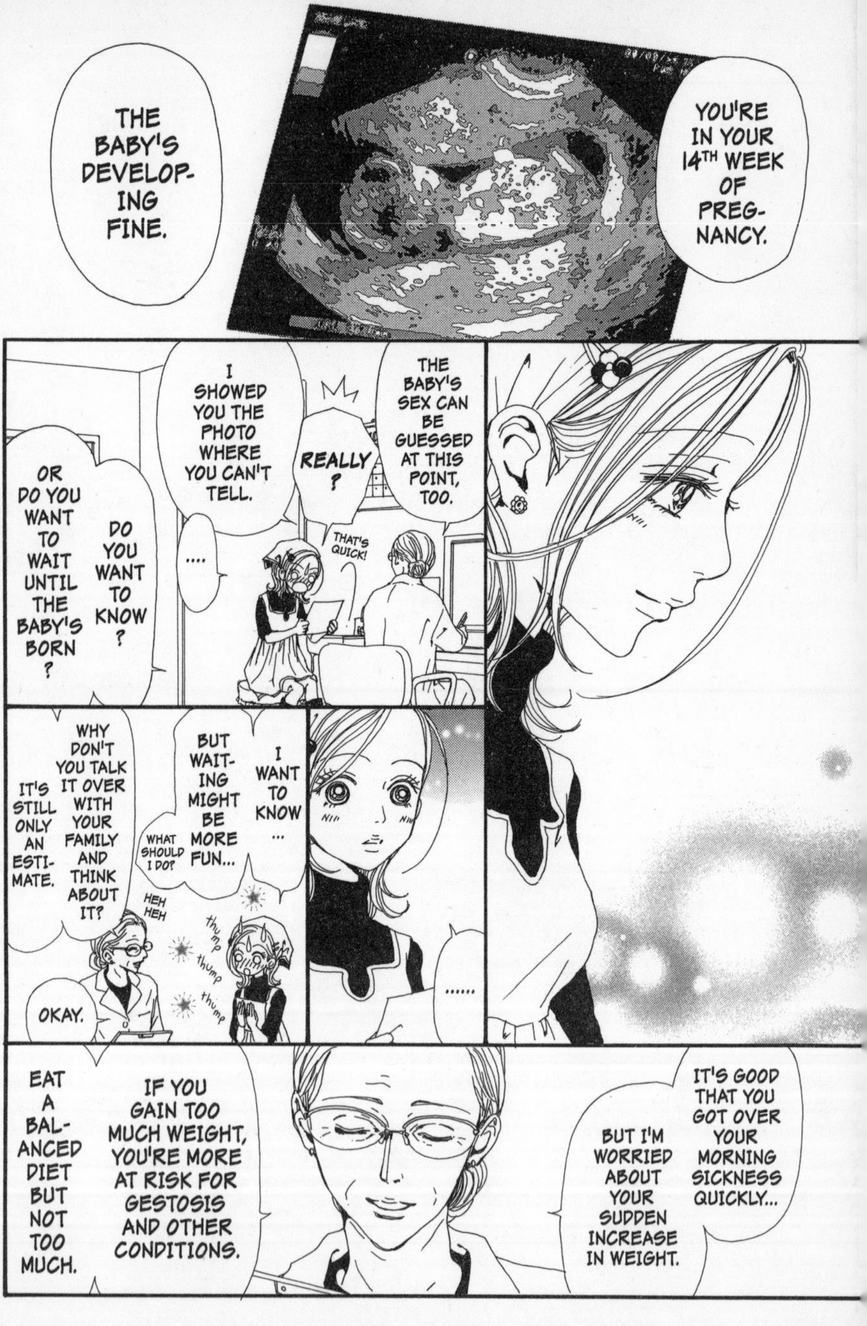
YOU'RE IN YOUR 14TH WEEK OF PREG-NANCY.
THE BABY'S DEVELOP-ING FINE.
THE BABY'S SEX CAN BE GUESSED AT THIS POINT, TOO.
REALLY?
THAT'S QUICK!
I SHOWED YOU THE PHOTO WHERE YOU CAN'T TELL.
....
DO YOU WANT TO KNOW?
OR DO YOU WANT TO WAIT UNTIL THE BABY'S BORN?
......
I WANT TO KNOW...
BUT WAIT-ING MIGHT BE MORE FUN...
WHAT SHOULD I DO?
WHY DON'T YOU TALK IT OVER WITH YOUR FAMILY AND THINK ABOUT IT?
IT'S STILL ONLY AN ESTI-MATE.
HEH HEH
thump thump thump
OKAY.
IT'S GOOD THAT YOU GOT OVER YOUR MORNING SICKNESS QUICKLY...
BUT I'M WORRIED ABOUT YOUR SUDDEN INCREASE IN WEIGHT.
IF YOU GAIN TOO MUCH WEIGHT, YOU'RE MORE AT RISK FOR GESTOSIS AND OTHER CONDITIONS.
EAT A BAL-ANCED DIET BUT NOT TOO MUCH.

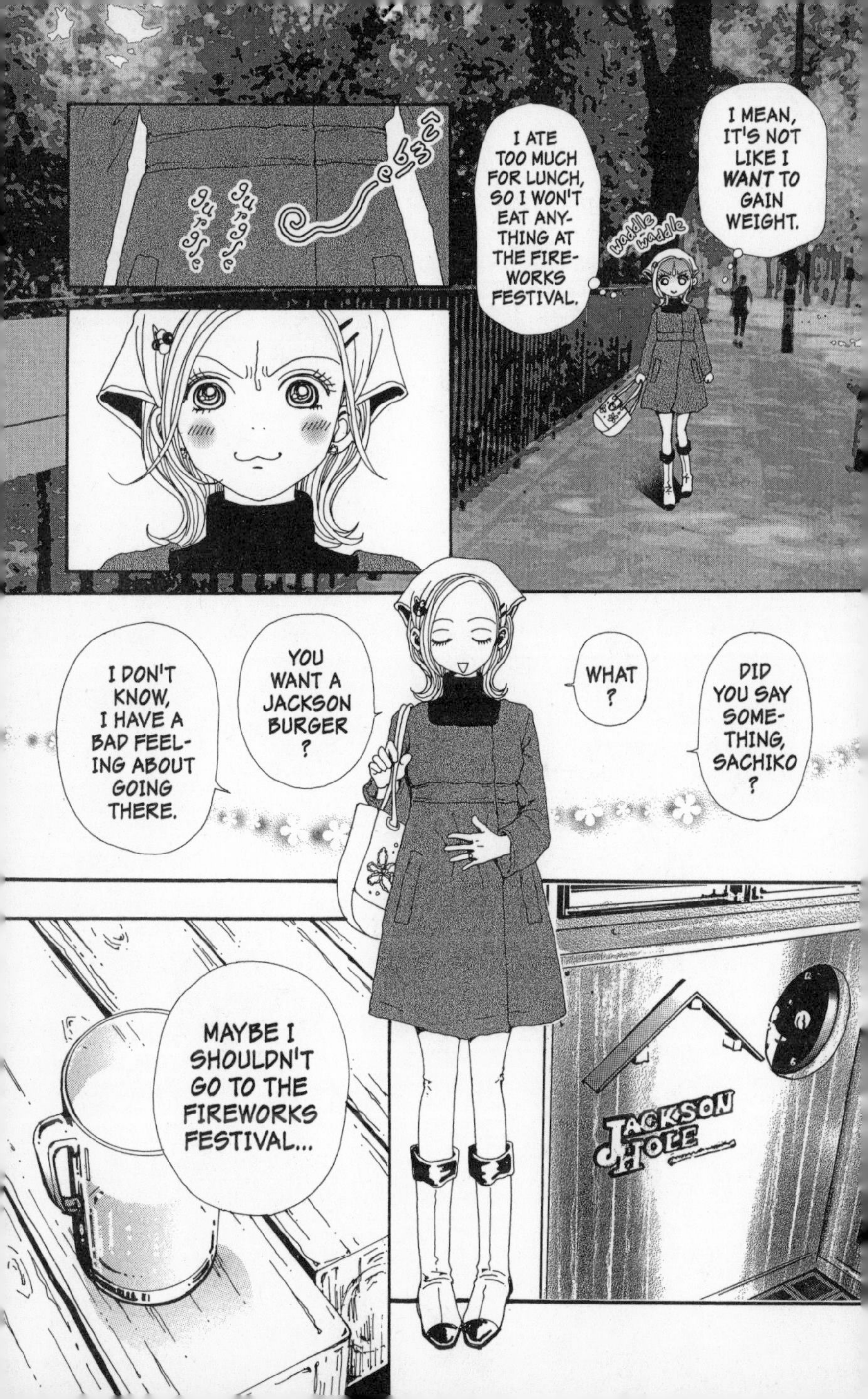
I MEAN, IT'S NOT LIKE I WANT TO GAIN WEIGHT.
waddle waddle
I ATE TOO MUCH FOR LUNCH, SO I WON'T EAT ANYTHING AT THE FIREWORKS FESTIVAL.
rumble
gurgle gurgle
DID YOU SAY SOMETHING, SACHIKO?
WHAT?
YOU WANT A JACKSON BURGER?
I DON'T KNOW, I HAVE A BAD FEELING ABOUT GOING THERE.
JACKSON HOLE
MAYBE I SHOULDN'T GO TO THE FIREWORKS FESTIVAL...

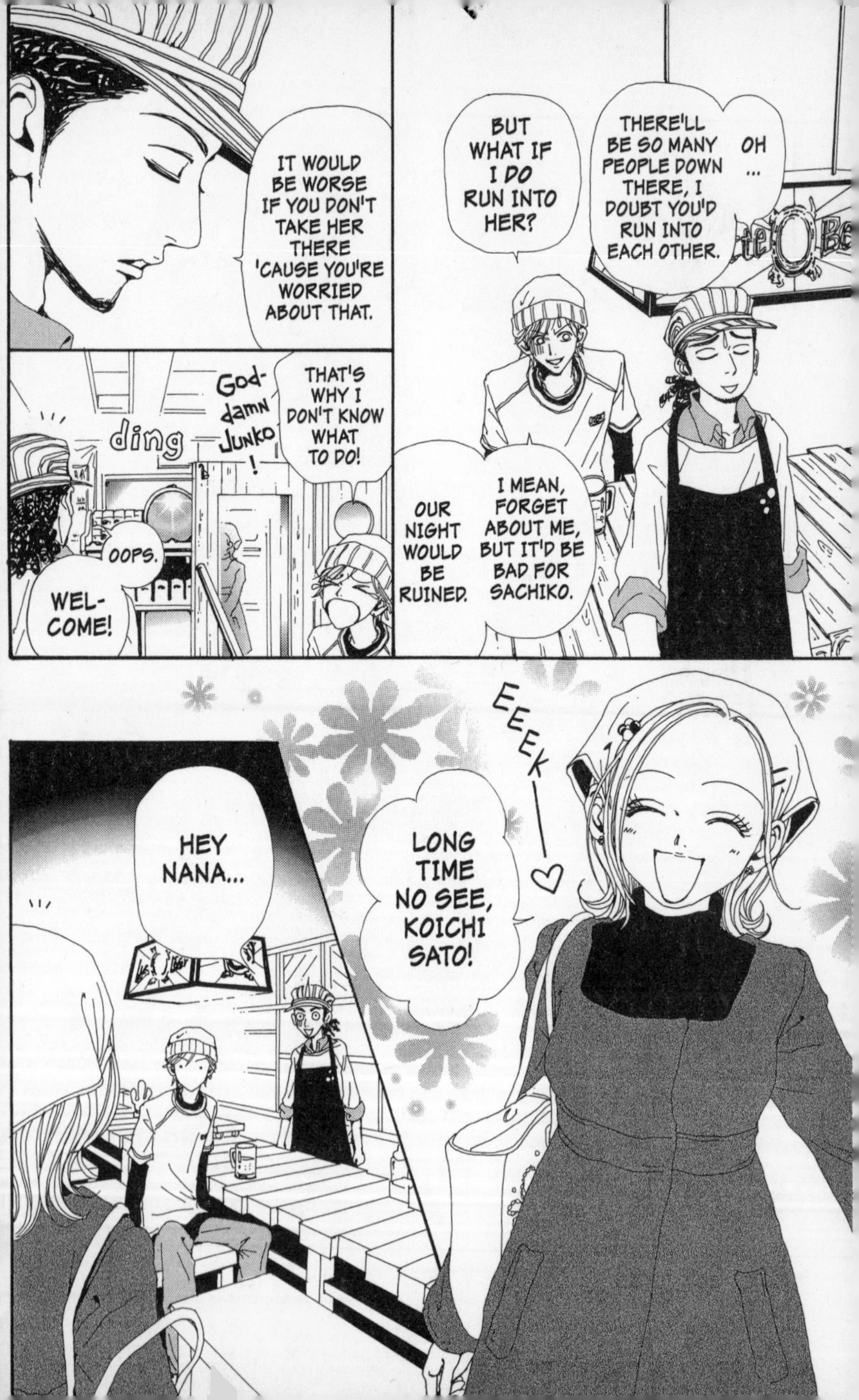
OH ...
THERE'LL BE SO MANY PEOPLE DOWN THERE, I DOUBT YOU'D RUN INTO EACH OTHER.
BUT WHAT IF I DO RUN INTO HER?
I MEAN, FORGET ABOUT ME, BUT IT'D BE BAD FOR SACHIKO.
OUR NIGHT WOULD BE RUINED.
IT WOULD BE WORSE IF YOU DON'T TAKE HER THERE 'CAUSE YOU'RE WORRIED ABOUT THAT.
THAT'S WHY I DON'T KNOW WHAT TO DO!
God-damn Junko!
ding
OOPS.
WEL-COME!
EEEK
LONG TIME NO SEE, KOICHI SATO!
HEY NANA...

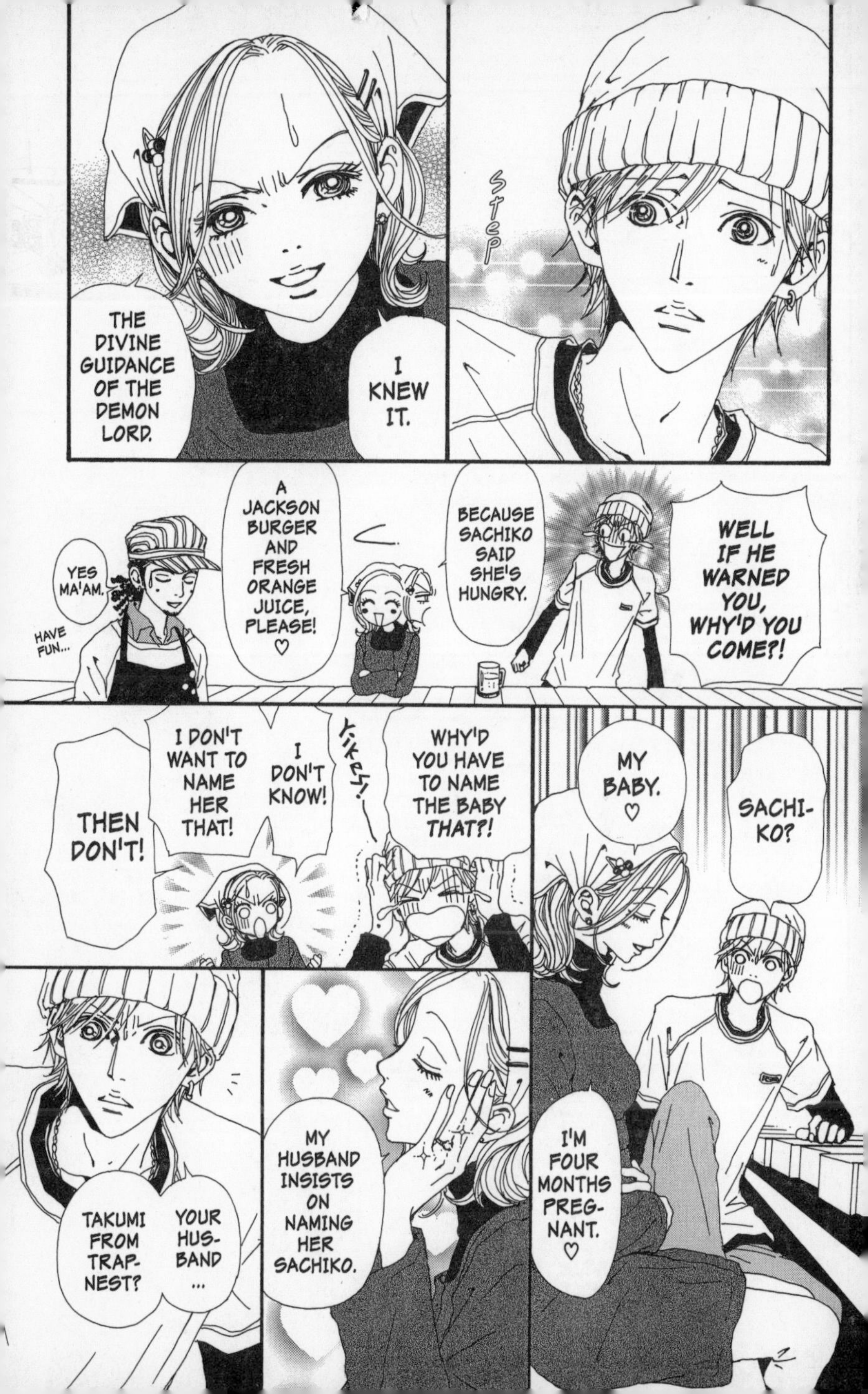
Step
I KNEW IT.
THE DIVINE GUIDANCE OF THE DEMON LORD.
WELL IF HE WARNED YOU, WHY'D YOU COME?!
BECAUSE SACHIKO SAID SHE'S HUNGRY.
A JACKSON BURGER AND FRESH ORANGE JUICE, PLEASE! ♡
YES MA'AM.
HAVE FUN...
SACHIKO?
MY BABY. ♡
WHY'D YOU HAVE TO NAME THE BABY THAT?!
Yikes!
I DON'T KNOW!
I DON'T WANT TO NAME HER THAT!
THEN DON'T!
I'M FOUR MONTHS PREGNANT. ♡
MY HUSBAND INSISTS ON NAMING HER SACHIKO.
YOUR HUSBAND ...
TAKUMI FROM TRAPNEST?

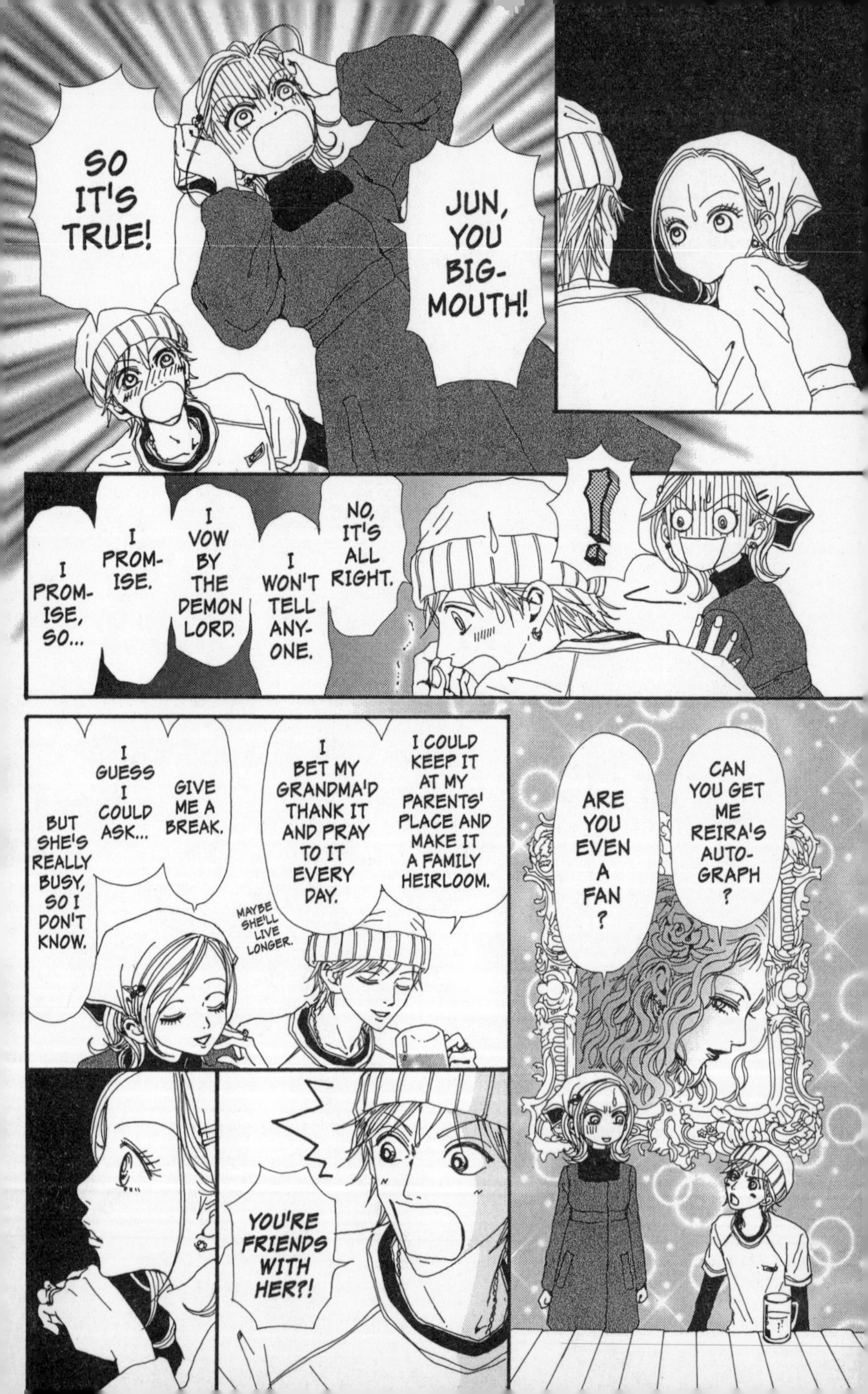
JUN, YOU BIG-MOUTH!
SO IT'S TRUE!
!
NO, IT'S ALL RIGHT.
I WON'T TELL ANY-ONE.
I VOW BY THE DEMON LORD.
I PROMISE.
I PROMISE, SO...
CAN YOU GET ME REIRA'S AUTO-GRAPH?
ARE YOU EVEN A FAN?
I COULD KEEP IT AT MY PARENTS' PLACE AND MAKE IT A FAMILY HEIRLOOM.
I BET MY GRANDMA'D THANK IT AND PRAY TO IT EVERY DAY.
MAYBE SHE'LL LIVE LONGER.
GIVE ME A BREAK.
I GUESS I COULD ASK...
BUT SHE'S REALLY BUSY, SO I DON'T KNOW.
YOU'RE FRIENDS WITH HER?!
...

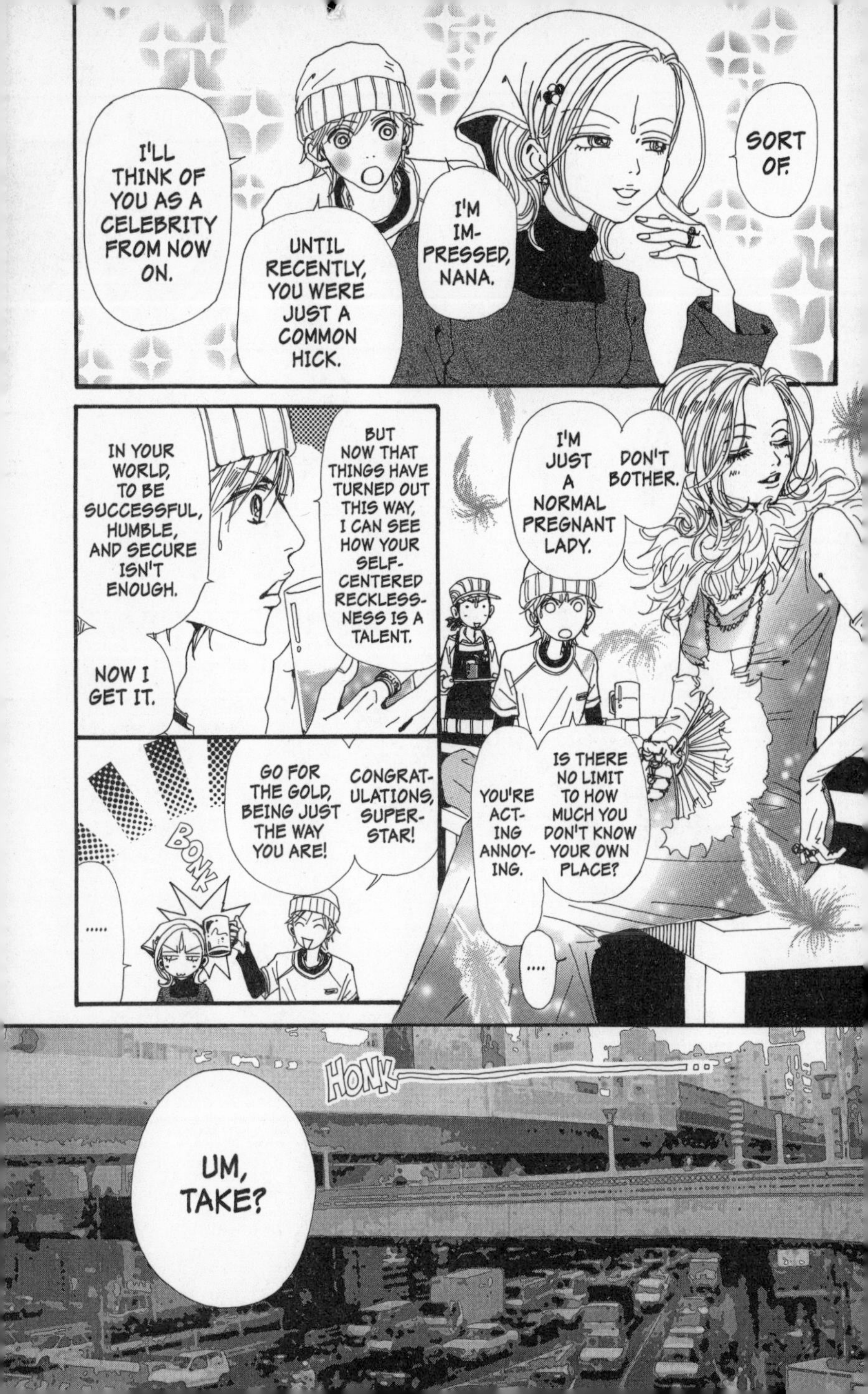
SORT OF.
I'M IM-PRESSED, NANA.
UNTIL RECENTLY, YOU WERE JUST A COMMON HICK.
I'LL THINK OF YOU AS A CELEBRITY FROM NOW ON.
DON'T BOTHER.
I'M JUST A NORMAL PREGNANT LADY.
IS THERE NO LIMIT TO HOW MUCH YOU DON'T KNOW YOUR OWN PLACE?
YOU'RE ACT-ING ANNOY-ING.
....
BUT NOW THAT THINGS HAVE TURNED OUT THIS WAY, I CAN SEE HOW YOUR SELF-CENTERED RECKLESS-NESS IS A TALENT.
IN YOUR WORLD, TO BE SUCCESSFUL, HUMBLE, AND SECURE ISN'T ENOUGH.
NOW I GET IT.
CONGRAT-ULATIONS, SUPER-STAR!
GO FOR THE GOLD, BEING JUST THE WAY YOU ARE!
BONK
.....
HONK
UM, TAKE?

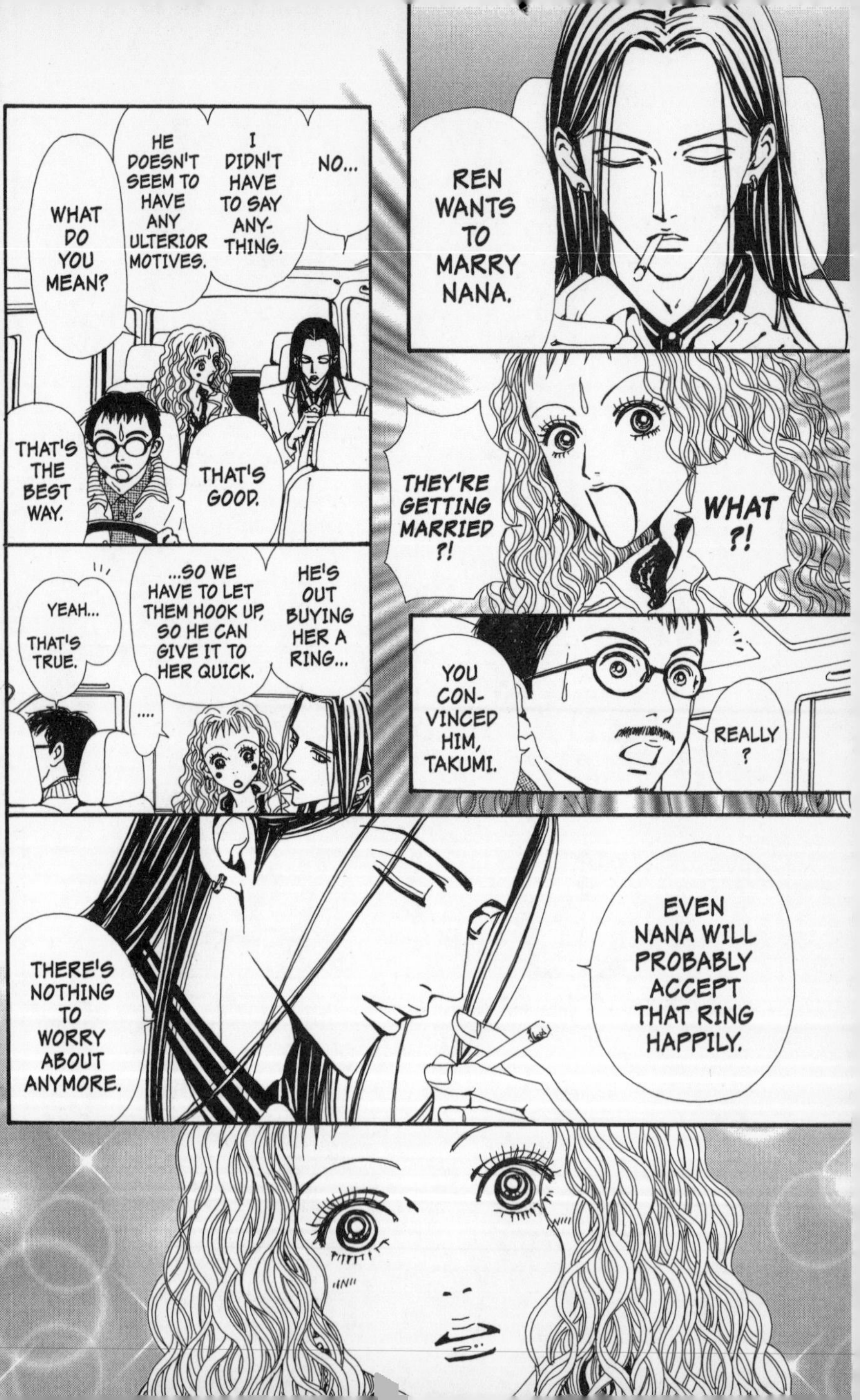

REN WANTS TO MARRY NANA.
WHAT ?!
THEY'RE GETTING MARRIED ?!
REALLY ?
YOU CON-VINCED HIM, TAKUMI.
NO...
I DIDN'T HAVE TO SAY ANY-THING.
HE DOESN'T SEEM TO HAVE ANY ULTERIOR MOTIVES.
WHAT DO YOU MEAN?
THAT'S GOOD.
THAT'S THE BEST WAY.
HE'S OUT BUYING HER A RING...
...SO WE HAVE TO LET THEM HOOK UP, SO HE CAN GIVE IT TO HER QUICK.
....
YEAH... THAT'S TRUE.
EVEN NANA WILL PROBABLY ACCEPT THAT RING HAPPILY.
THERE'S NOTHING TO WORRY ABOUT ANYMORE.

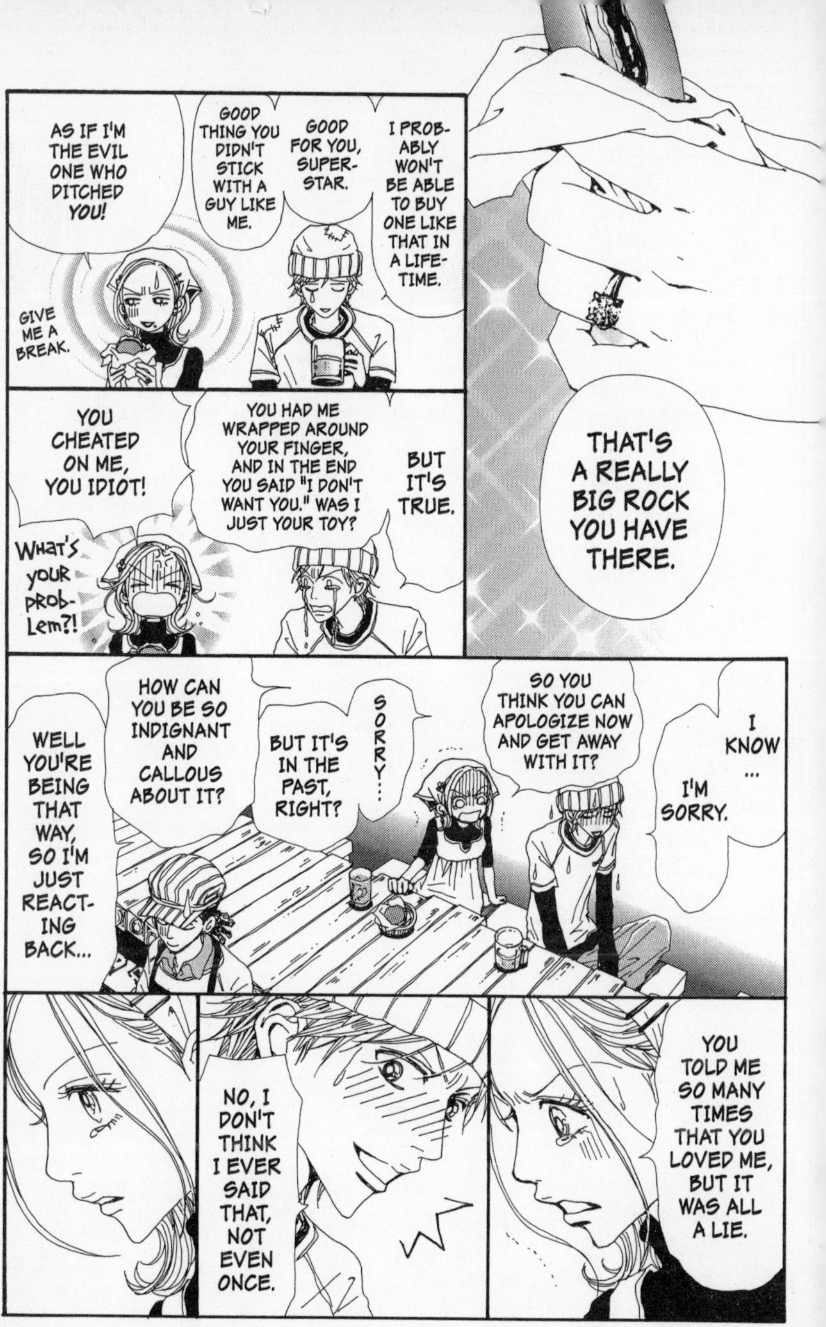
THAT'S A REALLY BIG ROCK YOU HAVE THERE.
I PROBABLY WON'T BE ABLE TO BUY ONE LIKE THAT IN A LIFETIME.
GOOD FOR YOU, SUPERSTAR.
GOOD THING YOU DIDN'T STICK WITH A GUY LIKE ME.
AS IF I'M THE EVIL ONE WHO DITCHED YOU!
GIVE ME A BREAK.
BUT IT'S TRUE.
YOU HAD ME WRAPPED AROUND YOUR FINGER, AND IN THE END YOU SAID "I DON'T WANT YOU." WAS I JUST YOUR TOY?
YOU CHEATED ON ME, YOU IDIOT!
What's your problem?!
I KNOW ... I'M SORRY.
SO YOU THINK YOU CAN APOLOGIZE NOW AND GET AWAY WITH IT?
SORRY...
BUT IT'S IN THE PAST, RIGHT?
HOW CAN YOU BE SO INDIGNANT AND CALLOUS ABOUT IT?
WELL YOU'RE BEING THAT WAY, SO I'M JUST REACTING BACK...
YOU TOLD ME SO MANY TIMES THAT YOU LOVED ME, BUT IT WAS ALL A LIE.
NO, I DON'T THINK I EVER SAID THAT, NOT EVEN ONCE.

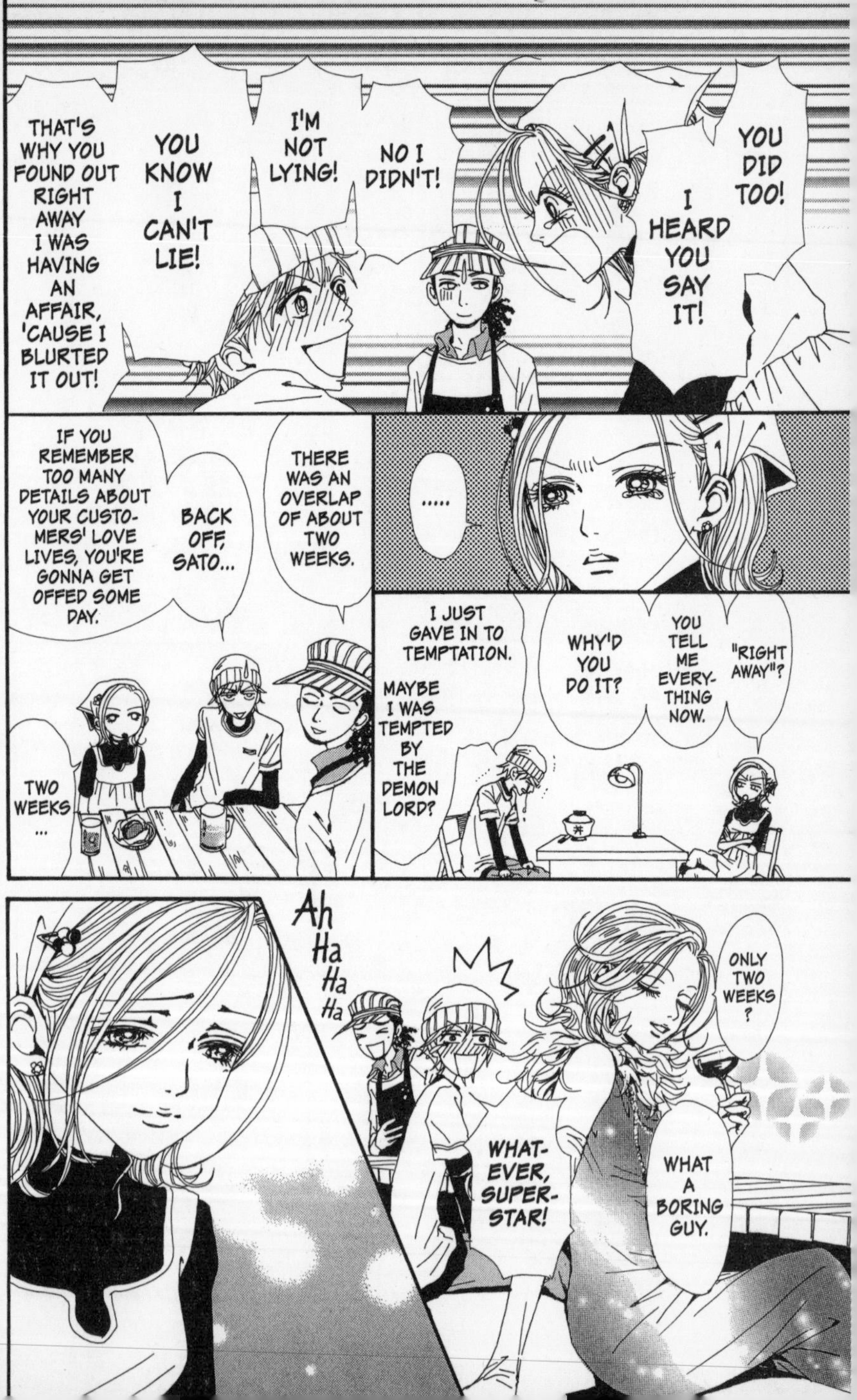
YOU DID TOO!
I HEARD YOU SAY IT!
NO I DIDN'T!
I'M NOT LYING!
YOU KNOW I CAN'T LIE!
THAT'S WHY YOU FOUND OUT RIGHT AWAY I WAS HAVING AN AFFAIR, 'CAUSE I BLURTED IT OUT!
.....
"RIGHT AWAY"?
YOU TELL ME EVERY-THING NOW.
WHY'D YOU DO IT?
I JUST GAVE IN TO TEMPTATION.
MAYBE I WAS TEMPTED BY THE DEMON LORD?
THERE WAS AN OVERLAP OF ABOUT TWO WEEKS.
BACK OFF, SATO...
IF YOU REMEMBER TOO MANY DETAILS ABOUT YOUR CUSTO-MERS' LOVE LIVES, YOU'RE GONNA GET OFFED SOME DAY.
TWO WEEKS ...
ONLY TWO WEEKS ?
WHAT A BORING GUY.
Ah Ha Ha Ha
WHAT-EVER, SUPER-STAR!

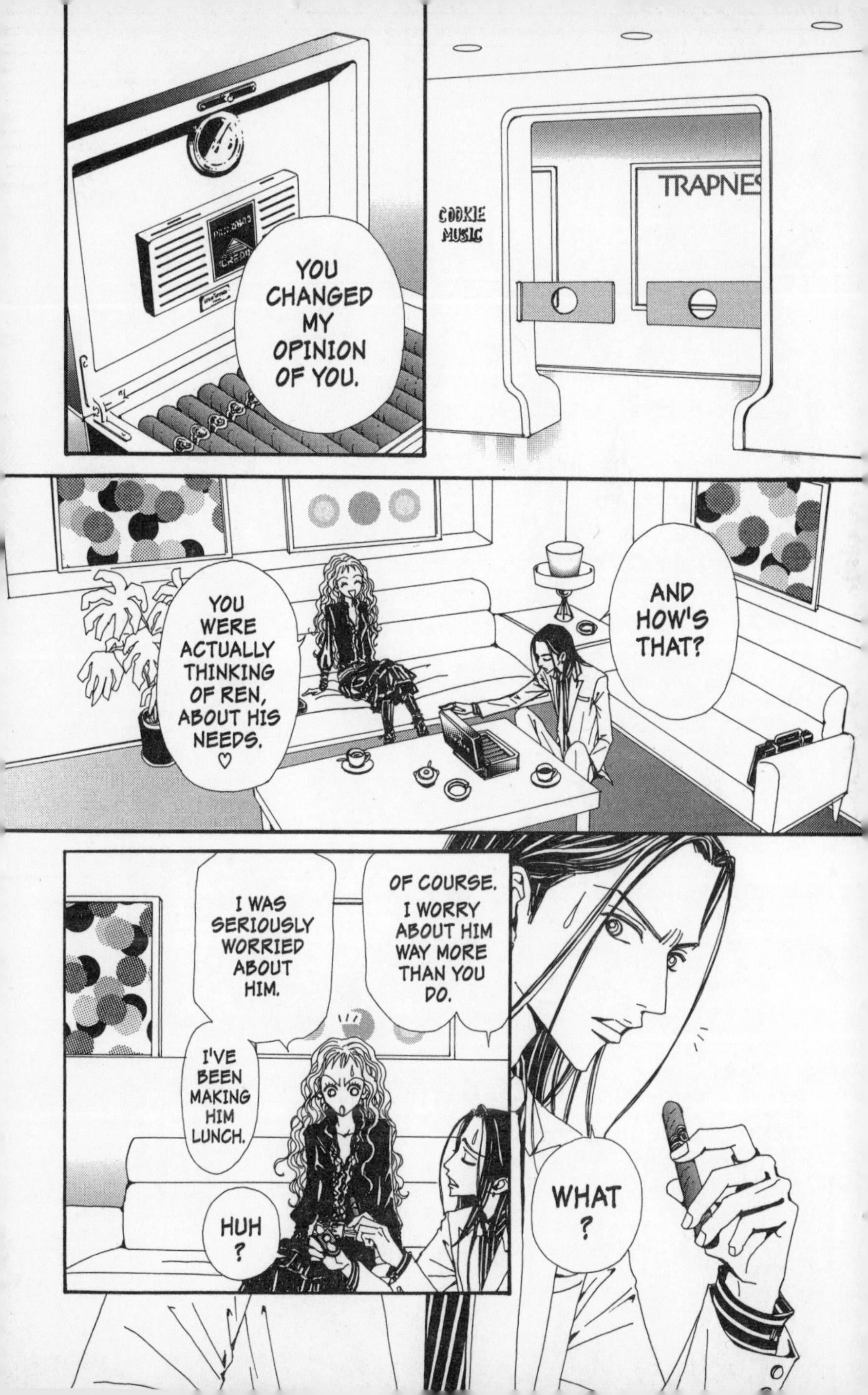
TRAPNES
COOKIE MUSIC
YOU CHANGED MY OPINION OF YOU.
AND HOW'S THAT?
YOU WERE ACTUALLY THINKING OF REN, ABOUT HIS NEEDS. ♡
OF COURSE. I WORRY ABOUT HIM WAY MORE THAN YOU DO.
I WAS SERIOUSLY WORRIED ABOUT HIM.
I'VE BEEN MAKING HIM LUNCH.
HUH?
WHAT?

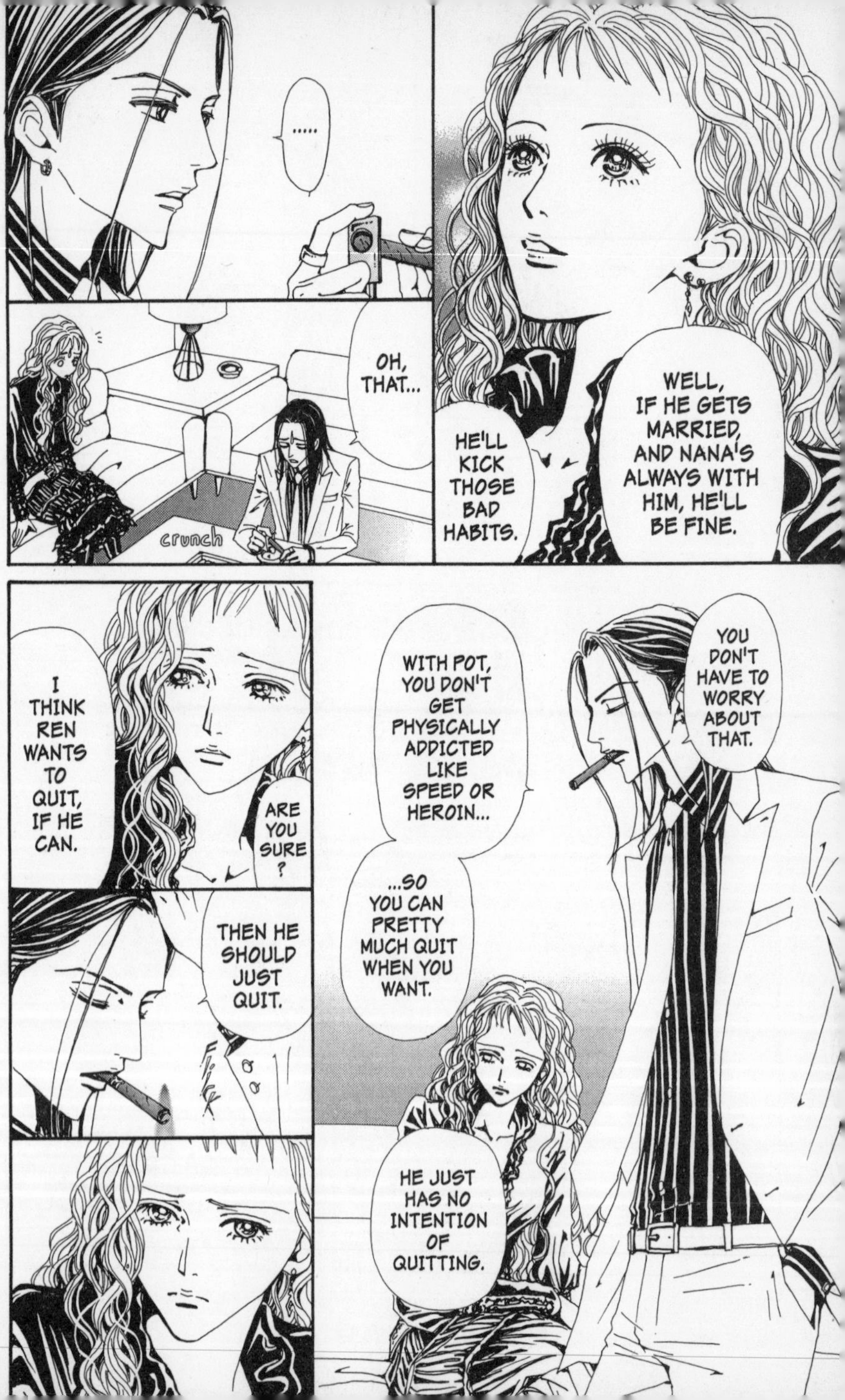
WELL, IF HE GETS MARRIED, AND NANA'S ALWAYS WITH HIM, HE'LL BE FINE.
HE'LL KICK THOSE BAD HABITS.
.....
OH, THAT...
crunch
YOU DON'T HAVE TO WORRY ABOUT THAT.
WITH POT, YOU DON'T GET PHYSICALLY ADDICTED LIKE SPEED OR HEROIN...
...SO YOU CAN PRETTY MUCH QUIT WHEN YOU WANT.
HE JUST HAS NO INTENTION OF QUITTING.
ARE YOU SURE?
I THINK REN WANTS TO QUIT, IF HE CAN.
THEN HE SHOULD JUST QUIT.

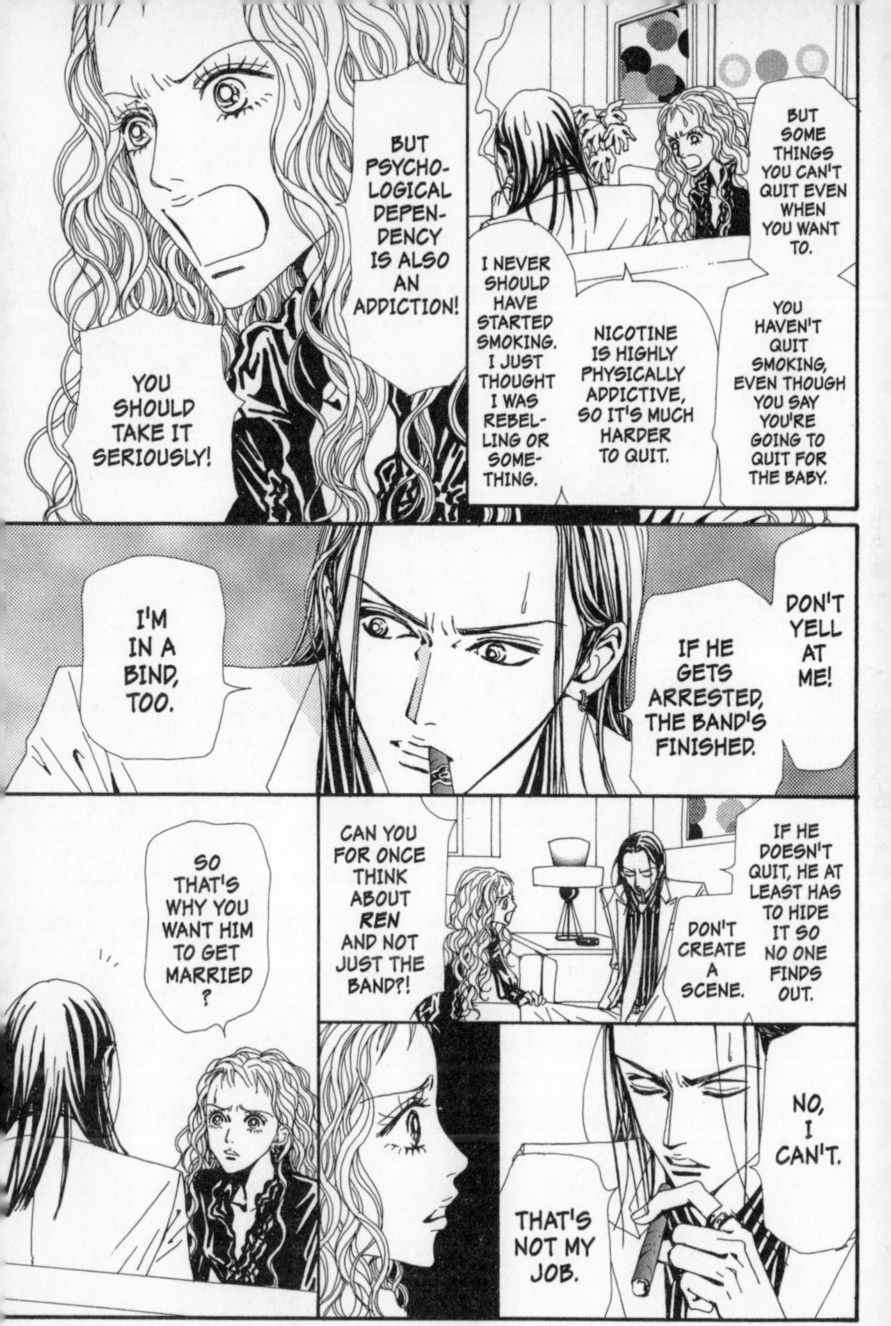
BUT SOME THINGS YOU CAN'T QUIT EVEN WHEN YOU WANT TO.
YOU HAVEN'T QUIT SMOKING, EVEN THOUGH YOU SAY YOU'RE GOING TO QUIT FOR THE BABY.
NICOTINE IS HIGHLY PHYSICALLY ADDICTIVE, SO IT'S MUCH HARDER TO QUIT.
I NEVER SHOULD HAVE STARTED SMOKING. I JUST THOUGHT I WAS REBELLING OR SOMETHING.
BUT PSYCHOLOGICAL DEPENDENCY IS ALSO AN ADDICTION!
YOU SHOULD TAKE IT SERIOUSLY!
DON'T YELL AT ME!
IF HE GETS ARRESTED, THE BAND'S FINISHED.
I'M IN A BIND, TOO.
IF HE DOESN'T QUIT, HE AT LEAST HAS TO HIDE IT SO NO ONE FINDS OUT.
DON'T CREATE A SCENE.
CAN YOU FOR ONCE THINK ABOUT REN AND NOT JUST THE BAND?!
NO, I CAN'T.
THAT'S NOT MY JOB.
SO THAT'S WHY YOU WANT HIM TO GET MARRIED?

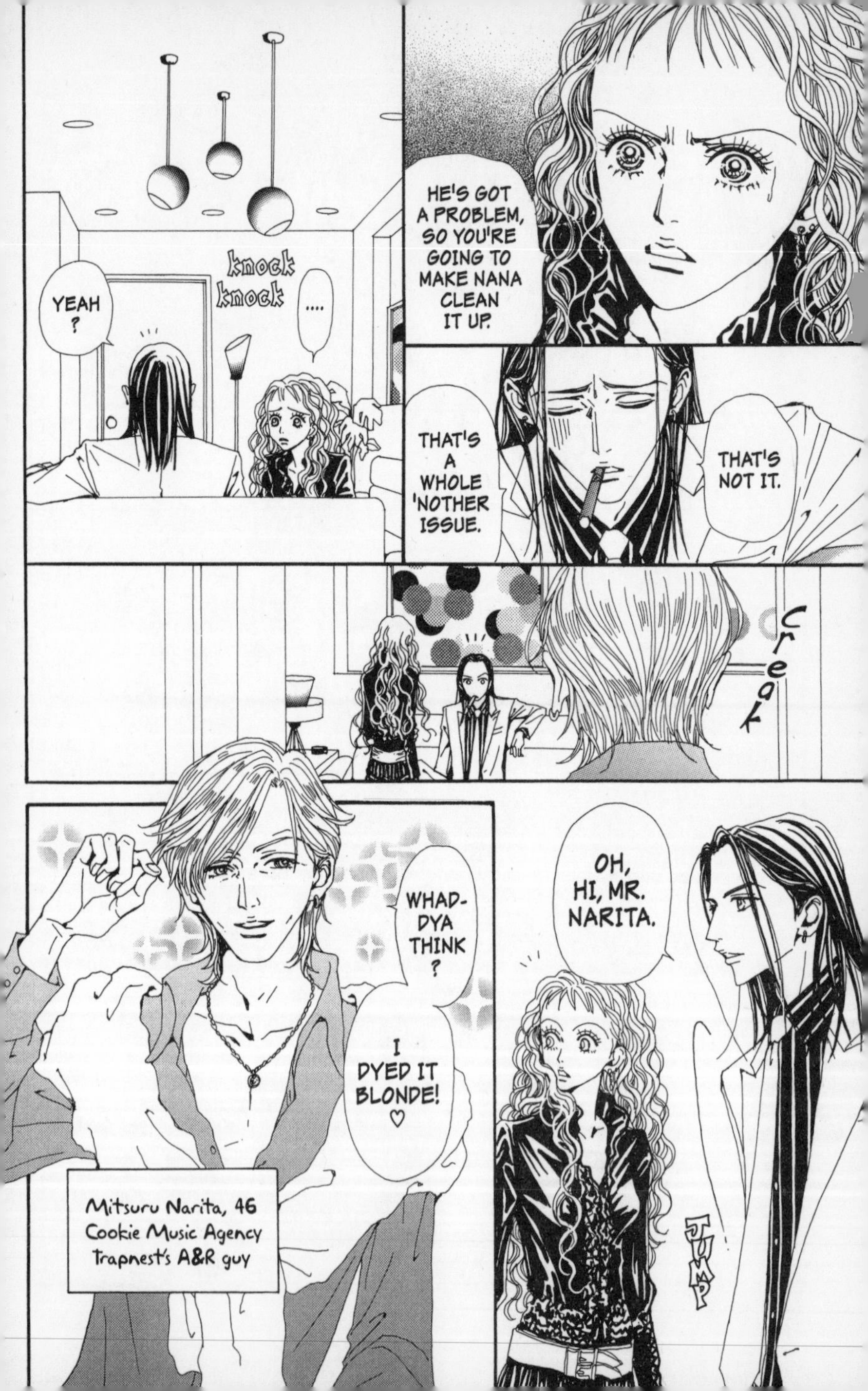
HE'S GOT A PROBLEM, SO YOU'RE GOING TO MAKE NANA CLEAN IT UP.
THAT'S NOT IT.
THAT'S A WHOLE 'NOTHER ISSUE.
....
knock knock
YEAH?
Creak
OH, HI, MR. NARITA.
JUMP
WHAD-DYA THINK?
I DYED IT BLONDE! ♡
Mitsuru Narita, 46
Cookie Music Agency
Trapnest's A&R guy

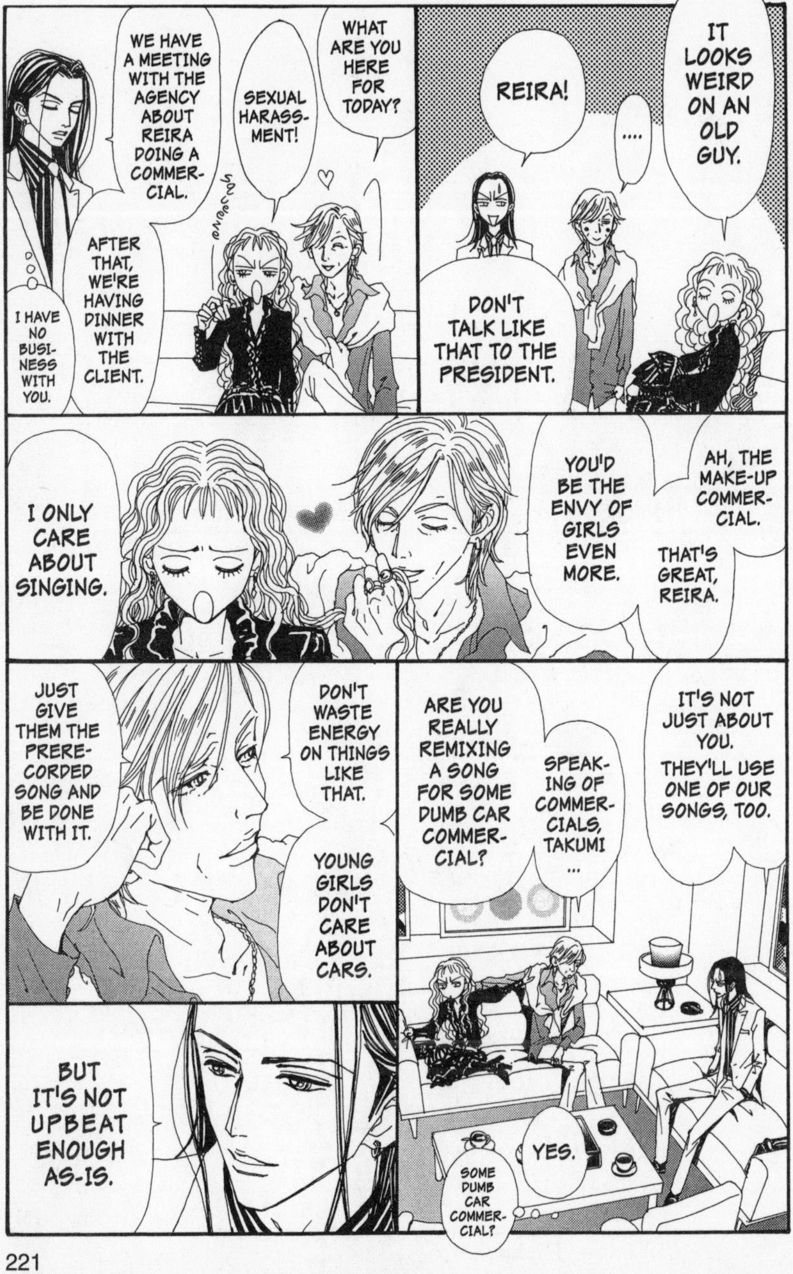
IT LOOKS WEIRD ON AN OLD GUY.
....
REIRA!
DON'T TALK LIKE THAT TO THE PRESIDENT.
WHAT ARE YOU HERE FOR TODAY?
SEXUAL HARASS-MENT!
WE HAVE A MEETING WITH THE AGENCY ABOUT REIRA DOING A COMMER-CIAL.
AFTER THAT, WE'RE HAVING DINNER WITH THE CLIENT.
I HAVE NO BUSI-NESS WITH YOU.
AH, THE MAKE-UP COMMER-CIAL.
THAT'S GREAT, REIRA.
YOU'D BE THE ENVY OF GIRLS EVEN MORE.
I ONLY CARE ABOUT SINGING.
IT'S NOT JUST ABOUT YOU.
THEY'LL USE ONE OF OUR SONGS, TOO.
SPEAK-ING OF COMMER-CIALS, TAKUMI ...
ARE YOU REALLY REMIXING A SONG FOR SOME DUMB CAR COMMER-CIAL?
YES.
SOME DUMB CAR COMMER-CIAL?
DON'T WASTE ENERGY ON THINGS LIKE THAT.
YOUNG GIRLS DON'T CARE ABOUT CARS.
JUST GIVE THEM THE PRERE-CORDED SONG AND BE DONE WITH IT.
BUT IT'S NOT UPBEAT ENOUGH AS-IS.

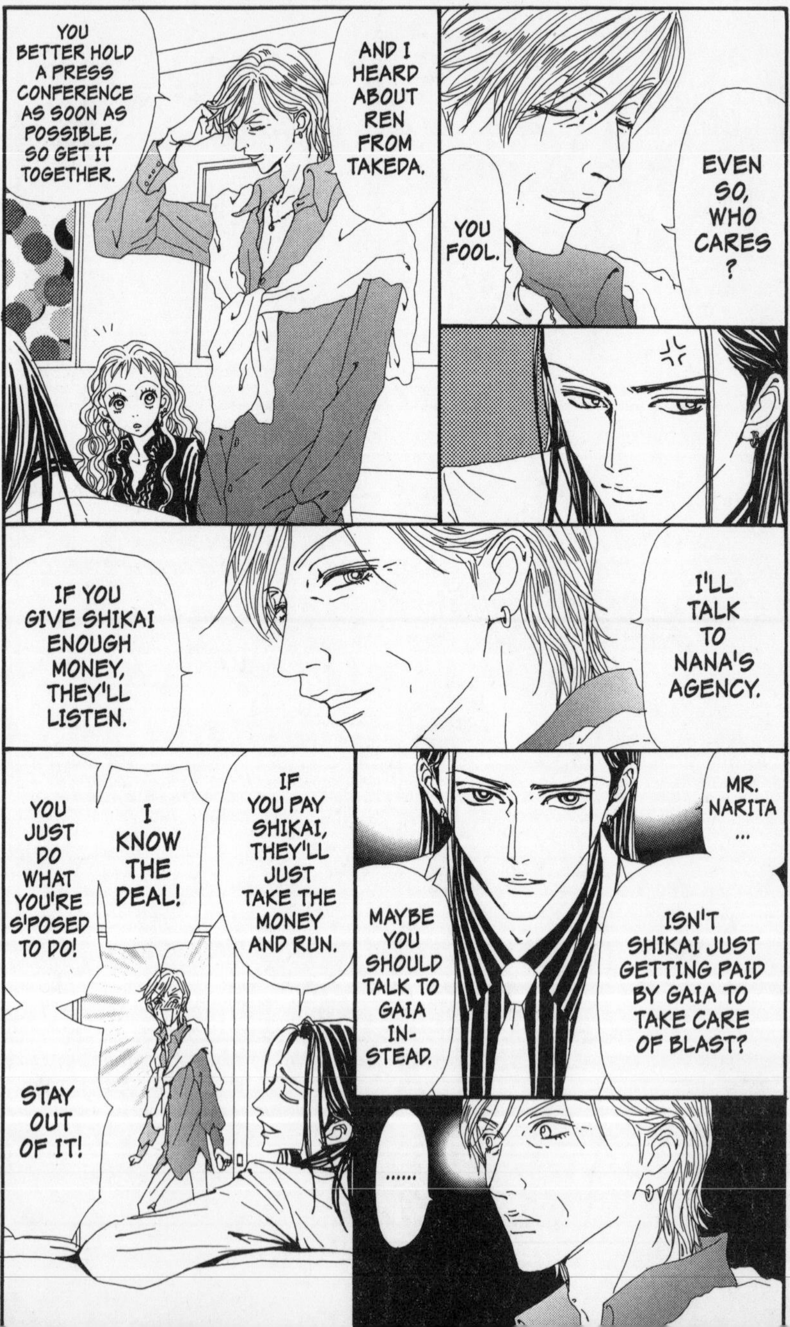
EVEN SO, WHO CARES?
YOU FOOL.
AND I HEARD ABOUT REN FROM TAKEDA.
YOU BETTER HOLD A PRESS CONFERENCE AS SOON AS POSSIBLE, SO GET IT TOGETHER.
I'LL TALK TO NANA'S AGENCY.
IF YOU GIVE SHIKAI ENOUGH MONEY, THEY'LL LISTEN.
MR. NARITA...
ISN'T SHIKAI JUST GETTING PAID BY GAIA TO TAKE CARE OF BLAST?
MAYBE YOU SHOULD TALK TO GAIA IN-STEAD.
......
IF YOU PAY SHIKAI, THEY'LL JUST TAKE THE MONEY AND RUN.
I KNOW THE DEAL!
YOU JUST DO WHAT YOU'RE S'POSED TO DO!
STAY OUT OF IT!

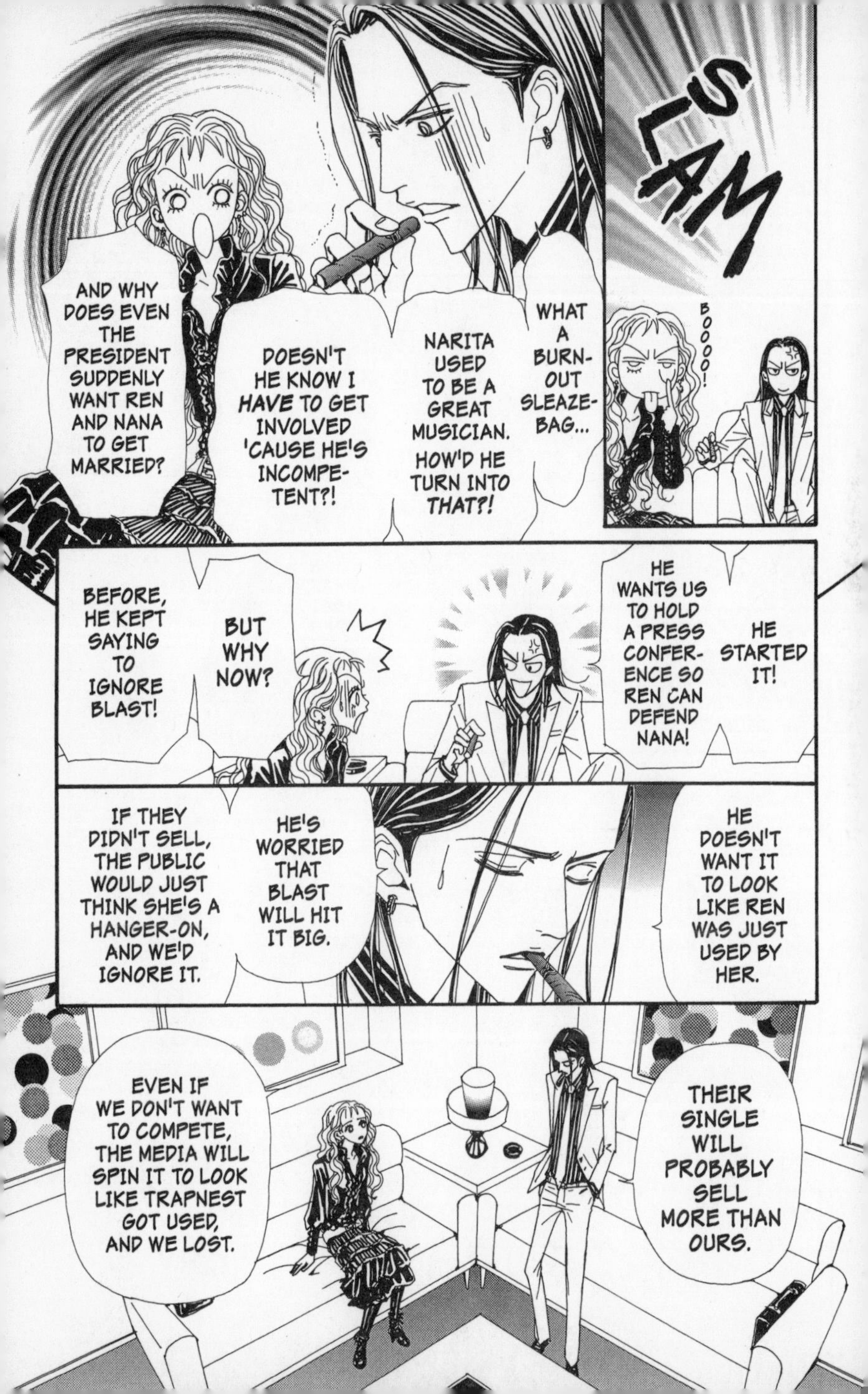
SLAM
BOOOOO!
WHAT A BURN-OUT SLEAZE-BAG...
NARITA USED TO BE A GREAT MUSICIAN. HOW'D HE TURN INTO THAT?!
DOESN'T HE KNOW I HAVE TO GET INVOLVED 'CAUSE HE'S INCOMPETENT?!
AND WHY DOES EVEN THE PRESIDENT SUDDENLY WANT REN AND NANA TO GET MARRIED?
HE STARTED IT!
HE WANTS US TO HOLD A PRESS CONFERENCE SO REN CAN DEFEND NANA!
BUT WHY NOW?
BEFORE, HE KEPT SAYING TO IGNORE BLAST!
HE DOESN'T WANT IT TO LOOK LIKE REN WAS JUST USED BY HER.
HE'S WORRIED THAT BLAST WILL HIT IT BIG.
IF THEY DIDN'T SELL, THE PUBLIC WOULD JUST THINK SHE'S A HANGER-ON, AND WE'D IGNORE IT.
THEIR SINGLE WILL PROBABLY SELL MORE THAN OURS.
EVEN IF WE DON'T WANT TO COMPETE, THE MEDIA WILL SPIN IT TO LOOK LIKE TRAPNEST GOT USED, AND WE LOST.

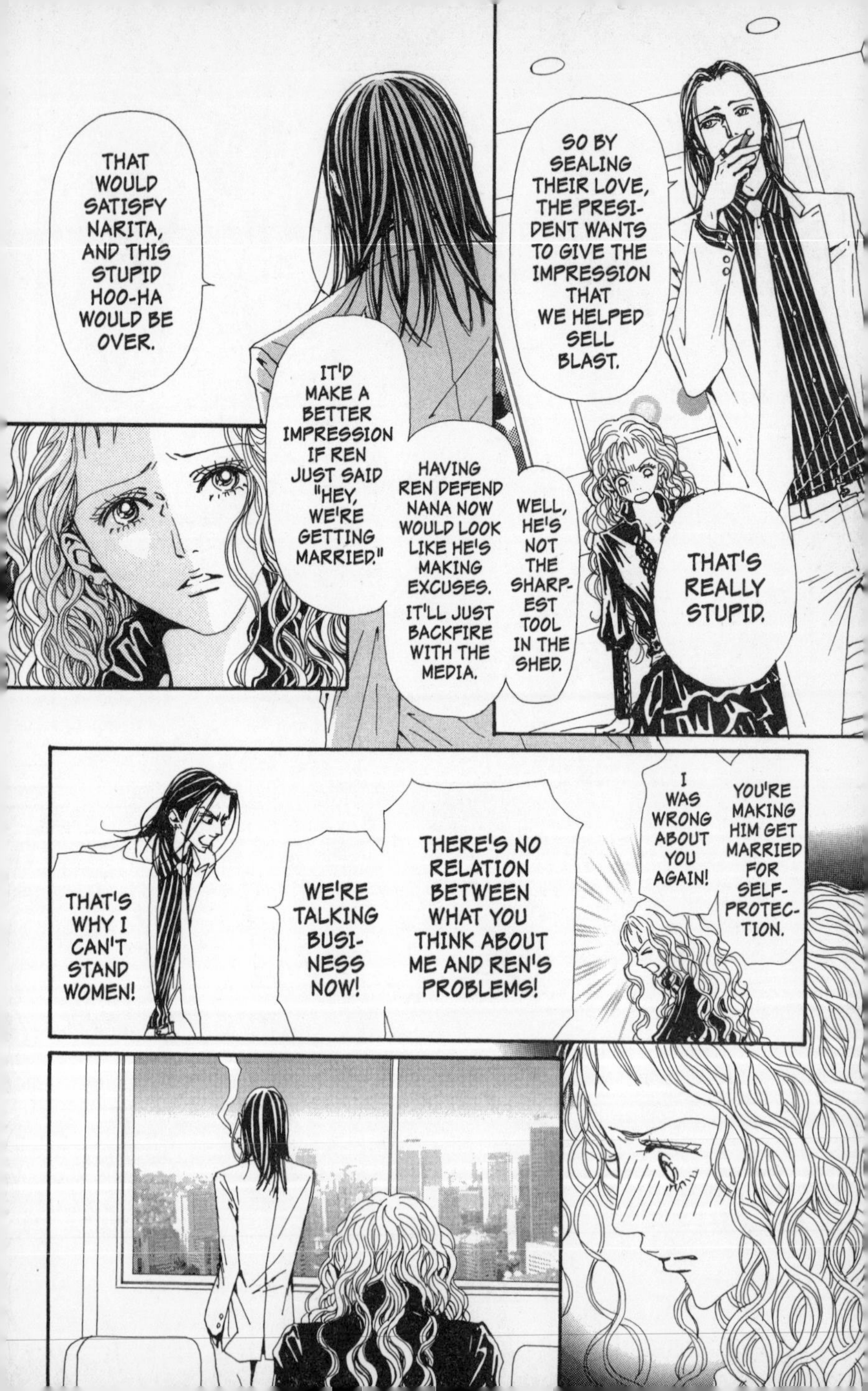
SO BY SEALING THEIR LOVE, THE PRESIDENT WANTS TO GIVE THE IMPRESSION THAT WE HELPED SELL BLAST.
THAT'S REALLY STUPID.
THAT WOULD SATISFY NARITA, AND THIS STUPID HOO-HA WOULD BE OVER.
IT'D MAKE A BETTER IMPRESSION IF REN JUST SAID "HEY, WE'RE GETTING MARRIED."
HAVING REN DEFEND NANA NOW WOULD LOOK LIKE HE'S MAKING EXCUSES. IT'LL JUST BACKFIRE WITH THE MEDIA.
WELL, HE'S NOT THE SHARP-EST TOOL IN THE SHED.
YOU'RE MAKING HIM GET MARRIED FOR SELF-PROTEC-TION.
I WAS WRONG ABOUT YOU AGAIN!
THERE'S NO RELATION BETWEEN WHAT YOU THINK ABOUT ME AND REN'S PROBLEMS!
WE'RE TALKING BUSI-NESS NOW!
THAT'S WHY I CAN'T STAND WOMEN!

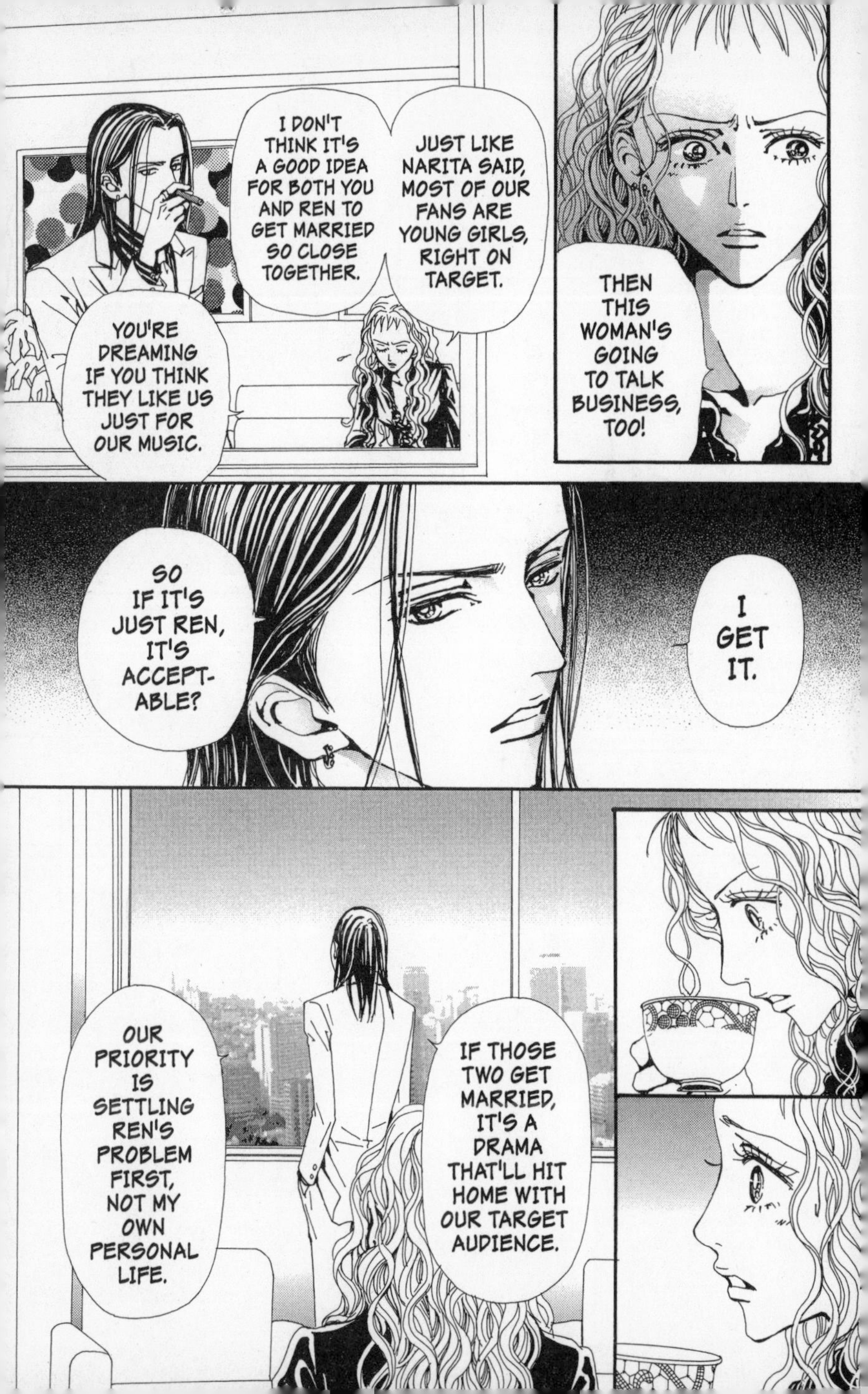
THEN THIS WOMAN'S GOING TO TALK BUSINESS, TOO!
JUST LIKE NARITA SAID, MOST OF OUR FANS ARE YOUNG GIRLS, RIGHT ON TARGET.
I DON'T THINK IT'S A GOOD IDEA FOR BOTH YOU AND REN TO GET MARRIED SO CLOSE TOGETHER.
YOU'RE DREAMING IF YOU THINK THEY LIKE US JUST FOR OUR MUSIC.
I GET IT.
SO IF IT'S JUST REN, IT'S ACCEPT-ABLE?
IF THOSE TWO GET MARRIED, IT'S A DRAMA THAT'LL HIT HOME WITH OUR TARGET AUDIENCE.
OUR PRIORITY IS SETTLING REN'S PROBLEM FIRST, NOT MY OWN PERSONAL LIFE.

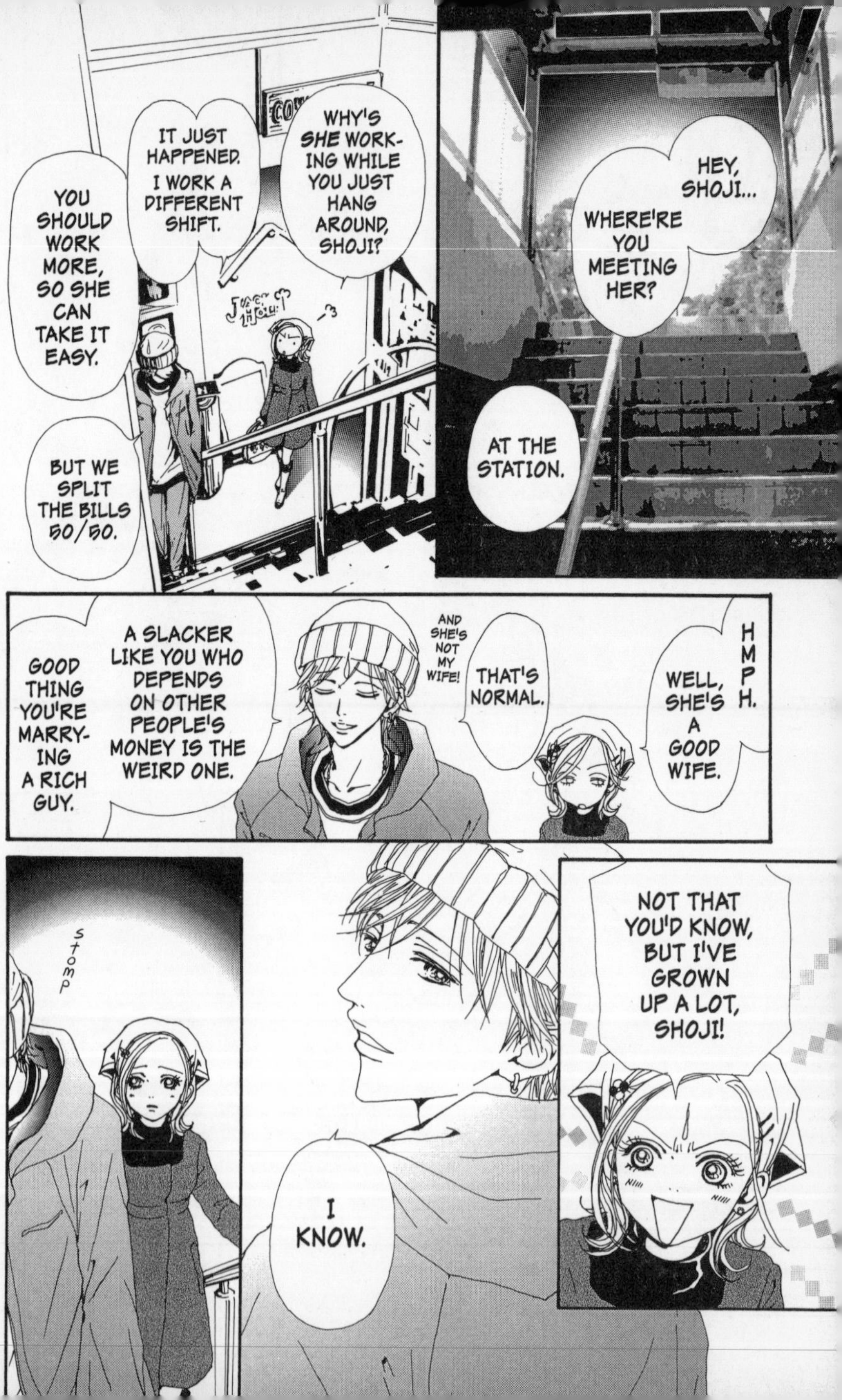
HEY, SHOJI... WHERE'RE YOU MEETING HER?
AT THE STATION.
WHY'S SHE WORKING WHILE YOU JUST HANG AROUND, SHOJI?
IT JUST HAPPENED. I WORK A DIFFERENT SHIFT.
YOU SHOULD WORK MORE, SO SHE CAN TAKE IT EASY.
BUT WE SPLIT THE BILLS 50/50.
HMPH.
WELL, SHE'S A GOOD WIFE.
AND SHE'S NOT MY WIFE!
THAT'S NORMAL.
A SLACKER LIKE YOU WHO DEPENDS ON OTHER PEOPLE'S MONEY IS THE WEIRD ONE.
GOOD THING YOU'RE MARRYING A RICH GUY.
NOT THAT YOU'D KNOW, BUT I'VE GROWN UP A LOT, SHOJI!
I KNOW.
stomp

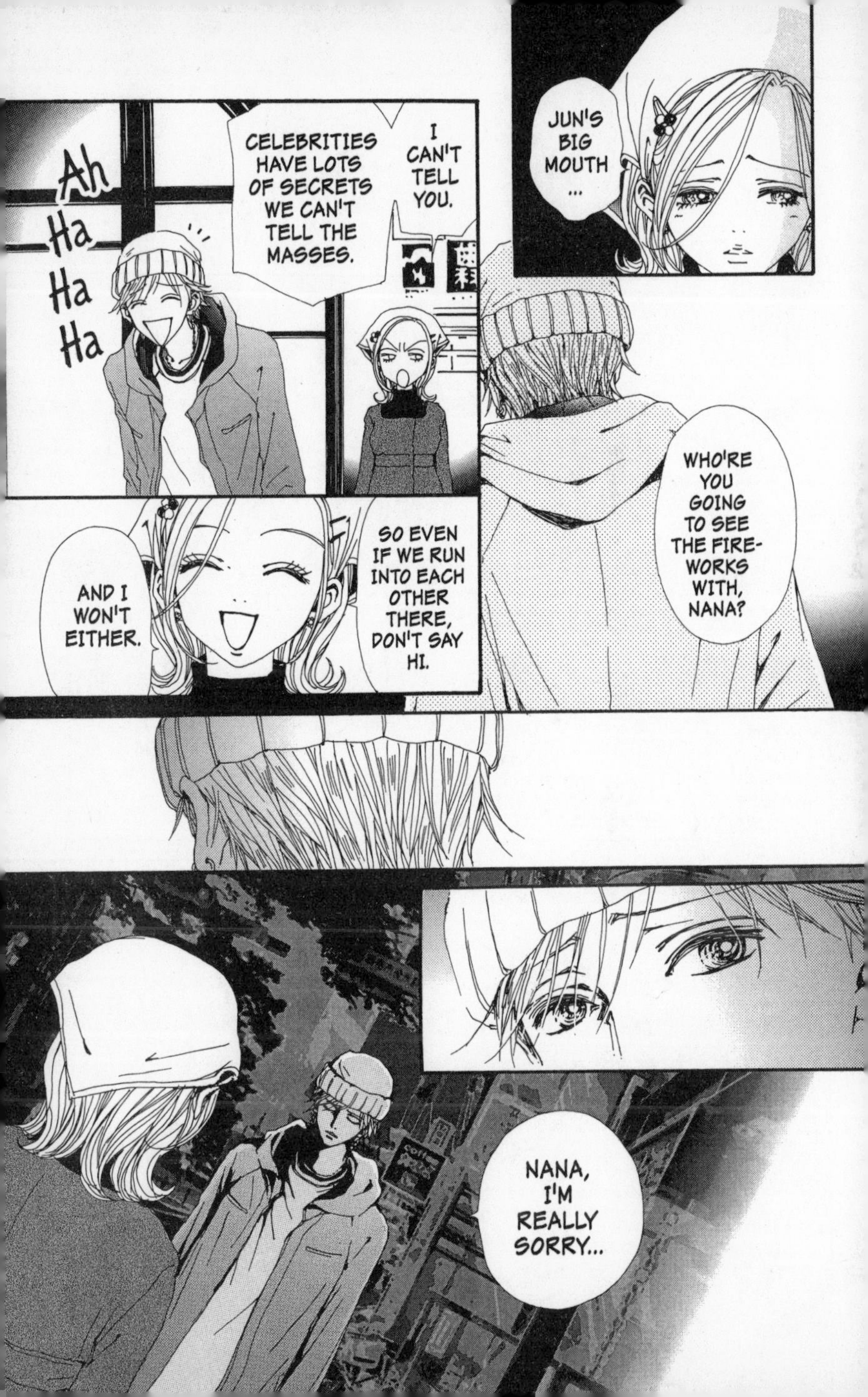
JUN'S BIG MOUTH ...
WHO'RE YOU GOING TO SEE THE FIRE-WORKS WITH, NANA?
I CAN'T TELL YOU.
CELEBRITIES HAVE LOTS OF SECRETS WE CAN'T TELL THE MASSES.
Ah Ha Ha Ha
SO EVEN IF WE RUN INTO EACH OTHER THERE, DON'T SAY HI.
AND I WON'T EITHER.
NANA, I'M REALLY SORRY...

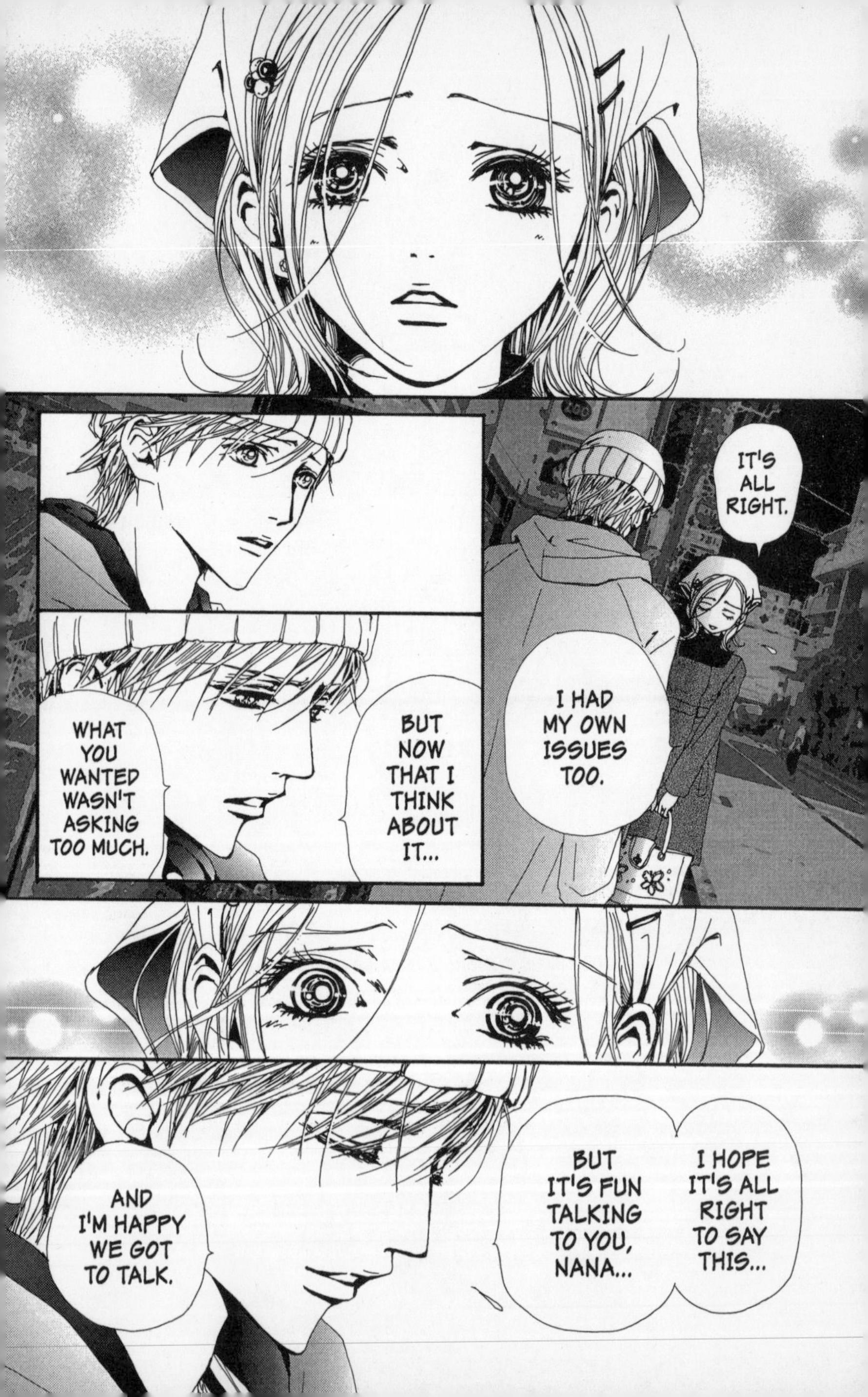
IT'S ALL RIGHT.
I HAD MY OWN ISSUES TOO.
BUT NOW THAT I THINK ABOUT IT...
WHAT YOU WANTED WASN'T ASKING TOO MUCH.
I HOPE IT'S ALL RIGHT TO SAY THIS...
BUT IT'S FUN TALKING TO YOU, NANA...
AND I'M HAPPY WE GOT TO TALK.

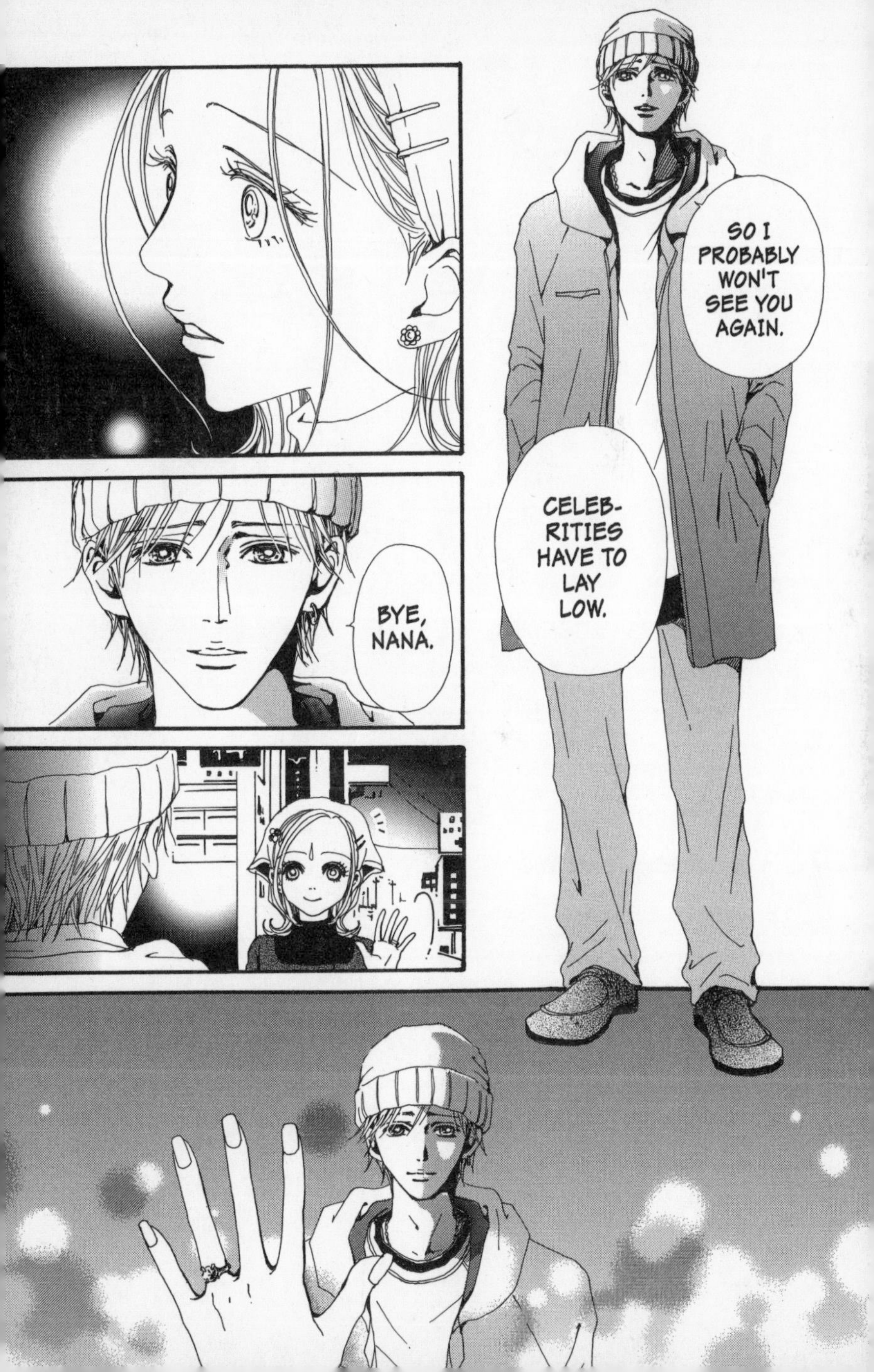
SO I PROBABLY WON'T SEE YOU AGAIN.
CELEB-RITIES HAVE TO LAY LOW.
BYE, NANA.

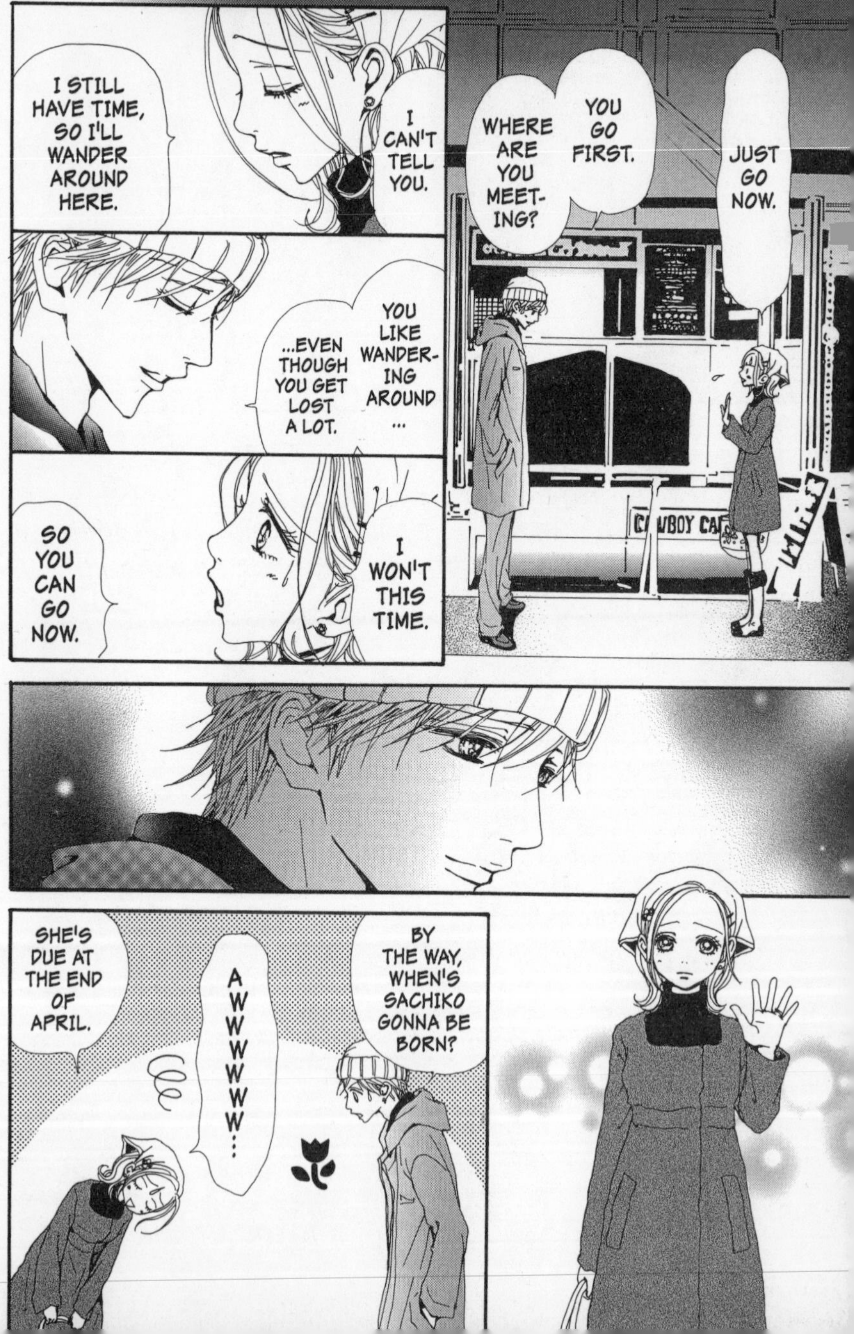
JUST GO NOW.
YOU GO FIRST.
WHERE ARE YOU MEETING?
I CAN'T TELL YOU.
I STILL HAVE TIME, SO I'LL WANDER AROUND HERE.
YOU LIKE WANDERING AROUND...
...EVEN THOUGH YOU GET LOST A LOT.
I WON'T THIS TIME.
SO YOU CAN GO NOW.
BY THE WAY, WHEN'S SACHIKO GONNA BE BORN?
AWWWWWWW...
SHE'S DUE AT THE END OF APRIL.

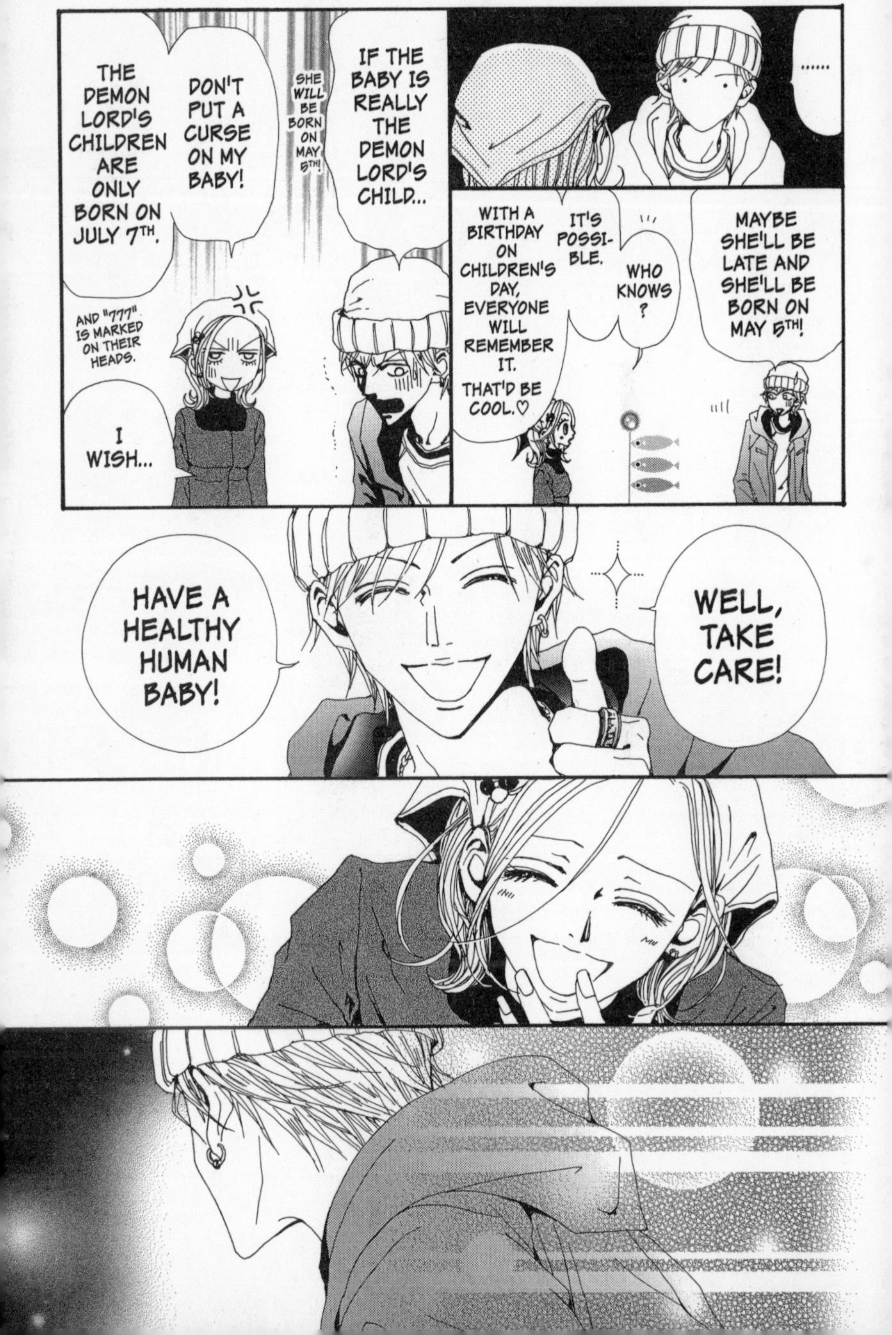
......
MAYBE SHE'LL BE LATE AND SHE'LL BE BORN ON MAY 5TH!
WHO KNOWS?
IT'S POSSIBLE.
WITH A BIRTHDAY ON CHILDREN'S DAY, EVERYONE WILL REMEMBER IT.
THAT'D BE COOL.♡
IF THE BABY IS REALLY THE DEMON LORD'S CHILD...
SHE WILL BE BORN ON MAY 5TH!
DON'T PUT A CURSE ON MY BABY!
THE DEMON LORD'S CHILDREN ARE ONLY BORN ON JULY 7TH.
AND "777" IS MARKED ON THEIR HEADS.
I WISH...
WELL, TAKE CARE!
HAVE A HEALTHY HUMAN BABY!

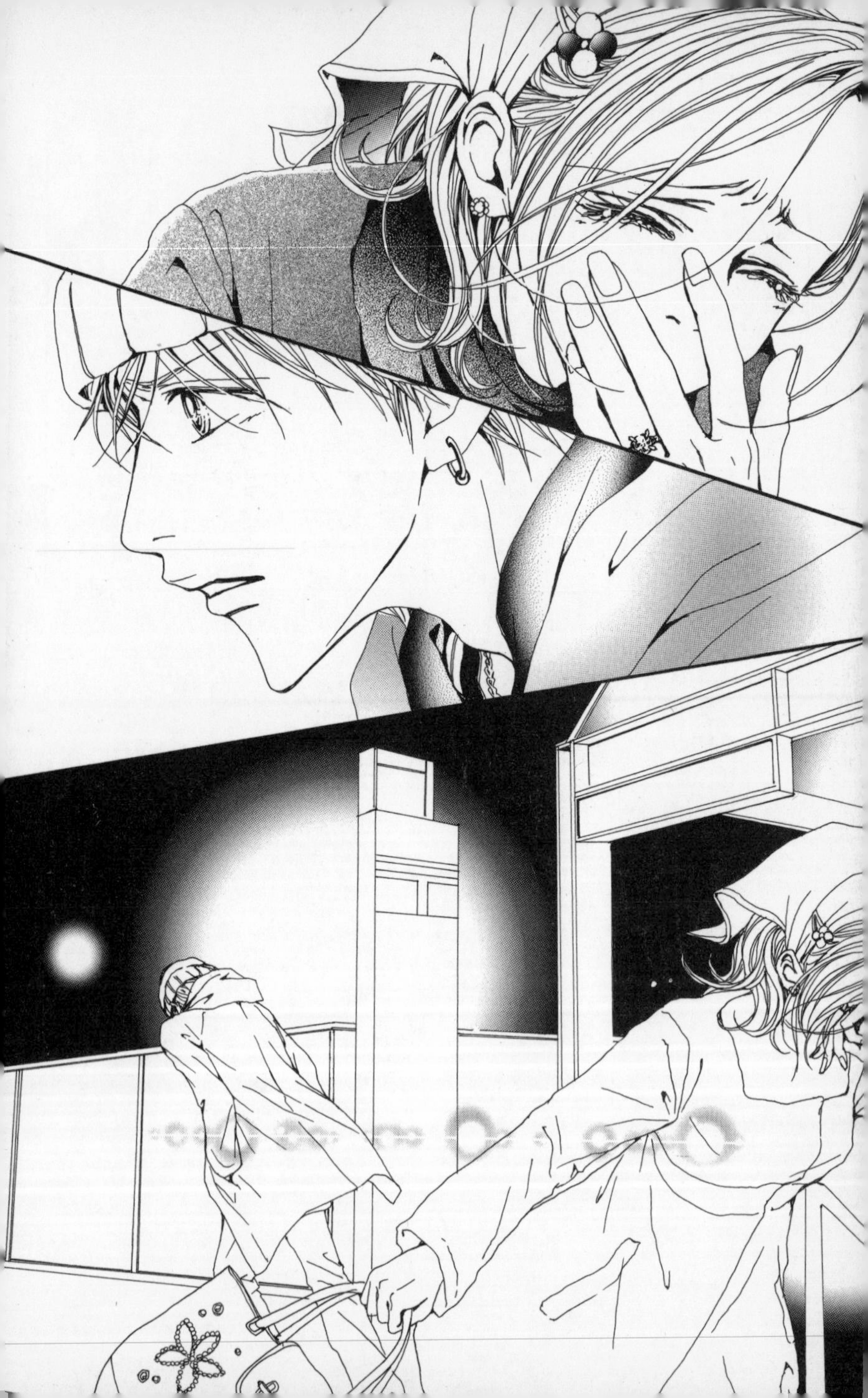

BUT NOW THAT I THINK ABOUT IT...

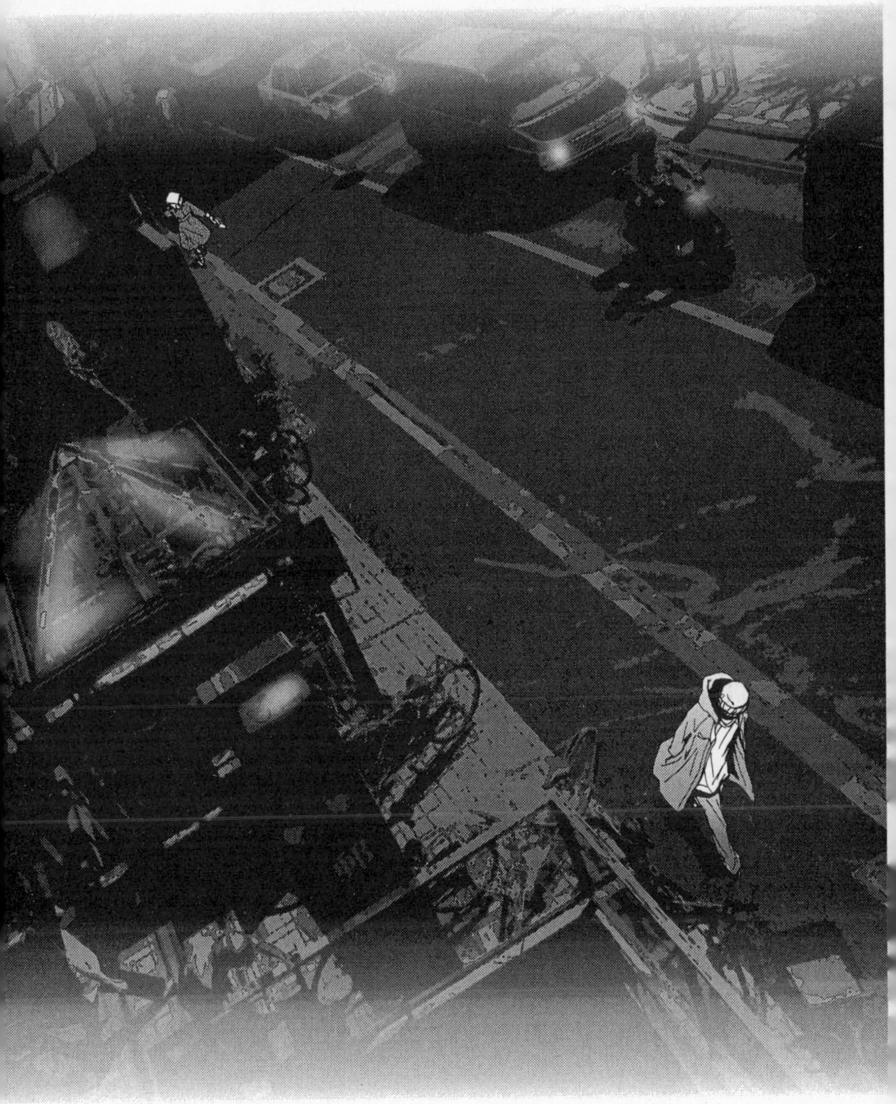

...WHAT YOU WANTED WASN'T ASKING TOO MUCH.

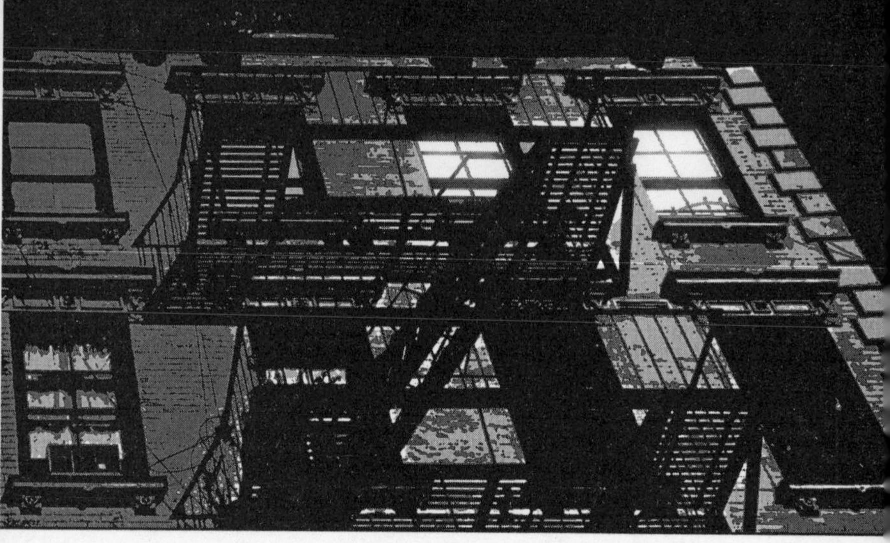

707

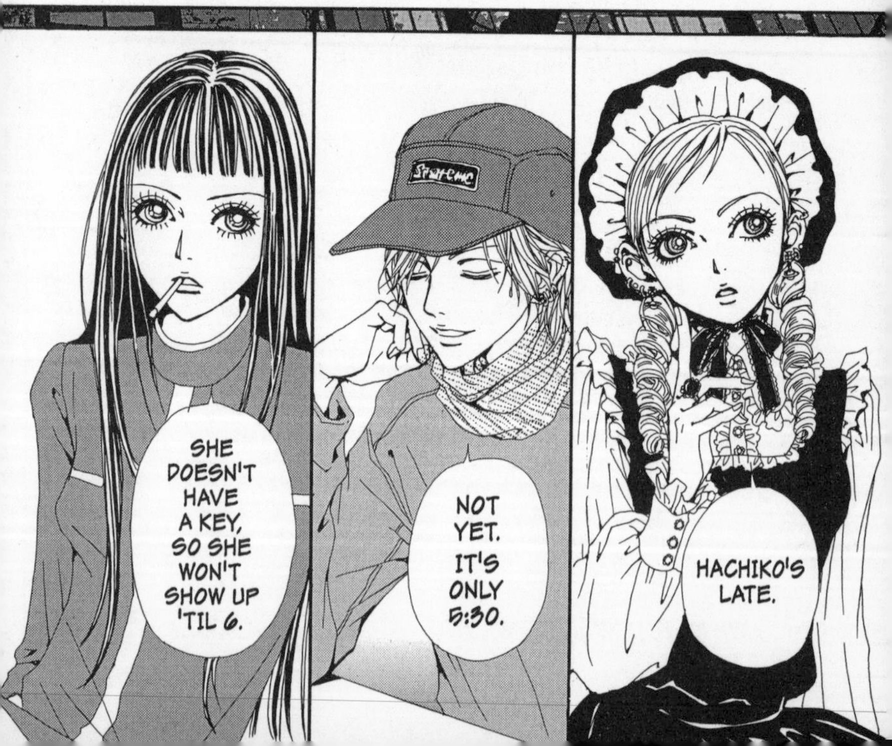

HACHIKO'S LATE.
NOT YET. IT'S ONLY 5:30.
SHE DOESN'T HAVE A KEY, SO SHE WON'T SHOW UP 'TIL 6.

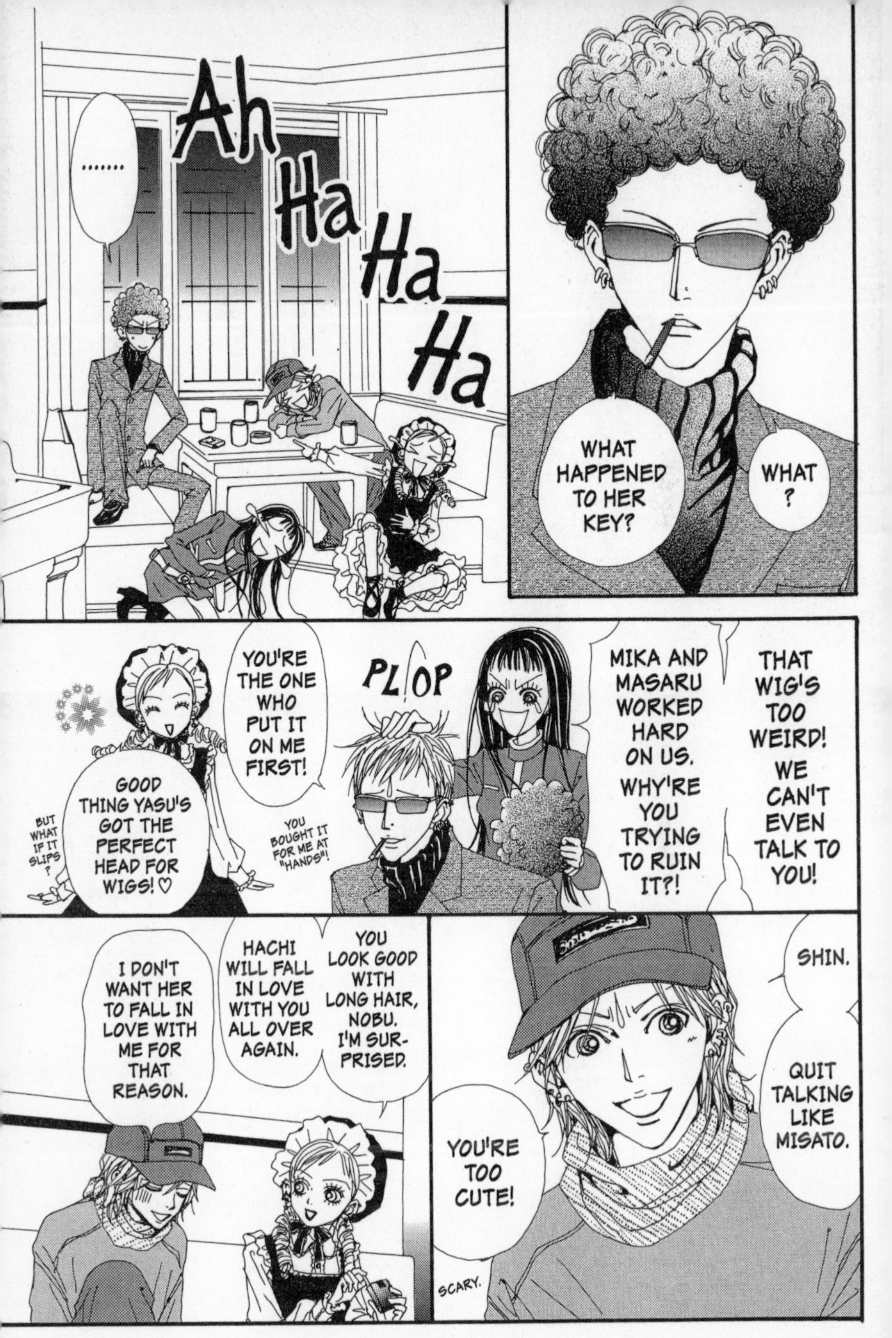
WHAT ?
WHAT HAPPENED TO HER KEY?
Ah Ha Ha Ha
....
THAT WIG'S TOO WEIRD! WE CAN'T EVEN TALK TO YOU!
MIKA AND MASARU WORKED HARD ON US. WHY'RE YOU TRYING TO RUIN IT?!
PLOP
YOU BOUGHT IT FOR ME AT "HANDS"!
YOU'RE THE ONE WHO PUT IT ON ME FIRST!
GOOD THING YASU'S GOT THE PERFECT HEAD FOR WIGS! ♡
BUT WHAT IF IT SLIPS ?
SHIN.
QUIT TALKING LIKE MISATO.
YOU'RE TOO CUTE!
SCARY.
YOU LOOK GOOD WITH LONG HAIR, NOBU. I'M SUR-PRISED.
HACHI WILL FALL IN LOVE WITH YOU ALL OVER AGAIN.
I DON'T WANT HER TO FALL IN LOVE WITH ME FOR THAT REASON.

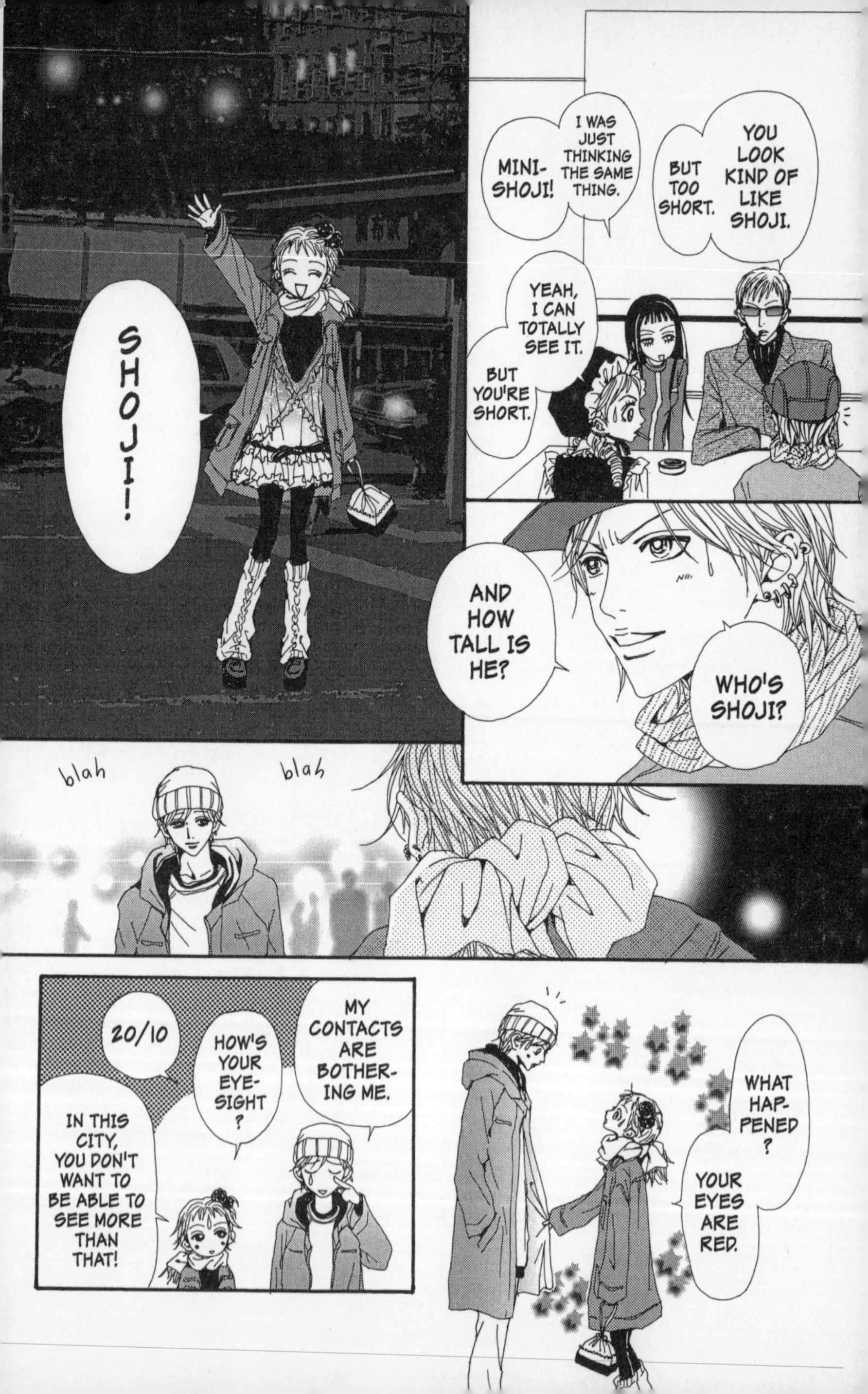
YOU LOOK KIND OF LIKE SHOJI.
BUT TOO SHORT.
I WAS JUST THINKING THE SAME THING.
MINI-SHOJI!
YEAH, I CAN TOTALLY SEE IT.
BUT YOU'RE SHORT.
WHO'S SHOJI?
AND HOW TALL IS HE?
SHOJI!
blah
blah
WHAT HAP-PENED?
YOUR EYES ARE RED.
MY CONTACTS ARE BOTHER-ING ME.
HOW'S YOUR EYE-SIGHT?
20/10
IN THIS CITY, YOU DON'T WANT TO BE ABLE TO SEE MORE THAN THAT!

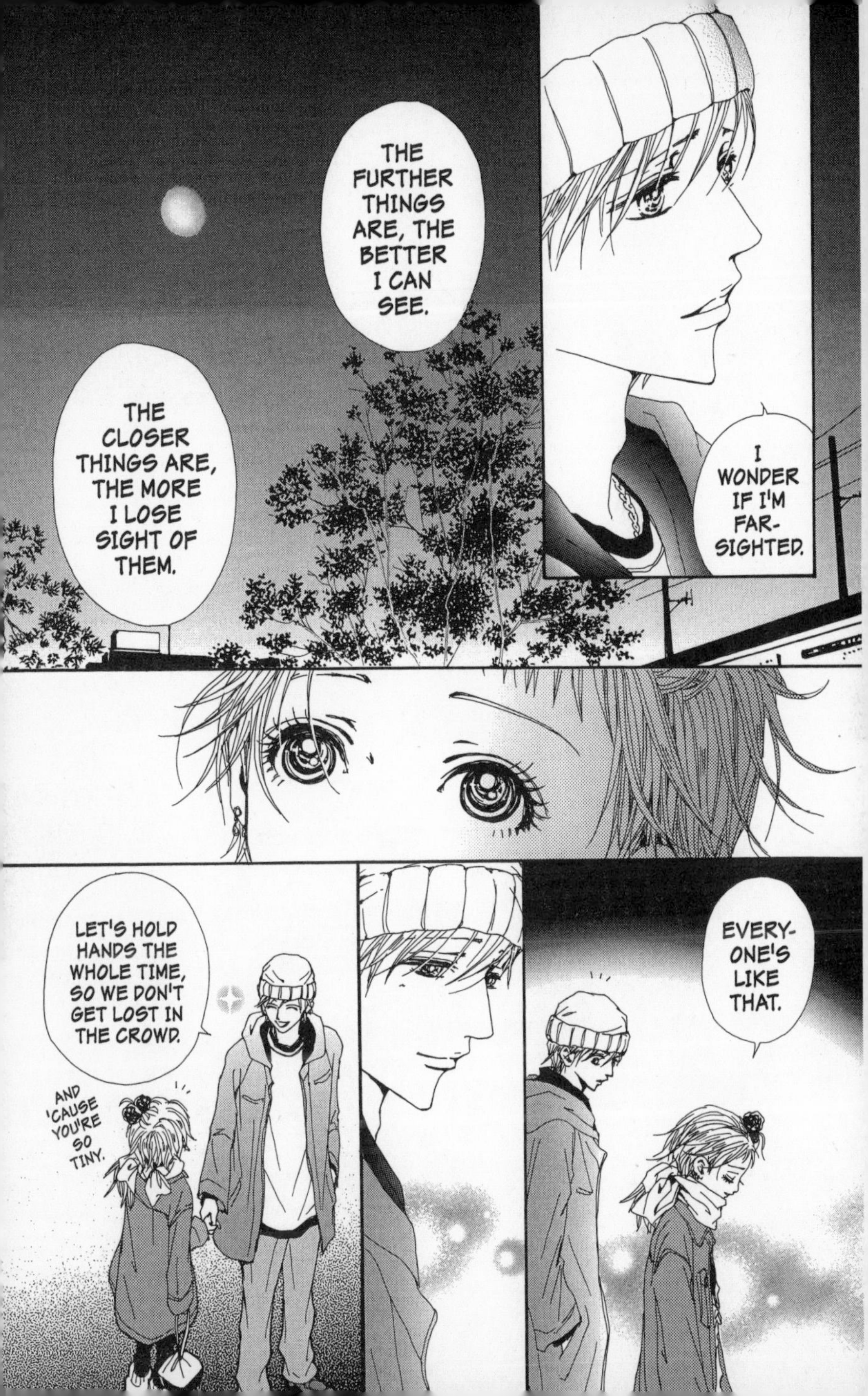
I WONDER IF I'M FAR-SIGHTED.
THE FURTHER THINGS ARE, THE BETTER I CAN SEE.
THE CLOSER THINGS ARE, THE MORE I LOSE SIGHT OF THEM.
EVERY-ONE'S LIKE THAT.
LET'S HOLD HANDS THE WHOLE TIME, SO WE DON'T GET LOST IN THE CROWD.
AND 'CAUSE YOU'RE SO TINY.

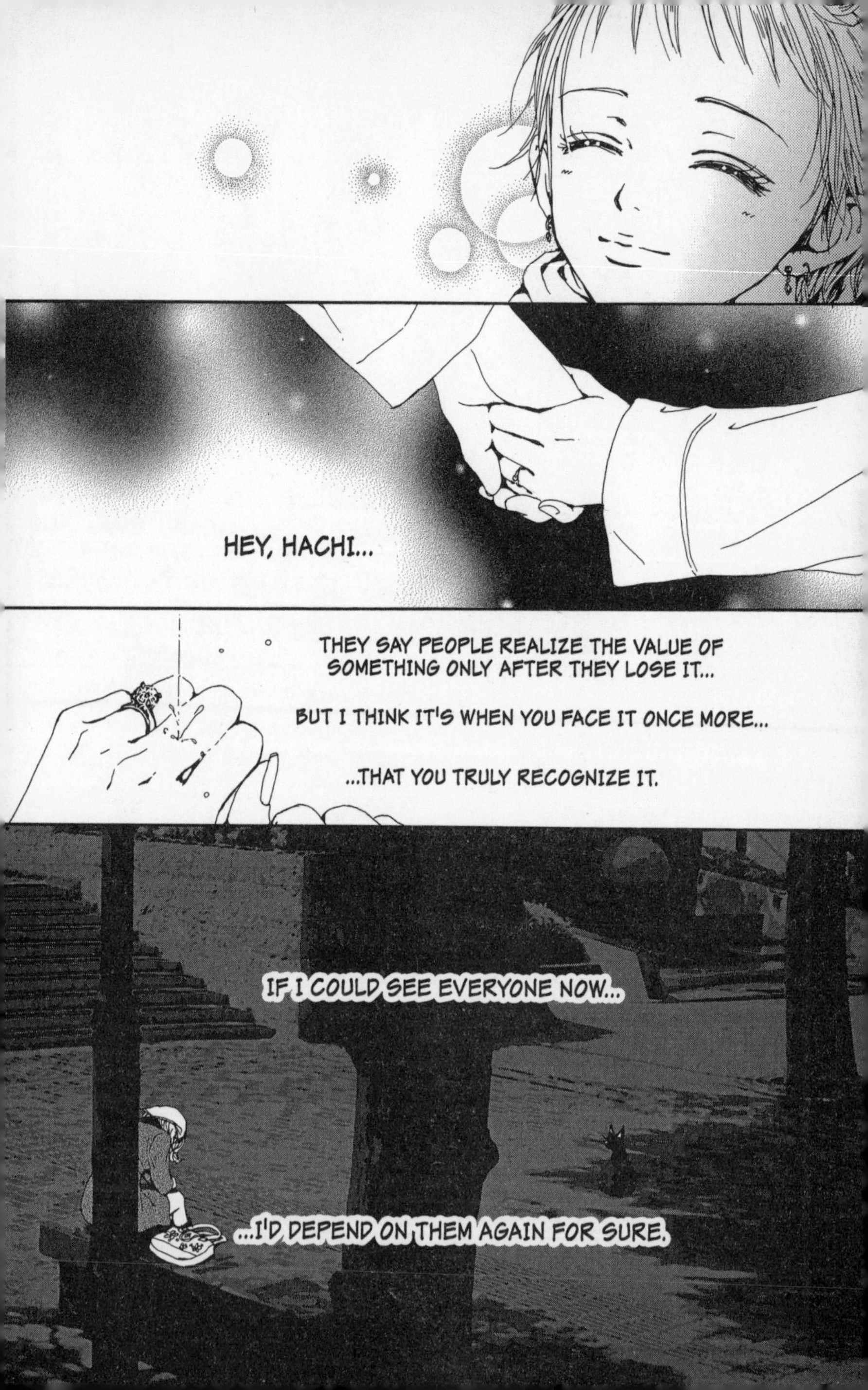
HEY, HACHI...
THEY SAY PEOPLE REALIZE THE VALUE OF SOMETHING ONLY AFTER THEY LOSE IT...
BUT I THINK IT'S WHEN YOU FACE IT ONCE MORE...
...THAT YOU TRULY RECOGNIZE IT.
IF I COULD SEE EVERYONE NOW...
...I'D DEPEND ON THEM AGAIN FOR SURE.

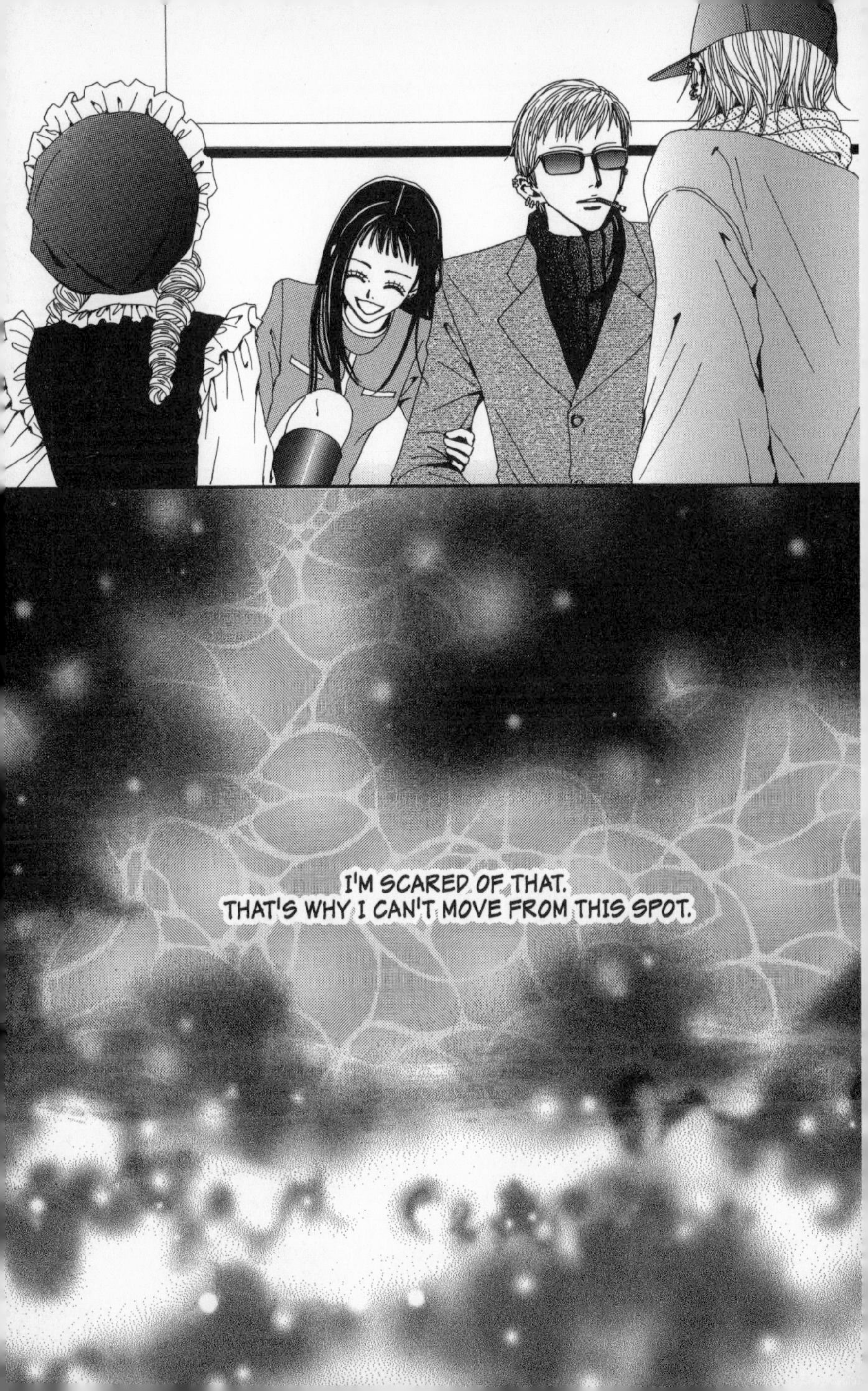
I'M SCARED OF THAT.
THAT'S WHY I CAN'T MOVE FROM THIS SPOT.

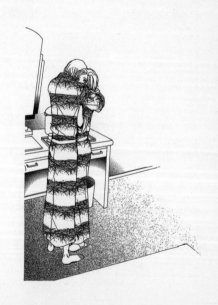

Bonus Page

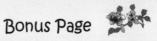

7F SNACK BAR
Junko's Place
Failed actress
Li'l rich boy
603
602
601
empty
Nobu
Myu
6F
503
502
501
Yuri
Nana
Yasu
5F
Unli-censed lawyer
Porn star
403
402
401
empty
empty
Me
4F
Hot guy
Domi-natrix
303
302
301
?
?
?
3F
Laundry
Rec Room
Vending Machine
2F
Parking lot
Entrance
front desk
Gin
Mr. Yamagishi
Elevator
Total queen
Just sprung from prison
I THINK THAT'S IT.
BUT LOOKING AT IT NOW, ALL THE CHARAC-TERS SEEM REALLY WEIRD.
IF A MURDER WAS COMMITTED IN THIS BUILD-ING, IT'D BE HARD TO TELL WHO DID IT, WHICH WOULD BE KIND OF INTERESTING.
THAT'S WHERE THIS MANGA SHOULD GO.
Murder in Room 401☆Who killed the hot guy?
creak
HEY SHIN—GREAT NEWS! ♡
OPEN
HON-EY, I'M HOME!
OH?
WEL-COME HOME, JUNKO.
CAN YOU TAKE A LOOK AT THIS?
WHAT?
A MUR-DER?
I DREW A DIAGRAM OF SHIKAI'S DORM, TO SORT OUT THE MAIN STORY...
BUT I GUESS THE MAIN SUSPECT IS YASU. ONLY A SMART CRIMINAL CAN COMMIT A MURDER IN A LOCKED ROOM.

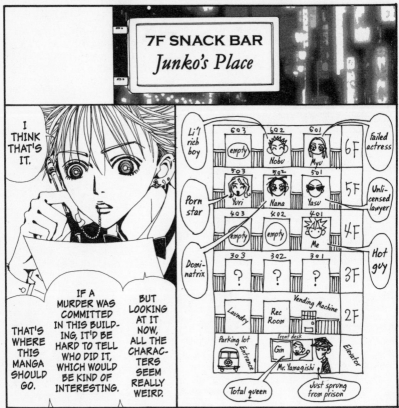

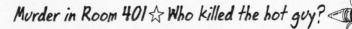

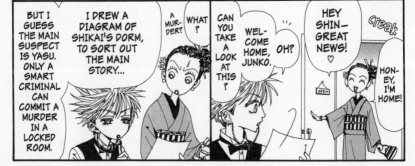

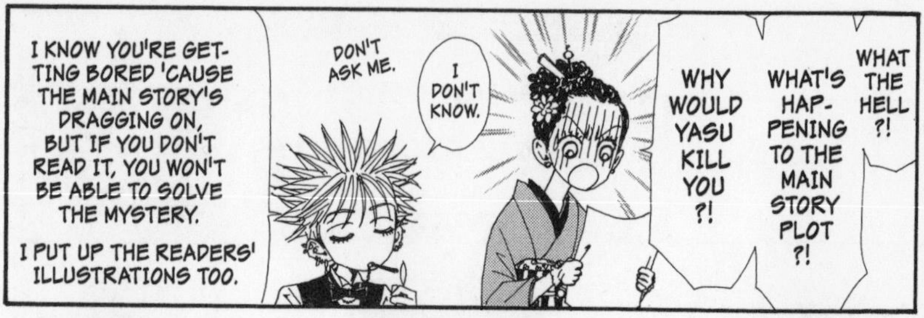
WHAT THE HELL?!
WHAT'S HAPPENING TO THE MAIN STORY PLOT?!
WHY WOULD YASU KILL YOU?!
I DON'T KNOW.
DON'T ASK ME.
I KNOW YOU'RE GET-TING BORED 'CAUSE THE MAIN STORY'S DRAGGING ON, BUT IF YOU DON'T READ IT, YOU WON'T BE ABLE TO SOLVE THE MYSTERY.
I PUT UP THE READERS' ILLUSTRATIONS TOO.

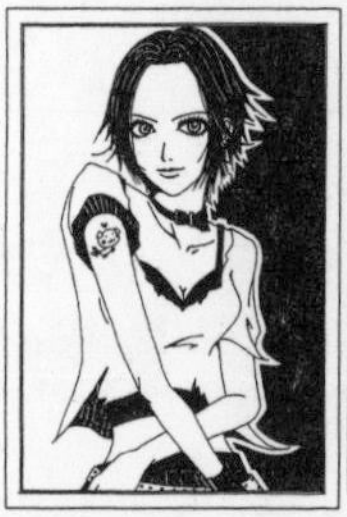

Kobe
KUCCHANE MASATOMO

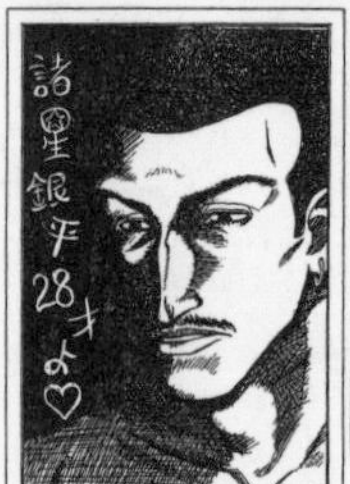
諸星銀平28才よ♡

Hyogo
TETSUYA HANADA

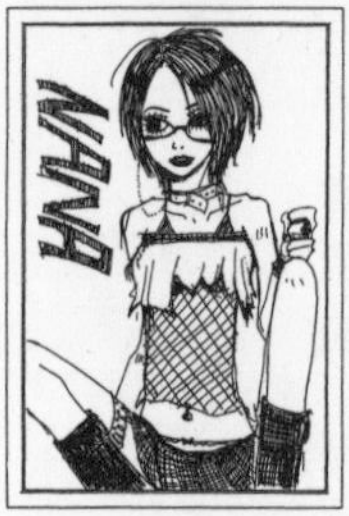
NANA

Miyazaki
HANA

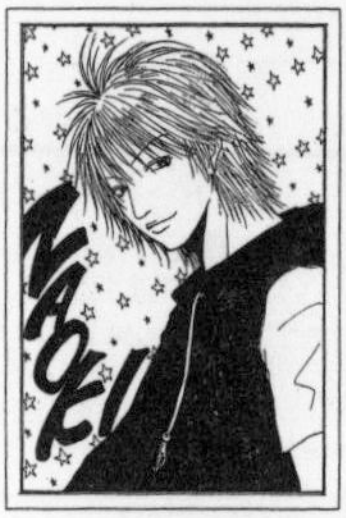
NAOKI

Saitama
TOMOKO KUZUMI

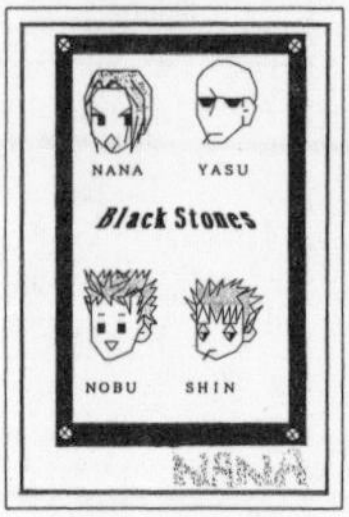
NANA
YASU
Black Stones
NOBU
SHIN
NANA

Chiba
WHITE STONES

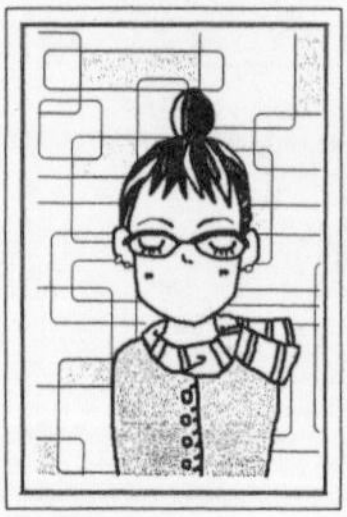

Fukuoka
AYUMI HAMAGUCHI

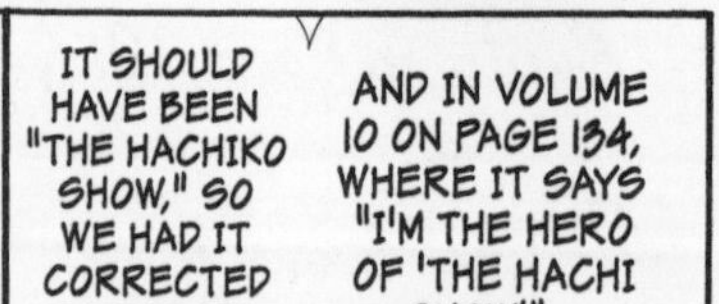
AND IN VOLUME 10 ON PAGE 134, WHERE IT SAYS "I'M THE HERO OF 'THE HACHI SHOW'"...
IT SHOULD HAVE BEEN "THE HACHIKO SHOW," SO WE HAD IT CORRECTED IN THE 3RD EDITION.
THE MEANING'S THE SAME, BUT NANA'S ANAL, SO JUST IN CASE.
I'M THE HERO OF "THE HACHI SHOW."

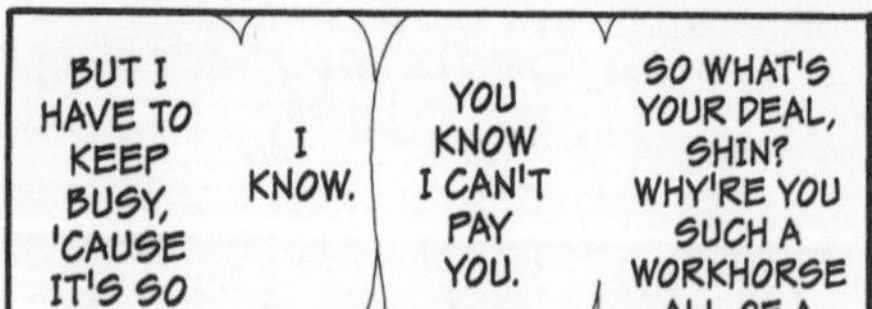
SO WHAT'S YOUR DEAL, SHIN? WHY'RE YOU SUCH A WORKHORSE ALL OF A SUDDEN?
YOU KNOW I CAN'T PAY YOU.
I KNOW.
BUT I HAVE TO KEEP BUSY, 'CAUSE IT'S SO DEAD IN HERE.
SO WHAT'S THE NEWS?

It's correct in the English version, too.

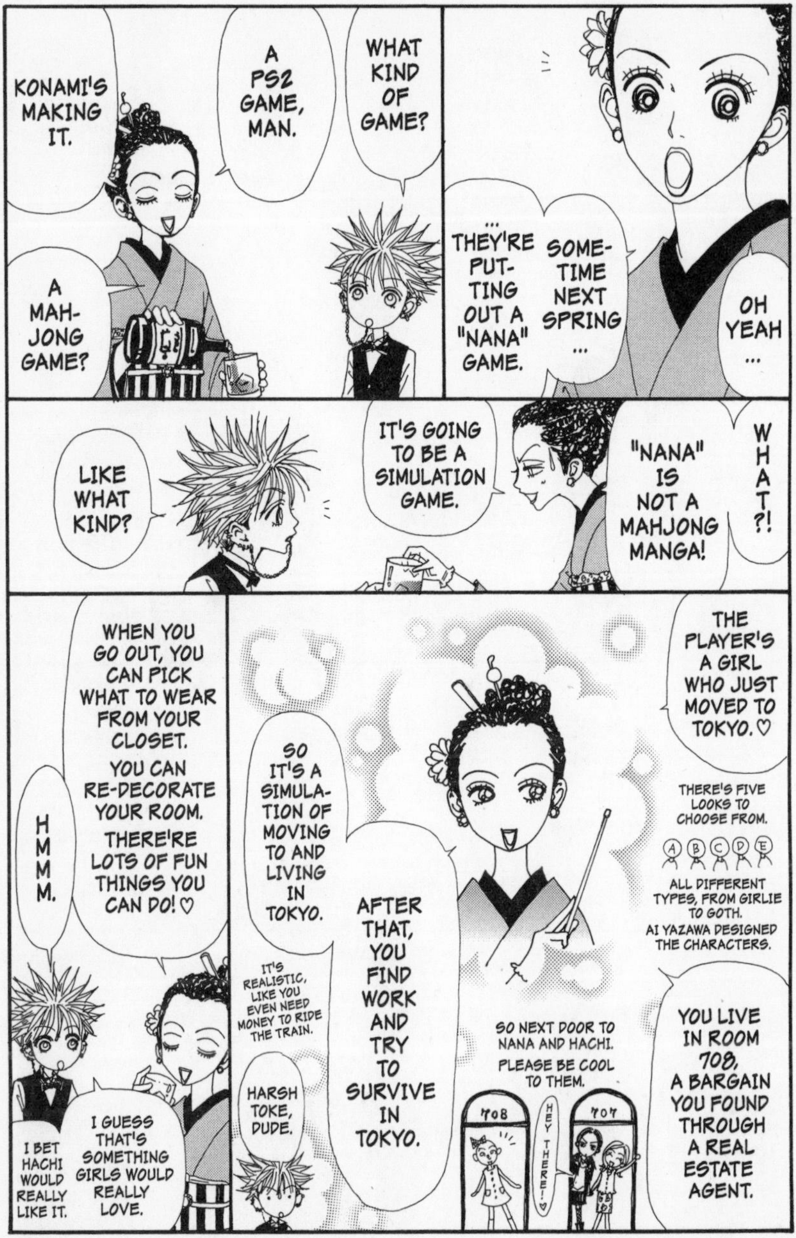
OH YEAH ...
SOMETIME NEXT SPRING ...
... THEY'RE PUTTING OUT A "NANA" GAME.
WHAT KIND OF GAME?
A PS2 GAME, MAN.
KONAMI'S MAKING IT.
A MAHJONG GAME?
WHAT?!
"NANA" IS NOT A MAHJONG MANGA!
IT'S GOING TO BE A SIMULATION GAME.
LIKE WHAT KIND?
THE PLAYER'S A GIRL WHO JUST MOVED TO TOKYO. ♡
THERE'S FIVE LOOKS TO CHOOSE FROM.
A B C D E
ALL DIFFERENT TYPES, FROM GIRLIE TO GOTH. AI YAZAWA DESIGNED THE CHARACTERS.
YOU LIVE IN ROOM 708, A BARGAIN YOU FOUND THROUGH A REAL ESTATE AGENT.
SO NEXT DOOR TO NANA AND HACHI. PLEASE BE COOL TO THEM.
707
708
HEY THERE! ♡
SO IT'S A SIMULATION OF MOVING TO AND LIVING IN TOKYO.
AFTER THAT, YOU FIND WORK AND TRY TO SURVIVE IN TOKYO.
IT'S REALISTIC, LIKE YOU EVEN NEED MONEY TO RIDE THE TRAIN.
HARSH TOKE, DUDE.
WHEN YOU GO OUT, YOU CAN PICK WHAT TO WEAR FROM YOUR CLOSET. YOU CAN RE-DECORATE YOUR ROOM. THERE'RE LOTS OF FUN THINGS YOU CAN DO! ♡
HMMM.
I GUESS THAT'S SOMETHING GIRLS WOULD REALLY LOVE.
I BET HACHI WOULD REALLY LIKE IT.

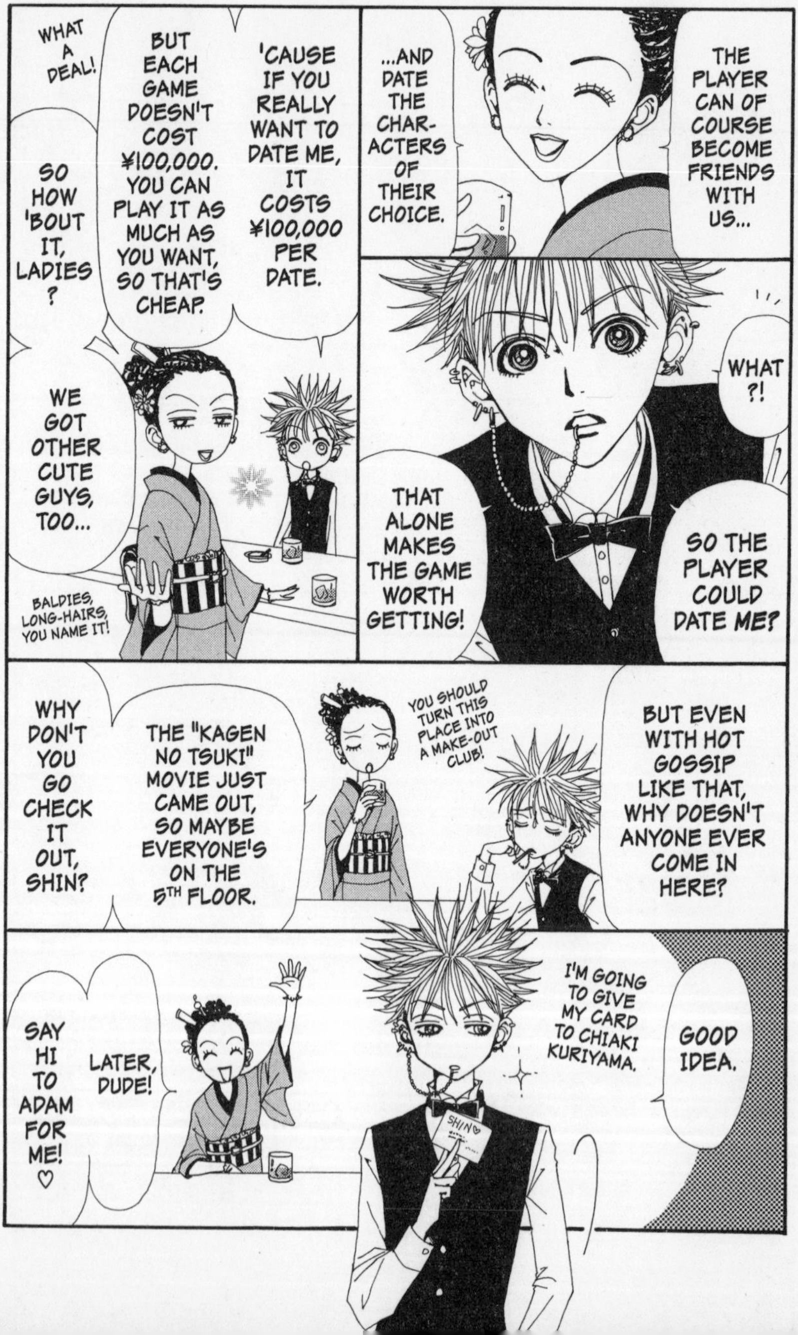
THE PLAYER CAN OF COURSE BECOME FRIENDS WITH US...
...AND DATE THE CHARACTERS OF THEIR CHOICE.
WHAT ?!
SO THE PLAYER COULD DATE ME?
THAT ALONE MAKES THE GAME WORTH GETTING!
'CAUSE IF YOU REALLY WANT TO DATE ME, IT COSTS ¥100,000 PER DATE.
BUT EACH GAME DOESN'T COST ¥100,000. YOU CAN PLAY IT AS MUCH AS YOU WANT, SO THAT'S CHEAP.
WHAT A DEAL!
SO HOW 'BOUT IT, LADIES ?
WE GOT OTHER CUTE GUYS, TOO...
BALDIES, LONG-HAIRS, YOU NAME IT!
BUT EVEN WITH HOT GOSSIP LIKE THAT, WHY DOESN'T ANYONE EVER COME IN HERE?
YOU SHOULD TURN THIS PLACE INTO A MAKE-OUT CLUB!
THE "KAGEN NO TSUKI" MOVIE JUST CAME OUT, SO MAYBE EVERYONE'S ON THE 5TH FLOOR.
WHY DON'T YOU GO CHECK IT OUT, SHIN?
GOOD IDEA.
I'M GOING TO GIVE MY CARD TO CHIAKI KURIYAMA.
SHIN♡
LATER, DUDE!
SAY HI TO ADAM FOR ME! ♡

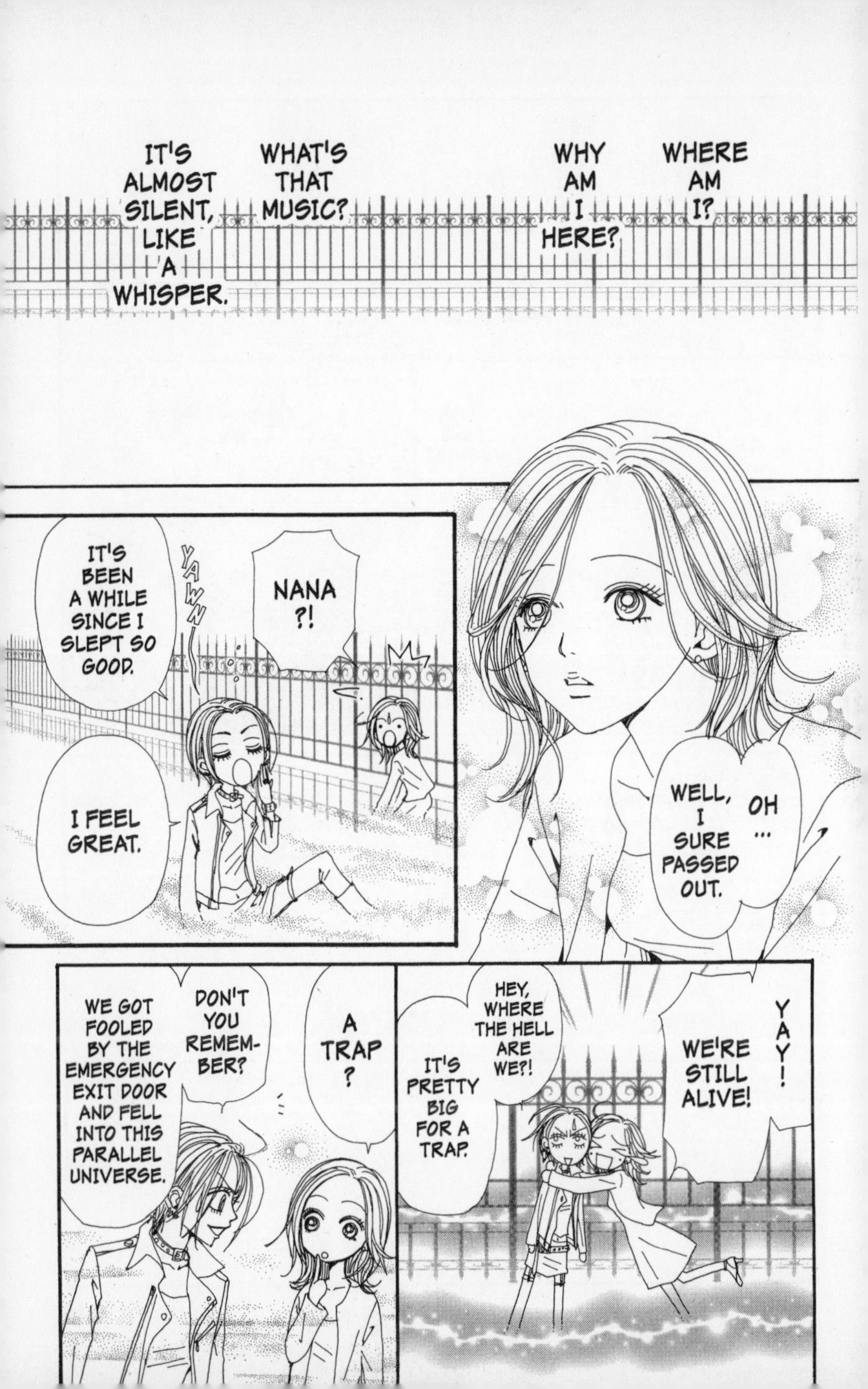
WHERE AM I?
WHY AM I HERE?
WHAT'S THAT MUSIC?
IT'S ALMOST SILENT, LIKE A WHISPER.
OH ...
WELL, I SURE PASSED OUT.
NANA ?!
YAWN
IT'S BEEN A WHILE SINCE I SLEPT SO GOOD.
I FEEL GREAT.
YAY!
WE'RE STILL ALIVE!
HEY, WHERE THE HELL ARE WE?!
IT'S PRETTY BIG FOR A TRAP.
A TRAP?
DON'T YOU REMEM-BER?
WE GOT FOOLED BY THE EMERGENCY EXIT DOOR AND FELL INTO THIS PARALLEL UNIVERSE.

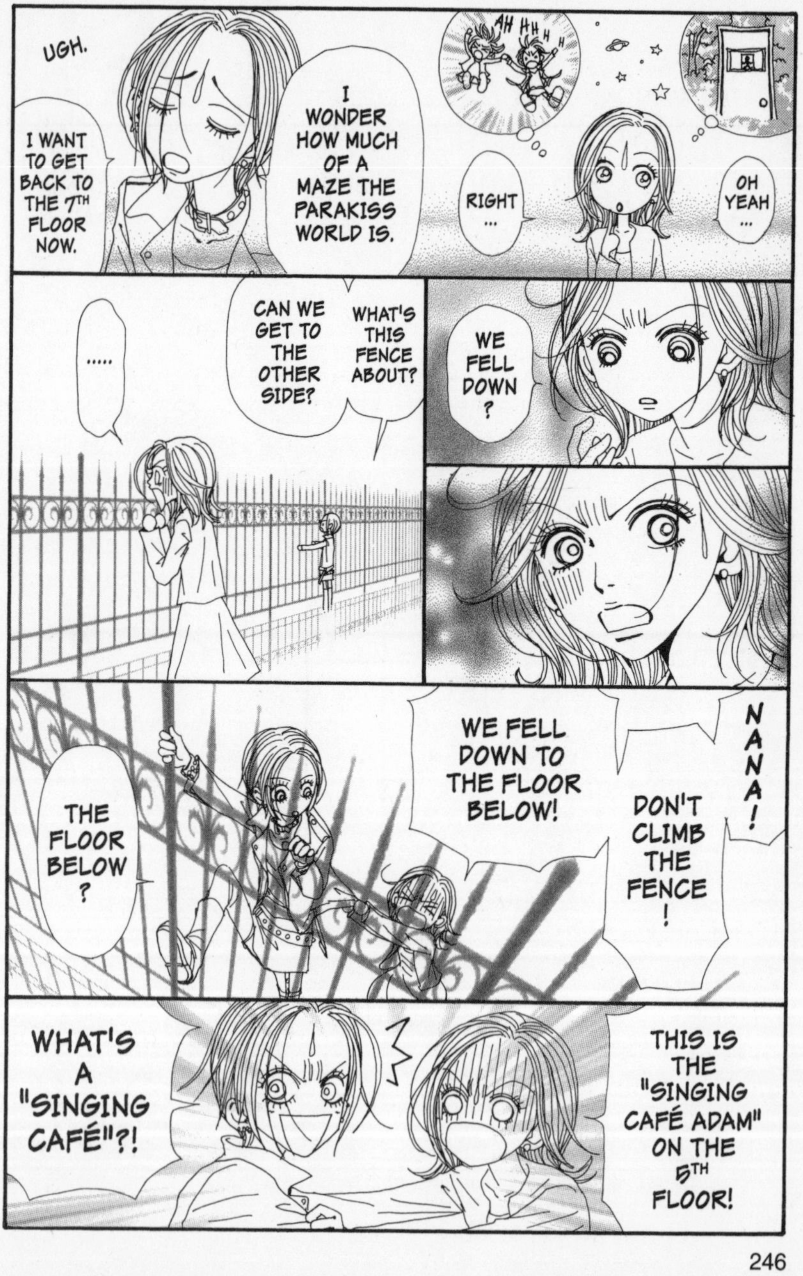
AHHHHHH
OH YEAH ...
RIGHT ...
I WONDER HOW MUCH OF A MAZE THE PARAKISS WORLD IS.
UGH.
I WANT TO GET BACK TO THE 7TH FLOOR NOW.
WE FELL DOWN ?
WHAT'S THIS FENCE ABOUT?
CAN WE GET TO THE OTHER SIDE?
.....
NANA!
DON'T CLIMB THE FENCE !
WE FELL DOWN TO THE FLOOR BELOW!
THE FLOOR BELOW ?
THIS IS THE "SINGING CAFÉ ADAM" ON THE 5TH FLOOR!
WHAT'S A "SINGING CAFÉ"?!

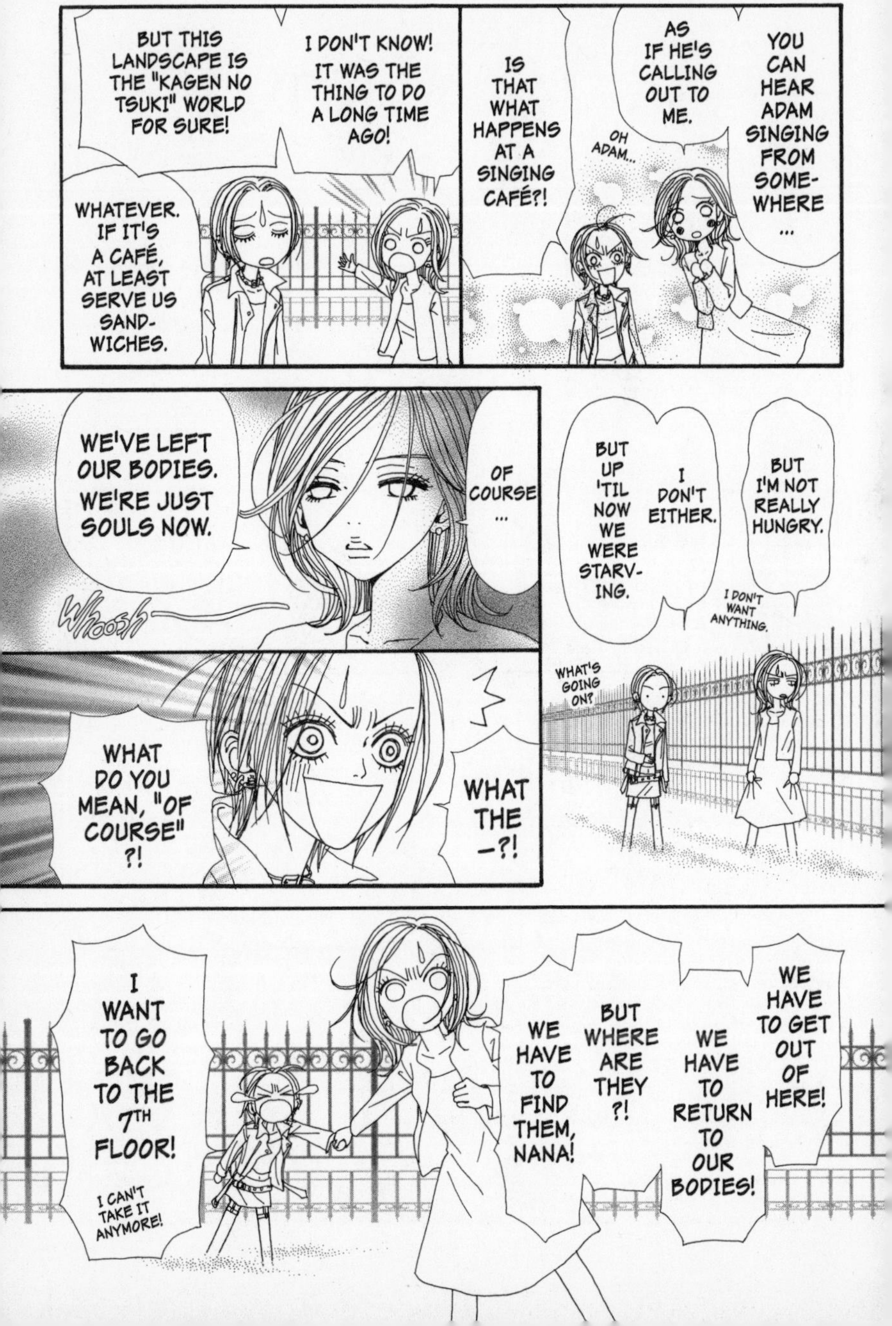
YOU CAN HEAR ADAM SINGING FROM SOMEWHERE...
AS IF HE'S CALLING OUT TO ME.
OH ADAM...
IS THAT WHAT HAPPENS AT A SINGING CAFÉ?!
I DON'T KNOW! IT WAS THE THING TO DO A LONG TIME AGO!
BUT THIS LANDSCAPE IS THE "KAGEN NO TSUKI" WORLD FOR SURE!
WHATEVER. IF IT'S A CAFÉ, AT LEAST SERVE US SANDWICHES.
BUT I'M NOT REALLY HUNGRY.
I DON'T WANT ANYTHING.
I DON'T EITHER.
BUT UP 'TIL NOW WE WERE STARVING.
WHAT'S GOING ON?
OF COURSE...
WE'VE LEFT OUR BODIES. WE'RE JUST SOULS NOW.
Whoosh
WHAT THE—?!
WHAT DO YOU MEAN, "OF COURSE"?!
WE HAVE TO GET OUT OF HERE!
WE HAVE TO RETURN TO OUR BODIES!
BUT WHERE ARE THEY?!
WE HAVE TO FIND THEM, NANA!
I WANT TO GO BACK TO THE 7TH FLOOR!
I CAN'T TAKE IT ANYMORE!

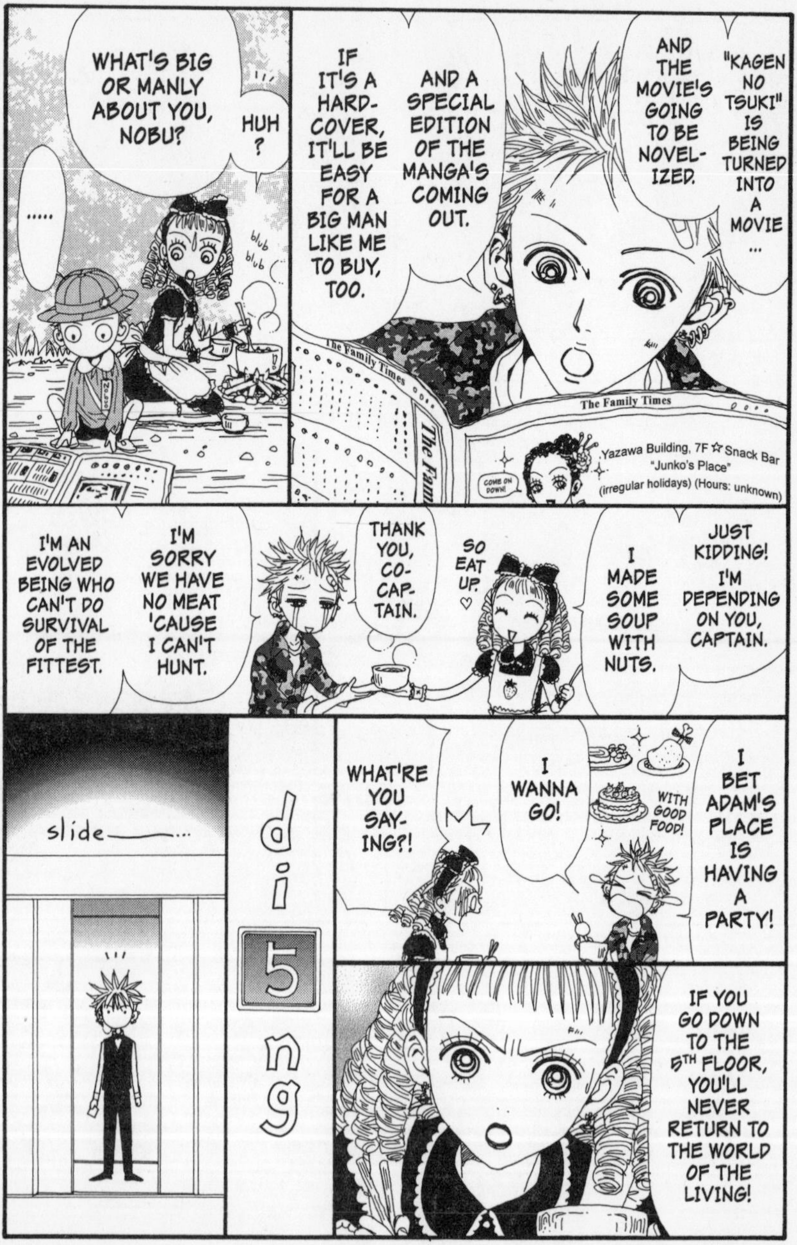
"KAGEN NO TSUKI" IS BEING TURNED INTO A MOVIE...
AND THE MOVIE'S GOING TO BE NOVELIZED.
AND A SPECIAL EDITION OF THE MANGA'S COMING OUT.
IF IT'S A HARDCOVER, IT'LL BE EASY FOR A BIG MAN LIKE ME TO BUY, TOO.
The Family Times
Yazawa Building, 7F ☆ Snack Bar "Junko's Place"
(irregular holidays) (Hours: unknown)
COME ON DOWN!
WHAT'S BIG OR MANLY ABOUT YOU, NOBU?
HUH?
blub blub
.....
JUST KIDDING! I'M DEPENDING ON YOU, CAPTAIN.
I MADE SOME SOUP WITH NUTS.
SO EAT UP. ♡
THANK YOU, CO-CAPTAIN.
I'M SORRY WE HAVE NO MEAT 'CAUSE I CAN'T HUNT.
I'M AN EVOLVED BEING WHO CAN'T DO SURVIVAL OF THE FITTEST.
I BET ADAM'S PLACE IS HAVING A PARTY!
WITH GOOD FOOD!
I WANNA GO!
WHAT'RE YOU SAYING?!
IF YOU GO DOWN TO THE 5TH FLOOR, YOU'LL NEVER RETURN TO THE WORLD OF THE LIVING!
ding
5
slide——...

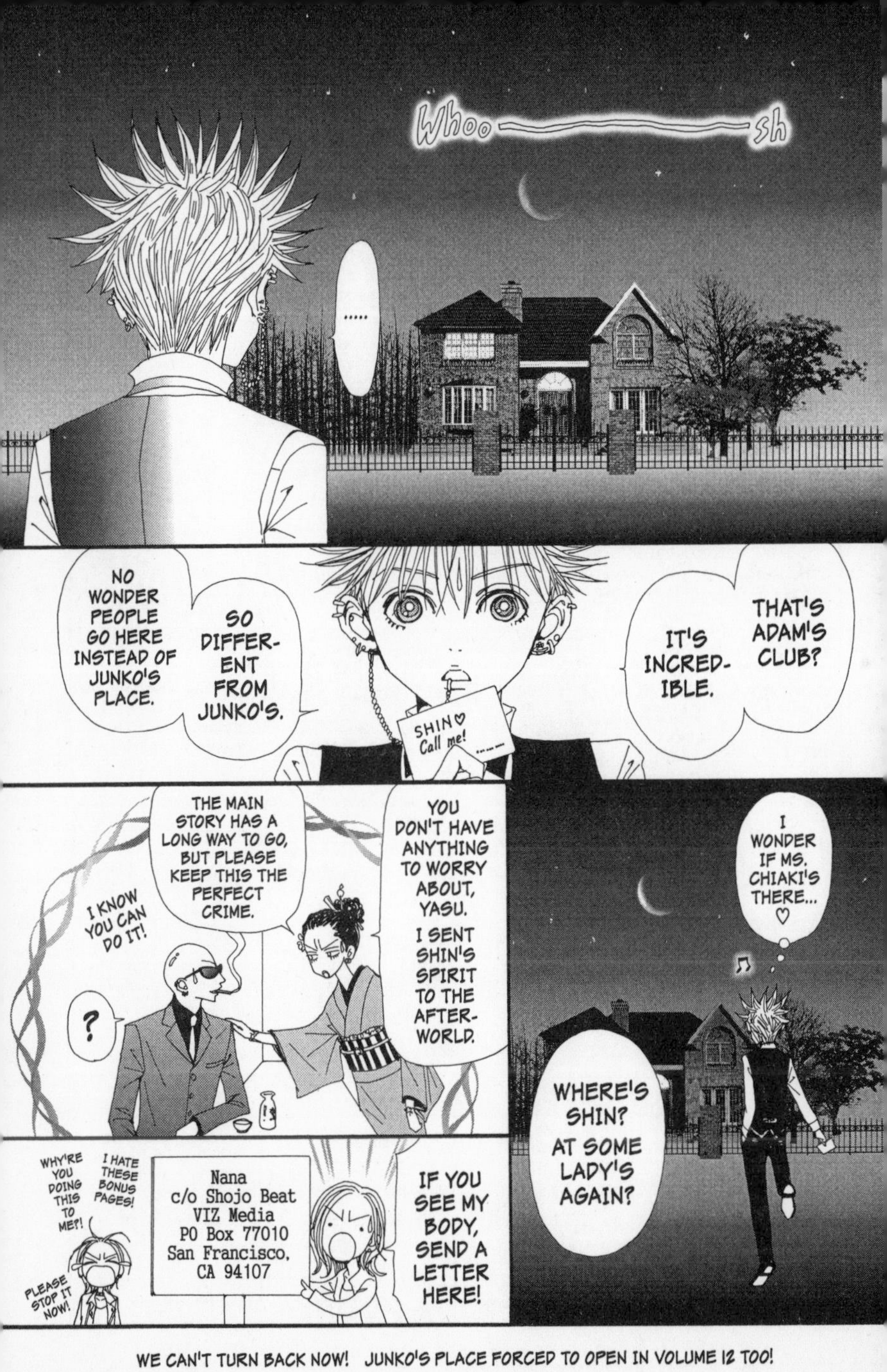
Whoo——————sh
......
THAT'S ADAM'S CLUB?
IT'S INCREDIBLE.
SO DIFFERENT FROM JUNKO'S.
NO WONDER PEOPLE GO HERE INSTEAD OF JUNKO'S PLACE.
SHIN♡ Call me!
I WONDER IF MS. CHIAKI'S THERE... ♡
WHERE'S SHIN? AT SOME LADY'S AGAIN?
YOU DON'T HAVE ANYTHING TO WORRY ABOUT, YASU. I SENT SHIN'S SPIRIT TO THE AFTERWORLD.
THE MAIN STORY HAS A LONG WAY TO GO, BUT PLEASE KEEP THIS THE PERFECT CRIME.
I KNOW YOU CAN DO IT!
?
IF YOU SEE MY BODY, SEND A LETTER HERE!
Nana
c/o Shojo Beat
VIZ Media
PO Box 77010
San Francisco,
CA 94107
I HATE THESE BONUS PAGES!
WHY'RE YOU DOING THIS TO ME?!
PLEASE STOP IT NOW!

WE CAN'T TURN BACK NOW! JUNKO'S PLACE FORCED TO OPEN IN VOLUME 12 TOO!

The Family Times Aug. 11, 2004

"NANA" Vol. 11! Another fat volume with Five whole chapters!

NEWS!

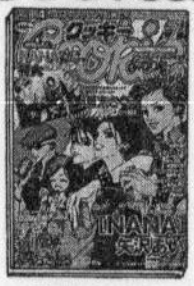

Cookie on sale the 26th of every month!
http://cookie.shueisha.co.jp/

You can read the continuation of Vol. 11 in "Cookie"! Good news for people who bought "NANA" Vol. 11 right when it hit the stands! "NANA" in the October issue of "Cookie", on sale August 26, continues where Vol. 11 left off! And the story enters a new chapter! Why don't you start reading it regularly now?

The Family Times

Aug. 11, 2004

"NANA" PS2 Game in the Works!

★ Go to http://www.konamijpn.com/NANA/ for more information about the game!

Konami will come out with a "NANA" simulation game. It will go on sale sometime next spring. The price is not yet set. Anyways, go buy the hardware first. This year's Christmas gift should be a PS2! Hey guy over there! Buy a PS2 for your wife and daughter!

"Kagen no Tsuki" Special Edition!

With a new design that looks like real literature!

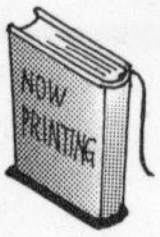
NOW PRINTING

—Author—
Ai Yazawa
—Price—
¥1200 each (incl. tax)

Shueisha

Both volumes on sale September 17! Cashing in on the movie? Even if you already own the manga, you should check this out! Full color illustrations that weren't in the tankobons are included in the illustration gallery at the end of each volume. It's like a small illustration collection. ♡ People won't know the books are manga, 'cause they're novel-size, grown-up-looking hardbacks. Buy both volumes together!

Read the novelization of the "Kagen no Tsuki" movie!

On sale September 3rd, before the movie's released!

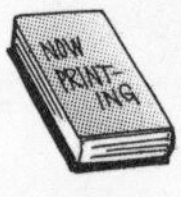
NOW PRINT-ING

—Author—
Kanae Shimokawa
Suggested —Price—
¥780 (incl. tax)

Shueisha

Beautiful prose and masterful psychological descriptions. Ms. Kanae Shimokawa, who's novelized many of our family's manga, has done a fabulous job on the "Kagen no Tsuki" novelization! The book contains many stills from the movie. There's also a three-way discussion between the author Kanae Shimokawa, Ai Yazawa, and the grand director Ken Nikai who also wrote the script. The book is a stylish paperback.

"Have You Seen Me?"

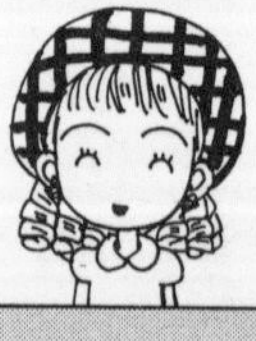

Misato Uehara (alias?)

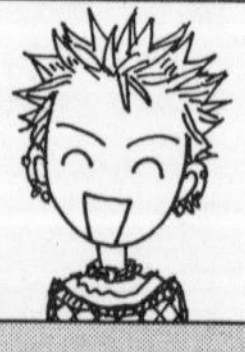

Nobuo Terashima

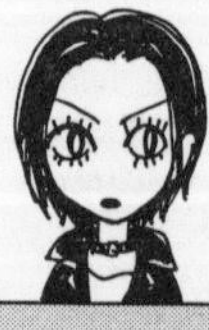

Nana Osaki

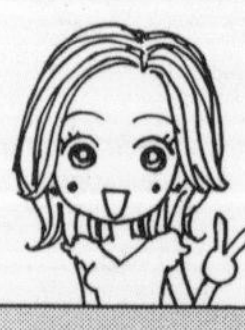

Nana Komatsu

The Family Times Aug. 11, 2004

First-run screenings nationwide October 2004!

Mobile Site: kagen@dwango.tv

URL: www.kagen.jp

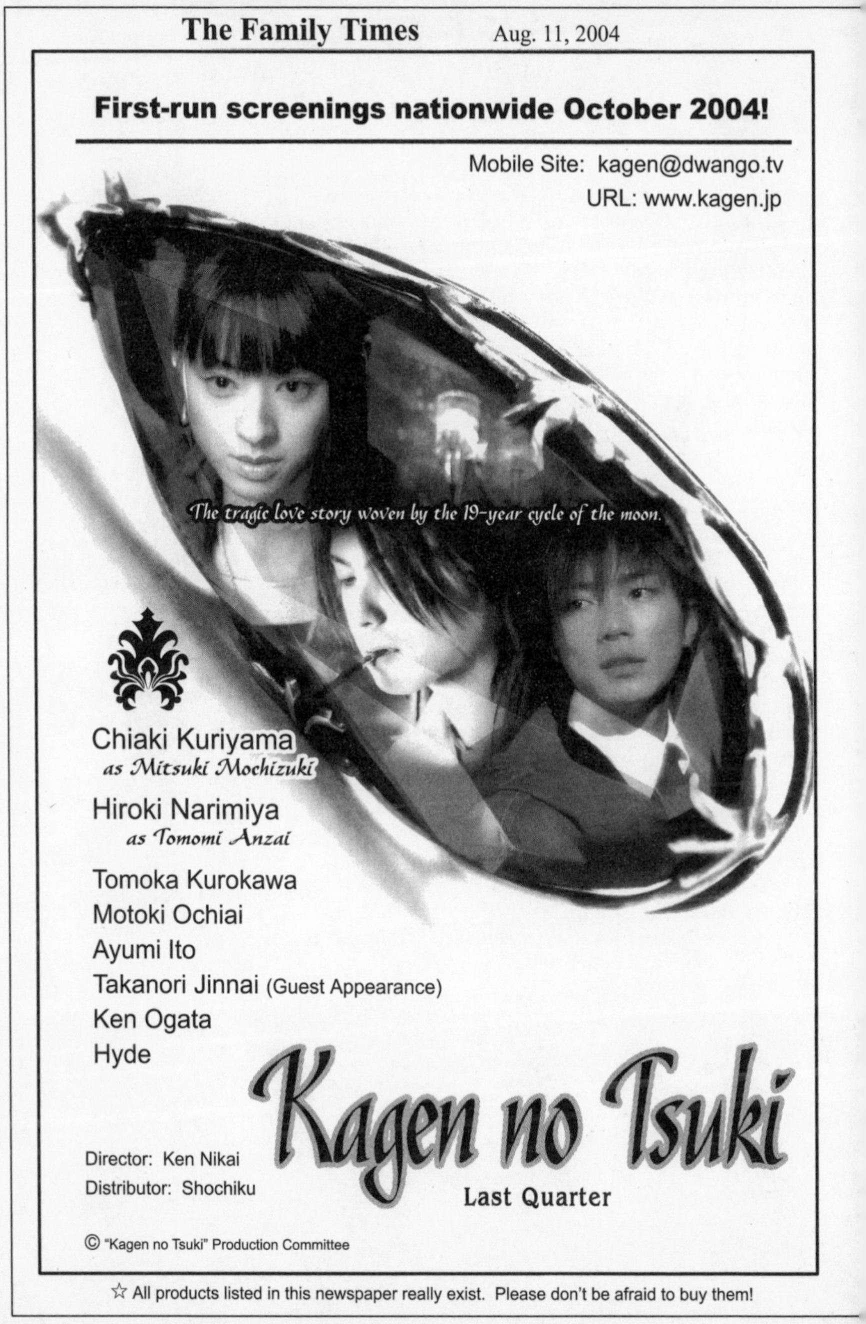
The tragic love story woven by the 19-year cycle of the moon.

Chiaki Kuriyama
as Mitsuki Mochizuki

Hiroki Narimiya
as Tomomi Anzai

Tomoka Kurokawa

Motoki Ochiai

Ayumi Ito

Takanori Jinnai (Guest Appearance)

Ken Ogata

Hyde

Kagen no Tsuki

Last Quarter

Director: Ken Nikai

Distributor: Shochiku

☆ All products listed in this newspaper really exist. Please don't be afraid to buy them!

The 2001 Chofu City Hanabi Festival was really postponed 'cause of a typhoon and was rescheduled for October 27. When I was taking photos by the Tama River, an old man started talking to me and told me that "the fireworks festival that was cancelled is going to be held soon." The entire fireworks arc was born that way. A uniquely precious encounter. It came out of this chance encounter with that man. Thank you very much. –Ai Yazawa

Ai Yazawa is the creator of many popular manga titles, including *Tenshi Nanka Janai* (I'm No Angel) and *Gokinjo Monogatari* (Neighborhood Story). Another series, *Kagen no Tsuki* (Last Quarter), was made into a live-action movie and released in late 2004. American readers were introduced to Yazawa's stylish and sexy storytelling in 2002 when her title *Paradise Kiss* was translated into English.

Nana has become the all-time best-selling shojo title from Japanese publishing giant Shueisha, and the series even garnered a Shogakukan Manga Award in the girls category in 2003. A live-action *Nana* movie was released in Japan in 2006.

NANA
VOL. 11

The Shojo Beat Manga Edition

STORY AND ART BY AI YAZAWA

English Adaptation/Allison Wolfe
Translation/Tomo Kimura
Touch-up Art & Lettering/Sabrina Heep
Cover Design/Courtney Utt
Interior Design/Julie Behn
Editor/Pancha Diaz

Editor in Chief, Books/Alvin Lu
Editor in Chief, Magazines/Marc Weidenbaum
VP, Publishing Licensing/Rika Inouye
VP, Sales & Product Marketing/Gonzalo Ferreyra
VP, Creative/Linda Espinosa
Publisher/Hyoe Narita

NANA © 1999 by Yazawa Manga Seisakusho. All rights reserved. First published in Japan in 1999 by SHUEISHA Inc., Tokyo. English translation rights arranged by SHUEISHA Inc. The stories, characters and incidents mentioned in this publication are entirely fictional.

Printed in Canada

Published by VIZ Media, LLC
P.O. Box 77010
San Francisco, CA 94107

Shojo Beat Manga Edition
10 9 8 7 6 5 4 3 2
First printing, July 2008
Second printing, October 2008

Tell us what you think about Shojo Beat Manga!

Our survey is now available online. Go to:

shojobeat.com/mangasurvey

Help us make our product offerings better!